SOMETIMES...

I DON'T REMEMBER MUCH OF THE

'70s

For information about permissions to reproduce selections from this book, translation rights, or to order bulk purchases, go to drnormjohnson.com.

Cover art by Jon Baker
Cover design by Lindsay Gatz at vonRocko design
Publishing management by Bryan Tomasovich at The Publishing World

Johnson, Dr. Norman P.
Sometimes...I Don't Remember Much of the '70s
978-0-9990992-1-6

1. Fiction / General. 2. Fiction / Biographical. 3. Fiction / Political.

Use your phone camera to scan the QR codes and enjoy the songs and videos that start every chapter.

Printed in the U.S.A.
Distributed by Ingram

SOMETIMES...

I DON'T REMEMBER MUCH OF THE '70s

DR. NORMAN P. JOHNSON

SOMETIMES...

Author's Note

This story is primarily a work of fiction, though it is based on actual events, people, and places. Names, characters, businesses, places, events, and incidents are pretty much either the products of the author's conniving imagination or used purely coincidentally in a fictitious manner. Any resemblance to actual persons, living or dead, or actual events, real or imagined, is not only intentional but more than likely, the mad ravings of a drug-addled lunatic in his final days of lucidity. Enjoy.

CHAPTER ONE

WAKING UP IS HARD TO DO

"Now he's comin' down the mountain goin' fast, fast, fast…"

New Riders of the Purple Sage
"Henry"
1969

Damn, if I don't love driving my big blue 4-wheel drive truck!

It's a '66 Chevrolet K10, better known in the identical GMC version as the "Gimmy."

Take a regular windowless delivery van, put windows all along the sides, bolt in up to three rows of bench seats, or just use the open eight feet of covered cargo space. Then, for us extreme drivers, four-wheel drive with over-sized knobby mud and snow tires all around. These were the granddaddies of monster trucks—and all the accursed soccer mom SUV's of the far distant future.

Fuck the future, we said, this is the '70s! We are the future! At least if we lasted that long.

Why I had an interest in going where there were no roads, I couldn't really say. Maybe it was symbolic rebellion against the fact I always found myself following someone else on civilized highways going nowhere in general. I guess I just liked the idea of taking roads less likely to be traveled, especially by two-wheel drive plastic-cage cars carrying idiots lost on the trail of life.

Anyone growing up in the '50s logging forests of Oregon learned quickly this was the truck of choice for anybody needing to go damned near anywhere, whenever they damned well pleased. Besides loggers, there were miners, prospectors, and ranchers all needing reliable, dry, rugged, roomy, and powerful trucks for going places and carrying workers and loads where roads were dubious propositions at best.

Gimmy's, also known as *Jitney's* in logging lands, were literally created to haul workers and their tools to those pesky, past-the-end-of-the-road job sites. These sites were normally attained by traversing some butt-fucked hell-hole of someone's demented nightmare of what might be facetiously referred to as a passable road but was really intended for only mules. This might mean anything from floating adrift in a sand dune sea, to climbing rocky trails that could easily intimidate a mountain goat.

The other nice thing about a Gimmy was they could seat up to nine big guys with all their required gear and tools, out of the rain and in relative take-it-like-a-man comfort during the often hours-long, sometimes brutal commutes. They functioned both as trucks and small buses with the added advantage of an over-built gas-guzzling monster American V-8 under the hood and the all-important four-wheel drive that fed hundreds of horsepower to four giant deep-tread mud and snow tires that could both dig it out of a hole or into one depending on the luck or skill of the driver. It could handle steep, often muddy, rocky, rugged, barely definable, dicey trails that back in Oregon were laughingly called logging roads.

It was in this strange collision of marketing hype, and an otherworldly setting of glowing yellow instrument lights, I found myself immersed in a comfortable feeling of warmth and optimism. I drove along quite happy to be traveling the road of dubious destiny.

At first, and as usual, I felt cool, comfortable, confident, strong, and right at home at the wheel of my big blue truck. It was dark blue, no doubt, to match the U of M colors, blue and gold, as it had been previously owned by the geology department and used to transport students and equipment to remote research sites in Mexico. Now it was mine, except I needed to replace the woefully worn-out six-cylinder with one of Bill Smith's custom rebuilt 350 big-block V-8 engines.

As the big 4x4 roared up a twisty mountain road that seemed to be getting markedly more narrow and precipitous, winding higher and higher into some ill-defined remote snow-covered mountainous pass, I wondered where the fuck I was. For some reason, I had no idea why I was here. I was enjoying the view and warm feeling of hearing the roar of exploding dinosaur juice.

Pretty soon though, I found myself straddling deep muddy ruts crisscrossed with snow drifts. The fishtailing truck danced haphazardly all over the narrow ridge road. I wondered calmly just exactly why I was at this stupid place at this particular time. An exceedingly vague and innocuous voice emerged from some dark foggy depth telling me it wasn't real, but I had to keep on truckin' anyway.

The road morphed mysteriously into a narrow set of intertwined, gouged-out wheel channels atop a featureless snow-blown, ever-narrowing ridge devoid of any familiar sight that might clue me into this location. I looked down the left side of the truck and only briefly could make out a river shimmering with ice far below. On the other side was nothing but the icy matching colors of cold and threatening clouds.

"Damn!" I swore to myself. I could feel the sweat break out on my forehead and neck. I felt throat-squeezing stress building as my muscles tensed for the preventable yet inevitable crash. "How the hell did I get into this mess? Where the *fuck* am I?"

I felt totally isolated in the truck and intensely aware of what seemed to be an insane sense of dread and urgency; wanting to get somewhere badly but not quite sure exactly where it was I was going or why with such urgency. I just knew I had to get there or I was going to be dead, or maybe something worse. This damned road was probably a summer short-cut that now I cursed myself bitterly for taking. When will I ever wise up?

"Why the hell do I always get myself into this kind of shit?" I felt somehow this scenario was all too familiar. I simply had to stop repeating this vicious cycle of stupid naïve optimism followed by inevitable disaster.

The truck tipped dangerously toward the edge overlooking the river. It was a long way to the bottom and if I went over the edge now, it would be certain doom and destruction of both me and my beloved truck. Death seemed to loom over me like a dark and heavy shroud, like a tongue lapping my truck down into the gnashing maw and rocky teeth of a hungry canyon maw. I felt abjectly helpless, miserably trapped.

I became literally paralyzed with fear. I couldn't move a muscle, though I desperately wanted to claw myself violently out of this hellhole of a mess. I was stupefyingly helpless to do anything. There was no wide space to turn around or even a spot to slow down safely. I didn't dare stop for fear of being sucked over the icy edge toward a bottomless pit and an instantaneous crushing plunge into the big hurt. I could see no way out. My guts started churning tighter as if a boa constrictor inside me was squeezing my heart like a helpless, dying rabbit.

I pushed hard on the accelerator, but nothing seemed to stop the slow but inevitable slipping sideways toward doom. My muscles tightened as the truck tipped even farther over the edge. I could hear the grinding noise of rocks sliding under the belly of the truck as wheels came off the ground and it tipped ever closer to a fatal plunge.

"Shi-i-i-i-i-i-i-t!" I screamed, as my body jerked stiff in the anticipation of sudden weightlessness followed by the big gravity hammer and ultimate hurt. Through the wall of noise however, I swear I heard Katie cackling a derisive, almost dismissive laugh, like losing a loveable but nasty pet in a fitting manner that released her of all blame.

I gulped for air and blinked rapidly a dozen times as the scene suddenly went black. Slowly, I realized I had been dreaming. The screeching sound of rocks on metal was replaced with the deep-throated relaxing drone of a smooth-running engine. There was a bright glow in front of me but otherwise there was clueless darkness. Then I noticed the glowing objects separate and become an instrument panel glowing brightly with dials and switches.

I was in a small plane. The cabin seemed to be tipped a little sideways, just not as much as my truck in my nightmare. But that was rapidly becoming just a hazy vision. I straightened my head from an awkward angle, causing some neck pain, as everything surrounding me started coming back to more-or-less level and recognizable reality.

Then it struck me with a flash that made my stomach turn a couple of flips. I had fallen asleep while flying at night! I should be crashing and dying!

What? Why?

"Holy shit!" I muttered to myself as I fought back the fuzziness in an attempt to figure out what the hell was happening.

"Fuck me!" I cursed, as I wiggled my sore ass in the seat while desperately trying to figure out where the altimeter was located. My eyes seemed to be under someone else's control. Everything looked both strange and yet very familiar.

I first focused on the big blue instrument right in front of the control column.

"Whew," I said to myself as I noticed the artificial horizon was steady and oriented like a real horizon with blue sky above and brown earth below, just as I remembered it should be. Brown over blue, on the other hand, is definitely not a good thing.

Outside of a small banking turn to the right, the plane seemed normal and about where it was supposed to be, flying almost level in a big circle waiting for the stupid pilot to wake up. At least the plane wasn't stalling or diving out of control. Finally, I found and focused on the altimeter, calibrated in hundreds of feet, indicating 54.5. I had been flying at 5500 feet heading east, so apparently, I had the plane well-trimmed and it was flying along just fine while I had taken a little nap. I looked at the clock: 4:45. But I had no memory of the last time I had read it. The gut-squeezing-shit feeling began to noticeably lessen as I took control of the stick, straightened up the bank, and rolled out on a course of about 60 degrees.

I felt indescribably exhausted. My brain seemed wrapped in a thick sticky goo similar to tar pits sucking up dinosaurs. Slowly, scattered and drug-fogged memories of my recent business venture started rearing their ugly little heads. We had been flying on our last leg between Kansas City and Ann Arbor. I checked my watch again. We had taken off from Kansas City at around 2 a.m. after refueling. It was now about five in the morning, just before sunrise. So we must be somewhere around Indiana or the Michigan-Ohio border.

"We?" I repeated out loud and realized there was someone else here in the plane with me. I look at the seat to my right and indeed there's a dark body with black hair, sound asleep, head leaning sideways against the passenger door with an ugly drool coming out of one side of his mouth and dribbling down the window.

I remember more now. It's my dorky partner-in-crime, Rob. A graduate student in math and computer science who like me worked at the Space Physics Lab while studying under a NASA grant; just like mine, it was in jeopardy of being taken away at any moment by that shithead Nix-goon.

I made friends with him because he seemed as intelligent as me and he was a PhD graduate student. I didn't fully trust Rob, however, because he had medium-length hair, almost conventional, and belonged to a fraternity. If you didn't have the guts to show the world who you were, you were a phony. He was sort of a phony, but so far, a tolerable one who liked to smoke dope.

I had joined a fraternity for a short spell just to see what it was all about. In short order, I realized they were pretty much what I had always suspected: sick, shallow, corrupt, nepotistic, salacious, and just plain dumbass, kiss-ass, bullshit-eating, snob suck-ups and dilettantes. At least Rob seemed to be smarter than the average idiot and sort of cool; he laughed at all the right topical jokes, which was usually a good measure of a proper counterculture sympathy. Still, he might be motivated by suspect forces that I still wasn't sure of. He looked a little shady, especially with his neatly trimmed goatee, but I couldn't hold that against him. We were all a little shady to the self-respecting white-washed masses.

Fraternity clowns were usually idiots trying to get a degree by any means that money, persistence, or influence could buy. Their one redeeming quality, at least for me, was their need for almost continuous partying while stuck in the four-year-degree scramble. I could relate to the consumption of copious quantities of beer, liquor, and various illegal substances. That's where Rob apparently stepped in.

Rob wasn't as rich as most of his brothers so that was in his favor and maybe that was why he came up with this crazy idea of flying to El Paso, buying some quality weed directly from the growers, and bringing it back to Ann Arbor's famished fraternity row. As I'd just gotten my pilot's license and liked to smoke good weed, Rob thought it would be a great way to top off our summer before school started up again and, of course, make a little bread on the side.

Neither he nor I had the money to finance such a trip, but his fraternity brothers did. He raised five grand the first afternoon. How foolish was I to have thought that they only did beer and the occasional sorority girl while watching mostly football on TV? Apparently, it took a lot of weed and cocaine today to get college girls in the same mood that beer and cigarettes seemed to provide in high school.

I jabbed him hard in the ribs.

"Wake up you bastard!" I yelled as I poked him in the ribs a second time and checked the compass heading again. Rob straightened up slowly and grunted something ugly but thankfully unintelligible.

"Fuck! You! You were supposed to keep me awake you scum-dog." He just sat there blinking in confusion and looking straight ahead into the dark void.

"A lot of fucking good you are," I shouted again. He looked as if he was still half asleep. I became conscious of my heart pounding furiously as I slowly realized how close we had come to being just another country newspaper headline: *Mysterious Airplane Crashes in Swanson's Back 40.*

If we ended up ashes, we would make it onto the obituary page sometime after they eventually identified us by our teeth. If we just crumpled in, then we'd probably make the front page because of what we were carrying.

"Where are we?" Rob finally muttered, as he wiped the spittle still hanging from his chin. He stared around dazedly, mostly outside the cabin but, like me, couldn't make out anything except for a few randomly scattered farm lights.

"I think we're somewhere over Indiana. Where's the map?" I demanded.

I checked the two navigational radios but wasn't sure what FAA stations they were tuned to or what radials we might be currently flying on. Rob shuffled through some papers in his lap and finally came up with a sectional for the upper Midwest. "Is this what you want?" he asked as he handed me the chart.

"Grab the stick you worthless frat-pig and hold her steady on this heading." I pointed to the gyro-compass, which now indicated the correct course. "I've got to figure out where the hell we are and whether we have enough fuel to make it home. I fell asleep too, and I'm not sure how long we've been flying in circles."

"Shit!" he screamed as he finally jerked fully awake. "We could have crashed!"

"No shit, Sherlock! But we didn't," I yelled back. "Now just hold her steady while I figure this out."

I consulted the map and kept looking outside to see if I could spot anything familiar that might correlate with the map so I could determine our general location. There were a few scattered lights, but nothing like a line of moving lights indicating a freeway, or a cluster of lights that might indicate a small town or city.

There was a faint orange glow to the east indicating it wouldn't be long before the sun lit up the horizon in a blaze of clouded, polluted glory. I started fiddling with one of the navigational radios and dialed in the frequency for the Fort Wayne VOR, hoping we were somewhere near.

A VOR radio transmitter sends out a signal that tells a receiver onboard what direction the aircraft's position is from the transmitter's location. Tuning two receivers to two different VOR transmitters and drawing lines on the map along the two indicated radials, or direction lines; will show your current position, exactly where the two lines cross.

I didn't have to draw actual lines on the map. I just needed to know our location roughly. The other radio was still tuned to South Bend and so I could just about imagine where we should be by tracing along the two radials with my finger. It seemed we were just northeast of Indianapolis and not very far from the Indiana-Michigan-Ohio border. That meant we had only about one more hour of flying time before reaching our destination. I checked the fuel gauges and saw that we had more than enough left to make it home. Fortunately, we hadn't been asleep very long.

"Hell!" I exclaimed with smug satisfaction. Rob was concentrating on keeping the wings level, the altitude constant, and the compass glued to 60 degrees. "We only have about another hour or so to go before we get to the Ann Arbor airport. We're almost home free."

"I'm worried," he quietly announced, as he made yet another small correction to our heading.

I was the trained and licensed pilot-in-command, but when I got busy navigating or talking on the radio, Rob knew just enough to steer the plane and keep it roughly on course. The old wood and fabric plane we borrowed for the trip had no autopilot or wing leveler, so outside of trimming the control tabs to neutralize stick pressure, it pretty much needed constant attention in order to keep flying straight and level. I must have done a damn good job trimming the plane before I fell asleep as it hadn't lost any appreciable altitude nor gone into a death spiral. It had just flown in a big circle patiently waiting for me to wake up or run out of gas, whichever came first.

"Now what are you worried about?" I asked slightly exasperated. Rob had been pretty enthusiastic about our little flying project when he first proposed it. But as we went along and got further and further locked into what at best was a dicey proposition full of twists and unexpected turns, he lost what enthusiasm he had and ended up sounding like an old crazy woman talking to cats in a bag.

"What if the narcs are waiting for us at the airport? What if we land and they jump out of the bushes with guns and dogs? Maybe we should land at a different airport like Kalamazoo or Ypsilanti."

Rob looked over at me; besides the obviously blurry bloodshot eyes looking back at me, I discerned another attack of paralyzing paranoia about to explode.

"You need to get control of yourself," I shouted back over the sound of the engine. I was too poor to afford headphones or an intercom, so we made do with the old style of cockpit communication. We yelled to talk and turned the volume way up on the two-way radio so we could hear it over all the noise. The giant, hand-sized microphone was straight out of some '50s TV cop show.

We did make one concession for our amusement and entertainment. I set a car cassette deck on top of the instrument panel and hooked up a couple of stereo headphones. At least we could enjoy some tunes while pretending we were counterculture heroes bringing back the gold.

This little contraption almost got us killed when we took off from our first refueling stop in Illinois, however. As the plane pitched up taking to the air, the cassette deck slid off its perch on top of the instrument panel and hit one of the controls almost killing the engine. I jumped into full emergency mode and began my procedures. I could see there wasn't enough runway left to land, and off the end of the runway was a large mobile home park with nothing but silver-painted roofs in sight, barring any emergency landing. *Jeez, what a dumb place to build a trailer park. It could only be a matter of time before someone augurs in. What a mess that's going to be!*

Visions of flaming mobile homes and twisted aluminum wreckage flashed through my mind as I grappled with the controls, trying to keep it flying as I searched frantically for the knob that had been hit by the falling tape deck. To keep the airspeed above stalling, I pitched the plane down toward the rapidly approaching shiny aluminum boxes. Rob started screaming like a teeny-bopper at a Beatles concert.

Fortunately, I found the mixture knob that had been knocked in by the falling cassette deck. The plane started to sink sickeningly as it slowed and began fluttering slightly like a falling leaf. The controls lost their responsiveness and we were approaching that magic speed where the wings unglue themselves from the airstream flowing over them and the plane suddenly transitions from flying like a bird to falling like a rock. I felt a gut-wrenching stall coming on.

I jammed the mixture back to lean and regained full power. The little engine gave out a mighty mini-roar and we began to level out and climb. *Whew!* My butt unclenched about fifty pounds worth. Needless to say, at the next fuel stop, I dug the handy roll of duct tape out of my bag and taped the crap out of the tape deck in hope that no further white-knuckle events like that would ever happen again.

Hah, fat chance!

I always carried a full roll of duct tape with me while flying this plane. It was a very old cloth-covered Piper Tri-Pacer or PA-20, with holes appearing in the fabric on a regular basis. Before we took off from Ann Arbor almost a week ago, I had to tape up a big hole in the bottom of the cabin. A bird had already taken advantage of it and had started quite a nice nest inside for itself. I scooped out the twigs and leaves and put on two overlapping layers of my best duct tape. Last time I looked, it was still there.

"I'll tell you what," I said conceding slightly to his fears. "We can buzz the field a few times and look for any suspicious vehicles. It looks like we're going to get there just at sunrise, and on a Sunday morning there shouldn't be a whole lot of cars around anyway. We'll be just fine."

I patted him on the leg. He snorted like a pissed off horse.

I tried to maintain a calm manner at all times so Rob would more or less keep his nervous anxieties from exploding into drug-induced, raging paranoia. I suppose in this kind of business mistakes that lead to disaster or worse, like getting busted, are probably caused by losing your cool and doing something dumb or brash. We knew we had been skating on thin ice for the past week and it was only a matter of time before something unexpected became almost certain.

Stay cool, stay cool.... I repeated softly to myself over and over, as if it were my new personal mantra. I was nervous too but giving in to your fears is the first step in getting them realized. Rob practically made *stay cool* his mantra as well. He was constantly stroking and pinching his little black goatee, especially when he worried. He would crack a devious smile, making you think he was up to something with his world-class brain, when in fact he was about to implode with fear and cringing. He could look cool and calm, almost reflective, until later alone he might rip off his clothes, run in circles around the motel room, and howl out the window at the moon like some lovesick coyote. Fortunately, people in the Southwest apparently don't find this behavior particularly suspicious.

As the horizon ahead of us started to show color, my thoughts began to wander. I couldn't help replaying over and over like a tune stuck in my head our little flying adventure over the last week. Rob had proposed the idea a few weeks back in the middle of summer, when most local supplies began to thin out; the quality got poor and the price got high. Rob was still living in his frat house and knew a lot of trust-fund babies who liked to augment their usual beer and cheap Scotch diet with something they perceived to be more dangerous and seductive.

So Rob hit up his brothers for investment money and asked around about where the best place might be for making a buy. I was amazed when he was able to raise around ten grand in small unmarked bills in less than three days, plus he found out about an importer of sorts who we only knew as Nick. He worked out of El Paso buying from a Juarez gang that brought pot up to the border from growers in southern Mexico. Nick bought in Juarez and then hired young Mexican students who regularly attended El Paso colleges to haul dope across the most heavily patrolled border in the U.S. He normally ran it back east in a decked-out fancy white van with all the windows darkened to Secret Service standards. We were going to be his first fly-in customer, sort of wholesale cash-and-carry.

I was game. Being a poor farm boy from Oregon, and working my way through graduate school, fostered a strong desire to make a little cash whenever the opportunity might arise. Flying a plane to El Paso to pick up a few hundred pounds of pot seemed like a fun way to have a little adventure and line my pockets at the same time. I knew a big drug dealer in Colorado who flew the southern routes and he seemed to be well off, pretending to be a hip photographer and pilot with a cornucopia of drugs and skinny blonde bitches hanging off his every word. I could dig it.

Besides, I liked smoking pot. It was the only thing that kept me from shooting myself from all the nerve-numbing drudgery of doing space physics research with those new fucking computers. Don't misunderstand me, NASA was fun for a while, but it slipped badly after the moon shot and now was clearly on the outs. It couldn't begin to compete with dodging the DEA, playing cat and mouse with Mexican Federales, and flying an old crate through late night thunderstorms over Nebraska. What fun!

With fucking Nix-goon in the White House, it just seemed proper that I become an outlaw. It was my form of protesting against the incredibly ignorant and corrupt government brought to us by a massively gullible and terminally stupid electorate. The Vietnam War was a prime example of stupendous social lunacy. This among a lot of other things proved exactly why the ancient Greeks did not trust democracy even though they invented it, used it, and abused it just as we do.

The general public of anywhere or anytime simply cannot be trusted to make sound decisions concerning public policy or proper governmental conduct. Hell, if 1930s Germany, one of the most intelligent and well-educated countries of modern Europe, could produce a Hitler complete with Nazis, wholesale genocide, and a disastrous World War II, then clearly even Americans in the '50s and '60s could just as easily be misled or, to put it bluntly, brainwashed into being the biggest bunch of blindly war-mongering, phony-patriotic, nationalistic idiots ever to defecate on the stage of human history.

Fuck'em, I said. My own country was trying to kill me, so anything I could do to throw it back in their face or simply take advantage of their stupidity was certainly more than justified. So every time I lit up a doobie, snorted some dynamite coke, or tripped out on psychedelics like acid, mushrooms, or the sacred cactus, it was just my way of standing up for justice, equality, righteousness, and the true American way. The Constitution guaranteed personal freedom. I was simply holding up my end of the bargain by living it. Fuck'em if they couldn't take a civics joke.

So here I am, flying high (so to speak) over the heartland of America the Beautiful, bringing the next big load of shit-weed to her finest future hypocrites and professional thieves, like lawyers and politicians, who if asked would condemn drugs as a scourge on America while quietly financing some of the greatest and most powerful black-market criminal empires on earth. Hell, business itself is simply hypocrisy at its most refined level. Everybody lies, everybody knows everybody is lying, and yet such absurd conduct is still winked at and considered right and proper human behavior.

Such also is the thinking of the engaged, well-educated electorate who consistently votes for someone else's interests at the unbelievable expense of their own. It's just another oxymoron; voters are incapable of making rational decisions based on their own welfare. Just can't do it. Their one and only redeeming quality, which keeps the rest of us sane minority piqued with keen interest, is the voters' unfailing penchant for doing something really stupid like destroying themselves over some ludicrous poppycock idea of racial superiority, as the Germans did, or better yet, obliterating most of civilization as we know it because their god is better than some other god or their way of making money is better and more sacred than your way.

Don't do as I do but do as I say. If it wasn't so pathetic I would choke laughing. Actually, I do laugh a lot because if I didn't, I'd probably blow my brains out. But living a counterculture lifestyle while disguised as just another conventional shithead makes me feel all warm and fuzzy inside. I may not be able to change things, make them right, but I can live quite happily and satisfied while continually being at total odds with the scumbag oppressors. *Survival of the smartest* was my motto, and there were no laws against laughing while screwing with the jerks.

Light was gaining a hold on the eastern horizon, finally allowing some details to emerge from the flat darkness below. I could now discern trees, roads, telephone poles, and a few cars. The lights of a city appeared off to the north, which I presumed was either Jackson or Kalamazoo. No matter, it wouldn't be long before we'd link up with I-96, which would lead us straight to our destination. It was probably less than an hour before we'd land at our home airport just south of Ann Arbor.

The lab where we worked as graduate students was under the engineering department, but semi-autonomous with its own budget. Even though it was situated on U of M land and staffed by college administrators, some who held university appointments in physics and engineering, it was entirely funded by NASA and the National Science Foundation. The official reason for its existence was upper atmospheric research. But in reality, I think it was an excellent excuse for frustrated engineers to get their hands on surplus military rockets that they fired off gleefully like boys playing with incredibly big fireworks.

NASA required justifications before they would hand over the good stuff, so it was my boss's job to come up with real research projects that received funding from the NSF. In turn, that allowed the engineers to build electronic payload packages that got launched by the almost infinite supply of old 1950s Aerobee-Hi rockets. The data collected by the custom-built onboard electronics was radioed back to earth, where overworked and underpaid grad students like Rob and I would spend long hours deciphering, computing, and reporting on any scientific discoveries we might accidently make.

Our instrumentation consisted of lightweight, super-tiny highly sensitive mass spectrometers, developed in-house, that could detect the various atmospheric gases in the near-vacuum of earth's outer atmosphere. We quickly determined that one of the gases that measured far above its normal concentration came from the exhaust fumes of Russian Intercontinental Ballistic Missiles as they blasted off from secret locations in Asia. That earned us electronic card-locks on the doors and some very ugly guards who wore clothes with strange bulges in places human anatomy could not normally justify.

But 80 percent of the labs personnel were either young graduate students like us, or recently graduated engineers waiting for their next lucrative job in private industry. We all smoked dope and if we could afford it, snorted coke. On special occasions when available, we took that daring step up the ladder of more exciting and dangerous drugs that only the CIA had more experience with, but that's a different story.

We weren't just a bunch of drug-crazed lunatics working surreptitiously for the federal government. We were young kids, freshly graduated from college, having the best time of our lives—chasing women, getting drunk and high whenever we could, partying like there was no tomorrow, and digging on Rock & Roll and loud music. We didn't take ourselves too seriously and had no particular axe to grind against the university. In fact, we loved blowing off our multi-stage rockets carrying highly advanced electronic payload packages into extremely eccentric orbits that we launched from exotic places such as Kenya and Fort Churchill, Canada.

Flying an airplane was just one more thing attractive to bright scientific-minded persons like me, which I had to do along with shooting off million-dollar rockets and playing with the latest government-owned computers, all the while pretending we were some kind of daring amateur test pilots for DuPont Labs. On weekends we gathered in the local parks, where we set up portable stages with outrageously powerful PA systems and invited any and all Detroit-area musicians to come and entertain. Life was great. We were having a hell of a good time. Being wild and crazy gun-totin' drug freaks was just the entrance exam to the University of Rock & Roll.

So it seemed natural that near the end of the summer when the quality and quantity of dope bottomed out weeks before the annual harvest would show up from Mexico and South America, we took it upon ourselves in the good old American tradition of entrepreneurialism and take-charge attitude to just go down there and get first crack at the new crop. It all started that Friday afternoon a few weeks ago when Rob dropped by my office to shoot the breeze in anticipation of knocking off early and getting a head start on the weekend. Weekends were our only life outside the lab.

The crap we did weekdays like working at the lab, if you could call it work, and attending a class or two at the university was sheer boredom at best. I was in the physics group, which was staffed by what were then called Atmospheric Physicists, and later, Planetary Atmospheric Physicists. At best, atmospheres were messy subjects far beyond any conventional mathematical approach. Such dynamic soups of gases, thermal gradients, gravity, and solar-powered winds defied any closed-formula approach.

Fortunately for us, the computer age was dawning; so messy real-world problems like atmospheres and geology were being attacked by something called simulations which were huge ugly computer programs that attempted to imitate physical processes by applying basic mathematical formulas and real-world data to a tiny hypothetical box containing whatever one was trying to simulate. In my case, it was a box full of gases at different altitudes and different locations that, when taken together, mimicked the chemistry and dynamics of earth's upper atmosphere.

My handwritten program consisted of several long boxes containing hundreds of IBM punch cards. Each card had a single line of code. In these heady days before solid-state memory or cheap massive data storage, the cards held not only all the lines of the program, but all the data needed to run it as well. I had to patiently type the entire thing, one keystroke at a time at a keypunch machine setting outside the lab offices in an alcove under the stairs off the main entrance lobby. It was a shitty, boring job, but only I could be trusted to do it right, so no help. Besides, graduate students are helpless slaves anyway, so I slaved away on the IBM beast.

As it was the only keypunch machine at our lab, it was shared by everyone at the lab and busy most days. I found it easier and more convenient to use late at night when I was doing another project, developing rolls of 35mm film from an optical spectrometer located on the lab's roof. It took pictures of the entire atmosphere over the top of the lab, photographing the spectrum of light from any sources of glowing gas like what an aurora produces. It took pictures every five minutes all night long, every night. Part of my duties were to develop this film and scan it for any possible signals from air glow. However, we were located near Detroit, so far south of the Arctic atmosphere and fogged by city light pollution that for an entire two years of exposing and developing, the film never recorded anything other than a normal black or cloudy sky.

So while I waited for the various baths to develop the film, I punched cards. When I thought I had a complete set of cards that the computer could compile and run, I would pack up the boxes, take them across campus to the monolithic computing center where there resided a very expensive IBM 360 computer. There, I submitted my boxes of cards through an iron-barred window that reminded me of a walk-up liquor store just outside an Indian reservation.

The computing center resembled a typical county jail. It had no windows, and its doors were heavy steel that could withstand battering rams and several pounds of C4 explosives. It resembled a Nazi-fortified bunker facing the Western Front. If it was done to frustrate those who after years of stressed-out frustrating work with insidious computers might snap and attempt to take revenge on the enigmatic soulless machine, then it surely accomplished its purpose.

I knew this all too well, as I had been submitting my cards for well over six months with no results of any kind, whatsoever. Inside the blockhouse, at the narrow window with the huge metal roll-down shutter, I would hand my stack of boxes to an attendant who in exchange gave me a single card imprinted with a job number. I would return after a couple of hours to be handed back, if lucky, several hundred printed sheets containing nothing but zeros, or more likely, a single sheet with the cryptic message, *Failed to Compile.*

No reason, no error message, not even a clue as to why it had failed. I would then retreat from the alien bomb shelter, taking the walk of shame and humiliation that had been dealt out by the all-powerful machine of mathematically certain frustration and failure. After a few weeks of this ego-shredding exercise, I sought some words of wisdom from my project director. He pointed out that sometimes only a simple comma out of place could cause catastrophic results.

"You have to go over your cards one character at a time, making sure there are no missing characters of any kind and no spaces where they shouldn't be," he advised.

That was it?

No great words of wisdom. No discussion of programming secrets or simulation philosophy. Just one stupid little typo in a program of hundreds of thousands of characters causes a complete computing meltdown. Were computers that fucking stupid? It was then I realized that computer jockeys were not the brilliant professionals they pretended to be. First, they had to be fastidiously accurate typists, and only after that dubious accomplishment could they demonstrate any level of actual cleverness. But the clueless computer could only do what the klutzy programmer typed.

In my case, and I suspected in many others as well, tedious acuity and mental agility simply did not coexist in the same brain. Then it dawned on me with a jolt of abject despair—the age of computers meant the end of a thinking civilization as we know it. Computers make humans more stupid and mindless, causing a dumbing-down of the race to the point they can't create anything better, nor can they do without.

My dilemma was whether to cowardly assist our new master in its climb to world domination or be a sabot and throw myself into the bowels of the monster. Now I knew why the computer center job window looked like the back door to Fort Knox.

It was on one such afternoon of frustrating, mind-numbing, detailed examination of commas and spaces that Rob entered my cubical.

"Hey. Que paso?" he asked, without really expecting an answer. It was just our greeting based on a comic expression made famous by George Carlin's Hippie Dippy Weatherman.

"Que paso to you too," I answered. He stared at the stack of cards in the keypunch machine as he stroked his curly goatee and smiled his crooked little devious smile. His eyes twinkled with mirth as he saw me struggling and getting nowhere. Some people take great delight in seeing other people suffer, maybe just like them. It clearly wasn't empathy, but rather an honest enjoyment of others' pain you know well, close to some kind of twisted sense of revenge and shared punishment. Weird, but it happens more often than one might think.

"You ever get that thing to run yet?" he said.

"Nary a decimal yet," I said somewhat despairing. "Whoever said computers make life better should have his thumbs perforated by a keypunch machine then fed through an impact printer."

"You know what helps me a lot in debugging?" he went on, casually ignoring my complaints. "I set up a bunch of print statement cards and insert them at key spots to see how far the program is working before it fails."

"I did that," I said still frustrated. "It's getting through the main part but for some reason the numerical solution from the differential flow equations aren't converging. They either diverge to zero or infinity but never the right answer."

"Can't help you with that. Sometimes smaller steps work," Rob offered.

"If I took any smaller steps," I retorted, "the computing center would run out of printer paper."

"They can afford it," he calmly asserted, as if they needed to be taught a lesson.

"But they charge it to the lab account. My boss would have a cow."

"He seems to be having a whole herd of cows lately. Must be budget renewal time."

"No shit, Sherlock! He's locked up with the other department heads now trying to rationalize next year's budget cuts. The fucking Republicrooks and Nix-goon are squeezing the crap out of the NSF and even NASA. I even heard a rumor they may have to close the whole damn lab."

"Not until we graduate for Christ's sake!" he declared loudly. Then Rob changed the subject just as fast.

"So what are you doing this weekend?" he asked, hoping to get me off the unpleasant issue of looming disaster.

"Nothing planned. I'll probably just hang out on campus. Go to the Film Forum showing maybe." I finally looked up from the computer printout that was starting to go fuzzy on me anyway.

"Know where I can score?"

"Weed? Nope. It's getting pretty dry around town. There's always coke," I suggested thinking of Bill and his Corvette-powered pharmacy on wheels.

Bill Smith was the charismatic local drug dealer who almost always had some kind of exotic pharmaceutical for casual sampling or short test flights. The American pharmaceutical companies were all gearing up with lots of new drugs for fighting the Vietnam War, Bill had a link to them all. He sometimes had pot, but he preferred coke and recently developed a solid connection with some guy who worked on the inside at a big hospital pharmacy, so he had all kinds of strange and exotic pills—including some amazing reagent-grade pharmaceutical cocaine, guaranteed pure by the FDA. Just having the label from that squat brown bottle was a major coup.

Bill carried around a *Physicians Desk Reference*, or PDR, which looked like a giant bible the Pope might use. He kept current with all the formal chemical names, drug effects, contraindications, and adverse reactions, which was sometimes exactly what one was trying to attain from a good high. He was both a genius and a successful lawbreaker, not a common criminal, and therefore considered himself to be legal savvy and exceptionally knowledgeable on the ways of the modern police force. Bill was a part-time private eye and a large-event security expert. He was also a damned good engine mechanic and auto parts finder.

He often helped the local promoters organize and run security at the many rock concerts staged in town. It was fortuitous and quite convenient to have a security chief who was also the premier local drug dealer. It kept things absurdly simple and nicely under wraps. He had full backstage access, all the right connections, and more practical experience with illegal substances than almost anyone in town. Bill was the key contact for anything involving the young locals and he knew everything that went on in the dirty little underbelly of that prestigious university town.

"Naw," Rob said. "I just checked the fraternities and they're all out of weed and getting desperate. They suggested that I make a run down south and even offered to put up the bread!"

For a mathematician, there was nothing esoteric about Rob's predilections. He liked drugs, sex, and Rock & Roll, like everyone else I knew, just not necessarily in that order. More than that, he liked money. He was a frat boy after all, not really trustworthy.

I wasn't sure how he thought he was going to get rich being a math major, but I guess for now it paid the bills. Wall Street hadn't discovered computers yet.

Since the Space Race with Russia, many students who were perhaps more interested in the pedestrian side of life found that majoring in science and engineering attracted more financial support than business or accounting. That was all changing rapidly, since that goon posing as a human, Nix-goon, actually conned a bunch of dumbasses into voting for him and he stole the election again even after he was clearly guilty of high crimes and misdemeanors as well as significant crimes against humanity.

"How much?" I asked trying to appear disinterested, but willing to keep up my end of the conversation.

"I don't know but I'm sure it would be enough to make it worth our time."

"What do you mean *we*, white man?" I loved this line from the old joke about the Lone Ranger and Tonto being surrounded by hostile Indians. When the Lone Ranger tells him, 'We have to do something about all those Indians.' Tonto responds, 'What do you mean *we*, white man?'

"I figure we could take a week off from work and fly down to El Paso, where I know a guy who gets it directly from the Mexicans. You can get a plane, right?"

"I might know where I can find a plane. It's only a four-place, so we can't haul more than a couple hundred pounds," I offered halfheartedly, going along with the absurd proposition just to see how far it might go.

I had no idea it would lead to a week of drunken, drug-addled paranoia, raging lunacy, skirting the edge of every sort of comic-book calamity and probable disaster imaginable.

Sometimes we succumb to a great notion. Sometimes we become victims of our own hubris. In this case, neither of us was going to admit he didn't have the guts to do something we'd been daring ourselves to do for months. At the time, we were convinced that two graduate students with a combined IQ in the 300s could surely outwit a bunch of high-school-dropout narco cops. All we needed was the will and a plausible way. Now that the money issue was resolved, we had no excuses left. We were mutually trapped by our own phony male bravado. Testosterone was our inspiration and fate, our leader. Nothing could stop us now even if it sounded totally ridiculous and absurd. Which it did.

As we neared the end of this nefarious adventure, so many foolish and ridiculous things had happened. They all seemed like disconnected episodes of a weeklong comic nightmare that I would ponder for decades. How could we possibly have survived any of it?

We had enough screw-ups our first night out to kill a dozen would-be smugglers. After damn near crashing on our takeoff in Illinois, we almost ran out of gas over Iowa. We beat an oncoming thunderstorm at 2 a.m. by landing at Omaha International between 737s. Then we flew into an early morning fog over Wyoming, desperately searching yet again for an open refueling spot. We didn't even have drugs to blame at that point, as we wanted to stay squeaky-clean-legal for as long as possible.

Finally, we made it to Boulder, sister city to Ann Arbor, and another of the few oases of sanity in a world gone mad. I happened to know the big dealer in town. It was the ol' *my best friend married a girl whose best friend is...* story. In this case, her best friend was the favorite mistress of Jim Blake, Boulder's biggest drug importer and rich hippie photographer dilettante whose aerial photography business provided cover for his fleet of drug-smuggling airplanes.

Jim's only photograph that ever made any money had nothing to do with airplanes, ironically, but everything to do with illegal drugs. It was a great hippie poster that showed two skiers riding a chairlift in a snowstorm passing a joint. *Get High on the Rockies* ended up in every headshop in the country as pot, skiing, and running away to the wilderness became ultra-cool.

Rob and I spent the weekend resting up at an apartment Jim had hidden inside his hanger at the Boulder airport. On Sunday, he took us to a legendary mountain party thrown by some big rock promoters in town. It was held at the secret wilderness home of a rich patron of the new arts atop a nearby mountain with an incredible one hundred-mile view to the eastern plains. I vaguely remember seeing Kansas from the back deck, which also overlooked all of Boulder and most of north Denver. The view was mind-numbing, even without the aid of drugs; the vast distance and sharp detailed perspective made one feel like a giant striding across an anthill earth.

The party-favor dish on the coffee table had more colored pills than The Doors' backstage snack table. Rob, still battling airsickness after flying across Nebraska dodging thunderstorms, didn't indulge. I did and drifted into random thoughts on our condition as the sky lit up with intense colors. Rob had found the host's telephone and was busy talking to somebody in an agitated manner. He seemed to be doing a lot of that lately. Probably just trying to keep all the nervous investors back in Ann Arbor calm. He could use some soothing himself. He seemed much more nervous than the situation actually called for.

I found a big rock near the Coors keg and settled down to daydream about our era. We lived at a time when apparently only college students were left to stand up for freedom and fight injustice. America had somehow gone insane with redneck super-patriots who'd turn in their own mothers if they wore peace symbols or even worse, sympathized with commie-pinko-atheist-coward students opposing their sacred patriotic war in fucking Vietnam. Everyone had been brainwashed except for an intelligent few who clung precariously to reality with the aid of chemicals. It seemed like the only place where sanity still ruled was in the minds of a drug-crazed Rock & Roll freaks.

We weren't all hippies, but we were smart enough to know our government was full of lying pigs bent on creating wars, killing innocent people, and otherwise raping democracy in order to loot the national treasury for the further enrichment of bastards who thought they deserved unbridled wealth and power at the expense of nearly everybody else on earth. Nobody told me life was a zero-sum game! Was the only way to get ahead in this world, to knock down everybody else?

The Military Industrial Complex had swept away the last vestiges of freedom and democracy in the country. They took control of the Pentagon in World War II. They took absolute control when they assassinated both Kennedys in a secret coup. After that, the so-called democratically elected government became a sham where the public will have turned into the product of modern psychological marketing and TV news brainwashing. The American oligarch-aristocracy quietly and secretly took over the government lock, stock, and barrel, making it their private little feudal kingdom to use, abuse, and bleed at will. They called themselves *Republicrooks* but we just called them Pigs.

The reason cops are called Pigs is really simple. When cops put on their Nazi-like uniforms, they change into something other than human. They morph into something akin to animals, with nothing but raw feelings of hate, lust, and the hierarchy of a feeding frenzy. No morals, no human values, except to follow the alpha-male and establish their territory wherever and whenever possible. They became cops so they could continue being the bullies and thugs they always were. Now they get paid for it by whoever's in power, covering up real crimes by attacking innocent citizens and criminalizing those telling the truth. The Pigs were Nix-goon's antidote for truth, justice and the American Way.

Thus victimized, the vast majority of Americans became nothing more than complacent advocates for their wily new masters. Students and professors at a handful of colleges and universities were the exception, and we were flabbergasted! We could fight with these dumb bastards, but we'd never win. They cheated. They lied freely. They abused the law to cover their asses. We used logic and reason while they used guns and clubs. We were at a distinct disadvantage.

So we decided it was best to play along and pretend to be one of them, but be ready to strike with the legendary *sabot* at any time. Sabotaging the war machine was the unofficial goal, but if that didn't work out, we had small caches of guns and stockpiled ammunition to play with just for the sport, just in case. You never knew how sick these bastards could get. Look at Kent State.

The whole thing disgusted me. We were fighting the demon as hard as we could but he had the money, lawyers, politicians, thugs, and all the really big guns. What was left to us was just a secret campaign of a thousand irritants and the certain knowledge that the monster could actually be killed by making it bleed from a million tiny stab wounds. Buying pot in Mexico from independent producers, reselling at a sizeable profit, and bypassing the government-sanctioned warlords and mob-connected drug dealers was a stabbing well worth the trouble.

It's gonna work. All we have to do is stay small and not get greedy. We fly under the radar. We fly a paper airplane. The Piper was perfect.

"The sun is coming up," Rob declared, gesturing toward the east, which was now pretty much dead ahead anyway.

I shook my head to clear out the blurry memory of that golden Colorado afternoon. I was back in the darkened cockpit listening to Rob state the obvious.

I saw I-94 coming up ahead of us on the left and adjusted our course to fly parallel with it on the last leg in.

"How much longer to Ann Arbor?" he asked.

"Less than an hour," I replied.

I adjusted the VOR's again, finding new directional radials pointing to our current location. I held up the map I normally kept folded on my lap and pointed out roughly where we were.

"Looks like about another sixty or seventy miles. I think I see I-94 off to the left. At our present ground speed, we should be over the airport in another forty minutes or so."

"What are you going to do if we see a bunch of big black unmarked government cars hanging around the parking lot?"

The worried brow above his deviate's smile told me he was for real.

I shrugged trying to look as unconcerned as possible.

"I don't know. We can buzz the field, I guess, and if we see something suspicious we could try for one of those private fields off to the north or northeast."

"What if those rednecks back at that weird airport in Boise City get suspicious and trace our plane to Ann Arbor and call the Feds?"

He was referring to the little freak-out we'd experienced yesterday afternoon after making an unexpected landing at a small airport in Oklahoma's western panhandle.

We had successfully taken delivery of our pot in two large suitcases early that morning after it had been smuggled across the border in several trips taking the entire night. The guys we were working with in El Paso warned us that there were major roadblocks on every road and freeway out of town with Feds, stopping every single car and truck to search for illegal contraband of any kind—drugs or people. Never mind that illegal search-and-seizure was totally unconstitutional, the Nix-goons were in charge now so it was a battle between thugs and henchmen on both sides. An independent honest entrepreneur didn't stand much of a chance.

Fortunately for us, the DEA roadblock on I-25 heading north out of El Paso toward Albuquerque was actually located north of Las Cruces where we'd landed our little Tri-Pacer a couple days earlier. We had long ago nixed landing directly at El Paso International for obvious reasons. Las Cruces was a small university town like Ann Arbor, so I thought there we might at least have a better chance of blending in.

Hungover from the Boulder party the day before, I cut corners, literally, and crossed a restricted air zone somewhere near the White Sands proving grounds in southern New Mexico. Rob freaked out again, expecting to see fighter jets diving out of the sun at any moment to strafe our ragtag little plane. He was paranoid as hell when we landed in Las Cruces, but I felt more or less safe, having taken every precaution to appear innocuous and hopefully as innocent as Catholic School girls.

Just to be sure, I found a pay phone and quickly called Jim back in Boulder. I asked him if I should be worried about the Air Force coming knocking. He assured me that small paper airplanes are way below their concern.

"Besides," he said, "I cut that same corner all the time. It cuts about an hour off my trips to photograph farmland in Mexico."

I heaved a big sigh of relief, which I purposely kept Rob from noticing.

We rented an aging pickup from the only guy present at the airport. He apparently pumped gas, sold tickets, talked on the radio, and rented cars. Otherwise he appeared lonely, dumb, and happy. The old battered truck looked right at home on the desert roads, so it helped us blend right in with the local poor white trash who were generally unmolested by the pigs. So at least we qualified, by being white and not wearing ties.

The guy at the airport who tied down our plane and rented us the beat-up rusty truck was probably onto us from the start, though I dropped a few obvious clues from our cover story to allay any first suspicions he had. We planned our cover story all the way out from Michigan. After a lot of discussion during the long periods of boredom between the more entertaining parts of our takeoffs and landings, we finally came up with a story that we thought was close enough to real life to carry-off.

Our cover, which had served us pretty well so far, was sort of the truth. Truthful enough that it made it easier to tell without looking outrageously guilty or simply out-of-place suspicious. It seemed unique and therefore more believable. After all, would two drug smugglers come up with such an outlandish cover story and expect anyone to believe it?

We agreed to pose as a couple of grad students, which we were, on our way to the New Mexico State University in Las Cruces, where we landed, to consult with a professor there on NASA business, hence the flying part. We even had the name of a professor at Las Cruces who did NASA research, but had never heard of us; if anybody had called to check our story, we would instantly have been doomed. I cursed at this, probably the weakest part of the plan. But I also knew how hard it was to find a professor who was actually in his office and answering the phone, so I felt we were probably safe enough.

Nobody was even remotely curious. Looking back on it later, what surprised me the most was the fact that no one seemed at all interested in what a couple of goofy kids were doing flying around the southwest in a tattered old Tri-Pacer. Maybe our mission was more common than we thought. Maybe nobody really gave a shit.

The airport guy might not have bought it, but I think he was happy for the business and didn't really care where the money came from. All smugglers have stories. Ours was probably more boring and ridiculous than most.

We left El Paso three days later with much heavier suitcases than when we'd arrived. We made it to the airplane in Las Cruces without ever seeing a cop. That didn't keep us from freaking out every few minutes as we imagined all sorts of hidden plain-wrapper cop cars converging on us from all directions. There were audible sucking wind sounds every time we spotted a black Crown Victoria or Suburban with blacked-out windows.

We finally made it all the way back to the airport, apparently undetected. No suspicious cars in sight as we drove onto the ramp to where the little black Piper waited patiently for its trip home. Rob loaded the suitcases into the plane's back seat while I paid the airport guy for the pickup, gas, and tie-down fees. I even gave him a tip. He smiled. Who knew, I might be back some day.

I watched him very carefully as I walked back out to the plane, attempting to see if he was acting weirdly, tipping me off to an ambush. He seemed totally unconcerned. I felt a little better but kept looking around nervously as I walked across the hot and dry, sand-dusted tarmac. We were a long way from home. Anything could happen. It sort of did.

To avoid looking too suspicious on radar screens, we took off heading straight north, as this was the direction most small planes would fly from the El Paso area to, say, Albuquerque. I was positive the El Paso radar operators would regard anything heading directly east or northeast as a sure sign of suspicious activity. We flew low and followed the muddy Rio Grande as it meandered along a line of mountains to the east and deserts to the west. I was fairly certain they would lose us quickly behind the mountains and even if they did see a blip on their screens, they would hopefully assume we were a small plane heading north into Mormon country instead of where we really intended.

Much later I discovered the radar facility at El Paso couldn't have seen a flying battleship unless it carried a transponder to amplify its echo. The rag-covered Piper had no transponder and was simply too small and lacking enough metal surfaces to be detected and displayed on their screens. As far as they were concerned we were a flock of sparrows.

That explains the reason nobody gave chase when we flew over that restricted area on the trip down from Boulder. In reality we had nothing to worry about. With our level of raging paranoia banging against the brink of insanity, we probably wouldn't have believed it anyway and taken no comfort from that fact. When you know you're walking on the edge, you might as well enjoy the adrenaline. It's part of the scenery.

We had been very careful during our stay in El Paso not to smoke anything or get too drunk. Years before, I had come up with a little rule of crime that went something like this: *don't break more than one law at a time*. In my experience, you could usually get away with breaking one law. But when you start multiplying your risk exposure with more than one infraction at a time, well, the result was usually that you first got busted for the little infraction and then they slapped you with *The Big One*. Murder is easy to escape unless you have a broken taillight, which exponentially amplifies the probability of getting caught.

So when we were a decent distance from El Paso and well north of the restricted air space that blocks any earlier turn to the east, we finally set a course heading that would take us straight to southern Michigan. At this point, we felt we had successfully escaped the worst part undetected, so Rob decided it was time to sample our wares just to see what we'd acquired for all our efforts.

When we met the seller just outside the barrio section of Juarez in a very scary, seedy motel, we could tell from the odor and look that it was primo weed but we hadn't actually smoked any for a lot of reasons. Being in a foreign country and having to keep our wits about us as we took delivery of a goodly amount of illegal drugs under the nose of some of the most corrupt and criminal cops in the world was more than reason enough to avoid any sampling.

Spending the rest of that night getting it smuggled across the border via several trips driven by a young English-speaking Mexican teen with a beat-up old white Toyota pickup kept the fear factor at absolute maximum until daybreak. We had purchased about five times the volume that the hidden compartments in his pickup bed could hold. While Rob and I waited on the Mexican side in a '57 Ford Fairlane 500 with a trunk full of hopefully the best weed Acapulco farmers had to offer, our El Paso partners worked the other side offloading the product each time the little Mexican kid made the trip across the border.

We really had no great need to heighten our already raging fear and paranoia. Fear and loathing may have been quaint in Las Vegas, but in Juarez it was tantamount to playing with death. Or so we thought. A little bit of insanity can actually sharpen the wits, but you have to be careful because sometimes it will turn downright delusional and treacherously terminal.

So, I put a New Riders of the Purple Sage cassette in the tape machine, still duct-taped to the instrument panel, and it started pounding out a rock song about driving back to California with a couple hundred pounds of Acapulco Gold. My body tingled with excitement. For weeks we'd been out of weed just like the song. We took a trip down south. Now we're bringing it home. I was going to be a hero.

CHAPTER TWO

YE OLDE SHAKESPEAREAN TWIST

"And if you can't be, with the one you love, honey,
love the one you're with...."

Stephen Stills
"Love the One You're With"
1970

Rob dove into one of the suitcases and found a huge stinky bud peeking out of one of the neatly wrapped bricks. He proceeded, using the sectional map as a rolling table, to crush it, de-stem it, and dribble the makings along the length of a giant EZ-Wider rolling paper. He carefully twisted it into a big ugly-looking doobie like what Cheech and Chong made famous.

At first, we just coughed a lot due to the fact that our bronchial tubes had managed to heal up nicely during our unintended drought. That was over. Then I started smiling. The uptight mood that I had apparently gotten so used to over the past few weeks that it was my new normal began to shift slowly and pull my psychic pendulum back to the lighter, non-gloomy side, which would hopefully become a more permanent normal for a while.

The scenery was spectacular from our view five thousand feet over central New Mexico. The stunning mesas and mountains carved by millennia of wind, sun, and water in so many fascinating colorful shapes made it hard to concentrate on flying. The music beat a rhythm in sync with my pulsing blood that was both exhilarating and soothing. Layers of heavy anxiety simply peeled away, sculpting up my psyche in deeply satisfying, artistic, and wondrous ways. I began to feel at one with the patterned landscape below. God, I loved pot, especially good pot, and this stuff was great!

I noticed Rob had a huge shit-eating grin plastered across his face, which I hoped indicated a final release of his perpetually constipated paranoia. At least I was mature enough, if that was the right description, to try to keep a balanced attitude, apparently in complete control of myself and my surroundings, fully alert to all circumstances and possibilities. Rob was, at best, a walking time bomb of instability.

He was always deadly serious and constantly pointing out the millions of minute possibilities concerning anything and everything that could possibly go wrong. I constantly had to act as Rob's paranoia referee, pointing out the few fears that might be worth worrying about while discounting all the rest as the products of a screaming psychotic lunatic who was completely out of his ever lovin' mind. Gifted mathematicians do seem prone to this kind of behavior, so I cut him some slack.

The terrain quieted down as we flew farther east and north. We were entering the continent's huge Midwestern plains, a vast flat expanse of mostly treeless grassy plateaus that you could swear slowly rolled off in a gradual descent as one travelled eastward. From our vantage point of about six thousand feet above the ground, I swear you could see the earth in front of you disappear below the horizon into a grey smoky sky lingering beyond.

We passed north of a small town on the east side of New Mexico. I had a big bunch of dumbass relatives there. Several uncles on my mother's side ran long-distance cattle-hauling trucks based out of this windblown, eternally dust-bowl settlement. I wasn't planning to stop by to say hello for obvious and longstanding reasons. By and large, they were redneck Republicrooks. We had very little in common outside of some begrudgingly shared DNA. They never forgave my Democratic cow-punching father for stealing away their older sister. Plus, they had a deep-seated bigotry against all educated non-republican Yankees, and I had a deep-seated prejudice against blatant in-bred ignorance and chronic inexcusable flat-headed stupidity.

Rob rolled another joint, which set off a few mental alarm bells, but the Rock & Roll music blaring in my headphones successfully drowned them out. We were heading on a direct line to Kansas City where we were scheduled in a few hours for our first refueling. Then it happened.

I felt a sharp thump from somewhere below me and thought I heard a loud bang. My first thought was it felt like we hit something. But the engine kept on turning with no indication of any problem. I quickly tested the controls and scanned all the instruments but could find no abnormal readings that would indicate anything was going badly. Then I got scared. It's not what you know that kills you; it's what you don't know. Suddenly I felt stupid by design.

"Did you hear that?" I shouted over to Rob. He seemed to be soaring blissfully aloft, not on wings made of steel or stretched nylon, but on wafts of silvery billowing clouds of smoke. He opened his eyes and just looked at me blankly with that same big shit-eating grin wondering what it was that I was babbling about.

"Did you hear that?" I repeated. "Did you feel something?"

He sat straight up at the mention of something unexpected. "Hear what?" he echoed.

"I think we hit something or something came loose," I yelled.

I was still checking on things and feeling the response of the control yoke. Everything seemed normal, but I couldn't be sure. Even though we had flown this plane over three thousand miles through all kinds of conditions and strange circumstances, I still understood that I had a serious lack of expertise that could at any moment conspire to throw us a deadly curveball and I had no confidence that I knew how to handle such things.

Rob's eyes got wide and his shit-eating grin instantly disappeared. He began to look around frantically. What he expected to see or do if he actually did see something in those first anxious moments escape me.

Finally, he seemed to run out of things to look. "What was it?"

"I dunno," I shouted still searching for something wrong. "It seemed like something bumped us or something broke loose."

"Like what?" he yelled back sounding somewhat panicky.

I finally had the presence of mind to turn down the music so we could hear each other better. As soon as I did, we both held our breath and listened intently for any sound that might not have been there a few moments before. The engine seemed to be humming right along as usual and the plane appeared to be flying just fine. But moments like this, you do not trust your first impressions. You keep imagining a warning sound is out there just below your threshold of hearing. If you strain hard enough, it will magically materialize in all its magnificent horror.

"Maybe the front gear fell off," I posited more or less in jest.

The two rear wheels stuck out far enough from the fuselage that you could see them from the side cockpit windows. The front gear however was below the engine housing, totally out of sight.

"Shit!" Rob said. "Fuck!" He immediately tried to look out the window nearest him in a vain attempt to see the gear dangling by a brake line or something. He banged his head on the side window. Not once, but several times as he fought to gain a better perspective.

"Maybe we hit a bird," I continued to guess, ignoring his desperate attempts to see something, anything. "Maybe we hit a duck or a goose and it damaged our landing gear or knocked it off."

Now I was obviously exploring the same realms of psycho-dipshit-land that Rob normally held dominion over.

Out of complete desperation, with nothing further to speculate about, I grabbed the sectional chart and began frantically searching for a nearby airport where we could land and assess any damage. I plotted our rough position. We were just passing across a small corner of Texas and would soon be over the Oklahoma panhandle. The nearest town of any size was Boise City. They had a decent little airport just east of downtown that even had an FAA weather advisory station where pilots could get up-to-the-minute weather briefings over the radio or in person. I read the Boise info box on the map and found the frequency for the tower. Dialing it in, I leaned over and tried to explain my plan to Rob without sending him into any further realms of psychedelic hell.

"There's an airport up ahead. I think we should land there and check things out. But we don't want to cause any suspicions while we're on the ground, so just act like nothing's happening and we're only taking a little rest stop. Go to the bathroom, maybe get a Coke or something but don't talk to anybody about anything. If you're asked, just stick to our cover story."

He bobbed his head in silent agreement.

Rob had that blank look again. He absentmindedly stroked his goatee and stared off into space as if he were listening to directions in his mind from some ethereal spiritual master. That didn't make me feel a whole lot better, but then what can you do with a self-absorbed super-brain finally on good drugs and in a bad situation.

I picked up the mic, keyed the transmit button, and calmly announced, "Boise tower, this is Pacer eight one two niner, echo."

The tower didn't seem busy as they actually spoke slowly with a southern drawl that was surprisingly easy to understand. I told them I thought I'd heard a noise and might have a damaged nose gear. They seemed unconcerned about our plight but said they had us visual and our nose gear was still attached. They offered to have a mechanic meet us on the ramp if necessary.

I put the mic back on its hook and actually began to feel a little better in spite of no sleep in the last twenty-four hours, a nearly permanent adrenaline high, plus a couple of Ritalin's I got from my brother that he got in Vietnam.

We were also high on the experience alone. That high was more of a heart-pounding, chew-your-tongue-raw, constipated-for-a-week, hang-your-ass-on-the-line kind of feeling. Buying bales of pot in Mexico, transporting them through the heart of treacherous Juarez, then smuggling them over several hours across the most heavily guarded border crossing outside of Israel while sitting on hundreds of pounds of pot in a '57 Ford in a police state that could technically have you shot for such things would give anybody that sort of high. It would have been absolutely mind-boggling had we been straight enough to appreciate the fact.

The worst thing about it was the fact that two very bright doctoral students were doing all this without any expertise or finesse whatsoever. Luck favors the amateur and after thinking our plan to death we ended up surviving on nothing other than raw, pipe-wrench-gripping gutsy-luck and an overwhelming desire to see it through no matter what. I was actually super calm as I fine-tuned my senses for the predictably strange encounter just ahead. It didn't even matter that I was still on a stupendous weed high, giddy from lack of sleep, and possible lack of oxygen from flying a little too high and convinced I was hearing strange airplane noises.

I grabbed the throttle tightly and pulled it out slowly, bringing the engine to around 2000 rpm. The little plane began to slow noticeably. I pitched the nose down slightly with the trim control and began a calm descent to the runway. I was floating with the plane as I worried about what might be missing or damaged. Rob was still stroking his goatee, listening for additional instructions from the other side.

I had lived for a short time at almost 10,000-foot altitude in the Colorado Rockies and had learned all too well the effects of smoking good weed and breathing thin air. I guess the thin air gives the smoke more room to infiltrate the lungs, making the highs higher and the mental effects that much more intense. I was fighting this intensity as I tried to calmly control my brain and fly the airplane as I had been taught. Oh hell, I just wanted to get it on the ground.

I thought I had a bright idea just before landing. The sun was shining so I knew that just before we touched down I would be able to see the plane's shadow on the ground, showing whether we still had a front gear attached. I don't know why it didn't dawn on me that the guys in the tower had already told me we did.

When I finally saw the gear's shadow right where it was supposed to be, I let out a big sigh of relief. The plane didn't collapse. I felt much better. The Pacer settled solidly onto the runway and we slowly taxied over to the terminal building. I tried to act if nothing was out of the ordinary.

We parked a little way from the terminal where we hopefully wouldn't attract any passersby who might look in the cabin windows and see some very big suitcases taking up the entire rear seat area. I had to admit that some of the suitcases probably looked suspicious, especially the two old cardboard ones that probably last travelled on the Zephyr. We had scrounged what we could from friends and fraternities and this was what we'd come up with. All the little details that pointed to disaster raced through my mind as I tried to get straight enough to face straight people.

Rob wandered off to the terminal while I, as casually as possible, checked the plane for any possible sign of damage or reason why I might have felt and heard the now infamous *thump*. The mechanic showed up and I described what I had heard. He gave me a blank look and told me to fire up the engine so he could hear it. I did and we both listened carefully as I ran the engine speed up and down for several minutes. He looked it over, kicked the front gear, checked the oil, and said simply, "Sounds okay to me."

He turned and walked off without another word. He had to have guessed I was high and suffering from an all-too-obvious brain freeze.

"Shit," I muttered to myself, "I better go find Rob and get the hell out of Rednecksville before a crowd shows up with pitchforks and firebrands."

I wandered into the terminal trying to act normal and innocently blend in while looking for Rob and a place to whiz. Outside of his weird goatee, Rob was way more straight-looking than I was. His hair wasn't too long. He wore slacks and collared shirts while I had modestly long hair and dressed in blue jeans and T-shirts. Yet here I was trying to be the normal responsible one and get his sorry ass out of here before he answered someone's question wrong.

As I walked into the main building, I spotted the FAA weather advisory office at the end of the hallway right next to the men's room. I walked past the open door to the FAA office and went into the head. When I came out, I spotted Rob in a phone booth near the small ticket counter on the other end of the building.

He seemed to be in some kind of animated conversation as he was gesticulating so wildly that a lock of his dark hair had fallen over one eye. I didn't like this. He was acting a bit secretive lately and I thought he'd been paying way too much attention to my girlfriend Katie, who I had been living with for some time. She'd been acting weird lately too, claiming that when the lease was up she needed to move out of our house and temporarily into a place owned by one of her liberated and wealthy girlfriends. *I just need to find myself and she gives me the freedom to be me*, was her lame excuse as she tried in vain to avoid any refuting arguments.

Women were becoming liberated and I was all for it. Liberated women liked recreational sex. My Katie was one of the freest spirits around so a little reflective time sounded reasonable at the time. Later I would learn that the cloak of liberation was just another excuse for a perfectly nice girl to act like a whore or a slut. Remember that the difference between a whore and a slut is a whore will have sex with anyone while a slut has sex with anyone except you! For some unfortunate reason I seem to only attract the latter.

As a result, I had reluctantly agreed to rent a house on Whitmore Lake with Rob as my roommate and we'd already put down a damage deposit and the first month's rent. It was going to be cool at the lake where we could have great parties and I would be closer to Mauer's little float plane that I had been training in for a seaplane rating and his fleet of really fast catamaran sailboats. Katy could get her head together and then she would probably end up as my permanent guest at the lake house. That's how testosterone-poisoned young men think when their main squeeze no longer enjoys their squeezing. You think she will eventually come to her senses and capitulate with a weekend of nasty, sloppy, makeup sex. Clearly, I was making a lot of silly plans.

Rob seemed to be blending in with the local action at the airport so I casually wandered over to the FAA office, attracted by a console of radar screens and teletype printers. I thought I might as well check the weather forecast along our intended route ahead while I had the chance.

I stepped into the office and found the Midwest weather map posted on a bulletin board just to the right of the door. The walls and counter were covered with weather maps and teletype reports of every possible kind. There was one young guy with a crew-cut and the requisite bright white starched shirt and government-issue black skinny tie leaning back in a chair, feet on his desk, reading a book and seemingly unconnected with the rest of the flying world.

I wandered a little closer to his desk in order to see a weather report for the Kansas City area when I happened to notice the book he was so engrossed in reading. It wasn't really a book, but more like a large illustrated pamphlet. It was the title that tightened my sphincter two more notches past spinster librarian dry twat. Its title jumped out at me like a club to the side of the head: "How to Identify Airborne Smugglers!"

I just about crapped my pants. I tried to read more words on the cover but couldn't quite make them out. The guy reading it flipped a page and looked up suddenly, catching me staring. I glanced back to the weather map on the wall as quickly as I could. As I gazed at the map I could see that behind the desk was a window to the outside ramp and sitting off by itself in an otherwise completely empty part of the airport was our little Piper. The cheap flat black paint job made her stand out even more suspiciously. If I had been reading that booklet and looked up to see that odd-looking little plane missing only a skull and crossbones painted on her tail to complete the outlaw look, well, I probably wouldn't just sit there and explain to some long-haired weirdo that the weather in Kansas City was clear and calm.

"Howdy stranger. Can I help you?" he said in a friendly southern Texas drawl almost feigning interest.

"Who? Me?" I said, glancing around the office and noticing that nobody else was there but me. "Not really. I think I have everything I need."

I pointed at the weather map in an effort to keep his attention inside the room. I heard an aircraft radio in the back barking out orders to a commercial flight that was about to land from Amarillo. He must have heard me talking to the tower earlier when I thought I'd lost my front gear. What more does he need for Christ's sake! I could feel sweat beads beginning to trickle down my forehead toward my bloodshot eyes. We were doomed.

He looked back at his pamphlet and it was then I saw the cover photo. It showed a new bright and shiny twin-engine Comanche parked at a small airport with palm trees. Standing in front of the plane was presumably the pilot or drug smuggler dressed like a professional businessman, clean-cut, white shirt and tie, wearing cool mirrored sunglasses. He looked more like my friend, Bill Smith, who happened to be the biggest dope dealer in Ann Arbor and wore only dark grey Ray-Ban aviator glasses day and night although actually, because of his chosen profession, it was pretty much only at night.

That picture must have been some narco-pig's idea of what a high-end smuggler should look like. It was a long way off from depicting our impromptu ragtag operation. I was certain though the pamphlet had a section that described in detail how amateur smugglers flying old stick and cloth planes made lots of landings due to flying too high and imagining strange noises.

"Have you ever spotted any of those commie dope smugglers?" I said, regretting it almost immediately.

He looked up confused until I pointed to his book. He looked down and then back at me. This time I could feel him scrutinizing me more intently. "Not yet, but if they ever land here, it will be their last."

I felt the sweat edging closer to its goal.

"Y'all from around here?" he asked innocently.

Now I smiled. "Sort of. I live in Clovis and I'm taking a friend to Kansas City."

He stared a little more intently for a moment and then curled his thin lips into a small crooked smile.

"Weather should be good. No thunderstorms predicted in that area tonight," he said.

Figuring I had pushed the issue a little too far, I decided it was time to blow this pop stand. "Sounds great! Maybe I'll stop by on the way back. You have any good country bars in this town?"

"Do we? They're all country bars. You just tell any bartender in town that Johnny sent you and you'll get the royal treatment," he explained happily as his face lit up with talk about one of his favorite hobbies.

"I'll be sure and do that. Keep'em flying!" I said as I edged toward the door.

I gave a thumbs-up signal which he eagerly returned with a big smile. I turned casually and walked through the open door trying to inconspicuously mosey back to the main hallway.

As soon as I was out of sight of the FAA guy's open door, I ran over to Rob as he was just hanging up the pay phone. For some reason he seemed almost startled, like he'd been caught doing something. He absentmindedly started to slowly stroke his goatee. He always did that when he was concentrating or pissed or trying to think up a good excuse.

I grabbed him and whispered into his ear what I'd just experienced. He dropped his bag of six-month-old vending machine popcorn, scattering white kernels all around us. He finally stopped stroking his goatee and instead began tugging on one earlobe as his opposing eye began a rhythmic twitching.

Now there were two people in a distressed intestinal condition looking for a way to escape without losing it, literally. We turned and began slowly walking back to the plane. Every so often, one of us would momentarily lose function in his lower legs and have to be held up by the other as we valiantly wobbled our way back to the plane.

It didn't help to think that everyone in the terminal was probably watching us and trying to get to a phone to call the FBI.

We had a deep desire driving us on regardless of whatever might be happening behind our backs. We just needed to get the hell out of there as quickly as possible. We made it, I guess. At least we didn't have anybody looking for us later that night when we refueled in Kansas City.

Now we were about to land in Ann Arbor, one of just a dozen or so well-known destination points in the country for about 90 percent of all drug smugglers. I was still feeling no pain from the quality and quantity of dope we'd been consuming all night.

Other than that little episode over Indiana where we both fell asleep at the wheel, it looked like we were going to make it back home in one piece, with our sanity only slightly strained but our egos jumping madly for joy.

The sun was fully up, but lower Michigan was solidly overcast, giving both the sky and the ground below us a cold, washed-out gray feeling. We approached the field at pattern altitude and flew slowly around the entire area looking very carefully for anything on the ground that didn't look right. It was six o'clock on a Sunday morning and outside of our cars left in the parking lot, there wasn't another vehicle or person in sight. The place looked totally deserted from the air. But then, the DEA would probably make it look that way.

So nothing seemed to be happening on the ground and it was still too early for any normal activity at the airport. Nobody answered our radio call for an airport advisory, which meant the office wasn't manned yet. I lined up on final and slipped the amazing little Tri-Pacer onto the runway without so much as a tire squeak. We taxied up to an empty ramp where we found the Pacer's usual tie down spot. I shut her down, got out, tied her lines and loitered near the plane while Rob casually walked to the parking lot to bring the car over for loading. No weirdoes with machine guns jumped out of the bushes. No terrifying black choppers appeared over the nearby tree line spewing hot lead into the little Piper.

Rob grabbed only the bricks necessary to cover the loan from the frat brothers. We agreed to meet later that day at our new rental house on the lake where we would split up the rest of the weed and calculate our profits. I decided to stop by Eberbach's house first to let him know we'd made it back with the loot.

I got him out of bed too early for a Sunday morning, but he was happy to get high after such a long dry spell. After smoking a couple of wicked joints as I related our adventures, we went to brunch at the downtown Hilton before I headed out to the lake and my new home. I still needed to move most of my stuff from the house Katie and I had shared for the last couple of years, but I figured I'd get to that tomorrow.

I decided to stop by the house where Katie was staying to give her the good news and invite her out to the lake house for the rest of the day. I was feeling tired but elated that maybe things could be patched up with her now that I had some money. I pulled up in front of her rich friend's house and parked right behind Rob's car.

I had to sit quietly for a moment until the shaking of my hands gripping the steering wheel subsided and I slowly got them under control enough to loosen my grip. For a moment, I felt physically sick from the realization that I had not just been cuckolded by my lover and best friend but also by my trusted business partner, intended roommate, and criminal confidant. Betrayal couldn't even come close to what this was.

I was frozen. I couldn't drive away, though I felt totally out of place. It was all too real now, but maybe it wouldn't have happened if I had just passed on by. Now I was trapped. I had to do something. But what?

In my gut I realized any future with Katie was gone with tragic finality, like the certainty of sudden death. Emotional death caused by the shocking realization of how stupidly naïve and ignorant I was concerning the people I thought I knew best. It was just too much to take. I felt a hot reddening of my face and neck as I reached into the back of the truck to retrieve a box stowed under the narrow bed.

"What are you doing?" Katie said, her voice muffled slightly by the sleeping bag. My gut tightened like a dungeon torture rack as I reached into the box where I kept my .357 magnum long-barreled Ruger Blackhawk revolver. I couldn't afford a Smith & Wesson or a Remington, but the Ruger looked cowboy cool and it was powerful. I especially liked the fact I could overload the powder when making my own bullets. They would explode with a huge ball of flame blossoming out of the barrel like a horizontal mushroom cloud with tons of smoke and a sonic shock wave that could deafen anyone nearby. No namby-pamby guns for this Oregon cowboy.

"I'm just getting my pistol." I looked behind the seat again to where we'd shared a sleeping bag on the narrow bed in the back of my truck so many times before. It was hard to imagine how we could have slept on such a narrow platform, but we did. My one-person sleeping bag helped hold us together, but it wasn't actually needed. We simply held onto each other all night as our bodies welded into one. She was still snuggled deep in the bag but her silky golden locks spilled out the top with an inviting softness that made me want to touch, stroke, and groom that lovely fluff in all the secret places it grew.

"Come back to bed!" she pleaded still half asleep.

"Not now," I said softly, "I have something to do."

"What could be that important at this hour?" she mumbled back to me still making no moves to expose any naked skin to the cold Lake Michigan air. God it was enticing, but I knew there was an insurmountable barrier between us now. She didn't love me enough to be exclusive anymore. Her hippie lifestyle didn't fit what I thought a couple in love should do. I thought she had matured in our relationship to a point where "free love" referred to the frequency of sex with me, not the price of admission for everyone.

I put on my black hat. It's time to fix this cowboy style. "Good-bye, sweetheart."

They say that your life flashes before your eyes just before you die violently. My life with Katie began playing out on cue as I opened the truck door, stepped out, stuffed the long-barrel revolver down the front of my pants, and began the long walk to my destiny of shame and humiliation, hopefully followed by vindication. Katie and I had shared an exclusive bed for more than two years through some of the most tumultuous times and now, right in front of my face, she had blatantly and publicly fucked my friend and business partner.

When I first went to work for Space Physics, the apartment I shared with three virginal second-year graduate students broke up primarily due to all of them finding female roommates who quickly became brides. I had been obligated to attend the weddings with horrible forebodings in every case. How could they marry the first girl they bed? How do you know you have the right partner if you only check out one before buying? It didn't make any sense, but then most of what conventional people did was pretty much conventional nonsense.

Take for instance the super-patriot idiots who not only wanted the war in Vietnam to be victorious for the loyal tyrants but also wanted to crucify anyone who dared use their First Amendment rights and speak out against the insanity. Killing of the messengers is the first sign of totalitarianism and unbelievably it was happening right here in America.

I was offered a cheap apartment in one of Bill Smith's slumlord student houses. It was near campus, which was great, but lacked a bathroom on the first floor where my apartment was located. In exchange for cheap rent along with the incentive of not needing to constantly climb stairs just to piss, I agreed to put a bathroom in the apartment.

Katie rented a single room above my suite and it didn't take long before I got tired of the myriad of hippie types traipsing in and out at all hours, punctuated by raucous laughter and constant rock music. On my many bathroom trips past her door, I spotted multicolored lights, black-light posters, and the requisite lava lamp next to a bare waterbed mattress on the floor. What the hell was a waterbed and why did she have one? My thoughts turned to obvious sexual maneuvers accentuated by a huge oscillating bladder moving rhythmically in sync with naked bodies writhing in ecstasy. Katie wasn't just sexually free, she was an explorer.

It didn't take very long for me to be smitten by the gorgeous little hippie chick with a real job, something most of her friends didn't have. As a consequence, she often provided the drug money and transportation for the many flies buzzing around her. She had beautiful long wavy blonde hair, a big smile pretty much all the time, an obviously huge IQ, and an insatiable thirst for sex, drugs, and Rock & Roll that so far appeared to be unfulfilled. What the hell, I thought, even if it was only a Stetson I might as well throw my hat in the ring.

One night, she finally invited me up to her room for some smoke and coke. The lights were dim, I was high and stretched out invitingly across her bare waterbed mattress in the middle of her small room, and Katie was getting playful. While I wasn't paying attention, she jumped onto her mattress, the only furniture in her room besides a small table for the clock radio, tossing me into the air uncontrollably where I did a half flip and landed on my head against the opposite wall. I can still remember her laugh. It was intoxicating. We made love violently and passionately three times that night.

"Do you love me?" I asked half-jokingly. I normally didn't like to get serious, but I wanted to know.

"Sure," she said without even looking back at me. My heart skipped a beat.

"Let's rent a house and move in together."

I had visions of a happy comfy home, warmly lit with modern artistic furniture like claw foot bathtubs turned into love seats and colored bead curtains hanging everywhere. The hippie lifestyle could become mainstream. We just need to give it some respectability, like all the young professors coming out of Ivy League schools did, teaching in a new way with respect for all ideas and fostering open-minded, far-reaching debate. Normally rigid dictatorial academia was becoming human again.

But now our love was over, *kaput, finis,* dead like bugs on my teeth while riding my old Harley. Something had to be done.

As I climbed the steps of the porch I could hear her laughter in the distance, just like my memory of her so many times in the past. But now she laughed for *him*. My cheeks, throat, and neck began to burn as if doused with gasoline and set on fire. I imagined giant red and yellow flames dancing above me. Fire, I remembered, seemed to be what Katie liked to play with most.

She introduced me to the hippie art of tie-dying and batiking t-shirts into bright multi-colored swirls and splotches that were the identifying uniforms of the newly enlightened. The batik part of the process required a large boiling vat of molten wax. By the end of a dying session, Katie and her psychedelic co-workers would be tripping on some kind of natural or artificial hallucinogen that begged a sensual visual overload. Standing near the bubbling pot of leftover wax, they'd laughingly toss in cups of water and then immediately duck as a large balls of instantly vaporized water and wax exploded in giant colorful orbs of swirling flames that seared shafts through the limbs and leaves of any tree unlucky enough to be directly overhead. It was an extrordinarily impressive light show that could definitely hurt you if you got too close.

She listened to a lot of Cat Stevens, which I thought was sort of downer music only surpassed by that down and out Canadian loser, Leonard Cohen, whose song, "Suzanne" tore my heart out a couple of times while dealing with its namesakes. When Katie got into one of those downer moods, if she could afford it, she'd inject herself with some form of liquid cocaine or heroin. That's where I drew the line and with some love and strong coercion, I got her off the hard drugs, especially needles. I insisted we stick to the tried and true mix of alcohol, pot, and snorts if we could afford them.

But at heart, Katie was a real honest dyed-in-the-batik-vat hippie-chick flower-girl with all the necessary hang-ups like astrology, spiritual communion through drugs and, unfortunately for me, free unlimited sex and love. I thought I could satisfy her needs and keep her focused on one true love. Silly me.

She was a graphic artist for a one-man print advertising firm with only one client, a company that made the machines that produced plastic milk jugs. Talk about boring careers in plastic; nonetheless she worked hard, showed up on time, and otherwise displayed admirable traits for a responsible young lady. I thought she was great. I was a photographer, so her artistic talents blended beautifully with mine. We felt like a team.

I got her interested in photo journalism. Whenever I was called out on a film assignment Katie would take production stills. She liked it and she was good. I showed her how to use a darkroom for both developing pictures and having mutual darkroom naked body experiences while waiting for the prints to dry. She was especially good at this.

Then Sony unveiled a relatively cheap portable video camera and tape recorder they dubbed the Portapack, which was based on a weird new video recording standard called half-inch helical scan. I jumped at the chance to lease one for $50 a month, justifying the huge expense for a lowly grad student by hoping to find a commercial market for low quality black and white live video productions, like maybe advertising or training. To the professional world, it was just a novelty, a plaything that was totally incompatible with broadcast standards and therefore pretty much useless except for documenting low value events not recorded in any other manner and then hoping the videotape could someday be edited and converted to useable media. It was the Super 8 of video.

The big advantage for me was sound. The only option for live sound in 16mm required having a whole separate crew running a microphone and portable audiotape recorder, physically separate from the shoulder-held camera, but tethered to it by a highly restrictive synchronizing cable. Post-production equipment for syncing the tape recordings to the exposed footage during the editing process was expensive and difficult to operate. But videotape had sound built right in from the start, so now live events could be fully recorded by just one person. Holy shit! It promised a revolution in motion picture production. It was going to make me famous in the Rock & Roll world.

However, such grandiose expectations rarely pan out quickly enough for new technology and so it was with the early video recorders, which needed color and better picture quality before it could be used even semi-professionally. I ended up using the Portapack to document rock concerts in the park, some university art events, and a few anti-war demonstrations. Finally, live video recordings could be made by ordinary common folk and not just the elite rich bastards at the TV and movie studios. All over the country, freaks like me were videotaping important counter culture events and happenings. We were documenting our times in an unprecedented truthful manner, unrehearsed, unedited, live and real, with no commercial breaks. Vietnam was in dire need of such photographic truth.

The Portapack even gave Katie the chance to spend a few minutes interviewing Jane Fonda solo, when Jane hosted a feminist workshop on Women Against the War during a two-day teach-in on campus. The final big event was held outdoors at the Huron River Park, which would be used later for the Blues Festival. Jane had just gotten back from North Vietnam, which got her branded as a traitor in the American press, so she didn't trust the news media, or for that matter, most men at a time when they were fucking everything up right and left. She declared her workshop tent *For Women Only* and when they held the big final event that was later used for the Blues Festival, Katie videotaped the whole hour-long affair up close and personal. She was arguably the only recording news media present, as every other TV news team was all male. Katie had a blast and we had super-special sex that night. She didn't stop smiling for a week or more, and neither did I.

"Katie, I thought I made you happy," I said to the curls. "What the fuck went wrong? I just don't understand this. Why are you destroying something that was so good? For what?"

"I don't know. I just like to be happy. Don't you want to be happy?"

"I'm happy when you love me."

"You shouldn't need my love to be happy," the curls responded and moved delicately indicating she was turning over to her other side in the sleeping bag. "Don't you see that it's too much responsibility? I need to take care of my happiness and you need to take care of yours. You can't make me responsible for your happiness."

"Why? Because you have to hurt the one you love just so you can make yourself think you're making yourself happy? Self-indulgence is a fool's paradise. If someone makes you happy and you can make that person happy, well, I call that love and it should be encouraged, reciprocated, and held exclusive."

"I love you too. I just need some time to find my independent feminine side. I need to live with a woman who I trust and knows how to be self-sufficient. I need to be myself first before I can love you the way you want."

The curls disappeared into the bag.

Not long ago, she begged to go to Mardi Gras with her hippie friends when she knew I couldn't come along because of my graduate research work. After a week alone thinking all kinds of thoughts of Mardi Gras—wild orgies and drunken sex games—I had to go retrieve her from the house where she crashed after driving back nonstop from New Orleans. All she had to do was drive another five miles and she could have been home in my arms, but instead, at four a.m., I had to literally drag her out of a strange sleeping bag tangled up with about a dozen more bodies in bags on the floor of some hippie crash pad in Whitmore Lake. It was clear she no longer preferred my bed, but I tried to ignore it. She just needed to grow up some and get her baser desires under control.

I trusted her, probably knowing better at the time, and now as a result I felt like warmed-over chicken shit. *What can you do?* I thought and was reminded of the old red-neck saying: *If you love it, set it free. If it doesn't come home, then you're free to hunt it down, kill it and eat it.*

I stepped quietly onto the porch. It was late Sunday morning on this typical cheap 1920's-something imitation-Victorian-housed tree-canopied street in Ann Arbor. Nobody would even hear the shots, I guessed, except for the countless house dogs nearby. But nobody in nice suburban neighborhoods paid attention to barking dogs anymore. They were only there to chase off all the thieves and muggers from the adjacent black neighborhoods down the street, no doubt. Yapping dogs and guns going off were just part of the trendy new suburbia.

I peeked through the front door windows and could see all the way to the backyard through the front room and dining room. Nobody seemed to be downstairs; even better, neither were the two giant Great Danes that lived here with the woman who'd won the house in a divorce decree. Not much sympathy for ex-boyfriends here. I opened the door and slipped silently into the house.

It was perfectly quiet except for the ticking of the grandfather clock sternly watching over the proceedings. The dogs were probably on a long walk with their owner, so whatever was going on here could go on uninterrupted. I guess they hadn't considered me happening by.

I walked up the stairs, hugging one wall so the creaky old steps wouldn't complain and sound the alarm. The door to the master bedroom was open a crack and I could hear soft voices inside. I recognized Katie's sweet tones and that rat bastard Rob. At least they were just talking and not actually doing the nasty. That would have made me even crazier.

"This just isn't right," I mumbled to myself over and over again. I had gone from being a successful smuggler and faithful lover to a cuckolded idiot in less than a day. My equilibrium was totally disrupted. Someone must pay for this pain. Two people I had trusted and respected moments before just ripped my heart out, took a huge dump on it and stuffed it in my mouth saying *Thanks for the ride! Don't come again.*

I pulled my black cowboy hat down low over my eyes, which I set into a Clint Eastwood man-with-no-name squint. I kind of wished for a cheroot to finish off my look of righteous revenge. I pulled the big black ugly-looking cannon from my waist, pointed it skyward, and stepped through the door.

"Hi Katy. What's happening?"

Rob screamed like a little girl that just had her puppy run over. He quickly scooted down in the big four-poster bed and attempted to hide by pulling the covers over his head. Katie was lying on the other side of him with her breasts displayed so gloriously I wanted to cry just for the beauty. She stared at me with those big beautiful, now wide-open, blue eyes, but with no hint of her usual beckoning smile.

"What the fuck are you doing here?" she said rather loudly. Rob screamed again only this time it was more muffled as he tried to sink farther under the covers.

"We just got back and I thought you might like to celebrate our success. But I see Rob beat me to it."

"We were going to tell you later today. Besides, you and I don't live together any more so I can see who I want."

"Funny, it doesn't look like a first date. You two must have been fucking while we were still living together. Now I understand why Rob answered the phone when I called you from Boulder last year."

"I'm not going to argue about who did what to whoever. That's history."

I began to lose my patience and maybe some sanity, as well.

"I'm not as stupid as you think I am!" I yelled. I began to swing the gun around wildly pointing it all over the room and emphasizing my words by jabbing it into the air as if it were a sword. "There's apparently been so much screwing going on I don't know who to shoot first. You, him, or the water bed."

The traitorous lump under the blankets shuddered and let out another little girlish squeal.

"The question is," I continued in a lower more desperate tone, "why are you so stupid as to think I wouldn't find out? Do you have any idea of the intense emotions and psychic pain you're screwing with right now? You two have been fucking me over for weeks. Now it's my turn."

I paused but didn't really wait to hear an answer. My gut told me I had been fucked, virtually, a long time ago. The shame and humiliation were producing a bitter taste that I could feel crawling into my gut.

"In what universe is it okay for my lover and my business partner to fuck me over behind my back like a couple of sleazy slime-dog thieves stealing from the poor-box? You know, in most civilized countries in the world no one would condemn me for blowing you two traitorous pigs to dog-shit hell right now!" I pronounced sternly, this time gritting my teeth in an ugly grimace. I was rapidly running out of justifying arguments.

I cocked the exposed hammer on my Ruger six-shooter. It made a loud click-clack sound that reverberated off the high plastered ceiling. Rod resumed his muffled screeching under the blankets but Katy just glared at me, daring me to do something stupid. *Fuck it*, I thought, *Why disappoint them?*

I took careful aim at the chain holding the chandelier over the bed and fired.

The sound of an overloaded magnum bullet shattered the Ann Arbor Sunday morning calm with a sonic boom and reverberating echoes of exploding matter as it careened through everything in its path. The silhouette under the covers flipped suddenly and the screaming momentarily muted as Rob buried his face in a pillow. Katy threw the blanket over her head just as the gun went off, so she missed the best part of what happened next.

The bullet and its sonic wave tore through the ceiling directly above the bed. All around the chandelier, eighty-year-old horsehair-plaster as brittle and fragile as eighty-year-old sun-bleached bones exploded into clouds of dry gray dust and, like a crumbling medieval cathedral, ragged chunks of plaster the size of frying pans collapsed on the two lumps under the covers. Then, like a giant flyswatter, the wooden ceiling lath collapsed onto the bed, followed closely by the chandelier itself. I didn't stay for the applause.

As I turned to run, I heard Rob's girlish squeals turn into shouts for help. Katie just kept screaming the same thing again and again, "What the fuck! What the fuck!"

I ran screaming down the stairs like a crazy drunk cowboy right after riding the biggest baddest bull in the arena. "Yee-ha! Ya-hoo! Wee-ya! Yippie-ki-yo, ki-yay!!"

Two more bounds and I burst through the front door onto the porch and kept yelling as I ran across the grass to my truck. Dogs were barking, but nobody else was the least bit interested in the crazies who lived in that big old house, known for strange sounds and weird activity at all hours anyway.

I drove straight to the rented house at the lake. I had no intention of having anything more to do with those two shitheads so I grabbed my things, along with a few things that weren't mine, and headed back to town. It was a very long drive of shame. I had suddenly gone from being on top of the world to having lost just about everything except for my truck, my cameras, and the pot from the trip. I needed a place to crash. I needed a home to hide out in. I needed to get off the road. I headed to Eberbach's house taking every back road I could find.

I don't remember the rest of the trip because I was struggling to drive through a fog of tears that blinded me to almost everything. I laughed as I cried, thinking about how this situation was just another comical Shakespearean plot twist. How disgustingly typical for a daytime soap opera! I am not meant to be ordinary in any possible way! I'm special! I groped my way back to Eberbach's trying to spit the vile taste from my mouth. I parked the truck out back in a hidden lot and slipped into his house and my new bachelor life.

I kept a low profile for a while, watching the street for cops from Eber's second-story window, but nothing ever came of my little shooting escapade. It didn't even make the police blotter in the local paper. I figured the owner of the house didn't want any more attention and decided I had inadvertently provided her with the demolition part of a long-overdue ceiling renovation.

I kept all the pot that was left from our trip, fully expecting Rob to show up any day and demand his share. If he did, I didn't intend to honor any agreements with partners who violate the first unwritten rule of bro' business, that being you do *not* fuck your partner's woman without his permission. It was perhaps morally wrong to keep his weed, but I couldn't help it. Hammurabi would have backed me up. I was inarguably the injured party.

He never showed his face to me again. In fact, I heard nothing from Katy or Rob for quite some time until Eberbach told me they'd married soon after our breakup but divorced less than a year later. Rob disappeared from the lab and Ann Arbor, but several years later Katy was seen married to an older accountant with five kids and living in a split-level suburban home with a manicured lawn. My, how weirdly fate twists our lives, or, perhaps more likely, how our twisted lives produce weird fates.

CHAPTER THREE

TWO CAN PLAY THAT GAME

"Oooh, Superfly. You're gonna make your fortune by and by…."

Curtis Mayfield
"Superfly"
1972

I awoke on the third day, well rested and feeling pretty good considering what those two rat-bastards did to me. Eberbach had just lost his roommate, a space engineer on exchange from England, so I lucked out and picked up his room, eagerly and hopefully indefinitely. How long that would be remained vague. Steve was one of the cool guys at the lab and the price was right. He liked to smoke pot and snort coke, so my suitcases full of Mexican gold helped a bit with the convincing. He didn't like the risk of harboring contraband, but he sure liked the idea of a constant house stash.

I stuck mostly to my new bedroom on the second floor overlooking Division Street, wondering if the cops would show up hunting for the hand cannon that broke the Ann Arbor sacred Sunday morning brunch peace and executed an authentic, yet innocent horse-hair plaster ceiling. Everything was oddly quiet.

The university was getting ready for a new academic year and the drought was driving up the price of pot. My little trip to Mexico was proving quite fortuitous, particularly due to the timing of my partner's indiscretion and resulting forfeiture of his share for the sake of love. I became uncharacteristically grateful that some romantic stories don't end happily ever after.

But I wasn't about to start another career and become a local weed dealer. Joining the ranks of hipster dealers did have the allure of glory and popularity, as well as great profit potential. In terms of being a chick-magnet, it was as good as being a rock star. However, I knew my roommate and landlord probably wouldn't like it, and for that reason and many others, I preferred wholesaling it in more distant, perhaps quieter places.

I never dirty up the water where I swim. That's just common sense. To sell drugs in Ann Arbor right now would be very risky as well as extremely stupid. With the legendary amount of drug consumption going on at the university and all the anti-war activities, there were probably just about as many snitches and undercover narcs running around as there were legitimate drug-consuming students. Those pesky out-of-town turncoat busted-junkies can be a real problem. Trust nobody but those you have a long personal history with and even then, always verify, often, that they haven't been turned.

That meant literally that if you choose to live on the fringes of the law then you need to have the talents of a damn good private investigator, a hard-bitten man of the streets, a Sam Spade, knowledgeable in everything that transpires in his town and everyone who's doing the transpiring. Someone who knows who's sleeping with whose wife, who got busted and turned narc, and who has the best jack in town. In the absence of having your own history in town, a private dick can be most useful, especially if he's also a hipster dealer.

Dealer and private eye are a natural pairing. The dealer visits his clientele, making deliveries and checking on sources for new purchases every night. He likewise cruises the hot spots, the parties, and the secret social gatherings. He knows his territory exceptionally well and he's ready with money, contacts, fast cars, low rent housing, and quasi-legal legal advice for just about any risky venture or hare-brained scheme that presents itself. A good drug dealer had to be multi-talented if he expected to stay ahead of the game and the pigs.

Above all, he needed to always know who's selling what, for how much, and from where. It was an economic microcosm of what the big boys on Wall Street did every day and with a lot less compassion. It took a true renaissance man to do this job well, especially where 'well' meant simply surviving over the long haul and remaining untouchable by the pigs, narcs, and all their sick minions.

In Ann Arbor, there was one who stood out not only as a true renaissance man in a modern academic and technological world, but also as a certified expert in building powerful GMC cars, attracting beautiful women, hanging with killer attack-dogs, always having cocaine as a cool lifestyle, owning student-slum housing, and running security at Rock & Roll concerts, just to name a few. He exemplified the plain old basic American value of having the most fun and making the most money with the least possible effort. All that, and especially the girl-magnet thing, attracted me to him right off.

Charismatic has to be part of the description too. Watching him at work, he had almost a magical hold on people for no other reason than he was actually damned interesting, seemingly enjoyed a great lifestyle, and was fatally rakish to boot. Everyone who met him liked him, or at least respected him. Bill was unique even among a cast of characters encompassing a broad spectrum of characters from the highest brains at a major research university to the hustlers, common thieves, and pimps infesting the baser but inevitable student haunts.

I called Bill as soon as I felt human again and it looked like I wasn't going to be arrested for an ugly girlfriend-breakup incident. After trying to raise him for several hours with no success, I finally got his answering machine.

"Leave a number and we'll get back to you," his girlfriend Patti's voice announced. Bill must have turned off the machine while he was sleeping so this meant he was now awake, but as usual, screening his calls. Nobody answered the fucking phone anymore without first knowing who the fuck was calling. It's a hip etiquette thing.

I left a brief message for him to stop by Eberbach's, as I had some good news. We never discussed anything illegal on the phone unless the call was made payphone to payphone. He would infer from my short cryptic message that it had something to do with drugs, so I half-expected him to fit me in much later, on his regular nightly rounds. With Bill, however, you never knew exactly when or where he would show up. He didn't like to be predictable.

Bill Smith, who was without a doubt the biggest and best dope dealer in Ann Arbor at the time, didn't like to deal with lowly hippie pot. Not cool enough and way too risky for the rewards. That might sound strange with the huge demand for weed in his hometown, which included probably fifty thousand drugged-crazed students. His specialty was cocaine and other exotic and sometimes dangerous drugs like all those newly-crafted pharmaceuticals coming out of the Military Industrial Complex.

He didn't have anything against weed. God knows he smoked plenty and always had some of the best in town. He just didn't like the odds of dealing with a mass of potheads or the flaky clientele it sometimes attracted. He preferred to sit back and quietly tap into the underground drug trade in his corner of Michigan and use that information to match up big buyers with big wholesalers. Bill liked to be a middleman, or a *facilitator* as he called it, and in control with little or no risk. He specialized in white middle-class professional clientele—you know, the people with money and secrets.

He specialized even further by carefully analyzing his market and adopting a business model that minimized his risk and maximized his profit. Smart, and not at all like a typical drug dealer, Bill was more like a Hollywood dealer to the stars. He could get you anything you desired and make you feel really smart and important while doing it. That, plus the fact that he was cool as hell at a time when that seemed pretty much all that mattered, was why I liked him.

On the sex side, unlike most dickish macho outlaw types, he actually loved his skinny Nordic-looking live-in girlfriend. So much so that as far as I could tell he never cheated on her openly. There were rumors, of course, but nobody cared if they were true or not and probably assumed the most dramatic anyway. He had plenty of opportunities and lots of beautiful admiring, perhaps cocaine-crazed women hanging around, giving his male friends a welcome new pond to fish or, in my case, a long shot at women clearly way out of my league.

I wanted what all young men wanted. I needed the stuff celebrated in song and story for as long as poets waxed poetic. I wanted some of that Rock-&-Roll-groupie cocaine-blow-job messy-all-night-long sex-till-you-drop action.

Bill was also the first true entrepreneur that I could actually tolerate and even admire. He owned a couple of those old Victorian turn-of-the-century homes near campus that had been converted to student-rental housing some time ago. Now they just accrued value as the student population grew and rents constantly climbed. Unlike the normal fat-bastard, bald-headed thieving, scum-sucking slumlords who normally preyed on the students living off-campus, Bill was honest, hated the war, loved Rock & Roll, admired smart people and considered himself a freedom-loving, long-haired, drugged-out stone freak just like the rest of us. He never went to college, even though he certainly could have if he'd been so inclined. Being raised in a college town, though, meant a lot of the academic culture had been ingrained in him all along.

Instead of rejecting the business world like most of us pristine idealistic intellectuals, Bill embraced it and used all the street knowledge of a do-it-yourself MBA and paralegal to achieve his personal monetary battle for freedom from want. Freedom was what it was all about. Freedom for the blacks to determine their own fate, freedom for the students to study in peace the subject of Peace, and in my case and a lot of others I suspect, freedom from the constraints and restrictions of monetary oppression brought about by the corrupt capitalist pigs.

But to Bill, being a hipster freak and successful in business was an appropriate way of sticking it to the man. I had never met anyone quite like him. Who couldn't admire a smart, ethical, alluring criminal, trustworthy and honest, with devilishly good looks and one helluva fast Corvette? He could have easily stepped right out of the lead in a James Dean movie or a Fitzgerald novel.

I was nowhere near capable of being any kind of a charismatic drug dealer like Bill. I liked the fun and excitement of smuggling, but all that socializing, late night cruising, and hawking of wares seemed somewhat dishonest, even boring maybe, and downright scary when things go wrong. Besides, you have to know a lot of people to be a good drug salesman and I just wasn't into that kind of social lifestyle.

Bill had once tried to set me up by introducing me to the *Physician's Desk Reference*, a catalog, if you will, of all the finest drugs ever produced by the American pharmaceutical industry. In it, you could find uppers, downers, in-betweeners, and even some that could transport you to other worlds and maybe even back again. Bill worked up a big stand-up table-top display poster where he taped a real example of every pill he had in his arsenal along with a photo-copied excerpt from its matching entry in the PDR. It looked like a slick high school science fair project, only slightly bent and weird. Having close to fifty pills to pick from, laid out like a menu at Hunter Thompson's Fear and Loathing Café, or the mythical Alice's Restaurant, was truly scientifically awesome and recreationally astounding.

Bill never sold anything he didn't first try on himself and any willing friends such as me, Munsell, or Eberbach. The three of us became known as the *Merck*-y Test Pilots. Our motto was *Keep on truckin' through the drug-induced fog!* which pretty much summed up the times. And the times were ugly.

Between his volunteer tours of duty in Vietnam, my brother, a Special Forces Captain with several personally-collected matching sets of Viet-Cong ears, had introduced me to several drugs the Army handed out like candy over there. Apparently, the super patriotic pharmaceutical manufacturers were now stepping up to the modern medicinal plate of war and helping turn normal alcohol-crazed uneducated redneck killing machines into drug-crazed super-fucked-up uneducated redneck killing machines.

They had instant pep pills that could keep you awake for weeks at a time, or pills that could knock you out even in the middle of a vicious hand-to-hand Cong attack. They had other drugs that could dull a prisoner's senses and make him babble his guts out to his newfound American friends. Or, they had drugs that would just make you a complete emotional mess, susceptible to any foolhardy suggestion, like attacking a cave full of enemy tunnel-rats with poison gas where collateral casualties or the enemy dead were determined only by the fateful drift of the wind. Drugs were becoming essential for fighting stupid, unpopular wars.

Bill and I eventually found the civilian versions of most of these secret military weapons right there in the good old PDR. Better American living through modern organic chemistry!

I belonged to the NRA at the time, so I wondered whether these potentially lethal, mind-altering drugs should be covered by the Second Amendment, like the latest assault rifles. If I had the right to defend my freedom and security with gun ownership, I should also be able to defend my own mind from brain-sucking assaults by Big Brother. Good drugs might be our only defense against the mind-snatcher mentality of a desperate and corrupt government bent on turning us into cannon fodder.

Actually, most of us only joined the NRA so we could prominently display their distinctive round decals on our truck windshields in plain view of any cop approaching the driver's window. It helped keep the rural pigs off our asses when we went road slumming for nature trips. With long hair, we were obvious targets for any buck-toothed, language-challenged, redneck super-patriot cop to pull over and drug-search anytime we ventured off the beaten path and into their backwoods clutches. But with an NRA sticker and a loaded gun in sight, we were usually given a knowing redneck wink and told to get the fuck out of there, which of course we always did, laughing our asses off.

My personal favorite drug from the exotics menu was Quaalude. It was technically a sedative-hypnotic or downer, but what it did for most people was calm down their racing minds and allow them to concentrate better and think faster under pressure. Methaqualone, its chemical name, also made you feel really, really good. It was a big hit in high-pressure jobs like dealing with hard-boiled, bloodthirsty Hollywood producers, or clashing with ferocious little black-pajama-clad freedom fighters.

Quaaludes actually helped me overcome abject shyness and uncurbed anxieties that prevented me from interacting effectively with strangers. When making new business contacts or simply calling strangers for technical help or hustling money for my film projects, I would become paralyzed to the point of stuttering, babbling nonsense, or sometimes abruptly going totally blank in the middle of a conversation without a clue as to what I was saying, or why. In short, I lacked any semblance of charm or wit.

But with Quaaludes, I became cool, calm, and collected. I could talk to anybody about anything, anytime and banter with the best of them. Besides that, they made you feel intensely pleasant and relaxed. Hence the recreational use became quite lucrative for the drug companies until after the war, when the military stopped ordering them up by the millions. Then Quaaludes became very scarce and expensive on the black market. There were pirated, home-brew versions but nothing like the Merck 90 or the Rorer 714.

So, even though the exotics market seemed very alluring to a blossoming criminal business, it never worked out for me. I had to consume way too much product just to get motivated to sell what was left. As they say, *never hire a worm to sell an apple.*

I was pretty much a loner who didn't like to hang with the unwashed masses or party all the time. Besides, criminal dealers had a hard side that sometimes scared me. I just wanted to make some quick money, and smuggling weed using my newly-acquired flying skills seemed like a good idea at the time.

I met Bill Smith during my first year working at the space lab, before I got my pilot's license but after I met Steve Eberbach, an

MIT electrical engineering graduate from a wealthy Ann Arbor family, who owned the house I lived in, and Thom Munsell, another local who grew up hangin' with the many artist-types and musicians around the university. Munsell worked at the lab too, as a solder jockey, and he loved putting together and listening to high-powered quality stereo sound systems. Almost every workday afternoon Thom, Steve, and I shared a joint in the abandoned RF cage on the second floor.

RF cages give me the gut willies. No radio waves could go in and none could get out. It's a Faraday bucket for humans and human-sized equipment. Weed seemed to make it better, but I always wondered if the cage cut off something like your subliminal electro-magnetic wave connection to the universe and vice versa. Just a thought that eventually went up in smoke....

Thom had just married a cute little blonde, Margie, who loved making pottery. Ever the romantic, he hand-built a brick kiln in his backyard and set up a couple of pottery wheels in his basement. I helped build the kiln, which was amazing to experience when sitting inside and high on some form of mushroom smoothie as he removed the temporary arch support. We heard a little satisfying crunch of gravity-locking bricks seemingly in midair above our heads. Trippy!

I even threw a couple of pots there and eagerly helped him burn two hundred gallons of propane in one weekend, firing a huge load of misshapen, hence artistic, earthenware and extra-large organic coffee mugs in the roomy brick furnace. The roar, the flames shooting out every crevice, and the shimmering white-hot blandness of pots and bricks all glowing with the exact same color of the sun was intoxicating. Raw power of this magnitude couldn't help but impress a young atmospheric physicist. It must have seemed magical to the ancient potters.

Naturally, we hung out together along with a few more freaks from the lab, kind of a techie-nerd gang who all dug cool new micro-electronics, satellites, rockets, computers, and high-powered musical sound systems that could administer CPR at fifty paces.

Music wasn't just made for listening anymore. Rock & Roll had to be felt. NASA engineers, who made the loudest sounds on earth—five-stage rockets to the moon—should easily be able to make that happen. We just needed a new kind of speaker with, of course, a little more of what made America great—raw power. Lots more power!

Thom threw one of his frequent parties where Steve and I mixed with other cool university hangers-on: the usual crowd of local artists, technicians, struggling musicians, and grad students. Well after midnight, Bill and his drug troops finally arrived to hold one of his notorious back-bedroom cocaine courts.

Bill was famous for his late-night party favors. He didn't normally mingle with the commoners at parties for the obvious reason that he didn't need to have anybody else know him or what he did for a living. Instead, he held private, invitation-only aristocratic drug courts, usually in a secure back bedroom of the appointed party house. Just like royal courts of old, the king sat in a well-guarded crown room devoid of riff-raff, sucking down brandied wine amid pseudo-sophisticated suck-ups dressed like clowns. There, he would receive select petitioners, listen to their whiney pleas, exchange secret information about mutual friends and/or enemies, and share their best intoxicating booze.

The only difference I perceived between then and now was that brandied wine got replaced by crystal blow and drafty castles were upgraded to centrally heated tract-houses. Everything else, I'm sure, stayed pretty much the same, including the costumes. As a form of entertainment, dressing up and groveling for favors while high on the latest mind fuck never seems to lose its appeal.

After several hours of drinking beer and smoking what was left of somebody's dwindling seeds-n-stems stash, Thom finally pulled me aside and led me through the thinning crowd into his bedroom at the back of the small but charming rental house. Through an ever-present blue haze of exotic smoke and incense, about a half dozen people in various positions of courtly ease were strewn around the bed and on the floor. Some were talking, but most were swaying gently in time with the music while keeping a watchful eye on the lord of the highs.

At the center of attention, sitting at the head of the bed, Bill was working intently over a small mirror that held a respectable pile of lumpy white powder with a couple of snowy lines laid out next to it. Bill wore his characteristic broad, lopsided grin in the form of an exaggerated sly smirk—definitely a sign he was having a great time. The twinkle in his eye didn't detract any either.

A cute little girl with lots of black curls and a face full of freckles sat next to him. She was dressed in a Levi jacket and matching jeans. Scruffy cowboy boots and a T-shirt with R. Crumb's famous *Keep on Truckin'* poster of the Grateful Dead completed her unisex earthy-artist look. She was laughing at something Bill said while trying to hold her breath after obviously taking a big hit on the joint she was still holding. She handed it to Bill, who dropped his razor blade on the mirror so he could safely hold the glass and all it contained with one hand while somewhat awkwardly juggling the joint up to his lips with the other.

Bill still had his signature smile spread across his face as he peered through lavender-tinted, gold-rimmed sunglasses at the joint he now carefully held at the edge of his mouth where he could apparently suck more forcefully. He started coughing and laughing at the same time. Munsell rushed in and saved the joint as both Bill and the girl collapsed in laughter and smoke on the bed.

Bill's modestly-long light brown hair, about collar length, wasn't enough to be automatically hip or advertise that he might be countercultural like the rest of us long-haired freaks. It was, however, long enough to clearly exclude him from the ranks of rednecks and pigs, or, as we called them, skinheads, shitheads, and assholes. Nice people called them straights or squares, but we assumed anybody over thirty with short hair was either a narc, a Nazi, or a plain old ratfink and definitely not someone to be trusted. The hair thing just made it easier for us to identify the enemy. Unfortunately, it worked both ways.

The sly, lopsided, almost-sardonic smile that Bill sported sometimes made me think he was talking out the side of his mouth. One side seemed to do all the lip movement, while the other stayed relatively still. It was as if he were speaking secretly only to you while keeping an eye on everyone else in the room. When he spoke to me in that slightly subversive, yet intimate manner, I took it as a sign that I'd been accepted into his trusted private circle. It was how he made you feel part of his mystique inner-circle world of cocaine coolness.

Bill was in his usual attire, pastel-tinted sunglasses, a plain white T-shirt with faded blue jeans and an unbuttoned long-sleeve shirt with the sleeves rolled up to just below the elbow. His jeans covered the stovepipe part of his black engineer boots, which being somewhat worn, attested to the fact that he actually did something more physical than snorting coke or partying all night. He carried his slim frame lithely, like a prowling cat, and could just as easily have stepped out of the pages of a New York designer's catalog catering to the hip and cool. He couldn't care less. He didn't follow fashion trends. Actually, he unintentionally made them.

What I saw was a clever and intelligent guy who like most of us had no interest in typical macho-male crap like screwing people out of their life savings, watching gladiator football, and drinking sulfurous piss like Budweiser. That was the kind of shit that got us into this dumb-ass war and we had to break that vicious cycle of bullshit testosterone-induced, one-upmanship violence. Bill redefined the male image to be one of strength through knowledge and ability; fun through drugs, sex, Rock & Roll; and of course, fast sports cars, powerful trucks, and crotch-rocket motorcycles if you can afford them. He figured out how to afford them.

He owned a small garage just south of town where he built his Corvettes and other muscle cars, including the K10 four-wheel-drive monster trucks that he built for himself, Thom and, later, me. Bill also had a deal going with local insurance brokers where they totaled somewhat less than totally-wrecked cars and then sold them to him for pennies on the dollar and a small cocaine kickback, so he could either rebuild them with new titles or just strip them for valuable parts. Fixing up slightly-warm cars was a great way to grease the wheels of his many other enterprises.

Why Bill would even give me the time of day was somewhat mystifying. I didn't belong in his league at all, even though he always made me feel like I did. His disarmingly cryptic smile always kept you guessing, wondering what he was really thinking. But he made people feel important just by the fact they existed within his elite circle of friends. He was an acute observer and an even better self-promoter.

Bill knew his job was dangerous, but he wasn't a typical violent-prone dealer. He owned guns just like the rest of us, yet he did it quietly and without advertising the fact. He preferred surrounding himself with guard dogs that he personally trained to scare the shit out of any nosy intruders. He always traveled with his favorite, Puppity, a purebred Weimaraner who guarded his cars and presumably his trade goods with gut-clenching, bowel-cleansing ferocity.

Long before annoying car alarms, Bill developed a much better system. Anybody walking within twenty feet of his unlocked vehicle would instantly be shocked out of their mother lovin' gourd when Puppity exploded at point blank range, giving them a primordial vision of having been already half-eaten by some blood-starved, throat-ripping killer hound from hell.

Puppity always spiked my adrenaline to levels comparable only to falling into a roaring wood chipper. After spending some time with Bill and his ferocious canine, with Bill's tacit permission, Puppity showed me her sweet affectionate puppy side, hence her name. But she was fiercely loyal and would gladly rip off any arms or tear out any throats Bill might quietly signal for. He didn't need to carry a gun, and as far as I knew, he rarely did. He had Puppity and, at any given time, one or more of her more aggressive offspring-in-training.

He lived a damned exciting life, or so I thought, and anyone who met him almost automatically envied his clearly deep lust for life and its many diverse pleasures and, above all, his absolute freedom to live it entirely on his own terms. He was completely unconcerned with what the rest of us perceived as our biggest threat: our mind-numbing, soul-grinding, life-devouring careers from hell. Bill kissed no man's ass. No woman's either, unless of course they needed it for some entirely different reason.

Thom handed the joint to me just as Bill recovered enough to pass him the mirror. Munsell beamed at finding himself in his favorite position, passing a joint while sucking a fat fluffy line. The only time he was happier was when he was firing pottery in his giant backyard furnace or sucking nitrous oxide straight out of one-liter green industrial pressurized gas cylinders. He carried a tiny crescent wrench on his key-chain, not as a statement of his career choice, but as a tool to use when operating the tiny valve stems on these not-for-human-consumption inconvenient steel bottles. They only cost a few bucks at the local gas supplier and was intended for micro-welding tungsten and other metals used by NASA in building hardened spacecraft.

Bill got his crooked smile going, talking out the side of his mouth facing Thom, but watching me for any reaction.

"Who's your friend?" he asked no one in particular, while staring directly at me.

Thom introduced me as the new physics grad student working at the Space Physics lab. Bill liked techie-sounding titles and almost everyone thought physics was cool, or at least the more popularized versions of rockets and nuclear power. He already knew several people who worked at the lab, so anytime a NASA scientist wanted drugs, Bill took it as a prophetic harbinger of strange new worlds to come. Needless to say, his favorite book was *Dune*.

Bill stood up to greet me. He was as tall as me but thinner with a wayward lock of hair falling across his forehead which, of course, just added to his already cool appearance. We shook hands. It was firm, but not stupid macho *he-who-squeezes-harder-is-clearly-the-better-man* grip. Bill had no pretensions about anything. You got what you saw. What I saw was the embodiment of pretty much everything I considered cool and hip.

"Cool," was coincidentally his only reply.

Bill knew a little bit about everything and considered himself a master at building and driving fast powerful General Motors machines. Besides his Corvette, he had a Buick Riviera and a GMC K10. They all had his favorite engine, a 454-cubic-inch Chevy Big-Block V-8, coupled with one of his specially-modified automatic transmissions. Bill deemed shifting gears far too important to be left to some flawed human behind the wheel. When his automatic shifted, it felt as smooth as Mario Andretti shifting his 1000-horsepower Mercedes into third gear coming out of the back S-turns at Lemans.

"Here, have a snort," he said, motioning to Thom to pass me the mirror.

I took it and somehow managed to slip down into a cross-legged position on the floor, without jostling one glistening crystal of the finely-chopped coke out of its proper place. Bill handed me a rolled up hundred-dollar bill.

"Nice," I muttered to myself. "Haven't seen one of these in a while."

I sucked up half of one fat line into one nostril, moved the rolled up Franklin to the other, and polished off the rest of the line with an audible *swoosh*. I pinched my nose with forefinger and thumb while I passed the mirror back to Thom. He grabbed it just as I exploded with two powerful sneezes, which I just barely contained.

Phoot! Phoot! I went, letting a little air out, but still holding my nose tightly so no powder could escape. *Can't be caught blowing blow out your blowhole. Bad juju, and a sure indication of an amateur. So very uncool to blow snow, fool!*

Bill began asking me questions and pretty soon we were talking about cars, Newton's Laws of Motion, how an atom bomb worked, and what new drugs were coming home with the troops returning from Vietnam.

Bill signaled to the freckled girl who had remained nearby, quietly attentive throughout our conversation, dispensing a seemingly endless supply of joints that made their way around the room one at a time. The magic weed cornucopia appeared to be a huge macramé shoulder-bag she wielded like an attached ammo bag. It had the requisite psychedelic colors and feathered fringe that left no doubt as to what new culture it reflected. She reached into her bag of tricks and handed Bill a small bundle wrapped neatly in unbleached rice-paper with thin fiber strands tying it up like a miniature mummy. He loosened the fine strands and removed the delicate paper wrapper.

"Here, try this on for size," Bill said.

He held out a strange looking, wrinkled-up brownish-green dried weed concoction, tied with the same little fibers to a six-inch-long bamboo toothpick. It looked like someone had tried to make a cannabis shish kebab. "It's a Thai stick. Straight off a C-130 Hercules transport from Saigon, yesterday," he said with a wink. "Ever see anything like it?"

He handed it to me. I looked it over and realized it was the end product of a society that actually cultivated, pruned, and packaged its merchandise like some fat, capitalist-pig corporation, only this particular enterprise was probably a people's commune in rural Cambodia working to support rebel freedom fighters. That was good enough for me.

Bill offered a packet of EZ Widers with his other hand and smiled like I was being set up for the kill. EZ Widers were for amateurs who were so uncoordinated they needed a rolling paper the size of a bed sheet to produce a passably smoke-able joint.

"Here, you might need these," Bill said with a gleeful smirk and wink to Thom, who was now staring off into space with a grin covering more of his face than it seemed possible. Thom had hit the sky-zone quite some time ago and was, more or less, on high-altitude cruise control for the rest of the night.

"No thanks, I've got my own papers," I said, dutifully producing a package of fine translucent rice-paper Zig-Zags from my shirt pocket.

I grabbed a magazine from the nightstand, opened it to the exact middle and began crushing up half of the Thai stick. I used one of Bill's razor blades to scrape the crushed weed to one side and let all the seeds roll down to the fold separating them from the smoke. There were just a few, and strangely tiger-striped. I'd never seen this kind of sassy, mean-looking seed before. I dropped them into an empty cocaine bottle I happened to have and tucked it in my pocket for future reference.

I produced a passable joint after a couple of tries. The secret was in proper wetting of the fingers. Too much saliva destroyed the delicate paper, and not enough made your fingers lose their friction so, instead of rolling, the paper would just crumple up and dump its contents back onto the magazine.

I offered the slightly crooked but tightly rolled joint to Bill. He just indicated I hand it on to the cute little girl next to him instead. "This is Amy, by the way. She's my personal assistant."

She flashed me a big smile as she took the joint and lit it up. She waved her free hand at me in greeting.

"Hi," she said between deep drags.

After a long draw that I thought was possibly unladylike, or more than her small frame could handle, she held her breath with some difficulty. She sputtered a little and some smoke leaked out her nose as she passed it on to Bill.

Cute, I thought. *A girl with obvious talents.*

Bill took a more modest toke and handed it back to me with a nod of approval. I guess I passed the first test. Amy reached over and shook my hand. "I hear you're from out west."

"Pacific Northwest, actually, Oregon to be exact," I corrected. I noticed her nose freckles wrinkled up in a most curious way when she smiled. It just enhanced her alluring pixie image. I wondered if fucking Tinker Bell was considered statutory rape.

Eberbach appeared, and he had to have a toke, as did Thom again. By the time it got back to me, it was just a nubbin' of its former glory. I took a final hit off the roach, noting that even though it had burned down to some ugly looking, tar-soaked mouse turd, the flavor and taste were exceptional. I had to look into this Vietnam thing a little more.

"I see by your boots you're a cowboy," she declared, looking at my partially hidden boots. The sharp pointy-toe protruding from my jeans must have given me away.

"You could say that," I replied casually. "It's a forty-acre farm and the cattle are all milk cows. I ride the range on a John Deere tractor and shovel shit for fun."

She laughed.

I wore the clothes that a farm kid routinely gets for Christmas, so my look was not cultivated, but typical. It was natural for me to wear blue jeans, snap buttoned western shirts, a denim jacket, black cowboy hat when it was called for, and shit kickin', pointy-toed, high-heeled, fancy-stitched cowboy boots. I liked the unintentional disguise. I could blend in almost anywhere out west, except maybe a hippie love-in or a Jewish wedding.

"I see by your outfit that you must be a drugstore cowgirl from Brooklyn," I said, throwing it right back, looking directly at her blue jean jacket, which sort of matched mine.

She laughed again as did Bill. "Touché," she said between gulps of smoke.

"So what do you do at the lab?" Bill asked.

"As little as possible," I answered, "but right now I'm writing a giant simulation program modeling the upper atmosphere's chemical and energy flows. I'm trying to calculate the solar thermal efficiencies at 100 to 500 kilometers altitude."

Bill took a big drag on a passing joint and handed it to me. "And that's important because…?"

"Because someone pays me to do it and I need a job to survive," I responded as I took the proffered roach.

I took a big drag and between the coughs and exploding smoke I added, "The post doc (*cough!*) in the next office (*hack!*) found that chlorofluoro—(*ahaagh!*)" I paused gasping for air, "... carbons are eating up our Ozone."

"Yeah, we don't want to lose our Ozone," Amy piped in with a big grin as she reached for what was left of the roach I had just choked on. "Otherwise how could we get lost in it?"

Bill laughed. The back story, I learned later, involved George Frayne, a local musician needing a place to rehearse his new band. Bill gave them the basement of one of his slumlord houses and kept them well-stimulated for the time it took to put together Commander Cody and the Lost Planet Airmen and their first album and title song, *Lost in the Ozone Again*. George was experimenting with that new shit-kicking Austin sound that was splitting the CW creeps into two opposing camps: the Nashville-alcoholic, brain-dead, whiskey-drinking, redneck music-dinosaurs, versus the terminally-alcoholic, drug-crazed, loud-trucking, new-sound-loving irreverent rebel cowboys. Although we mostly hated C and W music, we loved the rebel-truckin', modern-day cowboy-rock tunes. Even though the Commander's music was a little twangy, the hard-driving Midwest rock sound we all liked was still there in his other modest hit, "Hot Rod Lincoln." They may end up as a shit-kicking, redneck bar band, but all of them had advanced degrees and came from America's most liberal university town outside of Berkeley. Fuck you, Vietnam-War-mongering Nashville shitheads! Two can play that game.

"What the hell is a chloro-bloro carbon?" Bill asked, exhibiting some tongue challenges.

"Freon is what DuPont calls it. But you know nothing good ever comes from DuPont. Shit, they're hell-bent on creating the world's first massive ecological disaster in Vietnam with that Agent Orange crap. We'll probably be treating veterans for skin and lung cancer for the next fifty years, unless they all die first."

"That's probably their real goal anyway," Bill offered casually with his classic all-knowing smirk. "Helps get rid of the witnesses."

"In the meantime, all the refrigerant leaks in the world vent huge amounts of this shit, which works its way up through the atmosphere very, very slowly until it finds ozone, which it destroys immediately upon contact."

I motioned toward the ceiling with waving hands, illustrating gases inexorably seeping upward to attack our favorite atmospheric layer after oxygen and nitrous.

"Ozone is the principle absorber of solar ultraviolet rays, and its disappearance could contribute to sterilizing the planet's surface of all life, including the idiots that caused it," I continued. "It sounds like a giant Darwin Award is in order for the entire human race, with the only downside being that we'll take most of the rest of Earth's life with us."

"What's that?" Amy asked.

She stopped momentarily chopping up another pile of white crystals. Bill was apparently tired of doing the honors and had turned the ceremonial mirror over to his curlier-haired assistant.

"The Darwin Award?"

"Yeah."

She went back to chopping, still listening intently.

"That's what we award to those individuals who perform some stupid death-defying stunt, voluntarily removing themselves from the gene pool and thus improving the intelligence of future generations. In this way, we honor those who make us a stronger species by deliberately exterminating themselves prematurely."

I clicked my heels and saluted German-style with a beer.

They just looked at me funny. I guess it was still too soon for Nazi humor.

Just then, Thom came wandering by with his prized possession, a tiny green industrial gas cylinder with a small wrench attached to the business end for a valve handle.

"Hey, I'll trade you a hit on the Greeny Weeny for a couple of bumps," he offered.

Standing beside him was a skinny hippie-looking kid who could have passed for a young Gandhi in a T-shirt, and next to him, an equally scrawny little girl half his height who could easily pass for a Dickens street waif with huge sink-pool eyes.

Thom handed his gas cylinder to Bill, turned to the new couple, and announced in a voice that could be heard clearly above the loud music, "And here's the great and wondrous Bill Smith," as he gestured toward him with arms extended like an eager artist presenting a prized piece of work.

I recognized the girl. Her name was Bambi, and she was one of the solder jockeys at the lab; she had been seen often in Thom's company. Actually, I hadn't formally met her yet, as she worked in production on the first floor, while I had a tiny cubical on the second floor where the scientists and engineers pretended to work.

The guy looked new to Ann Arbor, at least newer than me. His hair was still too short for the company he was keeping because clearly, he had only recently forgone upstanding American-type regular shearing. If you were in the Rock & Roll or drug business, you knew these things intuitively. Hair length was our way of profiling the friendly and the foe.

Amy handed the now fully loaded mirror to Thom. I hadn't missed the little nod Bill made in her direction, indicating she do so. Thom lit up with his usual ear-to-ear grin full of welcoming wrinkles on all sides, giving him that rugged, outdoor, handsome-as-hell look, even though he might otherwise be considered a little too pockmarked from an ugly attack of teenage acne. But it just made his smile look bigger.

Thom handed the mirror to the new guy, who promptly handed it to Bambi. A man with manners, I thought. Cool.

"This is Larry Monroe, the new late-night DJ at the local FM station," he explained. Ann Arbor only had two FM stations, one run by the university and the other a little privately-owned country station located in the sticks southwest of town, near Scio. Its daytime broadcast area covered mostly the Detroit end of the I-94 freeway with hardcore trucker country music.

But from midnight to dawn, when I guess all good little truckers are fast asleep in their truck-beds, they hand over the studio to long hair Rock & Roll DJ's, turn their backs to the candles, soft lights, and strange incense drifting from the control room, and basically let the good times roll for a vast majority of some fifty thousand area college students. They had no problem supporting the late-night handoff with radio spots from every pizza joint and record shop within ten miles of campus.

Larry stepped out and shook Bill's hand, then mine, and finally Amy's. Amy didn't look too pleased, I guess maybe from being last. She seemed to be as observant as I.

Bambi passed the mirror back to Larry, who definitely helped himself to the lion's nose share. After Thom, it went to me, and then Amy, who still looked unamused. The little green cylinder kept making the rounds, so there was a lot of up-and-down psyche going on in the group. Combining coke with nitrous was like riding a mental roller coaster. The long soothing mindless buzz followed by a lightning crash of rushing thoughts and ideas flashing by. What a ride!

In the meantime, Bill and Larry struck up a conversation about music and the local music scene, namedropping the who's who of the local music scene and the who's who of local drug dealers, who were often the same. Finally, Bill explained that he had been listening to Larry's show on the car radio, as I guess their work-times coincided almost exactly, and that he really liked what he did and needed to do more of it. I made a mental note to check out Larry's show next time I was awake at that hour.

During the namedropping, a local rock promoter whose name I recognized turned out to have a brother who was also in the business. Curt Andrews helped his little brother by acting as a road manager and technical director for the many bands Pete was trying to promote into clubs and music halls all over southeast Michigan. Curt's real interest, however, was in running the PA mix board at big rock concerts.

Larry mentioned a new name, Marty, that Bill didn't seem to know. Bill would never admit he didn't know something, he would just turn it around and get you to tell him what he needed to know without actually admitting ignorance. Bill was used to being top dog, so he never allowed the impression that he was second to anyone in anything. It just wasn't cool.

So the gist that I caught was that Marty and Curt were starting a new Rock & Roll PA company here called Fanfare. Evidently, Marty was a long-time roadie and road manager for various bands around the Midwest, the most recent being the James Gang.

Anyway, the word was out that they had some kind of deal going now with Grand Funk Railroad, a Flint-based band, who played large arena theaters, seating thousands. Apparently it was going to be a state-of-the-art solid-state mix board, full stereo with huge speaker stacks and thousands of watts of power. They were building the world's loudest PA system.

That last part caught my attention. It caught Thom and Steve's attention as well.

"How loud is loud anyway," asked Steve. "Do they want to make ears bleed?"

We snickered at the thought.

"The loudest manmade sound would probably be a rocket motor up-close and personal," I noted. "That's about 140 decibels SPL and it definitely causes damage to the unprotected ear."

Thom set us straight. "Anything above 130 dB is painful as hell, so I think they're trying to get to an impressive but nondestructive 120 dB SPL inside a 10,000-seat indoor stadium with hopefully minimal distortion."

"At that level, even without speaker distortion, the sound waves create so much secondary noise with echoes and rattling plaster that minimizing total distortion may be very difficult," Steven countered. "Besides, you would need a giant wall of speakers spanning the entire stage to handle that much power."

"I don't think you want to do that," I responded. "Sound doesn't radiate like a planar wall. Remember Huygens' Principle?

Sound waves spread out spherically, as if coming from a point source. If you force sound to come out of a wall, the waves would interfere with themselves horribly, causing all kinds of distortion, including destroying any and all source directionality. A stereo recording would lose the implied direction of sound needed to discern where each instrument is coming from. It wouldn't be crisp and clear."

That shut them up. The prevailing wisdom for making loud music was to go for bigger and bigger walls of speakers like the Grateful Dead's PA.

"Do any of you space junkies know anything about a blue box?" Bill asked, breaking the silence and changing the subject. Larry was taking advantage of the lull in conversation to wipe the now line-free mirror clean with his wet finger and liberally apply the accumulated paste to his gums. The gum hit was the *piece de resistance* of the cocaine ceremony.

"I think the blue box was invented by a student at MIT," piped in Eberbach eagerly. "It supposedly allows you to make long-distance phone calls for free."

"How does it do that?" Bill asked.

I hadn't heard of such a thing so I just listened as I sequentially puffed and passed on one by one a continuous stream of joints coming from Amy's deft fingers. They seemed delicate, yet dexterous, just the right size for rolling. She could make someone a very happy man.

"When Ma Bell went to DTMF signaling," Thom butted in, "they must have opened up their touchtone frequencies to do more than just replace the dial clicks. They probably also provide in-band signaling of some sort to the other end of a long-distance circuit. If that's true, then anyone knowing the secret tone frequencies would allow them to control the whole friggin' phone system!"

Bill's and Eberbach's eyes bulged noticeably as they suddenly perked up from Thom's comment. I had heard about black boxes that could tap phone lines but DTMF touch-tone dialing was something I hadn't thought about. Thom casually picked off a joint passing by and took a long drag while everyone waited for more. He finally passed it to Eberbach and continued.

"I also heard from one of the grad music students that a few years ago some guy was caught singing pure musical tones into pay phones and getting free phone calls. Apparently he had perfect pitch and had accidently struck on some tones that magically turned off billing."

Bill's normal casual smile turned into a devious grin as he contemplated what this could do for his business and prestige. Eberbach was grinning because he was realizing how much it would be worth if he built one. I was smiling because I might know how to find the right frequency.

"You're being awfully quiet."

I looked behind me and it was Amy with another joint. I could see she was red-eyed and having trouble focusing. She unsteadily held out another Thai joint.

"I might be a fool, but why open my mouth and remove all doubt?"

I took the joint but just pretended to inhale. I felt slightly giddy from all the loose smoke and exhausted Nitrous in the room. I could use another line of Bill's excellent cocaine.

Thom had returned to his group of artist friends in the other corner. They were taking turns sucking on a new gas cylinder, this time marked in bright green and yellow. Artists freed themselves from conventional trappings by not using a formal gas mask and mixing valve as was normally required for breathing in the correct gas and air mixture preventing accidental asphyxiation. Instead, they put the tank spigot directly in their mouths and turned the valve, with a monkey wrench, blasting a whirlwind of frigid silly gas directly into their lungs. One blast is usually just enough to take the patient right up to unconsciousness, whereupon they drop the tank, preventing any nasty overdoses, collapse in any nearby bean bag chair, and slowly buzz their way back to full consciousness and that pesky, much-overrated reality.

"So how did a nice little Jewish girl end up in a place like this?"

I handed the joint back. It was about half-burned, so plenty left.

"How did you know?" she asked defiantly, eyes flashing, as she took another of her loud sucking hits.

"My first girlfriend, who did in my virginity, was Jewish. You look a lot like her. Plus, to an Oregonian, being from Brooklyn means you're either Jewish, Italian, or Black. I ruled out Italian and Black right away."

"Oh shit, you nailed me."

She handed back the joint but I had trouble getting it loose from her Bogart-pinch. Her eyes were almost shut.

"You're very astute for a guy with no name. So how are all the Jewish girls back in Oregon?"

"You mean all three of them? Don't know. How 'bout where you come from?"

I finally managed to get the joint from her death grip, but it fell on the floor.

"You mean Long Island?"

She was already on her hands and knees looking for it.

"I think it rolled under the bed."

I got down, peering under the bed, but her head was already moving for exactly the same spot in time and space.

Whack!

I dropped like a bull that just got shot between the eyes. She reeled back against the bed stand.

"What the fuck Cowboy! Look before you duck," she yelled as she rolled about holding her head.

I didn't answer. She calmed a bit and then miraculously recovered.

"Physicist! Cowboy! You okay?" she asked as she rolled over to face me.

Someone else was shaking me. It was Bill.

"You look like you need a little bump."

I opened one eye just in time to see a small silver spoon glide into my slightly blurred line of vision.

"Hit it!" he ordered.

That was my cue. I sucked hard through my nose and was rewarded with a burning sensation in one nostril. I managed to get a thumb up there to close off that nostril as he commanded, "Again!"

This time the burn went deep in the other nostril and my other eye popped open.

"Is it morning already?"

Everybody was staring at me. It was a terrible breach of protocol when the dealer has to manually revive the acolyte. Thom, laughing from across the room, pointed to the compressed gas cylinder he was holding up and motioned for me to join him. Yeah, just what I needed, more states of unconsciousness like, well, the one that I'm trying to recover from right now.

"I seem to remember a loose joint somewhere," I muttered.

"Got it," piped up Amy as she held up the little roach now sporting partially burned dust bunnies like a furry fungus growing on week-old pizza.

"No thanks," I said as I climbed back up to the bed.

Nearby, Eberbach was sitting on the edge of the bed in his favorite posture. When Steve was thinking, he would set on the edge of a chair or couch or bed, cross his legs and cup the upper knee with clasped hands and rock back-and-forth rapidly as he thought or, more accurately, chewed on his train of thought.

Bill sat back down next to me.

"Eberbach may have it worked out already," he said.

"What?"

"How to build a blue box. Tell 'm Steve."

He motioned for Eberbach to go on. Steve scooted closer to us.

"There's a new chip that has just come out. It's a programmable multi-vibrator that can switch in microseconds all the way up to seconds. There are two of them on an 8-pin DIP. I can easily build a battery-powered box that you can hold up to a phone's mouthpiece and it will generate DTMF sound tones. It's really quite simple. Just need the secret frequencies. I don't know why everybody doesn't make one. It's crazy!"

His eyes flashed with excitement. When Eberbach caught a sniff of money, he became obsessed, if not downright psychotic, in its pursuit.

"I told him to find the parts and I'll pay for them," Bill added. "My friend Talbot, the lawyer I work with, could really use one of these. So could I. How many can you make?"

"I can scrounge most of the parts at the lab," Steve volunteered. "It might take a week to get the chip. If we build more than one or two, we should layout a printed circuit board. Then we can knock off hundreds or thousands! How many can you afford?" He smiled broadly at his joke.

"Let's see if you can make one work, first," Bill said, knowing that if anyone could, an MIT engineer and a NASA physicist should be able to pull it off. Bill was a professional outlaw who used advanced technology, so he leapt at the chance to work with the best minds to build a better larceny box.

"Oh, it'll work. If it's possible, and it sounds like it is, then I know I can build the box," Eberbach added with a shit-eating smile of certainty.

"Did you know that Talbot and I used to fly bodies around the country for a mortuary service?" Bill directed to me, as he changed the subject.

Bill went on about his adventures with this wild Ann Arbor lawyer. I couldn't quite make out whether Talbot was a lawyer-criminal or a criminal lawyer, but he seemed to move smoothly from one side to the other with relative ease. I wondered if this mentor to Bill was a product of the infamously progressive U of M Law School, or was he just attracted to the Detroit area for all the criminal and/or legal equal opportunities to be found here.

Drug busts were way up, due largely to the local pig strategy of keeping students under constant duress and bottled up on campus, quiet and compliant. Talbot no doubt had an endless stream of clients, mostly white middle-class students whose parents paid handsomely to keep their little darlings out of jail. Marijuana busts were starting to be quite profitable for both the cops and the legal profession.

Based on Bill's description, Talbot heroically defended innocent druggies, successfully keeping the cops relatively honest and a lot of bright young kids out of prison. Unlike most others of his reviled profession, Talbot was young, cool, smart, chased beautiful coeds, drove hot Corvettes (hence the connection to Bill), did a lot of coke (another connection to Bill), and, of course, he had a precise lack of key conventional morals that made him effective on either side of the cultural divide. He was expensive, but worth it. He was even known to take drugs in lieu of legal fees. *Quid pro quo*, I suppose, for the drug profession.

Bill made a request to me, while offering a couple more tiny spoonful's of white fluff behind a raised hand, I presumed, because he feared being overheard by some deaf lip-reading narco-snitch. Later I learned he did this maneuver with everybody. It was his way of giving his words added urgency and personal emphasis. It was also his way of asking a favor that you both knew could not be easily refused.

"I want you to keep an eye on Eberbach and make sure he stays on this job for me. There's a lot riding on it. You live with him; maybe you can help him when he gets stuck. Let me know how it goes and let me know if you need anything."

He slipped me a small brown bottle as an added inducement. I guess I'd just been hired.

"Sure, no sweat," I was able to respond. "I really don't know if it can be done either, but I can check the literature and see what I can find out."

He handed me the rolled-up Franklin and pointed to another fat line of little white crystals spread completely across the mirror. I was a bit jittery and felt a slight tic in one eye. *Oh hell*, I thought, *why not?*

For some reason, Bill took a liking to me almost from the beginning. I was nothing like the type of person he normally hung with. For starters, I was a student at the University. He was a local. Locals and students never mixed. He grew up the only son of a local dentist and knew everybody and anybody in town worth knowing, of course, including college students if the occasion required.

I also wasn't part of his cool crowd, although I buzzed around on the fringe. Quite a few of the professional technicians and staff at the lab were locals and also solid members of the local cool club. Hence, I found a few I enjoyed hanging with and that got me past the student vs. local divide. That and the work I was doing with the local music scene helped me get past other social barriers as well.

In Ann Arbor of the '60s and '70s, Rock & Roll was the central attraction that everything cultural seemed to orbit around. Doing drugs was the way we proved we were committed rebels against the mainstream culture, especially seeing how it carried stiff penalties if caught. Likewise, the anti-war movement along with Black Power and Women's Liberation gave us all a strong, self-righteous motivation for hanging together, while hopefully changing the world before the Nix-goon Nazi's decided to lock us all up.

Steve and I made it back home sometime after sunrise. When we awoke later that night, neither of us had any idea what time that might have been. I'm not sure it was even the next day.

Eberbach and I started working on the blue box almost immediately. He laid out the circuit with a plug-in prototype board while I went to the university's engineering library and researched AT&T DTMF dialing codes. I found the frequencies for all the digits on the touchtone pad but failed to find anything on tones used for signaling switches or trunk lines.

After several days of searching the card catalogs and citation indexes, I finally found an obscure reference to an article on how to build a "Blue Box telephone device," cited in an obscure little-known French-published magazine called *The Anarchist Cookbook.* I looked up the name and found it had been put together by some communist printer in Paris, supposedly for the IRA and various underground revolutionaries around Europe. It was purportedly a definitive collection of nasty recipes and sabotage tactics proven effective throughout a century or more of European hotheads kicking ass against their incredibly corrupt and decadent aristocracy.

I finally tracked down a well-used paperback copy hidden among the stacks in the central quad undergraduate library. It was the latest edition, although I noticed several pages had already been torn out. Luckily the section on electronic eavesdropping techniques was still intact.

After leafing through it briefly, I became astounded at all the neat stuff it contained. There were recipes for explosives, detonators, and all kinds of clever spy toys. Then I concentrated on the chapter about defrauding the Capitalist Pig phone company. Near the end, they spelled it out. If you could get access to a trunk line, simply sending a pure 2300 Hz tone would cause the trunk line switch to respond with a dial-tone that allowed inputting normal long-distance phone numbers free of charge. It was called "seizing a trunk line."

The best way to gain access to a trunk line, the article continued, was to dial any random 800-number. This immediately connects your phone to a trunk line, but before the opposite end starts ringing, you assert the seize tone. The switch will respond by connecting the call to a vacant touchtone-enabled trunk line. This was how the Wichita Lineman actually made phone calls while hanging from a telephone pole in the middle of Kansas. Apparently, once you seized a trunk line by this method, you could make successive calls one after another by just asserting the seizure tone and dialing any number in the world. Apparently, the IRA had not been paying for long-distance calls for quite some time.

Holy cow! This couldn't possibly be true. AT&T wasn't known for hiring idiot engineers, so I remained flabbergasted that this device could possibly work. Later, I learned a company full of the brightest engineers is never any smarter than their most incompetent manager. Check it out. This is exactly why airplanes fall out of the sky and ships that hit icebergs sink.

Steve was able to get the 555 multi-vibrator setup so it imitated the normal DTMF touchtone frequency codes used for push-button dialing and could also provide the 2300 Hz pure tone we hoped would do the trunk-line trick. He even found a 12-digit matrix switch pad that looked like something I had seen on one of the telecom units he built at the lab for signaling satellites. He put it onto a small box that contained the circuit board, batteries, and a speaker on the back where it could be held up to a telephone handset. There was only a single miniature spring-toggle switch on its side to activate the seize tone. Simple and clean meant nobody could tell what it was by just looking at it.

We had no intention at giving the pigs any opportunity to trace us if something went wrong, so we tried it out for the first time at one of our favorite secluded payphones on campus. Steve made up an 800-number, put a dime in, got a dial tone and then held the phone mouthpiece up against the speaker holes on the back of the box. We cocked our heads near the earpiece so we could hear what was happening.

He started punching the 800-number into the blue box keypad. When he finished, he counted to three while we heard clicking and line noises indicating the call had been put on an international trunk line and was about to start ringing. He pushed the toggle switch. Almost immediately, we heard a loud click then another dial tone. We looked at each other questioningly.

"Did it work?"

"I don't know," Steve answered. "Let's call someone to see if it really works."

"Who should we call?" I asked. We looked at each other trying to think of something fast.

"I dunno," he answered and then he laughed. "Shit! We did it! And we don't even know who to call!"

"I just happen to have the main security number at Argonne National Labs memorized," I volunteered with an oily smirk. "I did an experiment there in '68 for the Atomic Energy Commission and I had to call them often, pretending I was my professor and requesting clearance every time I wanted to go for a motorcycle ride outside the gate."

"Oh, perfect," he said and held out the box so I could input the number.

I punched the numbers into the keypad. We were greeted with the sound of a phone ringing on the other end almost immediately.

"Argonne National Lab Security. Captain Harmon speaking. Can I help you?" came the voice loud and clear out of the earpiece. Steve was about to lose it. We paused for a second not knowing quite what to do next. Then I spoke up.

"Is your cyclotron running?" I asked loudly so the mouthpiece still held up to the box might hear me.

"Who is this?" Captain Harmon demanded.

Steve started laughing out loud even though he tried to stifle it.

"You better run after it before it gets away!" I yelled. Steve almost doubled up, completely out of control. He tried hanging up the handset but missed on the first try. I could hear Captain Harmon screaming something threatening about a federal lab or maybe federal law. Not sure, as Steve finally found the hook and slammed the handset on it.

"Holy shit! It worked!" Eberbach screamed. I too was amazed. Things usually never just work on the first attempt. I seriously think Murphy's Law is so old that it predates the Egyptians when the first pyramid didn't work either. Look it up.

Bill was ecstatic. He ended up with about dozen boxes while Steve, Thom, and I each kept one for ourselves. For the next half-dozen years or so, until Ma Bell plugged the hole in her security, she inadvertently helped support any number of nefarious characters, all kinds of quasi-legal activities, and righteous anti-establishment causes that would hopefully someday make robber barons roll over in their graves.

Bill and I became close friends from then on. He helped me get my first four-wheel-drive truck similar to the big yellow one he drove. Thom found two K-10 trucks at the University of Michigan surplus warehouse with small cheap six-cylinder engines that were pretty badly worn out. They'd been driven by geology students from Ann Arbor to research sites in Mexico. We got them relatively cheap due to the copious amounts of blue smoke emanating from their tailpipes.

Bill found a couple of 350 engines with low time and rebuilt both of them with some good-old serious gas-fueled American horsepower. I had to add the new wide rims with knobby treads that just plain looked mean. When he was done, I felt ready to four-wheel something like a Rocky Mountain trail on the side of a craggy Colorado peak. No such craggy peaks existed in Lower Michigan, so the truck became a status symbol of independence and self-empowerment as I auspiciously motored about Ann Arbor in one of only maybe a half-dozen similar trucks. Who the fuck needs roads or society with a truck like that? Just the thought that I could go literally anywhere I damned well pleased gave me great satisfaction and security in a time of turmoil and trouble.

Bill owned several student rental houses which I helped him maintain from time to time, doing repairs, plumbing and electrical work, and sometimes collecting rents from the pitiful student tenants. I grew up being poor and cash starved, so the thought of actually owning property that generated a monthly income sounded like a great idea. Several of Bill's friends also had houses, some purchased by their fathers so they'd have cheap housing while attending the university. Jeez, it must be tough to be rich and make money investing in real estate as a student, while the rest of us poor dumb peasants pour our money down the rental sewer hole.

With the money I made at the lab and on the side helping Bill, I could finally afford to take flying lessons, which had been my dream for some time. The university had a flying club that owned a couple of Cessna 150s, which made it even more affordable. Life was more or less getting good for the poor broke cowboy from Oregon.

I was finishing up my last electives for a PhD in Atmospheric Physics. One was "Philosophy of Quantum Physics" taught by the philosophy department which, understandably, did not understand quantum physics and took that to be somehow fundamentally pre-eminent. Just because nature becomes probabilistic does not imbue it with conscious enlightenment. The other was "Beginning Filmmaking" taught in, of all places, the School of Architecture by the architect-trained professor turned avant-garde filmmaker and brazen self-promoter, George Manupelli.

The philosophy course was taught by a young unknown post-doc who probably understood Kierkegaard, but definitely didn't understand a lick of science, physics, math, or for that matter, quantum mechanics. We couldn't agree on anything, considering that he couldn't grasp why squaring the complex amplitude of a wave function and integrating it over all space yields only a dimensionless probability of finding the quantum state populated. Quantum Mechanics spelled the doom for exact science. Now nature looked fuzzy and gooey, just like most philosopher's thinking.

Some people just can't get it through their heads that God and nature like to gamble. Some may find this loss of determinacy disturbingly twisted gobbledygook, while others might find it an awe-inspiringly confirmation of mysterious forces beyond reality. I just found it really boring and delusional. Asking why nature chooses to express itself in these weird ways is like asking why God made man so creepy, considering all the talk of being created in somebody's image.

Manupelli, on the other hand, was a well-known local underground self-promoting artist, teacher, hippie mentor, and coed collector who lived in a little old converted school house just outside of town. Renowned for his debauched artist parties, female student seductions, and his marathon boring underground films, he practiced and preached the mantra 'more is less.' As a consequence, he might use his camera to pan a room in one agonizingly slow continuous long shot recording little or no action, imitating I guess, real life transpiring in some agonizingly slow boredom. One would think this kind of crap would require dynamite dialog to save it and they would be right, which is why *Dr. Detroit* ended up putting to sleep the entire auditorium full of snobby, well-snorted, cocaine-infused film geeks at its midnight showing at the Ann Arbor Film Festival, which of course was his one claim to fame at the university, being both its founder and self-proclaimed charismatic dictator.

But Manupelli actually owned a 16mm Éclair, the revolutionizing European camera used to shoot all those artsy-fartsy black-and-white films coming out of France and Italy in the '50s and '60s. It allowed the development of a new form of cinematography, *cinema verite'*, in which the camera is no longer a static window but an active participant in the story. Freed from the tripod, the film artist also felt free from the expensive and stifling studios—and the girls became even more free to any cinematographer carrying one around. It was like being Belmondo while really in America.

I knew this firsthand, having rented one a few years back to film a concert in Grant Park in Chicago with my partner at Warlock Productions, Bob Lounsbury. The pigs decided this would be a good time to try out their upcoming tactics for the Democratic National Convention to be held in town later that summer. We got great footage of cops busting innocent music lovers' heads because someone in the crowd might have been smoking pot and somebody at the microphone might have called the war in Vietnam *a fascist war of colonial aggression*. It didn't take much in the '60s to start a police riot.

By that time, I was well-experienced in the art of covering riots and avoiding those random late-night cop beatings, while all the time filming someone else who might not be so lucky. Bob and I got some great footage that Haskel Wexler later used in his dramatic film *Medium Cool*, the story of a calloused news cinematographer who is totally unaffected by the horrors he routinely films for the six o'clock news. Beating up innocent young Rock & Roll kids was just another day for pig work. And there seemed no end to it.

Later that night at a small bar in Old Town, several young ladies attracted by my camera listened raptly to our tails of heroism and terror in the park. All of them insisted on following us home and, one by one, each of them made their way to my bed and presumably Bob's that night. It was the only time I ever had to say enough is enough.

So after a two-day sleep marathon following the epic weed run to Mexico, I regained rudimentary consciousness, called Bill and left a message to stop by anytime. Predictably, he showed up at Eberbach's house way past midnight.

Steve and I were watching TV with my giant color-television projector, which was massive compared to normal televisions. The projector stood about four feet high and consisted of a conventional 1950s tube-type RCA color TV receiver chassis which, instead of a single large screen, held three miniature TV screens each showing the same image in a different primary color. The incredible optics that projected the three tiny red, green, and blue images onto a six-foot-wide movie screen to produce a full-color wall-sized television picture made the unit worth a mindboggling $50,000 when it was built in 1957.

I found this behemoth at the Michigan surplus store, too. I paid $200 for it. It looked like it came from some World War II bombsite surplus store, but it had actually been used by the university medical school to project live closed-circuit TV pictures from the hospital operating room into the classroom. It was a unique toy at the time because nobody we knew had a TV with a screen bigger than about 30 inches. Plus, it was on wheels so was easy to move if you had a truck and a hoist, which I did.

Bill showed up on our pitch-black porch wearing his pale purple sunglasses and usual shit-eating grin, which always made you think he was extremely self-satisfied about something, probably illegal, but definitely fun. He just smiled knowingly as I related the tale of my bizarre adventure, but I could see he was impressed, probably because he knew how slim our chances for a successful outcome had been right from the start.

Bill sampled the product and got a little fucked up. Steve and I were already pretty wasted from smoking all night waiting for him to show up. He hauled out some coke so we could even out a little. I asked if he could help me find some buyers for my newly-acquired product and he said he'd make a few calls. Hopefully my new gig was going to be highly prosperous and extremely temporary.

"Just hang out for a while," he advised as he paused between snorts. "Someone will give you a call." His big smile seemed somewhat more intense than just the usual plastered grin. Bill most likely knew something I didn't.

CHAPTER FOUR

I COULD GET USED TO THIS

"One toke over the line sweet Jesus, one toke over the line...."

Brewer & Shipley
"One Toke Over the Line"
1970

Cool people never made promises. Or for that matter, any kind of commitment to anybody for anything. Personal freedom was their first concern, and commitment to others somewhere near the last. If Bill remembered the conversation at all you could count yourself lucky. If you actually got a promised phone call within the next couple of months, it meant you were really special and you were probably now in his debt for some bizarre favor he might ask. But now I could consider myself no longer an untouchable student, but part of the townies and connected to what was going on in underground Ann Arbor.

Bill must have been bored or distracted from his usual prolonged aloofness because just a few days after he sampled my product I was brutally awakened from a not-so-pure and yet disturbingly agreeable drug-induced dream at three in the morning by a nerve-damaging ringing sound. My waterbed made sloshing sounds as I rolled over toward the side nearest the phone. The California king mattress sat directly on the floor and was surrounded on three sides with makeshift cinderblock-and-board bookshelves. The phone was near the open side by the magazine section at the head of the bed.

"Yeah?" I said fumbling in the dark and trying to get the damned phone to shut up while juggling the handset to my ear.

"Hey! You Cowboy?" somebody yelled into my ear. At least I had the phone aligned correctly with my head. I lay back on the pillow, kept my eyes shut, and wished it was some horny girl calling to see if she could come over and share my bed for the rest of the night now that I was so rudely awakened. My lascivious hopes were dashed immediately when I realized it was some strange male drunk calling.

"Who is this?" I demanded as I forced myself a little more alert.

"Never mind. You know Bill?"

I had to think a second before I connected with who Bill might be. "Maybe. What's this all about?"

"He says you have some pretty good hay. I've got a starving horse."

"I dunno, maybe," I admitted trying to gather a few strands of my vaporous three a.m. wits. "Who's asking?" God, I hated the hours these drug dealers keep. If they ever see the light of day, they'd probably explode like a vampire dropped off in the Sahara at noon. They deserved it, too, just as much as any other walking dead.

"Never mind that for now. I just happen to be in town looking for something and he said I had to check you out."

"How do I know you're not a narc or something worse?" I asked even though I had no way of dealing with either one even if I knew the difference.

"I'll tell you what. I trust Bill and if he says you're okay, then you're okay. I'll be there in fifteen minutes. Put a light in the window."

The telephone clicked. Dead silence.

"Oh shit," I thought. "Now I have to deal with this crap in person at this ungodly hour."

I rolled back over to my former warm spot, making another loud sloshing sound no doubt caused by the huge air bubble I keep intending to remove. My giant waterbed took up about 90 percent of the available floor space in my room, which kept most of the rest of my belongings well within arm's length. I gave up and rolled off the open side onto the floor just six inches below and slowly struggled to my feet. Standing finally, in all my naked, hairless-monkey gloriousness, I grabbed my bathrobe from a nearby wall hook, threw it on, and felt my way through the dark to the top of the stairs. I didn't want to kick on the hall light, which might wake Steve.

Eberbach's house was a typical turn-of-the-century basic two-story, three-bedroom, four-gable, cross-shaped, wood-frame home. It came with the characteristic fully covered porch spanning the front, high peaked roofs, tall double-pane darkened windows, replete with fading white clapboard siding and peeling white trim. The miniscule front yard was open on three sides with weeds bordered by bigger weeds trailing off toward the rear, which dutifully died off early each year, leaving mostly bare dirt mixed with something more or less straw-like. Tall trees bordered the lot, which pretty much kept the house and immediate surroundings in perpetual shade and made the struggling grass struggle even more desperately.

Inside, tall ceilings and pastel-painted plaster walls were originally bracketed by rich, dark, well-oiled, solid-oak trim and maple wainscoting that long ago began accumulating layer after layer of thick lead paint. The home's characteristic hickory-boarded floors were now mostly hidden by recently-added secondhand throw rugs. The downstairs was initially divided into four small rooms, but Steve removed a couple of walls and now there was one good-sized room all along the right side of the house. The kitchen was in a separate little room at the rear and connected to the enclosed back porch that led to a small shack in the backyard that served as a garage and storage area. The back porch and garage-shack now held a sizeable accumulation of the larger pieces of leftover junk from our past projects and future failures.

One end of the big room had a hand-painted mural of a road the width of the floor rising up and disappearing in perspective into the east-facing front window. The vanishing road was surrounded by an expansive desert scene of rugged barren mountains, burning sand, lizards, cacti, a few vultures in the cloudless sky, and one lonely scraggly coyote licking his balls. I felt right at home in spirit.

At the opposite end of the room was again the asphalt road painted in extreme perspective, disappearing behind the west-facing window. But this time, it's the opening of a giant suspension bridge disappearing over water leading into a megalopolis city skyline lit up at night. I'm not sure if this giant art project had any meaning, as it was painted by a group of lab engineers while in a drunken and drug-crazed condition requiring, I suppose, a commiserative expression of creativity. The fact that it turned out so well, I assured everyone who asked, was totally unintentional. So the murals stayed and became one of the underground cultural hallmarks in town.

It was our living room and general party room. This was where the giant color TV projector resided with a six-foot-wide movie screen on the opposite wall, bracketed by a giant stereo system. Next to the projector was where the keyboard console of a thirty-two-foot church pipe organ stood in all its stained and carved hardwood glory. Its pipes had been installed in the space next to the stairway, with the air bellows in the basement and the longest folded wooden pipes requiring holes in the first and second floors to allow them to poke out in the dark attic. When Steve played it, the entire house vibrated and rattled like a cheap Chicago apartment six feet from an El train passing at full speed. To the chance pedestrian passing by outside, it sounded like an entire circus had moved into the neighborhood, complete with honking clowns and blaring elephants.

We were actually using it to see if we could build a Fourier sound synthesizer that would reproduce the incredibly complex sound of a pipe organ. Not easy. There was no known electronic sound system around that could even play back an organ recording at the same volume and rich fidelity of the actual recorded instrument, let alone maintain its distinctively rich overtones in absolute directional phase linearity. Pipe organs are crisp and loud, while most studio recordings are weak and muddy at best. They just don't have the dynamic range.

I believed it was possible if we could just invent a programmable Fourier oscillator capable of reproducing any sound in any complexity and couple it to a whole new kind of powered speaker system that could reproduce it. What that might be we hadn't figured out yet, but it was just one of the long-term projects that littered our living room and basement with all kinds of interesting and queer-looking equipment resembling what a mad scientist's laboratory might look like in a cheap British horror film from the '50s.

In the exact center of the room, two large couches faced each other, framing a five-foot-diameter cable reel flipped on its side masquerading as a giant coffee table. Its surface was completely covered by newspapers, magazines, various electronic toys including a house soldering gun, an audio power-level meter, and of course, a fair assortment of drug processing and serving equipment, all looking well-used and caught temporarily frozen in some nefarious process of something or another always going on.

Cable reel tables, cinderblock bookshelves, and bean bag chairs were fairly typical accoutrements for an impoverished graduate student's house, even if we were technically working at jobs and bringing home paychecks. Money was short and needed for much more important things like beer and pot. Besides, we were all looking for our fortune so these projects had potential for getting us off the government tit and into some lucrative high-tech start-up business. At least that's how we justified living like extremely well-educated and talented slobs.

At the bottom of the stairs, I kicked on the lights and immediately dimmed them down to barely tolerable. I tried to keep quiet so I could meet this jerk without causing much commotion. Good luck with that. I turned the volume on the stereo to just high enough to confuse a wired narc but hopefully not loud enough to wake Steve. Then I waited...and waited. I'm about ready to go back to bed when I finally hear a familiar sound coming from the dark night outside.

There's not a lot of street traffic at this hour so the sound of a big V8 coming down the street was pretty easy to identify. Then there were two big V8's slightly out of sync but otherwise revved about to the max as they both came down the hill in front of the house. *Oh shit, there's two of them!*

I peeked out the front windows just in time to see two Corvettes, one white and the other black, pull into the small parking lot adjacent to our house. A couple of minutes later, I hear the footsteps of two men climbing the wooden stairs to the big porch. I opened the front door and ushered in Bill and some jovial-looking, red-haired stranger.

"This is Jack," Bill said as the stranger held out his hand to me. I shook it as I gave him the once-over. For starters, he had a huge illegal-looking, shit-eating grin on his face that made him look like a cross between Bozo and a punching bag. He was medium height, a bit heavy-set, with dirty red hair and a matching short, scraggly beard. His milk-white complexion was mottled with freckles giving him a phony Norman Rockwell look of youth and innocence. Unlike Bill, who was fashionably cocaine thin, Jack's healthy robustness indicated he's probably not a hard drug user. Instead, his drug of preference was more likely beer.

"I thought he was coming alone?" I whispered to Bill as Jack charged straight into the big room.

"He was, but I thought I better come along in case you tried to shoot him with that hand-cannon of yours. You Oregon cowboys are dangerous after dark."

He winked at me and then followed Jack. I closed the door, slightly bewildered.

"Jack's from up north but he comes down here to buy pot for his hick friends," Bill explained with a big slow grin.

We were used to the give-and-take of meaningless derogatory remarks; that was our twisted sense of humor. If you took yourself too seriously you wouldn't last long with us.

"He used to be a student here until he discovered it was more profitable to sell pot to rednecks and biker gangs. He's a good guy, though. He likes Corvettes."

I stared blankly at the two of them as they sauntered farther into the living room. Bill immediately took out his usual tiny brown glass bottle packed with the usual pristine white crystals that sparkled like midnight moonlight on fresh hoarfrost. This was powder snow. The cute little bottle came with an equally tiny silver spoon attached with an even smaller chain to the center of the black bottle cap. But this time, he didn't bother with the spoon.

Bill looked around until he spotted the pervasive mirror hiding under some papers on the cable spool table with a couple of short plastic straws and an old-style, single-edge razor blade. He scooped them up and carried them over to our big leather couch where he perched on the edge right next to the San Francisco city scene painted on the west wall. He began pouring the entire contents onto the mirror.

"Jack here is a pot-head like you," Bill said nonchalantly, with his usual sly one-sided smile and one leg crossed over the other.

He began to carefully chop up the coke on the mirror using the razor blade like a sous chef chopping spices and herbs with a prized knife and then using it like a miniature bulldozer, pushing and scraping the white snow-like powder all over the mirror until he had six lines evenly-spaced and equally distributed, all fluffed up and flashing tiny beams of light as alluring as the sparkle of scattered diamonds.

"He seems to have found a market for grass that doesn't include blacks, auto workers, musicians, artists, students, or hippies."

"Geez, what's left?" I cracked.

"You might be surprised," Jack added soberly, while Bill concentrated on his favorite activity. He continued. "Bill says you took a little plane trip recently and brought back something worth selling."

Bill handed me one of the straws as he gestured to the mirror. He made a sweeping motion over it indicating I could take my pick. I guess I was going to be up for a while. It was only 3:30 going on 4. My mind started playing a record: ...*Twenty five or six to four...or...or...! Yeah!* Then I hear Chicago's horn section blowing minds like elephants stomping on Bubble Wrap.

I got down on my knees so I could get my nose closer to the mirror and the powder. First, I pushed on one side of my nose to close that nostril while holding the short plastic straw in my other hand. Using the straw like a vacuum cleaner nozzle, I navigated back and forth down one of the lines with a loud sickening sucking sound that any Hoover would have been proud to make and any dog to bark at. I switched hands and mimicking the same action with the other nostril to even out the biting chemical burn on each side of my nose. Balance, according to Aristotle, must be maintained at all costs!

"Two down and four to go," I said as I got up and handed the plastic straw on to Jack.

I weakly smiled at Bill presiding over his signature ceremony. He seemed proud and quite satisfied with his ample offering. When Jack finished his two lines, he handed the straw back to Bill, stood up and advanced on me again.

"So do you still have any left?" he asked directly.

"Yeah, I've got a little left."

"Bill here said you flew a plane down to Mexico and picked up some Acapulco Gold right from the peasant farmers. Is that right? That must have taken some balls."

He was still massaging his nose trying to get some of those shiny crystals to just bore straight into a nasal artery where it might be directly flushed to his brain.

Where the idea came from that the brain was somehow connected to the nose, I figured, had to come from the Egyptians. Didn't they drag the brains out of a mummy's head through the nose with long hooked needles? They actually believed the brain did nothing more than make mucous and snot. *Were they all that wrong?* I wondered.

"That's about right, peasants and everything," I said as I let go a huge yawn. I wasn't bored, just tired. I hate waking up at this ridiculously early hour. As a Westerner, I was expected to be a hunter or fisherman like my Bambi killer older brother, but after I found out what time they have to get up to perform this slaughter in the name of masculinity, I switched to something supposedly more civilized, like building nuclear weapons for an iffier tomorrow.

"Great, I'll take all you've got. Do you deliver?" Jack asked in all seriousness.

"I don't sell pizzas," I said in a vain attempt to be funny as well as enlightening at three in the fucking morning.

"Ha," he grunted half-heartedly. "Good one! But seriously, I need you to bring it up to my place in Leelanau. There's a little grass airstrip just a mile from my house overlooking Grand Traverse Bay."

He was talking about the little finger peninsula that juts out into Lake Michigan as it wraps itself over lower Michigan to join Lake Huron through the straights of Mackinaw.

"How did you know I have a plane that can land on grass?" I inquired forcefully, somewhat suspicious that someone I didn't know was way too knowledgeable about my personal details.

"Your buddy, Billy boy over there," he indicated with a jerk of his thumb pointing behind him toward Bill finishing up the last two lines.

Bill always liked to go last so he could use his licked index finger to sop up the last few sparkly grains leftover on the mirror and then rub them forcefully on the outside of his gums, both top and bottom. It looked like he was brushing his teeth with his finger, which could be pretty gross.

I was fascinated by the strange custom, which I immediately adopted when the tables were turned and it was my turn to go last and sop up the few scattered flakes left behind. I liked rubbing them hard into my gums for that great tingling feeling of numb teeth, which I was not sure why, but it seemed enjoyable. Cocaine, according to Freud, can just be fun.

"I'll pay you for the trip," he continued.

"You haven't even tried it yet," I complained, although I realized if we went down that road the ritual tasting and haggling could go on for hours. It seemed strange he didn't want to haggle.

Hell, we even haggled a bit with our ugly-looking probable killer in Juarez who sold us the pot and who could have just as easily blown us all away without blinking an eye. I've found, however, that most criminals are basically honest when dealing among themselves. They have to be, otherwise very little successful criminal business could be done. They just hate to be cheated even though that's their chosen specialty, so they are very careful to not cheat a fellow cheater. Strange considering it's almost an oxymoron that criminals are actually quite ethical.

"Don't need to. Bill says it's good. My clientele never complains, so what the fuck. The better it is the more I get for it. Let's do this thing!"

I just stared past him as I witnessed the end of the weird social drug ceremony going on behind him. "I just don't haul that much that far in my 'vette you know," he continued his whiney weak excuse. "It seems to be a pig magnet and I'm just not safe driving it loaded anywhere outside Leelanau."

He stared at me for a second and then added, "My old lady and I will show you a really good time. She does a great Swedish barbecue."

"Five hundred bucks and I can fly up this weekend," I flatly responded flatly, wondering what the fuck had I just committed to.

"Done!" he barked as he grabbed my right hand and started shaking the hell out of it. I involuntarily and quite coincidentally sneezed, due to a slightly delayed reaction to the coke. Jack just got a big smile on his face as he reached into his pocket and pulled out an even larger vial than the one Bill had dumped on the mirror moments before.

"I think we need a little bump to seal the deal," he said as he wrapped his arm around my shoulder and guided me back to the coffee table where Bill was just finishing up his polish job on the mirror, no doubt clearing it for round two. I had a feeling this day was already a write-off even though technically it hadn't even started.

They finally left, a few hours later, after the sun rose into another clear grey Michigan sky.

So I sold most of my share to the crazy guy from up north who drove a black Corvette and peddled pot to high school jocks and rural rednecks, neither of which actually deserved such good weed, but at least my chances of getting busted hopefully were greatly diminished. He didn't really know me and I could care less about him. If he got busted, he could potentially cause some trouble but generally these yokels out in the sticks were pretty well connected to their town's good ol' boys club and therefore enjoyed a certain amount of immunity from the politically inspired drug-crazed mayhem going on at most major college campuses.

People actually thought that pot was driving students mad, which they believed was causing all the agitation and rioting. Quite the contrary; we were already mad. We were just trying to stay mellow as long as possible in the face of overwhelmingly psychotic behavior by cops, college administrators, draft boards, and sicko politicians like John-sucks and Nix-goon. (I refuse to pronounce those shitheads' names properly as they deserve no such respect. *Spit! Spit!*) Pot was self-medication required to preserve what little sanity might still exist in a world gone fucking nuts and most likely about to end in a self-emulating radioactive cloud.

I delivered the product just like I promised, flying up to the little-fingertip of the Lower Peninsula in the trusty little generic black Tri-Pacer. The trip up was uneventful compared to the weirdness that plagued my earlier trip to El Paso. On this trip, I flew solo and it was only about two hours total flight time. Piece of cake!

Jack directed me to a small private hunter's airstrip about a mile from his luxury hideaway in the wilderness forests of Lower Michigan's upper fingers. It was a short unimproved grass strip surrounded on three sides by thick forests of 120 to 180foot fir trees towering above it like giant castle walls. At the only open end, used for both takeoffs and landings, was a 45-foot vertical drop-off to the rocky shore of Traverse Bay.

I could just imagine what it was going to be like taking off. It reminded me of the classic movie scene where the airplane races down the airstrip heading for the edge of the cliff, with not quite enough speed or too heavily loaded with orphans, struggling to get airborne before the runway dropped out of sight. In a heart-pounding moment and as on-lookers gasp, the plane disappears off the end. Then a mighty roar is heard as the plane slowly climbs back into view, virtually clawing its way into the air. I didn't need any B-movie nightmares, especially since I was permanently drug-addled anyway, with constant fear and paranoia pervading every corner of my consciousness. Hunter Thompson in his best drug-addled Gonzo delusions had nothing on me.

Jack was waiting at the far end of the runway, buried in the darkest corner of the tiny strip. I did three or four fly-bys just to make sure there were no surprises lurking nearby in the woods and to gauge the length of the strange little hole-in-the-forest field I had to land on. I had a few more nightmarish visions as I did, some actually having me crash into the wall of trees after overshooting the approach and not having enough stopping distance or room to go-around. Shit, what did I remember from ground school when we calculated the additional stopping distance needed for a fully loaded Tri-Pacer? ...on grass? ...with bad tires?

Oh what the hell, I thought. Back at the Ann Arbor airport, the old instructor who checked me out in this rag-tag plane wouldn't let me land on the pavement anyway. He made me land on the grass beside the paved strip every time at the slowest possible speed so it basically just fluttered out of the sky, rolling slowly to a quick stop like a big pelican landing on a short pier. I was amazed at how the Tri-Pacer bounced a few yards and then just stopped. The trick is to stop the plane flying right before you hit the ground, not too high and not too low.

So I greased her in pretty slick and rolled to a stop about midway down the now seemingly even shorter runway. Ground-level perspective made it feel even more claustrophobic, with giant trees blocking absolutely everything in three directions.

I taxied down to the lone figure leaning casually against a dirty white Ford Econoline van with the faded inscription, *Jack's Fast Plumbing*; there were tiny wings hanging off the "*Fast* still discernible under splotches of peeling paint and rust. Corvette Jack, who just days earlier had attempted to get me hooked on copious quantities of cocaine and dreams of big money, stepped out from the shadows of the primeval forest.

God, did all these small-time pushers have the same mentality? If it wasn't for the skinny blue-eyed blondes, fast cars, fancy houses, and/or large vicious dogs, it would be hard to tell them apart from the common professional, white-shirted clueless drugless rabble.

"Where's the blonde?" I yelled out the open side-window as I coasted to a stop just past the van.

"Back at the house!" he shouted without hesitation. "Her name is Ingrid!"

But I had already shut down the engine so everything fell deathly silent just before he finished yelling her name at the top of his lungs. He froze for a second, realizing the plane noise had suddenly stopped, making his voice way louder than he'd intended. Regaining some composure, he said in a normal voice, "Stay put and I'll bring the truck over."

He got in the van and started it up.

I crawled out of the little plane and waited by the back hatch while Jack backed the van up to the plane. As soon as he came around the van, I started handing him suitcases like I was some kind of tourist and he was my backwoods taxi driver.

"So, you got the money?" I asked, while not quite letting go of the last bag.

"Yeah, not here," he said even quieter, absentmindedly looking around. "You're going to come on over to the house, meet Ingrid and her cousin Lena. Relax. Enjoy a free weekend in the woods. You look like you could use a break from that dismal university snob-town."

He took possession of the last bag, threw it in the back of the van with the others and motioned to the passenger door.

Why not? Maybe he has some more of that white stuff that makes you feel happy and indestructible. He may have been a backwoods dealer but he sure lived like an uptown pimp. They all pretty much did, no matter where they were from. It's a transcultural thing.

I locked the plane and got in the van. It might have been a short distance to his house but with all the twists and turns, let alone all the other crossroads we passed, I was pretty sure I wouldn't be able to find my way back to the plane without a damned good map or another guide. It had been a sunny flight up, but now that we were buried in a thick forest, it quickly became dark, gloomy, and foreboding.

That still didn't seem to dissuade Jack, or Bill, to remove his sunglasses when it got dark. I swear I've seen druggies wear sunglasses while driving with their lights off at midnight on a cloudy night during the dark of the moon. I figured it must be some kind of trade-union rule.

When we finally got to the long driveway leading to his house, he had to open a substantial iron gate barring any entry. He obviously did not want casual passersby to get lost on his property. As we approached the house, I saw his black Corvette sitting in the driveway with its rear-end jacked up in the air and a gas tank lying on the pavement nearby.

"Got a leak in my gas tank," he said anticipating my curiosity. "A .32-caliber leak," he said with a slight giggle. "But before I can braze it over, I have to fill the tank with water so all the gas vapors are pushed out. Don't want to blow my handsome head off." He laughed again as if losing his head was a big joke.

"Good idea," I said thinking how I probably would just go to the junk yard and find a replacement without a hole. Then I instinctively looked around cautiously, wondering how he might have gotten his Corvette shot.

Jack parked the van near the back door. He didn't seem to be in any rush to check the quantity or quality of my load and simply left it locked in the van. We walked around the side of the house to a large open lawn in back where smoke and delicious aromas wafted copiously from a broad concrete patio complete with outdoor furniture, tables, couches all flanking a central built-in barbecue station. Music was coming from two huge *Voice of the Theater* speakers flanking the lawn side of the patio. Steve Stills was singing about how great a Southern man was. I didn't buy it. I was a Neil Young fan.

Ingrid, however, was a tall blonde knockout, just as I had imagined and her dark-haired cousin wasn't bad either. Ingrid was preparing some giant Swedish-meatball-looking hamburgers on a propane barbecue, which I always considered a vicious crime against all of civilized society.

Outdoor grilling over anything other than a natural wood fire has to be a mortal sin sure to be punished by the fire gods with something like a slow, painful, and terminal case of eternal roasting on a proper wood-fired spit. The natural flavors and aromas released in cooking over an open fire seem to be dopamine stimulators just as effective as sex, drugs, and Rock & Roll. Must be those woody complex-hydrocarbons in the smoke or something connecting our DNA to a distant past when chewing burnt meat was a tremendous luxury.

Prehistoric man invented cooking over wood fires and that is what we should be perfecting, not replacing. Besides, burning hydrocarbons solely for their calorie value is an incredible waste of an extremely valuable chemical resource, not to mention just plain insane. You can grow trees but you can't grow crude oil. But then, pathological human pollution-insanity seemed to be a rampant plague of gargantuan proportions with no foreseeable end in sight. After all, I had helped calculate the effects of runaway atmospheric destruction when the chemistry is disrupted—like fluorocarbons eating the ozone or when the sun is blocked by a globe-circling nuclear cloud causing a permanent deep freeze.

Planetary atmospheres like earth's are extremely rare and most likely highly unstable and prone to becoming extreme in one way or another.

Jack formally introduced me to Ingrid and Lena. Ingrid was a former U of M student, while Lena was apparently visiting from Sweden. Ingrid had a cute broken-Swedish accent, while Lena's inflections had kind of a British tone that she probably picked up from an English teacher with a strong British accent, as many Europeans do, or possibly from hanging out too long with some Brits. I knew several Germans who spoke English with a curiously strong Brooklyn accent, although they'd never been to Brooklyn or even New York. It was hilarious listening to them speak with German authority mixed with American vernacular. Paradoxically, accents in a beautiful woman were absolute intoxication.

Jack beckoned me to a cluster of Adirondack lounge chairs around a low table. We walked past the two girls and they both looked up from their work to give us big smiles. Ingrid had long blonde hair which she wore in a single fat braid hanging down her back, giving her that enchanting Northern-European health-glow appearance portrayed in fairytale and fable. Her cousin's dark brown hair was cut shorter and appeared to be naturally curly. They both wore full aprons, but I could still see rosy-pink bare skin was peeking out of short-shorts and tank tops around the edges. They had intoxicating bodies: taut, tawny, and tight, with all the right curves in all the most entertaining places. I had to remind myself to keep breathing when I finally peeled my eyeballs off the luscious scenery.

Jack picked up two frosty Heinekens sitting on the table, already opened and ready for consumption. Impressive. He handed me one as I wilted from the smile Lena flashed me. Jack motioned to the chairs seemingly unaware of my ripening imagination.

"Have you ever been up this way before?" he asked as we settled into adjacent chairs.

"Once," I answered, looking around innocently while slyly lingering repeatedly on the girls cooking activities. I didn't fool anybody. They spotted me immediately and flashed their big smiles right at me, so I had to look away quickly and sheepishly back at Jack.

"A friend of mine with the mate to my Suburban likes to go four-wheeling and camping up here so one time we followed him up for some dune driving and a fish fry on the beach. It's nice, but I prefer bigger mountains and nasty big rock four-wheeling."

"Yeah, I hear ya," he said as he took a long gulp of beer. "I like it here. It's private, the money's good, the scenery's not too bad," nodding his head toward the girls, "and the cops are congenitally stupid."

"Geez. I would think rural America would be a hell hole of rednecks and assholes who hate dopers. Aren't they all preaching their rope-a-dope and nobody smokes marijuana in Muskogee crap? Aren't they all proud to be dumbass beer-drinkin', pot-hatin', Okies?"

"You're making the same mistake all you college boys do," he responded with a sly smile. "Rednecks hate hippies and college freaks because by-and-large they're just a bunch of spoiled-rotten rich kids still on the parental tit. You go to college after high school, they go to Vietnam. You all think that drugs are your exclusive rallying cry, which is just plain absurd. Rednecks mostly hate the non-conformist protestors because they know deep down they just might be right about Vietnam, but they can no more admit that than say God doesn't exist or book-learnin' is better than dumbass commonsense. Maybe they are a pack of mindless patriotic green-toothed squirrel-eaters, but they still like to get high just like everyone else. After all, alcohol isn't everything, especially when you're trying to impress one of those newly-liberated women like Ingrid over there."

He motioned in her direction. She saw it and waved back. I felt more beads of sweat forming on my forehead.

"But isn't it much harder to keep a secret out here than in the big city?" I asked. "Everyone knows everybody else's business in these hick towns. I know, I grew up in one. Aren't you afraid of an old jealous lover ratting you out or some jag-off who threatens to turn you in as a commie-pinko-queer?"

"And that's the beauty of living in the sticks. They may hate you, but they all hate the government even more. There's a much stronger loyalty here which protects the locals from the big bad government. You'd be surprised how little cooperation there is between local sheriff's deputies and the state police or even worse, the feds. We all kind of band together so in essence we're protected from Big Brother. You poor bastards in a college town attract narcs like pale city-skin attracts mosquitoes. Out here, you have to really screw up to attract any attention at all."

"You mean like cannibalism or something?"

He just smiled.

The dark-haired Lena appeared at my side offering me a big old burger dripping juices and cheese with lettuce, tomato and grilled onion peeking out of a crusty Kaiser roll. When I bit into it, I discovered the burger was really a large Swedish meatball in disguise, smushed into the Kaiser roll. What looked like brown mustard was actually a spicy version of Stroganoff gravy. After smoking dope all afternoon, I discovered yet another unexpected high.

"Thanks so much," I said as I smiled back at her. "These are great. You and Ingrid should open a Swedish-burger stand. Ann Arbor would be perfect."

"You are very velcome," she said answering my smile with a bigger one. "Ingrid makes ze burgers and ze boyz love zem."

She curtsied again and I felt cold sweat materialize in weird places. I glanced over at Jack and he was already gorging himself without ceremony. Strange, Jack didn't seem to have the body shape or expected lack of appetite of a coke dealer. Maybe it was the fresh air.

"Well, I'm a guy and I like the burger and especially where it came from," I said smiling devilishly.

She pinched my cheek as if I were the beloved village idiot.

Ingrid seemed quite talented for a backcountry drug dealer's girlfriend. However, any talent, besides looks, always deserves recognition. It also never hurts to compliment a good-looking host for being a good host. You never know what it might get you. What Ingrid didn't do superbly her cousin stepped in and did almost seamlessly. Jack was starting to look like a very lucky bastard who probably did very little to earn it. I sort of hated him and envied him, simultaneously.

"You vant one more?" Ingrid called from somewhere behind the thick column of smoke hovering over the grill. I bet she said that to all the guys and hasn't been turned down yet.

"Sure," I hollered and reluctantly turned back to Jack. "Bill said you'd been a student at the U. What did you study?"

"I got a PhD in Sociology. I did my field work in the Caribbean, studying indigenous tribes and their interactions with modern European civilization."

"Sounds like it comes in real handy now," I said with the straightest face as I could muster.

We enjoyed the lazy Saturday afternoon on Jack's back patio eating burgers, listening to Rock & Roll on his super-expensive and loud stereo system and, of course, drinking more beer. Once in a while Ingrid and Lena would dance together between the two black speaker-boxes where the music was loudest and most intense. The view from the patio, or what there was of it beyond the dazzling flesh of dancing Swedes performing some ancient rite of spring and fertility no doubt, overlooked a prim and lush green lawn that separated the house on all sides like a meadow curtained by a dark thick forest of spindly evergreens. It reminded me of a legendary primeval forest, the mysterious north woods of Hemingway's youth.

Jack's home was a lush verdant oasis protected from the prying eyes and ears of the world, secure, and well-defended by its natural forest walls. Even so, I could imagine how lonely, dark and isolated it might feel in the winter. In this part of the world, guys probably needed someone like Ingrid during those long cold winter nights to ward off fatal cabin fever. No doubt, survival of the fittest had something to do with it as well. College towns, however, were a whole different world where silent fortitude gave way to even the slightest social pressures. What I knew for sure was that I could never afford an Ingrid on graduate-student pay.

Later, Jack introduced me to Leelanau beer skeet. At first, it was just like shooting regular skeet; contestants used expensive Italian 12-guage shotguns to bust erratically flying clay pigeons of increasing difficulty, controlled only by Ingrid and her cousin. With Jack's version, if you missed your pigeon, you had to take a shot of tequila.

"Pull!" Jack yelled.

First, one clay pigeon flew across his aim to the left, just when another crossed in the opposite direction. He popped them as they both lined up with his sights for a fraction of a millisecond. He broke the gun open, throwing smoking cartridges over his shoulder. Dropping in two new ones, he handed it to me. I had already missed a couple and was feeling a little frisky.

"Pull!" I yelled. One flew almost directly away from me. Too easy I thought. I hesitated to see where the second one was going. Finally, it came flying across my field of view, almost hitting the first one. Too easy I thought. It passed the first one when the gun exploded and the pigeon jerked sideways, losing half its disc to lead pellets flying by. The big piece erratically ricocheted back toward the other one when the gun barked one more time and caught the wobbling piece just as it lined up with the first. They both exploded into black dust. Jack took off his sunglasses to make sure he saw what he saw. I was apparently the only one who knew it was a total accident. Lena hugged my arm as they all applauded my Annie Oakley shot, brought to you by just the right combination of alcohol, sun, and pot.

Then Ingrid and Lena tried their hand. Needless to say, it was impressive. Lena even busted a four-way with two shots. I had to have a drink each time just to celebrate the extraordinary demonstration of shooting skill. I asked them how it was that they were such good shooters from such a peaceful country.

"Vee haf to learn schussing and shooting at very young age," Lena said. "Zat is secret to our freedoms. No army ever defeat us in zee snow."

"Viva la snow!" I said, hoisting my drink on high.

As the sun slipped behind the surrounding barricade of trees, the air turned chilly and the sky, inky. The girls moved the food and drink indoors and Jack showed me his outlandishly expensive stereo system which was, of course, state-of-the-art and extremely uncommon. Usually, I only got to drool over this stuff in stores and catalogs. Jack owned the real thing.

The Harmon/Kardon preamp driving the McIntosh ultra linear tube-amp represented well over a thousand bucks alone. Throw in a pair of Voice of the Theater speakers for outdoors and a couple of thunderous Klipshorns for inside and you had the equivalent value of one nicely-equipped used Corvette. But when Jack cranked them up to Rock & Roll levels, the distortion became noticeable and annoying, just like all under-powered stereo equipment that still used tubes. Rock & Roll required a lot more muscle and big-assed RCA power transistors were the only way to go. It also needed better speakers and something needed to be done about that soon.

As a physicist, I knew that any speaker utilizing a horn structure like the Klipsch only increased the distortion, even though some preferred that sort of thing. Klipsch was trying to balance the low power of tubes with the dynamic ranges required for modern recorded music. So they gained efficiency at low frequencies but this added distortion, because even though it took very little energy to use a megaphone, the horn at the front of the speaker made it sound like blaring Paris taxicabs honking in the background. What was needed was a transparent sonic air-cannon capable of operating between 20 and 20,000 cycles per second.

After assaulting my ears for another couple of hours with Procul Harem and The Moody Blues at full volume, Jack finally motioned for me to follow him to his laundry room of all places. He carefully locked the door behind us, reached into a hole in the back of the clothes dryer and pulled out a wad of hundred-dollar bills that made my wallet start to swell with lust right there in my pocket. Lush and green was beginning to be the day's theme.

e HHe proceeded to count out hundreds in small stacks of ten each, which he then stacked crisscross on the top of the washing machine. When he got to ten stacks, he counted out five more bills and laid them over the last stack.

"There you go," he announced. "Ten grand and another half for all your trouble flying up here. Better count it. No complaints after leaving here."

He stood back satisfied with his performance and clearly amused at my unconcealed delight in finally making the big deal. So, this was what it was like to be a Capitalist Pig, and I didn't even have to wear the dreaded suit-and-tie to get it? I could get used to this.

I tried to stay calm as I picked up each stack, counting them as best as I could pretend and put them all together into one large roll. I didn't actually need to count them after watching Jack. Finally, I had them all bundled in one wad but it was too big for a pocket let alone my wallet. I looked up at Jack and out of nowhere he produced a large manila envelope and handed it to me.

I pretended to be cool and unconcerned, but the sight of me stuffing over a hundred Ben Franklins into an envelope as I shakily fought them into submission was surely not pretty. My hands were shaking and my nerves seemed numb. I finally got them sealed up and the whole thing crammed under my shirt flap and pants against my belly. Jack had to laugh as I obviously wasn't used to having this much cash. He led me out of the laundry room down the hall to a back bedroom.

"It's a little late to fly back tonight, so why don't you stay over. You can have this bedroom for the night and we'll hit a couple nearby roadhouses for some late-night fun? Do you play pool?"

I hated pool. "Sure, sounds great," I said. "The weather's good so no problem flying back tomorrow."

I didn't like flying at night anyway. Felt too much like driving in the dark without headlights.

Jack reached into a drawer and pulled out a little mirror already piled with white dust. He used a little penknife to drag some powder into a couple of long lines then handed it over to me with one hand and held out a rolled-up bill in the other. "How's about a little celebratory snort before happy hour starts?"

"This isn't happy hour?"

His situation here, in the sticks of northern Michigan, reminded me of recently being on the road with a newly re-assembled one-hit-wonder band called REO Speedwagon. The only promoters they could convince to book them on their first tour with a new lead singer were the young wannabees out in the sticks who'd maybe just hit a local gold vein selling drugs to pickup-truck cowboys, assorted green-toothed rednecks, and maybe a dirt-farmer or two.

New wealthy druggies out in the boondocks all over America somehow legitimize their newfound wealth, popularity, and cool reputations by bringing Rock & Roll concerts to their respective backwater burgs. After all, don't drugs, money, and sex go exceedingly well with Rock & Roll no matter where or when? It was a match made both in heaven and here, a.k.a. God's other country.

I was sent out with the newly built giant Fanfare PA packed in an eighteen-foot box truck and two roadies to do the grunt work. When our truck showed up in the first town a full day in advance of the scheduled concert due to the many un-booked travel days allowed on these short hick-tours, the local promoter threw a big party for all his new hanger-on friends and the recently arrived, presumably ultra-cool band's road crew.

They spared no expense and lavished their best drugs on us. We, in return, dutifully and unashamedly over-consumed with gusto. Jack reminded me somewhat of those fuzz-faced, newly-moneyed, drug-fueled country promoters. Young kids in their remote hamlets coveted the local dealer/promoter friendship as long as the good times rolled. But when the money and drugs dried up, however, or they got busted, dealer/promoters suddenly became hard-pressed to find a friend to lend a helping hand. They obviously know this and that's what makes many of them highly cynical, oversexed, and eventually babbling drug-crazed confirmed loonies which, of course, just hastens their inevitable cycle of self-destruction. Or they become real estate brokers or insurance salesmen and join the local Rotarians. Either way, they become lost to humanity.

When the tree shadows extended fully across the back lawn and started climbing the forest wall on the opposite side, the darkness growing from the ground up rapidly covered human foibles in the way that only the night can mask man's ugly intentions. Jack swore he could actually hear the Siren's Song beckoning him to happy hour somewhere out in those woods. Being sufficiently lubricated with depressants, stimulants, and various sideways-shifting experimental drugs, no doubt originating with Bill, I was in no condition to fight off the allure of a few more drinks and a game or two of friendly pool amongst the colorful locals. Socializing up-close and personal with the inevitable barfly rednecks never crossed my mind, but then I almost never say no to a beer-and-a-shot, although not necessarily in that order.

Besides, Lena had been serving me drinks all afternoon and now she looked like she wanted someone to wait on her. We'd exchanged back rubs earlier in the day right after the shoot-off, which immediately plunged me into a deeply-moving relationship with her amazing hands of sinuous bones and milky flesh. She had some amazing skills that apparently only surfaced when up-close and personal.

The stealth-mode plumbing van had only two well-worn seats up front and pretty much nothing in the rear. I had to find a rusty tool box to sit on while I offered Lena the upside-down five-gallon bucket. Since lunchtime, she had stayed close by, almost shadowing me, ready to join the conversation, smile, or just radiate a Nordic glow not unlike the Northern Lights I was supposed to be photographing in one of our experiments back at the lab.

Lena was the dark intrigue to Ingrid's playful blonde. That seemed to be the limit of their contrasts. If I had them both naked in a dark room, I seriously doubt that I could tell them apart without some serious Braille practice. Lena pushed her bucket close to my tool box and grabbed my arm in an attempt to stabilize herself in spite of the various vehicular forces unleashed upon us by a Corvette-obsessed van driver. Jack apparently drove all his cars as if they were Corvettes and always assumed local highway departments were hosting an ongoing Grand Prix Open on his particular piece of the road.

Again, we wove our way along tall narrow cuts sliced through the all-pervasive dark northern forests until the trees finally parted, revealing a relatively open slot near the lakeshore where shops and commercial buildings were scattered about haphazardly among thinning windswept trees. Jack pulled into a parking lot and found an open spot at the end of a line of motorcycles. They were parked right in front of, and almost blocking, wide steps leading up to a broad covered porch and the main entrance to Mad Jack's Leelanau Inn. I guess at one time it was supposed to be a hunting lodge, built out of giant native logs. Now it was a sad reminder of what happens to the wilderness when the frigging carpet-baggin' fruitcakes arrive.

I had been known to ride a Harley from time to time so at first, I didn't think much about the perfectly aligned machines forming an ominous warning to all latecomers without Harleys: *Caution: Green-toothed, slack-jawed, bug-eaters crazed on alcohol and testosterone are on the loose inside. For a bizarre time bordering on suicide, enter at your own peril.* I had a bad feeling creeping up my spine. Lena instinctively put her hand on my back, in just the right creepy spot, and I strangely didn't give a shit anymore.

Pure ugly assaulted my senses on every level as we stepped through the doors. The lighting was almost exclusively from ion-generating, multi-colored neon bent tubes telling all who looked directly at them, which few ever did, that some pale horse-piss of one sort or another had started out as pure mountain or spring water and therefore was far better than the artificial stuff that was presumably made from ordinary polluted river water which, of course, they all were made from anyway.

The usual offensive smells hit next, such as the all-pervasive bad bar stink, a curious blend of twenty-year-old-puke covered floors, stale and rotten beer-soaked timbers overlaid by *essence de Pinesol,* and of course that *piece de resistance,* acrid body sweat profusely mixed with stale tobacco smoke permeating every interior surface, and hence, the very air we had to breathe. The only thing that allowed anyone to ignore all this was the overriding stench of relatively freshly-evaporated alcohol itself. I needed to get drinking if I was going to last very long here.

The décor was as predictable as the smell and the IQ of its patrons. The lodge had a huge structure of open timbers holding up a massive roof that had probably been impressive when originally varnished a hundred or more years ago. Now the rafters disappeared into a murky overhead cavern coated in soot, smoke, tar and God-knows-what-other black and nasty gunk that had drifted up there over the decades.

Lower on the walls, a pathetic collection of rusty farm tools and fishing buoys separated sections where faded curling Polaroid photos hung commemorating innumerable past drunken and melancholy moments. Old dollar bills with names written on them were pinned to the walls along with gaudy glass Mardi Gras beads draped everywhere, especially from the few dusty and unopened bottles of premium liquor behind the bar. Genteel drinking was apparently not a local pastime. Neither was interior decoration.

At least the jukebox was blaring out some good ol' shit-stompin' Rock & Roll. The Bob Seger System out of Detroit, and now the Silver Bullet Band, were regulars down in Ann Arbor at the Sunday summer free park concerts. ZZ Top was hot with bikers and everyone else redneck, and even that weirdo Alice Cooper seemed to have a dubious following here. But when I heard the New Riders of the Purple Sage, I knew our culture was being flagrantly pirated without any understanding. None of these creeps knew that the NRPS were spawned by the greatest drug-band ever, the Grateful Dead, who were long-haired, dope smokin', intellectual acid-freaks just like us. The enemy was becoming harder and harder to pick out of a crowd of long-haired hippie freaks.

As we pushed our way through the crowd to the cluster of pool tables in the back, it was obvious from the stares of the unwashed hordes surrounding us that, in these parts, women like Ingrid and Lena were definitely not a common sight. I began to have a bad feeling, but it was way too late to get Jack to turn around now. He had already ambled up to the bar and loudly ordered four Heinekens. The staring increased noticeably and not all of it was directed at the girls. The two women closed ranks around me and I began to sweat visibly from the little voice inside me screaming like hell to run before the shit kicking commenced.

I noticed that about half the crowd wore dirty, sweat-stained baseball caps, while the other half wore Levi jackets, with their sleeves ripped off and covered by numerous patches and flags blackened with years of road grime and what I hoped was just petrified bug juice. It appeared tonight was the local working yokels versus the visiting motorcycle gang. A few more at the bar were harder to place, so I labeled them the local professionals who had actual jobs that paid money and could obviously afford cleaner clothes and better beer. Class distinction was simple in the sticks, Budweiser or Heineken.

Jack handed us our beers, we clicked them in salute, and then he sauntered over to the nearest pool table and proceeded to lay a ten-dollar bill near where the money went and the balls were dispensed. The four guys playing the table just watched with undisguised amusement. Jack paid them no attention, even though it was obvious that nearly everyone in the bar was undressing the two lithesome girls and relishing every piece of clothing as it was peeled off in their little pea-brains and tossed into the corner of an imaginary cheap motel room. Others were more likely thinking about tying me to a couple of pickup trucks and playing *hippie make-a-wish*. Jack turned back to the three of us, took a long swig on his beer, and then bent his head in close to share his strategy.

"When we get the table, let me do the talking. We'll throw the first game or two until we get them to cough up the big bucks. Then we take them."

I looked over at Ingrid and saw a sly smile spread across her angelic face. Something told me this wasn't the first time she and Jack had run a pool ruse with beautiful Ingrid as the unsuspected ringer. From the look of the crowd I was betting they weren't going to be terribly amused by what Jack had planned, especially with me in the mix. It was his backyard, so I guessed he could play by his own rules. But just in case, I started looking around for a quick exit or something bat-sized and not nailed down that might make a good head-bashing equalizer.

I had my belt-buckle knife, which meant I was never truly unarmed. But that was for extreme emergencies, which this had the potential of becoming, but somehow our afternoon of drug therapy made me think I was invincible anyway, so what the fuck. We'll see where this goes.

"Jack, you old pig fucker!" someone shouted above the jukebox and noise. I looked around to see who was yelling, as one of the biggest bikers I'd ever seen came waddling out of the back area, approaching us with arms outstretched like a bear about to squeeze the life out of its dinner.

"Hey Buddy! What are you doing in this shit hole?"

He grabbed Jack around the shoulders pinning his arms and began squeezing as he lifted him about two feet off the floor.

"Hey George, how the fuck are you? Meet my friend from Ann Arbor," he grunted out between squeezes with the last bit of air in his lungs. George dropped him and started for me. I braced myself for the inevitable crush, but at the last moment he grabbed Ingrid instead and began swinging her around in circles like some carnival ride.

"You going to clean these guys out?" he asked, referring to the men playing pool nearby.

They were busy ignoring us, so I don't think they heard his inopportune remark giving us away. He dropped Ingrid just as she swung a haymaker at him that intentionally missed the mark. This, I assumed, was a standard greeting in this neck of the woods for Neanderthals, Sasquatches, and other borderline quasi-Canadian animals.

He returned to Jack, slapping him on the shoulder which made Heineken foam fly in all directions. "So, you got anything new? We haven't seen any decent shit in months. The boys are getting edgy."

Wow, I thought, *as if that wasn't a normal state for bug-eaters.* George made a sweeping gesture indicating many of the big guys standing around wearing the colors of some local gang. *Mackinaw's Mechanics* the patch on the back of their jackets proclaimed. Really scary. What are they going to do, fix my wagon good?

"I've got just the thing," Jack was able to wheeze out between gasps from all the friendly pummeling.

George thought about this for a good ten seconds before he looked back at me and then it dawned on him. He turned back to Jack like a hungry lion startled by the sudden appearance of a gazelle.

"We gotta talk," he said as he grabbed him around the shoulders and turned him toward the smoke haze and puke fumes emanating from the back of the bar, where all private business affairs were formally conducted.

Jack was heard to say as they disappeared, "You have a way of saying just the right words, you smooth-tongued devil."

Ingrid and Lena lounged close together talking in muted Swedish, I presumed, as I tried to melt into the beer-baked wood work. Nonetheless, I heard the dreaded opening line to a show down or, more appropriately for this northern crowd, somebody threw out the first puck of a hockey fight. At this point in time, in this kind of bar, in this sort of location, with my long hair, it was bound to happen.

"Who the fuck let a hippie in here?" rang out loud and clear all over the bar. I ventured a quick look and spied a middle-aged dirty-looking greasy kind of guy standing in front of the bar yelling at the bartender, who seemed alert and busy but otherwise disinterested. It was apparently more the ramblings of a disgruntled drunk contributing his inner most prejudices to the world at large rather than a challenge to anyone's existence in particular. In any case, I took it for the latter, but continued scanning for a quick and easily accessible exit.

"Ah shut up Marvin! Your kid has more hair than this guy," someone at the bar yelled back.

I kept looking around for the inevitable advancing line of pool cue wielding rednecks about to wreak their pent-up vengeance long overdue from some old festering war or long-standing family feud. But none formed. The rest of the bar kept doing what it had been doing, only now there was a distinct pot component reeking its way out of the recesses at the rear of this cesspool. We might get lucky yet.

I turned around again and there he was staring at me from about two feet away.

"What are you looking at you commie traitor?"

He was only about 5'7" to my 6'2", so it was a stretch on his part to be seriously menacing while looking up. Somehow he pulled it off. My guts began to shrivel like well-aged Italian salami.

"What's this? A peace sign?" He grabbed at my silver peace-symbol necklace. I jerked back and swiped at his hand. I thought he was going to hit me. He didn't.

"You a hippie creep? Did you burn your draft card, coward, or do you just let your mommy do all your fightin'?" I was stuck on whether to hit him first and then run or just run and hope he's rheumatoid.

"You know you got a lot of guts coming in here you draft-dodging shithead. This is 'merica and we don't cotton to cowards and traitors."

His veins began to pop out on his shag-rug of a forehead, now turning a bright trailer-park orange where it would normally be red if not for the yellow sullenness of an alcoholic smoker living life largely without sunlight or vitamin D, which had turned his skin a sickly sallow salmon-pink. His eyes had flecks of jaundice as well. Fuck, I thought, what am I going to do? One good swing in his direction and the resulting breeze might give him an overdue heart attack.

"You want to step outside so we can have this out right now behind my truck on private property right next door? Nobody cares anyways."

He was starting to spit and drool. I expected foam to start spewing from the corners of his mouth next. They kill dogs that do that. I wonder if it extends to rednecks. Damn, I should have had a plan to bring my .357 along on these plane trips. Good thing I don't plan anymore.

"You be a man? Or are you some quivering little coward who shits his pants when mama ain't around to protect him?"

Now I could feel the whole bar watching us. He was beginning to get to me. My hand started quivering.

A red rash began to seep out of my rear area causing a burning sensation that spread like hot lava devouring all the helpless villagers on some tropical isle as it burns its way to the sea. I was never any good at wrestling in PE class, or any other body-contact sport. Touching other guys seemed weird. I just couldn't get physical, violent or otherwise. Therefore, I try to avoid this kind of shit. Sometimes it's unavoidable, though. Like tonight.

God damn Jack, where is he? Maybe he knows this guy and can talk him down. I scanned the crowd over the top of his head looking for Jack or maybe some help from the barkeep, but saw nothing helpful and both Lena and Ingrid seemed awfully close now to the babbling idiot. So if he tries something, I guess I'll have to offer my body for him to pummel and protect the girls.

"You know I'm about to call the Feds on you, doper. I bet you're carrying now. How 'bout we just search you right now and arrest your sorry ass." At the mention of dope, Lena leaned in just close enough to the clown to momentarily divert his attention. Next thing I know, the guy's slumping to the floor all rag-doll like. What the fuck? I look around but nobody seems to notice that this guy is suddenly just lying on the floor without so much as a whimper. Before I can figure out what just happened, Lena grabs me by one arm, Ingrid grabs the other, and we march back to the pool table that has Jack's ten-dollar bill.

The other side of the cultural gap was losing its grasp on cohesiveness. A year or two ago, when the Vietnam war was being fought by reluctant conscripts and macho killers, the couch patriots who were left behind howled for hippie-traitor blood. Then Kent State happened and Cronkite flipped after actually visiting 'Nam. Now they were slowly coming to the inescapable, inevitable conclusion that they'd been fucked, or to put it more politely, the victims of a great compromise. Vietnam was changing America from self-righteous, flag-draped paranoid bullies to dumbass Agent-Orange suckers. All the dead soldiers and slaughtered civilians were being sacrificed for nothing but the almighty dollar. They didn't like to think about it, but there was the truth in all its elephant-in-the-room glory. The 'merican public had just been duped, and duped good, by greedy corrupt war-mongers and power moguls.

The war was finally winding down and, now, the know-nothing rural rednecks were feeling lost without their sacred cause to help cloak and conceal, as if it were a national secret, their common unfathomable and profound ignorance. Hippie-bashing was good for only so long until your own children began to show hippie symptoms like long hair, independence, pot, sexual freedom, racial tolerance, intelligence, love of Rock & Roll, and ultimately culminating in the most reviled hippie attribute, peace-loving activist.

When children are subjected to all this, it isn't long before they develop a general fear and loathing for coerced obedience to blind senseless hypocritical authority. What the previous generation had held in unquestioning esteem now received the complete opposite from their children. Our elders may have occupied the moral high ground during the Big War, but now those same heroes were clueless groveling followers, like Nazi supporters, permitting great harm and evil in the misplaced name of patriotism. That's why we so proudly proclaimed the dawning of the Age of Aquarius and proudly wore the peace symbol. Who knew the very idea of peace would piss them off so much? They might have been the greatest generation in their youth, but after the war they turned to shit.

What was really weird though was the fact that drugs helped fuel the first round of rebellion among elite upper-class whites, but now it was filtering down to the unwashed buck-toothed masses with quite opposite and perhaps devastating effects. A social study graduate once told me that drugs and religion were traditionally used by all cultures to organize and control their own useless masses. To me, drugs were liberating and religion was IQ-suicide, so I'm not sure how the combination ended up building pyramids or fighting World Wars. In my mind, anybody today who's doing more religion than drugs should probably be considered a pathological enemy of sane humanity.

Later, it turned out, pot wasn't strong enough for them and coke was way too expensive, so rednecks rapidly turned back to good old belligerent mind-numbing alcohol, only now with a chaser of speed or Methedrine for that wide-awake drunk effect. I understood the meth thing. It came from long-distance truck drivers trying to find something stronger than boiled coffee to stay awake and, of course, returning Vietnam vets who had put to good use what Dow and the US Army handed out to keep the boys alert all night long so the sneaky little black-pajama freedom-fighters didn't cut their throats while they slept.

For college kids, speed was just something to help with an all-night study binge. But when we did it, we usually ended up in long, drawn-out philosophical discussions with fellow crammers after about 4 a.m. when we were at our drug-crazed sanest. On the other hand, rednecks just seem to go absolutely fiendishly depraved. So low it could only be effectively described as a negative pit somewhere beneath the bottom of the religious hellhole. Not sure why. Must be something in the water.

The good old cowboy shit-stompin' country music lovin' honky-tonkin' hard-runnin' entrepreneurial American independent truck drivers of the '40s and '50s morphed into the long-haired dope-smokin' coke-snortin' hard-rock music lovin' hocked-to-the-man-for-their-wife-and-kids kind of big-corporate patriotic truck driver in the '60s and '70s, just shit-eating happy to be employed and voting Republi-crook. You can lead a redneck to mind-altering drugs, but without a sane mind somewhere deep down inside to properly alter, they're still just plain stupid-assed jerks.

A small crowd formed around the limp loudmouth on the floor while Lena and Ingrid kept pushing me toward the pool tables. I still had a Heineken in my hand so I took a big gulp that mostly splashed my face as Ingrid yelled, "Comin ze throoo! Excuse'm wa, comin ze throoo!"

And like the sea parting for Moses, the mostly-male crowd split like an overripe melon sliced open by a machete.

Jack finally reappeared from the doom and gloom back area, seemingly unscathed and still lucid. He ordered more beers and rejoined Ingrid to watch the chosen table play out their game. I couldn't help but notice a slight change in the complex bar smells and the level of rowdiness.

The sweet smell of mellow-yellow now drifted into the mix. Guys not actively shooting pool were visiting the head at an amazing rate. Laughter seemed to erupt randomly for no reason. People were actually smiling. Jack seemed unaware of anything beyond the pool table. I noticed a couple of men had picked up the loudmouth and half dragged him outside, I presumed to send him home. Good riddance. Now I could enjoy the game. I chugged the last of the Heineken, whereupon Lena handed me another one. How did she do that?

Then the guys at the pool table finished their game and, as their apparent leader picked up Jack's ten-dollar bill, all eyes turned to our odd little group. We were up.

I tried to play my part well. After all, I was just the one-night-stand for the local drug dealer's girlfriend's girlfriend, the guy that everybody wishes he could be but just doesn't seem to have all the connections necessary to get there. Lust and greed were plainly palatable. The eyes of our new opponents seemed glued to the bare midsections of the two Swedes. I guess Northern Michigan girls can't take the cold.

I played last in the rotation, after everyone else. I was also clearly the worst. The beers and drugs weren't much help either. No pressure here. I watched with growing amazement as our side always just kept barely even with the opposing weirdo's score no matter how well they shot or how lousy I did.

The leader of the opposing pack of rednecks, or who I dubbed weirdo number one, would drop two or three balls. Then Jack played next, usually sinking a similar number. Weirdo number two might sink one, or not, followed by Ingrid who would make just enough shots to keep the score even. Weirdo number three usually had a hard time with Ingrid's leave, making him increasingly frustrated. Then came Lena, followed by weirdo number four and, finally, yours truly. Even though the local greasers were doing their best to humiliate our motley crew, they could only win each round by a modest margin, which they claimed was due to skill and we claimed was just luck. They were getting drunk, loud and cocky. I was starting to get a little worried again.

The evening dragged on like this for two more games, and in each one Jack gave up a twenty-dollar bill to the fearsome foursome. I was mostly joking with Lena about how badly I played and she had to agree. After my sixth or seventh beer, I noticed I was doing considerably worse than when we started. I also noticed that way too many other people were starting to watch us. Unless I'm separated from the audience by a six-foot-high stage, I tend to get nervous when unknown possibly malevolent eyes study me from the darker fringes of a room. I was beginning to feel like a tasty rodent-morsel wandering in the dark woods while shining eyes peering from behind a wall of trees followed my every move. Below every pair of eyes, I imagined hidden tongues licking hungry chops in greedy anticipation of a bloody kill.

Jack didn't seem too concerned, even though the girls were probably being scrutinized much more intently than me, and the tension was thicker than Vegan-constipated shit. The girls were intent on each other and the game and didn't seem aware of anything else. Comments about long hair, college scum, and hippie-commie-trash kept rising above the background noise along with macho innuendos, sexual overtones, and downright insulting gestures. Having grown up in a redneck logging community, I've found myself in touchy situations before, but I felt somewhat trapped here as I'd become a willing hostage to Jack's entourage and, somehow, a possibly fatal innocent bystander to his secret suicide pact.

Finally, Jack made his play. He slapped down two Ben Franklins on the edge of the table and much to my surprise, the idiots slapped down a fat stack of twenties that presumably matched it. This was my cue to start watching the exits, making sure they would be available at a moment's notice just in case things went dicey in a hurry. I had learned over the years that you can never over plan your escape from a bunch of liquored-up rednecks. Anything can happen and usually does.

It didn't take long. About the second go-round when Ingrid was up again, she began to run the table. I could see the jaws drop simultaneously on the Four Horsemen of the Apocalypse as she made a triple bank shot sinking two balls at once. The crowd suddenly came alive with her abrupt change in proficiency and, even though the noise level increased, I swear you could hear a pin drop from the shocked, mouth-gaping silence of our opponents.

I took another swig off my Heineken, finishing it off in one large gulp. I grabbed Lena by the arm and began to edge her toward the door just as Ingrid sank the last ball. It wasn't just a friendly game of pool anymore. Someone threw a beer bottle against the rear wall as Jack scooped up the money and fell in behind Ingrid as they sprinted to catch up to us. The Four Stooges just stared in amazement and then fury as it slowly dawned on them what had just happened.

One of the Stupid Brothers swung his pool cue in the direction of a departing Jack. It missed but Jack grabbed a stool by the leg and swung it back at the group causing them to all duck and scatter behind the pool tables. Then, just as some greaser came flying over the pool table, arms outstretched and looking for a throat, Ingrid stepped in front of Jack. Her next move left those nearby awestruck as she caught the flying jerk by his jacket and rolling backwards, redirected his momentum and head into a nearby post with an ugly *thunk* sound. The whole bar rattled and dust shook from the rafters as Ingrid bounced back to her feet ready for the next one.

The big motorcycle guy stepped out of the head and expelled a huge cloud of smoke as he yelled something about defending 'merica from Godless pinko-commies. He charged across the room like a mad bear, throwing wild-air haymaker punches apparently at thin air. But instead of going for us like everyone else, at the last second one of the four jilted pool-playing boys stepped a little too close to the bear. We could hear the crack of his neck bones being displaced by a well-aimed slug to the jaw. The redneck crumpled. Then and only then, did all hell break loose.

Jack grabbed Ingrid and shouted at Lena and I to get moving. I looked around just in time to see Lena flip some goon twice her size onto an empty pool table where his head made a egg-cracking sound as it struck the slate. Several nearby boys backed off as she looked for another target. Seeing no immediate threats, she grabbed my hand and started running after Jack and Ingrid.

Jack was laughing his ass off as he burst through the front door seconds ahead of the girls and me. A chair came flying through a window next to the door, exploding neon glass tubes, electric sparks, and flaming liquor bottles that all missed us by inches. I kept the girls moving toward the van as Jack grabbed the chair and threw it back through the now gaping window-hole. Screams and the sickening sound of wood on bone kept coming from the inside as we jerked open the van's side door and piled in. Jack made it to the driver's door just in time to see about half a dozen tangled bodies fall through the front door with arms and legs flying in all directions.

I struggled to get the big side door pulled shut behind the girls as I heard the van's engine roar to life. Something was different. I'd heard that sound before. Now it was obvious he had something more than a lame Ford truck engine in this crate. I swung into the front seat and held on to whatever I could find in anticipation of what I knew was coming next. Jack was still laughing hysterically as he popped the clutch and spun out in the parking lot, kicking gravel in a wide circle as he cut a donut right in front of the bar.

Then he took a larger swing past a row of trucks and bikes just to get into a better position to display more of his van's unique qualities. That's when I spotted it. One of the larger trucks near the edge of the lot suddenly lit up like an ELO concert. A blinding row of Argon lamps bolted to a crossbar above its cab stabbed out at our van like a laser spear, pinning us in place.

"That must be the redneck who tried to fight me inside," I yelled above the roar of the engine.

"What redneck? Aw, never mind. I know how to nail these clowns," said Jack.

I could see dust clouds rising behind the truck as it spun out trying to come for us. From the distant roar, it was obvious he had a few horses on us, too. I doubt if that even crossed Jack's mind. He got a glaze in his eye that wasn't the usual drug-glaze and he started counting down.

"Three...."

Now the truck was accelerating toward the lodge, between two rows of cars.

"Two...."

If we continued the direction we were headed, he could easily T-bone us right in front of the brawl that was now spilling out into the parking lot.

"One...."

Not cool.

At the count of one, Jack jammed the van into reverse and stood on it.

"Zero!"

A mighty roar was heard as we spun around with what I can only describe as a reverse-fishtail in a circle. Then he straightened out just in time to hurtle backward directly at the speeding truck. I don't think the redneck was expecting to see a van fishtailing in reverse, careening crazily around cars, as it found a way through the maze to get at his truck. The truck broke into the light from the lodge just in time to see a white whale with two blood-red eyes coming for him out of the dark. He jerked the wheel and his truck spun sideways to avoid the van when, in fact, Jack simultaneously shifted from reverse into drive causing the van to spit clouds of dirt and rocks covering its synchronized pirouette with the giant truck as we accelerated away from the truck in the opposite direction. Now blinded, it was inevitable that the truck's driver would forget about the line of bikes parked in front of the lodge.

He locked up all four almost getting it stopped in time, but the truck must have bumped one of the motorcycles at the end of the row, because right then I saw the slow-motion domino effect begin as one motorcycle fell into the one next to it and so on all the way down the line, creating a great wall of fallen Harley's. Beer bottles instantly began hitting the truck from behind the tangled hedge of bikes barricading the irate drunks from the parking lot and instant justice. It didn't matter; they were all locals and everybody knew everyone. They'd find justice eventually backwoods-style, in the back, at a more opportune time.

As we roared away in literally a cloud of dust, I saw George, the big biker-gang leader who'd hugged Jack and Ingrid earlier, pop out the door with one struggling baseball-capped head-locked under each arm. He was screaming something that I swore sounded like, "Thanks for the party, Jack! Come back y' all!"

The local population apparently considered this a very successful evening out on the town. Jack was ecstatic, as were the two girls. I was very happy to be alive but failed to find any humor in almost being the focus of some backwoods lynching attempt. I guess things are so boring out here in the hinterlands that their favorite entertainment is stirring up the natives for no good reason other than just wanting to witness wholesale mayhem, which I understand is a celebrated local sport like cockfighting or bear-baiting. I may not have understood this phenomenon, but I certainly did enjoy one of its consequences. Lena was especially excited by the events and spent the rest of the night making sure I was just as excited about her as she was about not dying in a bar brawl partially of her own partial making.

The next morning, after not getting a lot of sleep and still badly hungover from all the drugs and alcohol, I begged to be taken back to my plane. The girls came along to see me off and I tried to get my mental fog under control enough not to be a hazard to air traffic. Lena gave me a big hug, a long kiss, and a longing look as she said, "Don't be shy. Come visit us again real soon."

"You can count on it," I lied. I climbed into the plane, started it up, and while it was warming up, I swallowed the Quaalude I had pocketed from Jack's candy bowl the day before, just for this situation. Quaaludes were the best damn cure ever for a hangover.

They all drove down to the far end of the runway, the one with the cliff overlooking the rocks and the water, while I taxied the plane back to the trees at the other end in order to get the longest possible run before the cliff. I figured one way or the other I was going to be airborne. It was just a tossup as to whether I was going to be flying or falling.

As it turned out, I made a mighty rush toward the bay end and had a gut-wrenching, bowel-clenching reaction instantly as I careened over the cliff's edge and saw large rocks along the shoreline loom menacingly close. They filled the windshield as I pushed the stick forward in order to rapidly gain airspeed as I had been trained to do. The added airspeed from falling was all I needed to make the Tri-Pacer's fat stubby wings grab onto the air like Tarzan leaping onto a swinging vine.

I pulled up just in time to avoid leaving fabric on a piece of driftwood sticking up too high. The plane skimmed the rocky shore, scattering seagulls in all directions, before climbing slowly back into the sky. I dipped my wings at the figures below, now jumping and dancing and waving at me, as I made a lazy turn back to the south, over the heavily forested Lower Peninsula and flew southeast to Ann Arbor.

Actually, that's total bullshit! Being seriously low in weight after dropping off the load and burning off half the fuel, the plane popped off the ground like a black raven making off with a stolen French fry. I was already several hundred feet above the cliff when I flew over it with a mighty roar and dipped my wings at the trio waving on the ground. One of these days I've got to get my imagination under control. But not today, apparently

The lasting effect on my intestines, however, both from the night before and my imagined terrifyingly romantic takeoff today, ended up pretty much as one would expect. I did make it as far south as Lansing before I had to make a non-declared emergency landing. I spiraled down from 5,000 feet, shot a direct approach, taxied straight up to the terminal door, and jumped out of the plane as soon as it stopped moving but before the propeller stopped spinning, and hit the ground running for the restroom. I was going to have to learn to be somewhat kinder to my body and plan things a little better to avoid a nasty, stinky high-altitude embarrassment.

Maybe dope smuggling wasn't as glamorous as it was cracked up to be.

CHAPTER FIVE

IT'S JUST NOT AMERICA ANYMORE

"What a field-day for the heat, a thousand people in the street...."

Buffalo Springfield
"For What It's Worth"
1967

"Hey! Wake up! Did you hear about what's going on at the lab today?"

I snapped my two burning eyes open only briefly but ended up seeing the underside of a pillowcase in great need of a wash and maybe some bleach.

From beneath my pillow, I could dimly make out Eberbach poking his head into my bedroom at the ungodly hour of 8 a.m. the following Monday morning.

"The lab's closed today!"

It was news to me. I'd been a little busy recovering from some kind of drug and alcohol abuse problem that happened somewhere near Canada culminating with, and subsequently accentuated by, a nasty case of the shits. But then I usually didn't give a shit about anything before 10 a.m., and I was almost awake anyway, so why not go for the next step and see what happens?

Steve was employed at the lab as a full-time electrical engineer, so he was honor-bound to show up around 9 a.m. like the rest of the nine-ish to five-ish professionals. Technicians and hourly people like Thom and Bambi supposedly arrived by 8 a.m., but graduate students had no such working-class-driven schedule. We seemed to be either outside those social structures or simply didn't give a damn. I didn't want to be predictable so my day could start anytime, but it was usually timed to end after midnight so I could line up the closing of my workday with the start of Bill's and the rest of the local "Armies of the Night."

"There's going to be a big anti-war rally on North Campus today. The White Panthers and all the usual university groups are protesting secret government-sponsored war research," he continued, as if I needed the details. I didn't. Nothing surprised me anymore concerning student protest marches. They were getting progressively meaner and more violent, and that meant more excitement, more news demand, and maybe a little *dinero* for me. I didn't want to miss any sellable action.

"Dr. Crane decided it would be best if we could sort of get lost today and stay away from all the crazies that might show up. I've heard the cops may call in the National Guard and the White Panthers may call in the Black Panthers from Detroit. Who knows what could happen?" he added, no doubt beaming with excitement and anticipation.

There had been rumors for months that the local White Panther Party had been doing business with the Black Panthers just hoping, I imagined, that some of the latter's legitimacy might rub off and infect their own lowly, pale, self-righteous, guilt-ridden butts. Plus, for some reason, cops shit their pants at the idea of a pissed-off armed and dangerous black man like the persona the Black Panthers assumed. They weren't really Che Guevara revolutionaries; they just liked making the same fashion statement. They were actually ghetto organizers who'd recently decided to assume their Second Amendment rights, the very same privileges that whites had used for centuries to prevent exactly such organizing activities.

"What?" I yelled from under my pillow. "Are you crazy? If there's going to be a riot, we need to shoot it!"

I threw off the pillow and sheets as I let the daylight shock my eyeballs fully alert and burn like desert sand. A sportsman's excitement welled up in me at the prospect of documenting senseless violence, blood and possible gore, almost certainly eye-searing teargas and, if fortune smiled, a few broken windows and maybe a small fire or two. If the National Guard showed up and the Black Panthers did too, well, the carnage could outdo anything we'd seen so far. *Remember Kent State!* I yelled putting on my underwear.

I had plenty of experience with demonstrations and protests. In the '60s, any college student with a conscience couldn't avoid them. I cut my teeth driving around the South with some activist friends during the Civil Rights Movement, taking pictures for the school paper and helping organize Black voter registration drives. People were getting killed during this little episode in American politics, so my buddies and I went down there on slightly different terms then most of the other young, idealistic, and innocent northern college kids.

From the time I left the farm in Oregon, I packed heat. It was just something my brothers and I did. My ancestors settled the West. Everybody then carried a gun for lots of reasons. It was a basic tool for survival in a dangerous place, the wilderness. We didn't make a big deal out of it. It was something you did that was expected. I didn't see any harm and I reasoned if the enemy is armed, and you know they are, then don't be a sheep, standup and be an American. I considered at worst, the Second Amendment attempts to guarantee the rest of the document.

When we worked in South Carolina during our first college spring break in '65, all the guys I travelled with were discreetly carrying and enjoying their Second Amendment rights. We agreed we had to help out people struggling for their freedoms, but we were damned if we'd become martyrs so early in life without at least being able to put up a fight. Most of us were just freshly graduated from virginity and ardently looked forward to a lot more advanced love lessons.

So, when the local clean-white-sheet club came calling one night on our puke-green '65 Valiant with Massachusetts plates on a lonely stretch of South Carolina highway, a simple demonstration of Mr. Smith's and Mr. Wesson's classic Model 29 was enough to change their cowardly little minds about these drug-crazed long-haired hippie agitators from up north. *I walk boldly and am not afraid because I am the craziest son of a bitch with the biggest bang-stick in the valley.* That seemed to be something even subhuman KKK thugs could understand.

I marched on the Pentagon with Norman Mailer's *Army of the Night* in 1967 and thoroughly enjoyed every minute of it. I ostentatiously carried a press pass from U of M's student newspaper, *The Michigan Daily,* and that along with my big-lens Nikon FTN 35mm SLR camera usually bought me free passage from one side of the police lines to the other without much trouble.

Of course, once the police went into riot mode, then no amount of press passes or anything else could save a lone photographer from roaming bands of off-duty patriotic vigilante cops and other violence-prone concerned citizens out to clean the streets of those filthy purveyors of moral conscience and equal justice. After all, wasn't it the pigs' sworn duty to suppress the people—that is, kick the livin' shit out them—whenever they exercised their constitutional right to free expression by criticizing or disobeying the current assholes controlling our government and stealing our taxes?

I quickly graduated from amateur student protests when I accidently filmed a practice-session precursor to the infamous 1968 Democratic Convention's brazen all-out police riot in Chicago. I was in Grant Park for the April '68 Vietnam protest concert. It was a really mellow Sunday afternoon with a rare bright springtime Midwest sunshine, outstanding live music in the band shell and good peaceful vibes all around.

That is, until a squad of pigs showed up and unceremoniously started busting heads for no fucking reason other than they *could*. I turned our 16mm camera on the scene and captured the beginnings of a first-class bloody police riot.

A police riot is when the cops become so frustrated with peaceful demonstrators not showing the proper fear and obedience that they feel a need to bust heads so they can satisfy some kind of lust for busting heads, literally. Real macho of these tough jerks, seeing how nobody was armed in any way or protected by cowardly helmets and shields like these big tough Chicago-Bull cops. All it did was piss everybody off and, as usual, a one-sided fight would always break out. The next day's headlines proclaim the cops were surrounded and attacked by drug-crazed anti-war activists. They were, of course, only partly right on one count. There were five thousand long-haired freaks in the park getting beat to crap by a hundred cops. Who fucking surrounded who?

The footage I took was later used by Haskell Wexler in his film about an emotionally-dead TV news photographer who shot stories for the nightly news but failed to have any feeling for what he saw and recorded. The movie, *Medium Cool,* was based on Marshall McLuhan's analysis of modern media in which he states flatly, *the medium is the message. either cool or hot, mind numbing or stimulating.* TV was cool, radio was hot. We agreed. Underground radio stations were our voice, our glue, our culture. We hated TV for its bland inanity and gagging superficiality. We also hated the thuggish enforcers of the corrupted status quo: The Pigs.

I'd been chased by club-wielding rogue D.C. cops wearing civilian clothes during the 1967 march on the Pentagon, and now I was being chased through The Loop by rogue and this time uniformed Chicago pigs. Fortunately, I had the benefit of excellent instruction from a college buddy's brother who had gone through the Sorbonne uprising in November '67. He had tooth marks from some hapless French gendarme proudly imprinted on the case of his vintage Leica camera, which he carried everywhere like a beloved weapon or lover. He said he was an artist and his canvas was photographic truth.

It wasn't long until I could proudly display Chicago Police tooth marks on my Nikon. The challenge was to be able to take pictures continuously while using your camera like a small club or brass knuckles. A heavy Nikon with motor drive and a 300 mm lens was a good substitute for a No. 9 Louisville Slugger bat. One of my best pictures was a blurred close up of the contorted face of a Chicago bull expressing extreme surprise and perhaps even some dismay at seeing the fast-moving black box with a massive lead-compounded glass lens headed straight for his slack jaw. Priceless!

"So how many do they think will show up?" I asked as I pushed past Steve in the hallway, unsteadily making my way to the bathroom.

"They called off all classes today so they could have up to fifty thousand students on their hands."

"That's real smart. Just what they need. A bunch of out-of-class students with nothing better to do. Could be cool though," I yelled back through the closed bathroom door as I ritually purged myself from both ends.

"When is it going to kick off?" I spluttered through rabid tooth paste foam encircling my mouth.

"Thom said he stopped by the lab about an hour ago and he said the cops were already setting up roadblocks. He barely made it out without being stopped. I think the march is supposed to start around noon, but Thom said he saw a big crowd starting to surround some of the larger North Campus buildings near the lab."

North campus was in an industrial part of town, north of the main campus and across the Huron River. Since the beginning of the Space Race, the university had been buying up cheap farm land along the river's north bank and they'd started building engineering labs there, with diverse specialties, funded mostly by the federal government but administered by various U of M departments. The problem was that these research labs were also really cozy with defense corporations and secret quasi-academic war research. This funneled university talent and engineering discoveries almost directly into the private coffers of multi-national corporations and, of course, our ever-adorable Pentagon. One of our buddies would talk about his work on a wire-guided anti-tank rocket that couldn't miss. But we really didn't want to end up so desperate that we had to work for death companies like that.

These labs and research centers cloaked their activities in secrecy for lots of reasons, none of which made much sense in terms of educating students in a free and open dialog aimed at discovering universal truths. This was all new stuff for an esteemed state institution and it just didn't seem appropriate. Supporting the technological needs of an oppressive regime that suppressed people's rights and democratic will is the antithesis of the university philosophy. It violated the basic search for truth by confusing fundamental morality with might-makes-right machismo. Obviously, such efforts were on very shaky ethical grounds and that was what was pissing us all off. It was just plain un-American.

Numerous anti-war activists had for some time claimed that there was more than just government-sponsored academic research going on in several of these buildings. We heard rumors all the time about this part of campus, running the gamut from secret CIA labs where new drugs were being tested on locally-procured missing pets to super-secret, high-tech weapons, like a shoulder-launched, laser-guided anti-aircraft missile being developed. Talk of secret weapons research got everyone's attention, especially if it meant that the government wanted to expand the war in Vietnam and invade the other half of Southeast Asia, or some progressive Latin American country like Chile or Nicaragua.

Our lab was part of the North Campus complex, but the most dangerous thing we did was measure upper atmospheric constituents in real-time with miniature satellites we built and launched ourselves with equally tiny rockets the military gave us from their overstock supply of retired 1950s stage-three boosters for intercontinental ballistic missiles. Having been used for years to hold nuclear material in some Nebraska cornfield, these little devils were a little hot to just bury in a landfill, so the military gave them to universities like ours to blow up on the pad or be disposed of properly by launching them into space and letting them burn up in someone else's atmosphere far from American rain clouds.

Sure, we accidently discovered that our modest little satellite instruments designed to measure the different gases in the upper ionosphere could also detect tiny changes in atmospheric gases whenever the Russians or anyone else fired off one of their giant ballistic boosters. This meant we were inadvertently collecting secret information that our lab didn't really care about, but it made us a *de facto* Cold War spy organization.

The lab did basic atmospheric research that was published worldwide in the American Geophysical Union's research journal but our raw data was classified so, technically, I wasn't allowed to know those numbers although my computer program chewed them up regularly and spit them out onto my graphs as little noise blips that I had to ignore as *unexplained gas bursts*. You can fool most of the people some of the time, you can even fool some of the people most of the time, but you can't fool Mother Nature.

Our lab occupied only half of the building and we didn't have much security on our side, mostly just locked doors at night, which were no challenge to me or any of our gang. My friends taught me basic key-lock technology in undergraduate school, which I later perfected by designing and making my own special lock picks. The other side of our building had twenty-four-hour guards and electronic surveillance everywhere. I kept my distance from the strange Mormon-missionary-type, skinny-tie-toting men in black that appeared and disappeared at odd times.

We heard rumors they did some kind of interception of Soviet satellite communications, so the weird antennas on our roof and the innumerable 16-inch-diameter half-inch-wide data tape reels in unmarked crates coming and going from the rear loading platform pretty much confirmed everybody's suspicion that no possible good could be going on in that side of the building.

The Vietnam War had been raging for about a decade and we were just beginning to hear the first real horror stories of rampant use of indiscriminate Napalm or jellied gas bombs, Agent Orange defoliants, and brush-cutter cluster-bombs that, all and more, clearly violated every law in the civilized world and put modern military mass-destruction research projects into about the same category as performing Nazi medical experiments or developing innovative medieval inquisition techniques.

Students around the world were demanding that their institutions of higher learning restrict themselves to the peaceful and critical examination of the human condition and the unrestricted exploration of the laws of nature for the benefit of all earth's creatures, not just the greedy. Exploiting the human legacy of hard-earned knowledge for unrestrained profit, war, and oppression was simply counter to what the free pursuit of universal knowledge at public universities is supposed to be all about.

Unfortunately, universities had discovered that practical knowledge, especially the kind concerning capitalism, tyranny, and slaughter, can be very profitable and we know what profitable means, right? Money buys might, might makes right; and right, of course, guarantees and justifies having all the money and power in the first place. Hence, money absolutely creates oppression, pure and simple.

Money is just a score card, but power is the doorway to immortal history. Outside of hunting humans for sport, this might well be the greatest game on earth. War, on the other hand, merely takes the free enterprise system to its logical conclusion in which bullets replace the lawyers and death becomes the collection agency.

I didn't care so much about the moral uses of knowledge. After all, even da Vinci prostituted himself to the war generals of his day for, I am sure, a tidy profit. So, a lot of what my fellow students were protesting didn't really add up for me, except for the part about being forced to die fighting an illegal, immoral, and unnecessary war. The war we chose to fight was the one in the streets, where the pigs became paid security guards for the criminally rich and oppressors-of-the-poor and we, the liberating revolutionary army. The pigs saw us as fair game for developing new forms of crowd control like Billy clubs applied to the knees at close range, tear gas applied directly to the eyes and, if necessary, rubber bullets or real ones fired randomly into crowds just to provide them a dose of random gun diplomacy.

When we partied, who ruined it? When we got high, who drove us into paroxysms of paranoia? When we assembled peacefully to protest our evil corrupt government's racist and imperialistic policies, who bashed our brains in? They were no longer the friendly neighborhood cops on the beat. They were volunteer ghetto prison guards who had become professional enforcers, honing their skills at keeping a tight lid on ordinary citizens.

It was a time of 'Us versus Them.' After Kent State, until just recently, we thought we would have to take to the hills with our surplus WWII-relic rifles and defend ourselves against a new onslaught of brown-shirted, super-patriot fascist thugs and mercenary professional death-squads. In other words, it was boiling down to redneck cops against peaceful intellectuals, or thugs versus make-love-not-war organic flower-child hippies.

Right-wing military death-squads were appearing all over South America, eradicating free-thinking liberal university students, news reporters, intellectuals, and politicians who stupidly got themselves elected on the merits of serving the people instead of purchasing the franchise for intimidating and dominating them. In any case, we figured we were probably next.

America was no longer the land of freedom or the home of liberal human rights. It was now a place where rich bastards who wanted to loot the ultimate prize, the U.S. Treasury, did so freely under the guise of protecting us from the evils of godless, yet somehow unexpectedly popular, communism. This had to be justified by having our country's sons and daughters regularly and routinely slaughtered and sacrificed to support Big Government lies, big corporate looting of our treasury, and the raw political power required to guarantee the whole affair could go on unabated and unexamined for generations. People belonged to political parties like they did religions, selecting them for family social connections rather than a particular philosophy or take on reality and truth.

Hell no, we won't go! was the standard rallying cry from the students. I presumed this meant their primary concern wasn't the war's legitimacy but rather, who exactly was going to fight it. Any male over 18 could be drafted and sent off to die in Vietnam. About 300,000 or more U.S. soldiers had done just that and the body count kept growing. But potential draftees could get exemptions from the suicidal lottery laughingly termed 'compulsory service' and one of the biggest exceptions was simple for sons of the middle and upper classes. College students were draft deferrals and, as a result, attending college literally became a real-life survival strategy. Beyond having a good career, students had a strong new motivation for staying in school. It had become a simple matter of life and death.

The poor ghetto blacks and equally-impoverished, generally Southern-redneck or Midwestern-rural whites, provided most of the cannon fodder in Vietnam. But when it came to precious little white boys of promise and prestige, well, someone had to stand up and say *Fuck It! We Won't Go!*

The cops hated the fact they'd lost all respect from and control over an entire generation of kids they were supposed to coerce and control. The enforcers of the status quo were, as usual, fighting on the wrong side of the ongoing human struggle for freedom and western civilization's long arduous march to attain universal suffrage, equality, and justice. Hired goons suppressing the constitutional rights of law-abiding citizens seemed to be an ongoing battle, even in America's self-righteous so-called land of freedom and justice. It was one thing to read about it in history class. Now it was getting personal.

I showered and dressed as quickly as my two-day-binge hangover would allow. I grabbed my Nikon with a super wide-angle and a long telephoto lens from the closet and hurried downstairs. Steve was waiting near the front door with his Japanese twin-lens Konica hanging around his neck, looking like a common Asian tourist, except for his unruly shoulder-length hair, which gave him away. I grabbed my old, olive-drab skeet-shooting vest, hanging handy on a coat hook between the door and the stairs. Where I recently carried 12-gauge shotgun shells slung together belt-like, it now held dozens of 35mm film containers. My *Michigan Daily* press pass was pinned below the left shoulder where a soldier's name tag would normally be attached. We were the soldiers of the night and I was our self-trained gonzo journalist exposing the truth wherever it reared its ugly head.

We ran for my truck, which was always parked in the little empty lot next to the house. I headed north on Division Street until it joined Broadway and crossed the Huron River just north of the main campus. Off to the right, we could see the huge ten-story backside of University Hospital up on the hill overlooking the trysting area of the giant arboretum and the river below.

As soon as we joined Plymouth Road, which ran right through the middle of North Campus, we spotted a police roadblock. They were forcing all traffic to turn around and go back through town. I quickly swerved into one of the big parking lots that surrounded most of the buildings out here where there weren't any strolling students or quaint professors-on-bikes.

Steve and I had cruised around North Campus for years, so we knew all the hidden connections between the various parking lots, alleys, and long-abandoned farm access trails, now so overgrown with weeds that even the cops didn't bother with them. As we took the long back-trail to the lab, I'd seek cover behind whatever trees or buildings were handy so nobody would see us driving around where we obviously weren't supposed to be.

Our lab, one of the first built out here, was pretty much in the middle of the clustered build-out comprising the bulk of the university's newest suspect facilities. The buildings were all basically bland industrial design, brick and steel with windows provided only sparingly, if allowed at all. I've seen prisons and movie studios with more windows.

There were no cops that we could see as we skirted the research complex, staying as far as we could from the site selected for the anti-war rally and any probable action. I pulled up close to the rear of the lab so my truck couldn't easily be seen from any major roads on the other side. Steve unlocked the lab's back door with his key and we immediately headed for the roof-access ladder on the second floor landing.

I had a legal key to the roof-access hatch, issued so I could service the aurora-seeking spectrometer mounted on the lab's roof. In the two years I had been doing this, I never once recorded an aurora or anything other than a perfectly black sky and equally blank pictures. I didn't care because it put me in a well-equipped film lab for hours on end where I could work on my personal photography projects and get paid for it. An endless supply of free 35mm Tri-X film with black-and-white developing came with the deal, so I was in celluloid heaven.

We climbed through the hatchway onto the roof and walked over to the utility room housing the elevator equipment, a.k.a. *the penthouse*, then climbed the attached metal rungs to its roof. From this improved third-story vantage point we had an excellent view of the entire campus.

The first thing we noticed was a huge mob milling around one of the larger, darker, more foreboding buildings several blocks southwest of us. There were a number of police cars with flashing lights swarming around the same area like vicious black and white wasps looking to sting anything that moved suspiciously. Traffic may have been blocked from entering the area but we could easily see multiple bands of students crossing the river, near the arboretum and hospital, on a little-known footpath suspension bridge. So much for police crowd control. It was almost like they wanted something bad to happen.

"They're still coming," Steve said as he scanned the area with his huge 12X50 military surplus binoculars.

I mounted my biggest telephoto lens on the Nikon, an f/3.5 300mm hunk of heavy glass, and rested it on the parapet to steady it without a tripod.

"They seem to be converging on that one building over there."

He pointed in the same direction he was looking. "It looks like at least two or three thousand with more obviously on the way."

He swung his glasses slightly to the north to watch a fat line of students emerging from the trees across Plymouth road, near the river.

We could also hear a voice faintly booming in the distance from an obviously underpowered and fidelity-limited bullhorn. A distant screeching, scratching-chalkboard-sounding voice was reciting: *What do we want?*

We could barely make the words out over the bullhorn's whining, tooth-drilling feedback. I'd get pissed just having to listen to it.

The responding chorus came immediately and much clearer: *Peace!*

The bullhorn screeched faintly again. *When do we want it?*

A tsunami sound wave you could surf came rolling back Now!

Usually these things would get started with the concerned masses gathering to hear some student leader give a rousing speech condemning first the war, then the current bunch of politicians such as Nix-Goon or MacNa-Hitler, and finally, the nameless university administration that was deemed *bought-and-paid-for* by Pentagon puppet money or Wall Street mobster money posing as technology developers but who were, in reality, just plain old pillagers and purveyors of death and destruction in the name of the great American Dollar.

Whenever possible, organizers would find an eager local rock band to set up and play a few songs to get the crowd righteously fired-up with what the mainstream propaganda media referred to as 'that evil Rock-and-Roll-inspired hooliganism.' In truth, these peace rallies attracted more demonstrators who came to hear the music and watch the possible police violence than advocates who actually believed in the cause. Like sports fans at a NASCAR race, only there to see the fiery car crash.

Finally, after being righteously riled up and ready to protest, the crowd would typically mass into a formation roughly twenty or thirty people wide by as long as its ranks of demonstrators would extend, then march down the middle of some main thoroughfare obstructing traffic and hopefully halting commerce within the heart of the offending capitalist territory. Cops were always optional, as were violence and head bashing, but a protest would be considered an abject failure without at least some kind of incident. This event looked to be following the usual script.

The whole point, of course, was to get the message out to the largest audience possible. Mass media was the answer. What was bigger than the 6 o'clock news? If the pigs turned violent, even better; then it could hit the national news. Now that's effective advertising! If the Vietnam War was produced by the stroke of a pen, by God, it could surely be overthrown by the cold, dispassionate glare of all the cathode-ray tubes in the world.

Occupying buildings and throwing up barricades usually didn't come until later, after prolonged clashes failed to get the point across. In most confrontations where the pigs would overreact and attack peaceful unarmed protestors, a few overzealous demonstrators might take up the challenge and maybe put a rock through a bank window or, my favorite, brazenly screw their old lady in the middle of a downtown intersection in front of thousands. *Take that you uptight Puritan chumps!* I actually saw this happen one summer afternoon on a crowded main campus street, right in front of a smoking bank building that later replaced its shattered windows with what could only be described as gun ports. Shocking!

In response to the news stories, the pigs would always explain their actions as preserving the peace or protecting private property. But we all knew they were just there to assert their assumed God-given right to be bullies and enforcers of social and political conformity. It was hard to blame them. They were simply pawns in a much bigger game. Jocks in high school, followed by military training, makes a man qualified for only two careers: cop or criminal. We respected the criminal much more. Super Fly was our new hero, not Dirty Harry.

Pigs considered it their sacred duty to violently punish anyone who dared disagree with their self-anointed and rightful masters. It seemed strange to me the way criminal government goons always needed justification for their repression, which they usually accomplished by first controlling the national police so all others, guilty or otherwise, could therefore be declared traitors and undesirables at will. Absurd, but for some reason still effective no matter the size or outrageousness of the lie.

If violence is required to control the people, then I figure they've already lost the debate and, as a result, any legitimacy or respect they may have assumed. It's just a matter of how long they can survive once it becomes obvious to everyone else. *The times, they are a changin'!*

"Do you think we can get any closer?" I asked Steve as I changed lenses. I snapped off a few shots with the 24mm lens as I panned from left to right. I like making panorama prints, so I made it a habit to establish the surrounding landscape upfront at every new location by shooting as much as made sense of the foreground and horizon.

"Doesn't look good from here. I see an olive-drab police bus coming across the Huron Bridge. I bet ya it's either reinforcements or a portable jail. Either way, we might see some action today."

He began to bounce up and down like a little kid about to be given ice cream. Watching him anticipate the event's unfolding reminded me of the popularity of Roman gladiators, professional boxing, full contact football, and train wrecks. Call it an inborn fascination with fatal encounters and senseless violence, up close and personal. Or just call it natural human blood lust. I'm not aware of any other animal that kills for the entertainment-value alone. Except maybe cats. I like cats.

I swapped the normal lens for the telephoto again and began focusing on the activity of the cops who seemed to be marshalling their forces a couple parking lots away from the main part of the crowd. Most of the crowd were gathering around the guy with the bullhorn. We still couldn't make out his words, but he was clearly working the crowd into a screaming frenzy.

Then I picked out several small bands of protestors who seemed to be wandering off in different directions. There appeared to be at least one long-haired freak leading each group.

"What are those guys up to?" I asked Steve as I gestured in the direction my camera was pointing. He swung his big binoculars around and began scanning the area.

"Hmm," he muttered as he picked out the groups I'd seen and then some others.

"What do you think is going on?" I asked again as I, too, began to spot more splinter groups.

"Looks like an end run to outmaneuver the cops."

"The cops aren't even there yet. How can they be doing an end run when there's no line to run around?" I stopped taking pictures and turned toward him. "You don't suppose they're going to attack something?"

"Here come the cops!" he yelled. He turned his binoculars back in the direction of the squad cars, flashing lights, and now about four or five buses parked in a circle, all painted the same dull, muddy olive-drab and grey. Some had iron rods welded over the side windows. Otheres were apparently windowless but had long metal-covered indentations where windows once had been.

"Shit, that's way more cops than the Ann Arbor pig department," I observed.

I snapped a few more pictures of a uniformed mass of goons all tricked out in helmets, face shields, and riot gear. They were moving slowly across the parking lot in the direction of the growing crowd of protestors.

"Who the hell are those pigs?"

"I'll bet that's the new State Police riot squad they put together last winter after Detroit damned near burned to the ground."

"Check this out!" I interrupted. I pointed to a smaller structure along the riot cop's intended route. "It looks like one of those groups we just saw is hiding behind that building, waiting for the cops to pass them."

"Yeah, I see that. There's another group heading for the other side of the cops over by the river. Oh boy! This is getting downright interesting."

"That's a classic maneuver first described by Caesar during the civil war with Pompeii in Spain," said somebody from behind us.

We both damned near jumped out of our skins. I whirled around holding my big lens with both hands like a shield, just in case. Behind us and off to one side stood a tall straight-looking guy holding binoculars to his eyes and obviously following the same action we'd been watching. He was dressed like neither a student nor a cop. He was clean-shaven, however, which automatically put him into the category of either an undercover cop or an insurance salesman.

He was wearing nondescript street clothes: shiny black shoes, tan cotton slacks, a white shirt with sleeves partly rolled up, and no tie, dangling or otherwise. But his hair was cut short and well-trimmed, *clean-cut* I believe is the proper description, which immediately began setting off all kinds of alarm bells in my head. He clearly wasn't one of us, not even a university-type, administrative or otherwise. He had to be military or a fed, albeit a very relaxed one.

Steve paused, as I did, to more fully take in the stranger who had so deftly sneaked up on us without a sound and scared the living shit right the hell out of us. The worst thing that can happen during a demonstration, which could also be true in war, was a devastating attack from behind. Cold chills ran down our spines and our leg muscles tensed anticipating the inevitable surge of adrenaline signaling the onset of an autonomic *fight or flight* response. We had simultaneous drug-inspired visions of a James Bond-type character opening fire on us as we helplessly danced the "Danse Macabre" like Bonnie and Clyde. I probably need to stop taking drugs while watching big-screen movies.

The stranger slowly lowered his more modestly sized binoculars, revealing a broad friendly grin spread across a somewhat Rockwellian boyish, freckled face complimented by reddish hair clipped military-style, short and ugly.

"Hi guys!" he greeted us calmly. "Been here long?"

"Who are you?" I blurted out. "How did you get access to this building?"

We heard fresh sirens in the distance but ignored them as we waited for some answers.

"I work here just like you do," he replied in a matter-of-fact voice still holding onto his big ridiculous grin. He seemed to be looking past us at something even funnier.

"I've never seen you around the lab downstairs," I countered. I turned to Steve. "Have you?"

Eberbach looked hard at the guy and then admitted, "He looks familiar. I think I may have seen him somewhere."

"I work on the other side," he said.

He gestured with his binoculars toward the far end of our building, which was actually two buildings joined by a single-story common lobby with elevators and restrooms plus storage, janitorial, and shipping areas in the back. There was a small chasm between the two elevator penthouses, so he must have come up through the access hatch on our side of the building. Steve and I both followed his gesture and looked across the little canyon to the other rooftop. I looked back to him.

"So how did you get over here?"

He followed my glance at the other roof top and then looked back at us with a sly smile, making me think this guy was either playing us for fools or, more likely, had a few loose screws himself.

"I saw you park in the back so naturally I had to investigate," he said calmly as if this sort of thing happened all the time. "I followed you up here the same way you came."

More sirens came screaming from the area where more cops seem to be appearing like magic. The stranger put his binoculars back up to his eyes and began sweeping the area for more action.

He said, "I just got curious knowing your lab was closed today. I guess it's okay if you're here. At least you're not some network reporter looking to get more blood on the news. And you're definitely not an undercover cop cooking up charges with drugs they conveniently find in a student's back pocket."

Not knowing what the hell he was getting at; his last comment sounded a little scary. Could be just an obvious reference to the recent spate of prominent student leaders getting arrested on trumped-up drug charges, though the charges were usually illegal and bogus, with some victims even having oregano planted on them by cops who never expected to be challenged. The accused usually got off after years of expensive and sometimes dubious legal defenses, making the whole thing so overwhelming, expensive, and life-consuming that it effectively killed any further anti-war or anti-establishment activities on the part of any prudent man. We had our war casualties too.

I wasn't sure what to do with this interloper, but so far, he seemed to be non-threatening. I looked at Steve, who just shrugged his shoulders slightly indicating he had no clue either. I decided to play along, thinking maybe we could pry something revealing from him before we had to give up anything in return. Shit, it seemed like he already knew way too much.

"So how did you really get over here? We locked all the doors behind us."

I tried to be nonchalant about the questioning so I turned my gaze back in the direction of the slowly simmering conflict between students and cops and continued snapping pictures.

He didn't lower his binoculars to respond. "I have keys," he stated flatly.

"So what do you do on that side that requires you to have keys to our side?" I kept my eyes glued to the viewfinder, so I didn't see his initial reaction to my question. Steve picked up on my cue and began scanning the distant crowds again, trying to appear unconcerned as he carefully listened to every word we exchanged.

"Security," he declared.

A sudden flash of white smoke erupted from the vicinity of the escalating confrontation, followed a couple of seconds later by an explosive boom.

"We don't have security on our side," I said. "We are a civilian lab funded by the National Science Foundation and NASA. There are no military or government secrets here."

I could hear screams after the first explosion, so I put our conversation aside momentarily and tried to catch up with the action unfolding panoramically before us. It felt as if we were watching live TV news coverage or a long-drawn-out scene in one of those inscrutably boring European documentaries.

One of the squads had about ten or twelve cops, all smartly attired in their brand-new all black bulletproof vests, motorcycle helmets, and combat shields. The only difference between a Roman foot soldier and those modern-day imperial equivalents was that the former carried a mean-looking short sword, while the current-day pigs carried long, heavy riot batons backed up with plenty of tear gas and, whenever the cameras were looking the other way, guns, of course.

Today it looked like the classic *faint, diversion, isolation, and annihilation strategy.* Several separate groups had feigned attacks on other nearby buildings, causing the cops to react and disperse their forces as they ran to each rescue. Then other groups of student protestors would suddenly appear from out of nowhere and mysteriously coalesce on all sides of the now-isolated pigs. The surrounded pigs would react with tear gas and then make a mighty charge through the student lines in an attempt to retreat more-or-less intact back to their own ranks. In all the smoke and confusion, some of them would wind up in even worse circumstances, like getting gassed by their own overeager colleagues. We considered collateral fire as instant wartime karma.

It reminded me of the poor eighteen-year-old pimple-faced actual virgins of the Virginia National Guard who were absurdly called out to protect the Pentagon in October of '67, when a million or more students, citizens, and veterans descended *en mass* on Washington D.C., and the adjoining warmongers in Arlington, in an effort to shut down the lunatic war with sheer willpower. Fifty thousand screaming insane freaks surrounded the Pentagon and shut it down for a day. A squad of hapless young recruits was sent out into the overwhelming crowd, armed only with their abject innocence and blind dedication to following orders, no matter how stupid.

A photograph I took that day brought me a little notoriety. About a dozen fuzz-faced boys with army uniforms and olive-drab helmets, holding antique M-1 Garand rifles at the salute, were completely surrounded as far as you could see in all directions by drug-crazed maniacs, longhairs, hippie chicks, grandfathers, mothers, Dr Benjamin Spock, members of the 1938 Lincoln Brigade, and numerous others of equally inscrutable credentials.

I snapped a picture just as a beautiful girl dressed in a white cotton spring dress, with a crown of white daisies loosely encircling her golden hair, dropped the stem of a daisy down the barrel of a young, baby-faced soldier's rifle. The look on the boyish soldier's face was incredible. Right there was the whole problem and solution captured in a single image. Unfortunately, several dozen photographers took the same, or similar, shots all day long, so mine made it only as far as the *Michigan Daily*.

Most of the big demonstrations had been fairly peaceful, with maybe an occasional rogue band roving the perimeter looking for targets of opportunity. In more serious confrontations, good-sized rocks could occasionally appear out of the sky in response to the indiscriminate lobbing of teargas. *Going total,* as they called it, caused many to protestors to start outfitting themselves with helmets and gas masks. The anti-war demonstration technology race was on.

"There are always government secrets," the stranger calmly replied. "Actually, we wrapped up our operation here some time ago. With the war winding down, we have new objectives."

"So what are you doing here if there's nothing left to secure?" I countered, as I took another rapid string of shots of a small commotion erupting behind the police ranks.

"You could say I'm sort of between assignments, so they left me here to keep an eye on things."

Another cloud of tear gas exploded near the main group of protestors, which had so far been pretty peaceful and largely unaware of the confrontations going on around them. The roving bands were spreading out and actually herding the pigs toward the main crowd. The 6 o'clock news clearly needed a different perspective on this hoot of a riot.

"And what is exactly the thing that needs watching?" I kept digging.

New clouds of tear gas began erupting all around the protestors and other explosions could be heard as the bands of cops started moving aggressively toward the crowd. The wail of sirens became a constant cacophony of every conceivable type of siren used on government and emergency vehicles. I looked up quickly in response to a new sound, the now familiar *pockita-pockita* of Vietnam-surplus Huey's. Interesting and ugly photo-ops were about to happen.

"Oh, you know," he responded without taking his eyes off the scene unfolding in front of us. "The usual stuff like traitors, foreign insurgents, saboteurs, and of course your run of the mill long-haired hippie communist agitator."

I stopped taking pictures for a second while I looked over at Steve to see his reaction to his remark. We both had modestly long hair, slightly disheveled and over the collar. Nothing radical compared to most other college students and young graduates, but we both knew that when the authorities or the news media used the term *hippie* it was always code for "beat the insubordinate little bastards senseless."

That's why my friends and I never became full-fledged hippies. We considered ourselves to be Freaks. Freaks and hippies were similar, but different in a couple of minor ways. A freak wasn't a peace-loving vegetarian guru-following flower child. We didn't mind them. We even thought they were cute and needed protecting. They just didn't have a good grasp on reality, which is what a Freak was always supremely aware of, especially during massive self-administered drug therapy.

"I don't mean you, of course," he backpedaled. "After all, you're government employees too. I'm sure this whole thing about long hair and defying lawful authority will pass. Don't you?"

"Yeah," I answered, "freedom's just a fad. We both can't wait for the day that we cut our hair and buy a button-down white shirt with a skinny tie so we can look just like all the right people."

Steve burst out laughing and then caught himself short as he realized the guy might be taking all this seriously. We still didn't know who the hell he was and I was getting bored with this cat and mouse game.

"By the way," I said stepping closer to the guy, "my name's George and this is Harry." I held out my free hand in a gesture of greeting,

"Good to meet you, Cowboy."

He grasped my hand with a deliberately tight grip, I'm sure just to show off his military-inflated macho muscles. He let go of my hand, now highly compressed and hurting as the bones slowly popped back into their original positions. He stepped over to Steve and pulled the same stunt.

"Good to meet you too, Steve."

I could have sworn he looked back at me briefly with a wink, but I couldn't be certain, as just then I heard more explosions nearby.

I started to feel a slight tinge burning around my ears at being caught in such a bold-faced lie. I tried to get past it quickly by asking him a clever question.

"And you are…?"

"You can call me Karl," he responded quickly, holding onto his broad grin, which made me doubt him even more, of course.

Who was this weirdo who knew us by name and had apparently been watching us from inside the building?

"You don't have to worry about me; I have nothing to do with the local authorities. I was just curious about this demonstration. I've never seen one up close before. You know, been busy with bigger fish in a much bigger ocean," he explained raising his binoculars once more to study the western horizon.

"So you've been to Vietnam?" I hazarded and returned my attention to the sound of more distant explosions.

The crowd of students and protestors was starting to swell noticeably around the riot cops who were being backed into a small cluster of buildings belonging to Midland Chemical Company, a local mega-agriculture giant cloaked in layers of rumor and mongrels. A single jungle-green Huey circled slowly overhead, probably radioing the obvious situation on the ground to the poor bastards down there in the middle of what was clearly all hell breaking loose.

"Sure, I spent some time there along with a bunch of other places. Everyone who cares about stopping the communist menace has been there, except for you students with your disgraceful deferments. Some people think you're cowards and traitors for giving aid and comfort to the enemy."

I looked around just to make sure we were still alone and he wasn't pulling any hidden weapons. He continued to study the confrontation developing in the distance, seemingly without much interest in us. For a second, I caught Steve's eye. He just shrugged ignorance which I emphatically echoed.

"I don't think that, of course, but there are some people in very high places who don't appreciate the fact that you're so unappreciative of this glorious little war we've given you. You're missing out on a once-in-a-lifetime opportunity to make a heroic sacrifice for your country."

He took the binoculars away from his face for a second so he could beam his big handsome smile at us, letting us know exactly zilch concerning his veracity. I had a flash of a well-fed cat playing with the little-white-mouse birthday present from his sick owner. Instead of just dispatching the rodent naturally, the cat, having lost all of its killer instincts, played roughly with the lively little toy until he literally mauled it to death. Even then, the cat didn't eat the poor thing. It lost all interest when the mouse stopped moving.

"My brother's been to Vietnam," I volunteered without thinking it through. "He's a captain in Special Forces. He runs an A-team in the Montagnard region along the Vietcong trail."

"Yeah, I know," he replied casually, still studying smoky clashes in the distance.

That was unexpected. I wasn't sure what to say next. This was getting way too spooky for my taste. Steve nudged me out of my brief stupor and pointed up the hill to the north end where we could see some flags waving above a rag-tag group coming down the middle of the road. As I took pictures of this new development, I noticed it wasn't just a small group of demonstrators taking the long way around to North Campus. It was an organized march of about twenty people wide, spread across the whole two-lane road, with more protestors appearing over the hill behind them. Row after row of reinforcements were coming to the aid of their comrades under siege.

"So you know my brother?" I tried not to show surprise.

My brother thought he was hot shit in the Army, so I wouldn't have been all that surprised if this guy knew of him or had heard of his exploits in 'Nam. He'd bragged to me about how he sometimes spent nights stalking the Ho Chi Min trail in the mountains along the border where it popped out of Cambodia and into Vietnam. He claimed a dozen kills (verified by counting the ears he kept on a string and dividing the total by two) up close and personal with nothing but blackface and his favorite combat knife, dispatching teenage recruits with little or no military training as if it were a great feat of heroic proportions. Obviously, he hadn't read the part about desperate citizen soldiers defending their homeland against a wicked colonial military threat from beyond the sea.

"Not professionally, you understand, but we've talked on occasion. You know, shooting the breeze about work-related stuff after a long day. He's an officer and I worked there for a private contractor."

"So, you met him at the officer's club in Saigon?" I blurted the obvious.

My brother was known for his use of the officer's club to further his brazen self-promotion with higher-ranking officers. Most people just called it sucking up.

This time I studied him slyly out of my non-camera eye as he glanced deliberately in my direction with just a hint of surprise. He returned quickly to his nonchalant surveillance of the distant action. I concluded he was a government professional all right, but I couldn't tell what kind.

"How did you know?" he finally responded.

"Lucky guess," I explained calmly. "My brother likes to hang out in the officer's club of whatever military hellhole he ends up in, especially if it's a war zone where you're only a heartbeat away from hero status, depending largely on who you regularly get drunk with. He never let a drunken career-suck-up moment pass him by."

There. I said it. I had a sour relationship with the military going all the way back to when I was forced by threats of imprisonment to register for the draft at age eighteen. I tried to convince my local draft board that they really didn't want someone like me to be given orders to die or be killed after he was trained to kill dispassionately and then armed to the teeth. Who knows? I might think the guy behind me yelling insane orders is the most direct threat to my well-being and, understandably, I might mistake him for the enemy. Happens all the time in the fog of battle. It seemed obvious to me and everyone who knew me that I was not good military material.

Basically no one in their right mind has ever put his life or fortune in the hands of soldiers forced to fight against their will. Putting your life on the line for an idea you disagree with is nuts; it can only end badly. Real soldiers should either be highly trained well-paid professionals, or citizen-soldiers defending their freedoms and homes. To us, dying because some old fart decided it was your turn was crazier than the worst acid trip imaginable.

Forcing young men to fight against their will, especially in the name of some insane excuse like political dominoes, was just plain un-American to us, the true sons of liberty and guardians of freedom. We weren't about to become ignorant sheep led to the slaughter. It was clear they needed the war to fuel their corruption and cover the government looters' tracks. Nonetheless, here we were in the last half of the twentieth century with the entire Pentagon, White House, Capitol Hill, and the whole military-industrial-complex, seemingly dumb as dirt but getting away with the biggest scam in history! Obviously, someone read Orwell's *1984* and thought, *why wait another ten years?*

Their bloodsucking business plan was as old as the hills and just as simpleminded. Keep the people's attention diverted by trumped-up wars—ritualistic or full-blown—then loot the national treasury at leisure, and usually with the full cooperation and support of the so-called democratic electorate. Yes, that same government described in the Constitution: the one sworn to protect our lives, our liberty and our pursuit of profit; the one we trust with our taxes, to spend them wisely and use for the good of all the nation's people. Was it possible that government might actually be a tyrant disguised as a super patriot? Could the unthinkable be true? Could we be as gullible as the German people of the 1930s? I was beginning to think Hitler wasn't a uniquely random occurrence as we all might have assumed.

Besides, I came from a long line of closet anarchists and pacifists. You know, the same ideas that in the last few centuries got a lot of people kicked out of the Old World and sent over here in the first place. Ever since my great-grandfather volunteered for the Civil War and got his horse and leg shot out from under him, captured, leg amputated, thrown in Andersonville, and finally escaped, my family has subsequently tried to stay as far away from war as practicable. Then my insane brother became a career Army officer and decides I need to be turned over to the FBI for suspicion of providing aid to the enemy and possible sedition, whatever that fucking means. I guess we basically just disagreed on who the real enemy was.

So I didn't pay much attention to my brother in these matters. After all, I'd seen him soil his underwear one time when he accidently blew a hole in the roof of his car with an 'unloaded' double barrel shotgun. I thought I'd never stop laughing at the time. You just can't take a bumbling car-killer seriously when it comes to defining higher-level concepts, like patriotism and duty, or survival of the fittest, all of which he was convinced he exercised unique control.

Steve jabbed me in my ribs while I was trying to ignore our uninvited new friend from across the chasm. He pointed to an apparently lonely patrol car with its flashing bubble machines turned up to carnival-ride level, off to the south of where the demonstration was growing even more chaotic. The squad car was rapidly being surrounded by roaming bands of demonstrators, making its escape impossible. I focused on it just in time to snap a picture of the officer, who looked embarrassed, making his undignified getaway on foot. It didn't take the crowd long to start rocking the cruiser back and forth until it rolled over on its top, whereupon the flashing lights and new artificial electronic siren stopped their pitiful demands that all must fear and obey authority.

"It's property destruction now," our friend concluded coolly, with no discernible emotion one way or the other.

"Like you guys need a reason to arrest anyone," I countered.

"I told you I'm not in enforcement. I'm in security and mostly just the intelligence side. I leave the enforcement up to trained professionals."

"We know how that works. The cops come from the same class of people as those who become violent criminals. The only difference is one kind of thug does it for the government pension and immunity from prosecution, while the other does it for fun. Haven't you read *A Clockwork Orange*?"

"I would be shocked to think that all you demonstrators are doing this just for the hell of it."

"You could say that, but we also care a great deal about two things you probably can't even imagine."

He paused. "What, pray tell, would that be?" he almost sneered back.

"Equal rights and justice," I fired back. "You know, all that stuff contained in something called the Constitution."

"The Constitution is whatever our side says it is. You should know that. Equal rights and justice are just technical terms. It's up to the powers-that-be to define them as they see fit."

I started to feel uncomfortable with this crap. He was beginning to preach the same line of bullshit lies that got our country into this mess in the first place. I might as well try to carry on a coherent conversation with a foul-mouthed brothel parrot. I'd learned early on that once someone becomes a *True Believer*, factual reality and logical reasoning are no longer necessary thinking tools.

The stranger let his binoculars drop and dangle around his neck as he turned to stare directly at me. Then he very deliberately took a small notepad from his shirt pocket, fiddled with a ballpoint pen, and finally wrote something in his little book.

Steve took his binoculars off the action, which was now just a couple of buildings away from ours. He looked at the intruder, then turned to me with a slight grimace. I nodded and made a surreptitious motion indicating it was time to leave. The tear gas was beginning to drift up to our level and was now spreading in all directions. We could smell the acrid chemicals long before the greyish-brown cloud drifted close enough to trigger any gagging reflex. We quietly headed for the ladder.

"Don't forget to lock the door behind you!" I hollered out as I ducked below the parapet and out of the weirdo's view. Steve's head disappeared into the access hatch as I ran across the gravelly roof to catch up.

"Take it easy," the stranger yelled down at us as we fled into the stairwell. "If I see your brother again, I'll give him your best!"

I didn't answer as I was already through the hatchway taking three rungs at a time and sliding down to the second-floor landing. I caught up to Steve bounding down the stairs to the back entrance and my truck parked just outside. As we left the building, Steve carefully locked the big glass double doors and I scanned the area trying to spy a car belonging to the weirdo government guy who knew way too much about me. I couldn't see any other vehicle anywhere near the lab, at least not on this side of the building.

"Do you see any cars around that might belong to that character?" I asked as we settled into the truck. I started the engine and kicked on my stereo, which just happened to be playing *Sympathy for the Devil.*

"Nothing over here. Maybe he parked it on the other side of the building, or in some other parking lot," Steve said

He jabbed his thumb toward the front of the building, which also included the general direction of the mounting action. "Where to now?"

I gunned the engine squealing the tires some as we exited the rear lot onto a side street. At ground level, we couldn't tell where the demonstrators were congregating anymore but we could definitely see two distinct clouds of sickeningly grey-green haze hovering over two different areas to the west.

"Grab the film camera and we'll go in for some dramatic close-ups."

"We don't have gas masks. You're crazy!" Steve yelled back.

"We'll stay behind the police lines. We have press passes and they usually toss that crap downwind so they don't gas themselves. Besides, if there are any masks lying around, perhaps we can expropriate a couple."

"I'll stick with my crazy assessment anyway," Steve countered.

I threaded the truck through several parking lots, trying to stay clear of the main roads that skirted the edges of the modern park-like setting. Occasionally, I had to navigate over concrete medians or landscaped strips between adjacent lots but eventually we spotted a crowd of police vehicles parked haphazardly around a few of those mysterious grey-green buses. We had arrived at the center of the action.

I had a wooden trap case mounted partially behind the passenger seat and accessible from the front through the gap between the seats. I'd replaced the original bench seat shortly after installing the big V-8 with two very nice leather bucket seats from a Mazda sports car that my friend Bill was chopping up for parts in an insurance scam. I had to mount them on short steel rails to get the height I needed to see over the steering wheel in the big truck. The gap between the two seats gave me easy access to the rear compartment where I'd installed a raised platform bed with storage underneath on one side and on the other, a gadget box/table where I kept my essential gear including cameras, lenses, and film.

I pulled out a leather case where I kept my old beat-up Bolex H-16 motion picture camera. I already had it loaded with some free, out-of-date 100-foot Kodachrome daylight film given to me about three months earlier by a local NCAA photographer; it was probably long overdue to be exposed. I wasn't sure where I'd get the money to develop it but since it was just lying around our basement slowly getting fogged by the constant bombardment of cosmic rays, I figured I might as well expose it if there was any suitable action justifying the cost. This little demonstration appeared to be shaping up in that direction.

I handed Steve my Nikon. "Cover my ass as usual," I reminded him. I'd learned from the pros that you never go into a volatile situation alone. They can come at you from any direction, so you always need to work in pairs. Back-to-back, we could cover the whole 360-degree view and not get ourselves waylaid while focusing on other people getting beat to shit.

"Here." I handed him a bright yellow badge with a big blue M, boldly proclaiming Working Press across its front. "Pin this on your shirt where it can be seen."

It also carried the University's official seal so the local cops usually thought we were just paid administration spies. But in fact, in a way, we were spies for the other side. At least our sympathies were always with the students, even when they were bratty, little spoiled, white middle-class punks vandalizing the very same institutions their parents had sent them to at great expense. Some ancient Greek had cautioned people about getting what they think they want. But on the contrary, I found it far more interesting than working for a living.

I screwed on my favorite 10:1 zoom lens and gave the spring motor a final crank to make sure I had the full 20-second run time. The Bolex was made in Switzerland by precision clockmakers who built mechanisms that could work on the moon. Who the fuck cared, but it was rugged and portable, which is what it was all about and why it was the favorite 16mm film camera for *National Geographic* expeditions or covering wars. Besides, at a thousand dollars, it was about the only 16mm camera I could possibly afford. I had one of those new Japanese high-tech Super-8 movie cameras too, which was way more affordable, but the recorded image quality was way too fuzzy to use even on tiny boob tubes.

"Okay," I said to Steve as I opened the truck door. "Let's do this."

He had an unusually grim look on his face. We'd seen lots of demonstrations in Ann Arbor over the last few years, but this one was big and more chaotic than any we could recall. The cops were getting better at busting them up; this one, however, seemed to be in freefall.

The Vietnam War might be winding down, but the atrocities and our country shenanigans still seemed to multiply under the Nix-goon administration; a new crop of Green-Peacers and anti-government anarchists were stepping in for the old-guard civil rights activists and student anti-war groups. The message was getting diluted, but the movement was getting bigger. Big enough to goad the federal government into sending military-style weapons, riot gear, armored assault vehicles, and even helicopters to college-town police departments.

The local cops were arming up as if there was a revolution coming. Little did they know how close they'd already come to starting one and how much they were overreacting now at this demonstration. We were just happy not to see the student-hating, trigger-happy National Guard who'd already shot four dead in Ohio.

I headed toward the near end of the police line facing the marchers. The cops were lined up two deep in ranks about fifty or sixty wide, spanning the main road. They were blocking a crowd of several thousand demonstrators also aligned in sixty-foot-wide ranks, but whose depth stretched into the distance. Apparently, the crowd wanted to march down the road that the cops were blocking.

This kind of situation happened often with demonstrations. Somebody would forget to get a parade permit or describe the wrong route for the march or, more likely, the demonstrators would decide they didn't need no stinkin' permit and the cops would decide to cut the crap and just bust some heads. This one seemed to be shaping up as the latter.

Steve closed in beside me as I started holding the camera up to my face, pretending to be filming. Usually people didn't get overly frisky with the cameraman when the camera might be already recording their behavior. In a war zone this doesn't work so well, as they are much more inclined to just shoot you and run a tank over the camera. In America, both sides still respected the 5 o'clock news and didn't want to see their actual actions displayed for everyone to see for themselves.

"Follow me close," I said as I sidestepped a small mound of trash. "Keep using your camera like you're some rich magazine reporter with an unlimited film budget."

"Gotcha!" Steve hissed back without taking his eyes out from behind the camera. I could see, however, that one eye was looking through the lens while the other eye was actually scanning everything else peripherally. He had learned the war-cameraman technique.

I spotted a short line of patrol cars parked off to one side where the cop defensive line was nailing its left flank. Demonstrators on that side were thin so I decided to move up to a gap between the patrol cars to see if I could get a shot from no-man's-land, between the two sides. I wanted to capture both the pig's indistinguishable uniformed robotic menacing appearances and the brazen bare-chested, long-haired agitators opposing them armed only with their ideas and social consciousness. A caption like 'Jackbooted Thugs Advance on Concerned Students" with shots of fully armored Storm troopers attacking peaceful kids always made good copy, sold lots of newspapers, and made TV news sponsors happy.

I felt a jab in my back. I turned to Steve and he simply jabbed his lens in a particular direction. His focus ended abruptly about five hundred yards away at as curious cluster of out-of-place people standing in a tight little group facing us and, apparently, all staring right back. They looked like suits, except perhaps missing important parts of their uniforms—like jackets and ties. Couldn't be feds, I thought. Too much diversity.

More screaming and shouting started across the street and on the opposite side of the police line. Something was happening. As we neared the patrol cars, I spotted the gap I'd seen earlier, between two of them, and motioned to Steve to check it out. I focused my camera meanwhile on the group of suits behind us and squeezed the shutter button. The distinctive whirring sound of Swiss precision machinery overrode the noise of the surrounding mayhem. I slowly zoomed in as close as the lens would allow. What I saw made no sense.

I had a nasty thought that this was becoming a little too surreal, with strangers on rooftops who knew my name and academic-types convening for a seminar amidst a riot. It instantly brought to mind Hunter Thompson, *Fear and Loathing* and Dr. Gonzo.

Was I recording the event or was I actually the event? Only drugs and intense alcohol analysis would tell.

I counted a total of five people, two young men, two older men and one stout but young-looking female. What looked so odd was the fact that one of the younger guys had really long hair. Not the kind of hair you could grow in just a couple of years, and definitely not a wig. It was black, actually stringy, and interlaced with naturally spiraling curls separating long, windblown strands. The only other such people with that kind of hair and the tall skinny build were either rock musicians or one of their cocaine-riddled promoters.

Steve jerked me around toward the confronting lines of cops and students just as the Bolex's spring motor ground to an abrupt stop. A speed-governor instantly shuts down the camera movement if its spring-driven motor can no longer maintain the required 24 exposures per second.

Damn! I looked up from the viewfinder just in time to see the two opposing lines make contact. I began frantically rewinding the spring motor and both of us instinctively ducked behind the nearest parked patrol car just as a barrage of tear gas canisters came flying from the ranks of regular uniformed pigs dispersed behind the rigid wall of riot shields and heavily armored riot pigs. The tear gas assault was immediately followed by the distinctive sound of aluminum bats hitting flesh, like cannibals drumming to a feast, and intense grunting sounds accompanying each sickening thud of a club crushing flesh and bones.

The rapidly rotating tear gas canisters left ugly brown spiraling smoke trails as they arced high above the struggling front ranks, now locked in a *push-me push-you* schoolyard game of carnage. As they hit the ground, cans of caustic poison exploded amid demonstrators, pushing puffy clouds of greenish-grey smoke into every bodily crack and crevice within range. The stench hit us like boiling battery acid.

Waves of demonstrators radiated away from each cloudburst of poison like swells emanating from boulders dropped into a lake. The wave that moved in the direction of the front lines created just enough impetus to push some battered and bloody bodies right through the cop lines. The Zombies were loose and behind the pig line!

Nothing puts the fear of failure into a pig's heart more than having a pissed-off, wounded student-agitator behind his back. If they can isolate you, like clever predators that separate a lame buffalo from the herd, a surrounded cop is going to get punished, both now by the crowd and later by his own kind as they instinctively devour their weak.

We had a great vantage point as we carelessly burned film. The tear gas was beginning to spread viciously, repelling demonstrators and pigs in all directions. The cops were quickly sealing the holes in their skirmish line with additional reserves arriving from the direction of the parked buses.

Steve stopped to tie a neckerchief around his nose and mouth like an Old West bandito. It didn't really help all that much, but you felt a need to do something to show you were doing what you could to bear the stench and not run like a chicken. I didn't have a neckerchief, so I had to brave it out barefaced, occasionally poking my nose into the crook of my elbow to breathe through my shirtsleeve. We decided to attack in another direction, specifically the way we'd just come. We looked around for a safe escape route devoid of warring parties and, hopefully, noxious gas, but could see very little.

"Let's head over there next to that building," I said, nodding in the direction I thought might be right. "It looks a little upwind and it should lead back to the truck."

"Sounds good to me," Steve agreed, coughing.

We began moving out carefully, dodging a few fleeing demonstrators being chased by roving gangs of riot cops employing the classic tactic of *divide and beat-the-crap out of anybody you can catch*. We started running, zigzagging, staying low and holding our cameras high as a flag of truce, hopefully for both sides to respect. Or not.

"Hey! Stop! Stop right there!"

That was too loud and obviously directed at us. It came from a non-riot-geared cop, lightly dressed actually, as if he'd just stepped out for coffee and donuts. He was looking directly at us, not ten yards away. The working press, however, never assume they need attention from the cops. It was best to ignore them and go on about your business. Besides, I could always claim that I couldn't hear him for all the noise.

"Hold up, I need to talk to you two," he yelled again, as he hurried toward us.

Steve looked over at me with a question in his face. I looked back stupid-like, shrugging my shoulders, but still secretly hoping we could somehow make good our escape. I accelerated my rapid gait while panning the camera and ignoring the pig, hoping he was after someone else.

The cop continued hollering at us and suddenly broke into a run at a trajectory designed to intercept us alongside the last building. *Damn!* I did the mental calculation, coming up with a unfavorable result: *He was going to cut us off.*

"Hold up a minute! I just need to talk," he yelled again.

He closed the distance between us and our only obvious escape route.

I reached over and grabbed Steve by the same arm as he was carrying the Nikon with and pulled him up short. I stopped to accommodate the pig and find out what the hell went wrong whereby I attracted such undivided official attention in the first place. I just hoped it wasn't some forgotten old arrest warrant from some forgotten former life.

I whirled around with the Bolex to my face and pressed the shutter button. I caught about five seconds of the dogged pig running headlong toward us looking straight into the camera with a bemused look on his face, realizing too late that he was rushing headlong to nowhere for nothing and having it all recorded on film. As he made an ungainly stop, he obviously wasn't happy; nonetheless, he appeared to be under some kind of remote control that prevented him from losing his schooled composure and lashing out as the naturally violent psychopath he probably was—seething just barely below his phony façade of cop professionalism.

"I work for the Mayor," he said after catching his breath. He held his hands up, palms out, to show he had no concealed clubs or brass knuckles. I couldn't help but take notice of the big .45 auto holstered high on his hip, clearly to accommodate someone who normally sits at a desk. So he was a desk pig, not a street thug pig. *He's out of his territory!*

"We're on official press business," I said reciting the standard immunity mantra that almost never worked anyway, "and people know where we are." It was more of an empty epitaph or famous last saying, rather than an honest excuse for being in the right place at the worst possible time.

"I understand that," he said as he continued approaching us, waving extending arms palms down in an exaggerated calming gesture. "I just need to deliver a message and give you this."

He reached into his breast pocket with his left hand. I flinched and Steve cringed visibly as we both anticipated possible tear gas spray. He pulled out something smaller and offered me what looked like a business card.

"The mayor and his select committee on university relations saw you roaming around down here with a film camera. One of his members apparently recognized you and requested that you give him a call."

He held out the card and approached me slowly. Steve edged off to one side and took a couple more shots of the advancing pig with the Nikon.

"Cut that out!" the cop demanded as he stopped and glared at Steve. Steve looked over at me nervously and I shrugged again. Cops in the middle of a near, or developing, riot usually aren't prone to handing out business cards. I was nervous too, but now more curious than wise.

"Who's this guy hanging out with the mayor's select gang?" I asked as I boldly stepped up to him.

He ignored my question and again held out the card in my direction. I took it. He just glowered at me then turned and hurriedly walked away as if he was actually needed somewhere. I looked back at the grassy knoll between parking lots where we'd seen the suits, but observed it was now empty. There was nothing to see but blue and dark grey uniforms running in every direction, chasing loose students. The pasty brown and yellow cloud seemed to be slowly dissipating.

The crowd on the other side of the police lines, or what was left of them, was steadily growing noisier. Now I heard the sound of breaking glass. Lots of glass. I turned to Steve and motioned toward the hordes of demonstrators streaming past a line of riot police. Clearly outnumbered by hundreds-to-one, and probably soon to be completely surrounded by protestors, the cops looked as menacingly, as they likely could muster. If they didn't attack in some other direction soon and get the hell out of here, things could get ugly. I already had most of it on film and wasn't inclined to wait around to find out who was going to win. It wasn't about that anyway.

Another tear gas bomb came wobbling over the crowds in our general direction. Steve yelled, *Let's move it*, and began running low and zigzagging to avoid pockets of gas and struggling combatants. I *whooped* in agreement and quickly took off after him, heading for the corner of a building that concealed a parking area just beyond, where we'd stashed my truck.

We made it to the truck just in time to see the unmarked military helicopter swoop down low over the same area we'd just photographed and escaped from. I was able to take a quick shot of the Huey's open door at the moment some guy started throwing out what looked like large canisters. The first explosion was loud and accompanied by a brilliant flash of yellow light that illuminated tops of surrounding buildings and trees. Then several more detonated in quick succession.

I yelled over to Steve, "Phosphorous flash grenades! Time to get the fuck outta here!"

We jumped in the truck and took off on the most direct cross-country route I could think of to get us back to the Huron River bridge. I skirted around the police lines by making a wide sweep through the outlying areas of North Campus, four-wheeling over numerous parking lot islands and grassy median strips. Steve kept up a constant excited chatter, pointing out any suspicious groups of people wandering within our view, which I did my best to avoid. We were both so high on adrenaline we could probably have run a four-minute mile backward.

Each time he pointed and yelled, "There's another bunch over there!" I'd react by swerving in the opposite direction, which would usually take us over sculpted concrete obstructions designed to prevent exactly what we were doing. I didn't have to, but it seemed totally appropriate to leave a few tire tracks across the military-industrial-complex's precisely manicured grass.

Steve continued taking pictures out his open passenger window as I drove like a backwoods four-wheel maniac looking for the fastest way out of the parking lot rat-maze. Curbs and grass knolls were mere inconveniences for the big truck and we were soon headed south on Huron Drive back to the main campus and Steve's house.

I lit up a big doobie as soon as we were safely out of the riot cop's grasp and across the river. Cop cars were buzzing around town like bees after their hive's been kicked over, even here on the peaceful side of the river. They seemed to have no interest in us as we slowly cruised back toward the main campus and relative sanity.

We could see few students on Main Campus and surprisingly few vehicles. I guess everybody was watching the live entertainment from better vantage points. I turned into the alley behind one of the main administration buildings, which also housed the offices of the *Michigan Daily*. I stopped at a large rear fire door and hit the horn in three short blasts.

Steve hurriedly unloaded his last roll of exposed film from my Nikon while I grabbed a changing bag and immediately began to work on unloading the Bolex. By the time one of the copy assistants made it down from the third floor and opened the alley door, we both had our film in cans, labeled and ready for the lab. I had a standing agreement with the *Daily's* photo editor that they could forward without my approval any shots he deemed suitable for the wire. I hadn't made the local news yet, except for some still shots now and then. But this 16mm footage might be a strong candidate for the Detroit TV news later tonight or possibly even the national news.

"I think its Coors time," Steve said.

We pulled out of the alley and headed back to his house and my rented bedroom. I heartily agreed and parked the truck in its usual spot, behind a big tree in the small lot next door where it couldn't be seen from the street. Any pissed-off cops out cruising with my truck's description would have a little harder time trying to shoot out my tires or towing it for public safety. No sense giving the enemy any advantage if I could help it.

The film turned out to be very useful. We'd actually documented some extremely vicious actions on the part of the newly hired Gestapo-looking riot cops. It turned out later, a newspaper reported, that they'd been cast in this new role with little or no training and most were barely cooled down from escaping Vietnam alive. Kent State was not an unfortunate accident. The fucking Ohio National Guard was lethally armed and completely out of control.

These poor bastards were probably high-school-dropout killer vets, most likely from remote rural or inner city high schools, still not old enough to drink yet each one a budding alcoholic who didn't particularly discern any significant difference between American college students and the Viet Cong he was recently trying to kill. Trained killers finally had a professional career path. I put it on a par with throwing gas on a Boy Scout's campfire after it's already burning.

Kent State had just happened the previous spring so it was still on everybody's mind. It was the primary reason my friends and I became interested in, of all things, the NRA, cheap WWII Argentine Mausers, cases of dirt-cheap Canadian military-surplus ammo, Ruger Blackhawks and Super Blackhawk magnum revolvers and, my favorite, the good old standby Colt Commander .45 caliber semiautomatic pistol, accurized if you could afford it.

Most of us knew lots of returning Vietnam vets, including some with monkeys on their backs and a spare M-16 or souvenir AK-47 they were willing to trade for one more poppy fix.

We considered ourselves to be armed and dangerous flower children. We believed in peace, love, and harmony as guaranteed by those great American purveyors of equality and justice: Messrs. Smith and Wesson.

Most of our big bad nasty rifles were safely stashed away in unmarked cairns scattered around the county, usually among friends. But we liked to sleep up close and personal with our favorite pistols. The times may be changin', but I believe it always pays to be a fully prepared hippie-freak boy scout.

CHAPTER SIX

CLOSE ENOUGH FOR ROCK & ROLL

"But first, are you experienced?
Ah! Have you ever been experienced?"

Jimi Hendrix
"Are You Experienced"
1967

More important than who won the Battle of North Campus, the business card turned out to be from Pete Andrews, the young local Rock & Roll promoter, booking agent, and wanna-be band manager. Pete's territory was staked out early in life when local high school Rock & Roll bands started playing student bars. He provided all the rock talent that appeared in literally every venue in town, mostly bars, a few coffee shops that featured live music, and a dancehall or two, as well as the odd fraternity party, wedding, or funeral.

Pete's covetous eyes, however, were glued to the U of M budget, which allocated a huge amount each year for student entertainment. The university not only had the booking money, they also had the largest auditoriums in this part of the state, not to mention a 13,500-seat indoor arena and a 100,000-capacity outdoor stadium. The problem was their internal booking agent was still stuck in the '50s and scheduled shows that were now spectacularly unappreciated and similarly unattended. Teens simply had no interest in seeing how long someone could keep a plate spinning on a stick or glitzy Las Vegas family acts out on tour. It was budget murder by bad art.

Pete was never one to think small. He wanted to stage another Woodstock-type rock festival except he was convinced that, unlike those hapless promoters, he could make money doing it. He and John Sinclair, leader of the radical White Panther Party, were scheming to bring a giant music festival to Ann Arbor featuring the only bands they could afford: big city blues bands, Deep South Delta blues bands, and any funky old Black singer this side of New Orleans.

After all, Ann Arbor was virtually next door to Detroit, one of the hottest cities in the country for Rock & Roll. Home to Motown plus Bob Seger and the Silver Bullet Band, the James Gang and Grand Funk Railroad who were knocking them dead on the radio, in record sales and, now, national concert tours. Kids would drive hundreds of miles, camp out in the rain and put up with otherwise intolerable conditions just to see their favorite performers live in concert, with one of those new high-powered stereo PA systems that could blow your ears right off your head while blowing your mind into another reality.

The front of the card had all his business information, but on the back, I found just a simple hand-scrawled phone number with the arrogant, terse message: 'call me.'

Steve laughed when he saw the card. "That doesn't sound like Pete. If it is, he's keeping some pretty strange company. His hair alone should put him solidly on the pigs' radar. And, the only reason we pay so much for drugs around here is that he and his entourage consume them all."

"Yeah. I wonder if his pal, John Sinclair knows about this. Might seem to John that his business buddy's cavorting with the enemy."

"What 'n the world could he be up to?" Steve asked, although he knew the answer no doubt had something to do with money. Unlike most counterculture types who, like us, spurned the relentless quest for greed-money, Pete, with his long hair and penchant for expensive drugs, seemed to be someone simply disguised as one of us so he could cash in on the local movement by fulfilling its unmet needs and desires. Like a music pimp to the culturally starved natives.

John Sinclair might have been only marginally better, as he made money off both a head shop/record store he ran in Dearborn and the White Panther Party, a political group he ran as a student commune in one of Ann Arbor's old fraternity houses just south of campus. He later rebranded it the *Rainbow Peoples Party* after the Black version of his first-choice name got a bad reputation for actually standing up for their legal rights. The oversized Victorian house on Hill Street that accommodated the commune quickly became the focal point for a multitude of radical activities supporting righteous causes such as achieving equal rights for blacks, women, and all minorities, and exposing the military and industrial corruption of our democracy. The Party also needed cash, so they put on loud raucous rock concerts and, like most of us, made quiet drug deals on the side.

We'd photographed some of Sinclair's people earlier in the day when we were covering the confrontation at North Campus. The juxtaposition of their roles sort of tripped my head and left me wandering in fields of bewilderment and non-drug-induced delirium.

Steve and I agreed the rest of the day was pretty much shot. There was a good chance our pictures would make the five o'clock news, but that was several hours away. I pulled out my last two hits of Owsley windowpane acid, laid on me by someone in Ken Kesey's Prankster bus when it rolled through town recently, and gave one to Steve. A little chemical assistance in ironing out our confusion might help shed some light on this recent turn of events.

I popped a couple of beers for us as Steve downed one pane and I the other. *Cheers*, we said, bumping our Coors cans and guzzling heartily. Then I kicked on the six-foot video projector as Steve hit the lights. We spent the rest of the afternoon watching cartoons as we debated all the ramifications of this recent revelation. Something was afoot and it looked maybe like we were going to be a part of it.

The intense colors of Bugs Bunny and Yosemite Sam began to dance off the screen as we settled in for a little trip down

Psychedelic Lane. LSD and big-screen animation were made for each other. Together, it all made sense somehow.

The City of Ann Arbor didn't get a whole lot of praise for its botched handling of the previous day's demonstration at North Campus. Charges and countercharges were flying fast and furiously when I showed up at Pete's office later the next afternoon. There was a crowd of people in his little building, a small single-story white clapboard house converted into low-rent offices, all coming and going with great purpose as if some kind of major event had either happened or was just about to. Suzanne, his super-efficient secretary, was busy as always, coolly and calmly directing the chaotic scene, seemingly with great ease and even poise.

She was a substantial woman who never got rattled or intimidated by all the activity associated with Pete's business. She handled everything with amazing professionalism and diligence, particularly considering who she worked for and what he did, patiently dealing with spoiled imitation superstars in addition to making sure that every little detail of a 10,000-attendance show went off without so much as a hiccup. Pete would obviously be totally lost without her.

Suzanne spotted me as soon as I entered the outer office and waved me over to her desk. She had a phone in one hand with its mouthpiece pressed tightly to her ample bosom, which was her version of putting someone on hold, as she finished giving instructions to somebody standing nearby. When I was able to squeeze through the crowd and get within hearing distance, she pointed at the door to Pete's office and said, "Go right in. He's expecting you." Without so much as a pause to catch her breath, she went right back to giving orders, dispatching people and warming callers on hold with unrealized pleasures.

Without a doubt, she was the brains that kept the reality of doing business in this insane world of loud music on a reasonably straight and even keel. She could deal equally well with longhaired weirdo's, ridiculous egos, irate building managers, lawyers, accountants, and all the rest of the straight and semi-straight people one had to deal with in order to pull off music events for today's demanding, drug-crazed masses. From one perspective, it was all about money, but many others saw it as an exciting revolution not just in music and culture but conceivably even a political one. That's what scared the hell out of the cops. The thought of another street riot like the Chicago Democratic Convention or another concert fiasco like Altamont made everyone very nervous.

As I approached the inner sanctum, the door swung open, revealing Pete himself in all his longhaired glory. Without a pause, he motioned me in. "There you are." He pointed to John Sinclair sitting in one of several well-worn overstuffed armchairs clustered near a huge wooden desk, a relic of another century. Its surface was littered with thousands of scraps of paper, two or three inches deep, presumably notes and memos requiring his immediate attention.

"You know John, right?" he asked. John made a boy-scout salute indicating his presence.

Without waiting for an answer, he continued, "Have a seat," and indicated one of the empty chairs next to John, who seemed to be in another world. John smiled and nodded, rising slightly in his seat. He held out his hand and I shook it.

"Sure," I said threading my way around to my assigned seat.

The place was a mess, with boxes stacked upon boxes of advertising flyers, posters, and who knew what else. In the middle of the whole conglomeration was a low glass coffee table with years of accumulated clutter and what I imagined would be the dregs of innumerable lines of coke and countless amateur attempts at rolling perfect joints. John, sputtering and coughing out a cloud of blue-white smoke, extended a half-smoked joint to me as I sat down.

"Hey," he said in a way of greeting between gasps for air.

"Hey," I said, acknowledging the fact that we'd acknowledged each other.

"Have a hit." He was still offering me a bent ugly-looking doobie of questionable character.

I took the joint, sucked mightily and watched cross-eyed as the bright orange glow ran rapidly down its wrinkly white paper skin to about where my fingers were starting to burn. Pete sat down in a chair across from the two of us with his usual cockeyed smile unfurled across his pasty-white, yet eternally stubbled face. I handed him what was left of the conceivably once-proud joint. He looked at it and promptly dropped it into a giant overflowing ashtray full of roaches, sitting in the center of the coffee table. He reached into a small beaded box next to the ashtray and extracted another pre-rolled gagging-ly huge white cylinder that I can only describe as a marijuana cigar rolled by a taco machine.

"Good shit, huh?" he asked, eyes twinkling, probably thinking I was impressed to be in their presence and sharing the sacred herb.

"Not bad," I said politely while thinking how cheap this crap was compared to the quality buds I'd just flown in recently from Juarez.

"So, what were you doing at the demonstration yesterday?" John demanded.

"I didn't see you there," I answered. "But Pete seemed to be chumming it up with a bunch of pigs," I added, gesturing in his general direction.

When he heard that, Pete almost dropped the giant joint. But he recovered quickly, put on his cordial business face again and proceeded to light the giant joint.

"I know," John said. "I set it up. And for your information, I was there yesterday. I never miss a chance to harass the oppressors."

"From where I was filming, it wasn't all that clear who was harassing who," I countered.

Pete took a long drag on the white cigar and handed it to John who deftly picked the doobie out of Pete's fingers and stuck it in his mouth. He kept looking at me, waiting for some kind of reply, but I was in no hurry to play their game, so I just looked back at John with my usual shit-eating grin. Maybe the half-joint they'd handed me earlier was sort of working because I felt relaxed and ready to play darts with these two half-assed hippies. Their hearts, I guessed, were in the right place, so the rest was probably immaterial.

John passed me the now half-smoked joint and I casually put it to my lips and took another of my famous *suck till you feel purple and turn dizzy* hits. When I finished, I handed it back to Pete who looked at how little was left, again, and casually dropped it into the roaches' graveyard of honor.

"The reason I asked that guy to give you my card," Pete began, "is I recognized you from some of the Sunday concerts in the park. I thought you were helping with the PA there, but when I saw you with the film camera yesterday it dawned on me that you might be just the person we're looking for."

"So why were you filming yesterday's demonstration from behind the police line?" John interjected. "Are you working for them?"

I looked him squarely in the face and did my best to give him the evil eye. "You've got to be kidding. If I worked for them, I'd have much longer hair and I'd be filming you from your side of the street."

Pete let out a loud laugh. "He's got you there, John."

John got a scowl on his face as he reacted to what Pete said. "So you're just freelancing for the highest bidder? Is that it?"

I reached into my breast pocket and brought out a joint of my own.

"Here," I said, holding it out to John. "Light this up. I hate to be wasting your pot on trivial conversation. Let me contribute something to the cause."

John hesitated, looked me in the eye, leaned over and smelled it, caved, then took the bait. "I guess a narc wouldn't be carrying unless he was going to plant it after the bust. And, narcs won't ever smoke in front of a suspect. You're probably cool."

"Trust me," I replied with a sly smile and a wink. "No narc would waste weed like this on the likes of you."

John laughed as both of them visibly relaxed and, discovering his lighter had run out of fuel, fished in his pocket for another one.

"So let me explain," Pete said, easing back into his chair and lacing his fingers together in a pose of sober contemplation. Not a good look for him. "The new mayor is under a lot of pressure from the university to defuse the tension between the students and the city. He asked me if there was some way we could work together to ease the tension and prevent anything from getting out of hand like, you know, like what happened at Kent State."

John took a big toke on my skinny joint and held his breath as he passed it over to Pete. Then he let out a humungous explosion of smoke as his lungs convulsed violently, turning his face as red as a boiled lobster. Pete barely caught the joint before John completely doubled over in a coughing fit. I smiled quietly. The sacred cannabis oil always gets 'em in the end.

"He could call off his dogs and leave us alone," I said with the straightest face I could muster. "The students are just trying to exercise their First Amendment rights of free speech and free assembly. They need to be protecting the demonstrators, not beating them up."

"You don't need to...." John had to pause to cough a couple more times. "...lecture us on the Constitution. Parents are on his ass, the university administration is on his ass, and of course the FBI and state government are on his ass. They all just want it to go away, quietly." He emphasized the quiet part.

"Must be a big ass to accommodate so many people," I noted.

Pete made a muffled choking sound while trying to hold in the smoke. He was still convulsing as he passed the joint over to me. I wasn't sure if he was laughing at what I'd just said or whether he, like John, was coughing from the strong pot.

"The point is," Pete continued after recovering from his little choking spell, "that if the mayor doesn't get things calmed down, the state will step in and God knows what those creeps will do. They have the National Guard who, as you know, are a gang of nasty redneck, hillbilly punks with rifles who'd like nothing better than a clean shot at a bunch of rich longhaired college kids."

I took another one of my famous long drags and prayed my lungs didn't break into spasms like Pete and John's. I could feel my eyes start to water from the intensity of the smoke and I noticed they were both having difficulty controlling their bodies as well. Pete's eyes were seriously watering and noticeably turning red. John was trying to look away as he let out another series of short rasping coughs.

"Looks like we need to grab our six-shooters, Paw, and head for them thar' hills," I said in my finest fake western drawl.

I decided to bogart the joint a bit. I didn't want to have to explain any premature coronaries to the coroner if one of these old hippies croaked on my weed.

"I think (hack!) we have a better (hack!) idea," Pete sputtered between raspy coughs. I loved the contorted looks on their faces as they pretended to be immune to the effects of asphyxiation.

"Can you make a documentary film?" John probed, while Pete got up and headed for a refrigerator that stood next to the door.

Pete was finally able to croak out two more words as he opened the fridge door. "Wanna brewski?" He pulled out two bottles of Bud and looked my way but when I saw what he had, I shook my head.

"Jeez," I muttered under my breath, "haven't these nimrods heard about Coors yet?"

"What kind of documentary?" I asked loudly, perking up and looking back at John.

"We need a film that shows how we run the summer rock concerts in the park," Pete jumped back in,

He popped the caps off the beers with an opener that hung from a string on the side of the fridge. He walked back to our little circle-jerk, handing one of the beers to John as he took a long swig on the other. A noticeable purple haze wafted about chest high in the room.

"Sounds interesting. Who's the intended audience?" I asked.

John took a big gulp of his beer while Pete settled back unsteadily into his well-worn armchair.

"The city needs a documentary film," Pete explained, "so they can advertise and brag about how progressive, effective, and successful a city-sponsored concert series, featuring local Rock & Roll talent in area parks, can be for improving youth relations." I took this to mean, *dampening and diverting student unrest with the only mesmerizing bait that wasn't technically illegal.* At least not yet.

I looked over at John and said, "Is that what you really want to do? Calm the collective outrage? Stifling protests isn't exactly what I thought the Panthers were all about."

"We're not," he said succinctly. "But Pete and I have an idea about how we can make some bread and put Ann Arbor on a map that doesn't involve rioting or shooting students. And, there could be some federal grant money involved."

There it was. The giant pie-in-the-sky for intellectuals. Federal grant money or as we called it, the *Federal Tit-for-Tat.*

"Sounds like you want to do another Woodstock," I conjectured, "only this time with government support. Cool. You do realize, though, that Woodstock didn't make any money and they're still in court fighting over all the damage claims."

"Is that true for the movie, too?" Pete countered with a sly knowing smile.

I thought about it for a moment, staring blankly at the burned-out joint in my hand.

"It was a great film that will someday be a classic," I admitted begrudgingly, as I contemplated my insane jealousy of those bastards who'd scooped the entire underground film industry by simply being in New York when it all came down. Hell, I would kill just for one of those Éclair cameras they used. I was in Chicago at the time, making stupid underground art films that couldn't even get much attention at the Ann Arbor Film Festival, which was famous for the fact they pretty much accepted any film whether in focus or not or whether it was shot with enough light to even expose the film.

"The movie probably didn't make anything directly, but someone down the subsequent ownership rights trail probably will," I conceded.

John leaned over to me and flicked his Bic, which didn't light.

"Need a lighsssh?" he slurred, repeatedly clicking it. But it was hopelessly dead until, magically, it worked one last time.

I looked over at him and saw a shit-eating grin on his face. He was obviously pretty wasted and looking for more. "Okay," I said and leaned over so I could light what was left of the joint I'd been holding. I took a quick puff and handed it to him.

"That doesn't matter to us," Pete continued. "We won't have superstars at a blues and jazz concert, but we need the film so we can convince the city that we can organize and produce a major outdoor event without cops all over the place trying to bust everybody for smoking weed and drinking electric Kool-Aid. We'll control it and keep everything contained inside the fence. They save a hell of a lot of money and we get a helluva party. What more could you ask for?"

"You already do that with the Sunday park concerts," I countered. Then thinking better of it, I added, "I mean, I'll be glad to do the film but it just seems like it may be a big waste of energy for someone."

John had nearly finished the joint I handed him, but as a token gesture he offered what was left to Pete, who waved him off and went on, "We're having a hard time convincing the cops we can pull it off without a major incident. They're convinced it will attract bikers or drug-crazed hooligans, like Altamont, who'll shoot up the place or rape the city fathers' daughters."

"Altamont happened because the idiots hired the Hells Angels to do their security. It doesn't take a fucking rocket scientist to figure that one out. Using Hell Angels was about as smart as using a starving coyote to guard the henhouse."

"You got another one of those?" John asked, indicating the burnt roach he'd just dropped into the overflowing ashtray.

"You really think you can handle another one?" I asked right back.

"Shit," he said, "The day I can't handle another one will be the day I'm dead."

"Okay, it's your funeral."

I handed my last joint to John who promptly lit it up.

Pete laughed. Both of these hippies were getting more stoned than they were used to and that probably was not a good thing. I decided to see if I could pump them for some more information.

"So are you going to hire Smith to run security for this major concert event?"

John took a long hard toke, burning a run down almost half the length of the joint. As he took it from his mouth and leaned forward preparing to hand it to Pete, a huge glowing ember cascaded down from the run and disintegrated on the front of John's shirt and pants. There was smoke everywhere and a frantic little scramble as both John and Pete tried to beat out smoldering cinders on the front of John's clothes while successfully handing off the remains of the joint. What deft and grace! They put out the fires and simultaneously passed the joint like trained professionals.

In awe, I yelled, "Olé!"

"Holy shit, John!" Pete bellowed. "Do I need to get the fire extinguisher?"

"Like you'd know how to use one in the first place," John retorted, still wiping the front of his smoking T-shirt, which now featured several small brown-ringed holes displaying hairy skin behind each crater where the marijuana meteors struck. Pete took a drag on the now misshapen joint and tried licking the hot spot to slow it down while the other side caught up.

"So is Smith going to do the security?" I probed again.

"Not sure," Pete finally gasped after finishing his turn trying to tame the joint. "He may not be acceptable to the cops for maybe obvious reasons."

Everyone pretty much knew what Bill did for a living, though his front was pretty well established. Any casual observer could reasonably conclude, in fact, that he was legitimate businessman. He handled all the little Sunday concerts and had his own organization of supervisors who could effectively herd the Psychedelic Rangers like professional cops, only this time biased in the right direction.

The only seemingly strange thing about Bill was maybe his junkyard dog, Puppity, who he took almost everywhere he went in his white 1972 454-cubic-inch V8 Corvette or, alternately, his gold 1972 454-cubic-inch V8 Buick La Sabre. Puppity was a full-blood Weimaraner, personally trained by Bill to strictly obey his every command up to and including unswervingly ripping out the throat of anyone he might indicate with a casual but meaningful glance. She also hated any stranger who came anywhere near her car and would bark ferociously, snarling and baring a frothing mouthful of jagged pearly whites to snap viciously at the glass from the other side; it always terrorized the shit out of everyone, including nosy cops.

"I'll see what I can do. We may have to organize a superficial group to appease the overlords while we quietly put the right people in all the right places. The main thing is they're giving us more control over running these events."

"Since when do the cops get a vote when it comes to your deal with the mayor?" I asked, attempting to get some intelligence I could share with Bill. "You know he has the contacts and the experience. He monitors the cop radios with an expensive scanner and knows their secrets better than the mayor or even the police chief."

I was disclosing this tiny bit of information as bait in an effort to get Pete to open up. He was in no condition at this point to keep a secret anyway, so I thought it was a good strategy.

"I told the mayor he was the best organizer we had for these events and he said the cops had been watching his house for a few weeks and didn't like what they were seeing."

"What were they seeing?"

"Nothing yet, except Bill seems to keep very strange hours. He leaves the house every night around midnight in his white Corvette and usually doesn't get home until around noon the next day. When they try to follow him, they usually lose him within a few miles of his house. They think he's running drugs in and out of town, but they can't get the goods on him. They even tried to search his house one night while everyone was gone, including the dogs, but still couldn't find anything. Now they think he's probably dealing out of his garage but they don't have anything for sure on him there either. There are rumors that the garage is an insurance chop-shop. He never goes anywhere without an attack dog for company. Do I need to go on?"

"He's got connections and he knows a lot about security and being discreet. He likes his privacy. I'll bet you do too. Sounds like an obvious choice unless you prefer burr-headed patriotic super-paranoid alcoholic semi-psychotic Vietnam vets with uncontrolled acid-type flashbacks, probably armed to the teeth with plenty of old axes to grind."

"You've got a point. I'll see what I can do. Tell him to lay low for a while so nothing jeopardizes our pitch." He looked past me at John with his head slowly nodding off to one side, apparently about to fall asleep. "So, what's a half-hour film going to cost us?" he asked, staring at me pokerfaced.

I tried to explain to him about shooting ratios, location costs, and post-production. Making a professional 16mm color film wasn't cheap, but we were about as cheap as anyone could get. Bottom line, my partner in Chicago and I could guarantee him a finished product at around five thousand dollars a minute.

"Do it for a thousand a minute and we've got a deal."

He held out his hand to shake on it. I just stared at him, flabbergasted at immediately being squeezed beyond belief.

"A thousand dollars a minute isn't even underground student-art-film money! Developing Kodak color motion picture film is expensive. I'm not sure we can even develop it for four thousand a minute!"

"You're a smart guy. I'm sure you can figure it out. We don't have the money to do it Hollywood style. Can't you do it like those guys in New York? I hear they use handheld cameras with that new European film that comes in a green box. What's it called, *Agatha-something*?"

He was probably referring to Agfa-Gevaert film and the underground art nuts in Greenwich Village who didn't even bother to use a camera. They just exposed Agfa film with flashlights and colored cellophane, then foisted it off as New York avant-garde modern art crap. I could do that for a thousand a minute.

"If we can shoot it at 4-to-1 with minimal post-production, I might be able to squeeze it down to twenty-five hundred a minute but I can't guarantee the highest quality."

"There you go," he said gleefully, "close enough for Rock & Roll. You go back to wherever you do this stuff, think about it, and see what you can come up with. In the meantime, I'll see if I can get the city to cough up an extra few grand so you can afford the good stuff."

He held out his right hand again and this time I got up and leaned across the table to shake it.

"I'm not guaranteeing anything but I'll do my best. How about five thousand down now, just to seal the deal and get us started?" I held onto his hand in tight anticipation.

He grabbed my outstretched hand with his left hand too, and began pumping all three and declared, "I can do two now and two more in a couple of weeks. In the meantime, I need you to get started by shooting one of my bands I'll have at the Sunday park concert in two weeks. I need a short film of them performing one of their best numbers to show to promoters and record producers."

"Isn't that extra? You don't expect the city to pay for a promo film as part of this project, do you?"

"Don't worry about the city. You can work it into the film and I'll take care of the rest." He barely paused then added quickly, "You have any more of that weed to sell?"

"I'll see what I can do. Ask me again when you cut the first check."

I turned to leave and noticed John slumped down in the overstuffed chair, head on one shoulder with his tongue hanging out the side of his mouth, drooling spit onto his shirtsleeve. His guttural snoring sounded like a dog trying to growl and gnaw on a huge bone at the same time.

"How much is that going to cost me?" Pete added, as almost an afterthought, as he picked up a couple of rolled joints lying near the overflowing ash tray. He shot me a questioning look as he moved toward John's slouching body.

"I'll need at least five grand to get my partner in Chicago working on finding some equipment and film so we can start shooting right away. I imagine you're going to want us to shoot the rest of the park concerts this summer and, if you pull off the blues festival this fall, then you'll probably want us to include that, too, right?"

"You got that right," he agreed as he slipped the two joints into John's shirt pocket. "This stuff was beginning to give me a headache. John can give it to his minions when he gets back to the Rainbow House. So how much should I add to your check to get a quarter-pound of that stuff right away?"

"Throw in an extra hundred bucks and I'll label it as 'dichroic filters' on the invoice. Nobody, unless they're extremely film knowledgeable, knows what they are anyway and even then they're a little-known but very necessary consumable on every film project."

"I said just a quarter. I can find pounds at that price," he protested.

"And you'll smoke five times as much and still not get as high," I said.

He looked at me a little oddly, probably wondering what the fuck I was doing trying to hype a hipster. Little did he know that what he heard was about as deep as I could shovel it. I'm just not a salesman. I can't lie and get away with it.

"Okay, but I'll remember this." His smile was noticeably strained. "And don't forget to buy enough film to shoot my band doing their latest hit."

"Two takes or three?"

"What?" he asked, straightening up after giving John's shirt pocket a little pat to flatten the two joints and remove any distracting bulges. One could never be too careful during these Nazi police-state times.

"Do you want us to shoot the song twice, first with a long shot and then a second time for close-ups? It usually takes three shots to get the minimum number of alternate viewing angles in order to cut a continuous sequence into something that vaguely resembles an interesting way to waste time staring at a screen. Assuming the song is about three minutes long, we have to either shoot it with multiple cameras synched together, and you won't like that price, or just stage it like a studio recording session and do take after take until you have enough footage to properly mix the shots."

"Four minutes," he corrected. "So, shooting the song three times is better than once? What about four?" he asked casually, winking at me and not really expecting a response but giving me something to think about if I wanted to get paid on time. He walked around behind John's chair and motioned for me to come closer, clearly indicating he wanted to share something private. John started to stir from his little nap as Pete moved toward me. He caught me by the arm and led me into a corner away from the snoozing revolutionary.

"I wasn't going to tell you this, but have you heard of Don Kirshner?" he whispered.

"I've heard of him," I answered carefully, wondering where the hell Pete was going with this. "He's some kind of flashy Rock & Roll promoter in New York."

"He is also a rich son of a bitch, and he and I have been talking about producing regional rock concerts that he'll put on national TV. Do you realize what that means?"

"No," I lied. I had been hearing about this Kirshner guy for some time. Outside of LA, he was probably the most well-known promoter in the country. He had something to do with promoting Woodstock, and that little rain-soaked fiasco was rapidly rewriting the history of rock music, film documentaries, and over-the-top spontaneous musical events.

As he continued, Pete put his arm around my shoulder in a fatherly fashion. I looked at his scrawny pale arm and wondered if maybe he was being just a little bit too friendly. I recalled Bill's assessment of Pete as, "… a sneaky bastard, so watch him."

"There's a new late-night timeslot opening up on NBC on Saturdays that Don is planning to fill with live bands from all over the country. He told me he wants to display Motown talent prominently and the Michigan sound. He likes the fact that I'm a close personal friend of Bob Seger who plays at our outdoor concerts anytime I ask. I can get him Grand Funk, James Gang, and lots of other big-name musicians. With all the Detroit blues and jazz talent that John knows, we can't miss."

He looked just like Sylvester the Cat contemplating how wonderful it would feel to bite off Tweety Bird's head.

I felt my heart high-jump an inch or two. National TV definitely grabbed my attention. He was saying all the right things I'd hoped to hear someday. I would kill for the opportunity to do live color TV originations of large events, even Rock & Roll concerts. This could be the big break I'd been hoping for. So I ignored my first rule of doing business which was, *never believe somebody who tells you exactly what you want to hear*. All it really means is that a salesman has read you like a rookie poker player and now he's playing you like a cheap French horn.

"You can consider this first film you're going to make for me as an audition tape. I'll make sure that Don sees it and knows who can do more of the same," he added, not really needing to say anything further. I'd already caved when he mentioned network TV.

Pete guided me toward the door as he continued offering further inducements, including a shot at doing video projections for some upcoming university concerts that he was personally booking with some of the biggest talent in Rock & Roll. I was a little numb from what I was hearing but I could make out some of the acts: the Allman Brothers, Johnny Winter, and Grateful Dead, just to name a few. He stopped at the door, opened it and kept up his banter without dropping a syllable or slowing down his pitch a beat.

As I followed Pete to the door and out of the fogbank his office had turned into, I looked back and deliberately memorized that little scene and what happened there. I was finally a professional! I'd actually landed my first gig as a serious filmmaker. The carrot had been properly dangled in front of my nose and I was greedily nipping at the air in anticipation.

There was Pete's broad silly grin creeping across his face, eyes wrinkled and clearly sparkling, about to close the door on his mystical inner sanctum where I'd just been handed my dream on a silver platter. I had an equally goofy grin that belied any common sense whatsoever on my part. All I could think about was that I was going to be on network TV! Wow! Heady times!

I glanced past Pete and saw John struggling to get up out of the big overstuffed chair, probably still groggy from some bad combination of drugs and/or ideas. Little did I know that it was the last time I would see him in the flesh for a couple of years. I turned around to force my way through the crowd still milling about in the outer office. I had to get to a phone to call Bob in Chicago, my business partner in Warlock Films.

CHAPTER SEVEN

SHE'S PROBABLY WAY OUT OF MY LEAGUE

"Wanting just to stay awake, wondering how much I can take. Should I try to do some more, 25 or 6 to 4?"

Bob Lamm, Chicago
"25 or 6 to 4"
1971

I couldn't believe it. I was going to get paid to do something that wasn't physics. I was going to make a film about Rock & Roll concerts. Support of the basic sciences had been rapidly disappearing ever since the U.S. landed on the moon and the damned Republicrooks took over the government. I knew it. I'd seen it coming for years and surfed it like a rogue wave through college and most of graduate school, but the wave was waning now and it might be time to go looking for another ride.

The snobby little liberal arts school north of Chicago where I received a full scholarship to study physics also had a vibrant drama department which, for a budding young scientist from the backwoods of Oregon, was like oxygen for an amateur mountain climber or maybe Peruvian Pink crystalline coke for a first-time marathon runner. I lost my virginity in the school theater's green room in the first month after arriving from the squeaky clean prudish West. It happened as if I'd planned it even though really, it was just dumb luck. My mother knew I was doomed when she saw me off at the bus station, crying for my innocence. I'd left home for the big bad city that corrupts good boys from the farm. Absolutely.

Soon after that life-altering occasion, I happened to notice that the key system on campus had a business-style hierarchy. If there really was a hierarchy, then a master key had to exist. I sampled a couple of lock tumblers from different campus buildings under construction that had random locks lying around. I stole a couple, opened them up, and plotted the various tumbler increments, which immediately revealed all the other common keys cut for the lock—including the building-master, a core-puller and, of course, the entire system master-key increments.

Then, using a small triangular file and a blank key, I hand-carved a master-key and disguised it with a different head, carefully soldered onto the blade, to make it look like a normal house key instead of one for campus facilities. It opened every door on campus. Now I had late-night access to my own private trysting boudoir: the theater department's costume storage room. Here my lovers and I acted out every bawdy scene we could possibly imagine from Shakespeare to Wilde. I introduced numerous coeds of the '60s to the newly permitted hidden pleasures of previously forbidden sex, often and repeatedly, thanks to that fine little drama department and the wonderful playground it provided.

And for a couple of years, I screwed many young and beautiful student wannabe-actresses, usually in a darkened theater on mounds of folded velvet curtains. It was a romantic setting that could get any college girl's heart pounding in those heady times of sexual freedom and legal birth control.

In the green room below the stage, I installed a refrigerator stocked with wine and beer, a color TV with a nice stereo console, and two full-size couches, which made it the best make-out lounge on campus. But the drama students kept it pretty much our secret room, just for the thespian clique. Here we turned down the lights to barely discernible, put Ravel's "Bolero" on the turntable, and allowed its pace, rhythm, and length to provide synchronizing accompaniment to the obligatory foreplay and coaxing of the coy young college girls to that all-magical moment when they finally whisper, *Yes, I want you inside me!* And I would thankfully and dutifully comply.

For longer interludes and more luxurious settings, we made love to that lusty new classical piece, "Carmina Burana," which most people think is about the futility of life. But we knew the whole central theme was one of drinking and lovemaking by horny medieval Latin poets and their alluring young groupies. I didn't miss the fact that nothing much had changed over the last thousand years or maybe even much longer. What Rock & Roll stars do to groupies today has pretty much been going on since we climbed down out of the trees to build our first performance platform and attract admiring fans.

Anyway, during my senior year, when I was pretty much the mysterious BMOC who had something going in the drama department and the physics lab, the school got one of their famous movie-star alumni to come for a visit. They planned to have him appear in a recruitment film dreamt up by some young overzealous marketing whiz bent on attracting new students by using famous old students.

To produce it, they hired an ex-WWII Luftwaffe pilot, who in a former life was supposedly a promising young filmmaker in pre-war Germany, and now was either partially retired or in hiding, we never quite knew which. Gunter didn't talk much about his wartime experiences and of course denied he was ever a member of the Nazi party. But if you suddenly clicked your heels behind him, he would stiffen and almost throw a one-armed Nazi salute before catching himself.

"I know nussing about ze Nazis," he always protested to the innocent young ladies admiring his yellow Corvette. "Zhey forced me to join ze Luftwaffe. I vas very bad at fighting but I like to go fast mit ze Messerschmitt," he admitted with a crooked little Germanic smile and a faraway look in his clear blue eyes.

He explained to us, his student volunteer film crew, that near the end of the war, he'd landed his fighter at the wrong airfield by mistake, claiming the Americans had captured his base while he was in the air. It wasn't really his base that was captured but he was flying one of those new He116 jet-powered fighters so, consequently, he was allowed to work for the American military teaching them how to fly jets. He was later sent to a prisoner-of-war camp in Wisconsin. As Wisconsin was already full of Germans and had not been bombed into rubble, Gunter talked the American military into letting him stay in the U.S. after the war. He ended up making 16mm documentaries and promotional films in Chicago and was well known to the Chicago police as having the fastest-clocked Corvette on the Lake Shore Outer Drive for ten years running.

I was selected not only to work as a gaffer and lighting assistant on the film, I also starred in it as one of the students shown off by the college president to the visiting celebrity as an example of a bright young scholarship student: ...*and we wish we could afford more like him*. I was instantly a star and the darling of the administration's efforts to recruit more paying students but not necessarily needy ones like me. After all, a movie is a movie, so suspend all thoughts of credulity at the door.

So when the celebrity stepped out of the administration building, supposedly to take a short campus tour with the college president, he walked right onto a film set with mikes on booms, lights on stands, a giant blimped motion picture camera on a steerable cart and, parked nearby, a small postal delivery van containing a giant console Ampex four-channel ½-inch tape recorder with tape already rolling.

Surprise! said the new marketing director, expecting the celebrity alumnus to be impressed by the professional-looking film crew. To his complete shock, the celebrity didn't appreciate being ambushed into a movie of somewhat embarrassing quality when in fact his film persona was his only asset. You don't surprise or commandeer a million-dollar movie star. His image was how he made money after all and he wasn't going to let just anybody, especially not some ex-Nazi fighter pilot turned commercial filmmaker, or even his old alma mater, screw with it. He begged off, saying he didn't have his makeup artist travelling with him and he was under an ironclad contract for something or other.

After much gnashing of administrative teeth in front of an expensive waiting film crew, he finally agreed to do a simple voiceover-only role. We had to re-compose the entire film so it was shot from the mysterious over-the-shoulder perspective of his faceless, never seen stand-in. Everyone played to the camera as if it and the audience were the recognizable Hollywood star narrating the film. Weird, but it sort of worked.

As a result of this endeavor, I fell in love with filmmaking. I tried like hell to make it a career option for nearly a dozen years after graduating, while I labored through physics graduate school just in case my dream job fell through and somebody still wanted to make bigger bombs.

I began to fantasize about being a great director someday, filthy rich and surrounded by adoring young starlets throwing themselves on me. Bob and I learned early on that all you had to do was walk into any random bar and/or grill with a 16mm motion picture camera on your shoulder and, almost instantly, you had friends buying you drinks and cute girls hanging on every word you drunkenly sputtered. Our first independent underground art production proved this theory with outrageous consequences.

We ended up with the local sheriff's daughter shacked up with one of our producers, accompanied by her girlfriend, the wife of a wealthy Lake Forest family's son who was busy making millions cheating stockholders out of their investments and workers out of their pensions. Meanwhile, his wife was being fought over and screwed several times a night by our leading man, the director, and the insanely rich producer and former Hell's Angel from Boston. I even got in a few licks myself.

I still fondly recall the night the producer was comically chased out the back window of his motel room at 4 a.m. as an irate father and her 300-pound former football-star husband were breaking in the front door trying to rescue their wanton property. I passed the producer speeding away from the motel in his Z28 Camaro at about 120 miles per hour as I turned in, expecting to join the party. I barely made it out of that parking lot alive myself. Then after the filming was done, we had to cool off in a secret hideaway in the Colorado Rockies while proper female subjugation and marital peace returned slowly to Chicago's exclusive North Shore.

Life was good as a pretend-to-be artist. Life was also miserable as a poor, broke grad student on the verge of losing his fellowship stipend. I was still waiting for Plan B to kick in but so far no instant film stardom had materialized to take the place of my stipends, until *maybe* now. Documentary films featuring Rock & Roll stars and other famous musicians could just turn it all around.

I had to get the word to Bob as fast as I could. As soon as I got home from meeting with Pete and John, I called him to announce our big breakthrough. He didn't seem very impressed. Especially about the fact that we were only going to get about five grand up front to get the ball rolling. He'd been living on pretty much nothing but his menial trust fund for the past two years, after the huge debacle of our first production. There would be no more artsy-fartsy films that made no money. He instructed me to go back and get the cash first, then he would start buying film and renting cameras and lighting equipment again.

"We can't keep this business going without some real film projects with real money," he said with a slight whiny undertone, in contrast to his normally jovial demeanor.

"This is real money! This is going to be as big as Woodstock. These guys are going to put Ann Arbor on the map. Look at Motown and all the bands coming out of Detroit. We're going to be right in the middle of it. Think of the possibilities. Television!"

Now I was just ranting with the same lame arguments Pete had used on me. Dangling the celebrity carrot was way beneath my normal cynical response to the old celebrity promise ploy. Even if there was money behind all this, which I seriously doubted, there was still the off chance that something might skyrocket from this, like making rock films or getting hired to do closed-circuit video projections at big Rock & Roll concerts.

"All right," he finally conceded. "I'll go along this time. But if we don't get some regular work here pretty soon I'm going to have to find a real job." *Ye gads!* The threat again. His girlfriend was probably putting on the thumbscrews and it wasn't his thumbs she was bent on squeezing.

"Listen, we have a long weekend coming up and no Sunday concert. How about I fly over to Chicago and we start the planning for the first shooting date?"

"If you do, bring money. I can't even afford a beer at happy hour anymore."

He was referring to our three-year record of making it to The Lantern nearly every afternoon during college so we could buy 99-cent pitchers of beer. Happy hour lasted from 4 till 8 p.m. every weeknight, which was perfect for college students because it gave us time later to finish our homework and still get some sleep. My buddies would wait outside the classroom where my last class of the day, Thermodynamics, was held. Since I was the only guy in our group who actually had a car, it was my job to get everyone to The Lantern as close to four o'clock as possible so we could get maximally inebriated before the prices increased and we had to leave.

I assured Bob that I would arrive bearing gifts from the east. As I hung up, after committing to landing at Meigs Field by roughly 8 p.m. on Friday, I had a sinking feeling that Pete's promised check might not materialize by then. I thought to myself that I'd better bring something else that could be turned into cash, at a minimum, and into a damned good time no matter what.

I took off early from the lab on Friday and drove straight to the small airport south of town where I'd reserved one of the university flying school's four-place Cessna's, an older 185. To help offset the cost, I'd found a couple of other people willing to pay for a quick roundtrip to Chicago for the weekend.

They were waiting at the flying club's little office when I arrived. It turned out to be a lovesick fraternity brother taking his girlfriend home to his parents on Chicago's North Shore for a little introduction to the family. I shook hands with the brother, looking past him to his good-looking girlfriend. My immediate guess was that she's probably pregnant and ready to run away with a handsome young film artist to a cozy little cabin in the snow-covered Rockies. I smiled and she smiled back. It was going to be a nice little road trip, or, actually, air trip.

It was a bit cloudy, scattered and broken, so we'd probably be dodging clouds all the way across southern Michigan. I planned to fly around the southern tip of Lake Michigan and then up its western shore past Gary and south Chicago, hanging slightly offshore until reaching the tiny downtown airfield built on a small landfill peninsula sticking out into Lake Michigan just south of where the Chicago River dumps into the lake. It's a real handy little business airport, sitting within walking distance of The Loop.

All the other Chicago airports were miles away to the west, where the city finally gave way to the endless prairie that had plenty of space for airports. Landing at those monster airports was like a pigeon landing in the middle of a freeway at rush hour. Instead, I liked the idea of landing on a small strip surrounded by water and a dramatic Chicago skyline so close you could wave to the people in their offices as you flew by on final approach. I knew the cute girlfriend would be impressed too.

"Ever been to Chicago?" I asked her once we were airborne with nothing to do but make idle conversation. I find I'm able to listen to the plane's radio for other pilots sharing this vast expanse of vibrant greens and brilliant whites, with glimpses of a dark blue peeking through from time to time, and carry on a half-decent, perhaps even witty, conversation. The Cool Pilot image was the gift of years of bad Hollywood writing. Everyone expected handsome pilots who could fight off squadrons of Zeros while cracking jokes a mile a minute over the radio and were the very definition of cool. The over-sized Bausch & Lomb gold-framed aviator sunglasses helped a lot as well.

"No, this is my first time. Jake here is taking me to his home in Wilmette to meet his parents. I hear it's very nice."

"How close is his home to the lake?"

"Pardon me?"

Her boyfriend had conked out in the backseat as soon as we'd gotten airborne. But, excited to see everything she could along the way, she'd gotten in the front seat next to me. I don't think he gave it any thought that we could be carrying on a conversation about him obscured by all the engine and air noise. Obviously, he wasn't that excited about the pregnancy while she literally glowed. I fell instantly in love with this luminous vision.

"How close is his parents' house to the lake? You know, Lake Michigan."

"Does that make a difference?"

"In Wilmette circles it does."

"So what?" she said indignantly. "The closer to the lake the higher-priced the property? I know they're well off and live in a very exclusive neighborhood. I don't care if they are super-rich."

"In Wilmette, a few extra yards between you and the view of million-dollar yachts motoring by can be all the difference in the world. It will determine what schools your kids will be qualified for. It will certainly define your circle of friends, since there's no social class mixing in Wilmette. And, it can even define what bankers you have to deal with when it comes time to buy your own little piece of white American heaven."

"Why you sound almost like a communist. Are you a hippie or something like those White Panthers back in Ann Arbor?"

"Actually, they're the Rainbow Peoples Party, and no. I'm just another graduate student hoping to make my fortune and get out before this whole house of cards collapses. Either that or run away to the mountains and become an artist or a hermit, whichever happens first."

She laughed. I still had it. I had to admit I was still hurting after my last breakup and it was always good to have a pretty young girl talk to you. I had enough painful memories of high school, where I couldn't get the time of day from the spoiled rich bitches on the cheerleading squad. I guess I wasn't athletic enough or from the right money or social class. Now with the Space Race and the nasty Russkies scaring the shit out of everyone with their super-smart comrade robots, brains were becoming somewhat more desirable than money or brawn—even considered sexy by some college girls.

Activists like me and many others had torn down the walls restricting sexual freedom and obstructing equal rights for blacks and women as well as getting the hell out of Vietnam. The '60s had been heady times. I'd seen many social changes that we all hoped would become permanent, creating a new and better world of intelligence, peace, and freedom for everyone. Quite opposite from the way we found the world in the '50s. The greatest generation may have won the big war, but they lost the larger battle for freedom and justice. Now it was up to us, the Baby Boomers, to fix it.

"So what are you going to do for the weekend?" I asked her as Lake Michigan came into view.

We were still dodging around massive, brilliantly white, puffy clouds as I swung the craft a little farther to the left so we could follow the coastline as it bent down into Indiana's far northwestern corner, just east of the Illinois border.

"I guess we're just going to hang out with his parents in Wilmette. I think they're planning a big Sunday dinner just before we have to head back to the airport. We are leaving about four in the afternoon, right?" She looked over to me waiting for confirmation.

I drank in her youthful, glowing loveliness for a moment before answering. A little voice inside me suggested she might not be quite so radiant when we met next, on Sunday. Upper middle-class douchebags from the North Shore tended to be pretty class conscious and bigoted. She would need the right credentials if she was going to survive the inspection.

"That should be plenty of time to get back to Ann Arbor before dark," I said cheerily, realizing that I was in a great place to console her if things turned ugly at her exhibition on Sunday.

We passed huge rusting and decaying factories, clearly displaying the effects of cheap foreign labor and steel, as we flew west along the southern shore of Lake Michigan. This sad stain gave way to the even uglier slums of the south side as the shore swung to the northwest. We finally caught sight of the downtown skyscrapers dead ahead, with Lake Michigan on the right stretching off into the horizon. I was still dodging the puffy white clouds that temporarily blocked our path, but the golden spring sun was illuminating everything like a movie set and clearly both the girl and I were digging it.

When we came within range of the Meigs Field tower, I got busy with the landing procedure, which was followed after landing by a lot of talking on the radio to locate a place to park and tie-down for the next two days. When I finished everything, the frat brat and his girl were gone. I wandered over to the business terminal, enjoying the great rare view of the Chicago skyline backlit by a brilliant glowing sun and apparently abounding in mild spring weather. I paid for the overnight, phoned Bob, who said he would be right down, and again luxuriated in the unique lakeside view with the sun ducking behind skyscrapers as it sank in the west.

Bob soon showed up in his little yellow MG. I threw in my small overnight bag and off we went. I loved his little sports car but hated British automotive engineering, so I had some mixed feelings. I loved riding in their cars when they worked; I just hated having to work on them. They had poorly-planned construction that typically required a PhD in ingenuity just to figure out how to get a wrench, or what they call a spanner, onto a critical bolt only to find out there's zero clearance for turning it. They required all kinds of special tools and it was generally a horrible headache trying to keep the damned things running.

I did win a road rally one time in a beautiful '57 MGA sporting a loose electrical connection to the fuel pump. I acted as navigator and sometime *reach-under-the-car-and-wiggle-the-fuel-pump* person while my buddy drove like hell all over southern Wisconsin and northern Illinois. I have no idea why we won, as I was lost most of the time. Speed and luck is all I can suggest that might have distinguished our efforts.

Bob lived on the near north side in the Lincoln Park area, actually right across from the Lincoln Park Zoo. You could open a window at night and hear the lions roaring their satisfaction after feeding time. He lived on the top floor of a typical three-story brownstone that was by far the standard for virtually every living structure that occupied the north side of Chicago from Downtown to the Evanston border and beyond.

Bob told me he was planning to have some of our old college buddies over for a little brunch party on Sunday morning before I was scheduled to leave. In the meantime, he wanted to get down to solid detailed discussions on our upcoming film project in Ann Arbor. We popped a couple of Coors cans and settled into an ancient but comfortable couch where I proceeded to brief him on the nuances of satisfying a devious rock promotor while educating a jackbooted city council on the idea that hippies and hucksters, along with Rock & Rollers and other ne'er-do-wells, could come together professionally and put on a giant music festival that was both economically feasible and necessary to keep the lid on potential demonstrations. It was our shot at glory.

"No sweat," was his first comment. He knew the power of Madison Avenue all too well having grown up in its shadow, in a Manhattan eastside brownstone much like the one he now occupied in Chicago, with a father working in the advertising business.

Propaganda wasn't cheap, but if carefully crafted, it usually paid for itself. A big flaw in the nature of the human consumer made it all possible. Advertising and promoting might be nothing more than flagrant lying, but a lot of people seem to want to believe them anyway; anybody can be persuaded to buy anything if you just market it right. I hate to admit it but it's basically the P. T. Barnum proposition about a fool being born every minute. You can't cure stupid, and stupid will buy crap if they believe the crap is necessary.

We put a plan together that night in Bob's kitchen. We laid out the budget and the various expenses we couldn't do anything about, then we calculated back from a 20-minute final cut to how much footage we would need to shoot and how many days we'd have to be on location. I even threw in a small amount for administration and editing time just to sweeten his take on the deal. Normally he and I would simply split the net profits, but Bob had been stuck in dry Chicago making nothing; I'd at least been milking the Feds for a graduate stipend, which was about as close as anyone could get to having fun and still receiving a paycheck.

After about a case of beers and a full tablet of paper, we called it a night. I crashed on his couch and tried to sleep through the next morning as much as possible, although his apartment lacked blinds and the morning sun was peeking under the trees through unguarded windows and ultimately beating a marginally perceptible photonic drumbeat on my eyelids and causing me much head and eyeball pain. We spent the rest of Saturday putting our shooting plan together enough to waste the daylight, but by dark we were both ready to hit Old Town.

For the last ten years or so, Old Town was the place to hang in Chicago if you were white, honky, and from the sticks or 'burbs. It began with folk singing coffee shops, but soon settled into pot, coke, and jokes. It had exotic head shops, record stores, boutiques, bistros, live-music bars, and something entirely new—comedy review clubs featuring ad lib skits that were paralyzingly funny. If you were black or just wanted to hang with some of the greatest blues artists and whiskey drinkers alive, you went to the south side mostly around Roosevelt Avenue. Being as we were of the whiter predilection, from a prestigious liberal honky school, Old Town suited our tastes just fine.

I do have to admit, though, having a great time one Chicago night blues barhopping in the south with a philosophy major and a long-haired, blonde, 6-foot-2-inch Swedish fashion model. If I'd been a pimp that night and Ingrid, my bitch, we could have made some serious cash and God only knows how many dead bodies would have resulted. We got out alive on that trip but even with my ability to sense trouble coming from two or three feet away, and steering our entourage away from the worst, we still started quite a few intense discussions among the bar patrons as to who was going to kill the philosopher first, then rape the remaining white boy and his blonde-on-blonde girlfriend to death.

I had a little cash in my pocket, so after a grueling, all-day planning session, I offered to take Bob out for a little celebration and who knows, maybe a little action. Old Town was also where hippie chicks and wanna-bees hung out in hopes of meeting their own perfect flower-mate, or at the very least a misunderstood folk musician. Seeing how just about every corner in Old Town was occupied by a street musician or performer of some kind, our chances were actually pretty good. The sexual revolution was in full swing and we weren't about to let it pass us by without diving in once in a while. I had to admit the sampling had been pretty good lately, since we learned the camera trick. Bob just happened to have Günter's Arriflex movie camera in his apartment from a shooting job on Friday, so he threw it over his shoulder without any film and we headed downtown on the L.

Jumping off at the Wacker Drive station, we begin a slow saunter along various streets into the depths of Old Town. Soon, we breathed the heady air of unbounded freedom signified by the odor of sweet incense assaulting our noses in order to cover up the true smell of freedom, weed. The stores were brimming with psychedelic sounds, electronic synthesizers, exotic sitars, and the old standby, marathon acid rock. Incense and patchouli oil, the exotic smells of faraway places, wafted in the air like a fragrant fog. Black-light posters glared garishly at all passersby with vibrant and intense glowing colors that drilled into their soft brain tissue with ultra-violet light. It had everything anyone needed to take a full head-trip, or just get high and listen to music. Here dwelt the new culture of a strange new generation. Quite frankly, there hadn't been anything like this since the goliards of twelfth-century Europe.

Brilliantly colored light shone from every door and window along the street. Record stores, headshops, bookshops, and night spots all lit up as if to shout, *Come to me. I am beautiful. I am young and virgin. I am exotic and foreign. You are not alone. We are together. We are more than just a bunch of temporary freaks; we are a lasting movement. It is our new world and this is our parade ground.*

We felt completely at home with our people. Even the beggars had their rap down for guilt-ridden, white-cracker liberals. *Hey, man, can you help a brother get high? I've been oppressed by the man and need a little help from some friends.*

As we walked along the now crowded streets, the chatter was incessant as easily spotted newbies were hustled by every longhaired panhandler within a hundred yards.

"Hey brother," a tall gaunt longhaired freak beckoned to me. "Come here. I got something for you."

"Yeah, like what?" I said rising to the bait, mostly due to being slightly bored and hoping for some weirdness to help with the night's entertainment. You never knew where strange encounters could lead.

"Check this out," he implored, as he realized he'd actually gotten a reaction to his banter.

He held out a bag for me to look into and be impressed. So I looked, expecting to find the same dried parsley/oregano mix that most of these street punks try to pass off as smokable weed. I was more than mildly surprised by the dark green buds and their pungent odor as I contemplated the best-looking weed I'd ever seen in a plain brown paper bag held up to my face by a street person.

"This looks like the real stuff," I said, looking back up at the vendor. "Aren't you afraid of getting busted?"

He looked me right in the eye and proclaimed that he didn't give a rat-fuck because all he wanted to do was turn the world on so everyone would stop fighting and just love one another, right now. I looked at his gaunt face and blanched skin, wondering what crazy internment camp for the socially naïve he'd just escaped from.

"So, how much for an ounce?"

"Fifty bucks man, and that's what I paid for it."

For some strange reason, pushers never admit to making a profit. In all the rest of capitalist society, profit is not only expected from every transaction, it's considered, in fact, a noble pursuit like the American dream or apple pie or waving some idiotic flag. But not with drugs.

"You paid too much!" I yelled over my shoulder as Bob and I melted back into the streaming crowd. Saturday night was always the busiest in Old Town and this was shaping up nicely. We hadn't gone two more blocks before some clown in cowboy boots, an old straw hat, and well-worn jeans with a beat-up old 6-string F-hole Gibson strung across his back, stepped right in front of me.

"You owe me ten bucks," he said matter-of-factly.

"Excuse me?" I said.

I tried to sidestep him and continue moving with the flow.

"You dated my sister in college and I spotted you two six-packs one weekend a couple of years ago, so you two could get drunk and screw."

"I screwed your sister? You'll have to be a little more specific. Most of the girls I screwed back then somehow all had brothers."

"You may have to list all of your sisters. I think that's when he was into twins and close cousins, right?" Bob asked no one in particular.

It was clear he was not going to help me get rid of this guy. In fact, it seemed he might be throwing gas on the fire just to make sure it raged marginally out of control, probably for his own perverse amusement.

"My sister's name is Susie."

"Now, could that be Susie Cream Cheese or Susie the Slut?" Bob added, as I started to smell raw gasoline fumes.

"Don't forget Susie Slider. Nobody can forget the Slider."

The little pretend-to-be folk guitarist, or whatever he thought he was, was all decked out like a drugstore cowboy, straight out of some badly exposed underground gay porn film from the depths of New Jersey. I'd seen those films and my disgust was palpable. True *cinéma vérité* artists like me would never stoop to such depravity. *We, like ze French, adore ze love story and ze mystery wiz a leetle adventure on ze side. But depravity; we leave zis to ze Italians.*

"Susie Wilson. I'm her older brother, Ken. I was performing at a club in Evanston and she showed up with you in tow, demanding I buy you two six-packs so you could go back to my apartment and…well, you know the rest. But then, I'm presuming she did to you what she usually did with all the rest."

"All the rest? That didn't sound right," I said pretending to be confused. I knew exactly who he was now.

It was all coming back to me. Deflowering a virgin, I had madly fallen in love during my last year of college. She was my first girlfriend, at least the first who had really good looks, and was therefore way out of my league. She pounced on me, though, if I remember correctly. It was great. We were a well-known couple on campus the second half of my senior year. We did everything together. Even flunked a modern drama class together, spending most of the time in the back of the class brazenly fondling each other in front of a gray, balding unmarried English professor who still lived with his mother. Sure, I was a little shitty about it then, but when you got it, why not flaunt it? I got nothing from the virgin bitches in my high school, so I figured I was just making up for lost time.

Then Susie's parents found out about me and locked her up in a private loony bin so they could perform invasive medical tests on her, most likely to see if she'd been having premarital sex. My buddies and I smuggled her out of the crazy hospital one night and spirited her away to a philosophy professor's house I was minding while he was on vacation in Lake Bluff. There we lived like young artists, madly in love and inevitably doomed to play out a bizarre operatic drama in which the evil parents ultimately turn their daughter against her chosen lover and, in the end, it is she who tragically destroys their love for no reason.

For a moment I'd lost myself in a whirlwind of memories.

"Ken!" I yelled.

I reached out with my right hand and grasped the hand he'd just been shaking at me, now in a friendlier manner.

"Sure, I remember you. I thought you had a really good act. Your songs were real and honest. Where's that going now?"

"I get by. Where's my twenty dollars?"

He took a step back in an effort to adjust to the new situation.

"I thought you said it was ten bucks a moment ago."

"It's been a couple of years. Call it interest."

"What's Susie been up to?"

"Are you going to give me the money?"

He looked at me like he didn't really believe I was going to cave; he needed to see something reassuring in my actions. I flashed a big smile and looked back over my shoulder at Bob, who was pretending to film our little encounter. We couldn't afford to burn real film at two feet per second on Old Town panhandlers, even if they were related to one of my old girlfriends, albeit one I felt had shot me in the heart and left me alone to die.

I pulled out my wallet, opened it, and removed one of the few twenties I had left. I still had to get home and didn't have a credit card yet, so I had to plan carefully. Out of the corner of my eye, I saw Bob start one of his classic camera moves that he liked to practice whenever he could. It was an old maneuver Jean-Luc Godard had done in one of his pioneering films with a revolutionizing handheld Éclair camera, the 360-degree revolving pan.

True portability in a motion picture camera was still new and required a physically strong and fluid cameraman who practiced his craft whenever he could. As Bob moved sideways in a circle around Ken and me, he kept the camera glued on a shoulder-shot as he orbited around us. He could do six or seven revolutions before getting dizzy.

Ken started to back off as he saw Bob coming up on his left side, and possibly cutting off any possible retreat, in case we turned out to be crazier than he thought.

"Don't worry. He's just practicing. There's no film."

I held out the twenty and Ken stopped just short of running away screaming.

He stepped forward, plucked it out of my hand, and examined the twenty close up as Bob disappeared behind him and reemerged on the other side.

He quickly changed his attitude and muttered, "She talks about you all the time," pocketing the now unceremoniously crumpled bill.

"Really? The last time I saw her she was pretty certain I was a failure even as a cretin, which was all I was remotely qualified for in her estimation. She said she never wanted to see my shadow anywhere in the same hemisphere again."

"Oh, that was probably more her mother talking than Susie. Mother thinks she's a whore, headed for a career in porn and drug abuse if she doesn't marry the boy across the street, who she apparently was promised to a long time ago.

"Who the fuck are you people anyway?" I asked, slightly exasperated.

Even though it had been a couple of years, I had taken the break-up pretty hard. Up to this point, Susie was the best in bed of all the coeds I'd deflowered. She meant something to me. Like my philosophy professor had said, *Susie is way out of your league*, and she was. So I'd resigned myself to hanging with the counterculture dropouts or hippie chicks for my spiritual release.

Ken was just staring at me, waiting for some clue as to what I meant.

"Do your parents believe in selling their daughter to the highest bidder, like some Arab raghead?"

"No, no. My family is 100 percent American, White Anglo-Saxon Protestant shitheads from the suburbs with all the bigotries and intolerance you can imagine in a non-southern household. They just believe that if Susie wants to think for herself, she still has to come to the right conclusion, which is to marry the dork next door. He's respectable, shares their beliefs, and he probably won't venture very far from their neighborhood and continued parental influence."

"So how come they haven't ostracized you? Your lifestyle doesn't seem very compatible with country clubs, cracker-asses, and white shoes. Why haven't they had you kidnapped and sent to a reprogramming camp for wayward young Nazis?"

"Funny you should ask, like I haven't sometimes expected it. But deep down in their male-dominated theocracy, the male heir is always allowed to go out in the world and either find his way back home or be lost forever. Not so the *protected* daughter. She needs to be guarded against her own desires, or what they call *unearthly urges*, or otherwise you've violated some religious edict about protecting weak and naturally lustful women with mental incarceration and strict parental control."

"I offered her freedom. I could have taken her away from all that. Susie could have come with me to Michigan and graduate school. Finished her degree. Maybe got a job and started a career. Shit, if she wanted to, I would have probably married her. Although I am kind of concerned about any progeny of mine being related to the fruitcakes in ticky-tacky Shitsville, Illinois.

"I hear yah, bro."

He held up his fist in the universal salute of the brotherhood.

"I'm not your brother! At least not yet."

"So, do you want to see Susie?"

"Sure, where is she?"

"She's on her way to my apartment. My roommate's hosting a little after-hours party for the cast of Second City. Why don't you come?"

I looked around for Bob. He was nearby, already flanked by a couple of girls and having some kind of animated discussion most likely about movies and stardom.

"Hey! Bob!" I yelled.

He looked up with that familiar shit-eating grin that's always plastered on his face when he's being accosted by cute young cinema-groupies.

"You want to go to a cast party for Second City?"

First he gave me a quizzical look, followed by his *surrendering to something against my better judgment* look and shrugging of the shoulders, followed by his trademark wide grin as he nodded *yes* and turned back to the job at hand or, I should say, two hands.

The prospect of seeing Susie tonight was too much to hope for. I suddenly had no interest in the two bimbos Bob had waylaid. Normally I would've been all over them, like a water-logged T-shirt at a wet T-shirt contest. Thinking about Susie again, however, made something quiver deep inside me as I fleetingly recalled our last all-night lovemaking session.

"So why don't you stop by sometime after two?" Ken said. "Susie should be there by then and some of the cast members will probably be showing up soon after."

"Is that real funny guy still with them?"

"They're all funny. You'll have to be more specific."

"You know, the short little fat guy with a Burnside cut."

Ken just looked confused.

"You know," I said as I waved my arms around to help with the translation, "where the moustache and sideburns are connected."

"Oh, you mean John Boletski." He brightened up noticeably. "He calls them muttonchops. He's my roommate. He's the one throwing the party. It's kind of a going-away party because he's moving to New York."

"Burnside's an American general and Canadians eat mutton. Figures. Anyway, great. Always wanted to talk to him. I saw him at Second City a couple years ago and damned near cracked a rib laughing. What's your address?"

I had to hurry him along because I noticed Bob was on the move with the two girls. I needed to get moving with them.

Ken fished around in his shirt pocket, almost losing a pack of Bambu rolling papers. He finally whipped out a scrap of paper with some scribbling on it.

"I just happen to have it written down."

He shoved it into my hand as I broke into a run, trying to catch up with my group before they crossed the busy street.

The rest of the evening seemed to just drag by. I couldn't stop thinking about Susie, who I'd been deliberately trying not to remember because of the pain. Now I was wondering if she'd even speak to me. Her brother said she still liked me, but then what do brothers know? Especially drug-addled, street-musician brothers who may be reality-challenged at best.

I loved Old Town, especially in the evenings when multicolored lights blazed all around, revealing strange wondrous ideas and *objects d'art* from around the world. The crowds were mostly scruffy, unshorn, and clad in brightly colored swirling patterns that signified many hours spent practicing the ancient craft of tie-dying and, of course, shopping Goodwill. There were a few suit-and-tie types, probably from the financial district, which wasn't that far away, most likely doing a little weekend slumming and looking for a quick opportunity with a commune escapee or runaway flower child. It didn't matter. By and large, this was where members of the counterculture gathered to revel in their uniqueness and for others still inside the noose, to watch close-up with yearning eyes.

The mood always felt electric with exciting possibilities and undeniable new experiences. You couldn't help yourself. You might be homeless and down to your last dollar and yet, here you were, infectiously happy no matter what. Some even proclaimed themselves naturally uplifted by all the positive karma here, exuding from the vast multitude of in-synch Aquarian souls.

I believed it was only natural that like-minded individuals congregate spontaneously and feed off the effects of the *I'm not the only crazy mother around here...I have automatic friends who are just like me!* syndrome. Its imagined consequences can affect anybody with any fetish, once their like-minded associates exceed more than a few dozen in the same room at one time. That thought gave me the chills, thinking about all the creepy rednecks who probably do the same thing at stuff like tractor pulls and drag races.

I ran faster, weaving through the crowds. Finally, I caught up to Bob just as he followed the two girls into a pub. We luckily found a big round table inside where we had plenty of room to gather around and marvel at the amazingly intricate, precision-crafted motion picture camera now prominently displayed as our centerpiece.

The two girls turned out to be deaf coeds from a local college for the deaf. They could both speak understandably and read lips pretty damned well. But when they went at it using sign language, it was just a blur of hand wriggling, finger waving, and other assorted gestures too bewildering to even begin to follow. All their exchanges were accompanied by much laughter and giggling. *Too much*, so I thought, *to be just innocent conversation.*

It turned out later that they were doing research on society's sexual hang-ups about extending women's new-found freedoms to the physically disadvantaged. That made me think. Was I liberal enough to make love to, say, a paraplegic? Or would that not count because of the lack of feeling they experience below the waist.

Sorry, bad example.

Maybe it's better to consider situations involving amputees and other missing parts, as long as they aren't the important ones required for this sort of thing. One-legged girls might be very interesting, if you think about it, which I unfortunately did. In the case of beautiful young girls who happen to be deaf, it really didn't even figure into the equation. If it wasn't for the fact that I might be seeing Susie later, I was ready to make some serious hand-moves on these wonderful hippie chicks. It looked like Bob had no reservations either. He was already getting loose and more than friendly with his hands as he moved in for some friendly banter or close combat.

I couldn't get my mind off Susie. I thought I'd really loved her and I thought it'd been totally reciprocated. After all, our pairing had been her idea in the first place. But something changed right near the end that someone failed to inform me about or give me any chance at all of altering the inevitable consequences. She'd disappeared right back into the bowels of big-city, White, conservative suburbia—where I couldn't go without gagging and ultimately drowning in the swiftly raging river of greed, hypocrisy, and arrogant ignorance.

Susie was different. She saw something in me that I didn't even know was there. She was much better looking than the girls I'd been used to and she showed me I didn't have to limit myself to other minor-league matches. It was a modern fairytale where the ogre gets the princess then becomes rich and famous. With a beautiful girlfriend, I thought I had it made. I had arrived. I was finally getting the kind of sex and social recognition I thought I deserved and it felt absolutely right and honest all the way up to the dumping. Boy, did I not see that one coming! And boy, did it hurt.

I'll never forget the cheap taste of humiliation as it swept over me that bright, late-summer day in Illinois. Susie had disappeared right before graduation; for several weeks thereafter, I couldn't get her to return my phone calls, if she was even getting the recorded messages I left. I became convinced that she was being held prisoner by her parents, just like what they'd done over spring break several months before.

This time, Susie didn't seem to want to be rescued. On a warm August day, I put the top down on my newly purchased personal graduation present, a crimson 1966 Mercury Caliente convertible, drove out to her parents' house in the 'burbs on Chicago's southwest side and marched up to their door, valiantly expecting to be greeted as a liberator, only to have Susie herself appear and tell me to get lost. I was devastated and dumbfounded. I thought true love was forever. What the hell had just happened?

Meanwhile, the little Bistro we were hanging out in started its live music offering. A young country folksinger from Nashville, introduced as a rising young star, took the tiny stage in the smokiest corner. In Old Town, rising young stars came and went about as often as Chicago garbage trucks. I thought I heard her name as *Bonnie Riot* or something like that. She wasn't bad—not a Joni Mitchell or Bob Dylan—but what I liked best between her musical numbers was her refreshingly vicious banter bashing our criminal then-president, Nix-goon. It was all precociously true but fleeting, like nothing you could hear from the nightly news.

As midnight approached, Bob looked like he was having a bit too much fun learning the finer nuances of erotic hand-signing. Some of the signs just didn't seem right to me. Maybe it was my puritan upbringing surfacing through my intellectual façade of *anything goes* but some of their signs were just too graphic, at least I thought so, for a public place.

Of course, nobody paid a bit of attention to their little show. Every table and every corner had its own little drama transpiring, fully independent of anything else going on around it. We liked that. It was why we came. Old Town was the only place where people like us could feel comfortable. It was like being home, only a cultural home, a safe place to think and be anything you wanted. For a lot of us these days, it was our only home.

Finally, Bob turned to me, holding out his spare apartment key, and said, "Don't wait up. This could be challenging without you, but I think I can handle it." He winked.

He grabbed the camera, threw it on his shoulder, and, cupping a deaf girl under each arm, broke a trail through the crowd heading for the door. I sat for a while sucking on the last of our pitcher of piss, wondering if 1 a.m. would be too early to wander over to Ken's for possibly the second greatest humiliation of my life.

"Screw it!" I said as I stood up to leave. "I'm a big boy now. I can take it, no matter what happens," I lied to myself.

That's the way you start to think when you've been up for three days out of six, subsisting on cheap beer, a few nasal bumps from friends, and the ever-present killer weed. Optimism without a shred of evidence is a garbage pit, open and ready for business.

I walked along the still-crowded streets, soaking up the festive spirit that infused a warm Saturday night with few cares.

It's hard to be pessimistic with so much enthusiasm and mindless gaiety all around you. It's infectious. By the time I found my way to Ken's apartment building I, too, was smiling and actually looking forward to the prospect of getting shot down again by a beautiful sexy lady. Some men as ugly as me can never even boast of that much. Personally, I like to think of rejection as a tacit admission that you were at least in the game enough to receive an unmistakable *No!* A zero score is way better than a forfeit.

It's truly appalling how much men grovel for sex and, sadly, I wasn't any different. I knew I might as well shred my self-esteem into ribbons and throw what little dignity I had left into the Chicago River, like some common murder victim in a weighted-down plastic bag. In a way, men are all masochists hanging our asses out on the line, based on the premise that fish don't get caught without going fishing first. Plus, I wanted a marlin instead of an ordinary run-of-the-mill carp, hence, I was in for more psychological punishment for trying to haul in a monster predator fish, versus simply reeling in a lazy, greedy bottom-browser.

I spotted the brownstone that had to be where Ken lived. I could identify the numbers, which virtually lit up against the dark brown nineteenth-century bricks that probably had seen the Great Chicago Fire. They said that was what gave them their peculiar rich tones of fused glass and twice-baked brick. The Near North Side had thousands of brownstones made from the Great Fire's rubble, just like this one. The small crowd gathering around the entrance betrayed an even more crowded scene inside, indicating another successful Chicago party that just couldn't wait for a more respectable hour to get started.

Climbing the initial flight of stairs took me past the first tapped keg, surrounded by the young and tasteless on a quick quest for inebriation of any kind. As I ascended from landing to landing on the old creaky but sturdy steps, the partygoers' ages increased noticeably and the random crowd movement reduced to small static groups of seemingly serious-minded young professionals and freaks, with a healthy dose of long-haired artist-types mixed in.

The sweet tangy clouds of smoke limited visibility to just two or three people away, so I headed in the direction the smoke appeared to be growing thicker and more pungent. Out of the corner of one eye, I spotted a small group gathered around an individual doling out snorts with a tiny silver spoon and little brown bottle. Indeed, the trail seemed to be leading me toward an open apartment door on the top landing, where I spotted Ken and a couple other guys in some kind of heated debate.

A short fat guy with a big bushy moustache appeared pissed.

"Who the hell are you to tell me I'm selling out after all the shit we've been through?"

"Because you're selling out to the man, man."

"Who the hell is *the man*?"

"You know damned good and well who. NBC is *the man* and they're going to chew you up and spit you out like yesterday's ratings. You need to stay free and with the people."

"Listen bro', I have a chance to make it in New York. Do you know what that means to a fat Canadian comedian who makes squat?"

"Yeah, I know. Just look at how Lenny Bruce made it in New York. Or how that comedian before Cosby had his career trashed by the network executives because he had a conscience. Dick Gregory, I think it was."

"They all mixed too much politics with their work. How the hell do you think anarchistic comedians will be treated by fascist media bosses?"

Ken turned to me with an exasperated look, not unlike the one he'd shown me earlier when demanding I pay an old beer debt.

"Good, you made it. She's inside sitting on the floor," and he gestured in that direction.

Then he paused and looked back at me. "You're in the film business. Will you explain to this idiot what happens to creative people who go to New York?"

"They either overdose on bad drugs, get rich and famous, or they're never heard from again." I turned to the short guy and held out my hand. "Hi. I hope to go to New York myself, soon. I've been filming rock concerts and there may be a slot opening up late on Saturday night, where we'll do a live concert, every week, from somewhere in America. I think we'll call it, *Saturday Night Live Concerts*."

"Hi. That's nice. I'm going there to write and perform on a new late-night Saturday comedy show."

"I should have added that our show will be on NBC."

"So will ours," he said slowly.

I thought about it for a Detroit second.

"That's weird. Nobody mentioned any comedy show to me. We might have some standup comedians as a warm-up act, like George or Richard, but it will mostly feature up-and-coming bands from around the country either performing in the studio or live, on concert tour. Ever hear of Concerts East or David Geffen? This is big, big money with almost guaranteed ratings."

I was just bullshitting off the top of my head, still reeling from the fact that somebody hadn't told me we had competition.

"What's a rating?" he asked calmly.

I just stared at him as another joint made the rounds among those of us standing on the top landing. He had a shit-eating grin that reminded me of someone, or something. This guy really didn't look like he gave a damn about anything, except whatever was crossing his mind at that moment.

I finally broke the awkward silence. "Haven't I seen you at Second City?"

That was the name of the local comedy-improv club that had moved down from somewhere in Canada or maybe Milwaukee, not sure which, and had been packing them in like sardines for the past couple of years. Their out-on-the-edge comedy and improvisational theater-of-the-absurd was the counterculture's answer to insults to our intelligence such as Ed Sullivan and Jackie Gleason.

Second City had grown right along with Old Town itself and now they were almost the same thing. If you went to Old

Town, there were two counterculture focal points you would most likely also check out. Second City was one and the other was listening to WCFL's *Midnight Special*, broadcast live every Saturday night from the Old Town Hall. It was a whole new genre of entertainment, only this time with biting intelligence, social irreverence, and twisted humor. Everything was changing and I, for one, welcomed it.

I have to admit, when we first saw him at Second City, he blew our socks off with racy off-color humor. The whole cast did. That kind of real stuff was great in private nightclubs where the patrons paid good money to be titillated, but TV was different. Television tore everything down to a common level of boring inanity and caustic stupidity. This guy wouldn't be able to survive the sterilization of his material. I thought, *what a brave attitude to take right before being eaten alive by the New York machine. Only big money, like Rock & Roll, has any chance of surviving a pond of piranhas like that.*

"Yeah, I came down here with them from Toronto a couple of years ago, but I need to bust out and get into something more mainstream. I want to make movies, maybe start a blues band."

"Here, have some more dream smoke." I passed him a stubby roach, not worth the finger-burning. "You be sure and let us know how that all works out for you."

I edged past him and headed into the apartment and a very uncertain future. My guts were twisting themselves into knots as I slowly pushed past tight clusters of animated party-goers. The smoke blocked anything beyond a few feet, so I carefully crept and groped my way into the next room.

The darkness closed in, with only a couple of lava lamps casting an eerie glow of yellows and pinks on a group of people huddled on their knees around them in the middle of the floor. I stopped and listened to get the gist of the conversation as I carefully scanned each face and body for something familiar.

"My lottery number is 36 for Christ's sake. I may have to go to Canada until this damned war blows over!"

"Shit. You're too late for that. I hear the Canadians are cracking down on American draft dodgers and expelling them straight into the arms of the feds."

"I'd rather just disappear into the backwoods of Alaska or Montana. They'll never find you there."

The brave wilderness survivor then handed a joint to the next person in their circle and my chest suddenly tightened to the point where I could barely breathe. It was Susie. Unmistakably. My beautiful pert little Susie Cream Cheese, defined famously in song and fable by Frank Zappa.

She had on her favorite kind of clothes: men's stovepipe Levi's, a red and yellow flannel shirt, clodhopper boots, a scarf tied around her head that gave her a slightly rakish look, like some tough female revolutionary in a Hemingway novel—or a Northwoods pirate. As my eyes lingered hungrily on her body, which I had not seen but coveted longingly for years after graduation, she glanced my way and we both froze.

"You came!" she said.

"You're here," I said.

Everyone stopped talking and turned our way. Suddenly I felt like I was on stage without a script. What did that guy do, outside on the landing? Improvisation?

She got up slowly. "I thought you would never want to see me again after what I said."

"Why would I not want to see you when that was all I wanted, when I saw you last and you threw me out? Didn't you get my letters?"

I felt a little twinge in my gut as I remembered the sharp pain of my first love lost.

She walked right into my space without a hint of hesitation. "What letters?" she said softly, smiling as she gently found my hand and squeezed it.

Now she was looking up at me with those liquid blue eyes that had the power to make me violate puppies or heartily betray my country in a heartbeat. Before I could deliver an earthy quip, she wrapped one hand behind my neck and pulled my head down as she stretched up on her tiptoes and laid one on me. Tight, wet, and probing tongues is all I can remember.

It definitely was not a friendly kiss, like sister to brother, or between long-lost reunited friends. I felt her anxious lips working themselves into a sensuous formation of fleshly cushions, hungrily kneading my own lips in a provocative massage. Then her tongue poked through, seeking its own vision of gratification. It was like bumping, literally, into an old friend.

Memories flooded through my body, of strong feelings and emotions unleashed in the distant past, more recently suppressed but now eagerly accepted, without any thought of possible disastrous consequences. I greedily touched, twirled, and ultimately massaged her tongue, revealing in no uncertain terms of where my intentions lay. She seemed to be saying exactly the same thing. My dick perked up like a sleeping old hound dog that had just gotten the scent of a fresh rabbit in the woods.

Somebody muttered, "Get a room," which caused a sniggering of giggles from the now all-staring crowd.

"Do you want to get out of here and find a nice quiet place to talk?" I whispered in her ear, as soon as I broke loose from her lips for some air.

"Where are you staying?" she whispered, then glued herself to my lips again, preventing any intelligible response.

I tried to tell her I was staying with Bob, but all I could get out was a sound similar to a strangling mouse as it's being swallowed by a snake.

She gave me a parting twirl with her tongue as she withdrew it.

"Doesn't matter. Let's go."

She didn't need to say anything else. My spirits soared like an eagle. I was going to get laid!

We took the L back to Lincoln Park. Susie glued herself to my hip the entire distance, with one hand stuck firmly in the opposite back pocket of my jeans, clutching tightly and massaging my butt, which drove waves of pleasure up my spine. We could hardly navigate as a single entity, being so unused to having four legs and four hands, all working at different purposes.

By the time we arrived at Bob's apartment, my desires were raging like teenage hormones. We locked lips again as I fumbled to unlock the door. Bob wasn't home, apparently still out assisting the Helen Keller gang with their research. We fell into the living room and barely got the door shut behind us before clothes began flying in all directions.

A few hours later, during a necessary pause in the action, I innocently asked the obvious.

"So why did you throw me out of your parent's house on that infamous day in August?"

She looked at me with a flash of hurt in her eyes and paused as she gathered her strength. I almost regretted asking, but I was so burdened with having asked the very same question thousands of times over the past few years that it just came out.

"She was there that day, hiding behind the door while I spoke to you. I am so sorry." Like petting a nervous pussy cat, she massaged my neck in synch with her words. "I didn't have any choice. She heard your phone messages announcing you were coming, so she was ready."

She paused for effect while a tiny tear peeked out from a lowered brow.

"They'd found my stash the week before and threatened to lock me up in a psychiatric hospital if I didn't get rid of you. You know from the last time, they could do that. They kept blaming you for the fact that I wasn't growing up with their values and complying with their expectations. They said you were a bad influence." She smiled coyly.

I could see the hurt in her eyes, so I felt compelled to say something stupid in order to reduce the tension.

"Bad influence, huh? I figured as much."

I didn't really. All along I'd felt like Susie had performed one-half of an Aztec heart transplant on me that day, and I was prepared to never forgive her for it. But now I could feel my heart melting and regretted even bringing it up. Instinctively, I reached over and cupped her face in my hands, drawing her lips closer to mine. I could see the tiny tear had grown into a crocodile tear glistening in one eye as I closed my own and opened my mouth to envelope hers in abject contrition.

It was like that all-night long. Confessions, contrition, forgiveness, redemption, followed by guiltless dirty-dog lovemaking. I was in some kind of sex heaven, or so I thought, until dawn broke. I rolled over in the soft gray light filtering into the room so I could watch her twitch as I stroked the lovely concave curves above her well-sculpted thighs. I could hear the soft patter of rain on the window. It could not be more perfect.

Rain!

I immediately sat up in bed, muttering a soft curse.

"What's wrong darling?"

Susie rolled over, facing me in her full exquisite nakedness. I had to pause for just a second, to savor the view. God, she was beautiful. She was definitely out of my league. Or was she?

"It's raining."

"So?"

"I flew here in a rented plane and was supposed to fly it back today. I have to go to work tomorrow. I've got people to do and things to see."

She giggled. "What's the problem?"

"I'm not instrument rated. I can't fly in the clouds, at least not legally. I might be stuck here until the weather clears up. Dammit, the forecast called for broken clouds today. Nobody mentioned rain."

Susie swung one of her perfect legs over the top of mine in an obvious move to gain a certain amount of intertwining. I caught sight of her glorious folds hiding between soft curves of flesh and silky dark bushy hair. I reached down softly cupping her crotch in my hand as I applied motion and pressure causing a soft moan of pleasure to escape from her partially open, inviting lips.

I carefully searched with my middle finger for her clitoris, which I lightly massaged. She wiggled and squealed in pleasure. When Susie seemed unable to bear any more waves of pleasure, I slipped it deeply into her vagina. It still felt incredibly slick and slimy from our all-night love-making. Nothing even came close to this stuff for giving the greatest of sensations. Not exotic oils or even copious mucous could compare. If I could only bottle that stuff.

She arched her back, breathing heavily, and grabbed my hand to give it some preferred guidance. My finger felt all the different shapes and textures within its reach. Her cervix seemed small and tight as I remembered it. The small ridges along the top were tantalizing, even to just my finger. That comfortable warm glow began to envelope me as my penis began to swell once again. She moved on top of me pushing hard against my hand, caught between her pelvis and mine. With one free hand, she found my fully erect penis and gave it a teasing squeeze, which was exactly what I'd anticipated. I tried to keep my composure and continue her internal massage, but things were coming to a head, literally, beyond which I had little control.

My penis swelled up with even a greater state of tautness than before, making it a little painful, except now exquisite and marvelous pleasure masked everything. Susie didn't slow down, and in fact seemed to be getting pleasure from my loss of control. I bounced with every stroke she applied, giving back what had just been given. I could barely stand it anymore. I withdrew my hand from her crotch to an immediate groan of displeasure. I reached around her thighs, cupping her butt cheeks as I positioned her directly over my towering inferno. With one hand, I forcefully moved it against the length of her vagina until the top of my stiff penis pushed through her slippery flesh, causing both of us to gasp from the quick penetration.

She immediately rammed her whole body against my loins forcing me deeper into her, farther than ever before and more than I thought possible. I felt it almost double up inside her as it rammed up against a rock-hard cervix. My fingers danced all over her skin, massaging her most sensitive parts and in return, my pulsating shaft received overwhelming and exquisite pleasures of its own.

She began to cry softly each time she thrust down and forward. I moved my hands like a Mozart pianist, tickling her ivory skin, exploring every curve, every orifice, giving fleshy pleasure wherever I could. Cupping her gorgeous and perfectly shaped breasts, I deftly twirled her nipples between thumb and forefinger. I held her by the small of her waist and helped her move more forcefully.

Only when the intense pleasure and exquisite pain became intolerably mixed into a totally new, yet exquisitely sharp sensation did I finally explode another huge load into her belly. In response, she screamed out uncontrollably and began vibrating violently as she collapsed into a heap of sweating putty, still straddling, engulfing, and now squeezing and pulling on my spent member in a rhythmic pattern that literally sucked the jiz right out of my balls. I was almost crying with pleasure.

She fell on my face, cupping it with her beautifully shaped and well-proportioned breasts. I loved it. There is no greater sensation for two humans than to have a fleshy object from each buried deeply in the other. It matters little whether it's fingers, penis, breasts, vagina, mouth, or tongue, and, dare I should say it, a well-lubricated anus. Many believe humans were originally differentiated by their brain and verbal communication. Personally, I think we got started when humans began to make love facing one another. When screwing became a pastime, the complications of society and civilization soon followed.

After a long motionless silence, save for the tingling of our genitals, random twitching of muscles, and heavy breathing, I slowly squirmed from beneath Susie as I whispered my apologies.

"I'm sorry, but I have to find out."

"Find what?" she whispered back.

"I need to know when this rain will clear out," I said, easing from under her gentle weight and stretching a leg over the side of the bed in order to straighten up. "I've got to call the FAA Field Station at Midway."

"What are *we* going to do?" she demanded, in no uncertain terms, and rolled off the rest of me, then sat up cuddling the sheet under her chin in a pose of phony modesty. *What a turn-on!* She still knew just how to play me for a fool.

"What do you want to do?" I asked.

"I never stopped loving you. I want to be with you," she lied flatly, again with that damned coy smile that made my head spin like a Disneyland teacup ride.

I looked at her in the soft gray glow of an early morning rain and melted completely. Sure she broke my heart and then stomped the shit out of it, but now she's sorry. She loves me. This could work.

That's how a brainless idiot thinks after an all-night session of fucking and sucking.

"Then you're coming with me back to Ann Arbor," I pronounced. I sat up, still looking at her glowing countenance. "I love you too," I lied quietly.

She kept smiling coy, coquettish and possibly devious smile that sealed the deal anyway. I totally ignored the devious part. As I stood up to go into the other room, where the phone was, I leaned over and kissed her lightly on the forehead.

"Keep that motor running; I'll be right back."

CHAPTER EIGHT

TRY PLACATING WHEN SUPPRESSION FAILS

"I seen 'em send up John Sinclair, you know,
two joints is all it takes...."

Bob Seger
"Highway Child"
1971

The rain didn't stop for three days. I went nuts. I had to get the plane back to the University Flying Club and I needed to get started on the film. I also had a job I needed to show up to on Monday morning. I was sitting in Chicago twiddling my thumbs while dealing with my old—now new—girlfriend as she ran away again from her parent's house and started clinging to me like sap to a tree. It felt and tasted great, I thought, but, of course, was way too sticky for respectability. Even for a half-assed hippie cowboy.

Bob loaned me his car so I could take Susie out to her parent's house one last time so she could get her necessary clothes and some money. She had been staying a lot with her brother while attending a small state extension college in downtown Chicago, so they were used to her showing up at odd times to exchange clothes and beg for more allowance.

I had fears of a repeat of my last performance at the suburban hellhole she called home. She decided to do it late at night and in a manner to minimize any reactions from her tyrannical overlords. I parked around the corner from her parents' house while she went in for the pickup. We arrived around midnight and noticed with satisfaction that the lights in the house were out. The enemy was asleep. This was going to be a cakewalk.

After she went in, the lights came on and stayed on. I rolled down the window so I could hear better. I thought I heard some shouting, but when I concentrated on trying to decipher it, the Illinois cricket chorus of cloaking silence ensued. I felt an anxiety attack creeping up on my consciousness. I kept looking around for the expected patrol car that was probably being called to nab me. These suburban ultra-rightwing fascists have been known to carry guns and use them at the slightest excuse. I sank a little lower in the car seat as I tried to get my heart rate and blood pressure under control.

The lights went out after another half hour, but Susie still didn't come out. I got out of the car and wandered around to the rear of the house, hoping to see something inside. As I rounded the corner, Susie's leg was poking out of a window above some bags scattered on the ground below her.

"What are you doing?" I asked in a desperate whisper.

She froze halfway out the window. I could almost hear a sob. She looked down and brightened immediately.

"*Shush*," she whispered. "I thought you were my father. Help me down."

I grabbed her around her tight waist and lifted her clear of the window, setting her down in the middle of several suitcases.

"They're asleep, so we need to get out of here as quietly as possible," she whispered in my ear followed by a little kiss and a friendly bite on the neck.

She grabbed two bags and headed for the corner of the house where I had recently appeared from. I grabbed the rest and followed her as we darted from shadow to shadow, slowly and as quietly as possible, stumbling in the dark. Overloaded by pink and yellow suitcases, we made our way back to the car. What a bizarre sight if anybody had seen it.

I was very careful to keep the lights off as we eased out of her parent's neighborhood. A couple of blocks away, and with no police sirens, we both heaved a sigh of relief as we headed back to downtown Chicago—and a whole new life of some kind I wasn't sure was going to fit with the rest of my life. But what they say about desserts, *there's always room for more*, made me think a woman in my current life was going to be a good thing. I needed the sex to calm my frustrated nerves.

She called her parents the next day, telling them she had run away to Ann Arbor to be with me and to seek her own life. They reluctantly agreed to not call the cops. She was twenty years old, soon to be twenty-one, so it was pretty ridiculous to be trying to fight what should be obvious to anyone else as mortally inevitable and fatefully unstoppable. Children must find their own way, even if it is wrong. Just check out Shakespeare, if you don't believe me.

Meanwhile, we got stuck in Chicago for three more days due to bad weather. I was missing out on work both at the lab that paid my bills, but also with the film which was my Plan B in case the lab and Plan A failed. I didn't like to be away while things might be going south with rumors of layoffs and closures. I needed to be back there so I could advocate for myself and also get started on the film project that I hoped would be my savior if I did end up losing my pitifully low paying job.

It just made no sense to me why after investing three or more years in successful research and several cutting-edge reports on the dynamics of the upper atmosphere that anyone would be willing to scrap all that work, completely losing everything that had been hard won up to this point. But then I was still young and stupid in the ways of governments and especially corrupt conservative governments that are only interested in looting the public treasury for their rich military industrialist supporters at the expense of legitimate needs. After all, the conservative assholes say, *science should only be done if it is profitable. Let the market decide what we need to know.* Oh God, just shoot me, now!

They loot the treasury in the sacred but paranoid name of national security, trying to stop the make-believe communist boogie-man. They give the loot to the executives of big government contractors and war manufacturers for basically nothing, for which they are in turn rewarded with obscenely huge amounts of campaign money kickbacks, which the politician could either pocket or buy influential TV time to convince the electorate that it is in their best interest to continue letting them loot the government, enriching the already stinking rich at our expense. Sounds like a winner to me.

I guess the world of science hasn't learned how to buy off politicians yet. I wonder what kind of world we might have if they did. The possibilities could be mind-boggling. Imagine a wealthy and influential Einstein caught supplying hookers to senators.

The couple that flew out with me had to catch the train back with many recriminations tossed over their shoulders as they departed forever from my life. The money they paid me, which I partially refunded, hurt even more.

The girl still looked distant and nervous, like a newly caged jungle animal, but she managed to put on a brave front as she faced a life of looming mother-in-law inspections, mind-numbing boredom, and total life purposelessness—except for prompt and productive procreation. I wanted to be romantic and save her from such a terrible fate, but sometimes people jump overboard for lots of personal reasons, which even if they come to regret later are for the moment sacred and unapproachable. I let it go again. So much for knights in shining armor.

When all the bad decisions and lost dreams come to eventual and inevitable fruition, however, they can always justify their meager contribution to society by the number of children they have thrust into this world to continue their so-called legacy. Seems ugly to think this reason is the same one that drives religious fanatics to kill indiscriminately, or force whole populations into sub-survival poverty, disease, and starvation. *Yeah, I want to be remembered as a person who not only did not contribute anything positive to civilization's progress, but in fact mindlessly contributed to its ultimate demise. I made more idiots than there were before I started. I win, right?*

Susie moved into my bedroom at Steve's house. I could tell Steve was not happy. He didn't have a girlfriend and so having one around just made it more acute. Susie tried to blend in as best she could. With only one bathroom, the bachelor pad suddenly became liberated coed space, much to our chagrin at first shock, (*Oh boy, random skin!*) followed by amazement (*What the hell is she doing in there for an hour?*) and finally, topping off with just plain old inconvenience, (*What the hell is this and why is it here?*).

With a girl in the house, however, now we had more sit-down meals than ever before. Susie jumped in and started doing all the cooking and cleaning, while Steve and I enjoyed having a beautiful girl hanging around whom we could joke with and discuss women's issues without getting too serious. Only problem was she slept in my bed, exclusively. He tried to make the best of an awkward situation, but you could tell he was getting anxious.

Steve and I even cut back somewhat on our routine cursing and drug usage. We didn't want anybody to get the wrong impression, but Steve needed to get laid, and soon. I told him to stick with me for the upcoming festival and he would surely get laid; he would be part of the stage crew, and therefore desired by horny young nymphs out of their daddy's house for the first time looking for a nasty time with a Rock & Roll stagehand.

"Did you see this?" Steve casually mentioned the next morning while reading the *Ann Arbor News* at the little kitchen table.

Susie was busy making coffee and pancakes. I sat down in the only other chair and Susie came up behind me with a kiss on the neck and a steaming cup of pure black java.

"No, what?" I said, still uninterested in morning banter but trying to be polite.

Susie reached down and squeezed my crotch, almost making me spill my coffee on her hand and my junk.

"John Sinclair was arrested this weekend on marijuana charges. The cops stopped him on the street and did an illegal search and found two joints of dope in his shirt pocket."

Back during the peak of the antiwar demonstrations, cops looked for longhairs at night so they could kick the shit out of them and then arrest them for finding the planted cheap pot nobody in their right mind would ever smoke and then lock them up for years so other sick sons-of-bitches could get their jollies by butt fucking them to death for being queer. That's justice in Amerika, Nix-goon style. So many young kids fatally brutalized all in the name of fucking conformity.

"Wow!" I said. "That was quick. I thought they gave up using pot as an excuse to bust demonstrators. I wonder what Pete's going to do now."

"Pete will run the show without him for a while, I imagine," he said as he grinned wickedly.

"Actually, the thing I wanted to show you was this," and he pointed at a half page ad.

"A new business has opened up renting and selling the new Sony portable TV camera and tape recorder. They're advertising the complete camera unit for lease at $50 a month."

"Jeez, even I can almost afford that."

"What the hell would you do with one if you had it?" Steve countered.

"16mm film is so damned expensive! I'm hoping that portable video cameras will have the ability to take the studio and move it outdoors where only film worked in the past. It's cinema verite' without the fucking expensive film and the hassle of recording sound separately and synching to the film later. This thing records both picture and sound, already in synch! And, most importantly, I can erase the tape and record over it, making the tape reusable. Film will be eventually replaced by tape. Just wait and see."

"But look at this thing. The camera is only black and white and the recorder is so big you have to wear it like a backpack or drive it around in a small truck."

"I can also put it on a bicycle. It's revolutionary!" I retorted. "Up to now, only silent 16mm film cameras have been small enough to be handheld. The cost to expose film alone is prohibitive for me and the post production costs for developing, printing, editing, sound dubbing, and all the other stuff that makes film production so goddamned expensive severely limits what I can do. Portable video cameras are going to change everything. Besides, we can only afford a black and white video projector for the Blues Festival, so it might work out great there."

"So how is the gig going to come down?" Steve asked.

I could tell Susie was quietly listening to us as she started making my breakfast. It was fun playing house with my now slightly used girlfriend. We were liberated, but still bound by convention. She cooked and I washed the dishes, sometimes.

"We're going to rent an RV that we'll park right next to the stage. We'll set up the control room in it and it will also be a place where we can party and hangout backstage during the whole festival," I explained.

It was well known that one of the most important things to look for while at a basic booze festival is locating the nearest porta-potty.

"We'll have our own private bathroom right next to the stage. How cool is that?"

"Cool!" His face lit up like a like a Chinese lantern. "They have refrigerators too. We can have cold beers stashed."

The thought of partying backstage at the biggest concert festival to hit the Midwest ever was just overwhelming with exciting possibilities.

"Sounds like fun. What's my job?" His smile went from ear to ear.

"I'm going to hire about three or four cameramen I know over at the U of M television center and I'll call the shots from inside the van. I thought that seeing how you are our best MIT electrical engineer, we'd make you our Chief Engineer and put you on the projector platform."

I smiled wickedly. Steve loved pot and coke about the same as everyone else so the thought that we would be an integral part of the festival, hanging backstage with some of the best Blues and Jazz musicians from around the country, while consuming all our profits in drugs and alcohol seemed like a perfect way to spend a weekend.

"Projector platform? What the hell is that?"

"We plan to fly a giant projector screen above the stage. We'll have to elevate the video projector up to the same height so it won't *keystone*."

"Ooh, that sounds neat. I'll have the best view in the house looking down on stage from my exclusive box seat, high above front row center."

"Well, not exactly."

"What do you mean?" His smile faded.

"It's rear projection."

"What?" he muttered, almost disbelieving such a thing was even possible. After some thought, he added "Why?"

"I did the calculations. Reflective screens only return about 30 percent of the light striking them from the front, while transmission screens pass more than 80 percent of the light striking it from the rear. Outdoors we are going to be fighting ambient light, especially in the daytime, so we will need all the light we can get out of these primitive oil plate projectors."

"The projector platform will be behind the stage where I won't be able to see the stage at all?" he whined.

He had seen the design for the stage, which showed a huge multicolored flying canopy of parachute cloth suspended by tension cables strung between stubby, but fat telephone poles sunk eight feet in the ground and at an angle tilted away from the stage. It looked like a giant kite suspended over the stage, with signatory rainbow stripes for the Rainbow Peoples Party that sponsored the show with Pete Andrews. It looked really nice and even avant garde. A young mechanical engineer designed it and had a few thousand bucks riding on its successful erection.

"You'll have the screen to watch. We can even get you a monitor up there so you will have a brighter image to watch."

"This is beginning to sound sucky," he complained.

"I've allocated five hundred bucks to our party drug fund so I'll carve out a special picnic basket for you and anyone you can convince to go up the tower to help you. It'll be fun. Did I tell you about the view?"

"I'll volunteer," piped in Susie as she forked some fried eggs and sausage onto my plate.

"I've got plans for you. Steve is going to have to get his own girlfriend. He can't have mine."

When a girl moves into a bachelor pad, the sexual tension becomes almost palpably sour. The eggs even tasted different. Must be all the pheromones running around in the air.

To help bridge over the issue and introduce her to my many Ann Arbor friends, Steve and I decided to throw a house party. We invited all the best of the Lab's NASA engineers, some out-of-this-world university artists, and most of the Ann Arbor musicians who hadn't gotten their first recording contract yet, all of whom were cool, hip, and together when it came to sex, drugs, and Rock & Roll. I volunteered to rent that new Sony Portapack camera to record the party and Steve volunteered to play "In a Gada da Vita" on the pipe organ.

Susie cut up an old olive-drab Army wool blanket I carried around in the truck and made me a Monk's habit with the big hood that hides your face in darkness and mystery. What a better way to video the event than disguised as a crazed Monk recording souls having fun for later use in hell's exquisite tortures.

Susie was little red riding hood with a pistol looking for wolves to blow away. She actually did a cute Easter-themed underground Super 8 movie with the same costume and basic plot. They liked it at the Ann Arbor festival, but sadly nowhere else. Into the archive it went, another victim of love's art-labor lost.

Steve put on a Benjamin Franklin wig and went as PDQ Bach (Pretty Damned Quick). He was too, doing twenty minutes of "Iron Butterfly" in five minutes flat. He opened the attic windows so the sound from the thirty-two-foot folded pipes could get out better. The house filled up quickly with costumed and drug-addled first-comers, so we let it spill out onto the front lawn and finally into the parking lot next door. After a couple of hours, it morphed into a block party. As most people living along Division Street were students or young post docs, nobody complained about the loud music.

Next up on the pipe organ was George Frayne, or as we knew him, Commander Cody, dressed like some tinsel-covered astronaut wearing giant sunglasses. He did his rendition of "Hot Rod Lincoln" with the crowd filling in the sound of racing engines. After him, it became open mic night at the street party. Ann Arbor harbored a lot of talent, so a couple of aspiring local bands assembled some equipment from around the neighborhood and set up in the parking lot. My old friend Bob Webb was there with his latest band, and one of Pete's bands did a little impromptu performance for the video camera. I started to think they were doing all this for the camera and not the audience. I caught some of them making gestures at the camera that were not very artistic or subtle. Hams come in all shapes and sizes.

Alcohol flowed like a river and cocaine dust storms were whipping up everywhere. I took a break from doing long walking dolly shots and sweeping pans, all with glorious sounds being recorded. I glided the camera at cat's eye-level up to overhead shots with the ease of swinging a bat. This damned thing was going to revolutionize the film industry, as soon as they got it to play in color. Without color, it was just a high-tech toy and a great conversation starter at parties.

Donny, one of the engineers who used to work at the lab but had found a higher paying position with a military weapons developer on North Campus, noticed that when I recorded trees after dark, the leaves all appeared white. He asked to borrow the camera for a second. He started scanning cars arriving in the parking lot and he noticed that the ones with hot engines showed up bright, where small engines and parked cars showed no such brightness. The spectral response of the camera was clearly in the near infrared. It could act as a spy camera in the dark!

He handed the camera back and mumbled something about how easy it would be with a few lines of code, to make the camera literally zoom into hot objects. He was already working on remotely controlled anti-tank missiles, so his reference made me realize again the double purposes new technology could be put to. I wanted to make art films and the rest of the world wanted to turn art into a dangerous weapon. *Speak to Salvador Dali who knows all about art as a weapon.*

Don was a damned good NASA engineer, known for his circuits surviving rocket launches and the occasional dousing of water by airport security not believing he was carrying spacecraft modules for outer space. He agreed to build me a special battery-operated in-line preamp for the microphone side of the intercom headsets the cameramen were going to need. The sound levels were going to be so high on stage, we needed super isolating and loud audio headphones for the cameramen so they could hear instructions from me, the director. The *mambi-pambi* headphones they used in the TV studios plainly would not work in such live surroundings.

I slapped a 50-watt chip amp on the headphone line to the cameramen that could override a nearby jet engine taking off. Likewise, I needed to hear the cameramen clearly, so we had to amplify their microphones right at the headset before transmitting back over a long cable to the control room in the Winnebago.

Donny produced four beautiful little identical clear rectangular cubes of plastic with a phone jack on one side and a phone plug on the other. A clip was attached to the big side containing a 9-volt battery for power. I had just invented Rock & Roll cameraman headphones.

The solid clear cast Lucite protecting all the tiny components inside and holding them rigidly in place made the unit damned near indestructible. It clearly revealed the hand-wired microcircuit pre-amp containing multicolored strange objects and shapes in weird tangled positions that when casually viewed looked more like jewelry or weird abstract sculpture.

Neat, I thought, *someone should explore this idea.* Electronic circuitry was always something one could appreciate from the artful side—from the old friendly warm glowing radios with weirdly shaped tubes and lighted dials, to the now ultra-modern printed circuit boards with their patterns of lines, curves, and spots seemingly organized in patterns of random meaning, yet conveying hordes of indistinguishable information.

Bill found us downstairs looking at the video monitor displaying our playback of trees with white leaves recorded earlier. He picked up the camera and wanted to see what the camera was recording. I switched the monitor to live video and he got immediately into some kind of brain feedback. First, he simply jumped the camera's focus from object to object while rapidly moving the zoom lever back and forth. Hippies, we noticed, always tried this first.

Screech! Don started getting dizzy watching it. Then Bill wandered his attention down to the recording machine with the tape running from reel to reel while wrapped around a flying recording head. He seemed fascinated by the shimmering tape as it moved through the machine. Then he focused in on the monitor and started making real video feedback just like his brain. It was the infinite tunnel of monitor screens showing a monitor screen inside a monitor screen and so forth. Then he found a mirror. I was beginning to fog up so I went looking for Susie.

I found her with a group of hippie-looking guys in our bedroom passing a joint around while sprawled on my waterbed. She had the giggles and often fell sideways on the bed, causing a wave that jostled everyone else on the bed in delayed sequence like a human wave moving around a stadium full of spectators. I didn't trust Susie with hippies; after all, that was how I got her in the first place. She had a known attraction in the past, which I felt was unseemly now, especially in my bedroom. Wasn't one quasi-hippie cowboy good enough for her?

I grabbed her and headed back to the basement. She had obviously overdosed on weed and needed a hit of coke to calm her down. When we arrived, Bill already had some coke laid out on a mirror as he showed some tall, dark, long-haired furry hippie how the camera worked. He was using the camera to zoom into extreme close-ups where they could admire the many-colored sparkling lights bouncing off the tiny crystals. Close-up drug inspections; another use for this technology.

"This is Marty," he said calmly, as he handed the mirror to Susie. He knew what she needed just from the huge shit-eating grin on her face and squinty eyes. "He owns that Rock & Roll PA company, Fanfare. Pete's brother, Curt, is his partner. Remember? I told you about them at Thom's party."

All I could remember was something about a new stereo PA being built that could deliver full fidelity 120 dB SPL to a football stadium. This is what a Rock & Roll entrepreneur looked like. From his long black wavy hair hanging halfway down his back in a ponytail indicating he had been growing it for years, and therefore was an early member of the movement, to his long black beard, which said simply, *fuck you if you're hung up on hairless men, I don't give a shit.* Plus, the fact he was easy six feet tall, but couldn't weigh more than one hundred and fifty pounds, attested to a calorie-starved life of drugs and late-night roadie work. *My kind of man*, I thought.

I shook hands and he added the victory grip at the end. There was no doubt now, he was a brother of the movement. As most of us were revolutionaries, we seldom used the victory clench amongst ourselves, except when meeting new people to whom you wanted to assert your membership right up front, no bullshit. Marty was like that, so he instantly joined our little club.

I looked back at Susie and noticed her beautiful blue eyes were now wide open and her teeth were grinding. Looked like good shit, so I had some.

"Bill says you're a physicist," said Marty.

He took out a joint from behind his ear where it was nicely hidden by his long hair. He lit it and took a hit and held it out to me. Susie and Bill were already deep into a conversation about drugs, like *what's good for whatever, while doing some whatever's.*

"Yeah," I answered taking the joint. It tasted good. *He's no sloucher.*

"So, do you know about sound?" he asked.

"A little."

"Do you know what causes feedback?"

I spluttered a bit. Feedback was the key to loudness—that and fidelity. Everybody would like to solve that problem. I thought a bit and decided to give him the full technical argument without the normal dumbing down of science for the unwashed masses.

"Feedback happens when the amount of total positive loop gain at any one frequency exceeds one." In other words, when the sound you make at the microphone is less loud than the amplified sound coming back from the speakers, then feedback occurs at whatever frequency first gets to this level of loudness. A rock singer could easily produce sounds at the microphone in the 120 dB SPL range; thus, the PA should be able to deliver that much to the audience before it gets back to the microphone. "The key," I continued, "is an absolutely flat response over the entire sound spectrum and little or no phase distortions." Easier said than done.

I went on to explain that most modern practices for building loud PAs was all wrong. Flat was not enough. Speakers were notorious distortion makers, and that destroys the flat response, again causing early feedback. Large PAs kept designing with high-efficiency speakers because power amps were hard to come by. That means they had limited frequency response. Sometimes, up to five or six different kinds of speakers would be used to span the entire sound spectrum. That meant having to match the speakers at the point in frequency when one speaker took over for another as the sound changes frequency. This required a tuned circuit at the crossover points so the power for each type of speaker would be divided up according to the frequency it reproduces. This naturally produced large amounts of distortion and the possibility of early onset feedback at the crossover frequencies. No rock star likes that unless, like Hendrix or Joe Walsh, they use the feedback as part of their music.

Marty would agree to most everything I said but then would throw in the practical side; he knew that side all too well from his years on the road actually trying to nurse every last dB he could out of the equipment that whatever band he was with could afford. Basically, I said he had to find more inefficient speakers that have wider frequency responses, and thus less crossover points. Two was too many, but the five he was planning was way too much.

He said that was impossible. I told him it wasn't. We smoked a joint. I told him that with built-in amplifiers and just two kinds of speakers, he would solve his problem. He didn't need large woofers to make loud bass sounds. Many small speakers working in unison could recreate a bass wave louder and more coherent than a big floppy paper cone flapping in the breeze like a loose sail. He said the audience expected big things from the bass. We snorted some more coke.

All this time, Steve was listening in from across the room. He showed up when the coke came around the second time. He immediately got interested in our argument about speakers. He threw in his ten-cent MIT concept that the best speaker was the wall of speakers like what the Grateful Dead did with their wall of Marshall speakers. I said that works fine for very low frequencies, but when the wavelengths approach the dimensions of the speaker itself, then flat speakers started to interfere with themselves. Somebody handed out a bunch of Coors, probably the last of my stash.

I went on to point out that a certain MIT professor by the name of Bose had already built what I advocated, a speaker with a curved front. Only we needed to build a big one that a PA would require. *How about the obvious?* How about pie-shaped speaker sections that would stack up like cake layers to whatever power level you needed? Bill thought that was cool and broke out another gram. Susie hugged me in a hip-grinding manner, also unmistakably obvious.

We went on till dawn and when Susie and I finally decided to hit the hay, we had to throw a couple out of our room who was still groovin' on the music in their heads. It was a great party and, unknown at the time, one of the last before tragedy would strike.

After the party, it was time to get to work. I had some drug money, I had a regular squeeze, my truck ran great, and I had a film contract—actually two, one for the 16mm film documentary the city was paying for about the festival, and the closed-circuit video projection at the festival itself.

I wasn't used to having more money than rent and food required. Bill Smith was a pretty smart guy in this regard. Even though his main business was totally illegal, he didn't blow it all on drugs or pretty young blondes like Corvette Jack. Bill had a legitimate retirement plan. He invested in local real estate and even owned a small repair garage where he was the local car expert for the hip and connected in the community.

He helped me get my first 4-wheel drive truck. How great it was to drive a truck where you could look down on the Cadillacs of the world! Volkswagens were now perfectly good candidates for roadkill. I secretly prayed for ice and snow just so I had an excuse to shift into 4-wheel and go out where nobody else dare venture.

Bill also helped me become an Ann Arbor student slumlord. I took the cash from my trip up north and put most of it into a down payment on an owner contract for a hundred-year-old well-maintained two-story Victorian house near campus. I heeded the three rules of real estate: location, location, location. It was walking distance to the main campus and had student renters now that barely covered the mortgage payment, but I had a plan to add another apartment in the huge unfinished attic, thus increasing possible profits and hopefully making some big equity.

I bought it on an owner contract so no bank was involved. Banks wouldn't loan longhairs anything anyway, even if they had a decent job and good prospects like Donny. That was why Donny had to cut his hair short, though that wasn't the way he felt. Bill said *cash talks*, so I whimpered out five grand and surprisingly the old retired couple who owned it took it. I now owned a house, but still couldn't afford to live in it. All the rent money went to cover the mortgage and insurance. I felt foolish but kept up the charade of being a young independent business man. I bought an old 1957 white Alpha Romeo Spider convertible to celebrate my new status.

Bob had been up to Ann Arbor a couple of times to film the summer Sunday concerts, where Pete's band did a full musical number. Now all he had to do was film the Blues Festival and edit it all together with sound and special effects. I trained Susie to handle the microphone on a boom while I ran the audio recorder and Bob ran the camera. We worked pretty well as a team, moving from one set-up to the next with little hassle. It hadn't the portability of the little Portapack but the image quality was up to studio and broadcast standards which was what was needed and something the Sony couldn't provide.

As planning moved forward on the Blues festival, I had plenty of volunteer cameramen and gaffers who were well experienced in TV production. When Katie and I were a pair, we had both worked evenings part-time at the university television studio helping tape various professors telling the audience about their latest discoveries and academic researches. It was antiquated black and white, tube-type monster cameras man-handled around on big hydraulic pedestals on wheels.

The technology was not that great, nor were the artistic values, with mostly dark foreboding backgrounds sparsely decorated with old office furniture and fading plastic flowers that actually looked good in black and white. It was the studio procedures and various skills such as camera work, video switching with a plan and over all coordination of diverse efforts that was needed to do a video origination that interested me, even if it was only closed-circuit to a captured audience of maybe ten thousand.

At the same time as putting together the production crew for the festival, I proceeded to hire hippie carpenters to remodel the attic in my newly purchased rooming house. When I finished, I would be able to house fifteen students in a space that originally housed a family of six. My introduction to *American Free Enterprise* was apparently proceeding right on track, except for one tiny detail. When money flies in through the front door, you'd better start ducking any shit that's bound to start flying in from the rear.

There were rumors circulating at the Space Lab predicting it might close by the end of the year. A hundred or so engineers, physicists, technicians, and professors were all at risk—not to mention several lowly grad students like me. No more paycheck and no more PhD research work. My project advisor saw it coming and found an open position at the new Johnson Space Flight Center in Houston, Texas. He promised to take me with him if I wanted to continue my research and finish the doctorate degree I had started in planetary atmospheres. I shuddered at the thought of living amongst the hated war–mongering, anti-intellectual enemy who killed Kennedy. My professor's interests in life, besides being a decent physicist, were contract bridge and golf, both of which seemed to me an instant death sentence by a lethal volley of boredom.

On my physics front, I had actually gotten the atmospheric simulation software nightmare debugged and was racking up huge statistics on predicting how solar energy transported itself into, out of, and all around our upper atmosphere. I had calculated, with the help of that damned frustrating IBM 360 running Fortran 2, the magic number that many federally funded atmospheric geophysicists were inexplicably busting balls to find.

"Now," my advisor said in a manner similar to giving a stranger direction to the restroom, "it's just a matter of writing it up, defend it in front of your doctoral committee and finish your PhD. You could graduate within the next year or so, and then look for a post doc position."

Just write it up! he said, as if that was the most trivial part of the PhD program. Writing for me was like pulling basketballs out of a chicken's ass. Three years I had been working on this damned computer program, and yet I still had a hard time explaining to anyone what the hell I was really doing. I understood the program I wrote and realized it was the only successful simulation of the upper atmosphere at the time, but it just bored the hell out of me. It clearly was going to take a lot of cocaine to keep me from falling asleep every time I tried to write something about it.

First it took a year just to get the program written and debugged. Programming was a nightmarishly frustrating battle between human-speak and machine-speak when translations did not exist. Many times during that period I had wanted to just set fire to the *I. B. Mad 360* and run away to the mountains of Colorado where I could happily disappear into a hermit's mountain cabin. I would be so far away from civilization no one would find me until my bones showed up about a million years from now as a fossil on an eroding river bank in some ancient valley.

Call it wanderlust, call it my fatal Walden, call it what you will. Ever since my best friend from college and I visited his girlfriend for Christmas in 1968, where she was living in a little rental cabin located at a 10,000-foot altitude in an old Colorado ghost town, I became irrevocably possessed by the romantic idea of living in that place. Where else outside of maybe Nepal or Switzerland could you step out your front door, look in any direction, and see comforting craggy, snow-capped mountain tops towering majestically above you on all sides? This town was so shadowed by the tall peaks, sunlight was shortened by a couple of hours every day in the summer and twice that much in the winter.

But such barren rocky hideaways are fairly unique for this country, and totally captivating to my mind. No matter how downtrodden I found myself while being dragged through the muck and mire of graduate school, I could always dream of a romantic place, spending hours devising secret plans for running away to my own private little Shangri La. When the time came to disappear quietly from a collapsing civilization feeding on itself like some confused zombie, the high mountains offered peace and safety. I saw my future security net as a high-altitude refuge with mountain peaks as my new castle walls.

I guess everyone needs a secret refuge in the back of their minds where they can sneak off to whenever the stress and ignominy of life drags down what's left of any shreds of self-esteem and legitimacy one might still be harboring. When I was given the choice to relocate to Houston, where I could *just write it up*, I checked my options again and discovered I could neither run off to Texas, easily the most hated of states, nor to Shangri-La. I was an Ann Arbor property owner and tax payer. I had inadvertently put down roots in a college town. Somehow that didn't sound like me. I guess I was also engaged to Susie, but I tried not to use that word. *Committed* seemed more appropriate with women's lib and all that.

So, as any young man of the seventies instinctively knew, I opted instead to join a Rock & Roll band and go on the road where getting laid and doing copious drugs was essentially a job requirement. Probably the dumbest move I ever made, but at the time and under the influence of the number of drugs and alcohol I routinely consumed, it seemed pretty much the right thing to do. I could go on the road for a few weeks, make a bunch of money, hopefully get laid copiously, and definitely consume a lot of drugs. Then, when the tour ended, come home just in time to collect the monthly rent from my slum tenants.

On the ugly side, I would lose out on finishing graduate school with a PhD in Physics. I hated to give that up, but then with a PhD in Nix-goon's world I probably would be horribly over-qualified for any job I might need just to survive. Nobody needed an atmospheric physicist with a major in elementary particles at a time when the government was essentially burning scientists at the stake for the pretty colors they made, and engineers for their calorie value.

At least the damned Vietnam War was finally winding down. The government had apparently given up on killing me—at least my draft board's threatening letters stopped coming—so I didn't need the student deferment any more. Along with the war, the space race was apparently over as well. Our elected government had declared a clearly fictitious victory for the former, while barely accomplishing the latter.

After landing on the moon three times, we decided we better stop stretching our luck and just send all the engineers and scientists who had been trained by that monumental feat back on the open market to make a living presumably by inventing new and more profitable foot creams, or maybe developing the greatest pharmaceutical discovery of the century, say like boner pills. That would probably sell.

So, they closed our little NASA lab, put us all out on the street, so to speak, and created a local high-tech depression.

I had seen all of this unfolding over a long time and had tried to prepare for the time when I would be cast adrift in a leaky boat without a paddle or a bucket to bail with. At first, I tried the wonderful world of filmmaking. I envisioned myself as an independent film producer/director. However, with little money and equally sparse talent, about the only thing I could come up with, under pressure of feeding myself, was maybe a documentary or a new thing called live video projections.

So, when the opportunity arose, I had to give it a shot.

Everybody had been impressed by the Woodstock Folk Rock Festival a few years before, so why not an Ann Arbor Blues and Jazz Festival? By using old blues musicians and aging jazz bands the talent would hopefully be less crazy, the audience less destructive and, most important, cheaper than a bunch of bad-boy greedy rock bands. There was also the hope that blues and jazz lovers might be less socially obnoxious than the typical rock freak. They were also apparently shooting for an annual touristy rip-off event so this first festival had to go off professionally and without controversy. At least that was the story they were using to convince the city fathers and the pigs.

The intent, Pete said, now that John was in the state pen and could no longer be the spokesperson for the event, was to bring classic blues and jazz musicians from around the country to a pristine Midwestern college town and present to musical connoisseurs end-to-end classic American music acts in a large outdoor stage for three to four days in a row. They needed a city park just outside of town where the audience of ten to twenty-five thousand could be contained securely without dogs, tear gas, or electrified fences. The last thing the promoters, let alone the attendees, needed was an unwelcome visit by the pigs like what happened in Chicago's Roosevelt Park a few years back. So they sold the city on the idea of privately policing the event with local youth talent. That's where Bill came in.

Who better to run security than the one person who so far had avoided the clutches of the pigs and had all the high-tech equipment to create a little hippie militia? The Psychedelic Rangers were formed as the private security organization responsible for guaranteeing the Sunday concerts and the Blues Festival would be uninterrupted by overzealous pigs trying to bust long-haired pot smokers. The city agreed to back off and only deploy traffic cops—and then only miles from the event. Basically, they would look the other way as long as there was no violence. Our secret weapon became mellow-yellow pot and a system of two-way radio communications that put the cops to shame. We could respond faster and more appropriately than any fucking macho, violent, militarized pig.

Psychedelic Rangers handled everything from parking to hauling around large amounts of cash to making sure all drug dealers kept a low profile and nobody caused any bad trips. No bad drugs were allowed, so somebody with the knowledge and ability had to check quality before allowing anything glowing or electric inside.

That's where James Griffin came in. He was the genius organizer behind the Rangers and long-time friend with everyone involved. Son of a university professor emeritus, he grew up comfortable on both sides of the locals/student divide. If anything or something happened in Ann Arbor, James either caused it to happen or was there to watch it happen. James took care of the staffing and logistics, while Bill handled organization, communications, and drugs. He was also damned good at sampling drugs for an instant quality analysis.

The Rangers became key to the deal with the city. When the Rangers were under John's control, i.e., the White Panthers, the city cops had nothing to do with them, and likewise in return. But when a drug dealer and an academic brat took over the Rangers in the name of Sunday Free Concerts, and negotiated with the city through a rock promoter, well then, that worked. Who would have thought?

We fed the city leaders paranoia by intimating freaks without rock concerts might turn ugly like the hated anti-war demonstrators. Hippie freaks can be calmed by strange music when the cops are not around. *Play along or fight us at your peril.* They caved.

Little did I know that I was making music videos with a 16mm film camera and the new Sony half-inch videotape recorders a full decade before MTV and bizarre rap videos would become commonplace. As most innovators and inventors who are far ahead of their time discover, nobody sees the potential except them. As they fight to get their idea accepted, they end up usually wearing themselves out. After years of frustration, they give up just before it becomes accepted without much further fanfare or credit. You bust your ass to prime the pump and yet someone else gets to drink first. So it was with me.

Meanwhile, Marty was moving ahead with his PA business. He already had a medium-sized PA system using off-the-shelf mixers and speakers. He needed more money than even his wealthy partner could cough up if he was going to build his dream system. Pete and Curt grew up in a wealthy family living in Ann Arbor. Their father made a fortune with the Arthur Murray Dance franchise and then lost most of it when ballroom dancing died by Rock & Roll. How ironic that what killed the old man's business was now what the sons were doing.

So Marty ran across a couple of little weaselly roadies who audio mixed sometimes for Grand Funk Railroad. They formed an uneasy partnership, approached Mark Farner who loaned some bucks, which got the mix board and speakers built, and in return Marty provided PA services for just expenses on their big upcoming Phoenix tour. He rented an old repair garage building down near the river on the north side and began cranking out big plywood enclosures for a giant PA system.

They also needed a new mix board that was fully stereo and capable of not only mixing up to twenty-eight microphones on stage, but also fully equalize the audio output with a minimum of third-octave bands covering the entire spectrum from 20 Hertz to 20 Kilohertz. Outside of some really big recording studios in London, New York, and LA, this level of sophistication and technology had never before been available to the traveling road show musician.

So, we all went to work in our spare time after the lab closed every day and used the considerable resources available from NASA to build the stereo mix board. Thom built the preamp modules, one for every mic input, and Steve provided the design for the five-way electronic crossover feeding the amps to the five different kinds of speakers used in order to cover the entire audio band.

We also developed a special power amplifier which we prototyped for our personal use. For the professional system, however, Marty opted for a commercially produced power amp, the famous Crown DC300. This amp was manufactured by, of all people, a small company in rural Indiana that built PA equipment primarily for missionary use in Africa and other hostile environments. The Crown part was actually a religious symbol, but the quality and performance was all we cared about.

One of Marty's PA trucks flipped in a snowstorm in Iowa and damaged most of the amps, some squashed unrecognizable. To their surprise and amazement, every amp no matter how banged up still played at full power. That's clearly what's needed for Rock & Roll! We thought it was a big joke to be using God-endowed equipment for our godless performances, but it made the little missionary support company a lot of money over the years and to this day, they quietly keep right on selling their craft to both the off-key singing missionary and the devil's own off-key singing rock musicians.

During these heady days of beats, protestors, hippies, and acid freaks, music, especially loud Rock & Roll music, was the glue that held us all together. The industrial military power structure being super paranoid—as they should be—tried suppressing this right of expression until finally we convinced the local Ann Arbor city fathers that it was better to successfully placate then fail to suppress.

So for a pittance of money and lots of youthful volunteers, we put on ten to twelve free rock concerts every Sunday all summer long in various city parks all over town. It was at one of these concerts that we fired up Fanfare's new fantastic rock machine for the first time.

Bill had to find us a 20-kilowatt Army surplus diesel generator to provide enough power, since the park only had one 20-amp circuit. We hid the generator in a clump of nearby trees behind the stage where the sound could be easily over ridden by the music. Curt kicked on the power switch that sunny August Sunday afternoon, and for the first time we heard an ominous low frequency 'thump' as all the giant speakers responded together to the initial inrush of many amperes of electrical current from the bank of Crown amps. They had 10 amps on each side of the stage behind the giant speaker stacks, giving a total sound power capability of 6000 watts.

Bracketing the stage on both sides were stacks of newly painted black speaker cabinets towering over the audience by at least fifteen feet. The speakers looked massive and mean. The largest one at the bottom of the stack was big enough to actually crawl inside when replacing shredded woofers, which happened all too often. There were four more sets of speakers stacked on top of the giant bottom woofers, each tuned to a different frequency band leading up to the big array of aluminum ribbon high-powered tweets at the top, which looked wickedly like the business end of tiny jet engines ready to scream on command.

But the most impressive part was the custom-built mix board. All solid state and built with a surplus of linear amp chips, it was truly state of the art *and then some*. This one looked something like a Hollywood set for a villain's death ray machine, or the control room for a starship. They liberally used the new light-emitting diodes as indicator lights. It glowed with myriad eerie yellow, green, and red specks of light coming from the dozens of panel meters and indicator lights scattered all over the three-foot deep, six-foot-wide console. It was one of the first of its kind anywhere; like I said, *fucking state of the art.* I had only seen similar units in big professional recording studios in New York.

It sat on a table about waist high with a gently up-sloping panel loaded side-by-side with slider knobs for every one of the up to twenty-eight microphones on stage. It was crowned across the top by rows of VU meters for every input and output, along with the world's first 10-channel graphic equalizer for each of five crossover outputs to the speaker stacks. It was the first board capable of acousta-voicing or tuning the PA frequency response flat by compensating for the variations in environmental or acoustic responses of a theater or outdoor venue. It could match the acoustics of wherever it was used. And also, for the first time, it was fully stereo.

The twenty-eight individual microphone channels were divided in narrow columns from left to right across most of the sloping panel space. Above each channel at the top and vertical to the sloping panel were two VU meters that indicated the sound level being assigned from each microphone to the two stereo output channels going to opposite speaker stacks at the sides of the stage. On the right were the power controls and cross-over equalizers for the two main outputs connected respectively to the stage right and stage left amplifier racks.

There was a total of 3,000 watts of power available and Curt, with a mischievous grin, reached over and slowly advanced the two master power control knobs until they hit the stops at the end of their travel. I could hear a humming noise and strange crackling sounds, coming from the two giant speaker stacks, indicating a virtual opening of a floodgate of sound waiting for some stimulus to trigger the deluge.

Marty walked out on stage, also grinning from ear to ear, as he deliberately walked up to the front center stage microphone.

He bent into the mic bringing his lips to within an inch of the business end. Curt edged the microphone channel knob up to about half scale. The hum noticeably increased and a strange crackling noise that I had never heard from a PA before started to sound like a nearby forest fire.

Testing...One...Two... exploded from the speakers. Everyone in the park jumped noticeably from the unexpected blast of sound. I heard the phrase again as an unexpected radar echo coming back from a tall apartment building three blocks away.

Hello Ann Arbor! Marty said and the crowd began to yell in response to the unholy loudness they were witnessing for the first time. I noted with satisfaction that it was not only loud, but perfectly clean, crisp, and without so much as a tinkle of any squealing feedback. *Welcome to the last concert of the 1970 Ann Arbor summer park program!*

The crowd went nuts. Curt leaned over to me and said, "We just broadcast a voice message five miles without an FCC license."

The first band came running onto the stage eager to use this new wonder of technology. I noticed Curt turning down the output to something more tolerable.

"We just wanted to let them know we could do it. No sense tempting the man to try and shut us down though," he added, as the drummer on stage began to bang his sticks together for the start of their first number.

Curt was adjusting all their mic volumes as they started up. He leaned over to me as the band began playing.

He yelled into my ear, "You want to go on the road with us?"

I didn't need to think about it. I leaned over to his ear and shouted back, "Hell yes!"

I thought a second and then leaned back to shout in his ear again. "Who is it?"

He leaned into my ear and replied, "As soon as we finish the blues festival over Labor Day, Grand Funk Railroad is doing their *Phoenix* album tour."

He still had that devious smile plastered all over his face, like some Cheshire cat. It was the best offer I had heard in a long time and apparently a damned sight better then fucking Houston, Texass!

The rest of that month flew by as we all worked feverishly to get ready on time for the blues festival coming up in September. I found a giant projector screen so cheap that I bought it instead of renting one. It had a metal frame bolted together like ribs on a bridge and it came with two screens, one for front and the other for rear projections. The stage builders had put in two telephone poles at the left side of the stage where we would suspend the screen directly above and to the left of the stage. The offset helped keep spill light from the stage washing out our TV picture. It was not going to be the brightest of pictures anyway, and with the lack of suitable TV projecting power, every little bit helped.

Near the end, Susie and I were visiting the site on an almost daily basis, checking on the progress of the giant fence being built around the park. Bill and James were there setting up their command center tent off to one side and overlooking the entire park. They had scrounged about a dozen CB handheld radios so they had constant communications with the rest of the Psychedelic Rangers stationed around the park in key areas, such as the front gate and parking areas at a nearby school.

On top of a nearby hill, Bill pointed out a red canopy with several red-shirted rangers standing around it with binoculars watching over the entire venue. It was their Eagles nest, where trouble could be spotted early and senior rangers could be immediately dispatched by radio to intercede. Our main concern was rogue cops showing up and causing trouble. We had a deal with the city and we intended to enforce it. No cops on the grounds without a ranger escort. No drug busts unless we requested it. And that was not about to happen with Bill and James, two of the biggest druggies in town running the show.

The rangers oversaw activities inside the fence, keeping people with electric orange juice or other give-away treats to be honest about what they were handing out. *No bad trips allowed!* was one of their many mottos, along with the old standard, *Keep it cool.* With no cops in site, everybody felt safe, at home with their kind of people; the entire weekend went pretty mellow, except for the day before opening night.

The engineer contracted to erect the flying canopy over the stage chose the one day when the wind came up unexpectedly strong in the afternoon. We were there rigging the projection screen so it could be put up or brought down when necessary, or when the wind blew too hard. As his crew tried to connect the flopping giant canopy to the poles that had been sunk firmly in the ground, presumably to hold it up in case of a wind, the wind began gusting, causing the canopy to turn into a giant wind sail with the wing area of a 747. Soon we saw people being dragged across the ground who were holding onto the lines. Then after tossing a couple of long-haired crew members twenty feet in the air, lines started breaking, poles began to loosen, and the giant canvas canopy began to whip about in a huge circle.

We stood back in horror, wondering if it was going to destroy the stage under it, bust up the speaker stacks already loaded on each side of the stage, or demolish my screen and support pole right next to the stage. Pete was rather pissed watching all this but, I thought, awfully calm given the situation. In the rock business, I guess, you learn to take disasters in stride because they literally come with the territory.

Soon we heard huge ripping sounds as the giant tarp began shredding itself to relieve the extreme wind pressure trying to lift it and twenty or so wranglers off the ground. Finally, we could see the head contract engineer running from line to line trying to salvage something or chasing down flopping canopy pieces as they turned the backstage area into a giant fun land of flying colorful pennants and flags reminiscent of a medieval festival after a tornado.

Pete called a halt to the entire fiasco at this point and ordered everybody to stop what they were doing and get the damned canopy removed entirely. Soon, most of the canopy had been torn into long colorful banners; nearly everyone grabbed one, not able to resist the temptation to run around in circles trailing the streamers in the wind and playing with them as if they were ground kites, or some spring mating ritual. Pete just shook his head at the spectacle and went back to his office so he wouldn't have to be tortured anymore with all the last-minute craziness and the paralyzing thought that something was going to prevent the show from going on, on time.

So, the show went on without a rainbow canopy, the signature piece of the Rainbow Peoples Party Blues and Jazz Festival. I guess rainbows don't just happen on cue.

Being an experienced Thespian, I knew that shows in preparation were the next thing to pure anarchy and chaos. Somehow, though nobody knows why, but they usually go off right on time with most everybody doing their best. It just happens that way, so get used to it if you're going to be in show business. Otherwise, get the fuck out of it so someone who understands craziness and thinks they can control it can get shot down in your place.

The Winnebago showed up and we parked it right behind the screen support poles. My canopy-chasing crew finally showed up back at stage left and we finished stringing our power cables and camera cables around the stage. Soon, we had the control board and camera monitors installed, along with a half-inch Sony video recorder locked in the back bedroom, just in case we might need it. I wired my special Rock & Roll intercoms, ran a quick test, and a full day before opening we were ready to shoot.

From inside, I sat in front of a six-camera TV mix board, where I previewed the cameras before selecting which one to put on the big screen. Just like uptown, but portable and no fucking studio trying to make it better than real. This was going to be live and as real as it could get.

Fanfare had already set up their speaker stacks, which almost got wiped out by the flying canopy. Now they strung their main mic snake from the stage out to their mix tower. It took four guys to haul their big ass mix board up the tower, as Marty bit his lower lip in fear of it being dropped. Mikes and stands were showing up on stage along with stage monitors and a new little mix board behind the speaker stack where a tech mixed the fold back mikes to the stage monitors.

The lighting contractors were still hanging and adjusting lights. They would be up all night getting the lights set, as it had to be done in the dark and it was the last night before opening. We just needed to do a test run with the projector as soon as it got dark and we were done for the day. In the meantime, Fanfare was ready for a sound check, or so Curt said.

One other complication was that Pete and John wanted to release a live album of the event; they needed to do a mic split at the stage so each mic could be sent to two different mix boards, one for the PA and one for the recording truck. Fanfare built the mic splitter, but for some reason they couldn't get it to work at the last minute.

Sound check time came and went. A bunch of guys were under the stage working over a big box with dozens of cables going in and out of it. The smell of panic began to infuse the air along with a sharp increase in pot smoke since they had closed the main gates and applied security to the site for the first time. I was about to send Steve in for a look at the mic splitter when Curt called over the radio saying they had it fixed.

I had intended to take a mixed feed for our recorder from the PA mix board on the tower, but now I realized I might possibly get a better stereo feed from the recording truck, which was just a few feet from our Winnebago. I thought that would be way cooler for our video efforts. I offered them a closed-circuit feed from our projection system so they could watch the performance much better than their little static surveillance camera they normally used. They accepted the offer and so we got an audio feed cable run from the recording truck to our video van.

In retrospect, we should have stuck with the PA feed because the recording truck came under much scrutiny by the artist managers hanging around backstage with nothing better to do than try to protect their musicians from pirated recordings. Cables ran everywhere on the ground, so it was hard to trace any single one, but some took the effort.

It had dawned on us much earlier that we could record our live feed to the projector with the new Sony half-inch black and white videotape recorder. A memento could be had, if you will, of our brief fling in the big time. Pete automatically said *No* when I approached him earlier with the idea. I assured him the quality of such a recording would prevent any commercial use. It simply was incompatible with broadcast television standards. It literally had the jitters.

He said it cost too much. He also said he would look into it. I saw a gleam in his eyes when I mentioned he could have a copy video recording of the event.

He had not thought about video rights to the festival, except for his own little project; Bob was shooting exclusively with 16mm film for his Ann Arbor documentary. No songs at the festival could be recorded by Bob end to end without explicit permission of the performer. Pete got us Bob Seger's permission, and some of the local bands and other small blues bands, but the big acts kept saying no without huge sums of compensation. Musicians were spoiled by the likes of Ed Sullivan, who actually paid big bucks to perform on TV.

We didn't have the necessary film equipment to actually record sound and picture in sync as we had intended to only do mostly wild shots of people and festival workers. We got a few nods from the poor black delta blues players that would be there, but the main attraction, Ray Charles, flat out said *fine, 12,000 dollars please, plus residuals*. Pete choked and so we agreed to shoot the film around him, yet nothing was exactly said about his video projection performance.

Video was closed-circuit with no possible rebroadcast. Again, we didn't actually have the equipment necessary to do something remotely commercial, so we got everyone's permission for the closed circuit projection, even Ray, with the presumption of no commercial tape recording.

"Same for recording film," Pete added.

"Sure," I agreed, not knowing if I agreed not to, or to. With a professionally mixed audio feed and projection video somehow converging on the small locked bedroom in the Winnebago, it became real hard not to turn the knob to record. *It was for training purposes*, I told myself.

Bill distributed the many orders for cocaine the next day as everybody showed up backstage for the festival. I didn't know anyone backstage who didn't pause about every fifteen minutes while they found a secluded place to take another snort, or to meet up and share several toots all around. I told my cameramen they could only snort during breaks, no snorting on stage, and do it all in the Winnebago, preferably by sharing with me.

I didn't want the word getting around that we had any coke, otherwise all the bastards would be bugging us for toots by Sunday when they had all run out and were starting to crash. I bought enough to last my crew till Sunday, and even then, I had a small reserve so there would be some during the breakdown. None of my crew would feel like they had to leave early because they were crashing. *No crashing allowed on the job! Stay cool* also meant *stay high but be discreet.* Who knows, there could be undercover narcs sniffing around.

The next day, people began streaming in the big gates at the rear of the park after noon. Bill began a regular commute to the front box offices swooping up cash for the portable safe in the command tent. He used a plain brown paper sack to transport the money so it didn't look suspicious. A known doper carrying a bag, how suspicious could that be? One time he stopped by to show me what a full bag looked like. I had never seen that much used unmarked bills at one time, except maybe for our little purchase in Juarez earlier that year. God, I was beginning to like this business.

The first act kicked off later that afternoon, but since it wasn't dark yet, I wasn't needed to call the video shots for the projector. So, I let Kevin, my chief cameraman, run the board just for fun. Meanwhile, the recorder was running, just for fun and training purposes.

Craziness began creeping in almost right away. I climbed the PA tower and took a stint mixing the sound for a couple of songs. It was amazing how with a little bit of concentration I could pick out each individual microphone on stage and hear only *it* as I did minor adjustments and tweaks to bring it into better balance with all the rest of the mikes.

Fanfare never took a sound feed from anyone's equipment on stage. It was always changing and you never knew if it was reliable or compatible with their system. They miked the speaker cabinets for all the guitars and bass instruments, and they miked almost every drum in the trap set, sometimes accounting for up to sixteen microphones alone. Even there, I could pick out each individual microphone one by one and balance them so no one mic or one sound source dominated the others. Let the band decide who should be loudest at any given note, just make sure the mic is well balanced with all the others so you just hear the sound as it is played, and not the PA.

Word came over the radio that there was some kind of scuffle at the front gate. We were closer than anyone back stage so Curt said, "It's time for the professionals to sort this out. Come with me."

He handed the board over to Marty and we climbed down the tower and headed for the riot. I wasn't sure about stepping into a riot without my camera as a weapon. Curt was fired up and I could see steam coming out of his eyes. When roadies smell trouble, something goes off in their brain and they become raging monsters of Rock & Roll ready to toss fans off a ten-foot-high stage, or in this case, kick the living shit out of anybody spoiling the show.

By the time we got to the gates it was all over and everybody was singing "Kumbaya." Curt seemed disappointed. So was I. I wanted to see what he would do to another long-haired hell-raiser like himself.

I checked in with Bob, who was roaming around getting interviews for the documentary. He had Susie with him on the sound recorder and shotgun mic. He was headed to the ranger station on the hill to get an aerial shot of the park. Later, I was scheduled to take Bob to the airport so he could do an actual flyover in one of the university planes.

I hired my old black flight instructor, Clive, lately back from Vietnam, where he probably did strafing runs on innocent Viet Cong villages. He thought this was pretty much the same thing, except missing the key element of live bullets being shot back at him. *Piece of cake*, he said. I was just hoping nobody had given him any psychedelics that might cause a flashback. I could just see him with a wild look, screaming in low and fast while he tossed expensive film equipment overboard as if it were grenades. I had to go hide in the Winnebago bathroom to smoke a big joint just to calm down and get ready for the evening's performances.

The sun started to go down. We hoisted the projector screen high up above stage left. Steve climbed the projector tower behind and fired up the behemoth. The screen was twenty feet wide by fifteen feet high. Without the rainbow canopy, it was the biggest thing next to the stage seconded closely by the speaker stacks on both sides.

They kicked on the stage lights and we started broadcasting to the projector long before either could be seen in the waning sunlight. I took a quick tour out in the audience and could see an image begin to materialize that could be clearly seen from all corners. I went back and settled into the director's seat for the duration of the evening.

I was finally at home. Editing live on the fly was my *Jones* and I loved it. My concentration went into overdrive, while my image-processing brain started flowing and dancing with the six monitors spread out before me like a smorgasbord of tiny windows surrounding the stage, all vying for my attention and selection for the rest of the world. If it wasn't selected for the projector or the recorder, it was lost immediately to electronic heaven where all wasted video images go when they depart our existence. It went through my brain briefly and then gone forever. I didn't care.

I was into the stream of images, connecting snippets from whichever camera got my attention with a new view that fit the last, constantly moving the image along as it jumped from camera to camera. Two big levers let me fade a camera from one switch bus to another. When thrown together with another camera setup, one image would fade into the next. Great for blues numbers and soulful rock.

Double images were my specialty. Showing a singer superimposed over the blues guitar riff was powerful. My hands flew like a one-handed pizza maker. I constantly kept up banter with my cameramen, suggesting long shots or, *move left or tighten up, hold it, coming to you. Got it!*

Camera two, give me a head shot of the drummer. Great hold it. Take 2, you're on. Now pan slowly left to the bass. One, come in tight on the lead. Hold 3, take 3, zoom in one, take one. Whoa, what a shot! Ready two....

The music was great. Our sound feed was fantastic. I could mix the sound clearly onto the headphones to the cameramen, so soon we were cutting to the beat, moving the cameras to the sound and even zooming fast repeatedly when the strength of the music demanded it. I was a goddamned choreographer of dancing videos. It may have only been black and white, but we were sucking every ounce of psychedelia we could from the special effects. If we had color, we could have done color saturations keying that would absolutely blow minds into the fences surrounding the place. People preferred watching the screen instead of the stage, 2 to 1. We were making the show happen like never before.

The first night was over before I realized I had just killed four hours without leaving my director's chair except to pee and grab another beer. Two more days to go. Susie drove us home while I tried to deal with the shakes. All the anxiety, tension, and fear of failures had been beaten down by adrenaline and cocaine, but they had to come out sooner or later. Right now I was having trouble finding my own nose with the little silver spoon. There would be no sleep tonight. I hoped Susie was up for some massive sex therapy.

The next day went even smoother, comparatively. We made it back on site at the crack of noon to help Bob get more footage backstage and to film some of the delta blues acts during the day. Somebody had put up a small tarp overnight to at least keep the musicians out of the sun. I looked at a couple of them and realized they had probably spent way more time singing at night than ever in the daytime. That's why their sunglasses looked like No. 9 welding goggles and their bloodshot eyes glowed eerily red in the direct sun. Rumor had it they were getting soused in one of the trailers backstage and were having trouble keeping the beat or, for that matter, finding the stage.

Bill told me to go check it out because I knew more about alcohol than he did. Cowboys, especially cowboy physicists, certainly did know more about alcohol than big city druggies. I took it as a complement, put on my black cowboy hat and went looking for the hooch house. It didn't take long.

One of the trailers had a little more black traffic than its size would normally justify. I knocked and was ushered into a little room with about eight chairs crowded around in a tight circle. Some had blues harp players doing a little jazz session in one corner and the rest were all seated around Light'n Hopkins talking whiskey business. That was the business old musicians do when trading tails and stories with other musicians over a couple bottles of Old Crow or Jim Beam, if they could afford it.

He was due on stage in about an hour and there was no fucking way I was going to tell any of these Gods of music they had to stop giving whiskey to the younger musicians who might not be able to handle it, especially in the hot sun. Fuck it, I thought, they had to learn somewhere. *Where the fuck did you think the damned blues soul came from anyway? Happy white bitches? Not a chance.*

I threw a few down with him as he told me about Mississippi nights on the bayou. I told him about redneck white men who can't hold their liquor in Michigan. As I left, I promised to have another case sent over after his performance. Had to make 'em try to stretch it out. I didn't want any old blues singers dying at a white man's concert. Just wouldn't be right somehow.

Night came and I went back to processing images in real time. This night, Steve actually got some girl in the audience to go up the tower with him and watch the show in reverse. I had been kidding earlier about the roadie groupie thing. Maybe there was something to it after all.

When Johnny Winter got on stage he almost saturated the whites on our black and white cameras. That guy was so white he made marshmallows look healthy. He jammed with some blues bands and the house went crazy. I got it all on tape. It couldn't get any better. The music in my head just kept going on and on after the show was over. My images made sounds and the sounds became images. Everything was coming at me out of sequence and building to a crescendo of colors, voices, and complex sounds tearing the mind into timeless lumps of piled up pictures and twisted impressions. I was starting to lose it after three days of no sleep, constant booze, nonstop joints, and enough cocaine to win the Triple Crown. To me, I was just tuning my fine motor skills into artistic brain farts for the last night's show. It's how art is done, just ask Jerry Garcia.

I caught my second wind while doing the second ounce provided by Bill. Bill made sure all the key people were alert and awake for the final performance. As he administered another bump, I told him I hoped Pete was somehow paying for the extra drugs. He assured me it was being taken care of. Something about *carrying charges* and *first cut* sort of thing. I asked no further. Rock & Roll accounting bored me to death, except maybe for the part about counting the gate receipts. Lots of things can happen in locked back rooms or command tents.

Finally the stage hands rolled an all-white grand piano on stage, the lights came up bright, and Ray Charles entered wearing an all-white suit to match his piano. This was going to be a challenge to a black and white camera. We were dealing with it when he started and I was getting down right creative playing off some of the reflections and images reflected in the piano.

Then there was a loud banging on the rear door to the Winnebago. It was the door to the locked bedroom video recorder. I stepped out the front door and yelled, "What the fuck do you want? Don't you see the sign? Nobody allowed in during the program."

A skinny little black dude in a spiffy crisp brown double-breasted suit, which was way out of place here except for the black part, was holding up a cable and demanding to know where it went.

Busted!

He was Charles' manager and he had traced this extra cable over from the mix truck, suspecting it was being used to pirate Charles' music. I tried to explain it was non-commercial video tape and intended just for training purposes. He didn't buy it. He stayed till the end of the performance, looking over my shoulder all the time. How can an artist work under such conditions? I started dropping shots and switching to the wrong camera. Sweat was pouring off my brow. When it was mercifully done, the angry little dude took the tape and left in a huff.

Pete was furious when he heard about it later that night. Words were exchanged and threats made. He didn't need to call for any more appearances from Ray Charles because he was blacklisted. Ironic, huh?

I told my crew not to worry; we at least delivered our work to someone who could appreciate it. In the meantime, we had some sixteen hours of video tape from all the other artists at the festival. A damned good time was had by all and now it was time for bigger things.

CHAPTER NINE

ITALIANS PREFER SEX BEFORE COCAINE

"And when it was over it felt like a dream,
They stood at the stage door and begged for a scream...."

Buffalo Springfield
"Broken Arrow"
1968

After the Blues Festival fence was torn down, after the bills
were more or less paid, and after everybody ran out of what was
left of their festival stash, if they had any leftover at all, reality
slowly returned, as did the same old problems. I was getting sued
for not paying the building contractor the last amount due on his
remodeling job in my attic. *What can I say?* I ran out of big cash
and couldn't cough up the last payment. I wasn't the only one.
The Rainbow People's Party was suing the canopy erector for the
return of any advance monies given him before fucking up royally.
That's the problem with engineers; if they wanted something that
worked, they should have hired a cowboy physicist.

Susie moved out of Steve's house to an apartment across town.
Said she just wanted to have a place to call her own. We would still
sleep together, just not always in my bed. It seemed okay to me.
I wanted to earn enough money so I could afford to rent a house
where we could live together. It was just temporary, I told myself.
I loved her and was seriously thinking about asking her to marry
me, but first I had to get a career going so I could afford her. At
least she was away from the toxic influence of her parents, so time
was on my side.

I was hoping the video stage projection would take off and
I would get more gigs for a video PA system. Maybe take it on

the road with a major band. I did one more gig for the Rainbow People's Party when they put on a major concert in the U of M amphitheater featuring Greg Allman's first concert on his own after his brother Duane Allman died, thus breaking up the former Allman Brothers Band. But this time, there was no Winnebago so I had to set up my video switching console right at the corner of the stage in full view of the audience and performers. I was a minor stage star.

Nobody knew who I was, but I had the privilege to be working a major Rock concert with banks of glowing CRT's, a video mix board, and lots of idiot lights. Very techy and very impressive. My crew was different from all other backstage roadies because around our necks, like a doctor's stethoscope, we constantly wore super-big cushioned headphones with airplane pilot boom mikes we had adapted for loud Rock stages. We had clear voice communication to all cameramen even with the loudest bands. We were professional rock videographers and no one had seen the likes of the big screen video close-ups before, anywhere.

Almost like the Blues Festival, it was a wild night of free-form videographing. I was higher than a kite in a tornado on some kind of pink Peruvian flake that supposedly came to town in a truck with the rest of the band's convoy of instruments, staging equipment, lots of overhead bars of flying colored lights that danced with the music, and of course Greg's concert grand piano, complete with traveling full-time piano tuner. Now that's a Rock & Roll job I would never have anticipated. Who knew that Rock musicians worried about tuning their musical instruments? I never gave it a thought, since we considered rock, like government work, required only what was needed to get the job done. Half-assed became close enough for government work as well as Rock & Roll.

...you know there's only one way outta here, but I'm just not going out that front door. 'Cause there's a man down there, might be your ol' man, I just don't know! I screamed into the headphones, singing and dancing along with Greg as I did a triple dissolve into

a fade and then an overlay of the lead guitar strings and Greg's hands on the keyboard. Nobody had seen a video director do live switching while standing at the console. This was fucking mind-blowing!

Portable video existed just for this. This was live editing on the fly as an individual art form. I was digging it and so was the audience. I thought I could hear *oohs* and *aahs* once in a while over the sound of the band when I might be doing something intricate and scary like a shot of Greg keyed inside the bass drum. His head banged back and forth in sync with the big drum stick. I was hot!

When the concert was over, I wasn't. I wanted to go on all night. Video live mixing performances for a captive live audience with live sound, all in the same theater, was in short, incredible. It was my canvas for painting pictures. It was my orchestra for producing music. I'd found my muse.

Of course, we had a video cable snaking to the back-stage area where we had a half-inch Sony video recorder running in a small locked closet. No one was going to surprise us this time. Steve and his new squeeze volunteered to man the recorder and feed it tape. It was an historic concert and we documented it. Steve, as part of my elaborate benefit plan for missing the concert, got a blow job back stage, during the show. I heard that was incredible as well.

I became the unofficial Rainbow Peoples Party film and music video producer. I wasn't really, as I could barely stand going over to their former frat house, now a run-down commune near campus. Without John at the helm, it was getting lame anyway. Apparently, cooperation only thrives under the direction of a strong leader. Otherwise similar-thinking folks will find some inconsequential subject to disagree on. I hate having to watch flower children act like the white suburban spoiled brats that they really were just underneath all the flowers and Patchouli oil.

Between gigs and after work, I volunteered to run an underground film school. Several student organizations helped organize an underground university where grad students and experts could organize and run free classes for the masses. After all, knowledge should be free and open for all humanity to use and enjoy. Universities are places where the free exchange of knowledge is not only allowed but should be encouraged. The administration visibly grimaced at this insult to their mismanagement, but what could they do? The people are free to do as they wish as long as it's off campus. *Fat chance!*

We had a pretty good group and we actually produced a little Super 8 film about druggies having nightmares or something. I just acted like a stupid money bags producer and had my students organize themselves into a production team and get the job done, under budget and on time. Committee art is a necessary evil in the film business so, as an aspiring practitioner, you might as well get it on. Hands-on learning allows innovation based on reality. In the film business, there was only one reality and that was money, unless of course, you're independently wealthy like Howard Hughes.

I ended up having to sell my student apartment house just to pay off the contractor suing me. The buyers were a young lawyer couple from Detroit out to make their first slumlord million. Yuppies were making their first appearance, and it didn't look good. Selfish greed seemed to be the natural response to communalism. After I paid all the contractors off, with interest, I still had a small land contract that paid me a small monthly stipend. It helped put gas in the truck and food in the stomach, but the real estate business was going to have to take a back seat to my new career. What it was, I wasn't sure, but I needed more gigs and I wasn't asking too many questions.

Then came Detroit Purple.

I thought that so far, I had not shied away from dipping into the weird side of life and being pretty cool about it. I accepted pretty much everybody of the new age, except maybe rednecks, bigots, pro-Vietnam war mongers, and, of course, the whole rip-off evil corporate Amerika thing. Hanging out with the Rainbow People's Party certainly provided a spectrum of acceptable weirdos as wide in color as a rainbow implied.

I barely remember the week that Ken Kesey and the Merry Pranksters came through town. They parked the bus behind the Rainbow house and proceeded to set a record for being the longest continuous acid-high party, while tie-dyeing psychedelic T- shirts to be sold to tourists in Greenwich village. The waxigen bomb flames from the vats were so intense that I kept flinching for a week whenever something flashed near me. It was just more of the afterglow from a nervous system overload. It happened a lot these days.

Kesey was from Oregon, my stompin' ground. I grew up with the same people he did and yet here we were, two outcasts from the most outcast state possible, trying to discover reality from a chemically altered state of mind and perception. Most people we met while traveling in the East couldn't believe we were heading in the opposite direction from the rest of the sane world. Most people saw Oregon as a haven of liberal outcasts getting back to nature and purity. *You must be crazy for leaving*, was oft heard by both of us. We agreed with the crazy part, knowing the trip was just a personal crusade before he and I both would eventually be returning to San Francisco, or the Pacific Northwest, or somewhere in-between. It's just a lot better there, but he nor I could put our finger on exactly why. It finally came down to the fact that redneck Oregonians seemed more tolerant and viciously independent than, say, southern rednecks.

So I asked him why he did it. He could have young blonde starlets up and down Topanga Canyon, but instead chose an ancient school bus needing yet another paint job and young, unwashed, curly-haired Jewish girls from San Francisco. He said he could see where he's been better from a bus than a bimbo. I had to agree. The view is important.

With some well-earned trepidation, I stopped by the Rainbow house to pick up a photo of me from the concert. Their official photographer had the run of the concert and had shot hundreds of still pictures for use in later propaganda leaflets. Mine were seriously impressive. I was at the video controls in front of a bank of monitors wearing those giant headphones. Technology was bleeding all over Rock & Roll, and there I was running the cutting edge of mobile video projection. The photographer was a short, dark, curly-haired, very liberal and liberated Jewish girl from the upper east side. She preferred Nikons, as I did, so we had at least something in common. She preferred girls, also like me, which paradoxically nixed taking the *in common* thing any further.

She was a passable photographer who made up for quality by quantity. I liked to wait for the picture, like Adams or Wexler. She shot film like it was a war and all she had was a machine gun. Take enough shots and you're bound to get lucky. She mentioned that she had been invited to a party by some clown running around all the liberal campus organizations handing out white T-shirts with a big purple question mark on it. She held one up to prove her story.

"Is he the Riddler?" I asked with my best cowboy smirk.

"Could be. He was wearing a huge purple coat, just like some sick Detroit pimp straight out of some Black sexploitation movie," she said. Clearly she had something against sex and big black dicks, which I had no interest in exploring any further.

"He said he's looking for music, film, and dance artists to help launch some dumb-assed product or band or head shop, not sure of the details. Also not interested in going to this guy's apartment, even if he has all the cocaine he claims."

"Cocaine, you say?" I innocently asked. "Did he have any with him?"

"Oh he had plenty. Got half the fuckin' house wasted," she spit with a grimace like that was a bad thing or something.

New York Jewish liberal chicks just weren't what they once were, I thought. That's a bummer. I couldn't forget my first one who had consoled me so thoroughly and exquisitely the day that fuckin' Nix-goon had been sworn in for the first time, I actually woke up feeling so good I thought for a brief moment Kennedy must still be our president.

She had this huge open apartment on the top floor of a Soho tenement building in lower Manhattan. The entire room was

SOMETIMES...

surrounded by windows without shades, making sleeping in after a full night of sucking and fucking pretty damned impossible. Watching the winter red sun rise from out of a cold crystalline sea from my precarious pornographic perch atop her curving hips made me fall permanently in love with the entire Israeli-Zionist movement in one fell swoop. Unfortunately, twenty-four hours is the extent of most mutual misery commiserations, but even so, I still have a warm and longing feeling for the swarthy Mediterranean miss who took pity on a poor, battered liberal boy that cold day of infamy. I don't remember her name, but I will never forget her selfless contribution to the movement.

Back in Ann Arbor, this one rummaged around her desk and came up with a business card. She handed it to me without any ceremony, along with two of those silly purple question mark T-shirts.

"You got to wear it to get in."

There was a giant purple question mark on one side of the card like the T-shirt and an address on the other, but no name.

"So who is this guy?" I asked flipping it back and forth in hopes something else might fall out of it.

The address looked like an apartment somewhere in Bloomfield Hills. It was apparently out in the new Detroit expansion area where lots of condos, apartments, and strip malls were being built on top of old corn fields. Mostly middle to lower classes lived there, working the auto plants, and a few struggling start-up technology companies. I shuddered from the thought that this too might be my future.

"He says he's Detroit Purple, whatever the hell that is," she replied. "I think he's some kind of pervert, but that shouldn't stop you from sucking up his snow. Says he wants to recruit talent for producing rock shows and filming them for TV. Must think we know something about it." She winked brazenly.

"Is he black?" I asked innocently, thinking he probably had to be.

Motown had changed who was producing the best music and shows in Detroit. It would be great to get in with them.

"Are you crazy? No self-respecting ghetto black would be doing what this clown seems to be up to," she announced. "Blacks don't give away coke without the expectation of sex first. My guess is he's either Italian or Portuguese."

"Italians prefer sex before cocaine? That doesn't sound right, and I didn't know we had a lot of Portuguese in Detroit."

"Then I guess dago it is," she said, finally flashing a bright phony smile.

"You forgot about France and Spain."

"What?"

"Most people skip over France and Spain when they consider the swarthy Mediterranean types."

She looked at me with a screwed-up face in total confusion.

"I'm just saying, maybe he's French or Spanish. It's hard to tell the difference in that part of the world."

"Believe me; Jewish New York girls know the difference. Now take your picture and get the hell out of here. I've got work to do."

I admired her picture of me. I especially liked how my long blond hair flowed around my headphones, giving me a look of professional cowboy hippie power. Indeed, I felt like a video pioneer going farther than any other live video production had gone before.

I didn't know we had a lot of Italians here either. This needed looking into, especially if he had plans about promoting Rock concerts and videotaping them. Maybe there was some money to be had. Maybe it's a plant from the pigs. However, giving away massive amounts of cocaine is not normally what cops do, and, on the other side, not a particularly good way to do recruiting. Cocaine is usually for bribing junkies and disc jockeys, maybe a quarterback, but what the hell, it definitely needed checking out and Steve and I were just the guys to do it.

Saturday came right on schedule. Steve grabbed his Detroit map and plotted a route to Purple's address in Bloomfield. We had to take a lot of country roads to get there; I didn't want to have to drive all the way to downtown Detroit before catching a freeway headed back in our direction to Bloomfield. Besides, I liked the idea of sneaking up on his place from the cornfield side. *Always do the unexpected*, is what Bill advised me. Habit and convenience breed carelessness, which can get you caught.

It was a brand-new apartment complex, quite large with over eight three-story buildings covering what looked like a former forty-acre corn field. Freshly planted six-foot spindly oak trees lined the roads, held up by wire and stakes. Fresh paint and asphalt still couldn't disguise the fact that this was a scary future of concrete everywhere serving hordes of ticky-tacky houses. People living in little cages bundled tightly with lots of other cages just made me want to puke. *What the hell was wrong with these people? Have they no values? Have they no shame? Have they no drugs for enlightenment?*

Steve finally pointed out the correct building. All the buildings were color-coded with different pastel colors for each building. I giggled when I saw the building Steve pointed out, which was painted a nice pale lavender. This guy could not be for real. This has to be some kind of prank or stunt. But we were here and we were promised coke so I turned to Steve and said, "Let's do this thing."

I looked around the parking area near the lavender building, finding not too many parking spaces available for guests. Plenty of cars meant maybe it was a real party and we could filter anonymously through the crowd without having to risk actually talking to anyone. After all, who the hell would come to such a party in Detroit anyway? My mind raced with all the imagined possibilities, with most of them being quite probably unpleasant at best. Maybe there'll be a monkey.

Detroit was not clean like our giant college campus. Students could be trusted somewhat to have intelligence and honest values like peace, love, and brotherhood. There was a certain loyalty and trust amongst the persecuted intelligencia. Who the fuck knew where the long-haired freaks from the streets of Detroit had been? Or what the hell they might be capable of, like maybe narcs, gangsters, pimps, or undercover provocateur cops? The hairs on the back of my neck were already trying to stand up and make their escape.

We easily spotted the third-floor party from all the colored lights and strobe action leaking over the railing. Loud Rock music gave it away further. We found the outside stairs leading up to the top floor. Strangely, there were no people hanging out or coming and going. It all seemed to be happening behind the one closed door with a UV black light bulb glowing eerily deep purple above it. In its glow I spotted a single brightly glowing purple question mark pinned at the top of the door where presumably a door number should be found. Creepy.

I looked around the parking lot from the top of the outside stairway just to see the lay of the land. The parking lot below did look somewhat crowded with some vans parked along the side of the lot facing the rest of the threatened corn field. *Funny*, I thought, *there's no fence around the apartment property. Someone could 4-wheel their way out of here if they needed to.*

Steve knocked loudly on the door so they might hear it inside over the music. The band played on. He knocked again. I could smell dope. I looked around to case the immediate neighbors, but everything looked quiet. Maybe he invited the whole building, as I would do, in order to get them on your side in case the cops show up.

"Hey brothers! Come right in."

I turned back to the door to see a tall guy about my size, dressed in a giant purple robe with one huge white question mark monogrammed across the front. He looked thin, as I expected, a little gaunt perhaps with a mass of tightly wound curly hair dripping off his head in all directions. A white T-shirt with a purple question mark, like the ones we were wearing, showed through the loose purple faux-fur robe and, from the T-shirt down, the theme continued with a pair of lavender bell bottom pants, terminated by elevated purple suede boots.

The elevator boots gave him away as being actually a little shorter than me. He had on a pair of purple granny glasses that contrasted with the speckled grey, two-day stubble growth. He had a big bushy mustache fringed with sideburns that almost met in a mutton chop. His nose was large and narrow, reminding me of a miniature Nordic ski jump. Ugly curly chest hair popped out around the neck of the T-shirt and a huge gold chain hanging around his neck. He wasn't black, but he was certainly tall, dark, and maybe handsome to coke whores.

Steve looked aghast as he tried to take it all in with one viewing. We had to blink several times just to try and make sure our eyes still worked as expected. Wordless and dumb struck, we must have looked lost or high, or both.

"Que Paso mi amigos! Welcome. Enter at your own risk," exclaimed who we presumed must be Detroit Purple in the flesh.

"Do I call you Purple or Detroit?" I asked, still trying not to look too fucking foolish.

"You have found what you are looking for!"

DP put his arm around my neck and guided us into a smoke-filled dark room, fairly crackling electric with strobes, synthesized music, and glowing head posters. It was a hippie pad in the big city. I know this because I read *Look Magazine*, and they published these things to inflame the public against the youthful revolution. I never thought they really existed outside of maybe the mysterious back catacombs of a head shop. *Now I'm in one.*

"Need a drink," he asked? "How about a toke? If you want anything stronger, just let me know." He pointed to a hallway disappearing farther into the darkness. "We have bedrooms for each preference, but I'd stay away from the acid room. Too many weird vibes there," he said while staring sort of wistfully.

Recovering quickly he asked, "You want a beer?"

Without waiting for us to even shake our heads *yes*, he darted into a crowded kitchen area where several cases of beer were passing briefly through some ice on its way to eager lips. He came back with three Rolling Rocks, the pretend Coors of the Eastern pretend mountains of Pennsylvania.

He motioned slightly and the nearest couch opened up. Steve and I looked at each other and took a big long swig from our beers. It might be a longer night than we planned. He motioned for us to set down.

"Here's to us," he toasted, tapping our bottles with his. "So, what do you guys do?"

"What's a Detroit Purple?" I asked, as I took another long swig from the green horse piss bottle.

"Ahh. That's the whole thing. It's a brand. It's a philosophy. It's an image, an idea, a poke in the eye of the up-tight business world. We are going to revolutionize marketing by selling first the feel-good experience of buying from your own kind, and then the products that follow are only the products we need and desire for the new age living experience. People are tired of buying shit from the likes of Lawrence Welk. People are going to want what Jim Morrison and the Grateful Dead have to sell."

He let that set in and reached out across the coffee table to pull a decorative candy dish in closer. It was one of those pink colored Depression glass bowls on a pedestal with three compartments for different colored hard candies. This one held three different kinds of colorful pharmaceutical pills. I recognized the black and yellow capsules as *yellow jacket* methedrine, and the ever-popular little blue Valiums. The other kind looked like cheap white aspirin.

"What's this?" I asked pointing to the white pills.

"Ah, you'll love those," he said proudly. "They're bootleg Quaaludes from Pakistan. Did you know Quaaludes were invented by an Indian chemist? Of course, any time India invents something, or makes something new, the Packies have to prove they are just as good. So, they do knockoffs that drive the Indians crazy. Good shit though, try one."

He held out the candy bowl to me. I scooped up a handful of the white pills, dropping them in my shirt pocket.

"No thanks. I'm driving."

"So what do you guys do?" he asked again while he tentatively offered the bowl to Steve.

Steve and I were getting impatient. We had been promised coke.

"Where's the bathroom?" Steve asked.

He looked longingly at the back hallway as he scooped up some of the yellow jackets. Figures, engineers need speed to stay awake for those long basement development times.

"Down at the end of the hall."

He pointed in the direction of denser smoke and weirder lighting effects.

"Knock first if you don't like surprises."

"So what do you do?" I asked, trying to get the conversation away from us.

"Oh, I do a little bit of everything. I like to think of myself as a cultural revolutionary. I don't want to tell anybody what they should buy or how they should live like the rest of the establishment. I want to give the people what they want. What they want right now, I'm fairly certain, is sex, drugs and Rock & Roll," he said breaking up into a laugh. "Don't you agree?" he continued while making a fake elbow jab to my ribs.

"I see you've got the drug thing down. What about the sex and Rock & Roll part?"

"Come here and I'll show you."

He got up and headed for the back hallway.

Gung-ho, I thought, as I rose to follow.

Halfway to the glowing bathroom door at the end of the hall, he paused to knock softly at a door on the right. It opened slightly from inside and after seeing who it was, opened up wider. We stepped into a glowing purple room that I guessed must be Mr. Purple's bedroom. Psychedelic posters were on every wall eerily glowing from the several black lights scattered around the ceiling. On the bed stand, the requisite lava lamp was busy giving birth to blobs, which were immediately cast up only to float down again to be assimilated with the big bottom mother blob and then born all over again. *Must be some kind of metaphor*, I mused.

I made out four or five young girls lounging around in various poses of boredom. One had already rose to attach herself to his arm, guiding him to an open spot on the bed big enough for the three of us to sit down.

He motioned to one of the nearest girls. "Joanie. Could you help our friend here…" he paused and looked back at me.

"Cowboy," I said. "You can call me Cowboy, Miss Joanie."

I held my hand out. She laid a limp, boney hand in mine and I pulled it up to my lips. She giggled and smiled up at me as if a plan had just come over her. I guess that answered my question about sex.

"Could you help Cowboy here relax a little," Detroit said, waving his hand in my direction.

I sat down on the edge of the bed next to Purple, while Joanie crept up behind me and began giving me a slow and soft neck rub. If this was going to be a long night, he better start hauling out the coke pretty soon, or I might pass out from sheer ecstasy. Joanie's slender fingers proved uncharacteristically firm and strong. They glided across my skin applying just the right pressure and movement, making each muscle feel singularly assuaged where they lay which, of course, drove me nuts.

"So what do you do, Cowboy?" Detroit persisted.

"I'm a film…and…video…producer," I blurted out between small spasms of pleasure. "What do you do?" I countered right back.

"I make money," he said right back. "You like coke?"

Finally! Maybe now we'll be gettin' somewhere. Before I could get my next little spasm going, compliments of Joanie's tingly little fingers exploring more and more of my back and tummy, a tiny mirror showed up with precisely two well-manicured rows at least three inches long of what appeared to be Peruvian 'greasy white' flake. I had not seen that quality in quite a while. Bill introduced me to it once, which he described as the real thing, *straight off the tree.*

You could identify it because of the dull sheen it reflected, sometimes resembling natural mica flakes. I picked up the partially unwound hundred-dollar bill, rolled it tighter into a little green straw, stuck one end up my nose, and blew all the air out of my lungs. With a mighty Kirby snort of inrushing air mixed with coke crystals, rat hairs, spider mites, microscopic bugs bigger than a virus, anything else hiding out on the mirror, and only fate knows what else, I snorted up one line. I pause, as it all settles in that nostril, switch the straw to the other, and now sucking down the second line. I'm roaring like a lion after gorging on wildebeest. I heard a little applause from somewhere behind me. *Good coke*, I had to admit. The Purple wasn't being cheesy with the coke. That took care of the Rock & Roll part.

"So what kind of films do you make? Have I seen anything?" he kept pressuring.

"Probably not. My film company, Warlock Productions, has done one underground short subject film and one documentary. We also did the video projection at the Blues Festival."

"You did that? I saw that. It was great. How come you didn't do it in color?"

I was tired of answering the same obvious criticism everybody seemed overly motivated to tell me.

"It's because they don't make a color projector that size for less than about fifty grand. But it's coming. Soon every Rock concert hall holding more than five thousand screaming paying patrons will be able to see color close-ups of their favorite musicians, complete with star-studded sweat beads on their noses." I tapped my nose to illustrate. "Think of the possibilities."

"Did you videotape the Blues Festival? I bet that's worth some money."

"Maybe. So what did you say you were doing?"

"I might be able to use someone like you. I plan on promoting some local bands. Sort of like Pete and John there in Ann Arbor, only I'll market them under the Purple banner. Detroit Purple will have a national recognition label like Motown has today. It will be so popular we won't need any real talent. We'll make our own talent."

He paused to do some more coke with his girlfriend. Joanie's amazing fingers had been slowly getting closer and closer to my crotch. I tried to ignore it, maybe discourage it. I was still in a committed relationship. I loved Susie even when she was hard to understand. The skinny fingers began to poke ever so gently around my waist and under my belt. I leaned back slightly against her and felt even more relaxed.

"So, Purple, how did you get started in all this?"

"That part was easy. I'm just carrying on the family business. My grandfather came here around the turn of the century from Sicily."

I knew it. Italian. Mr. Purple was a Mafia trust funder kid.

"He started selling weed to all the blacks working the Ford plant. The blacks back then were mostly from the south and had been growing and smoking weed for hundreds of years. But my grandfather bought off the cops and company officials to the point where he was allowed to sell drugs openly and exclusively just outside the plant gates on every payday."

He beamed broadly showing he was full of family pride.

"He passed the business on to my father, who took care of the war-time workers just like his papa had done earlier. My dad gave me the General Motors plant in Flint, where I have been adding other drugs and services to the product line. I want to make the business more diversified, so I decided to branch out into new markets."

"Does Pete or John know this?" I barely struggled out before mumbling *Oh-ohhh*. A slithery finger found apparently a hole in my underwear. He laughed. His girlfriend clearly had her hand much deeper into those purple bell bottoms than Joanie was into mine.

"Sure. I offered Pete a chance to work with me. I could help him get the job procuring talent for the university's annual entertainment budget. I've got contacts in the music and show business that might be very useful to the right person." *Oh, oh!*

Clearly someone had made alien contact. He lost his train of thought for a moment, rolled his eyes gently, and then slowly refocused on the nearest black light poster.

"You see," he continued slowly, "I've made some new contacts that are willing to back my play. I have some friends in the Rock business you wouldn't believe." *Uh no!*

This time he visibly twitched, which must have been a cue to Joanie who gave me a corresponding pinch in an area that made me jump a bit as well. The briefs had been breached from the basement side. I tried to keep my cool but I didn't have the practice like someone like Bill. I bet he didn't jump.

"Listen," he commanded as he leaned in closer to whisper. "There is really big money in this business if you know what the audience wants."

His eyes rolled again, only this time they disappeared into his skull socket and rolled around until reappearing on the opposite side. He paused, staring blankly ahead while his eyes readjusted to the darkish scene; he had the look now of a clairvoyant going into some kind of trance. Who was pulling whose string now, I couldn't tell. I knew who was pulling mine, though, and promptly lost my train of thought once more. *Darn it!*

"You know someone big in the business?" I was trying to get him to tell me more. "Are they on the talent side or the money side?" Everybody knew you either had talent worth corrupting or the money necessary to do the corrupting. Either way, some innocent bastard with talent would be raped, ripped off, and if lucky, thrown to the Nashville dogs for pretty much more of the same, except done with a cordial Southern smile.

"That crazy Alice Cooper is stabbing dolls on stage with a sword while singing about dead babies for fuck's sake! What do you think those kids are going to need for that!"

He leaned over to the nightstand where the coke mirror sat, dipped his upturned overgrown pinky fingernail into the little mountain, scooped up a healthy snow load clinging to not only his grotesquely unclipped fingernail, but at least a good half inch of the tip of his finger. He lifted the whole sparkly goodness to the vicinity of his—only now do I notice—extremely enlarged Sicilian nostrils, where the powder disappeared immediately, sucked into a dark hole resembling Carlsbad Caverns in New Mexico.

"But to make it big in this business, you've got to offer all three. First you rent the band for a piece of the house, then you cough up the bucks to put the show on the road. At each concert city, we collect the bejesus out of all the screaming sex-crazed druggies by double billing. They buy the ticket and then you market the residuals, like T-shirts, albums, and all kinds of cheap shit, and then of course the drugs."

"What drugs?" I asked automatically. Joanie was dancing around but avoiding pay dirt, which just teased me crazy. I felt something like my morals melting away.

"That's the other part I have."

He leaned in closer still with a white mustache of sparkly powder; he looked like a kid after taking a big slug of milk. I tried not to stare. Joanie had gone unexpectedly quiet too.

"You see, there has been a change in this country. You wouldn't know about it but I do. I have to. It's family business. The old suppliers have been bought out and there's a new man in town."

"Who?" I barked out as I flinched. Joanie had suddenly collared the dog.

"Can't tell you. If I did, I'd have to kill you! HA!" He doubled up laughing. He acted like he just cracked the biggest joke of his life. "Get it? I'd have to kill you! It's a matter of national security!"

He buried his head momentarily in his girlfriend's ample breasts as he laughed hysterically, causing them to jiggle in some most intriguing ways. As a physicist, I was observing coupled resonance waves, which I was pretty sure had never before been described in a scientific journal, but now that I had seen them up close and personal, it's obvious these should be. Now Joanie was taking the dog for a walk.

After a short snuggle, Purple reappeared with red teary eyes, no doubt from crying with laughter. The amount of cocaine in his tears were probably burning his eyelids. "And you're going to get to videotape the concerts for television where we make even more money. Hell, I could get Ford and GMC to buy the advertising up front. If there were only a way for the television audience to just dial a 1-800 number and get their drugs delivered for the show, just like the pizza guy delivers for football."

He thought about this for a moment. I saw his girlfriend screwing up her face in consternation as she concentrated on feeling around in the dark for something lost.

"That gives me another idea. I wonder if a pizza delivery service has figured out how to deliver more than just pizza. I bet my brother would know. He delivers whores to expensive hotels. I wonder if he's thought of this?"

He was now off on a side trip mumbling about how to set up a call-in menu on new high-tech phone answering machines and tape recorders.

"Here's the coke supply. Make it last until I get back."

He handed me the mirror he had just double dipped into with that weird pinky nail and it was still covered in flake along with a razor blade and a rolled up hundred-dollar bill. His girlfriend, still with one arm buried up to the elbow in his purple bell bottom pants, led him out of the bedroom, presumably to a less-populated room. Joanie's lithe little fingers were still digging like sex-crazed earthworms looking for a warm wet place to commingle. I leaned back a little farther until I could feel Joanie's supple breasts cupping my head from behind. This apparently gave more room in my pants to the worms for more vigorous wiggling. Then Steve wandered in.

"There're girls here!" he said with a shit-eating grin. Then he noticed Joanie. "I see you already figured that out."

"Here," I said, picking up the candy dish with my other hand and holding it shakily out to him. "Have another piece of candy. I recommend the white ones but you might like the blue ones." Joanie pulled a hand out long enough to snag a blue pill, after which it promptly disappeared back down my pants like a rabbit returning to its hole. Steve took a couple of yellows again.

"Are you sure? Maybe take a couple of spares just in case."

He dipped again.

"They've got acid in the other room," he said flatly. "I met a DJ, a promoter of sorts, a couple of roadies, and about a half dozen girls high as a kite. Nice girls, I think. Where's the purple guy?"

"I think he's getting a blow job. Or at least he should be getting a blow job from all the coke he keeps handing out. Here, want some?"

I held out the mirror in my other hand, still half covered in flake. That wily finger came out of hiding again, this time dipping a wet tip into the flake and immediately darting back to its hole. I felt something gritty and wet being slowly massaged onto the tip of my now awakening Johnson. Joanie was applying her homemade recipe for desensitizing things that tend to explode prematurely.

Steve seemed to ignore this. He grabbed the mirror and proceeded to clean the other half of it with his not too small, but noble Germanic nose. After holding in a couple of imploding sneezes, he finally focused on me.

"There's another room. I gotta check it out." And he was gone.

Joanie was having trouble getting a hand on the subject, so I helped her unbuckle my cowboy belt and the top buttons of my Levis. She leaned back on a pillow, pulling me with her. My head was still cupped between Nina and the Santa Maria, feeling very soft and warm. Now she had the room to do her magic.

Masturbation, especially from a whore, didn't count against a loving relationship, right? It was nothing I wouldn't do in the shower and my right hand is about the same as a whore, right? Susie can't get jealous over a hand, especially the same hand that can take care of her so well. You could say I'm simply paying a professional trainer to improve my performance. It's educational! It's probably even tax-deductible.

"More coke?" I offered. I looked around and noticed we were apparently alone. I didn't care. This was incredible. She just pinched me in a wordless response meaning, *in just a little bit, when I get this thing to dance like Popocatepetl.* She played and we danced until I couldn't literally stand up anymore. She still cupped my junk in her delicate fingers, like a shell-shocked soldier returning from war needing lots of hugging and spooning. I wanted to turn around and kiss every naked spot I could find on her body, but, had to resist, for Susie. Joanie seemed to not care one way or the other. She had professional detachment. I appreciated that.

"Cowboy! You look tired."

Purple wandered in holding a glass of red wine and his girl. She had clothes on. I was somewhat surprised. I began to expect the beautiful people would soon congregate naked around the palm-lined pool. Society dictated it.

"Joanie, get us some more flake. You know where it is."

Joanie pushed me away as I got back on the edge of the bed more or less upright, but groggy as hell.

"I met your buddy in the pot room. He said you're going on the road with Grand Funk for the end of the Phoenix Tour. There's a couple more guys in there saying they are audio engineers for the same tour. You must know them."

He sat down while his girl went for another glass of wine. Joanie reappeared with a new mirror covered in snow, along with a couple of fat joints.

"I doubt it. I'm with Fanfare, the PA company touring with them. We're an independent, separate contractor. These guys must be band roadies; you know, they set up instruments and amps on stage, keep the drinks back stage full or something. My friends run Fanfare, and I don't see them here."

"Weird," he said. "We are about to do some business, but I need to find out more about them it looks like."

With that, he wandered toward the door to speak with some newcomers just arriving. Joanie seemed to disappear as well. Steve came wandering out of a back room holding a burnt-out joint muttering, *what happened to all the girls?*

I needed some air so we pushed past a new crowd forming near the door and broke out onto the balcony. The air was a cool and refreshing jolt to my mind, still fuzzy from the odd mixture of stimulants I had just been test-piloting.

The parking lot was still full, with only a few cars coming and going.

Then I saw him.

It was just for a second, but some guy in a bleached white shirt, black slacks, and short hair walked calmly up to one of the bigger vans parked along the back of the parking area, opened the sliding side door and ducked quickly inside. He looked familiar, especially when he paused, looking around in our general direction before disappearing. I saw his face clearly under the glare of the sodium vapor lamps. But what got me really excited was the fact that when the door to the van opened, I saw the distinct glow of nixie tubes and pilot lights. That damned van was some kind of electronic surveillance vehicle. The place was being watched!

"Fuck, we've been made. We gotta get the hell outta here!"

Steve looked at me like I had gone mad. He hadn't seen anything. I pointed out the van I had seen the instruments in when I realized there were two more identical to it. They were big black GMC vans with the extended top so you could almost stand up in them. The smugglers we worked with in El Paso drove a white one that looked pretty much like these. Only theirs was decked out with a bed and porta-potty for long-distance, nonstop haulin' cross-country. The vans all had the outside cool-looking sunshade hanging real tough across the top of the windshield. They were great for freeway-cruising smugglers or snoopy surveillance narcs. We had plenty of the test equipment vans at NASA, only they were cheap Econoline's without class or any headroom for standing up. Clearly this was a branch of government with money. Not good for the honest people.

We casually moved across the parking lot like we lived there and were just on a stroll before bedtime. When we reached the truck, I started the engine and drove slowly out of the complex without lights, while keeping our eyes glued to the black vans. It was then I noticed what looked like a small moveable spotlight, or what looked like a spotlight, only it was way too small in diameter to be much of a spotlight.

"What the fuck is that thing on the roof?" I asked.

Steve grabbed my binoculars from behind the seat for a better look as I slowed down, giving him more time.

"It looks like a spotting scope or a camera lens. Can't see anything attached to it though, like a camera or sensor," he said. "Now it's gone."

As soon as we were out of sight and there were no other lurking black vans, I turned the lights on and headed back to Ann Arbor. My mind was running wild with paranoia. It was heat, no doubt. But were they watching us, or Mr. Purple? He as much as said he was mafia, and therefore, above the local law. It had to be the ATF or FBI attracted by all the flagrant use of drugs and sex—fucking morals Gestapo.

And the guy with the short hair and white shirt somehow looked familiar. But I have no friends or acquaintances with a crew cut, and even the physicists I know don't wear white shirts much anymore. I don't like it when the enemy starts looking familiar. There were a lot of characters at the party besides us. The pigs might be after about half of them. I hope we aren't part of that half.

"How about a laser?" Steve offered as we made it to Brighton.

"What the fuck would the FBI want a laser for? Are they going to burn holes in his stash as he comes and goes?"

"It might be a listening device. I heard about an experiment at MIT where they bounced ultra sound off big glass windows and the reflected waves were modulated by the sound waves inside the building that vibrated the window. It got classified real fast if I remember right."

"That thing was pointed at the apartment, wasn't it? They were using a laser to bug the entire party!"

It sank in for a moment before I realized I had not used my real name while talking inside. *Whew!*

It still didn't make sense though. Why not just put mikes all over the place like the good old G-man days? If they wanted to bust Mr. Purple, they certainly could have more evidence than needed, judging from the amount of security we saw being exercised by the Purple gang. It was all too relaxed and sublime to be a major bust in the making. Something didn't make any sense.

In any case, I swore that was the last time I wanted anything to do with things purple except for maybe eggplants and frilly panties.

It took us both all day Sunday to recover. The hangover wasn't so much our concern, but rampant paranoia was. Who the fuck was that character claiming to be some kind of Detroit mafia kid with his hooks dug deep into drugs and the sex trade? And who were the pigs in the parking lot? Why did we go there? We both decided that Ann Arbor was a lot safer than all these fruitcakes stirring up suburbia.

CHAPTER TEN

OVERLOAD NEVER FELT SO GOOD

"Send lawyers, guns, and money, the shit has hit the fan...."

Warren Zevon
"Lawyers, Guns and Money"
1978

Monday came and the ax continued to fall. I was informed by my PhD advisor that there would be no further paychecks starting immediately. That just sucked the big one! I had no money and no decent income outside the lab.

I wasn't going to be able to finish my dissertation now. I had bet they wouldn't drop me so close to a formal publication. I lost the bet. Nobody apparently gives a shit about the science once the money stops flowing. I had important results that had already blown another research group right out of the government-funding water. It needed formal publishing so the lab and staff would get the credit they deserved and I the degree. They could always find a little money somewhere. Not this time.

I was fucked and would have to drop out of graduate school just months away from completing my PhD. Shit, with the way Nix-goon was fucking up the economy, even if I had a PhD, I wouldn't be able to get a post doc or teaching position —or anything else I might be qualified for. Academic research outside of the defense department had simply ceased. With long hair and an anti-authoritarian attitude, that avenue was also closed, even if I had wanted to join *the death society*. Shit, I couldn't even get a job pumping gas! *Over qualified* was the new unemployment *let-me-down-easy* mantra.

So, what does a young boy do? He runs away from home and joins a Rock & Roll band. I called Marty to see if the tour with Grand Funk was still on. It was, and he was very happy to see that I was unemployed and willing to work for roadie wages. One hundred dollars per concert and fifty per diem for expenses. Drugs were extra, but he promised to keep me awake and alert, at least during the concert, no matter how fucked up I might actually be. *Cool*, I thought.

My job was to tune the speaker stack, help set up and tear down the PA and, during the concert, be available for troubleshooting and monitoring the output equalizers and cross-overs for proper sound level and quality. I soon learned this meant replacing blown speakers during the performance and slapping the hands of the mix engineer when he tries to mess with the output equalizers.

When I met with Marty just before leaving, I got the lowdown on what was really going on. Fanfare had rented an old gas station on North Division near the river. The secret I learned really quick to building huge speaker cabinets was a six- foot cross cut saw. The old repair bays at the garage were perfect for laying out full sheets of three-quarter-inch marine grade plywood, which the saw chopped into big rectangles for the sides of the big speaker cabinets.

They also had another crucial tool. The cabinets need speaker holes, round holes cut in plywood as big as the speakers, in some cases up to eighteen inches in diameter. This was accomplished with a router mounted on the end of a motor-driven adjustable arm. The router dug a deep groove through the plywood in a perfect circle. With these industrial-grade toys, they quickly built enough road-hardened speaker cabinets to field two giant stereo stacks, enough to handle about 2,400 watts per side. Marty thought there was only one other PA in the country with that much power capability, and it was busy doing the new Bob Dylan tour. *Damn, folk music was even getting loud and obnoxious.*

I wanted to show him my two tools for PA work which I didn't think he had. One was a Heathkit portable Sound Pressure Level (SPL) meter, and the other was a pink noise generator I built myself, in a nice little battery-powered box you could hold right up to a microphone. At close range, and at the mike's acoustic maximum level, it could load the system with equal power across all the frequencies. Each microphone could be equalized for its unique placement in the room, and the size and shape of the room. Some called it acousta-voicing the hall. I called it flattening the mic, as that is what it did; it flattened each mike's response across the entire spectrum which would virtually eliminate high-pitched feedback and ringing. It also meant you could get the loudest sound possible for the hall from every mic that got equalized this way.

"I'm willing to bet we can get at least 120 dB SPL at almost every seat in a large arena theater."

That was about the same loudness as a full-throttle jet engine at 10 feet. There was an unspoken competition to see who could make Rock & Roll even louder than what was already considered too loud by most sidewalk critics.

He looked at me with his twinkly eyes while absentmindedly stroking his full black beard; he had a full head of black hair, amply bracketing and falling well below the beard, making him look like a wise holy man from Hoboken.

"I can already do that," he said. "You trying to take my job?"

"Don't you want to get it even louder than what your ear can do?"

"My ears work just fine, but I want to see if we can get more gain from the drum mikes, so we'll give it a try."

"Maybe we can adjust the mike's placement," I suggested. "Put them off-center from the drum cavity so they don't resonate so easy. Drums tend to vibrate with the PA sound, causing high gains at the drum's fundamental frequency. If we couple to higher harmonics, the power response will flatten out more."

"Sounds good," he said. "Do you know what's been going on with Grand Funk?"

"Nope," I said eagerly, "not a clue."

I made it a point not to follow celebrities. They didn't deserve extra accolades past their enormous pay, so who the fuck cared if they showered or not, and with whom.

"They did a big tour last year for their *Phoenix* album that culminated at the Madison Square Garden," he explained. "They fired their manager for cheating them on record earnings a few weeks before, but at the last concert he walked in with a court order and stole the band's equipment right in the middle of the show."

"Wow, what an asshole," I said, knowing that description probably fit 90 percent of the industry anyway.

"So, this tour is a little extension of that tour with just four dates in one week. I guess they need the money to buy some new equipment. We have the only available PA big enough to do the job. Also, because they're looking for a new recording contract, this tour will be managed by a new guy from Dave Geffin. So even though it's just a short tour encore, it's with pretty much wholly new band equipment, including our new mix board and speaker stacks. A lot is going to be riding on this tour. It's our first shot at the big time and an opportunity to show the big wigs in LA what we can do."

"No pressure," I declared. "Cool."

"By the way," I interjected, "do you know a couple of little Mutt and Jeff characters claiming to be roadies for Grand Funk?"

"Oh, you mean Tweedle Dee and Twiddle Dum?" He laughed at his own joke. "They were the ones who introduced us to Mark Farner. They think they're electronic engineers, but they mostly just ride along on other people's talent. We may have a problem with them, since they have Mark convinced to let them mix the PA. If they fuck up, we could get the blame."

"Just what I need. Secret Rock & Roll agendas being played out like cheap Mexican soap operas."

"That's one way to look at it. But from my experience, it's just show business as usual."

"Shit, what a depressing thought," I added.

He reached into one of the drawers on his desk and pulled out a black T-shirt.

"In that vein, I want to award you your first professional roadie T-shirt."

It was all black with white lettering, size X-tra large, with a handy front pocket. It only had a plain logo on the back with a miniature version on the pocket, simply stating *Fanfare*. "We leave tomorrow morning with the band on their private jet. The equipment trucks, the band's and ours, are already there."

I didn't even try to sleep that night. My life had just taken another big change with no clue as to better or worse. Only time would tell.

Steve drove me to the business terminal at Detroit International the next morning. I had never been on this side of the airport before. This is where they dispatch all the corporate jets and billionaires. It's my first time to rub elbows with the rich hoi polloi and enjoy a little of their lifestyle. I openly despised them and all the evil that put them there, but I couldn't help but be jealous of how high it was above us lowly peons. Money means success in Amerika, and you can't get invited to the real party without it… or perhaps some marketable talent for getting it. That's where I might sneak in.

I looked around the shining chrome and glass modernist building, wondering how many of the suits wandering through here were higher than a Himalayan Monk on Everest. Rumors that coke was getting popular with the Nouveau riche, the young trust funders and other beautiful rich people, excited Bill's imagination. More money usually meant higher quality drugs, and who didn't like that?

Soon, it was gratifying to see a bunch of long-haired freaks gathering in the sanctuary of suit exclusivity. *Fuck'em if they can't take a joke*, I always said. Marty showed up right on time. The band members rolled in fashionably late in a limo stinking of booze and pot. No waiting now; the stars have arrived.

Marty introduced me to Mark, Mel, Don, and Craig, the current band members. It would just be the six of us for the flight.

We all walked out onto the wet tarmac to a small commercial jet warming up on the ramp. The band members had on their Mod clothes, pink glasses, stovepipe hats, and other weird regalia that pronounced to the world, *Hey, look at me, I have no taste, but I refuse to wear your corporate costume.* To the rest of us, it just meant they weren't real freaks, just playing at it for the money. It made me want to choke, but I was getting paid so I let it go for now.

The first concert was in Richmond. The band's equipment truck and roadies along with Curt and Lenny, another grunt minimum wage roadie, and the Fanfare equipment truck was already there waiting for us. The flight only took a couple of hours—just long enough for the band to play a couple hands of slam dunk poker and smoke a couple of joints, while ignoring us. I sat in the corner with Marty, marveling at how far the long-haired freak thing had gotten. Here we were smoking dope in a big jet airplane on our way to a Rock concert. What more could you possibly ask for? *Mo' better drugs*, of course.

Marty spent most of the flight staring into his three-ring binder he used for all his notes and reminders. He seemed to only be interested in two things: getting the best sound possible out of whatever shit equipment he might be saddled with and whatever the fuck he kept in that binder. He had an old, beat-up, hard-side briefcase that looked like a well-used poster board, covered in layers upon layers of now unrecognizable tatters of past hall stickers, backstage passes, and band decals. It was always with him, and that binder its sole content. Well, that and the cash he always carried around.

We might be able to crash the Detroit business air terminal once in a while, but banks and credit cards wouldn't touch us. So, it was a cash and carry business. Marty got seven hundred dollars for every concert he did and was paid promptly, usually before the show was even over. The band was on a similar basis on this trip, as well. Apparently, the fired and disgruntled former New York manager had taken all the accountants with him. As soon as the gate receipts were counted, Irving, the new Geffen manager, would be right there in the same box office counting the tour promoter's share out in cash, from which he paid Marty and, presumably, the band members and their roadies. Rock & Roll economics reminded me of dope economics.

We rode with the band into town in the required limo that met the plane when it landed. When we got to the arena theater, they left us off and went on to the hotel. Marty and I went looking for Curt. As usual, we found him grinning like a fool at the console, located directly in front of the stage in a special fenced-off section of the floor. He was just powering up the stacks and had Lenny placing mikes on stage. I looked back at the stage and was blown over by the size of the speaker stacks on each side of the fifty-foot-wide stage. I had seen them many times before at the outdoor concerts on a park band shell, and at the Blues and Jazz Festival. I had never seen this stack inside before, however, and they definitely took on a whole new massive black menacing look that was really cool.

Curt punched up the tape cassette and the sound of Traffic's new album, *The Low Spark of High Heeled Boys,* came blasting out. The clarity at loud volume was absolutely stunning. This was not your daddy's high school gymnasium PA. Every instrument could be heard clearly, distinctly and, above all, very loudly. Curt smiled even more as he slowly cranked the volume up, pausing momentarily at every new level to adjust the electronic cross-over and the dual output ten-band equalizer. I pulled out my SPL meter and turned it on. He was already at 100 dB SPL and it looked like he had plenty more headroom. I detected no sign of any obvious distortion or clipping.

Marty looked at the meter, cranked the outputs another 10 dB, and I could start to feel the pressure waves coming from the big W-bottoms. Now I detected some erroneous sounds, but it wasn't coming from the PA. It was vibrating plaster, trash and loose seats scattered all around the hall making sympathetic noise from the low frequency pressure waves striking them.

"What was that bet for?" Marty yelled at me over the loud music. The guys working on stage had stopped and were just staring at us in disbelief.

"A gram of Peruvian Flake, I think," I yelled back.

He jammed it another 10 dB and now I heard something that didn't belong. It wasn't the amps clipping. It sounded like one of the mid-band speakers was pounding its speaker coil on the extreme rear of the magnet. It wouldn't be long before the cone began shredding itself from all the extreme forces of Traffic's sound being driven by raw power.

Gzhttt! and a couple of little pieces of the black cone paper came fluttering out of one of the black cabinets half-way up the stack on the right. Marty shut down Traffic.

"You can start work now," Marty said. "Replace the speaker that failed at 120. I may win the bet, but if I do, I will have failed too. We need that 120."

He wandered off looking for Irving, while Curt told me where the spare speakers were stored in the truck. Sound check was an hour away, so I got busy.

By the time I replaced the blown speaker, the guys with the band finished setting up their equipment. Now was my chance to acousta-voice every mic on stage. Curt turned on the 1-volt p-p calibration tone and adjusted the outputs to read 0 dB. I pulled the little grey box out of my briefcase and went directly to Mark's microphone position, center stage. I held up the grey box so its little speaker was held about a finger's width from the business end of the Sennheiser.

I squeezed the red button on the side with my thumb and a loud hissing sound came out of the speaker stack. Curt flattened the microphone preamp output by raising the level on each band of the mic equalizer until it began to sing near feedback. Now the mic was equalized flat with respect to the entire hall and the location of the mic and all the other objects in the hall capable of reflecting or absorbing sound. We did this in turn with every mic on stage, all twenty-eight of them.

I could hear the difference almost immediately. The artificial pink noise was exercising every speaker equally so no one speaker or one tone would hit the auditorium feedback level before the others. Now when the mic gain approached feedback, it didn't whine at a piercing single tone, but would sort of begin a subtle hollow growling sound, as many different frequencies from both the highs and the lows were trying to feedback all at once. We now had maximum headroom to crank the volume into for every mic on stage. I smiled secretly. I knew that when the hall filled up with soft pliable sound-dispersing bodies, the headroom could only increase. *Enough*, I hoped, *to win the bet.*

The guy with the band doing the remote-controlled spotlights cut the house lights and started going through some of his maneuvers. He had several banks of Fresnel lights on each side, pointing mostly down at the stage. There was one light bar, however, suspended over the rear of the stage with more fixed-colored Fresnel's pointing down, and four moveable parabolic spotlights capable of turning almost any direction desired and changing colors, all by remote control. They mostly pointed down and slightly toward the audience, really only illuminating the tops and backs of the performers, but they could be turned in any direction, either synchronized together or separately. I wondered how it was all going to look during the performance.

And then we waited. The band said they wanted a sound check at 4. It was now 5 and no band in sight. It became my first exposure to the typical star ego crap. *Fuck everybody else, I'm the star and I can inconvenience or fuck over whomever I please,* was the apparent attitude. The bigger they thought they were, the shittier they treated their own people for being beneath their station. Egalitarianism apparently had no place with giant egos and blatant buffoonery.

There was a strict class system at work here that seemed out of place with the times. I didn't treat my crews that way when running the video projections. This was the phony part of the Rock & Roll business. They professed idealism, liberty, freedom, peace, and brotherhood, yet in the trenches, they acted like self-centered egomaniacs too cool to hang with the common masses, even if they grew up as old friends back in Michigan. The whole thing began to stink of elitism and assumed Rock aristocracy. The band members were sort of dickish when it came to socializing with the adoring peasants who actually supported their shitty lifestyle.

5 o'clock drug to 6 and then on to 7. We waited in the partially dimmed auditorium with sound and lights ready, standing by for the final approval of the band. The gates open at 8 so they better get their act together soon.

Finally, they showed, but their mood was sour. They walked around the stage looking at all the equipment and placement of stage monitors and mikes. Mark did a little rearranging of his foot pedals for his guitar. The bass player, Mel, picked up his ax, which was about as big as he was and probably about the same weight, plugged it into the double Marshall stack behind him, and hit a few notes. The bass sound from the 18-inch Marshall cabinets, blasting directly into four EV150 mikes, came boiling out of the big "W" bottoms of the PA another ten-fold, rattling the thousand or so empty metal chairs on the floor in front of the stacks. It was loud but causing all sorts of sympathetic vibrations from its wake.

Mark stepped up to his mic and said softly, *Testing…One… Two….* He adjusted his guitar levels, struck a couple of chords, sang out, *I'm getting closer to my home…!*

It was loud and clear. He didn't smile though. He disconnected his guitar, stepped back, looked left at Don, the drummer, and then the new keyboard player, Craig. Don did a couple of drum rolls, smacked the crap out of his one bass drum, and hit the symbols hard. He had eight mikes surrounding his curiously small road drum set, totally unlike the trend toward trap sets larger than the stage. He started a little rhythm, sang a few words into his Sennheiser. Again, loud and clean, the sound came back at them with just a little reverberating echo from the empty hall, but otherwise fairly clean and loud.

The new keyboard guy, Craig, played a few licks and seemed the only one to smile a little. We took his sound feed direct from his equipment without a mic, making it a lot cleaner and louder than the acoustic feeds. It seemed downright magic when there's no hint of feedback. The loud sound seemed to reach right inside your chest and massage your heart with devout love and soulful meaning. *Rock & Roll* and *Loud* were now married and living happily ever after in our brave new world of in-your-face music with a message and a soul!

The band members huddled up to talk a little on stage while the guy on lights was going crazy, throwing his multicolored light beams all over the stage, including most of the floor seating area right in front. He was clearly winging it by hand (later we learned he was using an actual joy stick), so might have needed some rehearsal but the band simply turned tail on the sound check and went back to the hotel to get ready, I guess. Later, I learned, *getting ready* meant getting the right amount of drugs and alcohol in your system to just cut the ever-present nervous fear-edge and mellow out the brain memory banks for the coming high-intensity synchronized effort. Marty, Curt and I just looked at one another like *What the hell?* and, as always, again waited for the fucking pampered stars to get their infantile whiny shit together.

Later, while killing time backstage drinking free cheap beers and munching on dry, badly made submarine sandwiches, Marty clued me into some of what was going on under the surface. Apparently, the band had to find a new manager and road show promoter after the debacle in New York. They also had to earn some quick cash to help replace their equipment that was lost to the former manager and to try out this new PA and lighting gear they had helped fund. It was four dates in five days. Concerts East, David Geffen's east coast branch, was now handling the road show and it was strictly cash and carry. That was Irving's job, accounting for the ticket sales and reconciling the box office during each performance so the money was in hand before the band took the stage.

The other rumor was the band, or Mark in particular, needed to come up with a new album, fast, to cover their lost income from the court battle. They were said to be building a secret sound studio somewhere in the woods near where they grew up in Flint in order to develop a bunch of new songs for Capital and Geffen. Marty mentioned visiting Mark's farmhouse near Flint when they were cutting the deal for building the new PA, but he said he saw nothing there resembling a studio unless they had something going in the old giant red barn sitting behind the newly remodeled two-story classic Midwestern farmhouse Mark bought to relive his childhood Michigan farm dream.

Anyway, Marty made it clear there was a lot riding on this little mini-tour and he didn't want to fuck it up. It was Wednesday. After tonight's concert in Richmond, we had all night to drive the PA equipment truck to Columbia, South Carolina, for the next gig. From there, we had one more night's drive to Little Rock, which should be no problem, but the last date on Saturday night was in Omaha, which was a good five hundred miles from Little Rock.

"You know something about trucks and truck driving?" He held out a heaping coke-spoon to my left nostril. "Hit it!"

"Don't say it," I said as I held my right nostril closed while sucking hard through the one remaining. *Pfft! Pfft!* I sneezed trying to hold it in. "You're not making me go with the truck, are you? You promised I would be on the band's charter plane, you low life Rock & Roll scuzz ball."

"This is really important. We can't let anything go wrong with this tour if we are going to get any more gigs from Concerts East. Frankly, Curt kind of loses it under pressure. I'm afraid of what might happen on the road that could paralyze him with fear and possibly blow this whole gig. I need someone cool and competent riding with him. If we pull this off, there is talk of touring with some major new bands like the Eagles or maybe KISS. I'll make it up to you, I promise. The next tour you can fly, but I really need you to help us finish this tour and help Curt if there is a problem." He held out another heaping spoon to the right nostril and instructed again, "Hit it!"

About then, the warm-up band showed up. They were some kind of imitation greaser band doing old fifties Rock numbers, while all dressed up like cheap greasy Elvis imitators. They were so happy just to be appearing with Grand Funk that they didn't care about anything. We let them set up next to GF's equipment so we only had to reposition the mikes and strike their stuff during the intermission. A quick sound check and they were happy. By then the audience began streaming in. It was a sold-out show already. Little did they know that just about everything used in the previous Phoenix tour had been totally changed out. Except for the three spoiled Rock stars, damned near everything was new and untested.

Finally, the hall began filling with an amazing number of long-haired freaks from what I thought was a hotbed of redneck bigots, Richmond, Virginia. I was surprised. The smell of pot was in the air and the smoke was getting thicker. Curt manned the stage monitors from a small mix board behind the left stack. He had to wear big headphones with soft, water-filled cushions to help keep the ambient noise from blocking his ability to balance and control the sound being folded back to the stage so the musicians could hear each other and play in sync.

Marty and I mixed the first band, which was pretty much no challenge. They sang all tunes with the same loudness and intensity, leaving very little to do for the creative sound mixer. The crowd seemed to enjoy it and the pot smoke just got more intense. The smoky haze lit up along the beam paths to the lights, giving each one a colored shaft of light dancing in unison to several more lit up beams as they whirled, pointing this way and that, spinning and thrusting shafts around the stage and the whole hall to the musical rhythms being played. George, the lighting guy, was obviously having a blast.

As for me, I had to do some measuring. The band on stage was as good as any loud Rock & Roll band, so we should be able to get the performance we were hoping for. I took the portable sound pressure level meter with me as I climbed to the middle of the top balcony in the rear of the arena. I had a small flashlight with me to signal Marty at the board in the center of the floor. *One if by land or two if by sea.* If he could hit 120 dB SPL without encountering feedback, then we prove our case.

It was reading right around 115 when I signaled Marty to attack by sea. He began slowly edging up the outputs until I saw a change in the meter. It got noticeably louder to me, but I doubt if the audience was even that aware. It was loud and for the first time ever, pretty damned clean for such a huge arena theater. The Rock fans were obviously digging the shit out of it. So was I. I signaled for more sea.

The meter began bobbing its needle up against the 120 reading as I began to feel a little crinkling noise in my ears. That was the sound of my ear canal closing down its little sphincter muscle in an attempt to protect the inner workings from the extreme pressure waves being applied to the eardrum and every tiny bone, anvil, and cochlea downstream from there. That alone told me we were putting out the maximum any ear could tolerate, and yet still it was clean with no clipping or damping and above all, not a hint of feedback. All the power was going into moving speaker cones in response to all the sound being amplified, and not into oscillating at one brain-splitting frequency.

The dynamic range was approaching orchestral, but what brain-fuddled Rock & Roller would ever notice? The acousta-voicing worked. We had the only PA in the world at that moment that could shred cones in perfect harmony with the music. The new heavy metal bands are going to love this kind of power. Raw power for raw music and souls worn raw from all the shit.

A joint appeared in front of my face, gesturing in a provocative manner suggesting that sharing deviant behavior was not only allowed, but encouraged. I noticed earlier the distinct lack of cops inside the hall. Our Ann Arbor trick of using private security people, usually long-haired freaks themselves, inside the venues defused a lot of misunderstandings between dope smokin' Rock & Roll freaks and the jack-booted pigs. I took the obligatory deep suck on the fat joint, hoping secretly it was not acid-laced, and passed it on. I got the *two thumbs up* signal from the freak who passed it to me, which was all you could do to be understood with so much sound filling the air. It was impossible to even shout into someone's ear and still be understood.

When the needle was averaging 120, I gave the *one if by land* signal. I could see Marty's grin from ear to ear even from that distance. He raised one thumb up while still concentrating with the other hand on the board, getting a little more headroom for the guitar. When the set was finishing up, I made it back down to the stage to help with the changeover. My ears were still doing that crinkly sound thing as they tried to now open up to normal sound pressures. When Marty handed the board over to Twiddle Dee and Twiddle Dum, he was visibly smiling and noticeably feeling a lot better about our first performance. He hauled out the magic bottomless coke bottle for another round before the next big hurtle: getting paid.

"Keep your eye on those two while I go find Irving," Marty said.

He ran off toward the hall entrance clutching his one signatory feature— his trucker's wallet, the only official badge for all professionals who call the road their primary home—which said more about Marty than his perennial daily dress of Levi's with picture T-shirts, his freakishly long hair and beard, or his undying love of the Rock & Roll road show. I never saw him put a tie on for any reason, including funerals. I admired anyone who could do business with suits without ever having to stoop to their level. It was a new world and I liked it.

Marty's wallet hung permanently on a presumably unbreakable chrome chain locked to his wide, thickly embossed leather belt. It was made of thick, heavy-duty bull-skin leather, very rugged and ugly, stained visibly darker with hard road age, dirt, and sweat, large enough to carry a hefty wad of one-hundred-dollar bills, a small office filing system, respectable emergency pharmacy, and possibly a purse pistol for those inclined to violence. Nobody I knew on the road ever carried a gun although Curt once in a while wished he did. Marty was never seen dressed without his wallet, and one time in a Hyatt hotel hot tub, he was clearly undressed yet somehow still had it attached to himself.

Marty disappeared as he fought his way through the now agitated, freaked-out long-hair crowd toward the front ticket offices to collect his share of hot cash from the tour of the desperate and destitute.

The lights went down. The hall went quiet. Some noise was heard echoing from open mikes. Movement could be seen on stage but nothing recognizable. The quiet lingered expectantly a little longer. Mutt and Jeff were getting animated. They both kept glancing up nervously as they too tried to make out what was happening. I hoped Mark could find the mic in the dark.

The lights were cued and as they flashed on full power, the first note crashed the hall like an exploding runaway rocket. The band appeared almost magically out of the darkness already playing their asses off. The music was loud and for the first time, apparently surprisingly clear. I could see some amazement on the face of the band members before they went blank with performance face. Even Mutt turned to Jeff, fist bumped him and beamed him a big fat satisfied smile like some Cheshire cat munching happily on his own tail.

Boom da-da boom da boom.... Donny smacked the little base drum with the help of about sixteen extra drum heads in the form of 18-inch woofers being driven with kilowatts of pure, raw electromagnetic sound power, creating a drum beat sound that was truly seen and felt more than heard. It needed no air to get from instrument to ear as it came from small synchronous seismic events set off by the drummer and conducted to your ear through concrete, steel, flesh, and ugly bone.

From such a Midwest solid Rock beat, little Mel's bass guitar came thundering in just a little louder and little more gnarly as it played one-on-one counterpoint with Donny's bass drum. The seismic events now wore some flowing streamers—big bold streamers of clean, pure-throated basso profundo waves, like the roiling surf, powerful but smooth and extremely forceful, seeming to roll off the stage like giant boulders thundering across the floor, crushing bodies as they passed by, only to crash up against the opposite wall of seats full of screaming, freakish masses. Their drug-crazed brain goo was tripping on something they had never heard before, loud but undistorted base notes so low and distinct they simply had never been heard outside the studio.

All that and mind-boggling, whirly colored lights flashing mad patterns of light beams stabbing in every direction through the hazy smoke, like multicolored Damocles swords looking for heads to slice off. Every sense was getting its fair share of overload and the brain loved every second of it. Overload never felt so good.

I think I won the coke bet with Marty, with the unfortunate caveat that I was going to need it if I was going to help Curt and Lenny drive the truck between the next three gigs. *May not be enough* came the dreaded next thought. *Oh well, nothing I haven't done before* was the soothing lie.

Mark, the golden-haired and, I guess, the golden-throated barebelly warbler joined in with some wicked licks on the guitar. That completed the basic band and brought the audience to the floor, pushing toward the stage, where they stayed packed the rest of the night, shoved together as tight as cigarettes, but jumping and writhing in waves of connected flesh you couldn't believe actually worked under these circumstances. I came to call it the common frenzy mode, where everybody connects up like ants on pheromones, throwing their bodies into an uncontrolled mass, making a bridge for the rest of the hive to pass over unharmed. They perform as one entity with no centralized nervous system other than the smell of music and the sound of colors.

Fanfare controlled one of those aspects and therefore I was secure in the knowledge that I was making an important, dare we say, significant contribution to the betterment of civilization, or at least its swift deserving demise, (I didn't much care which at this point). I was hoping to add a video projection screen to the road-mix backdrop of special effects, lights, and staging, completing the new road show look for all the traveling bands for the next decade or more. That sounded like a solid business plan.

Now that my job was essentially done, I headed backstage to see if there was anything left to drink after the warm up band and GFR had probably cleaned out the serve-ur-self bar. I found a half bottle of black jack though, and some cans of moderately cool coke which I combined into a personal drink stash that would carry me through to packing up the trucks and hitting the road. I planned to pass out right away and get some sleep while the chumps did the driving.

For the rest of the show, I hung out in the wings behind the speaker stacks, watching the band perform from so damned close I could have spit on their shoes and they probably could have spit right back without losing a lick.

I was drinking on stage in Richmond fucking Virginia with Black Jack in a coke can, which was illegal as hell, and I was snorting coke every couple hours just to stay alert, which was even more fucking illegal, and I was zinging with the Funk, up close and personal. Every time I had to go to the head backstage to get rid of the jack 'n' coke, I took a big old mellowing hit on my new dugout one-hit pot pipe, which for some strange reason, seemed apparently even more illegal than all the rest. Between all this and maybe a few opioid pain killers, I was pretty much controlling whatever I needed my body to feel or not feel. Welcome to the new world of Rock 'n' Roll *Dune!*

Near the end I noticed the crowd was pushing in a little more toward the stage and the band roadies, all three of them pretty big bruisers, were now all around me in the wings watching Mark and the crowd right in front of him. A few arms were reaching within a few feet, of his feet but he seemed unconcerned. The stage was six feet off the floor with a fence in front.

The fence seemed to have disappeared. A freaky long hair with no shirt started pulling himself up onto the lip of the stage.

One of the roadies rushed out and in one fell swoop drop-kicked the furry head off the stage lip and back into the sea of churning flesh. *It was a zombie invasion! Every man for himself!* I started to back out of the way, but one of the roadies caught my arm and pulled me out onto the stage just as the hordes began to breach the sacred no-man's stage lip at several points.

The roadie next to me took out the zombie on his left, presumably leaving the one right in front of me as my problem. *Oh well, what the hell, it's either them or us and we've got the high ground.* But I hated one-on-one violence so I stepped on his hand instead. He screeched, or so I thought, but I couldn't hear a thing over the loud music. I bent down and offered my hand to his one remaining uninjured hand, looking like I was going to help him; instead, I just hoisted him up higher so he would fall back farther when I let him go.

Mark was screaming in my ear about his *captain*, and meanwhile two more try the climb of shame and we roadies are all over them, first hoisting them on stage where we could get a better swing at throwing them even farther off the stage, taking out the rear support zombies before they could reach the stage wall. We were building a wall of zombie bodies to help keep them at bay. I normally am repelled by violence, but righteous Rock & Roll violence in defense of the purity of the stage must be upheld at all cost! It was a sacred duty.

Rock & Roll Hierarchy Forever! Or so I was thinking while heady on all that stuff.

The sound stopped, the lights went out, and the band left the stage. I was still helping the band roadies defend the stage in the dark but nobody was doing anything other than yelling and screaming for an encore. I used the dark to make good my escape, getting backstage again where I had hid my stash of doctored Cokes earlier. All that heart-pounding violence built up a terrible thirst. I was just in time to see the band exit the rear garage doors and get into a stretch limo. Looked like no encore was going to happen in Richmond. That'll teach them unrighteous Rock zombies!

I sipped on my last coke-jack, or was it jack-coke, listening to the roar of an outraged crowd not getting its way. The house lights came on. That alone is a huge mood killer. The band roadies were still defending the dark and empty stage but nobody gave a shit anymore. The show was over and everybody knew they had to come down and face reality again.

The PA cranked up the approved *before and after* canned music of the *Spark Low Heeled Boys* and Curt and Lenny began the process of disconnecting every fucking cable, rolling them up, and storing everything for travel. I was getting so fucking drunk I wasn't much help, but I did twist my ankle when I jumped off the speaker stack after handing down all the tweets and horns. I found another half-filled bottle of Black Jack in one of the private rooms Irving had been using to count money during the performance and took it out to the truck. I intended to crash and nurse my ankle with alcohol and codeine like Mother Nature's pharmacy intended.

Curt was already there pissing and moaning about his missing stereo box. Back at the shop, he put together a little wooden box with an in-dash car stereo cassette player, a 12-volt power amp, and matching speakers in small tuned enclosures. It was a homemade portable Rock & Roll boom box he could take on the road with rental trucks. Clever and cute, but now *gone*—along with the passenger side window. He looked around the seedy neighborhood surrounding the arena; these were some serious downtown Richmond slums. It was the type of neighborhood that might erupt in flames and wanton looting at the sound of a good car door slamming or pig batons breaking bones.

"You Goddamned black bastards. Fuck you all!" he screamed.

I tried to cool him off with a shot of Jack-in-a-coke. "They broke a window and grabbed the whole thing. Probably didn't even know what the hell it was except it wasn't nailed down and it was in their neighborhood after dark!"

"I'm sure the Michigan plates didn't help either," I added.

It was a poor black neighborhood and it was a rich white boy's truck. At least they didn't take the tires. Seemed fair to me, but Curt was inconsolable for the rest of the tour. The only entertainment left in the truck was an AM radio. Not only that, but we had to tape cardboard over the window for the rest of the trip. I had been counting on using it as a headrest. Now I needed to call dibs on the inside seat. *Bad juju*, was all Lenny said as he lit up another joint.

At least Marty paid off the bet promptly. We had actually pulled it off. 120 dB SPL in every seat and no feedback. My little acousta-voice mic box actually worked, adding at least 10 dB of headroom to our bottom line. His payoff gram barely made it to Columbia South Carolina the next morning when we hit the motel around 11 a.m. We had a sound check scheduled for 4. I tried sleeping anyway. It didn't work. It never worked. When you need something, you can count on things conspiring to specifically exclude you from the very thing you need the most. Sleep, like money, I guess, is only for those who already have it.

So while not getting any sleep, I called my brother at his Military Intelligence office on the nearby Fort Jackson Army base.

"Hey, Bud, I'm in town on tour with Grand Funk. I can get backstage passes for you and the kids. Its only for tonight and we can spend some time together. Want to come?"

"How the hell did you get this number? Never mind. Damage done. What do you want?" he clipped off brusquely, then paused. "You're what?"

"A roadie," I said matter-of-factly. "I'm a professional sound engineer working on a concert tour with Grand Funk Railroad, the famous Rock band from Flint Michigan. We're in town for a concert tonight and this would be a good time to hook up for a quick visit. I hear you may be going back to Vietnam soon."

"I can't comment on that. You don't have the necessary clearance."

"Anyway, come on down to the municipal theater around 7 tonight and I'll have your name on the backstage list. Wander backstage and I'll see you or just ask anybody for Fanfare. Bring the kids. They'll love it."

"We'll see. What happened to your PhD from NASA?"

"Thanks for asking. I was laid off by your fucking Commander-in-Creep and all-time lame dick, Nix-goon!" I answered and hung up.

I took a cold shower, snorted a couple of fat lines, and headed with Curt and Lenny over to the theater. Everything was pretty much the same as the day before, except with a little less anxiety and a little more boring routine. Curt and Lenny set up the PA in quick order; I performed the acousta-voicing and ate another shitty cold-cut sub catered by Safeway, probably leftover from Richmond the night before. I drank a beer or two and, of course, we waited.

This time the band showed up only one hour late for the sound check and this time everyone seemed in a much happier mood. Maybe Irving decided to cut loose the good stuff after such a successful, nearly riotous show performance last night. They also probably got laid last night by some young groupie Richmond chicks.

I, instead, enjoyed listening to Curt all night bitching and moaning about the dearth of Rock & Roll on AM radio stations. He and I both marveled at how fucking stupid all AM trucker stations were for playing *alcohol-downer-old-lady-shagged-my-brother-dog-died* country music from midnight to dawn. Minds on this shit were surely doomed ultimately to produce nothing but trailer trash morality. I wondered if the government supported these brainwashing bastards so they could harvest the resultant idiot children for their zombie armies.

I mentioned this to my country-music-loving Army captain brother. "I don't think it's even music," he chortled. "Shit, I can't tell the difference between the guys and the girls."

"If that's your problem, you need to go back and repeat the seventh grade. Sexual confusion can cause all kinds of undesirable behavior, including misplaced hostility," I offered.

He seemed unamused. I thought I was hilarious.

My brother was currently based at Fort Jackson waiting for his next chance to go back to Vietnam for some more of what was much coveted by junior officer suck-ups: combat tours of duty.

"Combat ribbons mean a lot to those in the know," he said to me, like sharing some secret family knowledge. "It's going to be very important later when I'm in politics. Nobody votes against a hero."

He had it all planned out. Twenty years as an Army Colonel, retired, and running for federal office from Bend, Oregon. He said he couldn't lose. He was smart and he would have an unbeatable war record to run on. I thought I heard some ephemeral laughter after hearing this, and I'm pretty sure it wasn't me or the drugs.

My brother showed up right on time, which I learned about immediately when I was approached by a mildly sweating and agitated Irving. He asked me to take care of the uniform causing a ruckus backstage. I found the object of attention holding a beer, standing next to the ice tub looking smug as hell. Everyone else had taken up their favorite corner retreats or locked-door toilet stalls, plotting how to do their drugs and get around the guy in a military uniform guarding the beers. He was with my oldest nephew, Jay, short for Jessie Junior, his name linked forever with the shadow hero.

"Come on, Bud." I grabbed his arm and escorted them out to the stage. "You're scaring the natives."

The lighting guy was running through his routines testing all those cheap Japanese servos he was using to make the lights move. Jay liked the lights. I did too, secretly. Bud just looked out of place.

I put them out on the floor near the mix board where I could keep an eye on them.

"Best seats in the house," I shouted to Bud.

Marty had already turned up the PA as the first long-haired freaks started coming into the hall. Bud looked first bored, and later agitated, as he smelled the first whiffs of illegal smoke come drifting across the floor.

I leaned over and yelled in his ear, "Don't sweat the small stuff. Apparently, there's a truce here in the South when it comes to large groups of semi-depraved freaks paying big bucks to listen to loud Rock & Roll concerts. Think of it like the British did during the revolution: *Salutary neglect helps keep the peace.*"

He moved his head around to speak into my ear.

"It didn't work for them and it won't work for you." He paused and continued, "I hope you're not hooked on anything like these lunatics." He gestured to include the whole arena.

I thought about it for a second. "Just life, brother. Just life!"

He couldn't appreciate the fact it was just the sign of the times. An inconvenient fact. Kind of like taking a 10-point IQ subtraction in order to join the Army and serve the monster war machine. Only in my case, the effect wasn't permanent.

The house lights dimmed and the first band, Nasty and the Hooters, took the stage. The crowd went nuts when Marty cranked the PA on their first song. Even a bar band sounded better at high volume. Bud was acting pained.

"I don't think you understand what's going on," I yelled in his ear. "Nobody's going to be a hero from Vietnam. Vietnam doesn't make heroes, only dead-before-their-time gullible kids."

"That's traitorous talk, you little shit," he growled. "You're giving aid and comfort to the enemy. I could shoot you for this!"

"Army Captain shoots brother when brother reveals hero is an idiot. Captain said shooting his brother was justified for giving out secret military competency reports to the enemy."

"This is not funny!" he said. "This is war!"

"This is not war. This is just America gone insane and anybody who doesn't see this is no better than a true believer Nazi. Wake up! You have only your insanity to lose."

"You have no idea what you're talking about. These are not freedom fighters seeking liberty and human rights. They are teenagers indoctrinated to throw their lives away for some despicable tyrants by literally throwing themselves under American tanks in hopes their bodies will gum up the tracks. We are fighting for their freedom."

"No, you're not. You're just fighting for the freedom of some foreign devil to oppress him. They are fighting for the right to choose who they want to oppress them, and guess what? It's not going to be you, you fat, compliant, corrupt killer of freedoms and fun we haven't even enjoyed yet. Not by a long shot."

"Fat, my ass! Check this out!" he said as he lifted his shirt to expose a technically flat, sucked-in stomach big enough to hold a six-pack, only missing 5 of the bottles. No one around us, I noticed, seemed to care a military guy just flashed his gut at a Rock concert. I was shocked. Cheap beer will do that.

"Is this your brother?" Marty said as he came up behind me. The first band had finished.

"Not sure." Gesturing to Bud, I asked, "Are you my brother?"

"That's the story my dad sticks to," he said as he leaned over to shake hands with his first real long-haired freak ever, or at least one who he was actually being civil to. It strained him. I could see it in his face. I loved moral dilemmas. Just another crack in the thin shell of bigotry.

About three songs into the Funk set, Bud had had enough. "Gotta go. It's a school night for the kid here." I looked at Jay and it was clear he wasn't going to sleep anytime soon. "And I have to work tomorrow."

"Okay, baby killer," I said patting him on the shoulder.

"What did you say?"

The PA was cranked and Mark was getting closer to his home.

"I'll see you, I guess, when you get back from another tour over there? Better sprout eyes in the back of your head," I jokingly advised. "You really don't know who your enemy might be."

"Are you going to be all right with this?" he asked looking around, concerned as the crowd and the music almost shouted down his question.

"I don't know where all this is leading but I'm having a hell of a good time. I'll be okay."

"Call your mother," he yelled.

He slapped me softly on the head, messing up my long hair, waved good-bye, turned, and was gone. Although he barely survived two more tours in Vietnam, I never saw my brother alive again.

The concert ended this time with two encores. I was stinking drunk again, but with my already damaged ankle, I mostly watched while the equipment got packed up again and we headed out at around 2 in the morning for Little Rock. I still had plenty of coke and weed, but for some reason I felt a little empty that night as we drove west under an ink black sky.

CHAPTER ELEVEN

CASH, DRUGS, AND ROCK & ROLL SEEM TO GO WELL TOGETHER

"Booze and ladies, keep me right, as long as we can make it
to the show tonight...."

Grand Funk Railroad
"An American Band"
1974

I didn't get much sleep that night. We rolled into Little
Rock right around noon so we didn't bother checking into a
motel. I was a professional roadie now and soon would smell like
one too. We went straight to the hall and began unloading. I was
famished, so I went looking for the proverbial *green room* where
the food and drink should be.

I found it all right, those same damned Safeway white
glutinous subs again. *Did they get the catering contract for the
whole tour?* I wondered. I noticed we had apparently passed into
Shiner Bock beer territory. Good. I heard they were almost like
Coors. I used one to wash down about three Excedrin extra-
strength painkillers along with 5 mg of pure codeine. I wanted all
hints of that raging headache in the back of my mind to disappear
without a trace.

"Hi. Are you with the band?"

"Not really," I said through a mouthful of white bread paste
and beer, without even looking up. I hadn't missed the group of
chicks huddled in one corner of the green room when I came in. If
you look at a groupie too quickly she'll sense your unimportance
fast and bolt, scaring all of them like a bunch of chickens. Hence
the nickname, *chicks. Gotta play cool and un-needy.*

"I do the sound," I added, as I turned to face them.

She was a cutie all right. A knock-out actually. Small, but very well-proportioned, like a Playboy bunny. She had black hair, green eyes, and a slight little grin that immediately told you she knew stuff. What it was, I couldn't possibly guess, but she didn't look like a rookie by a long shot. I immediately wondered if she belonged to the local pusher; he'd probably backed the concert and gotten stage passes for his entourage.

"Hi, I'm Connie. Perhaps you've heard of me?"

"Hi, I'm Cowboy. Surely you've heard of me?"

She laughed. "I'm not Shirley, I'm Connie." She laughed some more. "I bet this is the first time you've toured with a big band to Little Rock?

"Actually, it's my first time to ever see Little Rock, let alone do a show here. I just helped build a new PA, the loudest by the way, which Grand Funk is renting for this tour. I'm just tagging along to keep it working."

"How fascinating. You must be the brainy one. Do you hang out with Mark?"

"Who?"

"You know, Mark Farner, the one with the dreamy long blond hair? Do you hang out with him back in Michigan, or wherever?"

"Oh. Him. No. We're not friends."

She looked disappointed.

"Yet," I added uncertainly.

"I hope I'll see you later. My friends are motioning me to go with them now, Mr. Cowboy Sound," she giggled.

She rejoined the larger group of groupies across the room. I tipped my hat as she departed and there were more giggles.

I grabbed a couple more torpedoes of death, a couple more Shiners, and headed back to the stage to share them with my other suicidal road buddies. Fucking Rock stars get all the chicks, for free even! Dumb-assed chicks don't know what they're missing. In a just and proper world, physicists would get laid before poets and musicians.

SOMETIMES...

The rest of the afternoon went according to the routine. Sound check done on time for once meant I could find a corner somewhere and relax for a couple of hours. But my head kept buzzing with road noise memorized from the night before. Or was the buzz some kind of drug reaction in the ears? Is this where sleep deprivation and drug overdosing make you hear things? Like God telling you who needs to be killed. In my case, I found it just fucking annoying.

I got bored and wandered out to the mix board where Curt was going over some presets with the manager of the warm up band. Curt had done most of the driving over the last couple of nights and yet he was still seemingly alert and aware of his surroundings. I was already feeling the burn and would probably crash sometime in the next twenty-four hours. Curt, on the other hand, acted so confident and assured we could only imagine he was getting somehow more out of the coke than we could.

"Can you believe this guy?" he started off.

He pushed me aside in the mix box and began fishing for his bottle.

"He wants us to put four mikes on his B3 so he can throw the sound around the arena like a surround-sound movie."

He fished out a tiny heaping spoon of fluff, which he sucked up noisily without hesitation. Likewise, with the second one, and then he professionally dispatched two more for me. I didn't suck as loud as he did. He may be having a sinus condition.

"It's not a bad idea actually, but we would have to prepare for it."

He fumbled a little trying to get the tiny cap back on the little brown bottle, but finally finished it off with a flurry as he dropped it safely back in his breast pocket.

"We would need some small stacks in the rear and we would have to run off another snake. Sure would be nice if it was wireless. Why can't you physicists figure out how to run wireless audio cables so people would stop tripping over them? Shit you put a man on the moon and all that shit. Now do a little something for your soul brothers."

"First of all, physicists didn't put men on the moon. Engineers did. We, if you remember, tried to put Hiroshima on the moon, but unfortunately it blew up on ignition. Tried it again on Nagasaki and gave up. So, if you want wireless, you'll have to find an engineer, of which there are plenty right now."

"Okay, get me an engineer," he demanded. "What about that goofy-looking kid you hang out with, isn't he an engineer?"

"Not the right kind. He built satellites. Wireless engineers are all working on building shoulder-fired rockets that never miss. I could probably fix you up with someone back in Ann Arbor, but you'd have to pay Defense Department wages, which I hear, are not cheap."

"Shit, what about the Japanese or something? Can't they do wireless for model airplanes?"

"I don't know, wireless seems prone to interference, and it bounces. It might not work inside an arena with all the metal walls and powered equipment."

"So, have you met Connie yet?" he asked, changing the subject and simultaneously breaking into a bright twinkling smile.

"Who's Connie?" I asked, taking the bait.

"She's the greatest of all the groupies. She's legendary. They did an article about her in *Rolling Stone*. She's entertaining the troops backstage as we speak. I just got mine about a half hour ago. I might go back for seconds here in a minute or two."

"What the hell are you talking about?" I demanded.

"That's right," he realized. "You're a rookie. First time in Little Rock with a major Rock band." He laughed. "Haul out that barrel of rocks you been hoarding and I'll tell you all about her."

I complied but it was no barrel. It was what was left of my bet with Marty. I had one more 8-ball stashed just in case, but I wasn't talking.

As I doled out a couple of heaping spoons, he explained that Connie held the world record for blowing Rock bands.

"She is credited to have serviced every major Rock band that has played Little Rock for the past five years," he added gleefully. "Some people say this is how you know you've made the big time."

This I had to see. I didn't want to seem eager, so I shrugged off what Curt said, stuck around the board for a few more minutes, and then wandered aimlessly straight backstage.

I couldn't discern if anything was different. The band members were lounging near the back where the beer and heads were. Donny was beating out a complex rhythm on a folding chair. A couple of their roadies were drinking beer near the ice tub. Mark was missing. Then I heard a loud bang like someone hitting their head on a toilet stall wall, followed by a loud gagging sound. Everybody looked back at the head where the racket was coming from and busted out laughing.

Then the low moaning started. It was somewhat muffled, like it was coming from underneath something. It got louder. The banging continued, only muted like holding a hand between the banging head and metal wall. More threshing about could be heard now as the sounds got mixed up with all sorts of other indistinct actions. Finally, it stopped and everyone started laughing again.

Soon Mark appeared, trying to zip up his tight stage pants without pinching or catching anything in the zipper. The cute girl from this afternoon appeared right behind him. Mark paid her no mind but headed straight for the beer tub.

"Cowboy!" Connie yelled. I looked around to make sure there weren't more of us. "Come here, you big bad sound man, I want to show you something."

I was thinking about running, but hesitated too long. She grabbed me by the arm and pushed me back into the head where she had just put on a backstage show with the star. I could hear a low humming sound coming from the audience as the door closed.

"Hi Connie, how's tricks?"

"Why you naughty little monkey. You've been told." She was smiling ear to ear, which I thought might somehow be the key to her other oral talents.

"Told what?" I shifted my voice to falsetto and asked, "Why Miss Connie, whatever do you mean by that suggestion. If I wasn't a lady, I would be horrified, horrified I say!"

I fanned my face with my hand, mocking southern belle innocence.

"I hope you don't find it intimidating," she said mocking a pout. "I'll be gentle. I haven't bit anyone all day," she paused, "yet."

"Yet, she said, as I contemplated a future nickname like *Shorty* or *Stubby*."

She laughed. I laughed. We looked at each other. The pregnant pause turned into a lapse. "You've got a girlfriend at home, don't you?"

She could tell I wasn't getting it up. I thought I wanted to but something was interfering. Maybe too many drugs and not enough sleep, although that didn't seem to slow down Curt, or anybody else for that matter.

"Yeah," I admitted. "How did you tell? Did winky give it away?"

"Most guys cover it up, even when they do have a girlfriend or wife at home. It's not like that. It's not love sex, more of a kind of admiration sex. It's not cheating anymore than petting the neighbor's dog."

"Petting the neighbor's dog. I don't think I've heard it described quite so quaintly."

She began petting my sniffling dog through my pants and he obligingly wagged his tail. Well, so much for '70s fidelity: *if you can't be with the one you love, then love the one you're with.* She began pulling me by the butt into a stall where she sat on the toilet lid and proceeded to add another major Rock band member to her record.

"I won't tell anyone when this is over. I'll protect your reputation," I said haltingly. I had trouble forming the words. She laughed and for a split second I thought I heard God whispering something about eternity. No, it was just Connie making yummy slurping sounds.

When we reemerged from the head, no one was paying any attention. *All that acting and nobody to appreciate it,* I thought. The band was about to take the stage and Connie wanted the best seat in the house, sitting next to Curt behind the left speaker stack.

SOMETIMES...

I felt relaxed for the first time in days, so during this performance, I hung backstage reclining in an old office chair, feet on a nearby table, with a coke-o-jack in one hand and a lit joint in the other. Only one more gig tomorrow night in Omaha and I could go back home and get some sleep. *Sleep with Susie,* I thought, and it sounded just a little strange somehow, after Connie and all. *At least Susie's not in that league,* I thought naively. *But wouldn't it be nice if she did it only with me.* It's hard not to be selfish when there's all this free sex being thrown around.

I could hear Mark looking for his captain again. Some say he was jabbing at Nix-goon, comparing him to Captain Bligh and *The Mutiny on the Bounty* or something, but when I considered the source and what the Flint boys were obviously about, it seemed a little disingenuous. Mark failed the rebel test. His tight white jeans fringed in loose leather strips just didn't scream authentic. He was just a poor country boy who could now afford fancy designer clothes on the ride of his life and one lucky son of a bitch. Imagine getting blow jobs wherever and whenever you wanted, and you didn't even have to pay for them!

For a brief second, I wondered if all famous people had to put up with this unlimited reward system. I thought of Henry Kissinger and concluded, *no, nobody could love that shithead, not even for money.* He had to get it from his Mideast oil sheik buddies lending out their excess harems for political favors. Suddenly the world made a little more sense.

My thoughts were in the clouds for most of the rest of the evening. But before the *Low Peep of Soundproof Boys,* the band came and went for two encores. They threatened to do more, but their road manager warned them of the long travel time ahead and how the trucks had to get moving. I saw Connie under Mark's arm as they got in the limo to go back to the hotel. Lenny and Curt loaded up the truck while I held the doors open. It seemed awful dark outside for some reason at 2 a.m.

Not two hours out of Little Rock, I was jarred out of a semi-booze-snooze with Curt cursing the truck like an unfaithful girlfriend.

"You bitch! You cunt! You filthy whore!"

"What the fuck is wrong?" I asked, still half groggy.

Then I notice Curt pounding the steering wheel while trucks and buses were passing us on the freeway. When one of them was a beetle bus, I came fully awake.

"This fucking piece of crap truck just suddenly slowed down and now won't go over 45 miles per hour. It's like the tranny or clutch is going out, except they seem fine. It's the engine, maybe. It just won't go when I floor it. It accelerates but won't go over 45. Son of a bitch, we don't have the time now for fucking truck trouble. We still have to go five hundred miles and its only twelve hours from sound check."

"Okay, calm down. Let's stop and take a look."

He jerked it over to the shoulder and pulled it to a stop. He tested the accelerator, but the engine just raced up and down smoothly with no sign of hesitation or misfiring.

"That's weird," I said. "Is the clutch working? Try holding the brake and letting out slowly on the clutch until you load the engine down to see if it slips."

He did and it didn't.

"What the fuck is going on?" Curt whined.

I was puzzled.

"Let me try it," I said.

We switched seats while Lenny looked on in confusion, lighting up another joint.

I ran through the gears while holding the clutch in. It seemed smooth. I put it in first, revved the engine, let out the clutch slowly, and it seemed to start up normally. I didn't feel any slippage, so I ran it back onto the highway and continued to accelerate through gears 3 and 4, but as the speedometer approached 45, the engine just seemed to disconnect from the pedal. I pushed it all the way to the floor, but nothing happened. It wouldn't go over 45 no matter how hard I pressed on the accelerator.

"What the fuck is going on?" I whined back, just like Curt.

Lenny laughed, blowing clouds of pot smoke all over the cab.

After a couple more rounds of cussing, stopping, looking under the hood, looking under the truck, giving each other hits off our coke bottle as we went over everything it could possibly be, and looking at each other with blank, blood-shot eyes, we gave up and found a pay phone. I used my little blue box to make a free call and woke Marty up at the hotel in Omaha, where the band had just arrived a couple hours ago. Marty had never heard of such a thing in his entire career of driving equipment rental trucks, either. Curt was sounding close to losing it again. Marty asked me if I could call Bill. Maybe he might know something. It was a GMC. I said I'd try, *but you know Bill*.

I tried calling Bill's home, knowing his chance for being there at 4 in the morning was slim, but what the hell. Surprisingly he answered.

"Yeah?"

I explained the predicament and he started laughing when I kept repeating the part about our speed limit of 45.

"You've got a busted governor locking pin. Some of those commercial model truck engines have built-in defeat-proof governors for big fleet buyers. They're normally defeated by a trained tech inserting a little slip pin inside the carburetor housing. I bet you've popped that pin and turned on your governor. For good."

"Can we get to it and replace it or something?" I asked, which perked up Curt briefly.

"Not in less than three hours if you have the right tools, which I bet you don't," he said. "You're basically screwed until you can get it to a GMC mechanic, which, seeing it is now Saturday morning, that ain't gonna happen before Monday," and he laughed again. "You can fly me out there in about four hours, but I don't think Marty can afford me." More laughing.

I'm glad someone can see the humor in all this. Marty was probably about to shoot himself before telling Irving that the PA truck may show up about six hours late, or not at all.

"Good luck! Let me know if you need me. Gotta go," and he hung up.

I turned to Curt, who looked like he had just lost his favorite Grandmother. Lenny was bored and I was furiously thinking.

"It is what it is," I finally said, giving up looking for a solution. "We'll drive 45 mph and get there when we get there."

"If we get there," muttered Curt. "Don't you realize that we are going to get pulled over by the state bulls sooner or later if all we can do is 45?"

I thought about it for a second and realized he was right. Friday night and a slow-moving rental truck on a freeway in Missouri? No fucking way would we survive until morning. We had to take the back roads. I studied the map for just a second before it hit me. Kansas roads are as straight as an arrow north and south with little ghost towns along the way, but otherwise pretty much abandoned to local traffic where a slow-moving rental would not seem out of place. The freeway paralleled the border all the way to Omaha and right across the border was a state highway running straight past Kansas City and right on into Omaha. We'd take it.

Curt and Lenny split the driving and I navigated. Curt seemed relieved now that he had something to do that didn't require thinking. I had navigated a couple of road rallies in Chicago and had placed second and first in each one. The secret was a piss bottle and lots of cocaine. I knew it, my winnings was doomed from the start. *Geez I hate being right all the time*, I thought.

Two grams and eight hours later we made it to Kansas City, where we had to stop to refuel. I made a hurried call to Marty to give him our progress and ETA. Curt pumped gas while Lenny tossed all the beer cans.

"Best guess at this point," I reported to Marty, "is maybe around 9 p.m."

There was silence and then just a fervent plea. "Get here!" and he hung up.

I could imagine Irving Azof and Mark Farner standing behind with hands around his throat about to strangle him.

For the next half day, I had to witness the slow panorama of flat fucking Kansas and Nebraskan empty corn fields pass by a truck window, in slow motion. Watching water freeze in winter or grass grow in the summer, without a doubt, was way more exciting.

The hours dragged on as we settled into a mood not far from suicidal depression. Curt was foul for many reasons but the absence of Rock & Roll on the squeaky AM radio just heightened his other pains. The muddy yellow stubby cornstalks stretched to the horizon in all directions. I imagined we were just a flea truck running across a giant's carpet attempting to make it to the dog before dying of starvation or getting stomped on.

Ahead was a straight ribbon of asphalt angled to a point on the horizon that never moved or got any closer. The only thing moving was the dotted yellow line emerging from the horizon, which seemed to be on an endless conveyor belt that passed unobstructed under the truck. I felt like we were in a Hollywood studio driving a phony truck on blocks while projected images on all sides appeared to creep by in excruciating slowness. *Still,* I thought, *we're a whole lot faster than pioneers who stole this land with horse and wagons.*

Rabbits on the side of the road had their timing thrown completely off by our slow speed. When they thought it was perfect for running out at the last second to be squashed flat by the raging monster, they ended up sitting in the middle of the road, waiting for a quick trip to eternity, only to be left hanging embarrassed and all alone. Most gave up and went back to the side to wait for a more suitable and dignified ending as we roared by with a mild breeze.

Unlike the truck, our minds were racing uncontrollably with imagined scenarios. We could just imagine how pissed everyone will be when we finally get there. Nobody waits that long to see a show, and it will be a disaster. First time Fanfare goes out on a big-time gig and we screw the hound.

With relief on one hand and the gathering dread on the other, we finally reached the outskirts of Omaha long after sunset. The directions to the arena stage were confusing as hell, but when we got within a mile, we could see the lights of the theater and the huge number of cars parked around it. The crowd had apparently waited. The show would go on.

We grabbed a second wind and went to work. It was the first time we had ever had to set up in front of an entire audience, already seated for hours. I expected a lot of boos and catcalls but was surprised how everyone was actually encouraging us with sports yells, arena waves, and lots of volunteers helping move equipment. It was like the spirit of the free concerts back in Ann Arbor. It was the universal family of Rock and it was alive and well in butt-fucking Nebraska. The concert started finally with a full house at about 2 a.m., only six hours late.

I finally felt much better when I heard the band at full Fanfare volume and the lights whirling madly all over the theater. I went looking for the beer tub and a Safeway sub when I heard a familiar female voice.

"Cowboy! Cowboy sound!"

There in the middle of the overflow crowd hanging backstage was Connie.

She pushed through and sauntered up to me. "I hear you kind of fucked up, Cowboy. Too much good times getting to you?"

"How the hell did you get here?" I asked right back with a scowl. "Did you join the band when I was otherwise occupied dealing with crappy corporate American trucks from hell?"

"You're blaming it on the truck? Why not get a better truck?"

There it was again. Every problem experienced by the man is easily fixed by any women pronouncing the obvious.

"They were all out at the truck rental store. All they had was a truck that ran on squirrels chasing nuts. Eventually, we were going to get here, just late. Late is good, right?"

"In this case I think it is," she said through a slight giggle. "When Mark heard you were going to be late, he decided to throw a party while waiting. He sent the plane back to Little Rock for me and some of my friends."

"I guess when the truck blows, Connie blo…uh…flies," quickly correcting myself on purpose. "How ironic. Sounds like you owe me one for the party."

"What can I ever do to pay you back?" she mockingly begged while batting her eyes. "Maybe I can relax you with an old tantric trick I learned while traveling in India."

"I thought you'd never offer!"

She again guided me to the backstage head where we repeated yesterday's meeting…which now seemed light years away and already a fond but distant memory. Time was clearly variable and Connie seemed to have found a way to slow it down to just a few minutes. Life was good and Connie was a champ. Connie mentioned there was another planned band party at the hotel after the show, room 511, right next door at the Hilton.

"Everyone will be there," she bubbled gleefully between slurps.

"That sounds like fun," I bubbled right back.

The concert finished around 4 a.m. The band played three encores, inviting the backstage entourage on stage for the last one. Everyone was singing and dancing and happy as hell that they had survived the concert that almost didn't happen. I spotted Connie sideling up to Mark and holding him by the waist as they finished up. The lights went dark, the crowd exploded again, but this time, they were only greeted by the *Low Spark of High Steeled Guys* and glaring house lights.

The place was a disaster area, with trash and metal chairs scattered all over the place. No-man's-land in World War I looked in better shape than that theater. They reported record sales at the snack bars and all vending machines were sucked empty, even for chewing gum.

Marty was finally breathing again and making plans. Everybody was going to hitch a ride with the band's plane, which had to pass through Little Rock on its way back to Detroit. He offered me an additional five hundred-dollar bonus and another 8-ball, so I volunteered to stay in Omaha for Sunday, take the truck to the shop on Monday, and drive it back to Ann Arbor next week. The full day of sleeping I had planned on Sunday was my only motivation and it had nothing to do with the fact Connie would be on that plane.

When Lenny and I finished loading the truck, we went looking for the band party in room 511. But something was wrong just as soon as we walked in. The lights were turned way down and a boom box was belting out the James Gang. There was only Donny and Mel, each with a cute little groupie under one arm and a drink in the other. We found some beers in a cooler, popped a couple, and hung in a corner waiting for some action. All we got were silent glares from the two groupies. Mel gave me a stare like *what the fuck are you doing?* He waited for a break in the music to say, "Mark's room is on the sixth floor. Maybe something is going on up there."

Lenny and I sheepishly slunk out and took the elevator to the sixth floor. When the doors opened, we saw two cops standing across the hall talking to a hotel waiter. The cops looked at us with a nasty glare so I punched the button for 8, where our rooms were located. Lenny and I gave up. It just wasn't like Ann Arbor. The Funk boys were pretty disappointing in the after-concert party category. We expect music, drugs, and fun till dawn and beyond without regard to social status or physical condition.

With the Funk boys, band parties apparently were only for band members to exclusively screw groupies. This wasn't the people's Rock & Roll. This was country club Rock where money talks and everybody else walks. *Fuck this shit.*

I'm going to bed for twenty-four hours and then I'm going up to the Hilton's penthouse restaurant, the most expensive Omaha steak house, and pig out on a 16-ounce T-bone smothered in mashed potatoes and gravy.

And that's what I did. I didn't give a shit as people in suits stared at my long hair and Levi's while I ferociously attacked a healthy hunk of Nebraskan feed-lot steer. The hundred-dollar experience was well worth it. My bonus covered it with ease.

The truck got fixed promptly Monday morning and paid for by the rental company in Ann Arbor. Marty had been calling almost continuously since Friday night. They promised all sorts of perks if Fanfare would keep renting from them. They even promised to have all governors removed from their trucks.

Marty was furious, but he knew you couldn't argue with rednecks renting trucks to Rock & Roll people. Money talked and the truckers wanted to make their payments. Marty paid in cash and they had heard of Grand Funk, so we received first-class service after this incident, which was going to prove invaluable very soon.

I had a leisurely two-day drive back to Ann Arbor averaging 65 mph on freeways all the way. Plenty of coke made it really enjoyable, especially after our ordeal in Kansas, where no amount of coke was going to squeeze any enjoyment out of that at all. Now, even the bland but green Indiana didn't seem so ugly. I even found some AM Rock stations out of Chicago that would have soothed the savage Curt. Life is good as long as the truck keeps on rolling.

After delivering the truck to Fanfare's garage, I hitched a ride back to Eber's house. He just had to hear all the details about touring with a major Rock band.

"What's it like?" he kept bugging me. "Did you see any groupies? Did you get laid?"

I tried to tell him about all the technical stuff I had learned and how we had made the 120 dB level in a fifteen thousand-seat arena theater. He wouldn't let it drop. He plied me with beers and some really good pot he had found recently.

"So, what happened?"

I told him about the drunken meeting with my brother. He sympathized with me about him, but still wouldn't give up. Like a bloodhound, he sniffed blood.

I finally gave up and told him all about Connie. He didn't believe it. But he wouldn't stop asking about the details of what he didn't believe. I couldn't take the risk with him, knowing Susie and all, so I watered it down to mostly observations backstage before and after the actual events, without mentioning any in-betweens. She was Mark's whore, not mine. I'm sure I just got a taste of the icing on the cake.

I tried calling Susie to see if we could hook up later, but her overweight radical feminist roommate answered the phone.

"She's not here. Who's calling?" she demanded.

"It's me." I let that soak in. We had spoken on the phone before so no reason to bust my balls now.

"She's working overtime at the weight loss clinic. I'll tell her you called if I see her." *Click.*

Susie wasn't overweight, but she thought she was since getting a job with Weight Watchers and hanging out with porkers at her job. I needed to make some money and get her away from those frustrated ball crunchers.

I thought about going over to her apartment and surprising her when she got home. Then I shuddered mentally when the thought of discovering her with someone else took me back to places I didn't want to remember. *She'll call if she gets a chance. I trust her.*

I went back to my routine, except now I had no job. I needed to find some work for the new Portapack camera I had leased. Unfortunately, I found all kinds of people wanting me to put them on tape but nobody had any money. Without John Sinclair stirring the university pot, there wasn't much happening there that required my recording or photography skills. I got some nice footage of a local band appearing in a new dance club around the corner from Flood's Party and some shots of Commander Cody doing a benefit concert in the Law School cathedral reading room. When the Law School went anti-Vietnam, it was a sure sign the suits were finally wising up.

The heat was cranking up all over the country. Nix-goon had to get out of Vietnam, but his crap about leaving with honor had a price tag a lot of young kids were going to pay with their lives. He and Kissinger needed to be tried, convicted, and hung for war crimes and high treason. Actually, the Senate was finally going to investigate Nix-goon after they found his tape recordings where he bragged about being both a criminal and an asshole, something we had figured out a helluva long time ago. In a just world, Nix-goons would be allowed to only eat shit, not spew it.

After a month or so, I was about to break down and call Marty about some more roadie work when I got a call from Bill, instead. Bill never called me, so I figured something strange was up.

"You doing anything?" He always got right to the point. "I need you to back me up. I just got a call from Marty. His equipment truck is missing with the PA system onboard."

I didn't hesitate. "I'm free. What did you say about the PA?"

"It's missing. He said two roadies rented it for a gig and it didn't come back. Marty just hired me to try and find it."

"Holy shit!" I yelled, guessing immediately what had happened. "It's those two creeps who work for Grand Funk. How the hell did Marty let it get out of his control?"

"He said they had a gig, set up by Mark, but needed to drive the truck themselves to save on money. He made them sign a rental contract, but now he can't find them, the truck, or Mark and the band. Nobody is answering their phone calls and when he called the police, they said it was a private matter and referred him to a lawyer in Flint."

"Shit! That's a bummer. What's he going to do?"

"I told you. He hired me to find the PA and get it back."

"Oh, yeah. So, what are you going to do?"

"I'm going to find it," he said firmly. "I need a backup guy and I know you can stay cool under pressure. Do want to help? I'll pay for your time."

"Sure," I said, not sure what I was agreeing to, but if it involved Bill, it was bound to be interesting.

"I'll be right over. Don't leave.".

Fifteen minutes later and the 454 Corvette came roaring up the street, stopping right in front of the house. He honked so I went out and got in the passenger side.

"I think I found the truck," he said, as he roared away from the curb. "There's a truck in the rental lot that is backed up to a tree like someone trying to protect what's locked in the box. Let's go take a look."

It was Sunday and the truck was supposed to be returned Saturday night. Marty was getting crazy because he couldn't find out what the hell was going on. Did they steal it or did they have a wreck and nobody knew yet?

Bill headed for the industrial area north of town where the truck rental lot was located. When we got there, Bill pointed out the truck in question, which indeed was backed up to the only tree in the lot. He pushed open a fence gate on the side and slipped inside. I followed, keeping an eye out for any junkyard dogs. It was pretty quiet around here on Sunday, so I went along without much stealth or protest. I was curious what Bill was up to. The truck rear door was not locked. He opened it and lifting the door, saw only stacks of truck tires packed inside.

"So much for that idea," he said, slightly embarrassed. "Let's go find Marty and see what else he can tell us about these clowns."

We went back to Eberbach's place, where Bill called Marty and asked him over for a strategy session. While we waited, I found some beers and Bill laid out some lines. He asked me about what had happened during the last tour with Grand Funk. I gave him the sterilized version, emphasizing the drugs and money and technology. He asked a few questions mostly about Mutt and Jeff and their relationship with Grand Funk. He also seemed interested in Irving and his penchant for a cash-and-carry business model. Cash, drugs, and Rock & Roll seemed to go very well together.

I hadn't paid that much attention to those details, so we snorted a few more lines while waiting for Marty. Marty finally showed and he looked bad. Gaunt and drawn like a dead lizard in the sun. Bill gave him a couple of 'ludes, which he immediately threw down with a full beer. I lit a joint and handed it to him first. After a few tokes and heavy breathing in between, he finally looked ready to talk. Bill handed him the mirror with a couple of lines and asked the first question.

"What does Farner have to do with these two clowns who stole the truck?"

"They didn't steal the truck. It was returned today to the rental office, empty. They delivered the equipment somewhere else."

He took a big hit off the mirror, which clearly burned as he scrunched his face in response.

"Now I can't raise them. They won't answer their phone. We may have to go out to their house and corner them."

"Not a good idea," said Bill. "They won't be so stupid as to hide it at their house. Showing up now will just scare them into hiding. They know that's the first place we'll look anyway. I think Grand Funk is involved with this. Those two roadies don't seem smart enough to pull off something like this. Clearly, from what I've heard, Tweedle Dee and Tweedle Dum are just schmoozing Farner for a job. Farner was the one who put up the money and he's the one to mostly gain from this heist. He probably thinks he can just bully a couple of broke hippies from Ann Arbor. *Possession is nine-tenths of the law* and all that. We need to get Talbot involved."

Marty looked blank. He was beginning to realize he could be permanently screwed.

"Do you know where Mark lives?" Bill asked directly.

"I visited his farmhouse a couple of times, at night, but I didn't drive," he recalled.

"Could you find it on a map?"

"Maybe, but he probably wouldn't hide it at his house," said Marty. "He'd probably store it at his studio or at his road manger's farmhouse not too far away."

"Can you find those places?" Bill pushed.

"Not sure, at least not from the ground anyway."

"I can get a plane for a little aerial surveillance," I volunteered.

"Can you?" Bill asked. He knew I could. He was just playing to Marty for some reason.

"That's a good idea," Marty exclaimed. "I'm pretty sure we can find his house from the air and we can look around there to see if we can find the studio. It's supposed to be in the woods nearby."

More drugs and beer just sealed the deal. I called my old flight instructor, Clive, at the airport and he reserved a 4-place Cessna 185 for 8 the next morning. I wanted to take pictures, so I wouldn't be doing the flying. Clive was experienced in low-level strafing and jungle surveillance; I knew he would be perfect for the job. He agreed, saying he loved every opportunity to fly low and slow.

We met for breakfast at the downtown greasy spoon railroad car diner the next morning at 6 a.m. and then went to the airport. We had the plane for two hours, so we loaded right up with Marty and me in the back seat and Bill in the copilot seat. To help sharpen our wits, we all did a round of coke hits before taking off. Bill offered some to Clive, but he turned it down with just one word: *Later.* I checked my Nikon one more time, thinking how this was indeed a gonzo moment in Rock & Roll. Hunter would be proud of us.

Clive took off, climbed to one thousand feet, and then broke from the pattern heading North. It was sunny but cold, with a slight wind causing a few bumps at our altitude, nothing to worry about. There had been a dusting of snow over the past few days so we could easily see tracks in the snow. Visibility was unlimited with no clouds to speak of. This was perfect surveillance weather. We could see for miles in all directions.

Marty gave directions to Bill, who consulted a road map identifying landmarks along the way. We flew due north until we could see Flint on the horizon ahead. Marty indicated he thought the house was somewhere to the west so Clive began a back-and-forth pattern, sweeping west from US-23 in the Linden area. It was thickly forested below with scattered isolated farm houses in small clearings. Being winter, the trees were bare and we had an unobstructed view of everything on the ground. I could see why Mark picked this area. It was remote and private.

Finally, Marty spotted something. It was an old two-story farmhouse, only this one clearly looked like it had had a lot of recent renovations. It was painted bright white with a new green matching roof on house and barn. This was no simple farmer. Clive circled above at a steep angle so I could take pictures out the left side window, which now looked straight down above the house. I snapped off a series of shots and then studied the scene. There were no trucks parked anywhere around the house. There was a tractor peeking out of a garage, but unless they hid the gear in the barn, we couldn't see anything out of place. I noticed there was clean snow all around the barn and no obvious tire tracks leading to it. Nothing had been in or out of the barn for some time, so it looked unlikely that they stashed the equipment here.

Marty indicated that the studio had to be somewhere nearby in the woods. Clive began flying in larger and larger circles, centered on the farmhouse, until Bill shouted and pointed to a shiny new tin roof tucked all alone in the woods just a mile or so southwest of the farmhouse. Clive circled this one tightly again and I looked out the side window through my Nikon viewfinder, snapping off rapid shots as the land spun dizzily below us. There was a long lane leading from the building and winding through the woods before coming to a paved farm road. I could plainly see a large iron gate across the lane at the entrance. Muddy tire tracks cut through the snow in the lane, clearly indicating somebody had been there recently.

I began to notice a churning in my stomach. I felt a little dizzy too. Those tight spins were having an effect. I asked Clive to fly straight for a while. He looked back at me and Marty.

"The bags are in the seat."

He immediately flattened out the plane. I looked at Marty, he looked at me, and then I noticed he didn't look good either. All of a sudden, he lurched and his cheeks swelled out briefly as he tried to keep it in, but then he began spewing before he could fish out the sick bag from the seat pocket.

Mangled eggs and hash browns flew all over the back of Bill's seat and Marty's legs. He finally found a bag about the same time the smell hit me like flung monkey shit and I began to wretch. I was faster and got a bag to my face when it finally exploded, but it didn't matter; the flow from our big breakfast that morning was overwhelming these little lunch bags for rats. Clive announced that there was a little crop dusters field nearby where he could land so we could throw up to our heart's content.

Just as soon as we touched down and taxied up to the ramp, Marty and I bailed out of the plane nearly bowling Bill over trying to get out his door before the plane came to a halt. We ran to the side of the nearest hanger and proceeded to wretch ourselves into a gagging sick sweat. All the time I was cussing to myself for being so stupid as to eat a big breakfast and then go acrobatic flying with a camera. Looking through the lens at the spinning ground was just too much to handle.

I felt like shit and Marty looked not much better. We stunk to high heaven so Clive spotted a water hose and taxied over to it. We followed weakly and used it to spray off the bigger chunks from our pants, wash our mouths, hands, and head and then Clive took it and washed out the backseat carpet area where most of my eggs benedict and Marty's triple omelet ended up. The bright sun helped warm and dry our clothes so after a few minutes we took to the air again. We all swore to never speak of this event again.

We took up the search southwest of Mark's farmhouse and studio until Marty recognized the farmhouse owned by Grand Funk's road manager. This time we hit pay dirt. Parked right next to the farmhouse and backed up to a big-assed maple tree was their band equipment semi-truck trailer rig. I shot more pictures, but this time Clive kept the spin above the target to a more modest bank. It didn't matter, as I had nothing left to throw up anyway.

Later at my place, we went over the freshly developed film with my light box and a magnifying glass. I would be able to see more once we blew up the pictures we liked from the raw footage. I didn't have the nice photo printer at the lab anymore so we took it to the primitive lab at the Rainbow Party house. After many bribes of cocaine and pot, we finally had a dozen 8 by 11s to study. After more drugs and endless speculation and debate, I decided the purloined PA equipment had to be in the semi-truck at the manager's house. Bill was convinced it was in the studio. Marty wasn't sure.

"They wouldn't just steal a big mix board with a shit load of mikes to leave it in a truck backed up to a tree," Bill argued. "They'll want to play with them in the studio."

He had a point.

"But look at all the footprints and truck tire tracks around the manager's house," I pointed out the house, holding up one of the aerial shots. "That truck was clearly moved around and a lot of people had something to do with it."

I pointed out the tracks. It looked like the truck had been loaded or unloaded about thirty feet away and then deliberately backed up to the tree in one movement.

"That truck must be full of their road show band gear. There's no room for a complete PA as well," Marty pointed out.

"That's a forty-foot trailer and it wasn't that full on the road," I said. "If they removed the band instruments, there might be enough room to put in the PA. They immobilize the truck, and the tree prevents anybody opening the rear doors. Just looks damned suspicious to me."

We all stared at the picture for a while. Then Bill held up one of the studio pictures.

"Look at all these tire tracks going into this place. There's activity going on here and we need to take a look inside. I say we hit the place after midnight, just for a look-see."

Eberbach had been listening to our argument. He always liked to ask obvious questions that embarrassed others for not thinking of it.

"Why don't you just put a recorder on their phone and they'll probably give it away in a conversation."

Bill looked at his gleeful face. "You can do that?"

"I can give you the recorder. You can put it where you need it." He kept beaming with a self-satisfied look.

He was right, it was simple. He had a Sony battery-operated cassette recorder that he modified with a little DC current relay.

The relay was connected in series with the phone line outside so when the receiver was picked up inside the house, the cassette turned on, quietly recording the entire conversation. When they hung up, it turned off until the receiver was lifted again. If they made a phone call, it would even record the number dialed.

Bill got very excited.

"We've got to get this tap on Mutt and Jeff's phone right away," Bill declared. "Who knows where their house is?"

Marty raised his hand with a smirk.

Later that night, we decided to pull our first hit on the enemy. No sense waiting for the lawyers in the morning. If we found where they were hiding the equipment, we could maybe steal it back. Marty gathered up some flashlights that we carefully taped with black electrical tape so they only threw out a small skinny beam, making it harder to see at a distance by casual observers. I pulled my Heathkit walkie-talkies out of my truck and put in fresh batteries. Steve found an old princess phone he added clip leads to making it a cheap lineman's butt test set—a portable phone used to listen in on phone lines or make illegal calls from someone else's phone line.

Bill split us up into two trucks, he and Marty in his and Eber and me in mine. The plan was simple; Bill and Marty would lead the way to the house. When they found it, they would cruise on by and call us on the walkie-talkie, giving the location. They would try to take up a position on the road so they could warn us if anybody got nosy. Steve and I would drive by slowly and try to locate where their phone line was. From there, we sort of left open how we would proceed. The technical term, *winging it*, was the way most Rock & Roll got done anyway.

We cruised around the area northeast of Ann Arbor on unpaved country roads with mixed trees and farm fields until Marty finally called on the walkie-talkie saying they had located the house and were driving by. I slowed way down, as I could see their taillights ahead. As they moved on, I approached where they had been.

I remembered now visiting this house last year when I was helping Marty build the board. Tweedle Dee and Twittle Dum had set up a small production line in the garage of this house to make the thirty or so plug-in mic mixer amps. It was a newer single-story ranch house with dark brown cedar shake siding, making it look like a giant do-do dump plopped among happily fed shrubs and weeds.

Lights glowed from inside the house but all the windows were covered, exactly what one would expect from a bunch of rocker dope freaks living quietly and privately in the country. Steve noticed that the phone line was aerial along the road but went underground from a pole by the entrance to their property. A simple phone splice block and grounding enclosure was attached to the pole about four feet above the ground.

"Perfect," I said. "I'll drop you off and you hook up the tap in that phone box on the pole."

"Are you kidding?" Steve replied with a minor panic whine in his voice.

"It's dark," I said, "nobody'll see you. If a car comes along, just duck behind some tall grass."

"I'm scared," he declared. "I don't want to get caught. You do it."

"What's going on?" came Bill's voice over the walkie-talkie. "Put the tap in and keep moving. You're going to attract attention."

"Okay, damnit," I said. "You scoot under the wheel and run the truck up the road where Bill's waiting. I'll install the tap and call on the walkie-talkie when I'm ready to be picked up."

I was out the truck with a box full of equipment when Steve squealed like a little girl. "Headlights!"

I scrambled and fell down the slope next to the road and fell flat in the middle of the ditch. Steve started to accelerate away when the headlights turned out to be Bill's truck.

"What are you guys doing?"

He couldn't see me but he knew I was there. Steve just kept going. I started to get up and he started laughing. I had mud all up and down my front.

"Fuck you!" I said as I tried to brush off the bigger frozen chunks.

Bill said something to Marty and then got out. He climbed down into the ditch with me while Marty took the truck off in the other direction.

"You okay?" he said still chuckling. "I figured it was going to end up you and me getting this done anyway. Too many pussies, not enough fucking. I'll hold the flashlight."

We found the utility pole in the dark without tripping over anything or stepping in something. I took the cover off the splice box and hooked up the little tap relay. There was no room for the cassette deck in the box so I hooked up a long extension cord we had made up for this possibility. Bill found some rocks nearby and piled them around and over the cassette deck, which he hid behind a clump of grass near the pole.

I hooked up the princess phone to the line going underground to the house. When I picked up the phone, the cassette deck started. *Testing one, two*, I spoke into the phone. The little signal level meter on the cassette deck wiggled, showing my voice was being recorded. I hung up the princess phone and the cassette deck stopped. *Ah it was a thing of extreme beauty!* My chest swelled with pride. Those fucking arrogant rockers have met their match!

"Car coming!" Bill whispered loudly. I dropped to the ground, as did Bill, and the car approached, slowed down, and began creeping along the road. My immediate thought was a pig mobile cruising along looking for us cause the bastards inside had seen us and called the cops.

"Where are you!" Steve yelled.

"*Shut the fuck up!* We're here," Bill whispered loudly. "Let's get the hell out of here," he said back to me, rose out of the weeds and headed for my truck. I followed, trying to get my heart rate back down to Ravi Shankar speeds.

Back at Steve's house, we calmed down with copious quantities of pot and beer. Bill commented how we needed to get our courage up and start acting professionally or we were going to fuck up or attract undue attention. He volunteered to be the first one to swap cassettes tomorrow night. We planned to swap tapes every night so we could know immediately if they spill the beans on the phone.

"Look," he explained. "I'll get Patti to drop me off in the dark. She'll go down the road out of sight, turn around and come back in three minutes. That should give anybody enough time to swap tapes."

He looked around at us accusingly, making the point his girlfriend was more reliable than a bunch of male stoners.

Our house became the unofficial war room. Bill started dropping by each night to check the tapes and report on the lawyer's progress. Bill got his lawyer friend, Talbot—the guy who defended most of the dope busts in Ann Arbor and who actually got most of them off. He contacted Grand Funk's lawyer in Flint and was informed about their claim.

According to Mark Farner, Grand Funk financed Marty to build them a PA and they were simply taking possession of it. He warned Talbot that any attempt to take it back would involve charges of trespassing and possible breaking and entering, a felony. They had cancelled checks proving they paid for its construction. The lawyer advised giving up fighting for possession, confident that we couldn't prove anything otherwise.

Marty was devastated. The tapes weren't yielding any useful information either. There was one call to Grand Funk's road manager, who mentioned the band had been working in their studio on a new album. They were under a deadline from Capital to get something out quick to cover costs after their expensive battle with Barry White. That gave Bill an idea.

"Let's go check out that studio," he casually suggested after hearing the tape.

"Are you crazy?" I said. "Didn't you hear them? They'll be there working."

"We can take a look. What's wrong with looking?"

"They call the cops and we end up in jail, that's what's wrong with it."

"Look," he went on holding up one of my aerial pictures. "The studio is only a short walk through the woods from this road." He pointed to the road. "We can approach through the woods from the road and take a look through the windows. Maybe we'll see something we shouldn't." He grinned deviously.

It was Friday night. More than likely, the Flint boys would be out getting laid and not working in their studio. I figured like Marty that they probably had separated the board and mikes from the speakers. Where better to put the board than in the studio? My curiosity got me to agree.

"Sounds romantic," I said.

"You still have your lock-picking tools?" Bill asked. "I'll bring a small crow bar just in case there's a combination lock."

"What the hell," I said, "you want to break in?"

"Maybe. Might as well if we can, just to make sure."

"At least there are a lot of trees to give us cover. Two things though. We use gloves and tie garbage bags over our shoes."

"Of course," he laughed. "We're professionals."

Bill used his big-block Buick Riviera and Patti as our getaway driver. He explained that if we did get spotted, he could take over the driving and outrun just about anybody, including pigs. The plan was simple. Patti dropped us off around 2 a.m. along the country road nearest the studio. We hiked in while she went out of sight and waited with one of the walkie-talkies. When we're done, we give a call, she picks us up, and we ride off into the sunset.

The snow had melted during the day and then refroze as mud at night so we left no obvious tracks. As we got closer to the building, it was dark and obviously empty of any people. It clearly appeared out of place, being recent cinder block construction, yielding an industrial-type building buried in a forest with only a narrow road winding out among the trees. We flashed our lights through a small window on one side and saw all kinds of musical instruments and recording equipment filling the inside space.

Nothing looked like Fanfare equipment though, but there were corners of junk we couldn't fully see.

"Let's go in," Bill whispered. "I didn't see any security system."

We moved to the road side where there were two doors, one industrial metal fire door and one overhead garage door for the bigger stuff. I examined the door and fortunately it was an easy lock to pick. After just a few minutes of raking and twisting, the lock pins finally hung up just right and the lock popped open.

"I'm impressed," Bill said as he stepped past me into the dark building.

I smiled as I put my homemade pick tools away in a little leather pouch. Compliments from Bill were rare. I stepped in flashing my light around the interior. It was a jumble of wires, mikes, small mix boards, guitar heads and a stack of Marshall's against one wall. Donny's small trap set occupied one corner while the opposite corner was filled with electronic keyboards and a Hammond B3.

Bill's flashlight was already moving around all the recording equipment setting on a table in the middle of the room. The centerpiece of all the gear was a new 4-track quarter-inch Teac tape recorder. I stared at it for some time. It had 4 VU meters spread across the base below two 10-inch reels. Beautiful. I appreciated quality audio equipment and this was state of the current fucking art.

"Take a look around and see if you can identify anything from Fanfare," Bill said, startling me out of my trance. "I don't see any speakers but you would know better what they have."

I reluctantly took my eyes off the Teac and started going around the room in a systematic manner that took me past everything at least once. I noticed out of the corner of my eye that Bill was now giving the Teac the once over. Sitting next to it was its younger brother, a stereo Teac quarter-inch deck with 7-inch reels. They sure looked impressive setting next to each other. Clearly, they were doing multi-track overlays with these two machines. *Nice.*

I found absolutely no trace of anything from Fanfare. Bill motioned me back over to the tape decks.

"Let's take them," he declared. "They're the most expensive and most portable of anything in here."

"That's stealing," I said, feeling it had to be put out there for what's it worth.

"They stole from us! All's fair in love and Rock & Roll and all that stuff. Maybe it will stir them up to spill the beans. What do you think? Can you carry one back to the car?"

Bill was already unplugging all the cords from the 4-track.

"If we lock the door behind us, the cops will think it's an inside job and not look very far for a victim," I said, in a vain attempt at justification. I started working on the stereo deck.

"Exactly," Bill agreed.

We quickly hauled the decks through the woods where we crouched in the ditch, called Patti on the walkie-talkie, and waited for the white Riviera. When it showed, the road was empty, which gave us plenty of time to open the trunk and load both decks inside. Bill took over driving and out of habit I guess, took all the freakin' back roads imaginable all the way back to Ann Arbor.

When we got to the house, I took the stereo deck, leaving the biggest prize with the guy who made it all happen. I stashed the deck in Steve's garage and didn't bother to tell him. He might get too worried. In the meantime, Bill and I hunkered down for the weekend and waited to see if anything happened. I stayed with Susie at her apartment for the duration, but kept an eye on the house, just in case. By Monday nothing had happened, and we didn't hear anything on the local news. Quiet sometimes is not a good thing.

It was Marty's turn to swap tapes, so when he got back late Monday, we finally heard what we had been wanting to hear for days. We gathered around as he played back the phone tap.

Hello.... Hey, did you hear?... What?... The studio was robbed. They got the tape decks.... Is that all?... So far that's all we can find missing.... Is the truck okay?... Nobody's been near it. What the fuck is going on?... Beats me. But we called the state police and they're looking for prints. They think one of us did it because there's no evidence of a break-in. They had a key or picked the lock, we don't know... Not a damned trace.... I'll drop by tomorrow and see if they found anything else... Sure... Later.... *Click*.

"I told you it was in the truck," I said. "They're keeping the equipment together. We still have a chance to nail it in one piece."

"I think you're right," piped in Marty.

I hadn't seen him this excited since the tour.

"What do we do next?"

"They have obviously immobilized the truck in some manner," Bill said. "I could probably get it going if I had the right parts that they've removed, or a big enough cutter if they've chained it to a tree."

"Isn't stealing a truck grand theft auto?" Steve asked.

"Not if we return it before they know it's missing," countered Bill.

"Oh yeah, I bet that makes all the difference in the world," I added sarcastically. "In any case, we need to do some on-the-ground reconnaissance tomorrow."

"Seeing how it's your idea, you can go up there and pay the boys a visit," Bill said. "I'll come with you. They only know you from the tour and they don't know me. We can just say we're in the neighborhood and stopped by to say *hi*. Maybe ask them if they have any weed for sale. Anything to throw them off a little and give me a chance to look at the truck."

The next day, Bill and I took my truck and went GF-roadie visiting. Boy, were they surprised when we showed up, seemingly unaware of anything that had been going on. The roadies living in the old farm house were the same ones I helped throw hippies off the stage in Richmond. They remembered me, but knew I worked for Fanfare; they were aware that I was there to spy on them, only they couldn't say anything in fear of causing a ruckus or fucking something up way beyond their pay scale. Like on stage, they looked mean and formidable, but now hesitant to take action with all the weirdness going on.

I talked to them about old times, drugs, and what happened to Connie. They seemed confused, disoriented, said little, and plied me with pot and pills in hopes that would satisfy me and get me on my way. Bill played it real cool, hanging in the background with his darkest shades on, all eyes and ears, yet so cool and unconcerned they thought he was just high on something. Before we left, we had seen enough to know we weren't going to get that truck away from that tree. They had truck tires stuffed up against the rear tires preventing them from moving and then there was the giant chain that went around the rear truck axle and the tree. We had to find another way to get the equipment.

The next day, Steve and I took our turn to service the tap. Steve was uncomfortable even just being the getaway driver.

"What's the deal?" I asked, while driving out to the tapped house. "You're not this uptight when we're covering a riot."

"Riots are easy," he said as a matter-of-fact. "You know where the cops are and you can always run. With this creepy crime crap, all I have is my imagination, and as you well know, it's formidable, and unbearable. I just don't want to end up in prison. I don't think my brains or MIT degree is going to be much good in there."

He forced himself through it, but I could see it was a strain. I flipped the tapes, he picked me up on schedule, and we headed back without incident. I bet he felt foolish for being so affected by such a simple deed.

When we got back, we played the tape: *Click click click click.* Pause. *click click....* Someone was making a phone call. *Ring... Ring... Ring....*

Hello?" *What the fuck is going on?... I don't know what you're talking about... Those assholes from Ann Arbor showed up yesterday and you let them take a good look at the truck?... So what, they can't do anything.... You better hope so. We've got some big gigs coming up and we need that equipment intact and secure, you got that?... Don't sweat it BoBo... And don't call me BoBo!... Click*

We just looked at one another and cracked up laughing. *BoBo and BooBoo!* How could we have missed it? They weren't liked by the GF crew either. But what the hell did they mean by *big gigs coming up*? We had to wait till the next day when we found out that through the lawyers, Bill and Marty were setting the idiot twins up for the kill.

CHAPTER TWELVE

ROCK & ROLL NEVER
SLEEPS, REALLY

"If you ever get annoyed, look at me, I'm self-employed.
I love to work at nothing all day...."

Bachman Turner Overdrive
"Taking Care of Business"
1973

Bill and Marty conveyed through the lawyers that before the equipment switched owners, Marty had signed a contract to do a Deep Purple concert in Macon Georgia. They had to do the concert or there were going to be problems—big problems from Geffin, the tour promoter. Irving apparently called Mark and told him to do the gig, or else. Mark called BooBoo and BoBo and told them to load up the equipment in a rental truck and get it to the concert in Macon. BooBoo and BoBo apparently decided it was time to happily show off their new toy to the English rockers, regardless of the threat from some Ann Arbor hippies. They were hooked into moving the equipment to do a show and in so doing, they knew there was a risk of losing it.

The Deep Purple gig in Macon was about a week away. Dingle-ling and Dongle-dong made the classic mistake right at the git-go. They rented a truck from the same rental company that Fanfare used. Marty made sure that the rental guy paid him back for the earlier truck disaster. The rental guy called Marty and said the two puke boys had requested a truck for the four-day weekend. Marty talked him out of a spare set of keys for the same truck.

Talbot recommended we do the job as far away from Michigan as we could get. With keys in hand, we put together a hit team that would fly to Atlanta, drive to Macon and somehow hijack the equipment and get it back.

SOMETIMES...

It was going to be Marty, Bill, Curt, myself, and Bill's chief mechanic, Arnie. Arnie was Bill's right-hand man at his chop shop during the day, and at night, his dope and rent collector. He would do anything for Bill and/or money, and he knew how to fix trucks fast that may be intentionally disabled. I had used him to collect rents for me so we were already friends. He had also worked the security side of the Blues Festival, so was without doubt a trusted psychedelic confidant.

Before I knew it, we were checking in at the Detroit airport for a flight to Atlanta with a couple of very heavy toolboxes: one full of spark plug wires, rotors, and distributor caps for a '67 GMC C350, the other full of tools that would impress any second-story man. Bill and Curt had moderate-length hair, so they mostly went unnoticed in the larger world. Arnie, Marty, and I all had long hair and still got stares and huffs from natives when we ventured out, especially the farther south we went.

However, surprisingly, nobody in Detroit seemed interested in a bunch of long-haired hippies traveling with suspicious baggage, so we amazingly got on the flight without any problem. At the opposite end, we rented two full-sized Ford LTD's just like the Feds use to bust dopers and a box truck like the C350, big enough to hold the PA. We told the people at the truck rental we needed to haul stuff to Orlando. Our brazen, yet improbable mission was off and running.

We had to drive about eighty miles south of Atlanta to get to Macon and the site of that night's concert. Marty rented us rooms on the top floor of the local Hilton so our walkie-talkies would have maximum range. Plus, the room overlooked the concert arena about a quarter mile away; we could watch the backstage area and see when the truck left at the end of the concert. Only problem was, we had no idea what the Rummy Twins were going to do after the concert. If we were going to do anything, we had to tag the truck discreetly and wait for an opportunity. We also didn't know if we were under surveillance or being watched by some cops. Or if we even knew what the hell we were doing.

370

Maybe the thimble heads had friends watching over them, or they warned the local cops to watch their truck. Paranoia began riding shotgun.

We had to wait about six hours until the concert was over and then try to intercept the truck as it left, follow it, and hope we got a chance to heist the PA. The list of *maybes* and *what ifs* got longer and longer. Curt caved right out the gate.

"I can't do this. I'm not some kind of tough guy like all you guys. I just drive trucks and mix PAs. You guys are going to have to do this. I'll drive. Just give me a truck to drive and a place to be and I'll get it there. But I can't do this."

Marty looked pained and slightly pissed. Everything he had was riding on this shaky scheme and his own partner was turning flaky on him.

Bill got quiet and said he needed to think. We purposefully left all drugs at home, except for some pocket bottles of coke to keep us awake, more or less. We needed to be clean, just in case. Bill and several others in the troop were coming down hard at just the precise wrong moment. He locked himself in the bathroom and drew a hot bath. After about a very quiet hour we got worried.

"You still in there?" I yelled through the bathroom door.

Nothing. We looked at each other in frustration.

Finally, we heard a soft voice, "Come in."

"What?" I said, cocking an ear to the door.

"Come in," he said a little louder.

I opened the door and found him sitting in the tub, hunched over looking into a lukewarm puddle, deep in thought.

"I've thought it out and here's what we have to do."

We listened with all due seriousness as Bill, naked as a jay bird sitting in a Hilton tub, explained how it was going to go down.

"We'll break up into two teams of two each in the LTD's. They'll stake out the two entrances to the arena parking area and follow the truck if it comes out their entrance. We have three walkie-talkies so each Ford will have one and Curt will have the last one here in the hotel room. We can keep in touch with everyone and see everything that's going on. Once tagged, we can radio their position and we can all join the chase. Curt will follow at a discreet distance in the truck. Hopefully, they will drive a while and then check into a hotel for the night. They have to be tired and there's clearly no need for them to drive all night, although that's a clear possibility we don't want to consider. We could end up chasing these bastards all the way back to Michigan"

He looked up for approval.

We looked at one another. "Sounds good," we all said in unison, mustering all the enthusiasm we could afford at the time.

Arnie and I decided it was better to act and get the hell out of the hotel of nervous ninnies and do something. We told Bill we should do some up-close surveillance just to check things out. So Arnie drove one of the LTD's and I rode shotgun with the map and radio. We cruised around the arena several times, making sure we had all entrances and exits noted. Then we turned into the parking lot and got close enough to the arena loading dock that we spotted the familiar GMC truck with Michigan plates.

I radioed a description to Bill, who confirmed with Marty that the license plate number matched what was written on the key tag he had from the rental company. The target was confirmed. There were at least two more hours until the end of the concert and Bill warned us to keep low. We didn't want to attract any heat while following the truck or tip off the Dumb Brothers.

Arnie and I cruised out and found a little hill near some railroad tracks where we could hide out of sight from the road, but still able to cover an entrance to the arena. Stakeouts are boring and prone to over active imaginations. We had them all.

After an hour or so, Bill and Marty called on the radio reporting that they were watching the other entrance and Curt was still in the hotel room watching the arena. We just sat listening to the radio, bored to tears, and looking like crazy for anything suspicious. Paranoia is a good thing when breaking the law, I decided. It kept your senses on a keen edge.

Cars started leaving around 11 p.m. Finally, the concert was over. From here, we figured another hour to load the truck and then the chase begins. We started getting anxious and began cruising the area again just to be doing something and to make a moving target for any snooping eyes. We drove through the now empty parking area behind the arena and noticed the truck was still parked at the loading dock. The two idiots were taking their sweet time loading out. I guess they think there's no hurry getting on the road. I wonder what the hell that might mean.

Bill and Marty were getting antsy as well. I spotted the other LTD across the lot looking just a little out of place for the time. If there were cops in the area, we must be setting off all kinds of alarms. It's a good thing they are apparently not as suspicious as we were. Still, we were kind of making it obvious. I called Bill and told him he was looking suspicious and to try to stay more out of sight. We didn't want the Clown Twins to see us and get tipped off that we were here. Surprise was absolutely necessary.

Curt started to freak out on his radio, not knowing what was happening or what to do next. We told him to just hang until we tagged and started following the PA truck and then he could bail to follow us at a respectable distance, but not too far to lose contact with the radios. They had ranges of up to five miles, but we didn't want to push it.

I could just imagine all the things that could go wrong if we lost contact or if one of us got collared. The basic rule of successful criminal activity was *don't break more than one law at a time*. The more laws you break, the greater the risk of being spotted and stopped for some small infraction that leads to something much more disastrous.

Curt called saying the truck had just pulled away from the loading dock. He was so excited we could hardly understand him. I spotted it moving about the same time and so Arnie and I pulled onto the road heading the opposite direction from the truck and told Bill to intercept it at the first major intersection. I heard Marty tell Curt to start following us in the rental truck.

When we got out of sight from the exiting PA truck, Arnie quickly pulled a U-ey and we headed back toward the truck, tailing it now from a respectable distance. Respectable for me meant at least one or more cars between us and the target. The more the better, just don't lose' 'em. When we went through the first intersection we spotted Bill's LTD. I watched it in the rearview mirror as it dropped in behind us, also at a respectable distance.

I had my binoculars out, but they were almost useless because of the pitch-black darkness. Low clouds and the threat of rain made night-viewing difficult if not impossible. At the second light, the truck just made it through a yellow light and we had to stop. On the other side the truck disappeared on the on ramp to the local freeway loop heading west to the major north-south freeway we had driven in on earlier from Atlanta. I bitched openly at the stoplight but we couldn't take the chance of running it. Bill and Marty pulled up behind us. The light changed. Arnie gunned the Ford. We couldn't lose them now.

Fortunately, big box trucks didn't go very fast anyway so we caught up to it in a couple of miles. Bill tagged us and we fell back immediately to let Bill take the lead for a while. Again, we didn't want the two blowholes to see a consistent car following them at a constant distance.

When we got to the major interchange, the truck took the exit heading north for Atlanta as we predicted. Marty called and speculated that we could be in real trouble if they don't stop for the night. So far, we had gone about twenty miles with no slowing down. I could just see the PA in the dark slipping away from our outstretched grasping fingers.

Marty then shouted over the radio, "They're slowing down. It looks like they're exiting!"

We slowed down and approached the exit cautiously. Marty called back, a little disappointed, saying the truck was pulling into a Howard Johnsons restaurant. Bill pulled into a gas station nearby and pretended to be getting gas by the time we caught up. We all topped off our tanks anyway, just in case we had some ways to go this night. Marty called Curt and told him to go past our exit, pull off at the next one and get topped off as well. It looked like the duplicate turds were having a late-night breakfast. So again, we sweated as we loitered around waiting, trying to look like we weren't loitering. It's not easy being innocent while feeling guilty as hell.

Curt began to freak again. Waiting was not one of his talents. "If I get stopped, what am I supposed to say I'm doing? Driving an empty truck around at 1 in the morning!"

"Tell'em you're on your way to pick up a dead horse," I said over the radio.

"Real funny," Marty said.

"It worked for me once," I lied. At least Curt's mood improved.

"What the hell am I supposed to do with a dead horse?" Curt asked, this time pissed instead of nervous.

"Never mind, Curt," Marty said, "you'll think of something."

Curt started cussing his fate and bad luck when Marty piped in with, "They're moving!" Bill watched them in the restaurant with the binoculars and they were now standing at the counter paying their bill.

"You and Arnie tag them for now. We don't know how far they're still going to drive tonight so hang back, don't blow your cover, and we'll tag you out in about twenty."

Arnie was anxious to show what he could do, so we watched the truck leave and get completely on the freeway again before we took out after them.

It didn't matter much because they only went as far as the next exit, where they drove about a mile down a parallel frontage road until entering a Days Inn Motel tucked off the road surrounded by trees. Not wanting to get spotted we drove on past the entrance and stopped out of sight behind a grove of trees adjacent to the parking lot.

We radioed Bill and Marty to stay clear until they got checked in and asleep, probably at least another hour. Curt found a rest area about three more miles up the freeway and was holed up there until further notice. Bill told him to get some sleep, but keep his radio plugged in; it could be a long night.

I was trying to see them through the binoculars and the trees and could just make out some movement around the truck. We parked on the side of the frontage road opposite the side of the motel building and the large parking lot surrounding it. Pine trees buried us out of sight of anything else, except the trees between us and the motel parking lot were thin enough to see most of the well-lit parking area.

True to form, they backed the truck up to a two-story blank brick wall at the end of the building so it would be impossible to get into the truck box without moving the truck. It was also parked directly under a huge sodium vapor lamp that lit up most of the parking area on that side of the building. At least it wasn't in sight of the lobby entrance on the other side.

I saw the hood go up on the truck for about a minute and then down again. It was too far to make out anything distinct, but dark little figures moving about the truck made me pretty sure they had removed some vital components, just as we predicted, disabling the engine.

Arnie saw headlights coming so he started moving again, hoping like hell it wasn't a snoopy county-mounty or something worse, but it turned out to be the other LTD with Bill and Marty. Everybody was getting jumpy. They had circumnavigated the motel and checked out some of the back roads nearby. Bill said they had found the perfect spot to make the swap.

"There's a dead-end road behind the motel," Bill said, pointing back in the direction from where they came. "It leads a short distance to a railroad track hidden deep in the trees. Nobody would see us except if a train came along, but the rusty tracks say *not likely.*"

I told them what I had seen and suggested we send in Arnie alone across the parking lot in the dark and try the keys. The parking lot was almost empty of cars, so it looked real quiet. Arnie could sneak across the lot to the truck, start it up, and drive it away quietly.

"If it doesn't start then he can check the engine to see what's missing," I said. "Then he comes back here and we'll decide what to do next."

"Okay but have him take a distributor cap along just in case that's all they did. If we can do it in one trip, why not? It's after 2 now, let's send him in about 3. But let's get out of here for a while so we don't attract any attention."

"You got it. Where should we go?"

"Just stay out of sight for half an hour. Stay in touch by radio," and he and Marty accelerated away.

I got back into the Ford with Arnie and asked, "Where do you want to kill a half hour?"

He slouched down in his seat. "This works for me."

"We can keep an eye on the whole parking lot from here and there looks like no traffic on this Georgia cow path except for us. Let's just sit low in our seats so nobody driving by will see us and think it's just a stalled car. I say we stay here and case the joint until it looks cool."

We were edgy again but now we were close to the prize. We shouldn't be worrying about all that could go wrong, which was plenty! Arnie looked like he was getting some sleep, slouched low in his seat, chin on chest, but I couldn't. God knows where Bill and Marty are. I kept staring at the truck through the trees waiting for some shadowy figure to appear lurking nearby proving we've been set up.

All was deep-night quiet, except frogs and crickets harping about their lack of sex. I could also hear the dull roar of trucks passing on the nearby freeway, but even that began to taper off with the night. I hated having to wait for anything, but it was a good time for thinking. Problem was I had way too much to think about.

What was I going to do about a job, or somehow supporting myself, now that I lost my small graduate stipend? Was I willing to go on the road with Fanfare and work for them? Do I have what it takes to start my own film or video projection business? Can I even find film and video production work? Am I going to propose to Susie and get married? Maybe go into business with Steve and make super speakers? Then there was the continuous beckoning from close friends for me to join them in the Rocky Mountains and be a recluse artist in exile.

Now that was romantic. To winter over in a mountain cabin buried in snow, reading all the great novels, while watching the seasons change endlessly right in front of my eyes, that grabbed my deepest desires. *Fuck the world, I want to get off!* A small ghost mining town surrounded by snow-capped peaks seemed to appear right out of a children's story of Switzerland and goat herders. It was enticing. It seemed like a warm and cozy place for licking wounds, perhaps romantically.

What am I going to do about Susie? She left her parents to come live with me in Ann Arbor, which must mean something. She loves me and I love her. She's great in bed and a liberal, left-wing revolutionary just like me. She likes folk music and Rock & Roll just like me. But for some reason, she seems lately distant and removed, like she's unhappy about something. She says she's fat and that, she says, depresses her. But she isn't fat. She is gorgeous standing naked in my shower. I love her body. She must be just acting coy and self-conscious. Love it.

Crackle... "Hey, you there?" came Bill's voice over the radio.

"Yeah, where are you?"

"Coming. Standby."

I saw a light shining on the trees coming from the turn in the road behind us. A car's headlights appeared and by their width apart I knew it had to be the LTD. Bill and Marty pulled over behind us and got out. Arnie and I got out.

"It's showtime folks!" Bill said as we approached. "We woke up Curt and took him to the transfer place we scoped out earlier. He's over there now in a dark truck buried in the woods freaking out. I hope he's still there when we get this truck going."

Marty opened the trunk of his Ford and started searching for something in his tool box. He pulled out a distributor cap with a set of plug wires attached, which he handed to Arnie. Arnie stared at it for a moment, probably wondering how to carry it and not have it interfere with his free movement. He stuffed it as best he could into his jacket, zipping it up enough to hold it in place but with black wires dangling out his jacket like a cartoonish hairy-chested man.

"I think they just took out the rotor, so here's a replacement," Bill said.

He handed a little black object to Arnie, which he in turn promptly stuffed into his jacket pocket.

"Okay, check first to see that the key works."

Arnie nodded in agreement.

"If that works, see if it starts. We know it probably won't, but why not give it a shot anyway?"

"Because it might make too much noise," protested Marty.

"Yeah, I saw them lift the hood right after we got here," I interjected. "You might as well get under the hood and see what they took. Got a flashlight?"

"Better," he said.

He opened his toolbox and pulled out a small flashlight with a head band attached for wearing like a miner's light.

"I have to use this all the time when I climb into a truck engine compartment."

He slipped it on and flipped a switch, causing it to light up the interior of the LTD trunk and his tool box.

"Cool," I said. "I need to get me one of those."

Bill checked his watch. "It's almost 3, so let's go."

We walked some ways into the woods between the cars and the motel parking lot where three of us kept to the tree shadows and Arnie began a hurried walk across the parking lot to the truck parked next to the building. I couldn't believe our luck; no window in the motel had a view in our direction. The only way to catch us now is if someone drives into the motel parking lot and sees Arnie skulking around.

Bill and I were keeping track of him with our binoculars.

"He's in the truck," Bill announced as he watched Arnie's shadow disappear. I couldn't see anything but the truck. I kept scanning the parking lot looking for anything that moved. *If I don't see anything move, that doesn't mean it's not there, it only means I haven't seen it yet.* I could feel the sweat building in my palms, though it was a chilly night in Georgia.

Crackle... "Key works. I'll check the engine," Arnie said over the radio.

"10-4," replied Marty.

We waited breathless. We could see a dark figure moving in front of the truck, in full sight of the rest of the parking lot. The hood went up and the dark figure disappeared again. I kept scanning the horizon looking for any other suspicious movements, but nothing was stirring, not even a rat. *Or two rats for that matter*, and I laughed silently.

Crackle... "*They took everything!...*"

Arnie sounded a little desperate. He has everything he needs. What more could they remove?

"*...Two of the spark plug wires don't fit...over...*"

Marty looked at Bill sort of bewildered. He whispered, "Why didn't the spark plug wires fit that we bought specifically for that model truck?"

Bill looked stupid for a moment and then just shrugged his shoulders. He motioned for the radio.

He spoke quietly into the radio. "What's wrong?"

"*Two wires are too short that go to number one and two cylinders... Crackle... over...*"

Bill paused to think. "Just come back and we'll sort this out here, over."

Zzzpht... "*Roger...*" *Pssttt*

Soon I spotted movement near the truck as a hunched-over figure walked rapidly toward us across the parking lot. I nervously scanned the lot again, making sure no one picked up his movement. Amazingly it was still dead still.

When Arnie made it back to our hidden position in the trees, he was all out of breath.

"The damned truck (deep breath) seems to have factory (exhales loudly) air installed. The added compressors (deep breath again) and hoses make the front (exhales again) two spark plug runs about six inches (breath) longer than the (exhale) longest one we brought (inhales)."

"Shit," cursed Marty. "What the hell can we do? We can't drive on six cylinders; the backfires will wake up the hounds!"

Bill stood silent for a second thinking.

"The little bastards thought it might be warm down here so they splurged on Marty's bill and rented probably the only truck they had with A/C."

"Son of a bitch!" Marty blurted out a little too loudly.

"*Shhhh!*" I hissed at everybody.

Marty was getting frustrated. "Can we splice together another spark plug wire?"

"What other spark plug wire? We only brought one set," Marty said.

"What about the LTD's?" I asked. "We can borrow a couple and maybe tape them together to lengthen the truck's."

"That's it!" Bill exclaimed. "I'll bet the LTD's have longer wires because they have A/C. We can probably use them directly without splicing. Come on Arnie, let's go check it out."

They all took off to raid the nearest LTD, which was the one Arnie and I was driving. I kept scanning the parking lot, at least the parts that were lit up enough to see anything. There was a lot of darkness out there, leaving all sorts of speculations of what I couldn't see. So far, not one car had come or gone, or for that matter, not even down the frontage road connecting it to the freeway. It was way too quiet, but then it was 3 a.m. on a Sunday morning in the sticks of Georgia. Maybe they really do roll up the roads at night in Macon.

"Check this out," Bill said.

He held up a pair of black wires that dangled almost to the ground.

"This should get that truck started. Arnie is going to install them and then he and Marty will drive it to the transfer place. You and I will follow in the one LTD still running."

"What if someone finds the other LTD while we're gone?" I asked.

"So, what," he said smiling, "it's undriveable as it stands. Let's get going!"

He handed the wires to Arnie and stepped back as Marty took a radio and followed Arnie toward the truck. We watched them move quickly across the lot. Using the binoculars, I could make out that Marty got in the driver's side, while Arnie opened the hood again. Crawling halfway inside, he struggled to get the new wires in place. After a minute, I saw him jump down, closing the hood quietly behind him and get into the passenger side. I figured they must have gotten the wires on and were going to start the truck. This was when things could get nasty if someone hears the truck leaving. I listened for the roar of the engine but was surprised to see the truck start to move silently.

Zphht... "We're coasting down a little hill..." came Arnie's voice over the radio.

I hadn't noticed it before, but there was a slight grade up to the building, leaving the truck on a little hill ready to coast down about halfway across the parking lot. It slowed to a crawl after going about a hundred yards. I heard the cranking of the engine and for a second, I thought it wasn't going to start; we were going to have to hightail it back to Michigan—abject failures at truck-jacking.

Then a low roar came rolling across the silent scene and the truck picked up speed, heading for the exit. Marty didn't turn his lights on until he turned onto the rural road leading to the transfer point. Bill tapped me on the shoulder and we ran back to his LTD to go help with the transfer.

By the time we got there, Marty was backing the truck down the dirt road leading to the railroad tracks. Arnie was walking ahead, motioning with a flashlight, making sure he didn't back the truck off the road and into a ditch. Around a short turn in the road Curt waited with our truck. Marty backed right up to our truck, leaving only a foot between the two back doors.

Just as we had guessed, the truck with the equipment had a big padlock attached to the door hasp.

"Just a minute," said Marty.

Again, he rummages around the trunk of the LTD and comes up with a huge pair of bolt cutters. In less than a minute, he cuts off the lock and whips it as far as he can into the woods. He's still holding the bolt cutters in one hand as he throws open the truck door, revealing his beloved PA packed to the ceiling.

Woo Hoo! he whooped.

Curt poked his head around the corner and literally jumped for joy.

"Come on everybody," Marty ordered, "we've got a plane waiting."

Curt and Arnie followed Marty into the truck beds now facing each other, one full, the other empty. They started grunting and groaning, moving cabinets and cases into the empty truck. Bill and I looked on, noting that if we climbed up there we would just be in the way. The way they were hustling, it wouldn't take long.

I looked up and down the railroad tracks wondering if we could get a surprise from that direction, but Bill was right. There were weeds and rust showing nothing had used these rails in some time.

The sky was still dark with clouds, but now and then a few stars poked through the scudding black pack. I sensed a calm satisfaction. By god, we just might pull this off. I could even get a little excited. Bill motioned me over to the car where he had his little bottle in-hand, doling out the last few grains. He offered me a snort and I accepted gladly. These damned all-nighters usually turned ugly around sunup, so might as well be prepared. It was so quiet we could hear the frogs singing in a distant pond. It was the sound of relief.

"Okay, let's go!" yelled Curt as he jumped down from the truck bed. Arnie followed along with Marty, who pulled the door down on the now empty truck as he jumped off the tail.

"As soon as I get this truck out of here, you get our truck turned around and headed south to Florida," he said to Curt. It was the first time in days I had seen Curt with a confident smile and without the fatal glaze of doom over his eyes. He was all Curt now and ready to drive this truck to hell if need be.

Arnie jumped in the car with Bill and me and we headed back to our other LTD. Marty drove the truck back to where we found it, carefully turning off the lights before entering the motel parking lot. We watched from our vantage point on the frontal road as he crept the truck across the parking lot to the building, where he carefully backed it up to the blank brick wall precisely where he had found it. After he removed the spark plug wires and distributor, he came running across the lot to us as fast as he could go. Extreme caution like what we had been doing for days suddenly burst like a flooded dam. Now it was time to boogie.

Arnie slapped the wires back into the Ford in ten seconds flat and we all took off for the freeway to catch up with Curt. After we passed the exit to Macon, we really began to lighten up. Bill only saw one more hurdle. If the Bobsie Twins wake up early and discover the truck is empty and call the cops, they could be watching for us at the state line.

At this stage, there was little we could do except get to that state line as quickly as possible without getting caught speeding. About ten miles farther on, we saw Curt's box truck ahead of us emerging from the predawn mists. Bill called on the radio and told Curt we would run interference for him. So we did a little bandit action as we chewed up the rest of the nighttime hours and headed into a foggy Florida morning.

We slowed at the border and spread out to go through the fruit inspection station. If there were going to be cops, this is most likely where they would be. I looked carefully to check for suspicious activity, but only got waved straight through by a sleepy agriculture cop. Curt did the same and sped back up for the downhill run into Orlando about a hundred miles ahead. Suddenly we could all breath again.

God, I could do with a big fat joint right about now. Bill did up the rest of his coke a while back and now was starting to look a little worn at the edges. But we kept on driving, knowing for certain there were rewards ahead for the righteous.

The road was fairly empty of traffic on an early Sunday morning. Just a bunch of trucks and dope-crazed weirdos trying to make time from a three-quarter crime. The orange glow lighting up the low-hanging clouds made the greens and the browns of the pine forest glow with a mystic, otherworldly Disney-animated look. It was all beginning to feel surreal, as if it all went according to a well-scripted movie, with no surprises.

As we neared Orlando, Marty took the lead and we fell back behind Curt. What a scene! A Ryder truck escorted front and back by FBI-looking slug cars. Oh, if Mark and his snooty band buddies could see us now.

Bill had been explaining to me all the way from Georgia how with his help, Talbot set up the other side, duping them into believing they had essentially won the case, but first they had to do the right thing and perform the Deep Purple concert—despite their better judgment.

"See what happens when you do the right thing?" he admonished. "No good deed goes unpunished. Remember that."

Out came that sneering smile on half his face again, flashing just below his official drug dealer's sunglasses, reflecting the now blazingly yellow sunrise. Cool and smug and dazzling. When the smug is well-earned, as in this case, it's justified.

The plan was to get the equipment out of Florida and secretly out of reach of Michigan courts for a while. Marty finally 'fessed up, admitting he just happened to know about an ELO concert in Boulder coming up in two days. Apparently, Irving was playing both sides. Smart. Any way it goes, he gets paid.

So he set Marty up with a concert, not knowing for sure whether Marty could produce the equipment in time, but certain he couldn't appear he had anything to do with the famous Grand Funk Grand Larceny. That was a different division of Geffen now.

He had a PA backup, I'm sure. I even knew a guy in Boulder who had a PA almost as big as ours. We partied with him while passing through Boulder on our way to El Paso. He and Jim Blake were buddies. Funny how college town dealers end up knowing the local PA company, and very well. But you had to give it to that little fat, balding, penny-pinching bastard, he always seemed to be on the winning side, no matter who won.

Marty firmly had his equipment back and he wasn't going to lose it again, even if he had to nail himself to it. He led our nefarious convoy on nearly empty early-morning freeways straight to the freight terminal at the Orlando International Airport. He actually found someone awake at Delta who showed him their standard shipping containers.

They were big aluminum boxes with an oval bottom that presumably fit the lower curvature of a big jet fuselage and big enough to put in at least one "W" bottom and about half of the rest of the equipment. As he had four "W" bottoms, it was going to take four of these containers to hold the entire PA. It wasn't going to be cheap getting everything out of town fast but at least, he said, the ELO concert would pay for the trip. He and Curt planned to fly out later that day after dropping the truck at the airport Ryder rental agency. They had to be there in twelve hours to pick up the equipment on the other end, rent another truck, and head up to Boulder for the concert. Rock & Roll never sleeps.

Arnie had friends in Tampa, so he took one of the LTD's and headed west. He said he'd get back to Ann Arbor when he could after dropping off the car in Tampa. That ought to keep the cops guessing if they were tracing our cars.

Bill and I checked into a hotel to see if we could get some Z's after all the excitement and abundant coke abuse. But we were too wound up and happy as shit as it sank into us that we had just pulled off the coolest heist in Rock & Roll history, getting away with it so slick that nobody would probably ever know what happened, except for us. I wondered what the assholes at *Rolling Stone* would say if they knew the truth. *Fuck'em, it's only Rock & Roll, and I like it, like it, yes I do!*

We booked a flight back to Detroit the next day. We couldn't just sit it out in a hotel room, so Bill suggested it was a Sunday in springtime and time for Daytona.

"What's in Daytona?" I stupidly asked.

"Only twenty miles of beautiful white sand beaches straight as an arrow down the Atlantic coast. They used to set speed records there fifty years ago. Now they race in a nearby oval track called the Daytona Speedway. But the beach is great. People can drive from one end to the other, or park, whatever. On a good day there could be a thousand or more cars lined up enjoying the sun and surf. There's always something going on and it's only an hour's drive away."

His eyes were bloodshot but his enthusiasm was catching. My body was screaming for a joint, a beer, a couch, and TV.

"Sure. Why not?" I said as enthusiastically as I was able to muster.

He was right, why stop the adventure now when we are just starting to savor the sweet fruits of victory? As a confirmation of our flaunting fate, the clouds completely disappeared about halfway to Daytona. By the time we arrived at the beach, we had stripped down to our T-shirts. Now I needed more than pot. I needed sunglasses.

Bill was right. We started driving south down the beach and it was lined on the right with an endless procession of cars, trucks, and vans parked under the shade of palm trees. On the left were beautiful bodies running or relaxing in the sun on bleach-white sand with a modest blue ocean stretching to the horizon, linked to an equally intense blue sky. Suddenly, we were moving at a pace somewhat slower than walking. Like the cars in front, in back and coming the other way, it was a sandy freeway all right, except nobody wanted to go the speed limit of 10 miles per hour. It was a walking parade at best, where the participants stood still and the viewing public slowly moved by. Weirdly, we fit right in with all the other Sunday gawkers.

So, we cruised the beach feeling pretty satisfied with our lives, except for the fact we didn't have a thing to fairly get us high. It's just not right to be celebrating without some celebratory substances. Beer was okay but just didn't hit the spot. On Bill's side of the car the wild and flirty bikinis wobbled along the beach, providing him with at least some eye candy. What I would give for a good joint right now gave me pause to consider.

Really? I had to look again.

I spotted a big white GMC camper van parked under the palms facing the beach with the cool sun visor shade hanging out over the windshield. Two couples were sitting at a picnic table nearby. I looked down at the license plate and it was from Texas. *Shit! Could this be for fuckin' real?* It was the guys from El Paso who helped us buy the pot in Mexico last summer! I recognize the van now.

"Stop!" I yelled at Bill.

He jammed on the brakes, digging a couple of small sand divots under each front tire. He looked at me and said, "So, where is she?"

"Park right here." I pointed at an open spot next to the GMC van. "We just found Santa Claus hangin' at the beach on vacation."

I jumped out of the car and walked rapidly around the van to the side with the open sliding side door when I heard it suddenly slide forward, slamming shut. One guy was left out of the group and he walked toward me with an ugly look on his face. I thought suddenly maybe something went wrong with our deal after we left and now he's jammin' for me. I started to back up, wishing Bill were closer by just in case this guy goes ballistic.

"What do you guys want? We're not bothering anybody." He looked sore and scared for some reason. I held out my hands to show they were empty.

Then it dawned on me that we had just scared the shit out of these smugglers by driving up and parking a big Fed-looking LTD right next to them. Then I boil out all excited to find a long-lost brother of the road, and they think we are trying to roust them for having long hair and a good time.

"Whoa, take it easy," I said. "Don't you recognize me?"

He squinted and stared at me through his dark glasses.

"Remember the racetrack in Juarez? The funky pickup from Las Cruses?"

He took off his glasses and gave me another look.

"Oh yeah. The Michigan guys. You're Cowboy, right?"

He immediately relaxed.

"That's right. And you're '57 Ford."

"Right! Dang brother, what's happening?" he said as he motioned to the people hiding in the truck. "You scared the shit out of us."

The door slid back open and the other guy and two girls got out. We greeted each other with the revolutionary handshake. It was a sign of the underground, brotherhood of freaks, weirdos, longhairs, and dopers. We didn't care which one. As far as the pigs were concerned, we were all the same anyway.

Like us, they had been concluding some business in the neighborhood and decided to take the day off and come down to the beach to hang. We all thought it was a pretty weird coincidence that with all the roads and all the beaches in the world, we would cross paths here and now. Strange how Karma works. We're on a righteous mission setting justice back on track and as a sacrifice, we gave up all stimulants for the duration. Now in victory over the forces of evil money, in our demonstrated need, fate brings two people together, though they come from the ends of the earth. All is made well again.

We needed drugs and they were still in the wholesale business and well-stocked. But for old times' sake, we got what we needed for nothing, except for a great afternoon at the beach shooting the breeze and enjoying the shear fact we're all alive and happy, warming ourselves in the sun at the same time. After we indulged enough to reset our brains, we related our week-long adventure in the land of Rock & Roll high jinx. They were so impressed by the story, and the coincidence of meeting, that they gladly laid all the weed and snow even Bill and I could handle, until we had to be clean for the flight back to Ann Arbor.

"It's not the same anymore, bro," '57 Ford lamented over his fifth Coors. "There's a new cop in town and they've got me scared shitless. I don't know who they are, but they dress like Mormon missionaries and carry some big clout. Many of my oldest customers are doing business with these guys now. They always seem to have the best weed and coke around at any time. Also, someone new is buying up my suppliers in Juarez, sometimes offering gold and guns instead of just ordinary cash. It's just getting too weird, man."

"I don't know what you're talking about," Bill countered. "I do mostly pharmaceuticals and I see just a lot of hungry customers and very little competition outside of the crooked doctor or two."

"I've been smuggling across a major border for five years," he bragged. "But I'm a firm believer in early retirement. Me and my partners have bought a little farm in North Carolina. After this trip, you won't be seeing us outside of a local farmers market or a bluegrass festival."

"Wow," I exclaimed. "That sounds great. Tune in, turn on, and drop out. Drop out to growing tomatoes and milking goats. Man, that sounds really romantic. Are you going to make it a commune?"

"Yeah, maybe," he admitted a little pensively. "My friends are great and we are really excited about living organically off the land. We'll probably have separate houses. I'm not interested in living in a dormitory and eating in a cafeteria like a kibbutz. I don't share my family."

"I hear yah, man." I held my Coors up in an agreeing salute, but I really didn't. Three days without good pot and now over indulging in the sun, I could agree with just about anything, and probably did.

The Allman Brothers came on the radio playing loudly inside the van, but covering an area including everyone in a hundred-yard circle. We sang along passionately:

You got to run to keep from hidin'! And I'm bound to keep on ridin'! And I've got o-o-n-n-ne more silver dollar! But I'm not gonna let 'em catch me, lord! Not gonna let 'em catch the Midnight Ri-i-der! No, I'm not gonna let 'em catch me, lor'! Not gonna let 'em catch the Midnight Ri-i-i-der!

Orphans of the road dream about finally getting home. I wondered if it was just a dream out of reach, like the golden horizon.

After that afternoon of sun and fun, I don't remember very much about the rest of the day. Sun, beer, and good pot sort of kill the long-term memory in preference for immediate self-gratification, stoniness, and navigating successfully as an aware human being in the land of the troglodytes and pigs.

Bill told me later we hit a few bars on our way back to Orlando. Not much happened he said, except for the occasional redneck bitching about my hair length or accusing us of being Northern Loving Niggers. Bill tried to meet some local ladies, but outside of accepting coke hits from him, they seemed more attracted to baseball caps and Bubba jokes; just not that relatable to a Northwoods Michigan kind of guy who actually knows how to read. But he seemed undaunted. What he saw in these Florida fuck factories escaped me. I had no right to criticize, however, as I had a bunch of retarded southern cousins. Perhaps I wasn't a totally disinterested observer.

Our natural exuberance from all our adventures slowly abated over the course of the next day as we caught the morning flight direct from Orlando, full of families coming home from Disneyland to Detroit. I was hung over and Bill was only talking monosyllabically from behind his welding lenses, so the trip back was like gladiators being tormented for some imperial slight by brain-eating children from hell.

On my quieter drive back from the airport I actually had a dip of solemn depression. I started thinking about Susie. I wanted to just feel secure that she was my love and that she loved me. I didn't feel good about her moving into an apartment with other girls, but I was committed to renting from Steve for a while and it seemed the best plan at the time. I wanted her to feel what it's like to be on your own, to be truly free from her parents. Every child who desires their own life must leave the nest and be alone on their own. I wanted her to come to me an independent free woman, a mind unencumbered, not straight from her daddy's house and self-destructive parental influence to mine. So why was I feeling shitty now that I had every reason to be euphoric? Surely, she understood this.

When I arrived at Steve's, the whole gang was there. Munsell had been spending a lot of time hanging around our basement, helping Steve get the commercial version of our speaker design ready to manufacture. They had come up with some pretty neat tricks while I was gone, especially in the cabinet design. My original concept called for the speakers to be mounted on a radius matching the natural radiation pattern of a point source, or in our practical world, a cylinder radiating as if from a slot or vertical line source.

So they developed a tall elliptical enclosure with the speakers mounted roughly on a radius that recreated a line source. They found large, heavy-duty cardboard tubes they could cut in half to make the rear of the cabinet. The front was three particle board faces glued together like half a hexagon, with the rear three faces replaced by the cardboard tube. It stood about a meter high to get the volume necessary to load the rear cones of the four drivers into a bass reflex system that extended the bass response to forty Hertz—performance unheard of from other commercial speakers. When it was totally wrapped in a foam black grille all the way around the cabinet, it looked cool as hell and sounded badass.

The crossover was highly dependent on the types of speakers we used. They had evaluated all the latest low-efficiency speakers, along with high-efficiency tweeters. The crossover had to separate the incoming frequencies into two outputs for each type of speaker. Most idiot designers had three or four different speakers to cover the sound spectrum. But we knew the more ways you diced up the spectrum, the greater the frequency distortion and the greater the muddiness of the reproduced sound. We were going to do it with just two speakers and thus reduce distortion by orders of magnitude.

"Have you tried applying a square wave of about 50 hertz to this thing to see how the phases from the two speakers line up in time?" I asked Steve.

"What?" he asked looking a little incredulous, like I was pulling his leg.

"No really. The Fourier components of a square wave are infinite and spaced at third octaves so they must line up in phase and time if you expect to recreate a sound wave in the room that looks just like the original input signal."

"I can't imagine a square sound wave," he complained. "What would make such a noise?"

"Farts come to mind, but that's not important. We have to do as little damage to the sound created by the artist in the studio and deliver it to a set of ears in a room untarnished and uncolored. A square wave is just a sensitive test for phase distortion. I'll bet that other speakers can only reproduce some high-frequency crap superimposed over a low-frequency fundamental with all the harmonics arriving whenever. I bet on a 'scope you won't even see anything close to a square wave. Have you tried this with our speakers?"

"No," he said quietly. "How the hell are we going to be able to pick up a sound square wave in front of our speakers? We'll need a very expensive calibrated microphone, for starters, and a huge anechoic chamber."

"The school of music has a five thousand-dollar set of studio Sennheiser's," mentioned Thom with a wink and a grin. "I could arrange for one to mysteriously get stored in the wrong place for a week or two."

Thom had found a new job fairly soon after the lab closed. He created an opening with the U of M School of Music running their recording studio at Rackham Auditorium He now had his hands on some really sweet recording equipment, including an

Ampex half-inch 4-track tape recorder and the latest thing in tape recordings, a Dolby dynamic compressor.

It was meant to cure the one big problem with mastering on tape: tape hiss. The Dolby device slices up the audio spectrum into smaller bandwidths where it measures the amount of music power in each one and then adjusts the gain only in that band; if there is no music power, then there is no gain noise to add to the output. Pretty clever, and the damned thing actually worked. It knocked down the hiss noise to almost imperceptible levels, but the high end then seemed muted and dead. I didn't like it. It colored the sound.

Thom though, had actually stumbled into the best job of a lifetime and he knew it. Lucky bastard. I, on the other hand, wasn't sure where my next meal was coming from. A drop-out PhD candidate is so over qualified that I couldn't get a job shoveling shit at a pig farm. Too damned smart to take orders and stand knee deep in shit all day. Yeah, but I failed to see the difference between shoveling shit and doing government sponsored science. I felt dirty either way.

Thom and Steve discussed for a minute how they could build an anechoic chamber in the basement for tuning their crossovers to produce square waves. Then out came the beers, pot, and coke and their demand to hear all about the Rock & Roll heist. I spared no details as we celebrated the return of Fanfare's equipment and the continuation of putting on big venue concerts. Pete Andrews had pretty much ingratiated himself with the university activities staff. He even got them to hire his secretary to manage the big concert events he was planning on booking for the university, a little quid pro quo for the Rock & Roll industry. It looked like good times ahead now that everything was back to normal.

When it wound down, I called Susie and asked her to come over and spend the night. She said she would. I had a lot of things to tell her and maybe even some plans for our future. All that craziness of running around the woods of southern Georgia had given me a chance to think about things. Maybe I didn't have a real job, but Bill kept telling me to go into business for myself and I did a little bit. He made his living by doing a lot of things. I wondered if I could.

"The idea is stay loose, be smart, and be flexible," he said with that sly one-sided signature smile below the black shades and wind-tossed Corvette hair. "I buy and sell cars and real estate when the price is right. When that isn't happening, I do other stuff. There's lots of ways to make money, just look around. You already do video projections and videotape recordings; find someone to pay you for it. Pete is a good sucker. He's been ver-ry ver-ry good to me!" That last statement he did with an overdone Jamaican accent, referring, of course, to his lucrative security gigs with Pete.

He failed to mention the repair garage and undercover insurance chop shop, but I got the point and had to admit, I did do pretty well last year. Maybe I just need a good woman behind me and I could get something going right here in Ann Arbor. Maybe even work with Steve on manufacturing the speakers and make some money there. I could roadie once in a while to get cash and maybe get contacts for my video projection idea.

I was excited to see her after my long abstinence and all the things we needed to talk about. I hoped she would be as excited as I was and maybe I'd pop the question. Maybe she needed some formality like that. I didn't mind. It was love. We needed to look for an apartment we could afford.

Later that night when Steve and his buddies went out for coffee and I was couch potato-ing in front of the six-foot color TV, she finally showed up. She rang the antique doorbell that most people never used because it had been painted over years ago, but surprisingly, it still worked. She twisted the big white handle in the middle of the white wall and a rasping ringing noise emanated from the wall next to the front door, it could only be compared to a giant dying cricket, or Nosferatu's fingernails scratching across a blackboard. I jumped up and ran to the door, flinging it open with flair and enthusiasm. I was trying to be frisky, but from her solemn look, I knew immediately something was wrong.

"Hi" I said a little less excited than the second before.

"Hi" she said, less excited by far than I. She brushed past me and headed up the stairs to the second-floor bedroom.

I stood for a second watching her butt wiggle up the stairs, wondering if I was supposed to kiss her before saying *hi* or what? Maybe she had a bad day at Weight Watchers. Better get up there for the emotional support and therapeutic sex. I had a purpose. I bounded up the stairs, rounding the corner just as she went into my bedroom. She had lived here for a month so she acted right at home.

I closed the bedroom door behind me and turned to catch her taking her shoes off and stripping off her pantyhose from under her skirt. I also noticed her panties came off with the hose. *Whew.* I approached her back and hugged her with a loving squeeze to her midriff. She froze. I turned her around slowly until she was looking up at me. She still looked a little sad but I saw a small smile, or so I thought, and kissed her quickly so she couldn't do anything but feel my lips on hers.

I held it long and hard while holding my body tight to her body. I felt for her lips and tongue with mine, trying to part her lips. She allowed me to probe her membranes like any lover would but didn't seem to respond like she usually did. She had been an eager mouth aggressor before, pushing even my limits for deep kissing without gagging. I pulled back my tongue, but nothing followed. I held her at arm's length for a second studying her beautiful face and deep blue eyes. I guided her to the waterbed.

"Boy," I said, "you must have had a really bad day. Here, lie down and I'll give you a back rub."

I rolled her onto the bed, causing a wave that died out quickly.

"That's okay, I'm not tired."

She stretched out beside me and propped her head on one elbow so she could still face me unobstructed. I rolled on my side and faced her, supporting my head likewise. She looked concerned. I looked concerned. I reached out again to stroke her side with my free hand. She accepted it.

"I've been thinking about us lately. All that adventure with being on the road and then working night and day for two weeks while tracking down Fanfare's equipment gave me a lot of time to think about us."

She started to say something but I put my fingers on her lips.

"I know it's been rough on you having to get an apartment and job but look at your independence! You've made your way in the real world without your mother or father telling you precisely what to do and feel. I really love you now! You're a real person now."

I pulled her close as I kissed her again just to seal the deal.

I started pulling her blouse out from her skirt. Once free, I slid my right hand up her back under the blouse to her bra strap. I was the master of the one-handed unsnapping of the mammary support prison. I could feel her left hand begin to work on my belt buckle getting it unhooked rapidly and then unbuttoning my Levi's. Susie was talented and experienced with my preference for button-up jeans and she began to pop them open one at a time working her way down to my crotch. *God that's sexy!*

I had her blouse off along with the rest of the confinements and she was prying my jeans over my hip bones, pushing them down far enough to get a choke hold. My prick was pulsing and pushing at the skin confining it to a smaller space than it wanted. My fingers started exploring her delicious creamy white breasts replete with targets. Her nipples stood at sharp attention as I caressed them into ecstatic expectation. I slid my hand down her back again, only this time I didn't stop at her skirt but pushed on through to her bare butt, which I squeezed like testing peaches.

"I need to tell you something," she whispered in my ear as she was licking it.

I thought it was a new turn-on, so I went along with it. I licked her ear giving her a wet-willy with my tongue. "I need to tell you something too," I whispered back. She gave my dick a little tug and then let go. She caressed my head as she gathered her strength. *What could it possibly be?* I thought. *Did she lose her job?*

"I wasn't going to tell you at first," she began hesitantly, "but I can't live with a lie. I have to be honest and forthright."

She looked into my eyes and I could feel her fingers tighten on my neck.

"I love you exactly for that," I said trying to give her encouragement.

I still had my hand on her butt so I gave it another little squeeze of reassurance. I tried to give her a little kiss but she went on.

"I met a boy last week and he spent the night in my apartment."

Silence.

I had to let it soak in a little bit just to make sure that was what I heard. Was I hallucinating?

"You let some schmuck stay all night on your couch? What did you do? Get him drunk and he couldn't find the door? You know that's not smart, especially in this town. Who was it?"

I stopped massaging her butt for a second.

"We slept together," she said flatly and then looked down to avoid my stare.

I let it sink in some more. She still had her hand on my neck. I finally took her hand off my neck and held it down to her side. While holding her by the wrist, I swung my body over the top of her rolling her on her back. I pushed myself up into a push-up position with her pinned beneath me.

"You what?" I said, becoming slightly irritated. "You fucked some stranger while I was gone?" I asked incredulously.

Silence.

She looked at me again, but this time I saw guilty defiance.

"What the hell were you thinking?" I went on.

My gut was tightening up like a twisted rubber band. I couldn't think straight. I was at a loss for words. It just couldn't be. We had pledged our love too much for this to even be a possibility. She pulled a soap opera drama on me twice now, and I was supposed to just roll over? Where did this come from? I had a whore for a lover? I suddenly wondered how many lovers she must have had during that year we were separated by her parents. Now I'm seeing a whole other side of Susie I flat never suspected before. Boy, she was good—for a whore that is.

I let go of her wrist and raised my hand just as I caught myself getting sucked into a blind rage. I was losing control. I wanted to hurt something. I wanted to get physical. I wanted to smash her smug shitty face. I formed my hand into a fist she could see. She just looked at me with simple acceptance. I could do what I wanted.

I still loved her. I couldn't hit her. I wasn't capable, only the desire was there along with thousands of other desires, but not the action.

I jumped up, sloshing the waterbed pretty badly and tossing her semi-naked body around as I pounded out of the room. I needed to be alone before I actually did something I wanted to dearly, but absolutely couldn't. I went down to the living room where I knew a joint, rolled earlier but not consumed, cried out to me, begging to sooth my mental state.

"How could she do this to me?" I yelled to nobody in particular.

I picked up the joint but when I grabbed the lighter it jumped out of my shaking hand and flew across the room into a pile of speakers, disappearing from my visual reality in some kind of Karmic convulsion.

"Damn it!" I got up and went into the kitchen to light it using the gas range. I got too close to the flames shooting up and singed my hair. Slapping my head to make sure it wasn't on fire made me even madder. My blind fury was simply replaying only one vision stuck in my head: someone else's naked body lying on top of my Susie with her writhing in his syncopated rhythm of thrusting a foreign dick into *my* love.

"*Arrggghhhh!*" I just wanted to curl up into a ball and cry myself into another reality. Not so easy.

I expected her to get dressed and leave after I blew up. I wasn't sure I wanted her around anymore under this cloud anyway. But will we get over this? How can I get over the girl who gave me her virginity, pledging her love not once, but twice, and now deciding I wasn't enough of a lover to be with me exclusively? What the hell was she thinking? Did she think I would just accept her taking other lovers? When did I give her the idea this was an open relationship?

After about a half an hour of smoking the joint and stewing in my own jealous juices I hesitantly went back upstairs. I opened the bedroom door tepidly, finding her under the covers with her back turned to the door. Her curves were outlined perfectly by the sheet draped over her, suggesting she was naked underneath. I stripped off my jeans and underwear and crawled naked into the waterbed with her.

"I don't know what to say." I whispered to her. She didn't move. "What the fuck did you do to our love? How could you do this to me?'

I waited for an answer but never got one. Finally, she slipped her hand behind her and grabbed my cock now erect as a skyscraper. I was mad, hurt, confused, and turned on as hell. I grabbed her hips from behind, pulling her butt toward me as I rammed my dick into something close to her cunt. She lifted her upper leg and helped guide my dick into her vagina. *Oh God that felt good!* There was nothing better than a well-lubricated pussy, unless of course it was a talented mouth and tongue.

I started pumping her as hard as I could from our lying side by side. I reached around her body from both sides and began flicking her clitoris with one hand while massaging her breasts with the other. I kept the thrusting action going as hard as I could. I wanted her to feel my hate and pain.

I pulled out and rolled on top of her grabbing her legs under both arms as I lifted her butt up in the air, from a kneeling position I thrust my dick into her now wide-open cunt, looking like some red monkey butt. I pushed down hard, doubling her up in the middle with her hips almost over her tits. I pounded hard and furiously. I wanted to get deeper and deeper inside her until I was a permanent part of her body. She grunted every time I thrust into her. Sometimes I would pull out so far it fell out, but she was ready with both hands to reinsert immediately. She was grunting and thrusting against me almost as hard as I, as I tried to punish her with violent love.

I pulled out again and this time I let her hips down as I crawled on top of her chest, pinning her to the bed with my butt. I dangled my cock over her mouth and leaned forward, pushing it up against her face and lips. She glanced up at me as if inquiring, *Really?* and then she closed her eyes and opened her mouth. Her lips grabbed onto my cock, sucking it forcefully into her mouth.

She began sucking, tongue lashing and chewing almost as if she knew what she was doing. It was our first time for her doing a blow job and yet she seemed right at home with a dick in her mouth. I leaned back and with both hands behind me I massaged her clit and vagina as she kept sucking my dick in deeper and deeper as she chewed on it like a cow chewing her cud. *Too much!* I exploded with my first orgasm of the night. She seemed to be having something of an orgasm too, but who can really tell with a woman. Sometimes I think they fake it just for the drama and entertainment.

We went on like that most of the night. We mutually avoided talking and just concentrated on fucking. We'd rest between bouts, sometimes getting up to get a beer from the fridge, but we just tried to fuck each other without mercy or shame. Anything apparently went, so soon we were exploring other orifices. With some lotion I was able to penetrate her anus for a wild ride inside a tight sphincter muscle grabbing onto my dick like a python with a strange new passion.

Along about 3 a.m. I fell asleep until I woke to a scratching noise. Cold early-morning light came through the window so it had to be around 6. I opened my eyes when I sensed she wasn't in bed anymore. I looked across the room in time to see her shadow opening the door to leave. She looked at me briefly without any emotion that I could detect, turned, and was gone through the door. I heard her go down the steps one by one and out the front door. The last I heard were her footsteps hurrying across the porch and down the steps. I turned over with tears in my eyes as I told myself I would probably never see her again. I didn't.

Several weeks of agony later, I heard she had moved out of her new apartment and back to her parent's house in Chicago. Apparently, the boy her parents picked for her asked her to marry him and she said yes. The part that really hurt was the fact he was military, enlisted. That was tantamount to philosophical treachery at the highest level. How could she, after all we had said and done together?

The thought crossed my mind that maybe I took too long to ask her to get married. Maybe I lost her because of something I did wrong, like treating her as an equal with all the responsibilities and duties thereof. I wondered if this was something we unintentionally unleashed with the sexual revolution.

Did sexual freedom kill off monogamy? I thought we were fighting for civil rights, not the right to be unfaithful for no other reason than one could.

I smiled as I thought of the cowboy philosophy of love and responsibility: *I found her, petted her, took her home, fed her, and named her. But all nature's children must be free. Wait for them to respectfully come home. If they don't, then you can hunt them down, kill'em, and eat'em!* This time, I swore, I won't come running back even if she apologized with sex. Even I have limits.

I felt more than confused. I felt betrayed. I know I'm a better potential husband than the wife-beating military clown she ended up with and she had to know it too. It really didn't matter now. She was gone forever and all I had were the midnight Rock & Roll memories. No matter how hard I tried, there was no way I could rationalize what she did. *How could she? How could anybody?*

CHAPTER THIRTEEN

BACH FLIPS WITH JOY IN HIS GRAVE

"Money, it's a hit. Don't give me that do goody good bullshit...."

Pink Floyd
"Money"
1972

The next few days passed in a cloudy haze. I wallowed in as much self-pity as I could muster. I also wallowed in whiskey, black coffee, and beer, not necessarily in that order. I made post-midnight phone calls to all the old friends I could find phone numbers for. Some were happy to hear from me at 2 a.m. and some not so much. I didn't give a shit. I had just suffered a great milestone in the life of the tortured artist and I was bound and determined to share it with all my friends perhaps in hope that, like cow shit, *the more you spread it closer to the neighbors, the less it smelled for you.* Or was it, *the more you spread it around the greener it got*? I wasn't sure.

Bill finally heard and swung by one night to cheer me up. I tried to explain to him that alcohol is the required drug for a jilted lover, not cocaine. He made a powerful argument to the effect it couldn't do much further harm. I had to agree. Broken hearts trump all drug downsides.

He laid out some healthy lines, which immediately and mysteriously attracted Steve and Thom from the downstairs shop. I wondered how they did it. Was it by feel, sight, smell, or sound? I wonder if this was a common problem among ancient Inca runners.

When everybody was well-lubricated, Bill pulled a cassette tape out of his jacket pocket.

"Guess what this is?"

We all stared expecting it to be some new song or band or album he had discovered. Bill, being the primary drug dealer to the local artist community, was the one to have new recordings and pirated tapes before anyone else. It was part of his *cooler-than-thou* image.

"It's the last tape," he announced finally.

"Who's last tape?" I asked, thinking this was a great lead-in to a Bud Abbot routine on baseball.

"It's the Tweedle Dumb Twins last phone tap tape we had in place while we were on vacation in Florida."

"Oh shit," I suddenly realized, "we left the phone tap running on their line while we were gone."

"Yeah," Bill added, "I was amazed the batteries were still working. Most of the calls were routine until we get to a week ago last Sunday. You have got to hear this. I nearly crapped my pants it was so funny."

Steve took it from him and put it in the cassette player. Bill had it cued to the phone call of interest so he just hit play.

Shhhshhhshhshhhs... Click... Ring...ring...ring...

Hello?...Wayne? Yeah... It's me, Barry... Hey!... Where you guys been? Your buddies over at funksville keep calling here for you guys. What's up?... What's up is we're missing the equipment. We don't know what the hell happened... You lost the equipment and the truck? Did you guys get robbed or somethin'?... Damnit, no! We just stopped to fill up with gas in Cincinnati and get some blow from the back when we found the truck fuckin' empty! Somebody got the equipment!... Jeez, didn't you guys lock it up?... Of course, we locked it up you doofus....

Bill was cracking up at this point. I couldn't believe I was hearing this either. They didn't notice the truck was empty for another six hundred miles! How fucking stupid could you be or stoned? You can't drive an empty truck without noticing it's empty. It drives different in so many ways you would have to be a rank amateur or a doofus yourself. All that worrying about getting caught was all pretty much for naught. They really were doofuses. We were getting drunk in Daytona by the time they even realized they had been taken.

"...I don't know what we're going to tell Farner. If it wasn't for the rental truck we ought to head straight for New Jersey and a new gig, if we can find it. Don't tell them anything. We'll be back tomorrow and maybe we'll come up with something by then... Well at least you got the money and the dope, right?... We got the money... What about... Click...the dope? Crap...."

Click)... Ssshshhshhshhh...

Everybody was laughing by the time it came to the end. What a perfect ending to the freak version of Mission Impossible.

I toasted Bill. "Nice job if I do say so myself."

Then I had to ask, "What did he mean by that *blow in the back* comment?"

"Oh, funny other thing," he said. "When Curt swapped out drivers in the W-cabinet in Boulder he found a little present from the Rock & Roll gods. Somebody left behind about an ounce of coke. I don't know who that could have possibly been," he added in a falsetto voice, clearly indicating the Doofus Twins.

"That's kind of a lot of money," I said. "What the hell were they doing with that much coke in the truck? They didn't need that much to do one measly concert. They must have been dealing, or transporting, or both."

"Wow, man," Munsell piped in, "maybe we misjudged these little pipsqueaks. Sounds like they were doing more drugs than Rock & Roll, never mind the sex part."

We laughed again at the sex remark. We never saw them with anyone other themselves or the guys in the band. But we didn't make any judgments. At least not by this criterion.

"I wonder what they were going to do with that much snow in Ann Arbor?" Steve interjected. "Which reminds me, what did Curt do with it?"

Everybody looked back at him dumb-like and then burst out laughing again.

"You gotta ask?" we responded in unison.

"The real question is how much of it made it back here from Boulder, and did Curt share it with anyone before announcing the discovery," I offered.

We all had to laugh again. The answer was as obvious as Nixgoon and his thugs being inept petty criminals. Like written in stone.

"Looks like someone is butting into your territory," I said, verbally jabbing at Bill. He got that crooked grin on his face and winked.

"There's never too much snow for Annie's garden," he announced, with quick agreement from the group.

With that, he laid out some lines while he told us what else was going on. His girlfriend was applying for medical school, so he was looking forward to taking her prescript pad for a spin around the block. Peter had successfully planted his secretary on the university staff as a talent coordinator and was booking major acts into university facilities. Sinclair was still in jail, but a lot of rumors were going around about a possible State Supreme Court appeal and maybe a fund-raising concert with someone big. Bob Webb and Joe Miller, a couple of local musicians we all knew, had put together a new band and were practicing in one of Bill's rooming houses. A new nightclub was about to open around the corner from Mister Flood's Party on Front Street. Bob's band would be headlining the opening on Friday.

"Why don't you videotape them?" he asked, while calmly carving out another line. "What do you think that might cost?"

"You know all I've got is that leased portable black and white Portapack," I said. "I need to turn it back in, too. I don't think I can afford to keep it any longer. But we can shoot Bob's show this weekend if you want."

"I think that would be a good hit." He held the mirror up to me with a straw in his other hand. I took both lines.

"I might have a few reels of half-inch tape laying around, leftover from something or another," I added.

"I'll volunteer to help," Steve said. I handed him the mirror.

"Me too," echoed Thom. "Does the new club have a decent PA?"

"I don't know," Bill responded, "but the rumor is it's backed by some serious drug money. I would expect something expensive."

"More likely an expensive piece of shit," I added. "I've seen what you guys spend on impressing people with a loud stereo Hi Fi." By *you guys*, I meant the rich freaks and drug dealers who didn't have to work to make a living.

"So make a better one," Bill challenged. "If it's all shit, build one that isn't and you could make millions. You know how much everyone is spending on stereo equipment. I hear the profits are as lucrative as dealing drugs, and, without a lot of the hassle." He smiled at me as he passed a newly lit joint to Steve.

"Yes, I know," Steve said gleefully.

He rocked back and forth on the edge of his seat giggling and shaking his head in apparent disbelief. "I can't believe how bad all the competition speakers are. We've already developed a speaker that reproduces a square wave. Nobody even comes close!"

He laughed some more, showing pity on all the poor fools. He passed the joint to Thom.

"We took our prototype down to the stereo store and did side-by-side tests on all their best speakers," Thom said while inhaling and exhaling a huge cloud of pot smoke. There were several sympathetic coughs in response. "I found this obscure Rock album with an instrumental cut where the bass was tuned an octave lower."

He passed the joint to me.

"How the hell could they do that on a vinyl record with the RIAA response curve severely limiting full fidelity?" I posed, as I drew deep on a very nice Jamaican blend. "Who brought this?"

I held up what was left of the joint.

"I did," Thom said. "They had to do a differential screw pressing to get enough room, between grooves in order to get it to record playback properly. Actually, some super lightweight tone arms couldn't hold the track and would sometimes skip a groove, but our Rabco straight-tracking arm did just fine."

"Where'd you get it?" I asked.

"The Rabco tone arm?" he asked as he took out another joint and lit it up.

Steve began to giggle along with Bill.

"No, the dope, dope. I know where you stole the Rabco."

"But the important part was that our speaker was the only one that reproduced the correct frequencies for the bass tuning," Steve interjected, while copping the new joint from Thom. "Other speakers just put out the harmonics with no fundamental." He took a big noisy suck on the joint. *Shlishshsh.* "It sounded really weird on all their best speakers."

"You could hear the correct fundamental on headphones and our speakers only," added Thom.

"My speakers," Steve corrected. "It's my business. I don't have a job and this could be a way to make some money. Money for everyone who works, that is."

Thom suddenly wrinkled up his already craggy face in contorted irritation.

"Actually, we all had a hand in their development," I interjected. "You were hung up on building speaker walls like the Grateful Dead, which would have gotten you nowhere. I had to explain how sound waves work, how to recreate a sound wave front and how to recreate phase linear frequencies across the band. Only then does one have a chance of recreating the precise waveform with correctly phased harmonics directly in the ear. In other words, speaker boxes should look like cylindrical columns or a section thereof, hence the pie shape. I sort of invented these things."

I found myself standing up and gesticulating with my hands and arms trying to illustrate how waves expand in circles and how phase linearity makes everything better.

Bill broke up laughing first, followed by everyone else.

"It's true!" I exclaimed. "That was fundamental to the design and Steve just engineered a crossover for two different impedance drivers capable of covering the entire band and maintain correct phase as close as possible to the crossover frequency."

I noticed their amused looks, gave up and sat down.

"How is it not a design?" Steve pointed out, "Besides, I filed a patent application."

Everybody made an *Ooooohhh* sound. "You know the patent process no longer requires a prior patent search besides your own efforts, which were less than exhaustive. Patents mean nothing now unless it is defended in a court. You just applied for a license to pay lawyers."

"Which I built," said Thom. "And, provided the calibrated microphone and low-loss inductors."

The story was that the expensive calibrated microphone purchased by the U of M School of Music was in the safe care of the guys running their recording studio—of which Thom was a notorious member.

"Yeah, and I only provided the lab and engineering," added Steve, referring to his basement and some spare time calculating complex impedances.

I looked around and saw that many of the smiles had turned serious.

"So when do I get to hear this super speaker?" Bill piped in.

"We've got a pair set up downstairs in the chamber," Thom volunteered. "We can kick some ass down there without rocking the entire neighborhood."

"I've got something in my car you might be interested in," said Bill "I'll go get it and be right back."

Thom brightened. I knew he probably thought it was more cocaine or something even better. I didn't guess.

"That sounds terrific. I'll get some beers and meet you down there," said Steve.

Looked like he thought it was coke too.

I followed Thom to the basement, where we had all helped set up a shop/lab some time ago for working on electronic projects, speakers, and another project Steve and I had worked on, a new kind of synthesizer with a proportional control keyboard. We thought it would be neat to build a synthesizer that could reproduce a pipe organ. That would be a challenge. The entire basement had been taken over for projects and toy development. It first housed the pumps and air banks for the pipe organ and now we were more or less trying to do the equivalent in high-powered, low-distortion speaker systems.

The weak points in developing a true electronic pipe organ were speakers which could recreate a pipe organ's dynamic power range and a synthesizer keyboard that had proportional control just like a pipe organ keyboard. From there, all we needed was a true Fourier synthesizer, which was easily achieved with computer logic chips. Imagine a synthesizer that could sound and play better than a real pipe organ and scalable to any size or power desired. Just the thought would make Bach turn flips with joy in his grave.

After the space physics lab closed, we picked up a couple of Tektronix scopes and set up several electronic work-stations on benches in the basement with all the basic audio test equipment. I was finishing my Mauer amp in one corner while Steve worked on his proportional keyboard in another. But since we got laid off, Steve and Thom were driven to get the speaker project off the ground and maybe make some money with it.

So they built a small anechoic chamber along the back wall of the basement. With the help of a very expensive calibrated microphone, they could actually do differential distortion testing that allowed them to fine tune the crossover and the cabinet reflex design. There was even talk about possibly manufacturing a consumer version, but first things first. We had to make it work.

Thom kicked on the lights as he went down the stairs off the kitchen. I followed, noting from the vantage of the stairs that they had been up to some serious testing while I had apparently been comatose in my room suffering from another bout of love's gut-ripping loss. They had two of the pie-shaped speakers set up pointing into the one open side of a black chamber about ten feet deep. A mannequin torso sat upright in a folding chair in the middle with two microphones sticking out of its head where the ears should be.

The chamber looked like a small cave open on one end and covered on all sides top and bottom with varying sizes of long, skinny pyramids made out of black open-cell polystyrene foam. There were a few open spaces on the floor placed strategically as places to step when entering the chamber. Two spots were placed at the foot of the chair so a person could sit in place of the microphone and hear directly what was coming over the speakers. I likened it to a giant headphone wrapped in a blanket and driven by full-blown room-sized speakers. *Killer!*

"I talked the music school into buying binaural calibrated microphones so we could precisely record what is heard by a real person in the audience. I love their love of pure sound." He made that big Munsell grin that meant he was in music heaven or high on his favorite drugs, or both. Mostly both in his case.

"Here, sit in the chair," he said as he carefully lifted the mannequin out of the chair and set it aside.

I sat in the chair while Thom cued the Rabco tone arm onto a record already on the turntable. I flinched when the tone arm landed on the record, suddenly sending a loud thump followed by tiny dust grains being hit by a micro miniature diamond tooth, causing sharp pings of static and pain. I was immediately struck by the obvious clarity. It was like being in the groove with the tiny grains being knocked about like trash cans in a New York alleyway, empty and hollow sounding just waiting for the next inevitable sound-drama to explode.

Dum-dum-de-dum. Duh-dum-dum-dum. I tried to follow the guttural notes being played on the base guitar but it was more than I could even air guitar to as it tore a whole new bottom in the audio spectrum. Just like Bach's "Great Fugue" and the lower third of the thirty-two-foot pipe standing against the opposite wall, one felt the low notes more than heard them. It was a rattling of guts while muscles involuntarily reacted to the earthquake-like vibrations. It was a far closer relationship to the music to be able to bypass the hearing process and go straight to the direct interpretation of a compression wave massaging your gelatinous body. Then the bass hit the low notes.

Dum-de-doom-doom-BOOM-BA-BOOM-BOOM. I was amazed to hear notes never before heard or recorded on a stringed instrument. It was deep—deeper than deep—and resonated profoundly with what could be our collective Rock & Roll soul. This was what *Gnarly* referred to. Our speakers were recreating the sound just as if the listener was in the studio at the time of the recording. Actually, it was better, because the musicians had obviously inferior speakers when they listened to their own playbacks. I was hearing something nobody had ever heard since the actual recording. It was like making a new scientific discovery. A Eureka moment: only in this case, the Eureka feeling happened damned near every time I listened to them.

It was like as if we lived in a closed-up room of dark and indistinct shadows only to have a window flung open, revealing brilliantly clear and colorful sunlight streaming in to illuminate intricate objects of joy and delight. Illuminate things we have never experienced before. I wonder what other LPs might realize totally unheard clarity since their recording. I knew that very expensive single-driver headphones could easily reproduce this sound for the ears, as well, yet only powerful speakers recreating the exact natural sound waves could deliver that reality of being there when it happened—gut-wrenching tsunamis of new sounds.

"What are you using for an amplifier?" I yelled out, trying to make myself heard over the sound of a *thirty-two-foot-long* bass guitar.

Thom pointed down at the floor between the two speakers, which were sitting on two small cable reel spools each bringing them up to about seated chest-level height, and thus, the best level to thump against the hollow lung chambers of listeners— like hollow logs beaten with sticks. I spotted what looked like a barebones Crown DC 300, except this one didn't look straight.

I mean the sides and top and bottom no longer looked like a 90-degree, box-shaped rectangle. The amp looked a little skewed to the right. I glanced back at Thom with a quizzical look, but before I could ask, he turned down the stereo preamp.

"It fell off a truck. Really! Insurance bought it for us from Fanfare. And it still works! "One of Fanfare's new roadies had flipped the truck coming back from Colorado in the snow last week, spilling several amps onto the highway where some got run over by other trucks unable to stop. The insurance company bought them all new amps so these literally dropped off the back of the insurance truck. Nobody bothered to see if they still worked or had any value."

"Amazing! Any more of those available?" I asked, wondering why I hadn't heard about this before.

"Nope. They were gobbled up in the first few hours. Most went to friends of Curt, but we were able to snag one for the effort."

"Nice," I said, still admiring the new shape of a modern art power amp. The music came to an end and the Rabco retrieved the tone arm from the test disc.

Steve showed up with two six-packs of Blatz. Cheap, but effective in a pinch.

"Did you see our new amp?" Steve said as he set the six-packs down, taking the first can out of the new six-hole plastic rings holding the cans together, instead of the old cardboard box.

"Yeah," I said taking the next beer hanging off the end of the plastic rings. "That form factor looks like some kind of abstract impression of an amp moving past us at the speed of light. It's a warped amp!"

Everybody laughed. Thom snagged a beer as Bill yelled out from the top of the stairs.

"Hey! Is it okay to let..." Muffled voices were heard in the distance. "Eric and..." More mumbling. "Sharon in?"

We looked at each other for a long second. Those two names didn't normally get put together. Eric was a lonely waif Steve brought home one night from the local coffee shop. He lived off his father's insurance policy after a fatal gyrocopter accident in Benton Harbor. The story he related was that his father was test-flying a gyrocopter that he had designed; Heathkit was going to sell it out of their electronic kit catalog. That didn't work out, so now his mother lived on Bainbridge Island across Puget Sound from Seattle, and he just hung out at the university library writing graphic novels about super heroes and weird fanciful aliens. He had published nothing yet but was adamant that there was a great future in writing fantasy crap and that he was going to be a part of it.

He didn't like drugs or Rock & Roll and he didn't seem to be interested in chicks, but he hung out with us anyway. His only common trait seemed to be a shared love of 4-wheel drive vehicles and a sense of good intellectual craziness.

He owned a brand-new Toyota Land Cruiser, a red and white fully enclosed aluminum box on a Jeep wheelbase. We made fun of it because it wasn't American-made with real American steel. I secretly admired it, though; its obvious application was for getting into remote places my truck simply couldn't traverse because of size, and neither could an aluminum British piece of crap Land Rover because of a distinct lack of reliability. The Toyota was proving more reliable than even a custom-modified Willy's Station Wagon.

But its price tag was way out of my range and there was not much chance of building one out of insurance parts. I had to settle for the fact I could pull the lightweight, under-powered tin can backward in a tug-of-war, but may need one if I ever get stuck in the wrong place.

Sharon, on the other hand, was a local slut whose hobby—and as far as I knew, only talent—was prodigious sexual prowess. I constantly scanned her almost always exposed upper leg for signs of some kind of scorecard. Her long legs were usually amply displayed in her signature denim short-shorts, and her full bosom was not too well hidden in a shear blouse tied high to reveal lots of flat, inviting stomach. She was both hot and available. I had many chances with her before, but I had been attached to Susie at the time. More importantly, I did not wish to dip my dick into a known, possibly toxic, public sporting arena.

"It's okay!" we shouted together back at Bill.

"Hi guys!" Sharon said, waving from the top of the stairs. "What's happening?"

Eric appeared with Bill right behind them as they all came stomping down the stairs. Bill was carrying a seven-inch reel of audio tape.

"They showed up on your porch while I was getting this out of my 'vette." He held up the tape.

Sharon ran over to Thom and gave him a big hug. He turned crimson as always. He remained staunchly faithful to his wife, which we all found quaint in this time of sexual exploration. She hugged Steve, who also turned red as a shit eating grin spread wide across his face. She hugged me and for some unexplainable reason, I hugged her back. She noticed and held me out at arm's length, most likely contemplating her new target for the night.

"You've changed. You're cuter than usual," she said, now fully aware of a possible conquest to add to her notches. She wrapped her arms around my right arm and stayed pushed up against my side, slowly grinding her body against mine for the rest of the night.

"So whatchya doing?"

She looked around the cluttered basement with five guys all looking back wondering pretty much the same thing.

"We just happened to walk by your house at the same time," Eric said with his whiney Midwestern accent. "I never met Sharon before. I knocked, but all we heard was loud music coming from the basement. Then Bill showed up and let us in."

"We're listening to our speakers playing this new album with an electric bass tuned an octave lower than normal," explained Steve. "It's really crazy! You can only hear it on our new speakers."

Now everybody who hadn't heard it yet crowded into the anechoic chamber to hear it all together. Sharon seemed quite happy to be sandwiched between two guys, even though one was a lot less good looking or cool. She had no apparent prejudices when it came to having fun. I kind of liked that idea, though it would be a big stretch for me to realize personally. Like the Methodists who raised me, fun is highly suspect. First be clean cut, and then let's never speak of real fun again. Here was the new age revolution in a nutshell. Fun was no longer immoral.

"Where is that tape deck you found?" Bill asked, loudly enough for everyone to hear. My purloined prize wasn't much news to this crowd.

"It's over there," I said pointing to the corner where I was working on the Mauer amp.

"I've got a tape that just fell into my lap," Bill went on to explain as he held up a reel of tape. "I think it's a new song being rehearsed by Grand Funk. You've got to hear this crap. Can you hook up your deck to these speakers so we can all hear it?"

"I can," Thom volunteered. He headed for the corner where my new Teac was stashed.

While Thom set up the deck next to the crooked Crown amp, Eric tried to explain how his latest story involved a new super race of alien-bred humans. He began to explain in much too much detail how aliens could interbreed with humans, creating a new hybrid human with extraordinary powers. Sharon asked him if the human females liked the hybrid experience or not, and if so, why?

Eric looked embarrassed and stumped for a moment, just in time for Thom to say he had it ready to roll. Bill produced a joint, lit it up, and handed it to me as Thom hit the play button and the tape began playing.

There were some indistinct voices in the background saying *Ready…one…two…*and then the music started. It began as a loud, hard-driving Rock & Roll riff that went on for a minute or so then suddenly broke into song:

Out on the road for forty days, last night in Little Rock put me in a craze!

Then they stopped. More mumbling in the background and they started again:

Out on the road for forty days, last night in Little Rock put me in a haze!" *tum-tum-tum-te-tum*, "Sweet, sweet Connie, doin' her act. She did the whole show and that's a natural fact.

Up all night with Freddie King. I got to tell you, poker's his thing. Booze and ladies, keep me right, as long as we can make it to the show tonight! We're an American band....

There were more mumblings and then the synthesizer hit about six hard notes in a row. Somebody said, *That's it*. Then it started again, only this time with the chorus first:

We're an American band, *tum-te-tum-te-tum-te-tum*, We're an American band. We're comin' to your town. We'll help you party down. We're an American band....

It stopped again. But everyone had gotten involved with the action behind the tape. It was a window on the creative process and we were listening in on a private session. It went on for another twenty minutes as the band slowly put the various pieces together. Near the end it made it all the way through without stopping or repeating:

Four young chiquitas in Omaha, waitin' with the band to return from the show. Feelin' good, feelin' right, it's Saturday night. The hotel detective, he was outta sight. Now these four ladies, they had a plan. They were out to meet the boys in the band. They said, *Come on dudes, let's get it on*. And we proceeded to tear that hotel down!

We're an American band. We're an American band. We're coming to your town, we're gonna help you party down! We're gonna help you party down! We're an American band! We're an American band, *wo-oo-oo*. We're an American band, *wo-oo-oo*. We're an American band, *woo-oo-oo!*

Thom stopped the tape machine before it ran out of tape and hit the rewind button. God, I loved the sound of a good machine whirring with such confidence and solid bearings; it made me warm just thinking that I owned something fine, and not the usual cheap crap I could afford.

"That was way too much *woo-wooing* there at the end, don't you think so?" asked Eric.

We just ignored him. Sharon thought it was cute.

"Well, now I know what happened with the hotel party I was thrown out of," I said.

"Jeez, do you think that's going to be a hit song?" asked Thom changing the subject. "It doesn't seem very serious for such an august group. They need to listen to some British bands who know how to use a complete orchestra. The days of shit-kicking four-man Rock & Roll bar bands is over."

"I have a lot of friends in the music business who would disagree with you," Bill pointed out. "There's always a big market out there for tasteless crap. Look at Nashville."

"It's well known there's no limit to bad taste when it comes to teeny boppers," I chipped in. "Look at KISS for god's sake. That's not music, just a continual scream-fest proposition for imitating orgasms."

Everybody laughed.

"So, what do you want to do with this tape?" Thom asked no one in particular.

"I'll put it in the archive box out in the garage with all the other pirated tapes I have from the Blues Festival and other university concerts. It might be valuable someday," I added, not really believing it. I just couldn't throw away anything remotely artistic. It would be like throwing away pieces of a person's soul, or worse, throwing away a Picasso before he became famous. *Bad ju-ju* for sure.

"What did you think of the speakers?" Steve asked the group.

"I loved them," Sharon bubbled. "When will I be able to buy a pair?"

"Yeah, everybody, when are you going to start selling these babies and make some money?" chimed in Bill.

"It's not easy. We need to raise a lot of money first." Steve responded with a slight whine.

The reality was that money was impossible to be had at this time, especially for freak projects. Most of the white shirt and tie people didn't even know about loud Rock & Roll not to mention anyone wanting to buy into a socially rejected business model. Freaks either found an angel trust-funder freak who understood the market, or they did a big dope deal.

"We have to find warehouse space, a power router table capable of complex circular cuts, and then we need an assembly line where it's all put together. It'll take hundreds of thousands of dollars."

"I heard your family has a little money," Bill brightly posed. "Why don't you ask them to invest in their boy having gainful employment?"

"Oh man, I still owe them for my college loans and this house. Now I have no job. They're more likely to foreclose on me rather than give me anything more."

I believed him but Bill didn't.

"Oh, come on. You know how to milk your family. You're just waiting for the right angle because they may not give you a second chance. Actually, you could just wait them out until somebody dies and the family inheritance starts rattling down to your generation."

"Man, if I keep hanging out with the likes of you guys, I could get disinherited anyway so I might as well get what I can."

"That's the ticket," Bill said. "Have another line."

He held up the little mirror he had been quietly working on.

"Ladies first." He shifted it to my direction where Sharon was also standing, slowly stroking my arm for some reason. She reached out and took it gleefully.

"Here, you hold it," she said as she handed me the mirror.

I held it for her as she devoured two fat lines. Then she took it, handing me the straw so I could take a hit. Finally, she passed it to Steve and Thom. Eric said *no thanks* when politely offered. Just more for the rest of us.

"You realize Nix-goon is kicking the shit out of the economy, especially science and technology," Bill continued. "You guys need to get your shit together if you plan on surviving. This poor excuse for a hippie commune invention factory will tear itself apart when greed and envy take over."

"We're not greedy," Thom said, "just hungry."

"I'm just saying that when there is money involved, friendships tend to get redefined in the order you think they're cheating you. It always happens and that's why I do everything myself. No partners, no broken trust."

Thinking about my recent violations of trust from business partners to girlfriends, I had to agree. Most of my downer conditions seemed directly related to trusting the wrong people to do the right thing. What was right for me seemed to be subject to reinterpretation, depending on how flexible one's morals happen to be. Sometimes getting fucked by a stranger is worth blowing a lifetime of dubious happiness with your true love. Maybe not.

"Well," Steve piped in, "I'm the one who has to make the mortgage payment every month, so I think I am the more responsible one of all of you. I provided the house, all the test equipment, and all the speaker drivers we had to buy for testing."

"Hey!" Thom spoke up. "I pay a mortgage and I have a job. And, I shouldn't have to remind you of all the stuff I've provided, including the microphone."

"See?" Bill interjected. "You need to figure out what you have to do to make money and survive, then worry about your friends."

"That seems brutal," I said. "I have a lot of fun creating things with my friends. It's why I love making films and video. It takes a crew to make a film happen and when they work together as friends and colleagues, magic happens as well. I just wish I had the money to do it all the time, but unfortunately, I have to compete with no-talent trust funders who have all the toys but none of the talent. I have nothing but my perspective and talent to sell, and nobody is buying."

There were the expected raspberries and nose-holding sour

looks at the mention of a perspective. Too big a word, no doubt, for this crowd.

Bill touched a nerve that nobody wanted to discuss. Money was something we had radically different views about. Bill was very practical and street savvy, always looking for the advantage. He maximized his income with activities that paid well. He had connections and cash, which he never shared with anybody, not even his girlfriend. Bill liked the big-city blues hustle.

Thom was actually a good ol' boy who happened to like hippie artsy chicks, 4-wheel drive trucks, nitrous, and long hair. He knew electronics, which all of us at the lab did. But deep down inside, I knew he was more country than big-city blues. He wanted money as well, but perhaps his was the nobler of reasons. He just wanted to make his wife happy and have a family someday. In the meantime, his wife had expensive drug tastes and living requirements that kept him busier than the rest of us. He clearly wanted to own something that made money instead of just working for the other guy.

I was feeling the pressure as well. I could barely afford to live in Steve's house and put gas in my truck. I made very little from the sale of the rooming house and all my other ventures seemed to be going too slow to pay for my minimal expenses. I needed a job, but didn't want to have to do something unpleasant, like selling things in a store or working for some defense contractor raping the world.

Pete wasn't calling about TV shows anymore and the word on the street was he had been stabbed in the back by his old secretary, Suzanne. He was having a hard time booking his acts. I could maybe work as a sound man for a new band, but the only one available right now was Bob Webb's band. That sounded too difficult, going through the *paying dues* thing from the bitter beginning. Startup bands are hell, especially if they go on the road semi-permanently.

Eric didn't need a job, but whenever we pleaded for a small loan, he claimed he barely had enough to buy coffee. I believed him. The Land Cruiser, he said, belonged to his dad before he died. He didn't feel right about selling it so he just hung out with the rest of us destitute and consumed little, nor contributed much. Funny how Eric's father seemed more interesting than he was. With such a father, I expected a son with more assertiveness and a bent for adventure. *Didn't happen*, as far as I could tell.

Sharon had no great plans that I knew of, but here she was anyway, hangin' with a bunch of techies getting high on sound and video with always the possibility of sex later on. Then I cringed slightly, thinking about how many men has probably marched with muddy boots between her legs and apparently, I was a reluctant next victim, or from her point of view, trophy. But after Susie and the pain she caused, I said *what the fuck, why not?* One bitch was as good as any other in a snow storm, I figured. *If you can't be-e-e with the one you la-ove, momma, love the one you're with!* Besides, isn't there a bible passage or something saying basically it's a sin to turn down a horny woman. It's just not right.

When Bill ran out of coke, he and Thom had to split. Eric and Steve went upstairs to have coffee and talk about comic books. Sharon made me show her my Mauer amp project. I got to the part about making a mistake and printing a mirror-image PC board for the left channel and getting it to work anyway; I had a unique amp that I called my *Alice in Wonderland* model. It had a stereo mirror-image board layout, making it look kind of weird, but not immediately obvious. I looked up to see if she appreciated the mathematical quirk when she grabbed me with some strength and our lips fell into each other like loose magnets seeking their opposite poles.

I swung around, grasping for a hand-hold to help me apply more lip pressure, but I needn't bother. She wrapped one of her long legs around my thigh, grabbing one buttock in a leg lock that forced more than my lips harder on hers. I responded by grabbing both of her butt cheeks, pulling them up and forward into my groin area, but I lost my balance leaning on the workbench, spinning off the end and onto a pile of boxed-up speakers waiting to be mounted in cabinets.

She went down with me, as we were pretty well locked together—both physically and with positive intent. As we rolled around on the hard floor, I felt her prying loose my belt buckle. Not to be outdone, I started tearing at her scanty clothes. When I unbuttoned her shorts and started trying to pull them down, I realized I was going to need both hands. She let go of my leg and I let go of her back. I was making progress when she suddenly let go of my lips and ducked down to use her teeth and both hands to unhook my belt.

I fell back on my butt, clawing to get her tight pants to at least roll down her legs like nylon stockings. Meanwhile, the belt buckle gave up with a loud snap, causing her to get hit on the lip by flying metal. She let out a little yelp of pain, which I mistook for pleasure. Redoubling my efforts, I was stunned to find she had no panties on. She jerked my pants down flipping me on my side so she could get a straight shot at pulling them off over my boots. I waved her off as I tried to pull off my boots with my pants down around my ankles.

"Is anybody down there?" Steve called from the top of the stairs.

Sharon and I froze. We didn't need to be seen in this state of affairs. If we're quiet he may go away. Then I felt a cold hand cup one of my testicles. I almost yelped in surprise.

"I guess everybody went home or went to bed," he continued apparently talking to Eric in the next room. "I'll just turn the lights out then." Everything went black. I almost thanked him out loud.

He didn't close the door completely so some light leaked in from the kitchen above. I could make out vague shapes next to me that clearly stalked my warm body like a creeping black panther approaching the quivering hare.

"Where are you?" she whispered. Before I could say anything, she said, "Oh, there you are." But there I wasn't. She was a few feet away as far as I could tell.

"Ee-ee-eek!" she almost screamed. I moved over to her to see what happened and found she was cupping the lower torso part of the calibrated microphone mannequin.

"I thought it was you until I found your lower half missing."

She dropped the mic and started crawling over to me. I was having problems crawling with my pants down around my ankles, held on by my boots. I gave up and pulled them back on.

"I say we make a run for my upstairs bedroom," I whispered as she stood up with me. Her shorts were twisted into a rag tied tight across her thighs revealing her ample pubic hair while she held one arm modestly across her bosom where her blouse should have been.

"I need my shirt," she whispered back.

"You need more than that," I said pointing to her rolled up shorts.

"Oh dear!" she said as she dropped covering her breast and tried to tug her shorts back up to her hips.

"It's okay. Steve and Eric probably walked down to the all-night coffee shop."

I grabbed her free hand and began moving quickly toward the stairs. The light from the open door helped us get up the stairs. I was still dragging her as she tried to at least cover her crotch with her other hand while having to trip along behind me restricted by her tight shorts squeezing her thighs firmly together.

They hadn't gone anywhere. They both looked at us with shock and horror as I drug an almost naked girl through the living room to the stairs and up to the bedroom. She waved with her free hand to the gawkers as we passed through. Not a walk of shame but more like the run for fun.

"Hi Steve," she whimsically muttered. "Hi Eric. Sorry."

They both grinned like idiots and only Steve had the presence to say, "Oh, there you are," as we disappeared up the stairs. I was pretty wasted, as was Sharon, but I didn't care and I didn't use a condom. Hated the damned things anyway, but with her reputation and the situation, that's what I should have done, but didn't.

I don't remember much else, but I think we only fucked for about ten minutes when I orgasmed all over her and she dutifully faked hers, so, well-satiated, we slept locked together long into the next day. I pretended to still be asleep when she gave up, got up, presumably found her blouse downstairs, and soon I heard the front door open and shut as she left. We never slept together again and we never spoke of this night again.

Later, I had to endure the actual walk of shame as I reappeared downstairs to face the guilt and humiliation. Steve and Eric were still there, although I don't think Eric stayed over. They just seem to have the same coffee drinking schedule. They didn't stop laughing out loud or chuckling every time they had to look at me that day and most of the next. After a while, it got irritating, but I had to admit it was still pretty funny.

It wasn't more than six months later before I noticed little warts starting to grow around the base of my penis. *Ah, there it is,' I said. 'I was warned, I knew it, I did it and now it's time to pay the piper.* Or in this case, the dermatologist, who got out his fucking scary electric torch and burned the little buggers off one by flaming one.

Probably would have hurt like hell too, if I hadn't laced my body from tail to head with painkillers, some administered by a doctor and some maybe not so much. I suppose I was lucky, considering all the other sexually transmitted diseases pubescent high school boys were warned about in health class that could have chosen Sharon as a home. Warts were almost a brown badge of courage in this day and age.

At least the concert coming up with Bob Webb's new band gave me a purpose other than worrying about where my next dollar was going to come from. I called him and he invited me over to their rehearsal session later that afternoon. He was still living in one of Bill's rooming houses where he and I met several years earlier when Katy lived upstairs and I downstairs at the same house. He and I crossed paths in the stairway many times until one night he overheard me singing falsetto through the thin walls of our tenement house while I was concentrating on one of my film projects.

He knocked on my door and invited himself in to tell me how much he enjoyed my singing, and to offer me a joint for the effort. Bob was without a doubt one of the truly cool guys. His first love was music and after that, just simple life fun; being high, and kicking back on good jams. I respected his immense musical talent and he and I became great friends.

Bob was prematurely going bald so maybe for balance and symmetry he developed long side burns that almost joined his full black mustache. He always seemed to have a twinkle in his eye, or he was just always tickled about something or another. He spoke slowly and melodiously, which I just ascribed to the fact I never saw him without a joint in his hand or freshly put out in the nearest ashtray.

His band had done some of the Sunday Park concerts, but he couldn't get any traction with Pete or any other local area promoters. He and his best friend, Walt Wilson, who played electric bass, had been playing together since high school in Dearborn Heights. They were determined to make it big so they recently recruited two new band members, a drummer and a keyboard artist; they were rehearsing for their first public performance this coming Friday. Bob was hoping somebody would see them and get them some gigs. Pete Andrews was supposed to be there, along with some guys from Motown.

"With you videotaping it, it should be an awesome concert," he told me when I showed up at the rehearsal. "Listen to a couple of numbers and tell me what you think."

They had stuffed all their band equipment into a closet-sized room on the second floor and were trying to balance their sound between instruments and vocals. Their two JBL monitors used for the small-band PA faced each other from opposite corners of the stuffed room. But the vocals were weak and tinny, almost ringing with feedback. I asked for some socks, but all I got was goofy stares.

"Put a sock in it," I said after hearing them struggle with getting any volume behind Bob's vocals. I pointed at their JBL

Monitors. "Literally, stuff a sock into those long throw horns in your monitor cabinets so you can prevent too much gain in the midrange, especially in these tight quarters."

Bob produced a couple of big wool socks he no doubt used when visiting his father's cabin in Northern Michigan. In the winter, when his retired surgical doctor old man was safely ensconced at his other home in Florida, Bob was free to have all his friends stay and party with him at the frozen lake-front estate. I had been there several times with him, along with Walt, Ned, and some of the others who used to play with Bob's band or hang at Bill's rooming house. We all had to do a snow trek across the hopefully well-frozen lake as a challenge to our drunken manhood. In Michigan, woolen socks were kept close like sacred cows and washed about as often.

I told Bob about Eberbach's new speakers that I had designed. He immediately invited us to bring them down to the club on Friday so they could try them out. *Man, that was easy.* Now to get Steve to actually do it.

"I don't think they're ready for prime time just yet," he begged off, while smiling coyly.

"Why not?" I asked. "This could be our big chance to show how good they are."

"What if they fail?"

"Why would they fail?"

"I don't know, but when I expect something to succeed, it usually fails. Remember the space lab and all those satellite failures?"

"What the hell are you talking about? We never had a failure. We put everyone else at NASA to shame because of our success record."

"Oh yeah, that's right. I was the freakin' design engineer, so I know all about all the failures it took to make the final shot a success. So in my case, I just assume every time I need to succeed, some shit happens."

"So what? Shit happens in Rock & Roll every day! It seems to actually make it stronger," I countered.

He smiled knowingly. "You're right, sort of. I'll do it anyway. Do they have an amp?"

"Yeah, I think I saw a new Phase Linear running their PA."

"That's 400 watts!" he exclaimed. "We've only tested them to 300 watts. That's its rated power. If these guys turn it up, they could possibly fry them, or worse."

"What's worse than frying them?" I asked slowly, so he had time to compose a believable answer.

"I don't know but with up to a 1000 watts flying around inside my speakers, shit could happen. I'm just warning you."

"What's a thousand or so watts between friends?" I patted him on the shoulder like a good soldier before the battle. "What could possibly go wrong that we can't handle?" I asked, keeping a straight face.

I had my own worries. For instance, how do I videotape an entire three-hour concert with only forty minutes of blank tape?

"Don't you just love Rock & Roll?" I didn't expect an answer.

On the anointed day, Thom, Steve, and I bundled up the speakers in Thom's truck while I loaded the Portapack into mine. At the club, Bob and the rest of his band were setting up on a small stage in the middle of the back wall.

The building had been some kind of garage or warehouse, but now it was just a big open area surrounded by old brick walls on three sides and windows making up the fourth facing the street. There were high-speed bars down both sides; there was no guessing where the owners expected to make their money. I counted about sixty tables, sitting four each, and a dance area big enough for fifty more couples. I figured a full house would be around three hundred and fifty or more, spending twenty or thirty bucks, add the cover charge, and it came to something like ten grand or more a night. Nice work if you could get it. I wonder what Bob's band was getting out of that, if anything.

Thom hooked the speakers to the Phase Linear amp and noted the output connectors on the back of the amp had fuses in line with the speakers, for some reason. Steve found a couple of tables to put them on so they would be about head high, pointing wickedly out toward the audience on both corners of the bandstand. Thom and Steve had stayed up last night to paint the cabinets flat black and cover the front speaker panel with a black open-cell polyethylene foam grille. Just looking at them made your ears grin and drool with the dark and ominous anticipation of pure Rock power about to gloriously infect your brain. I stood in front of the stage soaking in a view of the future.

No more ugly speaker stacks spraying noise in all directions. Blank black intimidating columns, in this case one pie section of a column, on each side of the stage looked clean, non-descript, and somewhat menacing. The sound, however, will be absolutely revolutionary, like Rock & Roll itself, pure and undiminished from finger to soul.

"Hey, Cowboy," Pete called from behind me. "What are you doing here?" I jerk out of my trance and turn to see the long-haired promoter walking toward me.

"What are you doing here?" I threw right back.

"I'm the club's exclusive talent agent." We did the usual revolutionary handshake. "You going to film this?" he asked, looking around at our equipment.

"Not really," I explain, "I can only afford to document it with my Portapack camcorder."

"Well, at least that's something," he said. "Can I get a copy?"

"If you can afford it," I said. "It runs about twenty dollars for a twenty-minute reel. I'll probably only shoot about an hour, since that's all the tape I have."

He gave me that crooked smile and wrinkled face indicating, *Are you sure? Are you fucking sure?*

"This high-tech crap ain't cheap. Which reminds me, how's your boys doing? You know, Teagarden and Van Winkle? Need any more promotional films?"

I had featured them in a short clip in the documentary film as a kickback for getting me the gig. But since then, he hadn't thrown a bone in my direction since the Allman Brothers concert—and he must know times are hard for an unemployed physicist.

"We've got an album coming out next month. Check it out. It's gonna be great."

Yeah, freaks have been waiting for an electric Wurlitzer slash drum combo who rocks them out like an old-fashioned old-maid tent revival. I wondered if Pete understood the concept of *lame*.

"Yeah, save me a copy," I said. "How's John doing?"

"Oh, you know. Prison sucks but he's having fun radicalizing political prisoners and other prisoners of conscience," he rambled, on brightening up a bit. "We're planning a big fund-raising concert to bring awareness to the injustice of our oppressive political system that make getting high illegal."

"Right on, brother!"

"Who the fuck is that?" Pete said.

He looked behind at whoever had crept up on us without warning. It was Larry Monroe, the late-night underground DJ I had rescued a couple years ago when he got snowed in for a long weekend at the rural studio/transmitter site. He set a local record by keeping the same radio show going for a continuous eighty-hour performance. It was pretty easy actually, considering the amount of cocaine and pizzas I was able to 4-wheel through the snowdrifts to his stranded studio.

"Oh, it's just Larry."

He stepped in front of me to get Pete's undivided attention.

"So who are you booking for the John Sinclair fund-raiser?" he inquired. "I hear it's going to be somebody big like Mick Jagger or Led Zeppelin."

Pete turned to walk away, but Larry stayed with him.

"I can't say anything right now; it's all up in the air and it's way too sensitive right now. But it will be the biggest thing that has ever hit Ann Arbor. I guarantee, it will blow…your mind."

I was beginning to think these two were a couple of long-haired hipsters who really didn't have any morals or righteous sense of justice for the people's revolutionary music. *Leaches on the ass of artists* might be a better description.

I turned back to the stage and found Bob Webb had been there for a while checking on his guitar amp. He saw me and plugged in his ax with a loud *buzzz honk* as it made contact with the high-gain amps inside. He looked at me, winked, and went into an incredible guitar lick that sounded more like Hendrix than a Midwestern boy from the snowy dark woods of Michigan. He went on for about another five minutes, running riff after riff of blues and Rock electric scales. Must be his sound check I thought. I looked back at the hipsters, now locked in tight conversation at one of the bars looking back at Bob with ugly faces; they gave up talking temporarily while Bob's guitar filled the room with piercing sixteenth and thirty-second notes ripping the air like machine-gun bullets.

Crap he was good. That boy could play a guitar. I bet he's going to go far.

He stopped abruptly, unplugged his ax with another *phhtzz* and motioned me over slyly while ignoring the ugly stares from his new promoter.

"Hey, man, I hear you're doing a video recording tonight. That's cool man, for sure."

"Yep, and we got you the very first pair of Time Window speakers ever produced," I said pointing to the nearest weird-shaped speaker cabinet sitting awkwardly on top of a table. "With your 400-watt Phase Linear amp, we should be in for a great sound treat tonight."

"Yeah man. Thom gave us a sample before you got here. The band never sounded so great. All the guys were blown away. Man, I hope we can make some money with this new band and we can eventually afford to buy your speakers. I'm really stoked about tonight. It's going to be a rocker. Thanks for all your help man, we really appreciate it."

"No problem, brother. You're fucking good and I just hope you'll remember me when you're rich and famous."

"Yeah man, the coke will be on me for once."

People were beginning to show up. Bartenders appeared and the door was blocked temporarily while they set up security to start charging a cover and checking for illegal drugs. Bob motioned for me to follow him. He led me to a back room set up as a liquor storage closet and the smallest green room ever. I guess the management figured Rock talent would be into more artistically stimulating drugs, so the liquor was sort of safe. I wondered what would happen if they had a big city blues band play here.

Walt, his long-time bass player was crammed in there with the other two new members: Gene the keyboard guy, and Ned the drummer. I pulled out the gram and a half I had been saving for later in case I found a young lady who would dance with the likes of me; instead, I poured it all out on the dirty little mirror setting on the nearest stack of whiskey cases. The lines ended up a little thin but like the fishes, it fed the multitudes. I lit up a fat doobie and started it around the group. I could tell they were really nervous and stressed over this first concert. They had a lot of themselves on the line, ready to be exposed for what they really have. *Do we have it?* hung in the air like a sour fog. When I left, however, they were all smiling.

I went back out front where I found Thom and Steve hovering over the borrowed mix board from Fanfare. The huge mix board was almost as wide as the tiny bar stage. The house lights were down and the stage was bathed in orange and blue light. Marty was not far away keeping a close eye on his equipment.

Larry Monroe was on stage giving the standard messages: no drugs and no drunks, which got loud catcalls, indicating nobody was intending to comply, Finally, he started the band introduction. I stood next to Marty so I could enjoy the same view. When Larry mentioned drugs, Marty took out his coke bottle and immediately spoon snorted Thom, Steve, me, and himself. God rewards a generous man.

The crowd went wild when each band member was named and he appeared on stage. Clearly the crowd was full of locals who knew these guys personally. They squinted at the intense close lighting, which just added to the impression these boys were marching to a different drum. Finally, Ned came onstage wearing dark shades and stumbling over equipment as he found his seat behind the huge drum set, He immediately began banging his sticks together.

Ding...ding...ding...ding ding ding dading ding ding...dading... dading...ding ding...dading...dading...ding ding...dading...

And then Walt jumped on one leg while he swung down on his ax and a deep resonant bass note came crashing out the Time Windows like twin turbines pushing tornadoes—as if sound were flying rocks from exploding dynamite.

Voo...voom...voom...va...voom....

Geez...I could feel it....

Thom looks up smiling. He's pushing it and it sounds crisp and clean like your head was inside the little holes in the guitar. "Great sound!" I mouthed so he could understand over all the loud music.

Now Walt starts twanging the bass notes in a very familiar way...the audience goes nuts with recognition.

Tawangwang...twang...tawang...twang twang....

Then the whole band jumped in with the funkiest sound I ever heard, so clear that I felt I was wearing headphones inside the bass drum this time:

When I get off of this mountain, you know where I'm gonna go. Way down the Mississippi baby to the Gulf of Mexico.

The crowd began stomping in sync with Ned which just reinforced the feeling of unleashed power on the upbeat. *Gutsy!*

If I spring a leak she mends me, I don't have to speak she defends me. A drunkard's dream if I ever did see one!

I spotted Pete at a corner table surrounded by fancy people. He flashed me the thumbs up signal like I deserved his recognition. I love head trips when I'm not even in the game.

Bum da da bum da da bum...

It was getting into my head so exquisitely. I heard sounds never heard before.

The crowd went wild after the first number. I fought my way

to one of the bars for a beer. No matter where I went in the room, the sound was clean and clear. I'd never heard anything like it.

"Two beers on the band account," I shouted.

Bartenders were deaf and could only read lips. *Good, I have excellent projection.*

The band slowed down with its second song. Thom was getting intense as he concentrated on the big bad board.

Well I came upon a child of God, he was walking along the road....

I loved the way Bob would add a little vibrato to his sustained notes by wiggling his guitar neck up and down rapidly. It put a visual emphasis on the music like an exclamation point. I broke trail to the sound booth, holding the beers high so everyone around knew I was on a mission from God. Bob and Walt were playing guitar warfare on stage, dancing, swaying, rocking, and bopping to every note and every nuance:

...going to join in a Rock & Roll band!

The colored lights were getting psycho right about now along with the entire room.

I handed Thom one of the beers. His flashed a smile wider than his face allowed.

We are stardust, we are golden, we are billion-year-old carbon....

He damned near drank the whole thing in one gulp, but he never let go of Bob's vocal pot. He went back to letting his fingers dance over the mix board as every note of music coursed through his head and then to his hands. He was separating sounds and assigning them to either left or right, creating a two-dimensional sound image people were hearing as well as seeing.

And I don't know who I am but life is for learning....

Bob was kicking ass, throwing in tiny little jewels of guitar licks that were masterfully mind-blowing. Timing was perfect, even slightly off just to add some funk.

Tum dittle de dum de de dit...

Each was greeted with wild screams, hoots, and whistles.

We were half a million strong....

The crowd went wild.

And we got to get ourselves back to the ga-a-ar...den....

The sound was perfect, the band impeccable. I was swept away. So was everybody else. The colors were getting intense and I was feeling giddily mellow. Really mellow. The drug mixture seemed to be just right between muscular dystrophy and the second coming of Christ. It was time to start videotaping.

I had earlier gaffer-taped my tripod to the floor right in front of the stage. I pulled out the camera and recorder from under the mix table where they had been plugged in for charging. I wanted the batteries topped off just in case I get caught up in the moment and need extended record time.

I fought my way across the dance floor, which was now so crowded that nobody could dance more than a massively synced group jumping in place. I took advantage of a pause in the music to barrel my way through the sweat and skin to the stage lip, where I quickly mounted the camera to the tripod and set the recorder down next to it. I started the recorder and put in pause mode.

From just three feet away and using the modest 4:1 zoom lens, I could make Bob's guitar neck and fingers fill the frame. Fingers flew, camera moved, like a second look, in sync, music boomed and image rang. Ned's dark glasses reflected bizarre images of the crowded and colorfully lit room, miniature receding, overlaid with droplets of sweat and in the background, wild eyes darting and hovering above it all.

I went nuts looking for these little intense pictures while the camera mounted microphone picked up the sound from the Time Windows as if it was a hard-wire patch from the PA, which it wasn't. *Amazing!* I thought, as I zoomed in on another little video weirdness tidbit and got lost recording some of the most amazing Rock videos ever made in a live concert. It was certainly one of the first. Too bad it was only black and white but I knew that even black and white could be more artistic and more impressive if done well. Editing was out of the question, so it was one continuous long shot following the music, the people, and the moment with a sense of being right there on stage with the band now suspended in time.

Then they started a medley of cocaine songs. First was Eric Clapton's "Cocaine," followed by "Casey Jones." The crowd went wild. I took a break while they did the Eagles' *Smuggler's Blues*. Surprisingly, Bill and a strange girl were standing right behind me. Bill made a motion to follow, so I triggered pause, set the camera down to let it cool off for a while, and followed them to the side bar and the other door backstage. I noticed Steve and Thom were now at the board seriously trying to concentrate while flying at ten thousand feet. They both looked stern and very professional in a sea of madness and chaos.

The green room where the band hung between sets was also off the hallway we were now in and the door behind the stage where the band could still be heard singing about *Coming into Los Angeleez, bringin' in a coupla keys!* Bill and the girl slipped into the empty room and I followed.

The girl was hot as hell, as any girl in Bill's company would be. Her tight blue jeans advertised a solid *Ten* without even considering the ample curves only slightly hidden above the exposed belly button. She was tall and thin, but full, like a weight-lifting bulimic model, but much softer. Her long, curly auburn hair made my eyes wander down to her waist again where I had started. My eyes were guiltily gulping in pure female beauty.

Bill had his little brown bottle out immediately, talking as he scooped out a heaping coke spoon full of white snow and administered it to her cute little dainty turned-up nose.

"This is Elaine," he said. She sniffed daintily. "She's a good friend of mine." She sniffed again. "I've known her a long time." She turned and smiled at me. "She's cool."

He took a hit on the bottle.

Being cool for Bill meant I could talk about drugs and other illegal activities with Bill when she was present. He didn't trust just anybody so I knew it was as good as religion. Something was telling me that worshiping was something a lot of guys probably did around her. For a moment I considered what being naked with her might be like, then immediately lost it thinking about how much coke that might cost. That's what they mean by *out of my league.*

"She saw you at the Blues Festival and thought what you did was really cool."

"Really?" She was still smiling at me and looking me in the eye. That doesn't happen very often. Usually, they're looking around for an escape route. I tried not to be too obvious and yet she seemed to ignore my poorly hidden crass desires.

"Elaine helped Webb's band get started," Bill went on, oblivious to my predatory stares. He gestured toward the stage door and the uncannily clear, but muted Rock sound coming from beyond. "Funny you haven't met before."

"I've heard about you," she added, still smiling demurely. "We obviously move in the same crowd, but just never had the chance to meet, I guess."

The sound stopped and was replaced with roaring applause as the stage door opened and the band came in dripping wet with sweat. Bob's tank top T-shirt was now totally see-through, while the rest of the band had shed their shirts on stage and were now carrying them backstage like sopping, used towels from workers coming out of a mine shaft after a long, hot, sweaty shift underground. Bill broke from me and Elaine to help the boys regain some energy. I noticed that Walt seemed to be fixated on Elaine without a hint of respect or desire. Something was afoot. I lit a joint and handed it to her as Bill hunkered down with Bob and the band.

"So, what are you going to do with the film you're shooting tonight?"

She tried to hand the joint on to one of the band members, only to be ignored by Walt, until Bob noticed and grabbed it instead. Bill didn't notice as he was busy snorting up Ned the drummer.

"Oh, it's not film," I said pulling out another joint and slowly leading her aside to the beer tub so she wouldn't have anyone to share it with anyone this time.

"It's video tape. This is the next revolution in film-making."

"You mean television?" she asked. "How is television going to make films better? I thought there was some kind of competition going on between them."

She paused to take a big hit on the joint while I popped a Coors for her.

"Private stash," I muttered as I handed the Coors to her and took the joint back.

"It's kind of both," I tried to explain. "Film and television are both locked up in studios with giant cameras, artificial lights, constructed realities, and lots of effort to produce simple results." I took a hit for dramatic interlude. "Film cameras are now hand-held with live sound so they can film in the real world. This Portapack camera is the same revolutionizing idea, except for television. Eventually, somehow, they will merge as one production medium, but in the meantime, I want to take film production and video production to the people using any new technology that's available."

"And you're making a living doing this?" she innocently asked, not really expecting an answer.

She took a long drag on the joint while I tried to do a little mental backpedaling.

"Not yet."

I took the joint from her pearly white fingers topped with deep red polish, almost blood red. "But I have some things coming up that might be the kicker."

About then, the stage door opened with a bang on a loud crowd and the PA playing New Riders of the Purple Sage with perfect studio quality in spite of all the background bar noise. In stepped Peter, followed like a puppy by Larry; following them was, strangely, Bill's live-in Nordic-blonde, model-skinny girlfriend, Patti. We rarely saw them out together, as Bill was usually seen doing business at night and he preferred to keep his home life separate. She was a pre-med student at the university and spent most of her time studying anyway while Bill made his late-night rounds.

My immediate thought was *What the hell was she doing hanging with that crowd?* Then Bambi stepped in, closing the stage door behind her. *Bambi and Patti must be friends,* I thought. *Also weird, but then who am I to spread that rumor?*

"How do you know Bill?" Elaine asked pointedly, prying my attention from all the activity now going on in the green room. She seemed to have little interest in the band. I wondered if her interest was Bill.

The band members were drifting around the room pursuing their preference for rejuvenation and inspiration. Bob seemed really happy about something, but Walt seemed to be pissed. Musicians are always criticizing their work way too deeply. I wanted to go over and tell him it's only Rock & Roll for god's sake. Bill snagged onto his fiancé and now was ensnarled with Pete and Larry talking about *who the fuck cared?*

"I could ask you the same thing," I offered. "I hang with a lot of Bill's friends, but never saw you." I looked back at her only to be met by two stunningly beautiful blue eyes drilling into my drug-addled soul. I wilted on the spot.

"Oh," she said slowly, while looking away toward nothing in particular, "I've been busy with my job and dealing with my former boyfriend." She sounded a little pissed, accentuating the *former* part which I thought was cute as hell.

"A real bastard, heh?" I mimicked a bad Canadian accent.

She looked good enough to have dated some glam rocker or lawyer, or some other rich bastard. Not much chance for me, but a guy can dream.

Bill and Bob Webb were now making their way in our direction. Patti was following Bill and Bambi was hanging onto Larry, who was hangin' on Pete and the rest of the band. And there was Walt, glaring in our direction again, pinching his nose in the après coke maneuver. Any leftover crystals were ground into the nasal membranes and delivered most likely directly to the olfactory brain. He might be smelling trouble two to three feet away.

"Aren't they all?" She let go my arm to embrace Bob. "You guys are sounding great tonight!"

"Aw gee Ma, I hope we made ya proud," he said with a twinkle wink and a sly grin underneath his signature handlebar. He looked at me and gave me a fist bump. He looked at Elaine and offered her one, which she daintily complied. Apparently, something was funny as he kept up his shit-eating grin for some time.

"I got some great shots until I ran out of tape," I said. "How's the PA sound?"

"Fantastic, man!" Bob said loudly. He leaned in to continue more softly, "I have never heard us play so well. It's either the drugs or your PA. What do you think?" He handed me a joint he had been Bogart-ing for some time. He put his arm around my shoulder and sort of turned me away from the rest of the crowd. I took a hit.

"I think you guys are just good enough to make the big time," I spoke into his ear and handed it back.

"You know of course, that Elaine was Walt's ol' lady since high school." He took a big sucking hit.

"Really?" I mimicked being stupid. I had figured there was something going on, just not this specific.

"He's been taking it pretty hard."

He handed back a dark gnarly nub. I took it carefully, trying to pinch it at a very minimal contact area.

"I'm sorry, I'll stop talking to her."

I tried to take a hit but there wasn't anything left. I tossed it.

"No. No. He's been writing lovesick songs and I like them. You're the stimulus he needs to create, so keep it up. If they want to get back together, they will. It has nothing to do with you."

He poked me in the chest as he walked away and I started getting that nauseated feeling that I was on a tight rope and could fall into a cesspool at any minute. A romantic cesspool, but still a shit pond. I needed to get my lust under control and find a nice quiet farm girl who knows how to slop the hogs.

"Did you know that Elaine lives out in the country in an old farm house?" Bill said as I turned back to the group. Elaine was smiling at me, standing next to Bill and Patti. Patti looked confused, or maybe high. Bill had on his signature number-9 welding glasses in a gold Ray-Ban frame sitting high above his permanent all-knowing smirk. Elaine was making little snorting sounds as she squeezed her nose in order to suck up or grind in any stray crystals.

"No, I did not," I answered.

She beamed at me. *That was it!* It dawned on me like a broken roller-blind, jerking violently out of my hand and spinning up tightly out of reach. This was a setup. Bill and Bob were helping the band at the same time as they helped a horny friend get laid and art be created. Sounds like a win-win situation, except for the poor fool who is found a week later with several bullet holes in his groin region. My hands began to sweat.

"Did you know she drives a 4-wheel truck just like yours?" This time I noticed she was wearing a Levi's jacket just like mine— and Bill's and Patti's and Amy's and Thom's and Margie's and just about anybody I knew who was close friends with Bill. Of course, I wore one ever since the farm where I grew up, but these city dudes were all following Bill's lead and adopting the Marlboro man look, or was it a country version of Shaft, as a sexy and desirable image? Just imagine, however, a fancy cowboy holding a joint instead of a cigarette. Maybe a shit-eating grin on his face too. Maybe the cows would look real content in the background.

"Again, I did not," looking at her with suppressed pride and lust. She had a very nice body, outlined in denim from head to toe except for the bare tummy that drove me crazy. No, her toes were covered by cowboy boots tucked under her pants the proper way. Good girl. I bet she liked horses.

"She likes dogs," Bill went on, as if owning the right truck and dog combination was the fashion statement of the new Ann

Arbor. "Their names are Snack and Doodle." *About as original as his Puppity.*

The band started to get their things together to begin the second set. Walt was guzzling down a beer as fast as he could before heading back out. Bob was getting a last snort from Pete over in the corner by the door with Larry and Bambi. I turned to Elaine and asked her what kind of dogs she had. I was imagining something cute like a poodle.

"Doberman Pinchers," she said with a sly smile. Of course, a beautiful girl like her, living out in the country, all alone and driving a big 4-wheel drive truck would need some doggy protection. A primal shiver began to twitch its way down from my now prickling neck to my yellow spine and ultimately to my weak knees. It hammered even on the door of lust, but so far, lust was still winning.

"Dobermans, you say," I said as cool as I could muster.

"Oh they're cute as two kittens on a pillow," she said still smiling like she knew something. "They wouldn't hurt a flea if I didn't tell them to."

Bill jumped in. "They have had professional guard dog training. I set it up myself with the kennel that provides all the dogs to the Detroit K9 squad. You'd be surprised how much drugs it takes to train a dog." He laughed as if killer dogs on drugs was a pratfall waiting to happen.

Elaine wrapped her hands around one of my arms and looked at me with those deep blue twinkles and smiled a wiltingly sexy smile.

"You want to come back to my house tonight after the concert and see my horse in the morning?" she asked, softly.

When I heard that, what could I say? I felt a warm tingling sensation course rapidly across my body. I was pretty sure what I was supposed to do, though. I bent down and kissed her ever so softly, with just a little twitch of a tongue. She made a little tiny squeak like a mouse and flicked her tongue ever so lightly across my lips in return. It was a spiritual connection. We had something else in common—tongues.

The concert finished up around 2 a.m. Bill and Patty escorted me to Elaine's rented farmhouse about six miles southeast of town. She had left right after the second set got started with just the cryptic comment that Bill was going to stop by later and I could follow him. I wanted to shoot up the last few minutes of tape and listen some more to those amazing speakers, so I shrugged her off. Bill was hovering around me and Thom, who never left the mix board all night long, and who he thought was in the greatest need of creative stimulation.

Steve was able to coordinate a couple of hits as well. One of the Phase Linear amps owned by the band fried about halfway through the second act. Direct-coupled amps are inherently unstable, unlike the Mauer amp, which could actually handle an overload without frying the output transistors. That was what those fuses were all about, trying to protect weak transistors from speakers that suck Rock power from them. Marty happened to have a spare DC300 in his truck, so the concert kept going.

The band was really fantastic. They could do just about any song from Buffalo Springfield, Doobie Brothers, Credence Clearwater, Neil Young, or the Grateful Dead. Plus they sprang a couple of new songs on us that were original and just gnarly enough to be popular. Larry the announcer disappeared as well after the first set, along with Bambi. Pete hung with some Detroit people at a corner table and seemed to be enjoying the music, but no producer showed up in the dressing room after the concert. Bob was happy with the performance and the fact that the hall had been standing-room-only with threats from the fire marshal to shut it down if they didn't get some people out of the building. It didn't work until the band stopped playing and a lot of overheated sweaty drunk students fell out onto the street.

I was feeling no pain and floated about two to three feet above what the hell I happened to be riding on as we drove out of downtown along Packard Avenue. My truck, like a good horse, seemed to autonomously follow its big brother, the larger K20 yellow truck that Bill drove. I didn't even pay that much attention to what was passing by outside or bother to memorize the route. I had a great night, great music, great taping and now I was going to get laid by a playboy centerfold. Life couldn't be much better, except maybe for the lack of cash.

When we arrived, the lights were on in the house along with a bright yard light that revealed outbuildings and barns on the other side of the parking area. Dogs, probably Puppity and one of her recent offspring, were barking in Bill's truck as he and Patti led me across the small lawn to what appeared to be the back door to the kitchen. All Midwest farmhouses seemed to have been built backward; the parking area always led to the back door instead of the front door, which was seldom if ever used. That, of course, wasn't the only thing they did backward.

There was an equal amount of barking coming from inside. Bill knocked and we heard a voice, "Just a minute. I have to lock the dogs up."

Bill turned around and looked at me with obvious pride. Another dog lover like him. *Wonder what else they had in common?* Apparently, they thought I had some love of horses, and that gave me a chance to belong. I didn't have the heart to tell my friends that though I dressed like a cowboy and called myself a cowboy, it turned out I had learned the rear ends of cows without the need of a horse. I milked cows when I lived on my parents' little farm in Oregon. If my Michigan friends thought I rode horses across the barren, windswept landscape to go to high school, who was I to correct them? Myths are fun and neat as long as they don't get out of hand. I was beginning to feel my hands get clammy.

Elaine opened the door, letting us into her well-lit, mostly pale-colored kitchen dominated by a big white antique oval dining table smack in the middle and an old wood-fired cookstove at one end of the room. Life here obviously revolved around the table so we each took a chair. The barking from the inside dogs was coming from somewhere upstairs like the rattle of machine gun bullets, constant and loud.

Elaine just smiled and reached out to kiss me as I found a chair. She stood next to me and Bill did all the talking while Patti looked on somewhat bored. Bill was bragging about the band and how everybody really liked them tonight and they would probably be signing a big contract soon to record their first album. Elaine produced a scratched-up mirror, apparently on a subtle Bill command that I missed.

He began laying out four lines and chopping furiously to get a better breakup of the crystals as he explained, "...lots of little needles that can jab their way through nasal membranes and slide directly into brain tissue." He was an adept student of the *High* and how to get there. He went on to brag that Pete had actually been partying tonight with a former Bob Seger producer slumming it in Ann Arbor.

Elaine sat on my lap as the mirror made its way around the table. I wondered why I didn't automatically just wear sunglasses all the time like Bill. Then when someone turns the light up, I can just relax behind a dark curtain that isolates and secures my eyes from jarring reality or mobs of photons. I took my snort after her.

She held the mirror so I could hold my nose and not bend over. *How thoughtful.* I wondered what else she could hold next to my nose, when I found out. As she handed the mirror to Patti on the other side of the table, her perky little tits brushed ever so lightly across my face. Was that deliberate? As she sat back down, it happened again. *That answers that.*

So, I began a little exploring of my own while Bill and Patty carried on a rather banal conversation with Elaine. I was still feeling very light, so light I could touch her body just enough to register, but not enough to actually feel skin. Considering the amount of drugs we had all done that night, it seemed like we were on a totally different plane of existence, where feeling good was not only okay but in fact encouraged.

I put my arm around her waist, holding the flat of my hand across her firm flat belly. Bill smiled, so I knew where his eyes were focused for a second behind his shades. Elaine hadn't apparently noticed yet or didn't want to. My next venture wrapped a hand around her equally firm thigh, Marveling for a moment, then slowly reaching around the other direction until it encountered a wonderful piece of flesh hanging out behind her other thigh. A chill shot through me almost slapping my dick up against the wall.

Adrenaline is a funny thing. That flight or fight conflict in the case of a beautiful woman becomes flight or fuck. Her hands started exploring me and I started my expedition up the Ubangem river with gun and camera. The conversation slowed to nothing. Bill and Patty excused themselves and let themselves out.

All the barking started slowing to intermittent half-hearted woofs. Elaine was delivering tongue like a dog eating peanut butter as she slowly straddled me on the chair and began rubbing her crotch up against my upper groin area. I was pretty sure what this meant.

I deftly pulled my famous *one-hand-behind-her-back-flip-the-bra-hook* trick. She complied and I feasted for a moment on the two most perfectly shaped tits ever produced for man's visual pleasure. I literally shook a little from the electric shock tingling my backbone and random muscles. She stood up proudly, like her tits, and pulled me behind her as she made her way across the kitchen.

She went down a short hallway and paused at the door to what turned out to be her bedroom, turning off the bright lights overhead and leaving a couple of glowing night-lights near the other door and the stairs. She led me into the room, pulling me into her body as we deeply kissed again. And again. And again. Finally, she pushed me onto the bed and bent down to kiss me one more time.

"I'm going upstairs to the bathroom to freshen up a little. If the dogs get out, don't worry, they're curious but they won't bite."

She pushed me on the nose, forcing me to lie back, whereupon she deliberately brushed up against my now pretty firm cock as she stood up and spoke directly to it: *See you soon.* She said it with a sexy tone that meant more than just *lay here and wait.*

She disappeared and I stripped. I took off my boots, Levi's, shirt and T-shirt. I didn't wear underwear because I figured underwear was a necessity only before showers. After showers, they really became symbols of prudish Puritanism, like the Mormons figured out a long time ago. Optional, in my case.

In any case, I was butt naked under a sheet when two very large and very loud barking Doberman Pincers burst into the bedroom, sliding sideways as they took the sharp turn from the stairway. I was already getting high on the adrenaline associated with exciting sexual expectations but now the pituitary gland went and exploded through the cranial nodule, blowing a wad of adrenaline into the blood that locked my body into a spastic matrix of twisted up muscles straining to get the fuck out of there.

In short, that's exactly what I did. When the two dogs jumped onto the other side of the bed, I threw the sheet over them, momentarily distracting them so I could grab my clothes and make a mad naked dash to my truck parked under that damned bright vapor light in the backyard. I suddenly didn't give a shit about the possibly greatest sex I might ever have; when it became clear to me that I was trespassing on a bro's territory and I needed to find a girl who defended herself the old-fashioned way—with a .44 tucked in her pantyhose that can be removed quietly when no longer required. I like dogs, but the thought of two of the scariest pointy-eared toothy killers watching us do it all night was just too much. I need privacy for some things, like sex and self-abuse.

IT'S NOT ALL SMOKE AND MIRRORS

"Bases are loaded and Nixon's at bat, playin' it play-by-play.
Time to change the batter...."

Joe Walsh
"Rocky Mountain Way"
1973

I had never been accused of taking the walk of shame before. Steve clued me in though as soon as I showed up back at the house way before dawn. The shame was not in being a dog but ending it unceremoniously way too soon.

"What happened?" he asked as I casually walked into the living room and through to the kitchen looking for a stray beer. "Did you run out of drugs or something?" he continued. He got up from the couch and followed me into the kitchen.

I understood the reference. They had all seen us leave together at the concert and certainly something had gone wrong. Nobody sniffs around a bird like what I did and then hardly spend enough time to get their clothes off. I didn't think it was anybody's business, but then entertainment is entertainment and I couldn't duck the momentary spotlight.

"She had dogs," I said, as I popped a Bush. He looked momentarily astonished.

Steve knew about Bill's dogs and their penchant for blood. He probably suspected, as I did, that there was more than just a love of animals between Bill and Elaine. Killer dogs don't fall too far from the paranoid tree.

"Besides," I went on, "she just broke up with Walt." I took another big slug of water-flavored alcohol. "You know'm. He's Webb's bass player. I don't need the testosterone drama or the midnight tire-slashing."

"What?" he countered, "You're going to respect some kind of male-female property thing?" He had me there.

"Listen, a girl that beautiful is nothing but trouble." I walked back into the living room and slouched into the couch. "I know this for a fact. My main squeeze from senior year college was way beyond my level and I was warned so by my philosophy professor. He probably learned it from experience, as his first wife was a looker too. That was Susie, as you already know. Burned twice, learn once."

"Since when did that keep you from planking any beautiful woman who asked for it, regardless of her romantic commitment status?" Steve was smiling now like he knew something for certain he didn't know a moment before.

"I had a moral epiphany."

He just stared for a few seconds and *harrumphed* himself up the stairs to bed. I had another Bush.

Bill called the next day to ask if something went wrong. I noted that he failed to mention Walt having a long-term relationship with the two Dobermans.

"That's history," Bill stated flatly. "She likes you and wanted to see what you're all about. I don't think it's about break-up punishment sex. But even if it was, you can't say no. It's a spiritual thing."

"I don't know," I continued. "Normally, I wouldn't say no. *Insult to nature* and all that stuff. I like Bob and I don't want to cause him or his band any trouble. My smuggling partner stole Katy," I paused, spitting to the side, "the bastard. Then I lost Susie to a total stranger." I spit again. "None of that's a valid reason for me to stick it to another chump. Rock & Roll brotherhood has to be thicker than sex or something." I lifted my fist in revolutionary salute. "All power to the amplifier! No power to the people at all!"

"Yeah, like now you suddenly get sex morals. Next thing you know, you'll be marrying the first girl who claims she's knocked up. You're a sucker for a damsel in distress."

"So where did she get the Dobermans?" I asked, changing the subject.

"Oh, they're from one of Puppity's litters a few years back when one of my friends had a male attack Doberman." *I knew it!*

"Did you meet them? They're really scary the first time they meet you. But they'll pick up on Elaine's emotions and act like little pussycats when you're making her happy."

I wondered how he knew that.

"That isn't why you ran away last night, is it?"

He just gave me that crooked smile of his like he already knew the answer.

"You heard my story and I'm sticking to it," I said flatly and tried to drop it.

The thought of two Dobermans drooling on my naked body while concentrating on appreciating pure aesthetic beauty made my skin wrinkle. I knew the dogs only scared me momentarily. Sober reflection of being Elaine's boy-toy, though under the watchful eyes of two vicious killer-trained dogs that could turn on you in a Elaine-heartbeat just didn't seem like a wise move for polishing off a great night of Rock & Roll, drugs, and hot jealous sweat-and-doggy drool-drenched sex. How depressing to realize my wild youth might actually be coming to an end. *Is this what happens when infected by the adult virus?*

But then, in the great scheme of things, all the little dramas that haunt our conscience usually shrink to insignificance when smacked by the giant fickle finger of fate. It wasn't two weeks after the concert that we woke up to an urgent phone call from Bob's girlfriend, Lacey.

The night before, Bob and the band were on their way to a gig at the airport Hilton in a nine-passenger station wagon. Their car was hit head-on by a drunk driver doing eighty on the wrong side of I-94. Two were dead at the scene. Bob was in intensive care at the Wayne County Medical Center with a mangled left hand, punctured lung, and severe concussion. Lacey was frightened he might not make it. We asked what we could do.

"I don't know," was all she said, and then hung up crying bitterly. I froze in disbelief. I had just been partying with these guys. *Fuck! Shit! Whore! Crap!*

Everyone's mood nose-dived to stunned but deliberate action. I called Thom and told him to come over. Bill called and we told him everyone was coming here to wait for the latest word from Lacey. Steve ran out to resupply our liquor, beer, and other emergency necessaries. Bill would bring plenty of snow, so I had to dig up the very last of my stash from Mexico, which I had been hoarding for some two years because of its unmatched quality. *Oh well, all in for the cause.* I did save a couple of pre-rolled joints for a special day or night, whichever came first.

The Wake slowly formed and progressed for the next twenty-four hours or so. I don't remember a lot of it, except for the eating of the worm. Apparently, it is a custom in Mexico, mostly I am told around Oaxaca in the south, where the friends of the recently deceased share a bottle of Mezcal, each in turn, until some lucky mourner gets to swallow the worm that has been lying pickled at the bottom of the bottle just waiting for such an occasion. The legend has something to do with letting the spirit of the worm and the friend be joined in paradise, where he can sample all the Tequila he wants, courtesy of the worm. They fail to explain what happens to the poor bastard who gets to actually eat the worm, but then that's the mystery of the worm.

At some point in the proceedings, I ate the worm. I thought for a moment it was going to provide enlightenment, perhaps of the kind Carlos Castaneda found in the sacred cactus and mushrooms found in the deserts of Sonora. There were only five or six people setting in the circle, each cross-legged with adjacent knees touching. The bottle was passed from right to left, signifying the direction one needs to go to find the river Styx. Each person would take a big swig from the bottle. Then as he or she swallowed, the bottle was held high, proudly displaying whether the worm was still in the bottle or not. Surprisingly it always seemed to still be there, swirling around, showing little or no concern to its imminent fate.

The tequila was getting dangerously low in the bottle, yet still the worm hung out laughing at us from his secure sanctuary. I started counting swigs and estimating from the level of tequila that it was going to run out about the time it passed me again for the fifth or sixth time, I forget which. Steve took a hit, held it high to show a partially submerged worm still clinging to the last remnants of its former liquid world. He swore something and handed it to me.

This is going to be easy, I thought. This worm has stubbornly held itself inside the bottle right down to the bottom. Clearly, I was going to be the direct benefit of surface tension, that wondrous electric force of liquid surfaces for holding onto stuff a little stronger than if fully immersed. I threw the bottle back with a swirling motion that accelerated the flushing action for the last of the tequila and hopefully stick the worm to the side. With a flourish like a toreador making a pass at the bull, I swallowed the last of the tequila and held the bottle aloft, showing the worm was clearly still inside. I smiled with confident victory and then noticed the bottle was empty. The worm was missing.

I dropped the bottle with an uncharacteristic scream suddenly realizing that there was more than just harmless tequila in that slug I just swallowed. *Holy Shit!* I've been violated by a pickled Mexican grub, and there was no going back. My worm virginity was gone and I'll never be the same again. I had to find other drugs to help me forget this first round of drugs. I might have found some acid.

Apparently, I did because I don't remember very much of that wake, or for that matter, the one I orchestrated in college when a fellow physics major hanged himself with an institutional plain white towel in the dorm room next to mine. The ensuing Wake occurred spontaneously when they found him three days later on a Monday morning, whereupon I donated a jug of wine, our local young philosophy professor, and the theater green room for which I had a key, so those in need of DIY counseling had a place to go.

One of the drama department bitches ratted us out to the dean of students when she saw a dozen or so people sitting in a circle passing a jug of wine talking about life and death in a campus building where such things were strictly prohibited. The dean called me to ask what the hell was I doing when he was trying to deal with grieving parents and the press. I assured him it was absolutely normal and proper and the wine was just about gone anyway. He could join us later if he brought more. He seemed satisfied that morals and laws were not being violated; no one else was going to die on his watch, and the press would never find us. We started locking doors after that, even if it was a totally innocent use of the facilities. Bad people see only what they expect, so why help them?

My head was swimming like a whirlpool in quiet waters, dizzy but still able to follow the action. More people came and went all day long. At one point, as I was gratefully fading into thankful oblivion, Bill came over and brought his little bottle. As he gave me a picker upper, he tried to express himself about something men are supposed to just accept and not be bothered with—death and *why am I here?* questions.

"Do you think there is a spiritual world beyond this one that we see and experience in real time?" he asked, almost too casually.

I looked at him and sure enough, he was dead serious. I took both hits first before answering him.

"Why do you ask that?" I asked right back.

I knew he was a basic atheist like all of us, but we also felt there might be something else going on with reality that we didn't understand yet. Hence, that is why a lot of drug use was going on among the intellectuals—a search for just that possibility. For example, Dr. Castaneda and Dr. Leary seem to think there is some other reality we normally have no access to, except perhaps with drugs.

"It just seems that a lot of things don't seem to be as random as maybe we would expect if…there was nothing going on except for what we can see and hear firsthand."

"There you go again. Stare at a blank screen on a TV tuned to no station for too long and you'll start imagining a picture hiding just beyond the snow and you think you see glimpses of it as it pops in and out." I kept to my normal cynical self about such revelations. "God is nothing more than us trying to make sense out of noise."

"But what if you could slip in and out of time and space at will? Wouldn't that be great!" he remarked.

"I don't know," I said trying to bring the mood back down to Wake level. "From a physics standpoint, you would probably need the power to move stars and galaxies around before you could open up space and time on a scale large enough to squeeze your puny body through."

I lit up a joint and handed it to him.

He took a giant hit and through the curling cloud of smoke now drifting around his cocked head, with red blinking eyes he said, "But if it's just perception that makes reality exist at all for us, then altering that perception should be like experiencing a whole different world of some other reality."

"Ah, I see your fallacy," I gleefully countered, as he passed the now furiously burning joint back to me.

"Is the lunatic in the asylum actually in another valid reality instead of being just out of touch with this one? Drugs I'm afraid are not portals to new realities, just minor scrapes with our own self-made insanity. Which I guess is why the lunatics are still in their padded cells when they are convinced they are somewhere else. Reality is a harsh mistress if you don't keep your head together."

He thought about it for a minute.

"Do you ever think about how just the wrong turn on a whim or being just a few seconds late or early and *boom*, something out of the blue strikes you down blindly. Out of all the possibilities there are, you are suddenly chosen to die instead of live on as expected."

"Fate," I simply stated. "Have you ever heard of "Carmina Burana?"

"What?" he asked. "Is that a Rock band?"

"Not quite, but the Goliard Poets who wrote it in the twelfth century certainly could have qualified for Rock status. They were the beat generation of their times. They were vagabond intellectuals and flower children wandering around Europe, singing profane poems about sex, love, the pursuit thereof, and taking drugs, mostly beer, celebrating life's pleasures just before the plague shocked everybody back to a darker, more stern reality."

"Here's to the plague," yelled Thom. He had been overhearing our conversation and had to make a comment. We all took a dutiful shot of whatever liquor was handy. I continued my story with Bill.

"Life was good for a while and they spent the time to enjoy it. Carl Orff found their writings seven hundred years later, which had been carefully and secretly preserved by generations of Monks at the Benedictine Buran in Southern Germany. I visited there in 1966 while helping the Germans build up their nuclear capability, but that's another story."

"Shit. You mean they have the bomb?" he asked.

"Not just the Germans this time, but the Israelis, as well. Fuck, before you know it, every little third world dictator will have the power to self-immolate not only his country, but probably everybody else around them."

"Fuck. We better start partying while we can," Bill said, holding up the last of the joint we had been sharing.

"I'll drink to that!" Thom said from across the room.

"So it's a choral piece," I continued with Bill as he lit another joint, "where the opening and closing songs are the same, celebrating or actually berating the concept of human fate and how it messes with us for an entire lifetime of unpredictable vicissitude."

"Tell me about it," Bill agreed ruefully.

Bill certainly could appreciate the fates, as he dealt with them every day in his world. He and I both probably didn't feel as bad as everyone else at the Wake. There was crying going on, as well as drinking to senseless unfeeling. He and I shared a sort of acceptance of the real world of man as something we couldn't change—only try like hell to stay out of its way, which is hard to do when you're young, talented, and restless. Dreams don't always come true, and in fact, dreams can evaporate instantly at any given time or place. We both knew of this universe's colossal indifference to life, which steeled us to its worst expression. Two young people were dead, and all for what?

We ended the Wake by replaying the videos I had just shot the week before when the band was unknowingly at the height of its popularity. Almost everyone cried during this screening, but we stuck to it all the way to the end. Things broke up quickly after that, but we all knew we had changed irretrievably—from being innocent to feeling deep pain. Not a good way to grow, but maybe necessary.

In the weeks that followed the accident, we visited Bob several times in the hospital and later at home as he recuperated. He would be disabled for life now, never to play the guitar again with his mangled left hand. His dreams had died that night and now he was trying to come up with plan B. Because he was awarded a big insurance compensation, he moved to Florida and started a Corvette repair shop. Sounded more like Bill's retirement plan, but Bob certainly earned it, in a sick way. We all hoped he would prosper anyway and be happy again.

The second Friday after the accident, we held a benefit concert at the same dance club as their debut. Pete provided talent in the form of Commander Cody and the Lost Planet Airmen along with Teegarden and Van Winkle as the opening act. Larry Monroe MC'd the event and was prancing around the backstage area like he owned the place. Something about him was making me nauseous. I didn't see Bambi with him and wondered if they were still a couple.

I bought some tapes and again did the black and white video recording of the event for posterity. I packed it away with all my other tapes for future use if I could process the low-quality tape format to play on standard TVs. Color was coming and other tape formats were on the horizon. I even heard of electronic format converters. These tapes might be an important document of the music world in Ann Arbor in the seventies. I was the only one doing this stuff so it was, in a way, unique.

The benefit was way more somber than the original concert, though everybody was trying to be positive and upbeat. We simply did our jobs and went home. It was a bummer having to grow up with shit like this happening. It cast a permanent veil over all our Rock & Roll souls and probably would haunt us for the rest of our lives. We couldn't help but wonder, *Only what if?*

A couple of weeks later, the word finally came out that the rumored benefit concert for John Sinclair was finally going to happen. John Lennon and Yoko Ono will headline the event, joined by just about anybody owing any favors to Pete, John, or the Rainbow Peoples Party and able to pull in some ticket sales. Bob Seger was booked along with Stevie Wonder, The Up, and Phil Ochs among others, and last but not least, our old friends Commander Cody and Teegarden & Van Winkle.

Also billed on the event were a lot of our revolutionary leaders like Allen Ginsberg, Jerry Rubin, Rennie Davis, and Bobby Seale. It was going to be an all-day and all-night affair. My eyes were watering with the thought of videotaping the event while providing video projection like the Blues Festival and The Allman Brothers Concert. I called Pete to begin the planning and negotiations, but he didn't call back.

Bill called later that night and announced he was again asked to provide security backstage and inside the Crisler Arena. I told him I hadn't heard from Pete yet. He just laughed.

"Pete's into this one way over his head. He can barely make any decisions. Since booking John Lennon and Yoko, he has more of a tail by the horns dilemma. They've got him by the tail and he keeps blowing his horn to stay in the game. Quite frankly, Pete didn't hire me. Suzanne did."

Suzanne was Pete's old secretary when he was up and coming. But she shifted over to the University Events Coordinator and now called all the shots for anything using university facilities, which this one certainly did. She controlled the show now and Pete was just another booking agent. She still used Bill because he could keep the lid on a potentially explosive political event without resorting to cops.

Later I got the call from Pete informing me that he had to sign away all the rights to the concert images, like film and video, to some clown diddling Yoko on the side and promoting himself as a documentary filmmaker. As it was a benefit concert, no one was investing in the budget for the production; if there was to be a video projection, someone would have to cough up the dough.

"Could you do it for free," he asked, "like a contribution to the effort?"

"You know me. I don't have any money," I retorted. "I do this for the glory and the honor. You need to stick to your guns about who is for the cause and who is just taking advantage of the cause."

"Sorry," he said complacently. "It's way out of my hands anyway. I am not proud about what I had to do to get this goddamned concert put together in the first place. But it got done and its going to happen—unfortunately without video projection. I'll see you have a full backstage pass and you can help out with the sound and *wink, wink,* security."

"Fuck!" I said.

"Yeah, that's probably what happened," he added.

I asked about the film rumors and he confirmed that some New York filmmaker already had the rights to film the concert and had sold off each camera position to anyone owning an Eclair 16mm sync camera, the camera that had made Rock & Roll history at Woodstock.

My old film nemesis, Manupelli, who just happened to own such a machine, was going to be one of the pay-to-work cameramen. I groaned out loud. His dry, slow, boringly stiff camera movements would fit *really well* with a Rock & Roll radical anti-government protest rally. Somebody had fucked up royally and I couldn't do a damned thing about it. So much for youthful idealism in the face of raw capitalism. I guess he who has the gold has the right to fuck it up.

Things were getting slim on the money side. I had a small income from selling my rental house but it wasn't enough to actually live on. I had to supplement my income somehow and drugs weren't reliable for paying the rent. I was beginning to feel desperate and perhaps ready to lower my standards and go to work with Steve building speakers for a living.

So far, he and Thom had built about a dozen of the pie-shaped cabinets and were using most of them to do experiments in the anechoic chamber in the basement. Steve was trying to perfect the crossover circuit to minimize the amount of distortion added by the speakers interfering. He wasn't even sure how to go about testing for distortion in free air with some instrument he might be able to afford.

I stepped in with my two-dollar physics analysis and simply pointed out that if his speakers could successfully reproduce a square wave out in the free air when fed a square wave audio signal, then he could be assured of less than a few percent distortion by simple inspection of the oscilloscope trace. The best frequency for such a signal would be at least one or two octaves below the crossover frequency. When he had both the woofers and the tweeters timed properly, then the woofer would fill in the big bulk of the square wave, while the tweets would chime in precisely at the leading and trailing edges of the square wave, thus sharpening it up and making it have a clean undistorted shape. It would be close to time phase synced.

Next thing I hear, he dubbed his latest design attempt as the *Time Window* where he proudly displayed an oscilloscope trace of a before and after signal showing a clean square wave in the first picture, the input to the amp and a somewhat ragged square wave in the second picture, captured by a microphone in free air. No other speaker maker could do the same, so the sound you heard from a Time Window was unprecedented. We had struck on an apparent hole in the design and manufacture of speakers and the only other company out there that could come close was of course Professor Bose's design, based on similar physics, but slightly different reflex geometry.

I suspected the only microphone within a fifty-mile radius that could even detect such a wave so accurately had to be something German with the U of M School of Music label stamped on one side. Clearly, without Thom's access to professional grade audio equipment, Steve probably wouldn't have had the results that he needed. I helped out by telling them what to do in the first place. I thought that maybe the three of us could form a partnership or something and manufacture high-quality speakers for a discerning and critical audience.

Steve bitched a lot about not having any money either. He made sure the mortgage was paid on time each month; I had to cough up my share as well or friction developed quickly. It was well known he came from a somewhat wealthy family of trades folks in town, but I never saw them the whole time I was there. I don't think he was an outcast, but he spent very little time with family and kept them strictly separate from his bohemian life down near campus, considered the student slums by natives.

I could tell that deep down inside he longed for the convenient life of a conventional family. The clean air of freedom seemed to wear thin on him. He was looking for something and no one else could go along. He was probably getting the mating urge to leave all the good times behind, cut off his balls, hand them to some woman on a platter, and never see his buddies again. Some called this abnormal state of humans *married and settled down*. I called them *the walking dead* or *Zombies squares* for short.

Finally, the day of the big concert arrived. I wandered over to the arena in the afternoon after it was well underway with all the padded low-class warm-up acts. This was the first concert where I didn't have to do anything and yet my pass showed I was a *concert coordinator* with the highest access permissions. Naturally the first thing to do was find a Psychedelic Ranger with a walkie-talkie who would know where Bill was.

I tracked him down in short order, got the scoop on the latest buzz. We walked out onto the main floor together and he pointed out the various camera positions, including the one on the left side where Manupelli in all his Italian handsomeness was squinting through the lens finder on presumably his one Eclair camera. Several of his groupie students were processing film cans, exchanging magazines so the camera could keep running almost continuously. Of course, the camera, designed to be handheld, was locked down on a big tripod and hardly moved an inch one way or the other for the entire concert.

Jesus Christ, how unoriginal. With fixed cameras, they might as well have used big-assed color television cameras like they use at NFL games. At least then, someone could be cutting the shots in sync with the music and giving it a live, *being-there* feeling, sharing the event with both the live audience in a video projection, but recording it in real time for release or broadcast later.

Quality would have been better, but then the phony artist ego behind the whole crooked setup would not have had the pleasure of setting behind a 16mm editing table for the next six months trying to put the excitement back into the film after they had so carefully failed to record it in the first place. It was dark in the hall and we were mostly hidden from the rest of the audience by the folded-up bleachers along one wall. He snorted me up and we shared a doobie I had brought along to help me stomach the disaster.

While we were huddled up on the side of the arena floor getting high and sharing last-minute horror stories about all the fuckups going on backstage, his walkie-talkie kept up an incessant chatter I could hear even over the loud music. Finally, he gave up trying to handle it over the radio and excused himself.

I hung out for a little longer, not really paying attention to who was on stage, or why. I wandered around some more, visiting the boys from Fanfare on the mixing platform. The hall was so dark, even with bright stage lights spilling all over the place, that the light from the LEDs on the board was lighting all of us up on the platform like we were the center of attraction for a cockroach-sized concert.

Marty was hovering around whoever the current band had sent up to pose as a sound engineer. He sometimes got some real crazies on drugs who, never seeing a 28-channel board all lit up like a starship and giving users a fantasy look at controlling the universe, would start creeping up the volume channel by channel, dB by dB, until he or Curt would have to reach over, slap their hands out of the way, and pull back on the controls. Even Marty knew that just cause you can make it louder didn't mean you had to.

Marty, Curt, and I formed a tight circle while Marty snorted us all up as quickly and surreptitiously as one can in the middle of twenty-five thousand screaming freaks and hippies. Curt mentioned in my ear how every band not from Michigan was a big pain in the ass and how he was going to cut off the hands of the next pansy boy in bell bottoms who touched his board.

Marty's long black hair with matching black full beard made him look like an anarchist about to self-explode. His stern looks often prevented official on-lookers from entering his side of the platform; instead, he kept them herded into a group around the lighting board where there was a lot more glamour and action to see and experience. I was beginning to see how musicians preferred the lights to the video projection. Stupid hams, always wanting to hog the limelight.

The stage crew was pretty good at running the bands off and on stage in record time. Most had gotten their training at the Blues Festival. Of course, here they covered up the changeovers with speeches about injustice and harrowing examples of our government's oppression of the masses. The fucking war was still killing kids to the tune of several hundred a day, sometimes with no plausible end in sight with that fucking crazy criminal Nix-goon handling things.

He keeps it going with continuous lies, cover-ups, and pleas for blind patriotism that kill off the impoverished and uneducated, while letting the rich kids, like most of the students at the U of M, escape senseless sacrificial slaughter. Nix-goon righted a perceived wrong, though, by getting rid of student deferments, which of course made him even more popular amongst this crowd. *He needed to just say no!*

The anti-establishment speakers got louder and more adamant as the day and evening wore on. They seemed to be getting more applause and noise than the musicians. Soon the sweet smell of smoldering cannabis began filling the air. I looked around the upper levels of the arena and nary saw one cop uniform. There were plenty of red shirts, the uniform of the Psychedelic Rangers, now pretty much staffed and run by the Rainbow Peoples Party, except for Bill and some of his key people. They still handled the technical stuff like special power requirements for security systems, communications, and interfacing with police radio protocols.

It all seemed to be working, but some shithead will almost certainly complain about the smell of dope at a pro-dope concert and it will get back to the university administration and ultimately the police, and then god knows where else. We all knew it was a huge conspiracy to use pure food and drug laws to target political dissenters and left-wing agitators, those inconvenient people who always hamper a good totalitarian scheme.

Then I saw him. He didn't have on his customary white shirt, but his haircut gave him dead away. He didn't belong here and that was obvious. Not only that, but he seemed to be standing in an upper-level entrance to the arena with a group of similar short-haired men: all tall, all somewhat muscular and all looking nervous as hell. Flanking this group on either side was an equal number of red shirts just milling around and looking as out of place as the group of short-hairs. The guy I thought looked familiar held up a pair of binoculars, but anybody could have told him they were useless in the darkened hall, except for getting a better look at rockers screaming out songs of rage and rebellion. I love it. When I looked back later, the guy and his escorts were gone.

Then a red shirt walked up to me and handed me a walkie-talkie. I put it up to my ear while holding my other hand over my other ear and squeezed the transmit button.

"What's up?" I said. "Over?" I let go the transmit button. *Squack!*

"It's me, Bill," the crackling voice responded. "I need you backstage right away. Don't bring anybody with you. Over?"

Screech! I squeezed again.

"Yeah, like I have an entourage hangin' on my every move," I replied sarcastically. "Over the line?"

I let go. *Phtzzt!*

"Stranger things have happened. We're in the hallway on the north side of the locker rooms. Make it snappy and be packing. And overboard."

He signed off and I handed the radio back to the red shirt.

Packing. What the hell did he mean? I hope it wasn't for cocaine. I ran out hours ago and only had a couple of joints left I was saving to smoke later if I found someone cute to share them with. Otherwise, and in spite of the backstage hostess cart full of liquor and beers—which are officially sanctioned, government taxed, and approved drugs—for a pro-drug rally, I was fairly straight. Don't get me wrong, I was high all right, just not making a big deal out of it. I think they called it *mellow.*

I wandered as best I could to the side of the arena. The floor had become a free-for-all a long time ago, except at the line defining the stage area at the front manned by ferocious psychedelic cops dancing and having a great time guarding the stage. I showed one my badge and he just jerked his thumb in the direction of the rear entrance behind the left rear of the stage. I knew that took me to the hallway at the northern end of the building, but after that I didn't know where Bill was. I peeked around the corner outside the arena area, looking down the hallway running along the entire north side of the building. I noticed one lone figure, looking familiar, about four doors down leaning up against the long, featureless, dimly lit cinder-block wall. Along the opposite wall he was facing were doors to classrooms and various other sports-related facilities housed in different rooms, some of which were being used for cycling the bands in and out of the hall. It was strangely quiet.

I stepped out and moseyed down the hall in full view of Bill. Most of the lights were out for the concert, but each doorway off the hallway had a little set of stairs, two or three steps only, leading up a short entranceway to each room. I noticed that some of the doors were open and the various band members and hangers-on were partying or just hangin' in each one.

Then I noticed a guy looking like a long-haired hippie peeking around the entranceway opposite Bill. He had a gaunt face with tiny purple granny-glasses that peered in my direction. *Who the fuck was that?* I blinked and looked again. I know that face from somewhere.

"Hi matey," he said to me, then to Bill, "This your friend with the boo?"

He had a strong British accent.

He was dressed like a normal mod: high-heeled boots, slick black leather pants with matching shiny jacket open in front to reveal only a plain red T-shirt. He wore those stupid dark purple granny-glasses, which I had to admit did look sort of good on the guy. Sitting right behind this gnarly little thing was a beautiful, equally skinny Asian lady with lots of long wavy black hair draped over his right shoulder like a mink stole. She had on a matching black shiny leather suit with identical red T-shirt underneath.

I looked back at Bill and he had a shit-eating grin all over his face like he'd just conned his way into a million-dollar coke deal. Bill was wearing his No. 9 welding shades, which added to the overall fashion statement. Shades in a dark hallway can only mean one thing.

"Yeah," Bill answered and then gestured to me. "Do you have any joints left? John here really needs a hit before he can go on. Yoko and John are so hot coming in from New York they had to travel super clean. I'll make it worth your while."

I looked back at the two of them and then it dawned on me. It wasn't just another groupie, this was John Lennon, the leader of our sacred Rock & Roll revolution. Good thing I'm mellow, I thought, or I would probably be freakin' out like a sixteen-year-old school girl screaming my ass off uncontrollably. Actually, not likely, but I was seriously impressed. I'm actually in the presence of fabled greatness. *They do exist. It's not all smoke and mirrors.*

"Sure," I said. "No problem. Anything for the cause."

"That's the spirit matey. Light that wanker up. I have to mellow out for the concert. I have trouble remembering all the lines sometimes when I'm nervous." He smiled at me expectantly while his girlfriend sort of studied me with mild disinterest.

"Here," I said as I pulled out the two joints I had been saving. I handed one of them to him and Yoko lit it up with a lighter she materialized out of nowhere. *She's good,* I thought.

"You don't know how much trouble your authorities give me when I'm traveling around the US. They are all thinking how great it would be to bust a Beatle."

He took a big hit on the joint, held his breath, passed it to Yoko. Yoko took a dainty hit, if anything, and passed it back to me. I handed it on to Bill. He had stepped across the hallway now and all four of us were huddled together, John and Yoko on the steps while we hunched around them. At least we were out of direct view of anybody looking along the hallway.

John finally let go and blew out a big cloud of smoke. "You Americans have to do something about Nixon. He 's real primitive. I'm surprised he hasn't started rounding up stoners into concentration camps."

"We're trying," I said. "That's what this concert's all about. Truth, justice, and the A-marijuana way." Bill passed the joint back to John. "We need to legalize marijuana. We figure if everyone got high, they would see right through all the absurd lies and shabby characters out there. How else can we defeat the old lies and the liars? Truth doesn't seem to work."

"Ah but weed uncovers the truth. That's why it's illegal, see? The system oppresses us for its very survival. Like a bloody vampire, it can't live without sucking your blood, but it can't do it in the light of day."

He took a big drag on the nearly spent joint and held it up to Yoko's mouth, who was now draped over his back with her two arms wrapped around his chest like a parachute harness. Her head rested on his shoulder. She took her dainty toke and blew the smoke in his ear.

"Yeah, concerts like this must drive pigs crazy!" piped in Bill.

"It's amazing you actually pulled this off. The last place for sanity in a world gone bloody insane must be the university. And there are no cops backstage! Bloody amazing!"

"That's Bill's job," I said gesturing in his direction.

"And you're doing a bloody great job, mate."

They gave each other the revolutionary handshake with fist bump. Never saw Bill being so cute before.

"So, what do you do around here matey, besides emergency weed runs?" he asked with a smirk, looking at me.

"Well, actually, that's what I need to ask you," I ventured.

I took the last joint out and handed it to him.

"I was in line to do a live video of this concert with a big-screen projection over the stage. And we would have been able to record it in color for turning into a movie or broadcast television later, maybe. What the hell happened instead are those clowns out there filming a concert with cheap 16-millimeter film cameras on tripods. If they think this is some kind of Woodstock, they missed the boat by a mile. Woodstock didn't have tripods!"

I lied, of course, but still, there were way too many button-down collars running around for such a righteous concert. Obviously, someone was involved who didn't understand Rock & Roll or avant-garde filmmaking.

"You'll have to talk to her," John said, motioning toward Yoko.

She was now kneeling behind him staring at me intently with that benign, neutral look of east coast disgust for outlying peasants. He took another long drag on my last joint and passed it to Bill.

"We have the same cameras as Woodstock," she said in her sweetest Japanese accent. "We have the best sound recording to go along with it. I have the best New York documentary filmmaker, Steven Gebhardt, directing it. Do you have fifty thousand dollars to negotiate the film rights for all these artists?"

I blinked. Bill passed me the joint. John was starting to smile from the pot smoking.

"I didn't think so," she answered herself. "We are all in the revolution and doing the best we can. Thank you for doing the best you can for us. All power to the people!"

She raised her fist like a black pissed off Olympic athlete. John and Bill raised their fists. I wasn't sure what to do, having just been put down by a five-foot-two meek and mild Japanese American semi-artist working for the cause—and who obviously had John by the short hairs and wasn't lettin' go. By short hairs, I meant blow jobs with extra rim licks. I raised my fist.

"All power to the transmitter!" I said.

It was time to bow out. This was becoming more than embarrassing.

A red shirt showed up warning John and Yoko that they had ten minutes before going on. Stevie Wonder was just finishing up on stage and we could hear the audience going wild way back here behind several concrete walls. I pocketed the roaches. No sense leaving any evidence around. John thanked me again and I told Bill I would look for him after the concert.

I wandered back down the hall in the direction of the arena, where I hung out with Curt and Marty on the sound mixing platform during the last act which, somewhat to my surprise, turned out to be dazzlingly bad. John looked high for some reason and Yoko ended up doing her own songs about Attica State and some other half-assed New York art-protest drivel. *Geez it was sad to see our hero lose his revolutionary fervor just for great sex.*

On the way home that night, I felt that if the documentary film she planned to make was anywhere near the quality of how she/they performed tonight, I was going to be ultimately vindicated but screwed anyway. Too bad nobody would know or care. Pete was the weak-kneed promoter who gave up too much for the deal. Of course, his boys, Teegarden and Van Winkle, were all over the stage, playing with Bob Seger and Stevie Wonder. He got them plenty of exposure. Not one lick for yours truly, who was *almost* a local and surely deserving of a break. Curse those indifferent Rock & Roll predators!

But it wasn't over yet. The next day I get a phone call from… guess who, Pete himself.

"Hey, can you get a camera up to Lansing by tomorrow afternoon?" he asked abruptly. I thought he might be calling about the pot I gave to John last night, and now he wanted some.

"Sure," I responded without really thinking. I glanced at my watch and noted that Bob might only have a couple hours left to get a camera rented and loaded with film on a Saturday afternoon. "But you realize it's going to cost something."

"How much?" he said. "Never mind, we need this done. The Michigan Supreme Court just handed down a decision overturning John's conviction on a technicality and they're letting him out tomorrow afternoon. Isn't that fucking great! We throw a benefit concert and he's let out almost the next day. Aren't you amazed?"

"Delirious!"

"Yoko's guy, what's his name?" he went on. "Never mind. The guy making the film called and said he wants us to get the footage of John being released at the prison. That is, if we can. I told him you could do it. Can you?"

"Five thousand dollars," I blurted out. There was an ominous silent pause.

"Okay," he abruptly said. "Just be at the state pen tomorrow at around noon or so. I think he's scheduled to be released sometime in the afternoon but we don't know exactly when."

"Oh yeah, and I'm going to need credit for Warlock Productions. In the finished film," I added quickly.

"I'm sure they will do that," he said. "No problem."

"I'll need a check today for the whole amount," I said.

"How about cash, half now and half when we get the film and you sign a receipt?" he said.

"That'll work," I said trying not to show too much glee. Now that the concert was over, the Rainbow People's Party was flush with mush. "I'll be right over. Start counting."

Sure enough, when I got to his office he had several stacks of wrinkled twenties already counted out in tens and laying crosswise for me to pick up. Counting as I went, just like a righteous dope deal. I appreciated the trust and open honesty.

"So just be at the prison tomorrow and film whatever happens. We'll all be there, including his wife and kids. Can you do sound as well?"

"I'll pick up some mag stripe film and rent a news camera. Don't worry, I know what I'm doing."

I knew what we needed: a portable news camera setup where the magnetic tape was printed on the side of the film and the tape recorder was built into the camera. It was a lot cheaper than the Eclair-Nagra combination and only required one person to operate. Quality was perhaps a little off, but what the hell did they expect at the last moment on a Sunday? The striped film was more expensive to develop and transfer, but that wasn't my problem.

I called Bob and I could hear him swearing directly when I told him what he needed to do in the next twenty-four hours. I offered him a grand in cash and all expenses. I told him it was for a John Lennon film that would make us all famous. After some strained silence, he calmed down slightly and remembered a friend he had at a local TV station who might help him get a news sound camera.

I gave him the address of the Michigan State Prison and told him we would meet there at noon. He agreed, muttered something to himself, and hung up. I think he said *never fucking again,* or something like, that but I didn't care. I just wanted to get my vengeance on the bastards who cut me out of the video job in the first place. Fuck that little art snob queen Manupelli and those no-talent rich New York filmmaker dilettantes.

The next day came off uncharacteristically hitchless. I met Bob at the state pen in Lansing around noon and just like all film projects, it was hurry up and wait, hurry up and wait, all afternoon long. Finally, we were allowed inside the prison with John's family. His actual release kept being put off from 2 to 4 and finally around 5 they let him through the iron-barred doors, signifying that he was free, and Bob and I were there burning film like it was video tape.

He also brought along a new sun-gun portable light that I held high over Bob's head, illuminating like a solar flare in stark brilliance the dark dank state institution of social vengeance and political punishment. We followed him through a brief news conference held impromptu in the prison yard and then later he made it to the hippie-painted Rainbow Peoples Party VW bus that was going to take him victoriously back to his commune in Ann Arbor.

I happened to look around during the crowded press conference and spotted some creepy looking shirt and tie short-hair goons lounging around with some uniforms; they stood back near a glassed-in holding cell or observation room, not sure which. I swore one of the shirts looked familiar, but the room was crowded. Every time I looked away from what I was filming, the group of shirts and uniforms kept stirring themselves into new formations. If they were FBI, which I presume would have the most interest in political protest, then they were being rather obvious and intimidating. Where were the good old undercover disguises of the fifties? Nobody from the People's side seemed interested, so I ignored them as best as I could. Still, they looked downright evil.

At the end, I gave Bob a stack of used twenties that made his eyes light up—greed and avarice finally realized. He gave me a box of cross-taped film cans containing the exposed film and recorded sound. Next, he said that he had moved in with his girlfriend and was going to get a job.

"Don't call me anymore," were his parting words.

That pretty much took care of Warlock Productions. I was on my own. That's okay, Bob couldn't handle the artist life style and besides, film was being replaced by video so I would have to pursue this thing on my own from here in.

I took the exposed film back to Ann Arbor and on Monday morning delivered the box to Peter, who paid me with more stacks of freshly wrinkled twenties. This wasn't even close to an illegal black-market deal, but it felt like it anyway. Just thinking that the money ultimately would be coming from Yoko and her art snob minions made me feel even more warm and comfy.

With no more film projects, and the video projection for Rock & Roll concerts pretty much dead, things got dull and desperate real fast. Here I was, a product of a deliberate national interest in promoting the sciences, but after we beat the Russkies to the moon, Nix-goon declared victory and turned us all out in the street to become unofficial unemployed veterans of the space race. Now that the Russkies turned out to be paper tigers, one too many physicists who knew how to assemble small tactical nuclear weapons somehow couldn't qualify to pump gas.

Once you're educated, you're now suddenly overqualified for any real available job and therefore by default, chronically unemployable. I went from PhD-published research on planetary atmospheres and programming huge computers to grubbing on the road for sex, drugs, food, and a little pocket change at the end, maybe. Kind of like commercial fishing without the fish.

The boys down at Fanfare were struggling too for some reason. The blowup with Grand Funk had apparently cost them some clients. But nobody is more loyal than money, and when Irving Azov wanted to do a quick Midwestern tour for Joe Walsh's new break-away album, *Barnstorm*, he had to pick somebody local and somebody he knew could do the PA work. Marty called and asked if I wanted to go on the road again, as a sound man.

"It'll be a lot more fun than Grand Funk," he declared.

He knew how my last tour had ended up in a disastrous truck breakdown and a driving marathon across Missouri and Nebraska.

"Joe was the creative force behind the James Gang and he likes to get high and party a lot. It will be a ballbuster cause they have us booked for twenty-six concerts in thirty days. But Irving is acting as his road manager—you remember Irving—and he'll be handing out cash and cocaine to see that it all happens on schedule, and hopefully no more screwups. Joe's new hit song, "Rocky Mountain Way," have you heard it?"

"Of course," I said.

It had become my favorite romantic dream song. I was thinking a lot about the solitude and romance of wintering over high in the Rockies. I mean really high! Ten thousand feet or more with snow up the yin yang.

"It's burning up the charts and they want to cash in quick. Besides, the word on the street is that Joe is proving himself to the big boys in LA so he can play with the Eagles and make some real California dough."

"Sounds like fun," I said. "How much does it pay?"

That is the wrong question to ask just before you run away from home to join the circus. I knew it was going to be minimal pay, but on the other hand, I didn't have to feed myself or worry about what I was going to be doing every night for the next month, so it sort of worked out. Again, it was like fishing, only this time we were going to catch a lot of rocker freaks out in the hinterlands of America and make them pay to see the fair-haired boy from the big city blow their minds. Fanfare had the PA that could do the cranial inoculation and Joe had a new instrument perfect for it.

The tour was sort of off the books so to speak—cash only. So, Irving booked a bunch of medium to small venues in a whirlwind loop through the Midwest, hitting some campuses and all the high spots like Grand Rapids, Sheboygan, Chicago, Waukegan, Milwaukee, Madison, and a shitload of others, ending up in all places, the Fitzgerald Theater in St. Paul. This was Rock & Roll at just about its grubbiest.

Like a circus, it came in with a proud arrival in broad daylight and ended skulking out in the dead of night to do it all over again the next day in the next village hopefully one step ahead of the law. Irving at least booked them in two hundred-mile or less increments, making it all very doable and still maybe get some sleep once in a while. If not, there was plenty of coke.

The music was slightly experimental. Marty had a brand new 4-track Teac quarter-inch reel-to-reel hooked up to the board so we could record as well as play back in four distinct channels. We dubbed it Quadra-sound. The board had been originally built with four independently equalized output channels just in case you wanted to do a separate stereo mix or a full 4-channel recording. But for all the previous tours, we only needed the first two channels for the normal stereo speaker stacks. Some of these venues however, like college basketball arenas, would allow using four stacks of speakers, so we could experiment with Quadra-sound effects.

Joe had done a prerecorded 4-channel tape at the Caribou studios in Colorado the previous fall while recording the first Barnstorm album. He wanted to play live against a backup riff of his big instrumental for "Rocky Mountain Way" in the road show. So when he does the instrumental part, the tape deck is rolling more or less in sync, playing background guitar sounds that go zooming around the room in sync with his onstage performance. At this point, Joe was playing his own invention, dubbed the *Mouth Echo* by some or *Eardrum Blaster* by others.

This special instrument made the weird synthesizer-like *wah-wah* sound heard on most of the *Barnstorm* songs. He would feed back his guitar amp sound into a high-power speaker driver, normally connected to a PA horn enclosure, but in this case, he simply attaches a plastic tube to the throat of the driver and sticks the other end in his mouth; weird contortions he makes with his tongue cause the guitar sound to take on an artificial synthesizer. It's a weird, but funky cool sound all controlled by his guitar playing and voice-mouth action.

This combined sound goes into the PA, where Marty turns down Joe's live stage guitar and instead picks up both from his voice mic. Then he adds a prerecorded background riff where Joe is playing his normal guitar in the background. Now all of that sound, plus the rest of the band, is sent to two speaker stacks up front and two in the rear, where the audience is treated to the very first ever (as far as we knew) surround-sound PA Rock concert, done *mostly* live.

Of course, we didn't bill it as such. We were just playing around learning how this new high-tech shit worked with big halls and lots of screaming drug-riddled maniacs. This was the fun part. Watching the amazement of the audience and the pleasure everybody got from hearing great new sounds being manipulated so easily and clearly for the first time was pure joy for us.

About this time, I started to think about changing from video to sound. If I had a shitload of money, I could build a studio like no other, maybe locate it in some nice scenic location where it's fun to create music and party at the same time. That's what I said about film and video not too long ago, and they probably cost a hell of a lot more than just sound—although five hundred dollars a pop for good microphones could make one poor fast.

And, as an added bonus, our illustrious jerk-off president, Nix-goon, was finally being hauled up before Congress on criminal charges, something we had been advocating since 1959. This time he got caught bragging about running a street gang of incompetent second-team guys pretending to be spies or something. Unbelievable, but since this clown had a reputation way back in California for muscling his poor victims into submission, we knew he was a punk shithead and needed to be drawn and quartered at the inquisition's earliest convenience.

Whenever Joe sang the part about "...bases are loaded and Casey's at bat, playing it play by play. Time to change the batter...", he'd substitute the phrase, "...bases are loaded and Nixon's at bat, lying it day by day, time to change the liar..." and every hall would erupt into stupendous yells, whoops, and hollers. Nix-goon was on most everybody's shit-list by now and even rednecks and bigots wouldn't admit they voted for him.

It looked like the national media finally were waking up about Vietnam and now bad stories were coming out. Instead of the whitewashed lies of the military, real correspondents were getting into the field and finding out the awful truth. The whole mess of lies and political corruption was slowly coming out in the nightly news. Walter was so flabbergasted that his government had actually been lying to him for so long about Vietnam he needed to go through therapy to figure out what the fuck was wrong with him. He recused himself from any collusion and handed the story over to his young hippie reporters who took portable lightweight sound and motion picture cameras into the jungle and brought back the truth that we had been telling for years.

The Pentagon Papers came out, proving that the military staged the whole Gulf of Tonkin incident just so they could get the power to go in whole hog on a lost cause with no possible good for anyone, outside of a few billionaires and crooked politicians wanting to be billionaires. Way before the papers were leaked we knew the truth, but nobody else could bring themselves to believe their own military and elected officials were the bad guys. We were fighting exactly what we thought we were.

We were putting down patriotic citizens fighting for survival and their human rights and dignity as a nation, resisting the imperialist raping by the greedy, power-hungry West. The whole war from the very beginning had been a pile of US-backed corporate lies falling on gullible ears, ultimately justifying the killing of fifty thousand young American boys and hundreds of thousands, if not millions, of innocent southeast Asians. My country had become the ass-holy Nazi's of the 70s but finally it looked like we, the real loyal opposition, were going to win on a technicality: the truth.

And then the big truth finally came out of the closet. Tricky Dicky was caught being the dick we all knew him to be and now he was doomed.

We were ecstatic. We were riding a wave of euphoria and newfound strength, and our righteousness allowed us to party accordingly. Nix-goon is gone, just before the firebrands and pitchforks could get to him. The Vietnam War was over and now the blame game was on to see who was going to take the fall. Even crazy Sinclair had beat the rap, and universities nationwide were opening up to new ideas in education and new involvements with society. The country was turning liberal and progressive, so on one hand we all felt victorious and justified. *Take that, corporate pigs!*

The road shows each night became a blur of mixed up memories. I discovered that the piano player Joe hired for the band always had a Coke can full of scotch setting on his grand piano throughout the entire concert. He seemed to play better with wet lips.

The poor bastard they hired to haul the grand piano from gig to gig hated the water rings that kept showing up after every performance. He would spend hours the next day tuning the poor abused piano back into *close-enough for Rock & Roll music* and rubbing out the polish so the piano looked like a shimmering black diamond under the garish Rock & Roll lights.

He had an extended-cab pickup pulling a goose-neck trailer where he kept two full Bergedorfer grand pianos and his tools. He slept in his truck and was always at the stage door before everyone else and the first to be gone after the concert. He didn't do drugs or party much; he was trying to save up enough money to buy his own pianos and make even more than he could by renting them. He was a great example of the entrepreneurial spirit one needed to survive alone in a cruel capitalist world caring nothing for your talent, knowledge, or abilities.

If I was to start a video projection company, I would probably do the same thing, hauling it around in a cheap trailer and sleeping in the car. The appeal slipped away silently as I watched Joe entertain a whole new generation of rockers who were not necessarily that politically active. They screamed like crazy for references to Nix-goon being run out of town, but obviously, anything deeper was simply off the radar. And they all had long hair, smoked dope, and looked just like us, but shallower.

While on this tour, I was able to experiment with how to properly mic a piano for an arena-loud PA setting. We tried strapping on a direct magnetic pickup device that stretched across the top of the piano strings and picked up their direct vibrations as a single audio output signal. This sounded just like we took the strings and frame out of the piano and plucked them like a harp. The sound was too pure and clean, lacking any semblance to a Bergedorfer, or for that matter, any real piano.

So, I went back to using four to six mikes, two underneath to catch the sounding board highs and lows, and then two or more mikes up above the open case where they catch the full sound of the reverberating and resonating piano as one instrument. When we did four mikes, we could assign them to a rotating quadrant of sound that went swirling around the arena as if you were being plunged spinning into the piano itself. I called it the *piano black hole*.

Joe Vitali, the drummer, an old friend of Joe's from the James Gang days and from the Detroit area originally, also got into the experimental spirit. He decided to tour with a huge drum set, something like thirty-six actual different drums and percussion objects within his striking range including a large gong standing right behind him. We ended up using a few sub mixers just to get the count down to about sixteen mic channels for the drums alone. We had twenty-eight mix channels on the main board, so he was getting by far the greatest share of PA sound power.

When we cranked him up in some of his little solos, everyone in the audience could feel the big kick drum pounding their chests with every beat. When we panned his mic channels in quadra-sound, things really got interesting. It was like being inside the drums themselves. I know, because I crawled inside once during sound check just to measure it with the sound pressure level meter. Talk about getting your brains scrambled and permanent eardrum damage, I didn't care. It was all for science.

Speaking of eardrum damage, Joe was getting earaches and headaches from his guitar-sound-in-mouth feedback instrument.

I measured the sound level two inches from the end of the plastic pipe he put in his mouth and found it to be in excess of 120 dB SPL. It was as if he had an entire speaker stack inside his head running at full volume. I didn't notice any bleeding ears like our backstage mix engineer, who one time failed to wear his headphones and ended up rupturing his left eardrum, the one facing the back of the speaker stack from where he sat mixing the stage sound.

Joe self-medicated with plenty of nose candy and pot to help with the pain; as a result, we had a star who was mostly happy as shit all the time and willing to party with the crew at the drop of a hat, even if he didn't have one.

After the last concert of this go-round tour, we ended up with rooms on the same floor of the St. Paul Hilton. Someone knocked on the door of the room I was sharing with Marty, so I answered. There was Joe and Joe, holding a big damned waste basket between them.

I barely had time to mutter *What the fu...?* when they suddenly threw the basket at me and a giant wall of cold fucking water hit me like the Bering Sea. They ran back down the hall cackling like a couple of teenagers at a pajama party while I stood wetter than hell halfway in the hall and a huge puddle of water spreading out around me.

I went back into the room to dry off and plot some revenge. It was clear we needed to get our wastebasket filled immediately. Moments later, armed with a leaky wastebasket weighing close to forty pounds, Marty and I knocked on their door. When it opened, we paused to get a good shot at the whole room; suddenly, they let go their wastebasket first, dowsing us and making us miss them with our belated counter-throw. Instead, we gave a good soaking to an artificial house plant just outside their door, it started to melt as if made of papier-mâché. We had to retreat for ammo.

Apparently those two clowns were going up and down the hallway, hitting all the crew and a few from the warm-up band. Everybody was arming up. Marty was refilling the wastebasket in the shower when I heard another knock. I looked through the peephole and there they were holding another heavy wastebasket.

"Just a minute, my little lovelies," I called out. "Hurry up!" I yelled into the bathroom.

There was now some more knocking, even more urgent. Marty came out carrying the wastebasket and I stood by the door motioning him to come over as I pulled the door open rapidly. Before they had a chance to dowse us, we blew them away with a mini-tsunami. I looked around the corner, ready to laugh my ass off, when I noticed the policeman's uniform.

The suit standing next to him was actually dripping water all over the place. They apparently had been called to our floor because of some kind of complaint involving water and an elevator and noticed the small pond outside our door. Marty froze. I couldn't help but laugh my ass off.

"I'll call Irving," I said to the still startled and wet officials. "He'll take care of this," and I closed the door.

Irving took care of everything. He could work wonders when it came to hotel damage and late-night complaints. I heard later that after it all settled down and Irving did indeed take care of everything, he was rewarded for his efforts with a four-in-the-morning wastebasket watering. The hall was dark and nobody could positively identify the culprits.

When I got back to Ann Arbor, I had a little pocket change but still no prospects. The local Rock concert scene was about dead. There were more concerts, but they were professional tours passing through with little or no local support or help required. Rock & Roll joined capitalism with a vengeance.

The university went to using a private security agency to replace the rangers because quite frankly, there were just too many concerts for the Psychedelic Rangers to keep volunteering their time and efforts; besides, the concerts were no longer spontaneous events, but carefully orchestrated money-making ventures, like drugs. There was plenty of money in the budget for security, just not any for special effects like video projection.

Steve and Thom were hard at work getting an actual production run of speakers built for the local market. It seems Thom had been pushing them to the students and faculty at the School of Music, where people with trained ears could easily hear the superior performance of the Time Window. Thom moved into a new house he bought with some inheritance money and was trying to get Margie pregnant when she suddenly disappeared with some surfer dude from California on his way back to the beach. Why a surfer dude would be found in Michigan is a real mystery, but there you have it. Thom was devastated by her infidelity, was trying to deal with it rationally and then he got whacked upside the head with a baseball bat when he discovered thieves in his house and tried to be macho and get physical with them.

He damned near died, but a young intern on his overnight shift at the University Hospital recognized a subcutaneous hemostasis in Thom's brain. He did an emergency trepanning procedure, relieving the blood pressure that was slowly killing him. Twice now in just a few months, something deadly has happened to two close friends. Something was going on that I didn't like and didn't make much sense. I was visiting too many hospitals.

Bill was back into living a strictly nocturnal Corvette life, dealing and wheeling. Patti was finishing up her BS before trying to get into med school. He was busy and hard to connect with, but whenever I did, there was faithful Amy eagerly waiting another order to better serve her master. Sometimes when I looked at her she started resembling a cute black-haired English Springer Spaniel, eager to please.

He offered me some interesting ideas to stick around and make some money, all illegal or should be, so I had to pass. Being a drug dealer just didn't develop the kind of people I wanted as a trusted social group. It wasn't the consumers so much as the suppliers; too damn paranoid. I liked the money but the life insurance was a killer. Also, I had to decide what to do for my next life as an artist. The world was clearly changing and I had to follow suit. Science was no longer my calling. Art was where it was at.

To get there though, was I going to be a roadie? Was I going to find some private business I could do like building speakers or doing portable video productions? Did I want to stay here in Ann Arbor now that I was no longer a paying student or should I head for the hills like my buddies up in Colorado? Hide out from this crazy fucking world for a while, or jump in and start grubbing money like a greedy pig? Marty did it with a clear conscience, so could I.

For my generation, clearly a road trip was the only way to get intensive, yet inexpensive therapy along with a chance to clear the head and think things over unmolested by the daily realities of life. I needed to think things over—and get rid of a hot reel-to-reel tape deck. It was time to go home to Oregon, visit family, maybe take care of an old military injury at a remote hospital, this way, I could avoid the embarrassing, but obligatory, visits by friends inquiring into your ailment as a shortcoming and showing overemotional, yet obviously shallow concern. I could take my time. I still had the real estate contract that paid a little stipend each month, more than enough while couching it with friends and relatives.

So, I threw my backpack and sleeping bag in the big blue '66 Suburban, which I could now call Suburban, as the name had stuck for its modern counterpart and was now part of the proper vernacular for 4-wheel drive, cab-over trucks. There was now the Blazer, the Bronco, and the Scout for short body 4-wheels, but only the Suburban, Travelall, and the Power Wagon had a full size ¾-ton frame. So I hit westbound I-94 late one afternoon in July with no intention to stop until I threw my first universal joint from the beating by the big V-8 installed by Bill gave to it, or until I arrived at my parents' house somewhere south of Portland, Oregon…maybe three days of driving later.

I had a nice new cassette tape deck installed before I left with a couple of tolerable bookshelf speakers in wood enclosures attached to the inside of the truck. Being a roadie for a short time had converted me to rocking my way across America with the best damned sound one could have inside the best damned noisy truck one would want while doing 70 miles an hour down the white-asphalted line. My favorite tunes besides Joe Walsh singing about getting high in the mountains, or REO Speedwagon riding the storm out, was Edger Winter only coming out at night. That's how you grind out the miles.

CHAPTER FIFTEEN

IT'S THE SEX, STUPID!

"Well, you walk into a restaurant strung out from the road,
And you feel the eyes upon you as you're shakin' off the cold..."

Bob Seger
"Turn the Page"
1973

Young Americans have always held the road trip as something sacred, like fasting in the desert in order to speak to God or running to the desert to escape the law. In my case, I viewed it as simple cultural heritage. When things get dicey, time to find new territory. Distance and time are great equilibrators that Americans find necessary for survival. That's what I needed, perspective. What better way to find such a vantage point than to blow this pop stand, follow the yellow-painted line, listen to the stereo blast out the jams, and watch the world pass by safely separated by a windshield, a steel cage, and three hundred horses of raging road machine?

I got into a careless attitude, too, that would prove to be cautionary. I knew I was about to leave town for an extended period of time, maybe not returning soon or if I did, not for long. I needed to find my next gig and things were looking slim where I was.

I happened to collect a parking ticket from the city of Ann Arbor; I just tore it up and littered the street with the remains. I considered it a political statement. Of course, fate would not let me get away with such hubris, it would just take a while for it to come complete circle and bite me in the butt later. At the time, I just didn't care about most worldly things. I had ugly dreams and nasty clouds to deal with. Where I was going and why seemed more important than where I had been and how tacky life can get.

I was looking for something because what I had in Ann Arbor was quickly disappearing. Peter Andrews and a lot of other people, including myself, had gambled with John Sinclair and basically lost the bunny and the market. He explained to me at the payoff for the film that Don Kirshner's proposed Rock & Roll concert TV series was not optioned by NBC and in place of solid American Rock music in the Saturday late-night time slot, they offered it to a live comedian improv nightclub act like Second City in Chicago.

I remembered talking to that fat fucker in Chicago who bragged about being part of such a show. It was all coming together, now but not making a whole lot of sense anymore. Comedy wasn't even a good opening act for most Rock & Roll concerts. How could it be favored after midnight on a Saturday night when people are looking to party down, have sex, and smoke dope in the privacy of their homes? Who wants to just laugh their asses off and go to sleep? That's what Johnny Carson was for. Rock & Roll seemed to be losing its cutting edge, or somebody just wanted to get farther away from reality than Rock music already provided. As Nero said, *It's better to laugh your ass off than fiddle your life away*, or something like that.

As for the speaker company, Steve in no uncertain terms said he would not take on any partners unless they could put up as much money as he and his family was going to put up. Boy, friendship doesn't go far when money gets involved. Money talks and everybody walks, so it goes. So without money and without lawyers, my contribution of inventing the Time Window was just going to be ignored and ripped off for a promised pair of demo speakers in the future. It was sad that all those evenings of fraternal idealism and conspiratorial scheming together came to naught.

He and Thom were having the most difficult relationship because Thom really had made contributions to the speaker development that involved real time, work, and money. Now Steve was making moves behind his back to effect manufacturing and marketing without a place for Thom at the corporate table. Thom was not happy about that and his private life was jacking him around as well, now that his wife fucked him good by fucking that surfer dude. That's got to hurt. Now she disappeared to California to pursue her dream of wet waves and sloppy wet seconds to the tune of the Beach Boys and the smell of phony Mexican fish tacos. *Ugh.*

I stored my big stuff in Eberbach's old garage out back of his house, which was already full of junk from most of our past projects and collections. I had a fifty-foot portable rear projection screen stored there and my six-foot color video projector, along with bits and pieces of my former stereo system and some lighting equipment.

I stored my personal papers, books, and archived videotapes in the basement of a close friend of Bill's, Steve Josephson, the rich bastard who owned his own house near campus while he attended law school. Bill even maintained a little cubby hole there where he could escape in privacy. They should be safe there, I thought; the guy is a paranoid New Jersey lawyer-type and keeps his house locked up tighter than a Hoboken whore. I told the people who bought my house where to send the next couple of payments and happily slunk out of town just as the sun was setting dead ahead of me.

The road, the road, the road! Nothing exudes the feel of freedom like moving down the road, passing scenery as monotonously as memories are passed into oblivion or re-colored to your liking. You occupy time and space so closely wrapped together as one so as to become both timeless and without tether.

My thoughts on the road wander all over the universe and back. My eyes are glued to the road and my muscles are geared to aiming the truck down the endless black ribbon. That is accomplished without thinking. *Monkey see, monkey do.* Someday cars will drive themselves. They have to. It's just too damned boring for people. Machines, and people who can act like a machine, can do it so much more reliably. But until then, I do it for the therapy. I doubt that without the driving part, it would be just like any other long trip, begging for sleep and for the torture to be over as quickly as possible.

When driving from the Midwest to Oregon, you know what you are going to be doing for the next sixty hours or more, so I settle in, choose my music carefully, follow along with a good map so I know where the fuck I'm going, and pace my consumption of alcohol and other depressants or stimulants as best I can as the miles ticked off minute by minute. Above all, I'm a captive audience to the whining howl of tires bending to the truck's weight while spinning their hearts out. In fact, every little *whir* and *warble*, every *pow* and *ping*, every *slam* and *slamming* that goes on while exploding gas chambers and intermeshing gears transfer the power of fire to the rotation of wheels, all this I am utterly in tune with. When a new sound appears, it stands out and I get nervous. Is this a pre-failure warning, or am I just hallucinating after twenty hours without sleep?

Jung thought the subconscious only made itself known to sane people during sleep when the brain is available for such distractions to come leaking out without conscious intervention. It must be the same here. Monotonous driving after a while makes the mind drift into areas usually never open for scrutiny. That's what I liked about long-distance driving. The self-examination never ceased. The past disappeared with the smoke trails left behind and the future beckoned with brightly lit green signs and arrows showing all the possible directions to the future. Socrates would have dug it.

The mechanical failures brought me instantly back to reality, however, and the dreadful inevitable feelings of failure and inadequacy also included the fear and loathing of spending money on repairs I could little afford. Halfway across Iowa, at around 4 in the morning, a new urgent vibration began to force itself onto my awareness. I denied it for as long as I could but finally had to admit that something was beginning to fail, and that something was one of the universal joints on my drive shaft running power to the rear wheels.

Finally, I pulled over from the now desperate vibration shaking my teeth in tune to the vibration of the road. I opened the big tool box I carried in the back and took out a half-inch open-end wrench and a short piece of baling wire. I crawled under the truck and quickly unbolted the broken universal from the rear shaft of the transfer case. I secured the now unsupported end of the drive shaft to the frame with the baling wire. Now I can keep driving on the front wheels only until I find a parts store open where I can buy a replacement universal. I then, in the parking lot, replace the broken one and reconnect the shaft to the transfer case. I once again found that my K-15 was a reliable truck that would not leave me stranded, even with mechanical failures that normally require tow trucks.

Something else, less obvious, seemed to be happening that I normally am prepared to deal with when forced into interacting with locals in the hinterlands of dullard America. But the guy at the parts store didn't stare at my long hair, or even snigger. He wore the requisite uniform of stupid advertising baseball hat above a saggy T-shirt above a big silver buckle on a wide leather belt holding up nicely faded greasy Levi's. Now, I naturally adopted some of the accoutrements of the road by wearing the buckle, wide belt and blue jeans, preferably Levi Strauss when I could afford them, but I hated baseball hats. I sometimes wore a black cowboy hat with my blue jean jacket, but I dropped the hat when I found out real sick rednecks were getting into it. But usually when I had to buy burgers, beer, or auto parts in butt-fuck nowhere Iowa, I got plenty of stares and many times outright nasty comments about my hair. That seemed to be changing as I noticed his hairline sticking out from behind his stupid hat and he didn't even bat an eye at mine. How the hell was I supposed to know what the enemy looked like now?

Pigs, cops, and military-types could still be spotted a mile away. The shorter the hair, the more compliant the brain. They kept an eye on us as well. When I stopped for gas in some bump-in-a-road of a town in Nebraska, a short-haired nutcase with more hair up his butt than on his head spotted a sticker in the back of my truck that said, *Nixon needs to pull out like his father should have.* He yelled at me while trying to remove it. He broke a fingernail clawing at the offensive words and finally left cursing the conspiracy that caused him to have a hangnail.

One thing I've noticed about the far right Nazi wanna-bees—no sense of humor whatsoever. That's the other way to identify the bastards; if they don't laugh at George Carlin jokes, then they should be disarmed and remitted to a retraining facility where they would be given a thousand mics of acid and made to listen to looped Grateful Dead jam tapes twenty-four hours a day. That'll clean the cobwebs out of anyone's brain.

The road cleaned out cobwebs for me just as well. Especially those late-night hours roaring down an empty highway in a flat land where lights on the horizon signifying the world's tallest broadcasting tower took sometimes hours to approach and then finally pass in the silent night as my truck kept moving as if standing still and the land slowly slipped by like a moving flat shadow. I could almost sense the earth rotating underneath me.

It's lonely on the road late at night, so the radio becomes an important companion to help while away the dark empty hours. At three hundred miles out of Omaha the FM and good Rock music fade from my radio's reception. Now it's AM time and trucker's Nashville *drunk on my ass and my dog's dead* music to tolerate or have plenty of tapes for listening. I had eight. At forty-five minutes apiece, that amounted to about six hours of unrepeated music, which was usually enough to make it to the next big city FM stations. Not so after Omaha. The next major city was probably Boise or Portland and they were about another day away.

The sun rose behind me as I shot across the top of the continent in Wyoming. It's high plains drifter flat with winds constantly blowing in from the Pacific crossing the continent at two relatively low paths north and south of the Rockies, which stood like a giant billboard of Rock blocking the wind and forcing it to go around either side. Why people lived here I could not fathom, knowing they rarely even had a tree to stand behind to help block the everlasting blow. My truck just shrugged it off as it whizzed on by the endless row houses appearing around places like Laramie and Rock Springs. From the highway overpasses, I could get a brief airborne view of the ticky-tacky invasion of pale-colored, neatly laid out rows of identical boxes spreading across the Western deserts like some alien fungus invasion. Probably smelled the same too.

Then there were the monotonous hours of driving through the featureless high plains windswept desert where the black ribbon in front of me was absolutely the only sign of civilization outside a fence or two stretching off into infinity. Everything else for hundreds of miles in any direction was nothing but scrawny jack rabbits, even more scrawny coyotes, and plenty of lonesome sage brush. Once in a while the sage dies, disconnects from the ground and starts rolling along with the wind. Many a cowboy compared his life and fate with that of the tumbleweed. It was sort of like Dylan's "Rolling Stone," a simple life of growing in one place and then letting the wind be your fate for good or ill from there on out. Sounds romantic but seeing huge piles of sage bush stacked by the wind against the lonely fences just made one wonder, *what the hell were we doing?*

I felt cast about by the winds in the same way. I tried to find root but it just isn't that time yet. Now it's time to roll and find new fields of opportunity. Besides, I didn't like the Midwest all that much. Too damn flat for one thing, long cold winters with hotter than hell summers, a few tornadoes, and too full of assholes for another. Of course, the assholes I grew up with had somehow faded to the point where I almost thought I belonged back in my home turf of butt-fuck Oregon. Maybe, but probably not the rural logging community where I was imprisoned for puberty; more likely the big city of Portland, or one of the serene university towns like Corvallis.

At the end of the second day, both my thoughts and a limited number of music cassettes became repetitious. The sun sat behind clouds hanging over the everlasting Mormon hills ahead as I neared Little America and the home of the Li'l Stinker giant truck stop and oasis. I had been reading the stupid road signs for miles, all with a clever saying and then pointing out how many miles to go before you could enjoy the Li'l Stinker gas station and an authentic American art icon located in the most unartful armpit of a desolate hole I could imagine. That's what I love about America—its sense of stupid, humorless humor juxtaposed with harsh, exacting environments. We don't just survive in the wilderness, we make jokes about it, dress it up funny, and generally show no respect whatsoever for what should be a serious contemplation of our temporariness, moderated and nurtured only by nature in all its rawness. Spitting in the eye of fate is certainly an American thing tantamount to flipping the bird to the iceberg as you pass by on the Titanic.

When I finally pulled my comparatively small 4X4 truck into the bright lights of a thousand tractor trailer rigs all bound in every direction but lined up perfectly in this oxymoron of road stop desolation, I realized I had just entered another redneck twilight zone of quiet bigotry and screaming ignorance. I didn't care anymore. I was hungry and tired and needed a little pick-me-up in the form of what every trucker uses to replace the love of a home on the road: chicken fried steak and mashed potatoes both smothered in white artery–clogging, pancreas-busting gravy. I still didn't care.

After thirty hours on the road, I felt a little wobbly and slightly woozy from sitting so long without moving. Now the partially atrophied legs had to work, but not so steadily. I found a table by the window where I could keep an eye on my truck and started poring over the standard road-slop menu I had read many times before at similar establishments. This one was still slick from the last guys greasy fingers, so I kept wiping my hands on my pants leg.

"What'll it be, Cowboy?" said the uniformed waitress. She was referring to my standard road dress of Levi's jacket, plaid shirt, faded dungarees, and pointy cowboy boots quietly tucked inside my pants legs. I wasn't really anything of the sort, but it was comfortable—not a suit—and it helped sometimes overcome the immediate reaction to my long hair.

I was startled by the suddenness of her appearance. Usually, they let you stew for a while before taking your order. She had on the standard ugly uniform dress, orangish-brown with a white blouse collar peeking out above and some kind of stupid cloth tiara indicating a servants' status, I guess. She looked to be the requisite age of around thirty-five going on fifty-five, slightly used around the edges, and now probably raising four kids alone in the wilds of Wyoming doing the only job she was still qualified for: waitress in waiting. Waiting for what exactly was the big unanswered question in her life and it showed, except for the big pasted-on semi-professional smile.

"How about some coffee?" she added cheerily, holding up a glass pot of some kind of black liquid.

"Sure," I said automatically. I was well into my second day of caffeine poisoning anyway so a little more couldn't possibly alter my state of jittery wakefulness. It was a fine balance most truckers and I went through, keeping liquids to a minimum so you don't have to stop to pee, but enough caffeine to stay awake two or three days in a row. Your body keeps trying to piss all those poisons away and you have to figure out how to maintain a blood level high enough to be therapeutic without overworking the kidney/liver thing trying to protect you.

"Hey Shirley!" yelled someone behind me loud enough to be heard in the men's rooms outside. "We don't serve girly-boys taking jobs away from real Americans."

She looked up and her smile instantly disappeared into a blaze of fury.

"Oh shut up, Joe. Nobody asked you!" she shouted right back.

Then she pasted on the smile again like nothing had happened and spoke directly to me.

"Would y'all like some cream or some sugar with that?" she said emphasizing the sugar part.

"Sure," I said again, automatically. I wasn't sure we were still talking about coffee. She smiled and poured about three-quarters of a small thick-walled mug of industrial coffee, pushed a miniature stainless-steel pitcher in my direction with a matching little pot and tiny spoon, and then turned to offer go-juice to everyone else in her section. With such small portions, she'd be back soon.

"Hey Hippie! Aren't you due back at the reservation?"

The other truckers snickered a few times and went back to their coffees. *Ah fuck! Are we really going to have to go through this shit again?*

Shirley came back, which kept the clowns at bay for a while. I ordered the standard truck stop meal because it would undoubtedly and literally stick with me all the way to Oregon with enough grease calories to start a small forest fire. Plus, it's quick out of the kitchen.

When the food showed up, she hung for a moment and asked, "I bet you work for a Rock band, don't you? You look just like the guys I saw working on stage in Rawlins when REO Speedwagon came through here last year."

"Do you like music?" I asked.

I kept eating while she talked. Never let conversation get in the way of sustenance. Kierkegaard did and look what it got him.

"Oh yes," she bubbled, "I have a stereo system in my trailer that causes the neighbors to complain all the time when I'm home. I'm learning to play the guitar, but I can't make all the chords they use on some songs."

"I'm sure you'll figure it out." *Burp.*

I burped from the mashed potatoes and gravy. The taste was designed for gluttony. It just slides right down the line taking everything with it to the bottom, where it tries to stay, sometimes for days. And then there are the gravy farts.

"I'm trying to write love songs, but so far I just have one," she reported proudly. "So who do you work with? I bet it's ZZ Top 'cause y'all have long hair and beards. They're so co-o-o-ol!"

"Yeah, that's us. Cool." I fished out my sunglasses and put them on and kept on sopping up the gravy with the remnants of the required two pieces of white toast cut diagonally and greased with something yellow that's never been close to coming from a cow.

"It must be so wonderful to go on a tour and be backstage at all the concerts with all the stars and their ladies. Are you on tour now? Are the brothers here?"

She started looking around but clearly, I was the only long hair male in the restaurant. Which was another way of saying I was the only idiot in this restaurant.

"I'm between shows. Sort of on vacation."

I finished mopping the plate clean dutifully. I was a twenty-year veteran of the clean plate club. My dustbowl parents made us kids waste no food, no matter what. Senseless, but what could I do. It was part of the DNA by now.

"I sang with my cousin's band over in Cheyenne at a high school prom. Everybody said I sounded like Gracie Slick."

"Yeah, just go ask Alice."

"What?" she asked with a wrinkled brow of confusion.

I stood up, pulled a $5 dollar bill out of my roadie wallet chained to my belt, kissed her lightly on the cheek, and slipped the fiver into her blouse pocket. "Keep the change sister and keep the faith."

She seemed shocked rigid for a moment while I made good my escape until I just made it to the door.

"Hey draft dodger hippie! How's it like being a traitor to your country?"

I turned and loudly proclaimed, "Excuse me, but I'm a four-year veteran of the Viet Nam war!"

Everybody looked up from their meals. The jerk yelling at me from a booth on the other side of the restaurant froze with indecision.

I let that sink in as they all sort of look at one another confused. "And I fought on the winning side!"

With that, I ran like hell for my truck, hoping I hadn't left the lights on or something making it fail to start in this critical instant. But it happily started up immediately and I slammed it in gear, spinning out in a hail of gravel as I noticed a small group of truckers in my rearview mirror emerge from the restaurant like pissed-off bees from a kicked hive. They were all commercial drivers so they didn't have the time to chase me down and kick my ass. Besides, I was turning off the freeway in about ten miles for the northern cutoff of I-80 around Salt Lake City on the older two-lane highway, US-30, and it was doubtful any of these yokels would be taking the same back roads.

This was the route followed by the covered wagons more than a hundred years earlier, followed by the railroad, which necessitated the requisite thirty-mile spacing between towns for refilling the steam engines with water. Now a two lane asphalt highway followed the lay of the land, instead of trying to defy it; it snaked its way between low mountains, following streams and small rivers until it popped out in the upper end of the giant Snake River Valley running all across southern Idaho. About every thirty miles, this ancient road would pass through one little dead town after another, sometimes with a lonely blinking stoplight marking the precise center of nowhere.

I drove this route most of the night, enjoying the curves and feeling the hulking shadows against an all-pervading darkness of trees and mountains on all sides. The defining moments came when I stopped by the side of the road to take a piss, Marveling at the dark night sky lit up like a starlit ballroom, only much more intense. I felt small and big. Big for the earth, small for the universe.

There I stood with my pecker in my hand, absorbed by the view of precisely one-half of the viewable universe stretching out a few billion light years. Awareness seemed dependent on perspective. No other animal on earth ever looked up at the stars with such understanding and deep appreciation for their place in it, realizing at the same time just how fucking infinitesimal they really are. Fuck, I wanted to scream: a primal *I'm here!* sort of scream, which I'm sure all the other animals within range knew exactly what it meant. Maybe it sounded like Tarzan.

I made it to Pocatello before dawn and then raced the rising sun across southern Idaho and into Oregon after rejoining I-80 North out of Salt Lake. The rest of the trip went by as usual, lots of boredom while Marveling at the desolation of the great western desert as it pushed up from Mexico all the way to Eastern Oregon and Washington. Sign posts were read, miles noted as they counted down, little dust stop towns came and went, and the twisting and turning of the highway was the only break from the boredom.

I wanted it to just end after two days of continuous driving, even though I had another day to go. I was also getting damned tired and needed some sleep, even if it was just a couple of hours. No problem in the truck; I just need to find a side road, drive some ways to get away from the highway noise, park out of the way, crawl into the back, stretch out on my foam pad, or in a sleeping bag, depending on the temperature outside, and grab some *zzzs.*

Up again before dawn, but at least I feel a little refreshed. Back behind the wheel, I rejoin the road and continue away from the pink sky forming behind me. I stop for a little pit stop, some coffee, couple eggs over easy, hash browns, and lots of Tabasco sauce. This time I wasn't hassled by any lost groupies. Must have been the hour and the fact that only farmers around this burg were up this early. They really could care less about the long-haired hippie in a Chevy truck. I liked the little town of Lava Hot Springs. I promised myself I would come back some day and try out their namesake.

The long lonesome highway gives me a chance to think. I keep coming back to what seemed like the root of all the problems: people seem to want to be stupid. They'd rather follow orders than think for themselves. Their desires cap out at the conventional. Vietnam was just an example of stupidity taken to the extreme, where the lies become so ludicrous one wonders what the hell is wrong with the constant defender of such blatant lies. What is wrong with people when they believe idiots—who are really out to rape, loot, and pillage—are somehow heroes in disguise? What the fuck is wrong with people when thinking is the absolute last thing they try?

The answer came to me as obvious and intuitive. Humans are gullible. It's an addiction. They want to believe shit they know can't possibly be true and yet will gladly fight and die for it. It's our fatal weakness. If I wanted to take over the world, all I would have to do is create such an outlandish lie that everyone secretly hopes would be true and as a consequence, they would send me money instead. Fuck! I just came up with the business plan for every two-bit shyster television evangelist that exists, and by last count, it wasn't pretty.

Speaking of crazy fucking nuts, the flat potato lands of southern Idaho reminded me of Jack Simplot, who became the potato baron and eventual potato despot of Idaho. He accounted for at least a ten-point drop in Idahoans average IQ by creating the world's most conservative state government ever attempted by man. He did this in order to guarantee his permanent despot status, while attracting other Nazi police-state, hyper-patriot bullshit artists and other criminal conmen to his private country. Idaho acted as if civilization was only an option and one that should only be exploited when all else fails. In this case, it was a failure that kept telling itself it was a winner. *See? King of the gullible!*

Boise flew by. Then Nampa and Caldwell. Finally Vale, the first city in Oregon. Oregon seemed almost the opposite of Idaho: liberal, intelligent, progressive, and the home of the greatest Senator ever, Wayne Morse. Senator Morse, so-called Tiger of the Senate, told the American people as early as 1959 that Vietnam was a political trap and a dangerous plot to corrupt the electorate by playing on people's brainwashed commie paranoia spread by the criminal war lobbyists of the '50s and '60s. In reality, we were the enemy of democracy, and yet a majority of the American voters were convinced we were helping the democratic side against the commie side when in fact we were accomplishing the exact opposite.

How could they be so stupid as to listen to these lies and actually believe them? What's worse in this case was the apparent desire by the duped to promote this insanity with a level of psychotic fervor usually reserved for extreme religious death cults bent on suicide. Where is our suicide salvation this time? Is there no cure for gullible?

That's how my thoughts wandered while driving. I could solve a lot of problems if I could just drive on it long enough. Soon I was passing through the cowboy country of northeastern Oregon, where beautiful green grass grew like a peaceful ocean with cattle spotting the green horizon enjoying the summer feast before roundup and slaughter. Just before entering the Columbia River Gorge leading to Portland stands the last bastion of cowboy mythic rodeos: the Pendleton Round Up.

Again, mixed feelings wandered around my brain, knowing the young cowboys were often simple rural athletes, while the animals were mostly unwilling victims. What was right? If humans need to beat up on something to prove their superiority, then why not keep it among ourselves. Why involve innocent animals? But that's war, so still no good. So besides gullible, humans were egomaniacs. How could anyone expect anything good to come from a mixture like that?

The run down the canyon through the Cascade Mountain Range is always nice even when it's icy and windy, which it isn't now, so doubly nice in the spring. The view is always spectacular, showing off the works of man such as giant, river-taming dams or the enjoyable structurally artistic bridges spanning the mighty river, bringing both sides into contact by human ingenuity and cleverness. Even in the dismal grey rain of the Northwest, these works of man lend a godly air to our interpretation of what nature should provide. Are we with nature when we only build and against nature when we destroy? The simple truth was we needed to find ways to build without requiring that something else be destroyed.

Finally, Portland that cute little town split by the Willamette River, came into view as the Columbia Gorge opened up to the inland valleys of the coastal range. Here is where the smarter and wiser of the European invaders came in 1840 to find a new life based on hard work and civic responsibility, farming these fertile untouched lands. The Californicators, instead, came at the same time to rip the gold from the hills with malice and greed. We end up today with different cultures scattered around the country based on the type of person each area attracted. In the case of California, it's a land of money grubbin' bastards out to steal your wife, child, and dog if they could get away with it. But Oregon has philosopher farmers, free yeomen, who prefer justice over advantage and truth over lies. I was home again.

I spent a few days visiting my parents, who were now retired and living quietly on a section of our former dairy and chicken farm Dad had eventually split up and sold off. All my childhood memories were now only that, as the old house was now gone along with all the barns and out buildings that I used to take care of as a child. So a little bit of me disappeared that I could never go back and see again, the repeated youthful scenes I remember in my mind were dimming and I felt I was losing a personal ethereal connection through time. My life was disappearing.

This is a hole in my life that Europeans, for instance, do not experience like Americans. They live in the same buildings their ancestors lived. We tear down our ancestors' buildings for newer, less connected ones. We end up unconnected to our past and heritage, and thus prone to being blown hither and yon, willy-nilly, with no solid foundation for supporting our values, our very souls, other than our music and art.

My next older brother, Bob, lived nearby with his four kids, all pre-pubescent but eager to hear about being a Rock & Roll roadie for the big bands. I brought along some color slides I took during the Grand Funk tour, which showed long-haired crazily dressed weirdos dancing around in the multicolored stage light making loud and obnoxious music. The slides were silent, and thus tolerable by the old and deaf.

I took the opportunity to drop off a still slightly warm Teac tape deck generously donated by Grand Funk Railroad for all my inconvenience in supporting Fanfare. The original studio tape of them rehearsing for the first time their new song inspired by Little Rock and Omaha, "We're an American Band" was still on the deck, so I knew my nephews would get some kind of inspiration out of it besides pissing off their parents.

A new generation of rockers were coming on and I was pretty sure by now that the next round of musicians wasn't going to measure up to the honest, home-grown bands I had grown to appreciate and respect. The new Rock was too much glamour and not enough revolution. We were losing our spirit of conquering new territory, defining new horizons by hanging our asses on the line and pulling it off regardless of the challenges. Now musicians sought ratings and profits by blow jobs, nepotism, and good ol' American bribe money. Rock was clearly headed in the direction of exploitation instead of experimentation, boring blandness instead of the excitement of birthing new ideas, new viewpoints, and new attitudes.

We were smarter and wiser now because of Rock & Roll, but I feared for the next generation. They seemed only inspired by a fulfilling bottom line rather than a fulfilling life of enlightenment. Just like a hundred years earlier, Oregon farmer philosophy Rock was being overrun by corporate California plastic Rock.

I spent a few days with my parents in a new strange house. I was still able to roam the woods of my childhood. Now they were mute evidence of the fact I once lived here but they seemed unconcerned of my returning, the woods that is. My parents were concerned. They had little appreciation of my current life. They, on the other hand, led a quiet life which was nice for me for a while, but there's just so much of *Hee Haw* a person can take and still keep some kind of grip on sanity. My parents were truly of another generation that I could neither understand, support nor tolerate. It turns out that about one week of *Hee Haw, Lawrence Welk,* and the *Grand Ol' Opry* was my personal best.

I was suddenly low on pot for some reason. I thought I had stashed a whole ounce up behind the heater in my truck, but it wasn't there when I went to retrieve it. My mom is a clean freak and she had vacuumed out the truck the day before; I got very suspicious that her Electrolux had swallowed more dirt than it was worth. A quiet search of the normal places where dirt from the vacuum might end up yielded nothing. I asked her if she found anything unusual in the truck when cleaning it and she just smiled.

"Why no, dear, what are you missing?"

I learned a long time ago that you can fool just about anyone except mother nature and Mom.

"Nothing, just a plastic bag of old dirty socks."

"Nope, didn't find any socks but if you do, I am doing a load of coloreds later today. Give them to me and I'll include them."

"I think they're too far gone to matter anymore."

So now I had an excuse to lookup an old high school buddy who I hadn't seen for ten or more years, now living and working in Portland as a pharmacist of all things. He was super straight with short hair and button-down collars, but he liked a little weed from time to time, He knew where I could buy something, *just don't get him involved.*

Now, here was the strange part. Even though he was, and always had been, straight as an arrow or boy scout, take your pick, he did like hanging with the higher side and had tried to find love and a wife the old-fashioned way: *get'em drunk, get'em laid, get'em coming back for more and pretty soon there's the sound of little feet.*

When he gave up on this, which I thought was way too soon, he turned to the gay lifestyle, which involved a lot more sex, drugs, and Rock & Roll. So now he was the closet queen running the super store pharmacy, straight by day, Portland swinger by night. I figured only in Portland's tolerant philosophical atmosphere would anything like this be remotely possible. Portland could be my kind of town, at least in case the spurned girls of the closet set were still available for the enlightened pickup.

He talked me into going out with him for one night, just as a friend and not as a date. I was glad he cleared that up. I thought gays were great, for gays that is. It's just that I didn't think I could swing that way, even with an unlimited alcohol and drug budget. The thought of me staring into the eye of someone else's one-eyed trouser-snake up close and personal would just be, well, it's just not for me. It was bad enough I had to learn to like sucking pussy, but sometimes the thought of my tongue going places another man's dick has been could be construed as being second-order gay anyway. I probably rejected trying gay out of some kind of ignorance, but I didn't care; I was not going to find myself in bed with a hairy-assed man if I could help it.

Maybe it was those Sundays as a child when my parents dragged me to the Methodist ritual where I had to listen to a female pastor—first in the West I was told—extol the virtues of doing things right and proper, according to God. Nobody mentioned screwing, at all, so I figured it was all either good or bad, without distinction of details. Later when they discovered there had to be a line, did they decide that maybe same-sex sex was not that bad. Anyway, I was liberal. I figured what two people do to each other behind closed doors is none of my business, the state's business, organized religion's, or anyone else's, for sure. So, what's the big deal?

Everyone should be free to be whatever they think they have to be in order to be human and true to themselves. The key here is not what you do so much as how what you do is received by closed-minded idiots. Moralists should just keep their noses out of some things. Methodists, unlike the Baptists, supported the equal rights movement and the sexual equality movement; they could at least claim the moral high ground if one kept such scores. Though they were superfluous, I was glad I was a Methodist heathen instead of just any ordinary bigot.

He introduced me to another friend that night who worked as a lawyer during the day and at night, besides hanging out in gay bars with friends, he rents apartments in the city and grows pot in them. He just harvested some plants and invited us over for champagne and smoke. I was intrigued, so we went, and while my friend and his friend got friendly in the bedroom, I checked out the pot he grew in the other bedroom. I opened the door slowly and felt like a fanfare was trumpeting a new day as the brilliant light spilled over me, blinding me momentarily. I was stunned. Here was a dreamland I could only wish I could do and this guy has done it. *Stupendous!*

When my eyes finally stopped down the iris to f-22, the whole room came into focus. The walls were lined with tinfoil to reflect the light back onto the plants. Several giant sodium vapor lamps hung from the ceiling, lighting up the room like the inside of the sun. Big pots of soil, each with a green plant growing out the middle, filled the floor from wall to wall. Small water lines came from a back bathroom and snaked across the floor to each plant. The plants were on an automatic watering system and automatic sunlight. And nobody knew it was here. *Genius!* I just sat down and went into some kind of temporary nirvana.

When they reemerged not the worse for wear, my friend was toking on a big-assed joint that was presumably from the latest harvest. I tried it and was immediately blown away. This stuff was as good as any Thai stick or Columbian sensimilla that I had ever had. *What was this stuff?* He just smiled and said it was his own breed he had been working on for a few years. He called it Skunk Weed because of the way it smelled when you crushed a bud. I tried it and it did smell stronger than any weed I had ever handled before. I asked for some seeds and he just laughed. I kind of figured he was being protective of his product, but in fact I learned later he was not even using seeds. He was getting a plant to spawn other plants just by getting cut sprigs to grow new roots. Weird. I had to look into this when I got back to Ann Arbor.

Anyway, I loaded up with as much as he had and that I could afford, which would probably just make it back to Ann Arbor if I hoarded it a little. I kissed my parents and their new color TV good-bye and headed up to Seattle, where I wanted to visit another old high school friend before heading back to business. This was an old buddy who was into sex, drugs, and Rock & Roll long before me and I considered him one of the true, trail-breaking revolutionaries who lived his life according to the new rules.

He tried college but decided it was too slow, went to New York, ended up in a white shirt and tie working for the biggest bull shitter company in town. He finally escaped IBM a couple years later, saving himself from probably becoming a heroin addict, moved to Seattle, and apparently found a way to make a living working for himself—and it didn't involve selling drugs. I had to find out his secret. I camped out in my truck in his driveway while I spent some time watching him enjoy his newfound life as one-half of a gay couple in the business of remodeling old, run-down Victorian houses in Queen Anne and Capitol Hill.

They were living in one of their houses being renovated on Capitol Hill, and after the first night of reminiscing and having a couple of drinks, I went to bed in the truck early. I had to let myself back in early the next morning to use the bathroom and make a cup of coffee while waiting for the city boys to get up. My friend's, I guess, wife came down and helped himself to the coffee, sitting down at the table where I was reading my book. If I'm not watching TV to waste time, then I always carry a book to accomplish the same mind masturbation value. It was probably something by Hunter Thompson or some other revolutionary writer.

"Did Don ever say anything to you about me?" he asked out of the blue.

I was reading and hoping he wouldn't make conversation with me. I don't want to say anything wrong in these unknown, perhaps touchy waters. But I had to be polite.

"Say wha?" I muttered, still trying to read. I looked up finally, from the silence.

"I mean, has he ever talked about me to you?" he asked.

This time I noticed his red eyes and maybe a tear or two.

"We really don't talk that much," I replied slowly, not wanting to seem too interested. "In fact, I haven't said *boo* to him for probably five or six years now, maybe. The fucker was supposed to go to the same snob college I got into and then bailed at the last moment. We haven't talked since."

I tried to make my story sound ordinary instead of anything exceptional. He was fishing for the exceptional, himself. I went back to reading.

"It's just that he doesn't seem to talk to me anymore and it really hurts. I love him more than life itself. But you pop up and he is way more talkative with you than we've ever been. I figured he and you might have something going, you know, from your past together."

I looked into his red swollen eyes and almost saw a jilted girlfriend. *Oh boy*, I thought. I had no fucking idea Don was gay when we went to high school, in fact, this whole thing is kind of a surprise to me as well. He always seemed to like the ladies and that's one of the reasons I hung out with him. He could pick up women like I might buy an ice cream cone. I just wanted to hang around and be near in case he dropped one. I wanted to learn his secrets. I had no idea this was the secret. He was good at this thing.

I looked up at him straight in the eye, and then I noticed he was out-'n'-out crying.

"Look, I have no idea what he's into anymore. Anyway, I don't want to be involved. I don't swing your way, I'm still a lesbian trapped in a man's body and I plan to stay that way for a while, so I can't help you."

He stopped crying as he wiped away strange tears. He wasn't getting any sleep, it was obvious. His old lady was breaking up with him. No. Wait a minute. Her old man is breaking up with him, I mean her. It was clear now who was on top and so forth in this relationship.

He had told me his story the night before when we were all too loaded to give a fuck. He started, I think, as a God-fearing, sober-straight school teacher or accountant or something equally boring in the bowels of conventionality and conformity called the rural West. After five wonderful years of marriage and family life in a tract ranch house, he woke up one day, said he was getting choked to death, politely excused himself, and headed for the nearest big city, Seattle.

He naturally slipped into the vibrant Seattle gay community immediately, so I'm thinking, 'he' discovers he's a 'she' or something like that. 'She' needs a 'he' to be complete, but in rural butt-fuck ignorant America, he was already the 'he' designated by his haircut and he had to have a 'she', designated by a frilly dress wearer, which he thought he was, or should be. Get it? I wasn't sure I did.

Anyway, I found it really strange to see a woman occupying a man's body. I didn't think of my friend Don in that manner so I just assumed he made the switch from girls to boys out of a desire for better quality sex. I could maybe see that after my bout with two Midwestern virgins, dragging them screaming and kicking to the joys of sexual freedom. Don always seemed like he loved a good romp. He still seemed every bit a male, just with different sex preferences than I. I could understand that. It's good to be a connoisseur at the things you appreciate. But this guy or girl wanted to be his wife in the conventional sense, or so he thought. He was trying to make everything else in the relationship work, just like a submissive female, and was missing the entire ballpark. *It's the sex, stupid*, but I couldn't tell him that!

Later that warm and sunny spring afternoon, I mentioned I had a couple of Owsley window pane hits on me and how pleasant it would be to walk around the Capital Hill neighborhood while smashed out of our loving gourds enjoying the sights and sounds of Seattle. Don was immediately up for it and his lover went dutifully right along.

"Now be careful," I cautioned them. "This stuff can do a number on ya!"

"Not to worry," Don said like a real trooper. "It took a lot more than this to keep me working at IBM."

"No problem," his live-in boyfriend said. Whenever I hear *no problem*, I get ready for the problem.

About halfway through our walk, we heard out of nowhere the sound of a big pipe organ playing Bach. The sound was magically winding its way through all the green trees and bright yellow sunlight we had been tripping on for the last hour or so. It was an added dimension to our high and we were now bound to follow it to its origin. A few blocks later, we found the sound coming out the open double doors to a Catholic church on Capitol Hill named St. Marks.

We wandered in even though we knew we could explode at any moment from being nonbelievers entering sacred territory. We decided the music was nondenominational and therefore okay for heretics to wander in off the street without all the fire and brimstone stuff happening. Sure enough, it was nothing more than someone practicing their recital on the brand-new wood organ the church had just installed. We sat in silence for a couple of hours listening to this guy go through his repertoire until he ran out of music and we ran out of special effects. *God, I love a pipe organ.* Wooden pipes are incredibly pure and mellow, almost like a feminine version of the more common lead monsters. It's just so expressive of the human will and self-determination. It's a little revolution every time I hear it.

When I think of pipe organ music, I think of the millions who quaked at its power and feared for their lives, that they thought the music was the voice of God himself calling them to obedience. Only pipe organs and big symphony orchestras can come close to the dynamic level and intensity of sound that Rock & Roll now produced. We felt that Rock & Roll was the next big sound that would carry us away from our human cesspool of muddled messages and bring everyone together again like the church did during the Crusades. Only our crusade is to free every individual from the shackles of religious and nationalist dogma, the exact opposite of what the other two had supported.

That's how you think when you're higher'n any Greenwich Village junkie. Don and I were constantly bantering back and forth about religion, God, and silly-assed gullible humans. He, like I, knew it was all a huge lie meant to control and contain the human spirit for some asshole's desires—for greed and avarice. But God was no longer needed. The threat was empty. We could handle the universe on our own now and we only needed churches and big halls for housing big pipe organs and for large revival performances of Rock & Roll music.

All day I could see the tension building between Don and his boy/girl friend. I wasn't about to get involved, so when we finally found our way back to Don's house, they were ready for a marathon relationship examination and I was ready to hit the road again while the hitting was good.

I suddenly decided to visit another high school friend living in LA. She was a PhD like me, only in psychology. She was spending her equivalent of a residency at a big psycho clinic where she administered sanity to rich bastards, Hollywood neurotics of which I understand there is a never-ending supply, and the occasional drug-addict millionaire. Perfect, we had plenty to talk about. And besides all this activity involving the wanton sex habits of the new sexual freedom age was making me horny as hell. Time to call in some old favors from an old trooper.

I blew out of town on the last ferry to Bainbridge. From there, I headed up to Port Angeles on the Straits of Juan de Fuca, where I camped in the truck for the night. That night, as I heard owls hooting all around in the woods where I parked, I consulted a map and decided to take the scenic route to LA and religiously follow America's highest numbered highway, US-101, from this end, next to Canada, all along the Pacific coast to Tijuana, Mexico. Shit, if Corvettes can make Highway 66 famous, why not a 4X4 Suburban on Highway 101?

When you drive from Seattle to LA, I sang. I needed a film camera and film so I could do a documentary, both of which I did not have. I did have lots more of Owsley's finest so why not instead do an acid trip down 101 and record it in my brain for history's sake.

When you fly from Seattle to LA, I sang again. That could be the name of the movie, *A Trip Down 101*, or would it be *Up on 101*? I decided to keep detailed notes in a journal, along with stills from the Nikon, which I would turn into a story book script later.

I remember the next day buying several cases of beer and toilet paper and heading off into the Makah Native American reservation where the members principally hunted whales, by hand, for a living. I thought about the first idiot who actually took on a whale in a little boat with a hook on a stick, or for that matter, the first land-locked idiot who took on a six-ton mammoth with a rock on a stick. *Jeez, we were daring monkeys!* Ego-driven, gullible, lying monkeys.

Like my brother the Viet Nam colonel told me: "The only animal worthy of our hunting down and killing are humans themselves, the ultimate prey and predator game." The flower children who turned vegetarian were right: hunting and eating meat is the root cause of killing millions of people in cold blood for no reason other than it it's possible. I'm sure that was the only reason the first idiot had when he actually succeeded. *It's in our blood. Bullshit!* The only thing valid in our blood is art. Pure, unadulterated art intended for thinking only. And whale watching, of course.

From that night in the extreme northwest corner of the United States, things got sketchy. I remember a night on the beach in northern California where there were people building a huge bonfire on the beach and spending all night dancing around it chanting weird stuff I couldn't quite make out from the top of a nearby bluff. I went down and spoke with some people standing around watching and I noticed one was filming it with a wind-up Bolex. He was really getting into the dancing as he was swinging the camera around the fire and up close to the flames and the dancers. He didn't seem to care about obvious things like framing the shot or holding the camera steady. He just got into the action and let the camera sort of come along for the ride. He was definitely a film artist. A Gonzo film artist.

It turned out to be Stan Brakhage from Colorado, filming some kind of white witch festival from a local commune. I knew about Stan from the Ann Arbor Film Festival, where he was always well appreciated for his advanced filmmaking style. I asked him what was going on and he just pointed at the bonfire and said, *Dance!* Stan wasn't big on explaining his work. That was what the camera was for.

When the dancers started getting naked and writhing with each other intimately, I started pounding my forehead against the rocks for not bringing any TriX film for my camera. Only TriX would be fast enough to shoot in the near darkness; so I had to make due with Ektachrome, under-exposed except for the burned-out flames. Finally, I stand back with the rest and watch lasciviously, but respectably. Something was going on in northern California that bared looking into later.

I don't know if I got laid that night or not, but I handed out some more acid to someone female-looking that I ended up dropping off in downtown Santa Rosa the next day, so I'm going to count it. I blasted through San Francisco heading for the Big Sur and some communing with Watermelon Sugar. I remember lots of yellow sun and blue sea and sunburn in the third degree. I kept up a steady stream of liquor and dope so I could see through the veil and experience what had made others trip out here.

I wanted to see what made Richard Brautigan tick. After communing with a wise old trout in a nearby stream, I was able to reconstruct that Richard was just plain crazy, but like us revolutionaries, in a carefully contained, almost silent and curiously intriguing way. For the first time maybe, we observing humans were experiencing and seeing other humans change in a fundamental way. Meanwhile, the sun shone down mellow, the sea radiated cool, and the waves beat a life rhythm unending.

Three days later, I found myself wandering around Venice Beach after midnight, stinking like an unwashed local hobo, looking for an apartment number only viewable from the boardwalk side of the street. I found it, but there was a body wrapped up in a cardboard blanket lying across the doorway just out of the rain. Linda answered the door, yelled at the poor guy trying to get some sleep after a long day in the hot sand looking for heroin, which he apparently found.

From there, I remember her holding her nose as she guided me into her bathroom, where she proceeded to strip me carefully while drawing a hot bath. I kept trying to tell her I was going to become a vegetarian and join a commune in northern California and she just kept telling me to use more soap. I asked her if she wanted to put flowers in her hair and get married under the Redwoods. I think she said yes, but I didn't ask again and she didn't volunteer, so it must have been mutually repressed by next morning.

She did take care of me like a woman takes care of the soldier just before battle and almost certain death. I tried to help, but she was the expert and was determined to try out some new moves she had learned since coming to LA. I enjoyed that night much more than I should have. But Linda and I had a little past thing going and we kept bumping into each other at odd times and under odd circumstances; we decided a long time ago to just take them in stride as best we could.

The last time had been in the barricaded administration building at the university of Chicago where she was one of the students occupying the place in protest over the war. I had been sent down by the *Daily* to shoot some pictures and find out what was going on. I wrote a nice little article about getting simultaneously revolutionized and laid on the president's desk but they didn't print it.

I do remember her stripping down and getting into the tub with me so *I guess* she could do more scrubbing in less accessible places. I encouraged her to rub it very clean, very, very clean. Later there were cool crisp sheets and lots of floundering in the dark. Linda was a big girl, almost my size, so there was plenty to fool around with for both of us. I marveled at how much she had loosened up since growing up in hometown Puritanville, USA. I couldn't get to first base at our senior prom after-party but now, after four years at Vassar and three at the University of Chicago, she was going to single-handedly make up for every moment she had been wasting during all those pubescent years of abstinence. *Good for her!*

I slowly came back to normalcy over the next couple of days. Linda let me hang out in her apartment, which was right on Venice Beach about twenty-five feet away from the boardwalk. The sun slowly baked the poisons out of my body and the ocean absolved my chemical imbalance. At night, Linda soothed my tortured soul, making me feel more and more like a normal human with normal feelings—like thirsty, hungry, and horny.

The first day off for her allowed us to spread a towel about a hundred feet due west from her doorway just above the high tide mark. I brought along a joint we could surreptitiously smoke if we were discreet. Most of the people hung out near the boardwalk, really just a skating and bicycling concrete walkway running for miles up and down the beach. After catching up on recent histories, I tried to explain to her what I was up to. I wanted to see if there was a way I could move to LA and try my hand at making movies here.

"That's what they tell me goes on around here a lot," she said smiling pleasantly.

She was an analyst to some stars and young *nouveau riche.* She didn't think very much of them like anybody with real values and intelligence. She was privy to the shabby world behind the glitz and didn't have much respect for blatant nepotism and rich little bastards complaining about their bad luck for not making enough millions to be noticed by those making billions. On the other hand, LA was permeated by no-talent hack actors, producers, writers, and wanna-be directors, all hustling each other like cheap whores arguing over a lucrative street corner.

"The newbie is eaten alive!" she pronounced knowingly. "If you plan on coming here, you better be prepared for the basest of human affairs. Backstabbing friends is the common theme and giving it double in return the religion. When they say someone is not going to work in this industry again they really mean, *you don't have the guts to come back for more abuse*, and usually, if they're smart, they go back to Nebraska."

"How do they expect any kind of significant artistic achievement from a cesspool like that?" I asked innocently.

"Oh, there are so many artists busy whoring themselves that some kind of art gets done in spite of anybody's true intentions. They all smile and hug each other like a bunch of commune hippies at a love fest while they are testing each other for flaws and weaknesses that will give them any kind of advantage. It's like feeding time at the zoo."

"Hell," I said, "that sounds like the cheesy little drama department at the private preppy college I went to. As for backstabbing, I've been cuckolded enough to be a Shakespearean comic character. I don't say *I love you* anymore, just, *I think I trust you to go to the next level.*"

"Please, still my throbbing heart," Linda said sarcastically while patting her left breast. "You do have a way with words."

"Yes, I do, don't I? I graduated from the Rock & Roll University of the Obvious. If we have to sing about it, it must be real. But really. I need to find something to do that will make some serious money."

"Have you thought about going back into physics?"

"I'd love to but all the budgets have been cut and I can't get into any programs because they are forcing students out of graduate school instead of in. They can't afford to keep them working on unfunded projects. I almost graduated, but the lab closed about four months before I could finish writing my dissertation. It was published in the *Journal of the American Geophysical Union* but most everyone else who did are now doing automotive engineering or bank programming, neither one of which has anything to do with planetary atmospheres."

"I have an idea. There's a party this weekend up in the canyon at some big Hollywood producer's house overlooking all of LA.

I know some of the people going and it will be exotic even for Hollywood standards. Why don't you and I go and you can check out the territory up close?"

"And intimate?" I added, as I rolled over to her side of the blanket ending up partially on top of her face-to-face.

"It may be more than a farmer from Oregon can handle," she said teasingly.

"How so?" I said smiling ear to ear. "Do they do it different here than on the farm?"

"You'll see," she quipped with a knowing look.

I gave up and kissed her long and hard. It's what beautiful people do, on Venice beach, in California, in the daytime. Michigan was becoming a cold dark distant muddy memory.

Come Sunday, we headed up into the hills north and above Hollywood to a place called Topanga Canyon. Most of the last few miles were on new dirt roads recently cut through the desert hills that surround LA. My truck felt right at home. Scattered along the route were all kinds of houses, from tarpaper shacks down near the bottom of the canyon where real green trees grew, ranging to designer concrete and glass houses at the top plopped right down in the middle of pristine desert where even starving jack rabbits wouldn't be caught dead. Actually, that would be the only way they would be found there. We climbed above the dark line of dirty air hovering just above the basin, and finally could breathe deep without choking as we broke out into bright sunlight and fresh air above the thermal inversion that trapped most of the LA city farts and other toxic gases.

Linda directed me into a driveway leading up to an empty ridgeline with a commanding view to the south, broken by some kind of concrete monstrosity of odd angled blocks stacked almost willy-nilly around a huge concrete pad, itself surrounded by a high chain-link fence laced with barbed wire at the top, separating the sterile concrete from the sterile baked sand and dead scrub brush on all sides. It could have been an abandoned military bunker for all I could tell. Linda warned me on the way up to use the ashtray and to not throw the roaches out for fear of causing a wildfire. I collected them in my ashtray anyway for in case I got desperate enough later.

Before we got to the fence, some guy in a thong and a big red bow tie holding a gaily flowered sun umbrella directed us to park behind about twenty other cars mostly new and exotic, except, strangely, no trucks like mine. We had to walk the rest of the way uphill past Corvettes, Jaguars, and a Bentley or two and through the rear gate in the chain-link fence into a large semi-walled patio and pool area. I noticed video security cameras all over the fence and roof of the blockhouse.

I brought a beach towel and a couple bottles of wine, one for us and one for the host. Linda did the honors and introduced me to a grey-haired hippie-looking wrinkled guy who apparently owned the house and who I knew by reputation to be a weird avant-garde movie producer. He apparently made a fortune off his latest movie and built this house, or fortress, to celebrate. Not bad for being an old hippie.

He was well tanned, probably from hangin' on his own deck around the huge pool. He had on a thong like the guy parking cars, but other than that, I couldn't find a tan line.

He showed us part of his house—the part where his giant sunken living room surrounding an open gas fire pit. There was a glass wall behind it, and like a giant outdoor drive-in movie screen, conveyed the best damned cinemascopic view of the entire LA basin I could possibly imagine. Behind and buried underground from this part of his bunker was a hidden thirty-five-seat mini-theater complete with 35 mm Xenon arc projectors with high-powered surround sound. I noted his speakers were shit 4-way horns and thought about hitting him up to buy a couple of Time Windows. But then I remembered, they weren't my speakers anymore, so why should I care?

He took the bottle of wine and disappeared, telling us to have fun and check out the swimming pool later for food and music. I thought I saw him pinch Linda in the butt as he left, saying, *I hope you forgot your swimsuit.*

Linda and I wandered a bit. I asked her if the guy we just met was a patient. She just smiled and said she couldn't say except if he was under court-ordered treatment, which he wasn't.

I noted some closed bedrooms off of hallways going back into the hill above the theater, A few scantily clad people were coming and going, indicating to me that important people were holding cocaine courts up there. Linda confirmed as much and mentioned most of her clients use cocaine regularly, which she has to warn them against. She warns them how to control the amounts of that type and other psycho-active substances so they can support and affect a healthy and properly functioning mind. She mentioned that after cocaine, the most self-destructive drug her patients had to deal with was alcohol.

"It's amazing how many people can't handle a shot and a beer here," she said. "Back home, I don't remember anybody who couldn't handle a little shot of hooch from time to time. Even Grandma Olsen. I could make a career and a fortune out of just finding almost any city full of drunks and opening an alcohol treatment center.

"It's not good to pump yourself up with drugs and then drag yourself down with mental anguish," she said. "I tell them to pick a direction so we can deal with that, but roller-coaster rides without end are not what most people would consider good mental health."

I had to agree, but still it would be nice to get into one of those courts upstairs and blow a few lines of LA snow, just for comparison purposes. I heard the market for coke out here was so great it sucked product from as far away as New York. I also heard that movie production companies often resorted to short-term smuggling and dealing to help pay the bills. Shit, not too different from the Rock business. If you're going to stimulate the drug market with your entertainment, then the entertainer should be allowed to get some of that action. It's just like taking a cut from the vending machines at the Super Bowl.

We wandered back outside to the brutal sun, where I was mildly shocked by several young ladies lounging around the pool stark raving naked. And fucking beautiful too. I looked at Linda and she just smiled back and asked if I cared to join them.

"You can do that?" I asked somewhat amazed. "I mean, you won't mind if I do a little sniffing around the bait to learn more about the big fish?"

"Knock yourself out," she said, smiling broadly. "I need to do a little cultivating myself for when you leave."

With that, she wandered off with the towel in the direction of the bar and a crowd of men. I marveled at how she had turned out. She was a lot more liberal than even me when it came to sex. I still had that built-in possessive jealousy thing going that all men apparently have and I had to learn to suppress it. I thought I was doing pretty well, but then I was pretty sure she would be going home with me, so maybe I could do a little reconnoitering.

I tried to make small talk with some of the naked girls around the pool, but they just bunched up like a herd of buffalo standing butt-to-butt facing down the wolf. More people started stripping down to various shades of whitish-brown skin, with curious pale white bands around waist and boobs, if they had them. I picked up a shot or two of whiskey from the open bar and before I knew it, I had my clothes off and was wandering around looking like everything was normal, like I always dressed this way at home, didn't everybody? The weird part was I still had my camera slung around my neck. I kept taking pictures of the people coming and going to the upstairs rooms in hope of seeing someone I might know. Turns out I did, but only in the movies.

The smell of burning pot lay heavy in the air. Most groups were either passing a joint or drinking the fancy mixed drinks with little umbrellas. I seemed to be the only one pounding down shots and beers. The open bar included a favor bowl full of something new, little black capsules with a sign saying *Beat the Heat* which turned out to be some kind of synthetic mescaline laced with Valium. Now that's what we called a *sideways drug*. The bartender said it helped prevent sunstroke. Funny, I thought that was what water was for.

I grabbed a couple of Heinekens and went looking for trouble. I finally cornered a cute blonde naked something separated momentarily from the herd. After plying her with Tequila, I found out Peter Fonda was the main character holding cocaine court on the second floor.

"Forget it. If you're not a bimbo or Daddy Warbucks Jew, then his entourage will kick your ass out for getting too close to the boy genius. Pig!"

She spit in the direction of the house. She seemed to know a little more than the common bimbo, so I thought maybe I should heed her warning.

After the shots, sun, and all the bare-assedness going on, it seemed quite acceptable to just find the bastard and demand a snort or two. After all, the son 'um bitch made plenty of money off the Rock culture he ripped off with his motorcycle gang bullshit twist on Rock & Roll revolutionary counterculture. No self-respecting Rock musician, hippie, or freak that I knew simply did not live to ride Harley's, drink beer, fuck fat mommas that hardly fit on the back of their bikes, and smuggle heroin anywhere near Mexico. I figured those guys were phony greaser punks and they deserved what they got. It did point out mindless Southern intolerance, but who didn't already know that from the Civil Rights Movement for the past one hundred years or so?

Needless to say, the entourage stopped me before I even got to the stairs. They had clothes on so I felt intimidated. They wanted to know who I was.

"I'm here to help him write his next script," I said with slightly slurred speech. I tried to show him my dick so he would understand what I meant by script.

"What's your name?"

He began looking down a list of names on a long piece of paper.

"Cowboy the wonder guy! I've got an idea for a movie about drug smuggling in airplanes, for real!" I said trying to explain my idea for a sequel to *Sleazy Rider*.

"You're not on the list. Get out of here."

He turned to deal with a naked blonde standing next to me. Not the same one in the pool. This one he ushered up the stairs and then just looked at me like I needed to be not so much there anymore.

I wiggled my dick at him and went back outside in search of Linda and my clothes. I spotted her bare ass on the other side of the pool with a bunch of naked men. *Figures!* I wandered about some more and started to feel a little uncomfortable about the fact that everybody was pretending it was no big deal and everyone should be doing it all the time. They weren't nudists, just politically correct liberals showing their support, I guess, for the sexual revolution and the equalization of all things sex. If you can ignore the nakedness as something normal than you have no built-in hang-ups about sex and can deal with the person for who they really are, sans ugly diverting and subverting sex. I wish it were so simple.

I stopped by the hot tub, which was slightly elevated for the best view of the rest of the back patio concrete slab, pool and people. I joined the crowd in the tub and started up a conversation with the guy next to me.

"Been here long?" I asked innocently.

"Here, like LA, or here like old powder puff's entourage?" he asked jerking his thumb over his shoulder at the main house and presumed owner.

"I take it you're in the film business," I said, trying to hold up my end of the conversation.

"My agent tells me that stuff, but it seems like the business does me more than I do the business. My name's Jack."

He held out his hand.

"Cowboy," I said, grasping his in return.

"Sure, that makes sense," he said referring to my black cowboy hat I still had on as a sun shade. He was wearing dark sunglasses so I figured we were even. He looked back at the cliquish groups starting to herd up like gazelles at the watering hole at sundown.

SOMETIMES...

"Have I seen any of your work?"

I decided to study the scene as well, not really knowing what to look for.

"Not unless you frequent Hill-Billy drive-ins or sleazy slum theaters. You might have seen me as a vampire or some kind of flesh-eating monster, which is ironic, as that describes exactly the people who pay me."

"So is this kind of party typical of Hollywood these days? I mean all the skin. Is this where the skin deals are made?"

I was just trying to make conversation now because drive-in movies were about as far away as I could imagine from the kind of films I planned making. If this was what Hollywood offers to young film makers, I was doomed. I couldn't see myself paying dues by doing trash films for ten more years. At least Rock & Roll had a soul and some kind of morals. I wasn't sure these people knew even how to spell morals.

"I have no idea where the fucking deals are made. All I know is they keep score by money, so the more you sell tickets, the more deals you get and the higher you go."

He turned to me and pulled down his sunglasses to look me in the eye.

"The tricky part is the selling of tickets to as wide a range of idiots as you can possibly find. Hence, the exceptional is expunged, the creative is crushed, and the great are made to grovel as we plunge to lower and lower depths of banality and irrelevant absurdities. If you want to make movies that count, go to New York. My first movie starred two giant tits that should have been in Ripley's, instead of film, but it made money. Lots of money"

"So you wouldn't recommend I move from the farm to LA to pursue my dream of becoming a great film director?"

"Cowboy," he said patronizingly, "Grab a camera and some film and then go on the road and film America at its worst. That'll sell tickets. There's a guy right now making a film about death and how it is celebrated worldwide. I hear it is really creepy and therefore attractive to thrill seekers. You really can't out-disgust the audience."

He wasn't telling me anything I had not already guessed on my own. My gut just wasn't in it, though I knew I could do it. I knew I could handle the challenge, but would my soul survive intact as it is now? My brother lost his soul in just such a bargain for money and success. He chose the army over a university and died a moral death in Vietnam as a result.

Jack excused himself, saying he had to go pee, but I noticed he went inside and upstairs to the cocaine court. I sucked on the last of my tequila-soaked plastic ice cubes and gazed back out over the crowd that had now gathered around the band and pool.

Some were differentiated by being more mature, and therefore the saggy-skin and out-of-shape type. They must be the lawyers and accountants. Then I saw the real fat, balding ones sitting down around one of the umbrella tables with younger females hanging around the periphery like vultures waiting to feed. They must be the power group. Then there were the obvious weight lifters or well-hung beach bums, who were strangely lacking in the expected beach volleyball matching girls. They were the *de jour* meat market of new talent. I was definitely not in Kansas anymore.

"Can you tell which group is more popular?" Linda said quietly right behind me.

She had climbed into the hot tub unseen, still naked as a jaybird. "Does it remind you of anything?"

I turned and broke up laughing. "You have got to be kidding me?" I blurted out, while still giggling. "You see it too! I was just thinking how this looks like a high school prom of some kind or maybe a mixer at a fraternity party."

"What do you think I have to listen to when these people come to me for therapy to improve their social skills? They seem to think that if they are not successful or fawned over for their amazing talents, then they must have a psychological problem that requires adjustment, as if we were chiropractors of the narcissistic ego. They seem to think there's a magic formula for being able to effectively communicate to anyone how great they are and how much they should be recognized and worshiped. It has something to do with the new social concept of networking where the successful person can cruise between all social cliques, becoming a natural leader and effective extorter of human talents. They seek to improve their self-worth by enlightened training of their mind, sort of like self-brainwashing so they can be become little Hitlers in their personal war of conquering Hollywood."

I was astounded by her insight and long-windedness. But then that was her training. For a little Oregon purebred virgin Vassar girl, I was impressed.

"You mean they are all improving their mental masturbation skills so they fit in better?"

"More like self-approval causes mental improvement, hence political correctness is their new language of power. Treat everyone like winners and they all feel like winners. Have you noticed how much hands-on there is with their social greetings? They now insist on cheek-kissing or hugging everyone they meet, just for the love-effect."

"While they are distracted by flattery, the enlightened one fleeces their pockets. But how can they all believe they can be winners?"

"Obviously they can't, and there's the anxiety."

"Sounds like you have a solid business plan. *Whew.* You want to put our clothes on and go make love somewhere? I think I need a bath."

She grabbed my arm as we left the tub and led me to the clothes check girl.

"I thought you'd never ask."

CHAPTER SIXTEEN

MY YIN WAS TOO YANGED

"'Cause as sure as the sun will shine,
I'm gonna get my share now of what's mine..."

Jimmy Cliff
"The Harder They Come"
1969

The next day, I used my black box to make a phone booth call to Bill back in Ann Arbor. I was running low on money and thought maybe I could combine my trip back by picking up a little something down near the border and hauling it back to help pay for the trip. It took almost all day to finally catch him next to the phone and willing to answer.

"Funny thing about that," he said. "Thom's wife Margie is out there somewhere and she called Patti yesterday wondering if there was anybody out there she could hitch a ride back with. I'm getting the impression she's getting tired of sun and surf."

"What about Thom?" I wondered why he didn't shoot the surfer who took his wife to California in the first place.

"What about Thom?" he echoed. "He's busy working with Steve on their first run of speakers. I saw him with another woman at Floods the other night. I think he has pretty much written her off by now."

"Wow," I said, "I thought they were the ideal modern couple: in love, high school sweethearts, part of the artists community, open and honest. They were the beautiful people we all aspired to imitate. What the fuck happened?"

"You hit it," he answered, "high school sweethearts. She was a virgin when they got married and so she never had the chance to enjoy her hard-won rights and privileges as a liberated modern young woman."

"You mean her running away with that surfer dude was just making up for lost time? Poor damn Thom. He really loved her. It's going to kill him."

"I know Thom. He'll find something or someone else. He's a survivor. So do you want to give her a ride back?"

"Actually, I was calling to see if you knew anyone out here I could use as a contact?"

"For what?" he asked quieter, indicating to use code talk.

"I can only afford peanuts."

"Check with 'J' when you meet up. I hope your connection is secure. Here's her number."

He rattled off a phone number that I wrote down on a torn-out piece of phone book.

"I'll see you in about a week," I said, and hung up.

Linda and I enjoyed another day and night together before I left for the surfing beaches of Encinitas. We talked about how hard it was to find true love. She had been dumped a couple of times like me and we both decided that we were broken somehow, but in a good way, so it was their loss while we only wasted our time again. We made a penis/pussy promise, sort of like a pinky promise, except more wet, that if we both make it to forty years old and we haven't found anybody, we'd find each other and get married. She was the kind of girl that grew on, you so maybe by then I'd be ready to buy the farm.

I thought about that a lot the next day as I fought my way through LA airport traffic heading south along the coast. I kept thinking it wouldn't be that bad, though she was maybe too independent for me and I would get hurt again. Or maybe she'll make a high-mucky-muck Hollywood contact for me so I could bypass the ritual we had been forced to witness in the hills the other day. But LA sucks, I thought, as I crept along with eight lanes of frozen freeway traffic. Why would I want to subject myself to this when a true artist can do his or her art from anywhere it feels right? *Art cannot be done right in a prison!* Besides, I'd have to add air-conditioning to the truck, and that's not easy.

Several hot hours later, I made it to Encinitas. When I finally found the address that Margie gave me over the phone last night, finally, after calling for several hours in a row, nobody was home. She, or whoever she was hanging with, apparently played the same game with phones and sleeping patterns as Bill did.

Okay. Two can play the game. I left a note in the door and spent a couple hours cruising around learning the neighborhood and parking at the beach for a while, enjoying the afternoon sun. About sunset, I made it back to her house and found her home, but totally unconcerned whether I would show up. She was learning *California cool and disconnected*. We got right down to business.

She had a contact where she said she could buy Mexican weed for a hundred dollars a pound.

"Okay." I handed her the last of my cash, about four hundred dollars. I drove her to another surfer house nearby, where she went in alone and reemerged twenty minutes later with a grocery bag. *Nothing suspicious going on here*. At least it was after dark and there were very few streetlights. I took a couple extra turns going back to her place, just to make sure we got away clean.

I wanted to get on the road right away. She wanted to stay one more night. I met the guy she was hanging with and he was tall, thin, blond, and really just a more handsome version of Thom who wore polyester instead of blue denim. I didn't want to know any more about him, so I spoke mostly with Margie. She offered the couch for the night and I accepted, thinking I hadn't gotten any real sleep last night so maybe eight hours in an undisturbed sack would be good before driving non-stop back to Michigan.

As soon as I brought my sleeping bag in and they retired to the bedroom, the noise started—first the low moaning and bedspring squeaks. Next came the whining, more bed thrashing and snorting, followed by more and louder moans and what I could only describe as epileptic voice box seizures while singing an aria from Wagner. Surely, they knew I could hear this crap. What the fuck was she trying to prove?

I took my sleeping bag and went back outside and spent the rest of the night sleeping in the truck. I swear I could still hear their wailing floating on the soft ocean breezes that night, which made the hair on my back curl. As soon as it was morning, I demanded we leave immediately. I got her in the driver's seat at about 9, just in time to hit the fucking traffic on the freeways out of town. She used to drive Thom's truck a lot so I trusted her to drive mine. Besides, I love just getting high, working the tunes on the stereo, drinking a beer, and watching the country roll by while someone else concentrates on where the fuck I'm going.

We drove along the old Route 66 to Missouri, where we took the road northeast to Indianapolis again, bypassing Chicago and the toll roads until joining I-94 near Jackson and then on into Ann Arbor. It dawned on me that this was almost the same route I had flown not too many years earlier from El Paso. How times had changed, and not necessarily in an upward-trending direction.

With a bed in the back we drove continuously for about forty-eight hours, arriving in Ann Arbor at around 9 in the morning. Fortunately, the truck didn't throw another universal so I was relieved there were no unplanned stops or maintenance costs. We shared the gas.

I couldn't stand it on the second day out and had to ask her about Thom.

"So, what happened between you and Thom? I thought you were happily in love, forever."

"I got tired of Ann Arbor. I need to go places, do things, experience life. Thom just wanted to stay in Ann Arbor or camp out in Leelanau. I found someone who is more exciting and I want to see where that goes. What can I say?"

"But true love—"

"Grow up!" she ordered, so I shut up instead.

I dropped Margie off at a friend's house with her share of the pot and then I drove to Steve's house, where I had to wake him up to get in. My key didn't work anymore. He said they needed more security with his speaker business in the basement. I hauled my belongings upstairs to my old room where the waterbed was still available, sans bedding, and stashed the pot and my bags for what

I promised Steve would just be for a short time. I needed a place to crash until I could decide what or where to go next.

He said something had come up about Bill in the last couple of days and I should check in with him as soon as I could. I started calling but got no answer all day long. I grabbed some much needed sleep and woke up two days later, much refreshed, ready to do business one more time.

It was a Monday, so I stopped by Fanfare and found Marty in town getting ready to go out on another tour. They had done one more tour with Joe Walsh while I was gone, but Joe broke up the band afterward and is now hanging out with the Eagles in LA, maybe going on tour with them. Meanwhile, Marty had landed a tour with KISS, which he thought was going to be really great with all their showmanship and special effects. He was in love with the road show and the bigger the show the better; it didn't much matter what the songs were about as long as they paid in cash. Poetry and protest were turning to brazen lust and bizarre shock rock.

"You want a job as a roadie for KISS?" he asked directly.

I didn't have to think very long about that.

"No thanks, I'm due back on earth soon so...."

Doing new and original audio work for upcoming talent was one thing. Tossing speaker cases around and driving a truck without sleep for forty days and forty nights was kind of a step down for me that I didn't feel I needed to do at this stage. I needed to get my head clear and find my next path, preferably in a nice atmosphere where I can relax and enjoy life while finding my art, my muse if you will.

"Okay, but KISS is really going somewhere and this is a great opportunity."

I looked him in the eye and he didn't seem stoned out of his skull so I had to believe it was the money again, the great arbiter of our values. I didn't blame him. He had certainly paid his dues and should enjoy some success, even if it was questionable morality with a bunch of zebra freaks.

"Do they want to do a video projection?"

"I don't think that would fit their stage presence. They're more into fireworks and strobe lights that I synchronize with the sound. You should catch one of the shows and see for yourself."

"I'll do that," I pronounced while thinking no fucking way would I go to a fucking KISS concert, even if every idiot in the band gave me a blow job while tickling my ass with a feather. It's a cultural thing.

I went back to Steve's and used his phone to put out the word I had some pot for sale. I just kept it to close friends, except I didn't call Thom for obvious reasons, and I couldn't find Larry Monroe to let him know. He was always good for a pound among his friends. I found Bambi and asked her where Larry might be. She said she didn't give a shit if he lived or died and she was doing tantric yoga now and had stopped doing drugs. She asked not to call her anymore. Apparently, my yin was too yanged or something.

Thom showed up at Steve's and he didn't seem the same anymore without Margie hanging around. His usual big smile was replaced with grim purpose. He looked a little gaunt, too. Probably lost a little weight recuperating from his attack. He talked a little differently too. Couldn't put my finger on it, but it just wasn't the bright and curious guy I once knew. Steve was a little strange as well. But I had been warned, and I had my own experiences, so I just wanted to keep out of all theirs.

Later that night, some friends who heard I was back stopped by and we were talking about all the neat things going on in Colorado and Northern California where freaks were forming up into communes growing dope and making music and art. I was talking about my friends in Colorado when Amy stopped, by driving Bill's truck. She seemed anxious about something and took me upstairs to tell me something in private. I followed, thinking this can't be good, but Amy's nice so who knows?

As soon as I closed the door, she turned, gave me an intensely serious glare and just spilled the beans.

"You've got to promise to keep this all to yourself. Don't tell anyone," she demanded tersely.

"O-kay," I answered slowly and warily. She dove right in anyway.

"Patti and Larry were having a secret affair behind Bill's back and about four days ago they disappeared together. Bill has locked himself up in a hotel room downtown. I'm taking care of him, but I'm scared he's going to hurt himself."

I love the way Amy, a four-foot cute little black curly haired Jewish princess from Brooklyn, could take on the task of both delivering disaster while saving everyone, all with the same cool professionalism. She looked so damn cute in her Levi jacket with matching pants and boots. Her big black curly hair made her look like an American Rose doll dressed up like the Marlboro man.

"Bill caught some cops snooping around his house the other night, so he cleaned his house of all drugs, actually I did, and everything is cool except his Corvette is at the shop. He wants you to bring it over to the hotel parking lot tonight just in case they pull a search warrant on the garage tonight."

"Oh great," I said. "I'm gone six weeks and everything goes to hell in a handbasket."

She cracked a smile.

The rest is a little hazy. I should have said no. But then he was a friend and he asked for help. I couldn't say no. Amy took me to the garage south of town where everything was quiet under a lone blue cone of light from a single sodium vapor lamp at the top of the only telephone pole alongside one corner of the metal building. She handed me the keys and pointed to the white '72 cop teaser on one side of the light pool.

I got in thinking, *this is going to be neat. Finally, I get to drive the fabled drug mobile.* I did and then while driving my dream carefully, with a big shit-eating grin on my face, all hell broke loose when halfway back to town red lights start flashing in the rearview mirror.

I'm clean and sober so I don't get excited. I'm just doing a friend a favor. I get arrested anyway. Not for drugs. Not for driving

Bill's Corvette, which they wanted to bust. I couldn't believe what it turned out to be.

They claimed one of the taillights was out. That's the standard excuse they give when they pull you over just for the hell of it. But the real problem came up after they ran a routine check on my driver's license. It was a little matter concerning an unpaid parking ticket.

"Are you fucking kidding me?" I yelled at the cop putting handcuffs on a dangerous parking miscreant.

Nonetheless, they hauled me downtown to the city jail, let me call Steve, who promised to get right over and bail me out, and then they left me alone in a small puke-green holding room. That's strange, I thought, though I had never been arrested in Ann Arbor so not sure how they would do it anyway. Needless to say, I was pissed and scared shitless. They had me and I was already locked up. I started pacing the tiny room, furiously trying to burn off the emotions tearing at me. *This is not where I'm supposed to be. I have go to get the fuck out of here.*

Then it happened. There was an intercom speaker on the single small desk along with an equally small wooden stool—the only objects in the room. Then it began talking to me.

"Bet you're not so brave now, Cowboy. In fact, I'll bet you're about to shit your pants over what I'm going to tell you."

It or he was wrong. I had already tightened my sphincter to the anaconda level and probably wasn't going to shit right again for weeks. I was petrified. What the fuck was going on? How the hell had I walked into this, whatever this was?

"Listen good. You're a very lucky kid. If it wasn't for your hero brother, you'd probably be harvesting potatoes at a federal prison farm in Colorado."

I'd never seen this kind of interrogation in the crime movies. Rubber hoses, yes. Bright lights and choking smoke, of course. Threatening intercoms, not so much. They said it was just a parking fine. A $100 bill will get me out. Who the fuck is this?

"We know all about your selling drugs to Rock stars. We don't like it. Normally we'd just have you arrested, but your brother said you could use a warning. Consider this your last and final warning, punk!"

"Wha'dya mean, punk, you asshole!" I screamed back at the intercom, all the while thinking how fucking silly this must seem to anyone looking in.

I looked at the only window, the small one in the door, and there was nobody there. I turned back to no place in particular and kept screaming anyway.

"And who the fuck is *we*?"

I never got any answers. Steve showed up about four in the morning, paid the fine, and they let me go without so much as a wink of conspiracy. He took me to where I'd left the Corvette and I completed my mission. I knocked eight hours late on the hotel room Amy had said they were in, only to be greeted by a pissed off Amy herself.

"What the fuck happened?"

I stepped past her into a dark room with the heavy blinds drawn and only a small desk lamp on in the corner.

"Someone needs to maintain their vehicles. They stopped me for a fucking taillight. Didn't Steve call you?"

"Of course," she said backing off the intensity, "We were just wondering what they had you on? Bill wanted to call Talbot right away, but I told him to hold off until we know for sure. So, what was it? Couldn't have been very serious if they let you out so quickly."

"Apparently the fine city of Ann Arbor has a long memory when it comes to marijuana joints for John and vehicular parking transgressions for me."

"Parking?" she said disbelieving, and then half-laughing, pausing to think: "Where's the Corvette?"

"Downstairs. Where's Bill?"

"Bedroom, sleeping."

She jabbed her thumb over her shoulder indicating the direction to a bedroom door.

I couldn't help but notice the temperature was somewhere near runaway sauna level, along with the humidity to match a

Tarzan jungle scene. I remembered this was one of Bill's ways of dealing with extreme stress. Turn up the heat, run the shower on hot to inject lots of moisture in the air, and then sleep for as long as it takes for reality to come around again.

"After discovering Patti's betrayal, he couldn't find out where they went and spent about fifty hours straight high as a kite on coke, making non-stop phone calls trying to pull in every contact and favor he could. He finally burned out yesterday and is now trying to kick his coke habit, cold turkey."

"You don't get hooked on coke by overdoing it for a couple days."

I looked around the room; it looked just like a typical no-taste hotel suite with a separate bedroom from a living area and small kitchen. Expensive, but apparently, he can afford it.

"It wasn't a couple of days," she said flatly. "More like a couple of years. Maybe spent more time doing coke than taking care of business."

"Hey, get in here!" Bill yelled, somewhat weakly through the partially closed door. "We need to talk."

"It's been coming for a while," she whispered. "He's been addicted since the Blues Festival. I told him to watch out for that scum Larry. He dumped Bambi just before they split, so they were both fucking everybody for some time."

I had no idea either. They both had me fooled. Amy must have been the only one to see it.

I went into the bedroom and it too was dark and dank. Bill was barely discernible as an outline under the covers of the bed. He seemed to be laying on his side. He stuck his arm out and motioned to a chair near the bed.

"So you heard about the bastard?" he said softly, as if taking it easy on the vocal chords from exertion. He didn't wait for an answer.

"I can't believe I didn't see it coming. That bastard was sneaking around behind my back all the time pretending to be a friend while fucking my old lady." He let that soak in with a pregnant pause. "I'm going to kill that son of a bitch. Believe me. I know how to do it. Nobody will ever know. Talbot explained it to me. He's gotten lots of guys off from murdering shitheads who deserve it, and he knows how to do it right."

"Are you sure you've thought this through?"

I was still in the dark, literally, about what the hell was going on. I pulled the chair out from the desk and sat down backwards so I could fold my arms over the back and rest my head and shoulders while talking to a pile of blankets. I was tired from the all-night pacing in the green room.

"You want to catch me up?" I asked. "I just got in from California after seeing things I probably shouldn't have seen, heard way too much in the new ways of sexually free women, and I ended up doing things out of a sense of embracing the new future I'm not particularly proud of. What's up with you, Bunky?"

"Didn't Amy tell you?"

"She mentioned you were trying to kick a cocaine habit, cold turkey. I had no idea you were doing that much."

"I wasn't until things started getting crazy last winter. Guess who Patti was hanging out with during the Lennon concert? She didn't come home after the concert for several hours. Said she got too high and was afraid to drive."

"I know the story. It's usually something so ridiculous you wonder for years afterward how you could have been so gullible as to buy into it. You didn't really. You just give them the benefit of the doubt because you're supposed to."

"Yeah," he continued with almost a snarl, "and we can't be possessive or show any signs of jealousy or rage at other men's attention to ma' lady. We have to trust everyone or no one, there's no in-between apparently."

"Out West, we have saying: *If it follows you home, you can name it, feed it, pet it, but you must set it free. If it doesn't come back, then you're free to hunt it down, kill it and eat it.*"

"The scum is not worth eating," Bill mumbled, "but watching him beg for his life would be nice."

I could just see his broad satisfying smile in the shadow of the blankets.

"Yeah," I agreed, "been there, seen it, done it and collected the T-shirt."

I paused but not too long. I didn't want him to go back to sleep without some more information.

"So why aren't you living in your house?" I asked pointedly.

"It's hot," he mumbled again, barely audible. "The cops have been watching it lately. A white van has been hanging around the neighborhood with shirts and short hairs inside."

"That's not good." I was sort of surprised the cops would have anything on Bill because, well because, he was righteous, always took care of the troops, and had his heart on the right side. Besides, he seemed to have a rapport with the local cops, being a hometown boy and working legal stuff with Talbot and all the concerts he helped run security. Maybe his reputation was getting out beyond Ann Arbor.

"I'm selling it," he said. "I bought a Winnebago. I'm going to live in it after I kick this thing. That's what I need you for. I can't leave here for a while, so I need you to help Amy get the rest of my stuff out of the house and other storage areas and into the Winnebago."

"What about the shop?"

"Arnie will take care of it for me while we're away."

"What do you mean by *we*, white man and what do you mean by *away*?

"Aren't you tired of these cold Michigan winters? How 'bout you and me go south where it's warm and where a couple of smart guys like us could make a buck or two. How about going to Key West?"

I hadn't really ever considered myself being anything like a beach bum or shirtless kind of guy. I was more into the high mountains where rugged men challenge the elements and disappear from the rat race and never miss it. Key West didn't sound like flying under radar. If I went to Key West, shit, who knows what the hell I'd get into down there. I was hearing stories of sunken golden treasure being used to buy cocaine in Columbia and fly it by the ton to Miami.

I liked scuba diving, but still, I'd heard that it was like Aspen: full of celebrities and rich assholes driving the price of everything up beyond the reach of the ordinary poor bastards like me. I already had a friend in Palm Beach who lived in his grandmother's spare house two blocks from the Kennedy compound where he shared the same walkway to the beach. The people I met while visiting him were basically the enemy. These were the bastards who corrupted governments and sent kids to be killed for their profits. If I had to live with them, I'd either have to be like them or kill them. Either way, Cowboy loses in the long run.

"No thanks," I finally answered. "Two guys in a Winnebago in Key West is bound to cause gossip. Why don't you take Amy?"

I heard something drop in the next room.

"I already asked and she said no."

The door to the bathroom slammed shut.

"What are you going to do in Key West? They don't have any roads down there going anywhere except into the sea or Miami. Try running from the state patrol there like you do here and you'll find few roads for making any last-minute escapes."

"I've got it all figured out. They have lots of inland coastal waterways cutting through the mangrove swamps. A fast shallow draft boat could evade the Coast Guard and just about anybody else down there. I plan to go night fishing for bales."

"Bales? What're you talking about?"

"Fishing boats are always bringing in loads of pot packed in bales and if they get chased by the Coast Guard, they dump the bales overboard. I'm going to go fishing for bales and make my get away in the mangroves." His voice was slowing down and getting too soft to hear well.

"Whoa there big fella! That sounds like a recipe for mixing high-test gasoline, highly flammable fiberglass, and immoveable trees at 60 miles an hour, just to get fire. Again, have you thought this through at all or are you trying to repeat one of Evel Knievel's stunts?"

"I shtook a couple Dilaudids before you came in...I'm beginnig to fade. A sneed you shta help Amy get my shtuff together.... We can shplit shoon azh ya'm better."

"Sure, soon's I sell some California shit weed."

He didn't respond so I figured he was done for now. I stood up and quietly slunk back into the living area where Amy was just reappearing from the bathroom, still frowning furiously.

"I think he's asleep," I whispered to Amy. "Can you drop me off at Steve's?"

"What did he say?" she asked pointedly. "Did he tell you about his latest scheme?"

"I think so, if you can believe he's serious."

"I've been telling him for months that Larry was up to no good. Does he ever listen to me? Fuck no! Dumb skinny blondes could start World War III and nobody would notice, but let one run off with the butler and it's the end of civilization."

She sat down on the couch and began rolling a fat joint from the paraphernalia spread out on the coffee table. That didn't seem to slow her down from relating the epic tale of Bill crashing and burning over a skinny dumb blonde, which Amy wasn't. Amy was smart, talented, passionate, and actually cute as hell. She was a girl I could relax with, like a sister if I had one. I didn't have to be careful of insulting her or saying the wrong thing. I wouldn't kick her out of bed either, but then I've only been picky about fat girls and girls with killer dogs.

I explained that to Linda, thinking she might have some insight that would cure my one prejudice.

"You know better, but your male DNA programming dominates," was all she said.

She recommended deprogramming me from fearing large women by purposefully immersing myself in them. Now, I have a fear of suffocating while trying to lick all the hot spots hidden under folds of flesh. I was not aware I had an innate fear of unknown engineering challenges.

"He listened to that asshole Pete Andrews and gave away his talents to making those concerts happen for very little pay or recognition, and now he's suffering for it. Those bastards made thousands in skimming the box office and selling drugs to the band and crew."

She lit the joint she had just rolled and took a big hit while still talking.

"I told him he couldn't trust skinny blondes. They're always holding out for a better offer."

"So I take it you're not going to Key West?"

"I don't know yet," she said less enthusiastically. "I might, but...."

She took another hit and handed half a joint to me with a precariously hanging ash.

"What are you going to do? He thinks you should come with him and help him smuggle dope."

"I'm not a dealer or smuggler or drug king pin like so many fucking people think. I'm an artist trying to make a living without selling out."

I dumped the ash on the carpet and finished it with one huge suck.

"Did I tell you about what happened at the jail?" I wheezed the words letting wisps of smoke escape while trying to hold in a lungful.

"What?" she asked. "Did they beat you with rubber hoses? I bet you liked it."

"I would have preferred it."

I related as best I could the events surrounding the holding room and the mysterious intercom. She just laughed and rolled another joint.

"You expect me to believe that? You were hallucinating from drug overdoses and lack of sleep. If they had anything on you, you wouldn't be here now. You know pigs. They don't give warnings or second chances. They just fuck you unannounced, like best friends."

I gave her my weird questioning look. *Really? You know about best friends?* I thought.

"Somebody knows more about my business than I do. I think it's a sign. I don't believe in that sort of thing but still, I think I'll do better hiding out in the Rocky Mountains making movies with my friends and learning to ski. I want to be a mountain man huddled around a raging wood fire in a cabin buried in snow, riding the storm out and higher than a Rocky Mountain goat."

"You're crazy."

She ignored me and scraped together a couple of lines on the little mirror.

"I've got a friend in Palm Beach and it's kind of hot down there right now and going to get hotter according to him. And I don't mean the temperature."

"Who the fuck wants to live in snow besides the poor dumb bastards who are born there?"

She hit one of the lines with a handy rolled-up hundred and handed both over to me.

"Call it the romantic in me."

I snorted up the line and it burned a little too much. Somebody's stepping on his coke. Another bad sign.

"Listen," I said, "he wants me to help you gather up all his stuff and get it stowed in his Winnebago. I don't even know where the hell it is."

"It's in his shop right now getting a new engine. Arnie will have it out later today, so when do you want to do it?"

"I've got some business to do first, but we can get on it tomorrow. Right now I have to go home and crash. This trip is getting to be too much for me."

She just frowned and let me out, carefully locking the door behind me.

I spent the next day trying to get caught up on sleep and money. I needed a lot of both. I called around the few people I knew who might be interested in cheap mediocre dope. They weren't. I called Margie and found out she wasn't having any better luck. I needed the money I had invested. Actually, I needed all I could get my hands on if I was serious about finally moving to Colorado.

I called my real estate agent and she mentioned the holder of my note might buy it back. I called them and they made me a cash offer I couldn't refuse. Really, I couldn't. I was broke. I stuffed a wad of hundred-dollar bills into my trucker's wallet. It was my entire fortune and it had to last until something new came along. It might get thin this coming winter.

Finally, I got a call from Jack up in Mackinac. He was sending down one of his lackeys to pick up my whole load. He didn't seem to care if it wasn't top grade.

"Shit, from all the beer they drink up here, they get high from just looking at a salad."

Later that night, some pimple-faced kid shows up in a Corvette. We go upstairs, do our business, he counts out the cash and before I can count it, he's down the stairs heading for the door with the pot. Fortunately, I count fast and yelled for him to stop. He actually did, which sort of surprised me. He had shorted me a measly hundred-dollar bill.

He muttered something about a mistake and thought it was a tip and coughed up the missing bill. I relaxed after having flashes of a shoot-out over a drug deal gone bad. I wasn't meant for this much adrenalin. I'd rather be directing the action than being it. In the front room, Steve had watched the whole thing go down. He later freaked at me to get my shit out of his house. I had to agree. This was not making me proud.

I guess the worst part of leaving Ann Arbor was what I found out the next day when Amy and I went to Josephson's house to retrieve Bill's stuff and all my books, tapes, and especially my flight bag with all my log books and FAA certificates. Bill's boxes were totally missing, as was mine. When we confronted Josephson about what happened he just said Patti had come by with Larry and taken it all away. He thought Bill knew about it. He didn't seem to care or know that half the boxes were mine. I was really pissed now. It was getting personal.

The work of over six years filming, videotaping, and recording original concerts, festivals, and events—all gone. Not a clue where they went or why. Considering Larry and his penchant for being a celebrity suck-up, he probably saw a chance to steal my work and claim it as his own. Nobody could legally use any of it because of liability issues. There were no signed releases, so the footage had no commercial value outside of archival and historical reasons. The greedy little bastard! He was just feeding his fucking ego with stolen blondes and videotapes.

This whole thing was beginning to leave a bad taste in my mouth. I did have one last thing. The video projector that I had stored in Steve's garage. I knew I could use it if necessary to make a little money. I could rent it out to bars for sports events on a big screen. I hated to prostitute myself and my stuff to the enemy, but if it meant survival, who am I to bicker. Live again another day to keep fighting the good fight. I sold the enemy drugs already, so not much formality to stand on here.

I loaded it into the back of my truck, which it pretty much filled, and stopped by the Hilton on my way out of town to drop off the keys to the Winnebago. Bill was awake, but still huddled under blankets in a human sweat terrarium.

"You heard that Larry got my stuff too, just because it was next to yours at Josephson's house? What's with your old buddy, anyway?"

"I don't know."

He really seemed mystified by the whole thing. It was the first time I saw Bill actually show vulnerable weakness. Normally he was on top of it all. Now he was just an innocent victim, if you can be such a thing. The worst part was being betrayed by what you thought were your friends.

"You really should come with me to Florida. You'll get bored, out in that damned wilderness."

"Yeah, that's the idea," I agreed.

Amy stepped out of the bathroom with a duffle bag over one shoulder and a suitcase.

"What's that?" Bill asked.

She walked up to me and simply said, "I want to go with you."

My immediate thought was that she wanted to move in with me and it didn't sound all that bad, at first. I felt a little tingle of excitement. But then she went on.

"I want to get laid by a mountain man. I want to be alone for a while. Can I hitch a ride to Colorado with you? I can help drive and I'll pay for half the gas."

My good feeling immediately disappeared. Another truck trip with a truck-driving girl looking hot, but not interested. Oh well, it could be worse, but I wasn't going to actually do any comparisons. The die was cast and the Ann Arbor adventure had come to an end. Somehow, I sort of felt lucky I was getting out finally. I'm not sure, but I think the Midwest is poisonous to a western cowboy-type like myself.

Later that day, the dark blue suburban rolled into a pink and red blazing sunset.

Amy said, "I never want to hear his name again."

"Who?" I said.

"You know," she said.

"Yeah I do."

And as far as I know, she never did.

I turned on the radio and lit up a doobie. The road took over like the smoky haze in my mind.

"Don't let the sound of your own wheels drive you crazy.
Lighten up while you still can, don't even try to understand.
Just find a place to make your stand and take it easy..."

The Eagles
"Take It Easy"
1972

AFTERWORD

Cowboy and Amy made it to a little abandoned mining town high in the Colorado Rockies. She got laid almost immediately by a local mountain man who hadn't taken a bath in several months, if ever. She went on to live mostly in the Southwest, selling real estate and cursing Bill Smith for ever existing.

Eberbach made millions off other people's work, screwed Thom, and they never spoke again for the rest of their lives, though they continued to live in the same town. He never compensated Cowboy for inventing the Time Window, except for giving him one pair of DCM speakers, which he paired with the Mirrored Mauer amp and both are still working after almost a half-century of Rock & Roll abuse.

Bill went to Key West and actually did what he said he was going to do. Eventually, he did *zig* with his boat in a tight mangrove swamp when he should have *zagged*, throwing him about sixty feet into a wall of trees. He decided to finally go back to Ann Arbor, while still having most of his bones unbroken, and retire to just driving and building fast Corvettes.

Fanfare and Marty disappeared into the bowels of 80s glamour Rock & Roll and were never heard from again. They supposedly did many tours with KISS but then, who cares anymore?

Larry Monroe and Patti successfully escaped to Austin, Texas, where he became a regular fixture at local music events and DJ-ing a late-night show on the UT radio station. Cowboy accidentally heard him one night several years later while passing through town and scared the shit out of him by calling the station out of the blue and letting him know that Bill now knows where he lives. He never slept well the rest of his life.

Cowboy's young nephew was the eventual winner of the hot session tape lottery of Grand Funk's "An American Band." He grew up in Oregon, moved to LA, and later became a true professional roadie, spending some forty years mixing the PA sound for premier Rock & Roll bands all over the world.

Cowboy retired to the Colorado Rockies, where he learned to ski and help start and run the Telluride Film Festival. He used his skills in video production and engineering to eventually get into the bourgeoning cable TV industry, building communications systems and satellite stations all over the world. He ended up making millions in Saudi Arabia working the oil trash sector, then lost it all on a crooked congressional election. He claimed he knew politics was dirty before he took the job. He eventually ended up founding a multimillion-dollar start-up wireless company, cashing in on the Internet craze. He pulled a stock scam on his partners and eventually retired spending his time in the Pacific Northwest, fishing for the ever-elusive king salmon.

Dr. Norman P. Johnson, a retired internet entrepreneur, lives in Seattle with his wife, two beautiful daughters, and Maggie, their cantankerous pug. Some of his former lives involved work in high-energy and theoretical particle physics, including a stint with NASA developing atmospheric computer simulations. He later helped design cellular and satellite digital telecommunications systems worldwide. He loves movies and has spent thousands of hours in obscure projection booths showing vintage 35 mm films. He is writing a sequel to "Sometimes..." and another novel related to internet hacking. In his off-hours, he enjoys hiding out in Hawaii, volcano skiing, raising chickens, deep-sea fishing, and scuba diving.

www.ingramcontent.com/pod-product-compliance
Lightning Source LLC
Chambersburg PA
CBHW051203120726
47905CB00004B/961